W9-CRG-901

EX LIBRIS

Romance
Treasury

THE ROMANCE TREASURY
ASSOCIATION

NEW YORK · TORONTO · LONDON

These stories were originally published as follows:

THE SPELL OF THE ENCHANTER
Copyright © 1972 by Margery Hilton
First published by Mills & Boon Limited in 1972

WHEN BIRDS DO SING
Copyright © 1970 by Flora Kidd
First published by Mills & Boon Limited in 1970

BRIGHT WILDERNESS
Copyright © 1969 by Gwen Westwood
First published by Mills & Boon Limited in 1969

ROMANCE TREASURY is published by
The Romance Treasury Association, Stratford, Ontario, Canada

Editorial Board: A. W. Boon, Judith Burgess, Ruth Palmour and Janet Humphreys
Dust Jacket Art by David Craig
Story Illustrations by David Craig
Book Design by Charles Kadin
Printed by Kingsport Press Limited, Kingsport, Tennessee

ISBN 0-919860-22-2

Printed in U.S.A.

CONTENTS

THE SPELL OF THE ENCHANTER

The Spell
of the Enchanter

Margery Hilton

CRAIG

On television, the eminent lawyer Sir Sheridan Leroy always appeared as a champion of the underdog, willing to help any good cause. Young Jo hoped to enlist his help to save the Marcombe Youth Center from the onslaught of property developers; she also wanted to impress Dave, the Center's director, for whom she would do anything.

She hadn't imagined it would involve stowing away in Sir Sheridan's car in order to win his attention—nor that the enigmatic lawyer would exact such a high price for his help.

It didn't seem fair that one man should be so brilliant, famous and powerful and appear so charming and attractive when in *reality*. . . .

CHAPTER ONE

There was no denying it: Sheridan Leroy had the lot!

Sir Sheridan! Jo reminded herself, scowling at the handsome image on the small silver screen and consoling herself with another forbidden chocolate.

The frown stayed on her usually good-humored brow as she studied the clever, mobile features of the eminent attorney and took in the salient logic of the argument those deep crisp tones were winning with such fluent ease.

Here was one victim whom no smart interviewer would ever succeed in tripping, she conceded reluctantly, aware of a slightly malicious longing to see this eventuality happen. It didn't seem fair that one man should be brilliant and famous and powerful and successful, *and* appear so charming and attractive when in reality he—

"Jo? Oh, there you are." The light flicked on, and Diane came into the room, fluttering slender hands tipped with wet gilt lacquer. With a gesture unconsciously imperious she thrust a small bottle at Jo and obscured the devastating personage who was the cause of her young friend's scowl. "Be a pet and do my right hand for me. I've smudged it twice, and I'm going to be late. You've a steady hand, and I'm in a bit of a flap," she added, perching on the chair arm and grinning appealingly.

"How unusual," said Jo in dry tones, taking the extended fingers of her roommate and preparing to remove the smudges. "Why don't you let the first coat dry properly before you apply the second one?"

Diane made a face. "What's the matter with *you* tonight? Dave stood you up again?"

"No."

Over the studiously bent head Diane frowned and did not press the question. Her glance went to the TV, and she said idly, "Who's that?"

"Mike Slater—I think."

"I know it's Mike Slater. Who does he have on the rack tonight?"

"Sir Sheridan Leroy—the Queen's Counsel," Jo said in apparently disinterested tones.

"And I always thought all Q.C.s were at least 60, waspish, bombastic, and pickled in red tape. Wow!" Diane sank back and gave a dreamy sigh. "Exactly what I've been looking for all my— I say!" she sat up again, causing Jo to swear under her breath, "that isn't the ogre you've been trying to beard?"

Jo did not reply, except for a disgusted exclamation, and Diane grinned. "Of course, I remember now. I wasn't listening properly when you told me about it and didn't give you the benefit of my expert advice. So that's the cause of the scowl. Wouldn't he play?"

"Wouldn't even see me and didn't even answer my letter," Jo said furiously. "I never even got past his secretary."

"Poor pet," said Diane in sympathetic tones, holding up her hand to study Jo's handiwork. "Does it matter so much?"

"Of course it matters. It's terribly important to save the Youth Center, and we need as many important and influential people on our side as possible if we're going to succeed," said Jo hotly if somewhat incoherently. "Otherwise it'll be sold to those property developers and pulled down to make way for some factory extension."

"I'm beginning to think it's a pity it wasn't pulled down in the first place."

The change in Diane's tone startled Jo. The shock in her blue eyes brought a faint smile back to the older girl's mouth. She said slowly, "That wasn't meant to sound so callous, pet, but I can't help wondering if it's been worth all the work and worry it's caused."

"Of course it's worth it!" Jo could hardly believe that Diane was serious. "You've seen it. You saw it two years ago when it was a derelict old warehouse, and you've seen it since we repaired it and painted it. The boys fixed the games room, and the candy factory donated the money to build our little coffee bar. We made it fabulous and now—"

"Yes, I know you did a good job—a very worthwhile one. I'm not disputing it, but where is it going to get you?" Diane looked down at her hands and back to Jo's indignant face. "The thing is, Jo, you spend every available minute of your spare time over there, trailing right across town to a seedy dump that's going more downhill every day. Yes, I know—the Center itself isn't a dump," Diane interjected quickly, "but the area is. Can't you see? What residential facilities Marcombe had are fast disappearing. Very soon the Center won't be needed in any case—not where it is at the moment—so why go on wasting time, money, and energy over a useless project?"

"Dave doesn't think it's a useless project," Jo said stubbornly.

"Yes—Dave. It all comes back to Dave, and that's what worries me." Diane frowned and glanced at her watch. "I wonder if you'd still be so keen if Dave wasn't involved."

The rush of warm color in Jo's cheeks gave the answer, and Diane said grimly, "Yes, I thought so, and that's why I'm concerned about you. You're in a dead end, following Dave Merrow like a little slave. He has you like he has the other kids along there, practically worshipping him, hanging on his every word, and I don't like it."

"But Dave's the most wonderful man ever!" Jo protested. "I don't understand your objections to him. You seem to like him enough on the occasions when he brings me home and stops for a coffee. You ought to be pleased I'm there with him and not hanging around with the fast crowd from the office. Why don't you like Dave?"

Diane sighed impatiently. "I don't dislike him, my pet, and heaven help you if I find you with Sue Barton's high-flying set. I promised your aunt I'd keep a friendly eye on you, and I intend to keep that promise. But I'm trying to tell you that you're wasting your time adoring Dave. Where will it get you? You should be forming other relationships, finding new friends, learning to assess this world—and some of the men in it, not living with a sterile devotion to a man who's too like a saint to be true."

With an impatient exclamation she stopped and shook

her head. "I'm late—I'll have to fly. But I'll talk to you about this tonight. Things have to start being different, my girl, soon." With this Diane departed, leaving a somewhat surprised Jo to get ready and make her way some ten miles across town to Marcombe Lane Youth Center.

As usual, the building was alive with activity when she arrived. In the games room an animated script conference and audition for the play were taking place; from the kiosk along the corridor the snack crew were dispensing badinage and bottles of Coke to a crowd of youngsters, and in the main hall the Filament, the center's own group, were setting up their sound equipment in readiness for the evening.

Jo hurried up the narrow iron staircase and along to the big bare room that served as an office. Three members of the youthful committee were sitting on the table and responded with friendly "Hi's" as she entered.

"Hi there," she responded. "Dave not here yet?"

"No, he phoned to say he'd be a bit late," said Muriel, a petite blonde whom Jo secretly envied because she did most of the center's secretarial work and thus was closer to Dave than any of them. "Well, anything to report?"

Jo shook her head. "I was hoping to talk to Dave before he started the rehearsal. I want to ask his advice."

Muriel shrugged. "He shouldn't be long. He's gone to see the editor of the *Mercury*—they're going to do a feature about the Center and send a photographer along, so that's one good start to the campaign."

"That's great," said Jo.

"And we have Pete Pilgrim interested."

Pete Pilgrim had been born in Marcombe. Now a tremendous success whose new record was almost at the top of the charts, his help was being anxiously sought by the Center in the fight to prevent its closure.

"And my father's trying to get the matter brought up at the next council meeting," said Roy, a thin, intense boy of about 16 who tended to take himself too seriously. "Have you heard from Leroy yet, Jo?"

"No, not yet," she admitted unhappily. "I did write to him and phoned his secretary, but I haven't been able to contact him personally."

"You'd better get a move on, then," Roy said in his precise voice. "We really do need a good legal brain on the job, and he would be ideal."

Muriel nodded. "Yes, he acted for those people in that road scheme and saved their historic street for them. They say he waived his fee as well. If he can do it for them why not us?"

But was it the same? Jo wondered. A tiny youth center in an obscure suburb was somewhat different from a beautiful old village steeped in history. A lot of extremely wealthy inhabitants had fought officialdom and the march of what was deemed progress, but even though a worthwhile principle was involved in keeping the center going in an area deprived of amenities for the young, would Sir Sheridan Leroy see it as worthy of expenditure of his time and specialized knowledge? And for free? For the Center was as poor as the proverbial church mouse.

Some of her doubt must have showed in her face, for Roy said with a trace of patronage, "It's pretty useless contacting a secretary in a case like this. These legal bigwigs can only be reached by a lawyer. It's all terribly traditional. You have to buttonhole them in person, at their club or something." He waved his hand. "You'd better forget it, Jo, and let Dave or me see to it. I said at the beginning that a girl wouldn't be much good, but you were so determined to take him on as your task."

"Yes, and I will get him to speak for us—just give me time," she protested. "I'll try again. I'll talk to him."

Roy gave his irritating smile. "I doubt it, and we haven't much time. I think—"

"My uncle said he would help," interrupted Muriel, "and he knows all about the lease."

"Yes, but he's nearly 80," objected Roy, "and he mumbles so much you can't make out half of what he says."

"What who says?"

They all turned as Dave Merrow came in, and Jo felt the rush of warm joyous pleasure she always experienced when she met him. Whatever Diane said, there was no one like Dave. He wasn't good-looking with his brown untidy hair, thin whimsical face, and the pleasant mouth that curled up at the corners even when he wasn't smiling, but there was something about him that made people feel happier just to be near him. And yet Dave wasn't soft. He could be unbending in an argument, adamant over a course of action, and scrupulously fair in decisions. Somehow people just gave up, smiled, and said, "Have it your own way, Dave old boy." No one knew exactly how old he was. He had one of those ageless faces that could be anything between 25 and 40, he was good-humored, and he had the magical gift of keeping discipline among the rowdiest and most aggressive crowd of youths. Marcombe Lane Youth Center would cave in without him, and he didn't have a girlfriend, thought Jo, ever hopefully.

The discussion began on the plan of campaign, and for once Jo hung in the background, bitterly conscious of a sense of failure. Black thoughts about eminent Q.C.s who failed to answer pleading letters with coldly repelling secretaries who promised to keep Sir Sheridan informed and did nothing of the sort filled her mind with indignation and brought a droop to her mouth. She had so hoped to be able to make a triumphant report of success, and next weekend she was due to start her holiday. She would have to go home to her aunt for a week, and then to Edinburgh for a week with her cousin. That was all she could afford this year. Oh, for a gorgeous trip to Greece like Diane was having next month, but Diane earned twice Jo's salary. She—

"Cheer up, Jo. You did try."

She came out of her reverie to find Dave smiling down at her. He put a friendly arm around her shoulders and squeezed them gently. "We are off to a far better start than I'd dared hope. And you must realize that everyone won't agree instantly to our requests. Some of them will say no—and mean it."

"But not to you—they never do," she said with unguarded candor, and he laughed.

"They do sometimes. You just have to be tough and bounce back, and certainly you mustn't take it to heart."

Jo nodded, but not very happily. The others were going

out, their feet clanging hollowly down the metal stairs. Dave straightened, and his arm dropped away.

He said, "I have to miss the rehearsal tonight, I'm afraid. Are you staying?"

She shook her head. "I was going to, but. . . ."

The words hung unfinished in the air, and Dave paused in his move doorward. "Want a lift?"

"Oh yes, please."

He grinned. "Come on, then, Tich."

Tich! Jo stifled a sigh as she got into Dave's old Morris. The affectionate reminder of her diminutive size would have sparked a flare of rage had it come from anyone else but Dave. She might as well face it; he would never see her as anything else than one of the kids. Diane was right. She was wasting her time hero-worshipping a man who was what Diane had once termed rather scornfully a "do-gooder." But he wasn't, not in the sense Diane had used the term. There was nothing patronizing about Dave. He was simply a kind and unselfish person who did things he believed in instead of merely saying they should be done and then leaving someone else to get on with it. She knew that if they failed to save the Center Dave would simply shrug and set about finding new premises. To begin again from scratch wouldn't daunt him in the least.

"You're very quiet, young Jo. Not still fretting because Leroy snubbed you? He did snub you, didn't he?"

"Yes," she said sadly. "When I didn't get a reply to the letter I wrote to him I went along to his chambers in the Inn and asked to see him. I thought the worst he could do was throw me out. His secretary—at least I assumed she was his secretary—looked at me as though I was playing truant from school or something and said Sir Sheridan was out. Then she said he was too busy to be bothered when I told her who I was. She said he'd had a load of requests from all sorts of people wanting grievances sorted out, ever since the publicity over that road scheme business, and that it had been an exception. As I apparently had no authority to brief him on behalf of the Center—she talked to me as though I was an ignorant kid who hadn't a clue about the correct procedure for approaching a Q.C.—there was no point in her making an appointment for me to see him, and—"

"Yes—I should have thought of that," Dave broke in. "Roy did, but we were all a bit carried away with enthusiasm last week, and I let you all gallop ahead your own way. Don't worry, Jo, we'll make out."

But Jo hadn't finished, and she was smarting again at the memory of the previous afternoon in those dignified chambers in Lincoln's Inn. "She was quite old, and really grim. She seemed to be in a tizzy about something or other, as though that was *my* fault! All she wanted was to get rid of me, and at that moment the great man himself stalked in. He looked about ten feet tall in those pin-striped drainpipe pants they all wear. He looked down at me and almost groaned. Before I could open my mouth he said, 'No more appointments this week, *please*, Mellie,' and she said, 'Of course not, Sir Sheridan, but Mr. Lyle is waiting for you,' and she brushed me aside, opened the inner door and sort of waffled till he went through. Then somehow I found myself hustled out and I never had a chance to say a word to him. Honestly, I feel awful, Dave." She twisted around and stared at his profile in the reflected light from the street lamps. "I've made a mess of it, and I did so want to help."

"But you do help." The indulgent note was back in Dave's voice. "You did your best."

"And I'm going on holiday next week," she fretted as though he hadn't spoken. "I don't like leaving this undone. After all, I did volunteer to make this my little job."

"So what? You go and enjoy your holiday, you've earned it." Dave slowed the car at the entrance to the road where she lived. "We appreciate all your help, and I know how loyal you are, so put it out of your head. I'll try and get in touch with the great man and see if I have any better luck."

The car stopped, and he waited for her to get out. Obviously he wasn't terribly concerned about the matter, and somehow this made Jo feel even more inadequate. She returned his good night and went slowly up to the apartment. This time she couldn't brush the matter aside and forget it; the sense of a challenge not met persisted, and the memory of Dave's indulgence only served to heighten the feeling of failure. But what else could she do?

Diane had hidden the box of chocolates. Jo hunted them out and sought consolation in the soft creamy sweetness; all very well for Diane to tell her she couldn't afford to gain a single extra ounce while she stayed at a brief stature of five foot two, chocolate helped her to think. . . . So Sir Sheridan Leroy was far too busy to be bothered. . . . So Roy thought a girl wouldn't be much use for the bothering . . . and there hadn't been a single word of reproach from Dave . . . she'd done her best . . . but had she . . . ?

Sir Sheridan's residence lay in a quiet cul-de-sac off Gilbraith Grove. The houses were all detached, standing in large, tree-shaded gardens. To Jo, shivering in the third rainsoaked night in succession, they evoked the conviction that a single peep from a transistor radio would probably have the same effect as a bomb on the inhabitants. A bomb was exactly what she would have liked to set off under the nose of Sir Sheridan Leroy.

There had been little difficulty in locating his private address. A couple of minutes with the telephone directory had supplied the information. (Why hadn't she thought of this in the first place—at least there was a chance her letter would have reached him personally.) On the first night of her vigil he had finally arrived home at ten-forty-five precisely. The car had swept up so quickly, and the tall figure had disappeared so quickly into the shadowy depths of the grounds she had barely had time to register her quarry. By then she was so damp and dispirited her courage would not carry her to the door, much less ring the bell at that hour.

The second night he had arrived at a much more reasonable hour; unfortunately he had not been alone. There had been a girl with him. A girl in an exquisite brocade tunic suit with a luxurious fur wrap thrown care-

lessly about her shoulders. A cloud of hair glowed like a
burnished aureole around a face that was undoubtedly in
the Helen of Troy class, even in the brief glimpse the
porch lamp afforded as the girl entered. It had been raining, as usual. The girl had exclaimed in light silvery tones
as her escort took her arm and hurried her the three or
four steps from the shelter of the car to the mellow
sheltering glow within the house. With a resigned shrug of
her damp shoulders Jo had given up for the second time.

Third time lucky, Jo told herself now. She mustn't miss
tonight.

The blue Citroën was already home when Jo reached
Gilbraith Grove, and as it stood outside the drive gates
she could only deduce that its owner intended further
journeying that evening. She looked at the imposing front
door and began gathering courage to march up and sound
an imperious summons. Surely he would listen. Five
minutes would be enough; she had the speech well
rehearsed by now. Jo took a step from her cover, and the
door swung open, flooding the drive with light from the
hall. Instinctively Jo retreated that one step as the tall
figure strode briskly out to the gate. He opened the car
door and slung a bag inside, then made to duck into the
driving seat.

Jo forced herself to move; another moment and he
would be gone. She called, "Exuse me, but—"

Her small summons was lost in a stronger, more urgent
one, as a woman hurried out. A couple of yards from Jo,
he made an irritable-sounding response and turned back
to the house to take his phone call.

Jo watched the door swing shut behind him and
checked the impulse to follow. He seemed to have strong
repelling forces about him in the guise of implacable
females; this one might be quite capable of shutting the
door in her face. A better idea came and without stopping
to have second thoughts, Jo scurried to the car. He hadn't
relocked it. It took only seconds to look to left and right
to ensure she was unobserved before she fumbled for the
inside catch of the rear door and slipped into the back.
Panting a little and tempted to giggle hysterically, she

crouched low on the seat and hoped the telephone call didn't prove too lengthy. Her courage might run out if it did.

But he would have to listen to her now.

The interior smelled soft and leathery, with the faintest redolence of perfume. An expensive one, she thought, to linger like that, and almost certain to belong to the gorgeous creature of the previous evening. Was she his fiancée? Girlfriend? Sister? Not that one, Jo giggled to herself as she rescued the briefcase she'd inadvertently knocked off the seat. Maybe he was on his way to meet the titian beauty now. Well, he'll have to get rid of me first, Jo reasoned, turning over the possibilities and deciding how best they could be turned to her own advantage. She would. . . .

His steps sounded outside, and she tensed. Now? But instinct kept her silent until he got in, apparently unsuspecting that he had a passenger. Let him start off, get occupied with driving so that he couldn't throw her out. Jo stifled another nervous giggle; he might think he was being hijacked.

The car was moving and slowing again at the end of the short cul-de-sac before moving out into the main road. It gathered speed very quickly, and she decided it was time to announce herself. Better do it gently—in case he had too big a shock. Wait until he slowed—there were bound to be traffic lights very soon.

When what she considered the suitable moment had arrived she sat up cautiously, peering at the lights flashing past and subconsciously registering the fact that he didn't seem to be heading for the West End. Then she saw the red splashes of light ahead, and he was slowing down. She looked at the dark, well-shaped head outlined against the glassy span of the windshield, crossed her fingers superstitiously, and opened her lips. At the same moment the brakes slammed home. She was thrown forward, and a furious voice ejaculated, "*What the devil!*"

The head turned, and she fell back with shock.

"What—? Who are you? How—"

"No! It's all right! I—I—" Jo thrust her hands out,

convinced that a furious man was about to launch himself over the seat-back and wreak vengeance on her hapless person. "No, please. I'm sorry I—I wasn't going to—to steal your car, or—or anything. Please listen, Sir Sheridan. I only wanted—"

"Good God! It's a girl." His face loomed pale above her. "Are you crazy? What's the meaning of—?"

"I just wanted to talk to you. Honestly, I didn't mean to—"

A furious blasting of horns stopped her, and he exclaimed again, seeing the build-up of impatient drivers behind.

She said in a small voice, "I think the lights have changed. You're holding up the traffic."

"I—!" Words seemed to fail him, and he jerked back to the wheel. The car slid forward, half-way across the intersection as the amber flashed, and a quick-off-the-mark sports car shot across from the left. There was a little more hornplay, and then in the comparative quiet of renewed peace Sir Sheridan said icily, "Your explanation had better be good. Who are you?"

"Jo—Johanna Medway. I—"

"It doesn't mean a thing."

"Well, it should," she said with a sudden flash of spirit, "if you read people's letters."

"What letters? What are you talking about?" he said irritably, swerving to avoid a jaywalking black cat.

"I wrote to you, then I telephoned your secretary, then I went to your office and you walked right past me," she said, regaining courage, "so this seemed the only way to make you take notice."

There was a short silence, then, "And you think *this* is a method likely to inspire a benevolent taking notice?" The cold clipped tones were those of the prosecuting counsel now, and Jo bit her lip. She sought for words of mitigation, but the quelling voice went on, "Your behavior is not only preposterous but downright idiotic. I believe myself in an otherwise empty car, and suddenly I see from my driving mirror that I have a passenger. What other conclusion am I to make than that I'm carrying a prospective thief—or an imbecile? And you inform me you want me to 'take notice' of you." The dry tones checked while some unseen driving hazard was noted and skilfully dealt with, then they continued, "I can assure you, Miss Johanna Medway, you have succeeded. I can also assure you that I shall have no hesitation in taking suitable action should your explanation fail to be very, very convincing."

Jo swallowed hard. She felt very small and unhappily subdued. She was not imbecilic enough to fail to realize that the sight of her through the driving mirror was bound to cause a start of surprise, if not shock, in even the most steely-nerved of drivers, but did he have to be so acid? After all, he'd got over the shock very quicky. Didn't he have even the slightest sense of humor? Or humanity? Hadn't he ever acted from desperation or done something silly?

He seemed to be waiting for the very convincing explanation. There was something about the outlined dark head that suggested he had meant every word about the suitable action—whatever that might mean. Suddenly Jo wished with all her heart she had never embarked on so childish a scheme; she also experienced an urgent and imperative desire to escape. She clutched at her purse.

"I—I think it would be best if I asked you to accept my apologies and forget about it for now. I—I realize it wasn't the right—the right approach. Dave would— He was right, I should have left it to him. He—"

Her voice trailed into silence. There was no sense of any lightening of the atmosphere, no indication of any helping out being tendered.

"Well?" he said.

She sighed helplessly. "What else can I say? It's quite obvious that you—" Again she faltered. To say that he was obviously not in the mood to listen to reason would be asking for trouble. Instead, she ended, "You're very angry. It's understandable, I suppose. So if you'll stop and let me out I'll not bother you any further, and you can get on to wherever your destination happens to be."

There was a long silence, then, "I have every intention

of reaching my destination, despite either help or hindrance from you, young lady."

"Yes, well—" Jo leaned forward and grasped the back of the front passenger seat. "I—I'm not sure where we are, but anywhere along here will do. I'll find my way back. The next set of traffic lights will do."

There was no response, no slackening in the speed of the car, that, she suddenly realized, was traveling extremely fast. Jo experienced a spasm of unease. She had to find her way back, and the car had come quite a distance by now. She took a deep breath. "Sir Sheridan—?"

"Well?"

"Could you stop now, please?"

"No."

Jo recoiled, wondering if she'd heard that calmly spoken negative, then decided she hadn't imagined it. She looked at the immobile profile, faintly illuminated in the reflection from the dash, but not sufficiently to be read. The spasm became fear. Was he mad? A lot of brilliant men were said to be cranky, autocratic, and this one was certainly reputed to be both brilliant and autocratic. But. . . . If he didn't intend to stop, how else to explain it? Wild thoughts of opening the door and leaping out ran through her mind, then over his shoulder she caught sight of the green circle of the speedometer—with the needle hovering at 70.

She sank back, aghast, and he said coolly: "Stopping is forbidden on a throughway—in case you didn't know."

"Are we on a throughway?"

"We are."

"B-but," Jo stammered, "does that mean—? How far does it go?"

"About another 15 miles."

"Fifteen miles! Before you stop! But you can't!" she wailed. "I'll never get back! You—you can't mean it. You must be joking."

"I've never been more serious in my life," said the unmoving voice. "I am merely driving to my country home for the weekend, as I'm in the habit of doing most weekends."

"But I don't want to go to your country home. I didn't know!" Panic came rushing, and she clutched at the seat again. "You must stop. There must be a bus stop somewhere."

"As a member of the law I must uphold it myself. And kindly refrain from bouncing against the back of this seat, young lady."

"Oh!" she gasped. "But you don't seem to realize what you're saying. You're refusing to stop and let me off until you finish your journey. How am *I* going to get home?"

"By train."

"Train? But I—I don't even know if I have enough for the fare. And the time!" she almost screamed. "It'll be midnight before I get home."

"Not exactly. You won't be in time for the nine-twenty, but you should be in ample time for the six-fifteen tomorrow morning."

"Tomorrow!" she gasped. "Oh no!" She sank back weakly, wondering if she'd strayed into a nightmare. He must be mad. There couldn't be any other explanation. He—

"I believe the fare is about 80 pence, but it is some time, several years, since I traveled by rail. There may have been one or two increases since then. I believe one now pays on the train—British Rail's streamlining policy, you know."

Jo wanted to scream at him to shut up about British Rail's streamlining policy or any policy—except one that was going to get her out of this car and home. Then the wild words died on her lips. Had there been the faintest trace of ironic humor in his voice? Or was she imagining things? She said desperately, "Oh please, Mr.—I mean Sir Sheridan—you can't mean this. Oh, I'll admit I gave you a shock, hiding in your car and—" she gulped, "but it was only because I couldn't get to talk to you any other way. But this is too much. You can't strand me all night in a railway station. It's inhuman! It's heartless. It—"

"It may be a lesson to you, young lady," he broke in, "one that you seem badly in need of."

"What!"

"If nothing else, it may teach you not to stowaway in a strange man's car."

"B-but you're not a strange man," she quavered. "You—you're an eminent, highly respected person. You're—" She stopped as he gave a grim, derisive chuckle.

"You don't believe I'd be heartless enough to strand an unwanted passenger at the nearest railway station, without her fare home, and leave her at the mercy of the night?"

"Are you—heartless enough?" she whispered. "I don't believe it."

"It makes little difference what you believe," he said curtly.

Jo took a sharply indrawn breath, then made an attempt at bravado. "No, it doesn't, does it? You're just trying to frighten me."

"Am I? Now you do surprise me. I didn't believe that the allegedly gentle, but in truth the toughest and most mercenary of the two sexes, still cherished such old-fashioned and naïve illusions. The veneer of liberation and equality is still somewhat frail. Tell me, young woman," he went on in the chilling, implacable tones that were reputed to make the most ruthless of prosecuting counsel groan with secret despair, "why should I inter-fere with my plans for this evening and go out of my way to return one silly, prank-playing little girl to wherever she belongs?"

For a long moment Jo was struck silent. Then a surge of rage drove out dismay and the last shreds of discretion. "Yes, I'll tell you!" she cried, clutching the back of the seat. "No, not why you should, but why you won't! Because you're a prime example of what makes people lose their illusions. Everybody thinks you're a champion of the unlucky victims of circumstances. They admire you because you come over on TV and in the press as an understanding person as well as a fighter and an avenger.

That's why we wanted to get you interested in our cause. We hoped you would advise us, even if you didn't have time to help us. But we were wrong, stupid to imagine you'd ever bother about a little thing like a poverty-stricken youth center in a backwater I doubt if you've ever heard of."

Jo took another sobbing breath and sank back limply into the corner. "You're just another façade," she said scornfully, her anger spent. "You don't really care, and you don't really feel for people. It's just a part you play. Your way of enjoying power. If you cared just one little scrap you wouldn't talk like this. You—you could be a wonderful person if you weren't such a—a beastly bighead in reality."

There was an appalling silence after her outburst. Sir Sheridan continued to drive smoothly into the night as though she hadn't said a word. Only a slight increase in the car's speed gave any indication that he might be affected by any reaction.

Jo began to tremble. The dreadful accusations she had hurled at him seemed to reverberate with increasing force in the stillness around her. She opened her mouth to say something, but nothing would come, except for a small choked sound at the back of her throat. She stared at the back of his head and wished with all her heart she was anywhere else in the world but here. An icy coldness pervaded her as he moved his head, and she felt the forward thrust of braking pressure. But he was merely taking a side turning, down toward a small cluster of lights winking in the velvet darkness.

The car slid to stillness, and the interior light sprang to life. Jo shrank back as the dark head turned and an immaculately tailored arm came to rest along the seat back as Sir Sheridan turned around.

The lean, well-known face appeared. A dark, ironic gaze searched out the small figure huddled apprehensively in the back of the car. Still he did not speak, nor did the unreadable lines alter in his grimly etched countenance. Jo blinked, swallowed hard as though to break the frozen vice holding her mute, and abruptly he swung out of the car. His shadow loomed at the window before he opened the door with a mocking gesture. Obviously she was to escape at last.

"Is—is this the station?" she asked in a voice that didn't seem to belong to her.

"Does it look like a railway station?" he countered, reaching in to assist her with a hand that almost hurt as it closed around her arm.

It was very dark, but not dark enough to obscure the round fat billows of thatch against the night sky, or blur the glints on diamond-paned windows framed under dark old timbers. The scent of roses came subtly on the air; and the sensed presence of floral profusion, a high hedge, little winding paths and an arbor; all waiting for sunlight to waken them from night's drowsing. The jingle of keys jolted her out of her daze.

"Where is this?" she cried. "What are you—?"

"But surely you've worked that one out," came the calm reply. "You have the facts already."

Without waiting for any further protest he walked past her, pushing open a small gate in the fence bordering the drive. The outline of his figure vanished around the angle of the cottage and utter silence returned. Panic flared again in Jo and she cried out, thrusting through the little gate.

A trailing rambler scratched her hand, making her exclaim and gasp again as light flooded the darkness. Sir Sheridan loomed again so suddenly she almost crashed into him.

"What a panic-stricken creature you are," he said, steadying her. "No, I'm not deserting you. This way."

"Yes, but—" She hung back. "I don't understand. Yes, I realize this must be your weekend cottage, but why have you brought me here? I thought—"

"But I didn't bring you. You brought yourself." A delightful oak-beamed hall with copper and pewter gleaming warmly against white walls swam into Jo's bemused gaze. An exposed brick fireplace welcomed at one end. On Jo's left a fine old period staircase rose square around a niche that held the only modern touch of the inevitable telephone. He moved to a door, touched a switch, and a clinically modern fitted kitchen appeared beyond. He gestured, his features still expressionless. "Make yourself useful. Everything should be ready except for the coffee. I have to make a phone call."

Jo couldn't move. She could only stare.

His brows flickered slightly. "Is there some difficulty?"

"No," she took a step back, "but I—I don't want any coffee. I—"

"I do. I am also very hungry. But please yourself," he said indifferently, turning away. "Perhaps you will marshal your facts while I make the new arrangements."

Before the bewildered Jo could find a reply to this he had picked up the receiver and begun to dial briskly.

Jo opened her mouth, and as though he sensed another frantic spate gathering he held up one hand in a gesture so autocratic she was silenced in spite of herself. "Yes. . . ." his head curved to the phone, and his profile softened. The autocratic hand dropped to the edge of the little table, and the cool little barrier of privacy seemed to isolate him.

She shook her head, trying to think clearly. What on earth was she going to do? Where was she? What did he mean by his odd remarks and even odder reactions? And who was Mattie darling . . . ? Who was coming here? To whom he was *apologizing*! And who was the unexpected guest? It was just dawning on Jo that this last could be no other than herself when he replaced the receiver and swung around.

"That's fixed," he said calmly. "But I can see the coffee isn't. Oh, you may help yourself if you want to call anybody.

"Let anyone know where you are," he elaborated as she stared afresh. "They may worry and report you as a missing person."

With an effort Jo got a grip on herself. With an assurance she was far from feeling she said quietly, "Listen, Sir Sheridan. I know I did a stupid thing tonight, and I know it made you very angry. But I think you've had your revenge. Now if you'll be kind enough to let me call for a taxi, or direct me to this station you mentioned, I'll make my way back without wasting any more time—yours, or my own."

For a moment he looked steadily at her, then the first trace of a smile touched the corners of his mouth. "The taxi service is a bit thin around here, and the station's three miles away."

"I'll walk."

"No, I think you'll stay."

"Here?"

The shock in her face brought the smile to a brief if somewhat sardonic completion. "Isn't this your original objective? Or was it all a mere kick?"

"A kick! Do you think I'd do all that just for a kick? You must be joking," she exclaimed bitterly.

"I rarely joke—it does not become bigheads. Or eminent, highly respected persons," he said dryly.

It was borne on Jo that he was laughing at her. "All right," she said between compressed lips, "I suppose I deserved that. But whatever it is, joke or not, it's time it ended." A sudden weariness washed over her, and she turned away, feeling more forlorn and helpless than ever before in her young life. Her steps lagged as she made for the door. Her voice was thin as she said awkwardly, "Forget it, Sir Sheridan. I'll go now. Good night."

"Are you going to give up so easily?"

The dry tones arrested her, and she looked over her shoulder. "I don't know what you mean."

"You should." He was leaning against the carved newel post. The sardonic humor still glinted in his gray eyes. "Do you always waste such herculean efforts—even though they are somewhat misplaced?"

"I'm tired," she said simply, "and you're just making fun of me."

"Crusaders must always be prepared for ridicule."

She heaved a sigh. "I'm not a very good crusader."

"It's always something to aim for, isn't it?"

Subtly his voice had altered. The mocking note had disappeared, and the expression was that of the man the public knew. Jo stared at him, her disillusion too deep to allow her to warm to a charm so obviously facile. Before her suspicious stare he gave a small shake of his head.

"Listen, young woman. You've gone to inordinate lengths tonight to make me listen to you. Well, I'm listening. . . ."

CHAPTER TWO

"So you see," Jo leaned back without taking her earnest gaze from Sir Sheridan's face, "we haven't much time. This Wincroft man is determined to buy the land and pull down the Center, so that he can build this new block and make a killing. And now that Mr. Jackson's died, and his widow needs the money, naturally she's going to want to sell to Wincroft."

"Can you afford to match his offer?"

Jo shook her head. "Not a hope. Mr. Jackson always promised that he'd give us a new lease. He was very interested in the Center, but no one knew he was going to die so suddenly. And that horrible Wincroft hardly gave Mrs. Jackson time to get over it before he was swarming around, trying to persuade her to sell to him."

Sir Sheridan set down his coffee cup and looked reflectively past Jo. "Yes. I know Aldo Wincroft."

"Do you?" Jo sat up sharply, hope lighting her eyes. "Could you speak to him? He might listen to you. He—"

"I doubt it." Sir Sheridan pursed his mouth. For a moment or so he was silent, then his expression softened. "Does it mean so much to you? Because, from what you tell me, the Center's in a dying area, residentially that is, and one marked for redevelopment in the future. You appear to have gained a great deal of local support and interest, but is it a wise move to save the Center? You may find it is only a short while before some other redevelopment scheme threatens it again. Why not consider a move to newer, more permanent premises? It shouldn't be impossible."

"No," she sighed impatiently, "you still don't understand. There's another youth center only two miles away. It was new a few years ago when they built the big new estate, but the kids like ours. You see, Dave reckons we've found the secret of what they want."

"And what might that be?" A trace of the sardonic smile touched the well-cut mouth again. "No one else seems to have solved the problem of what the younger generation *does* want."

Jo looked at him sharply, instantly defensive as she sensed the eternal gap in understanding looming again. She bit back the urge to start telling him the answer that the older generation seemed too dense to see and tried to keep indignation out of her tone as she responded. "It's quite simple. There's a church center in Marcombe, but the kids feel they're bound to look pious while they're there. Some of them have their own strong religious beliefs, that's okay, but some don't. And they're sincere enough not to want to be hypocritical. And the other place on the new estate organizes them. They don't want that. They don't want to play games, join organized outings, and jolly pursuits. They want somewhere to go where they can make their own amusement, just talk and make music, make a noise if they feel like it, and not have adults looking over their shoulders making suggestions and spying."

"Spying!"

"You needn't mock," she flashed. "That's what it feels like sometimes when you're young. They're all watching you, waiting to say 'I told you so' and 'Don't.' And disapproving."

Sir Sheridan looked amused. "It may surprise you, but I do have a few hoary memories of a similar nature. I too was once young, though no doubt that would seem an unconscionably long time ago to you."

The sarcastic note was not lost on Jo. She flushed. "I'm sorry. I didn't mean to be personal. I mean, I know you're not old—probably about the same age as Dave, and he isn't very old, really."

"And how old is this fascinating Dave, whom you revere so greatly?"

"Thirty-something, I think," she said vaguely, still aware of color in her cheeks under Sir Sheridan's gaze. "But that doesn't have anything to do with it."

"I quite agree. More coffee?"

"No, thanks. I've had plenty." She looked around the attractive beamed lounge and added politely, "It was very kind of you to feed me and bring Mrs.—er—Mattie to see to everything. But I hope it wasn't dragging her away from anything."

He shook his head. "Mattie finds the arrangement suits her very well. She was with my family for years—she practically brought me up while my parents were abroad. When she was widowed about five years ago I'd just bought this cottage. She came back to look after it and me when I'm here. So she divides her time between here and her son's home a couple of miles away. That way she doesn't feel dependent on her son and daughter-in-law. Two women in a kitchen don't always mix, as you probably know."

Jo nodded absently, her mind already wandering. She was conscious of a distinct sense of comfort. Although a cold one, it had been a very nice meal and all the nicer for being unexpected. Sir Sheridan had certainly changed his tune. Why, she couldn't imagine, for looking back on the events leading up to it her behavior *had* been a bit "off"—from his angle, anyway. Maybe his TV image and reputation weren't misleading. Otherwise, why should he take her in and feed her, get his housekeeper to fix the guest room? Wait till she told the others about this! Glee bubbled within Jo. It looked as though everything was going to work out after all.

"Why the grin?"

"O-oh—!" Jo tried to wipe it off and assume a winning expression. "I was just thinking. . . . You *are* going to help us, aren't you?"

"I'm making no promises." He stood up and went to the liquor cabinet. "I shall need more facts, and I have several other problems. What would you like?"

"Nothing. I don't—drink makes me go a bit silly so I don't bother. What—?"

"Wise girl. What were you going to say?" he was helping himself from the decanter as he spoke.

"I was going to ask what facts you wanted. Dave would like to meet you. He could deal with it better now that I've—"

She stopped, but before she could re-phrase what she had nearly said he broke in dryly: "You have me interested?"

She colored. "Something like that. We'd be terribly grateful if you would help us. We're not asking you for money. Only to use your name in our publicity campaign and be able to call on your advice, and—well—" she gestured, "have you on our side. Quite a lot of people have sent us donations, but they haven't time to—fight for us."

"And you think I have?"

"N-no, but people listen to you."

"Ah, the big sentimental sell to the public. What about poor Mrs. Jackson?" he reminded her. "Isn't it going to be in her interests to sell to the highest bidder?"

"No! It isn't!" Jo exclaimed. "I'm surprised that you ask. Aldo Wincroft won't give her anything like what the land would be worth to him eventually. I'd have thought you would know that," she added disgustedly.

Sir Sheridan was silent, cradling the fine crystal brandy glass between well-shaped hands. There was a slight furrow between his dark brows, and for a moment Jo was able to study him discreetly. He was a sincere and thoughtful person, she decided suddenly. A genuine person, after all, but he'd had to acquire that hard, cynical shell during his career. The shell the world forces more of us to grow for sheer protective purposes, she thought with a flash of youthful cynicism. Like Diane wears to hide her feelings about—Diane! She'd be worried sick.

Jo looked at her watch and jumped up. "I forgot. . . . Can I use your phone? To let Diane know where I am. She'll—"

"Think you've been abducted?" He waved his hand. "Help yourself."

He was still sitting in a mood of abstraction when she returned after reassuring an anxious and somewhat suspicious Diane as to her whereabouts. Fortunately, Mattie—or Mrs. Matilda Blair—had come out into the hall, believing she was being summoned. The background exchange of an older woman's voice convinced the doubtful Diane that her young roommate hadn't been involved in an escapade.

Jo went silently to her seat in the inglenook and looked hopefully at her victim. In the space of a few hours he'd given her the fright of her life, only to end it by mellowing to the astonishing extent of feeding her and putting her up for the night. She had to admit he was making up for his earlier ruthlessness. The six-fifteen tomorrow morning. . . . Jo shuddered at what-might-have-been, even if she'd had only herself to blame; but was he going to grant her request?

He looked up. "I'd like to help. I'm not in the habit of ignoring people's letters, but at present there are difficulties."

Jo nodded, and waited hopefully.

"For one thing, my secretary goes into hospital on Monday to have a troublesome appendix removed, and life is going to be very difficult without her."

Jo brightened. "It doesn't take long—having your appendix out, I mean. I was up the next day and out by the end of the week."

"I'm afraid poor Mellie won't be quite so fortunate. For one thing she's been having these attacks for years and ignoring them, until this last one gave her a fright. Her doctor told her flatly she'd regret it if she allowed it to grumble once too often. And Mellie isn't exactly young," he added wryly, "so I shall insist that she has a complete convalescence before she comes back, even if it is inconvenient without her. Also, I was hoping to fit in a holiday after the end of the Assizes next week. If I don't get away then I've had it. And there are other problems giving me concern."

"I see." Jo drooped. It didn't look so hopeful now. "We could wait a week or two," she suggested. "As long as we knew that you are—that you're sympathetic to our cause."

He gave her a level look. "You're not going to trap me that way, Miss Johanna Medway. I never make promises unless I'm pretty certain I can fulfil them."

"Oh." She tried, not very successfully, to hide her disappointment.

He went on, "But I'll think it over and perhaps have a talk with this Dave of yours. And that is all I can promise."

"Thank you." She smiled. After all, it was better than nothing. If she couldn't push the business on a bit, having had one foot in the door, so to speak, then she was certainly slipping. "Dave will be delighted and terribly grateful," she told him. "We were getting so worried, because I'm going on holiday next week. I'd feel awful if I hadn't made some small contribution toward the—the crusade."

He smiled faintly, obviously relaxing now. "Are you going anywhere exciting?"

"Not really. Just to my aunt's in Barnstaple. I can't afford to go anywhere. Wish I could," she said wistfully, stretching out her toes and regarding her own slender limbs. "I'd love to go to Capri or Malta and just bake in the sun all day."

"Wouldn't we all?" It was merely a polite rejoinder, and Jo stayed silent, realizing that he wasn't really interested. And why should he, she asked herself in a small inward whisper.

Nevertheless, the silence made her conscious of him—and herself. He was so different from Dave, or any of the boys she knew, or Mr. Thirle for whom she worked at the office. But of course he was different. For one thing he was an attorney, and they were a race apart—or so Diane said. And he was also a celebrity. Suddenly Jo wished she could summon up some scintillating small talk. If Diane had been here she would have been sparkling with wit by now. Diane had that gift as well as her natural dazzle in the glamor department, and men seemed to fall over themselves to please her. Like Helen of Troy. A mental image of the beauty he had been escorting the previous evening flashed into Jo's mind and she frowned, experiencing a distinct sense of displeasure. It wasn't fair that some girls had everything; instead of a snub nose, a tendency to chubbiness around the chin that men simply grinned at, and an annoying way of getting a bit tangled up in what she wanted to say just when she was most anxious to express herself in crisp, telling terms—

"—be others whose word carries more weight than mine?"

Jo started out of her trance. "I'm sorry—I didn't quite catch—"

"You mean you weren't listening." He surveyed her guilty expression somewhat derisively, then smiled. "It's an expression I see quite frequently on various faces in court, usually those of colleagues who ought to know better."

"I'm sorry," she repeated in a small formal voice. "What were you saying?"

"I was asking, why pick on me?"

"Well, you—you're so articulate. You're strong." Jo waved her hands, making a determined effort to be concise and articulate herself for once. "When you state something it sounds convincing, and people take notice. You don't 'em' and 'hm' after every other word like a lot of people do, and—and get lost in the middle of it," she finished firmly.

"Hm," he said after a brief silence. "Is that a compliment or mere flattery?"

"No, of course not!" she exclaimed indignantly. "It wouldn't do us much good if we picked somebody who just talked, but never did things. And I'll bet that if you decide you want a thing you get it," she added with unguarded frankness.

"Just like that! Do you believe that it's a good thing for the human species to get everything it wants in life?"

"Yes, provided it has the sense to want what's good for it," she said firmly, suspecting that he was laughing at her again.

"Ah, but that's its weakness. It rarely does." He stood up, glancing at his watch. "And now I have some work to do. Will you excuse me?" he asked gravely.

"Oh yes—" A little flustered, Jo also started to rise, wondering if this was his polite way of chasing her. But he waved her to sit down again.

"No hurry. Enjoy your little daydreams by that fire if you wish. Mattie will be in her sitting room next door if there's anything you want."

A murmured good night, and he drew the door closed behind him.

She sat there a little while longer, tempted to break into small soft giggles as she went over the events of the evening. Just wait till she told Diane, and Dave, and that know-all Roy. . . . Suddenly feeling inordinately pleased with herself, Jo put the gilt fireguard in place and without disturbing her host or his kindly housekeeper she tiptoed solemnly upstairs to the guest room.

"Well, well!" Diane exclaimed when the recital was almost over the following morning. "I wouldn't have thought you had so much craft in you. Stowing away in his car!"

"It was worth it—even though I thought he was going to murder me!" said Jo dramatically. "But it's going to work out. I know it is. He—"

"Oh, never mind about the youth club business," said Diane impatiently. "Tell me about *him*. What was he like?"

"Well, I've told you practically word for word."

"I don't mean that. I mean what was he like as a man? You know," Diane grinned, "the man-to-woman impact."

"Oh, *that*." Jo suppressed a smile, suddenly conscious that her stock seemed to have gone up in Diane's estimation. It was a new experience to have the sophisticated Diane curious about her experiences, and it was unexpectedly satisfying. "He is rather special," she said after a pause for reflection. "Exactly like he looks on TV but more—more—"

"Potent?" suggested Diane.

"Mm, potent." Jo nodded, wishing she'd been able to think of that herself. It exactly described Sir Sheridan Leroy. He was potent—especially close to.

"I must admit I wondered what on earth you'd got yourself into," Diane said after a moment. "I mean, staying there for the night. You're sure this Mattie person was there?"

"Of course!" Jo looked horrified. "What *are* you suggesting?"

The other girl chuckled. "Even you must know that. But I'm only teasing. I should imagine he has a very sophisticated taste in women."

"Yes—I've seen one of them."

"You have?" Diane seized on the unguarded admission, and Jo had no choice but to recount the initial stages of her tracking down of Sir Sheridan.

"I think she must stay there on weekends," Jo said thoughtfully. "I know I shouldn't, but I couldn't resist looking in the dressing table drawers. There were two packs of panty hose, and some fabulous perfume. There was a white housecoat in the closet."

"You nosy child!"

"Well, I had to open the closet to hang my clothes up, didn't I?"

"Oh, quite."

"So she must be his fiancée or something."

"Or something, I should say," said Diane with faint derision.

For some reason Jo was stung to defense of her host-victim. "I don't think so," she said firmly. "I'm sure he isn't like that at all."

"No?" The small negative said a great deal, and Jo glowered.

"No. Actually he's very nice when you get to know him."

"The worst ones always are. Tell me," Diane did not lose her teasing expression, "what did you do for overnight kit? Or did he provide that? The classic thing is his pajama jacket."

"You're not very nice!" Jo turned away, suppressing a startling desire to pretend that Diane had actually hit on the truth. "If you must know, his housekeeper loaned me one of her own nightdresses. It was pink flannel with little blue forget-me-nots on it. The only thing it didn't cover was my nose."

"How disappointing." Diane turned away. "You'd better take me with you the next time. Where are you going now?"

"To see Dave and tell him." A fresh light came into Jo's eyes as she forgot the enigmatic Sir Sheridan. "He'll be thrilled, I hope."

"Are you going all the way across town to tell him?" Diane exclaimed. "Can't you phone him?"

"Yes, but I want to go—I've nothing else to do."

"You must be out of your tiny mind." Diane returned to her preparations for her date and dismissed the matter in favor of the much more important question of whether to wear her lilac suede gear and be casual, or her new tip-to-toe stark black outfit. "What do you think, Jo?"

"Don't ask me. I'm not back into my tiny mind yet. See you later." Jo shrugged into the nearest garment to hand, that happened to be her old red jacket and set off for Dave's house.

Dave lived on the top floor of a gaunt Victorian terrace house on the far side of Islington. Five families lived behind the façade of windows facing the tall tower blocks in the distance. Five different batteries of sound assailed Jo's ears as she climbed the four flights of stairs to the wide top landing. She banged the brass lion knocker and almost instantly the door opened.

"Jo!" Dave fell back, surprise on his thin features. "What brings you here?"

"News." She hesitated, suddenly sensing that Dave was not alone. "But if you're busy, Dave...."

"No—come on in." He waved her into the large room that stretched the depth of the house and served him as living, sleeping and office quarters. "Meet Paul Mannel and his sister Judith—from Community." He drew her toward the dark-bearded young man and the tall girl with raven hair braided close to her well-shaped head, adding, "This is Jo, my little helper at Marcombe."

Paul nodded, and Judith smiled. "We've only just been hearing all about you."

"I hope it wasn't too awful," Jo returned tritely, warming to their unassuming friendliness and recognizing Paul Mannel from a picture seen recently in a magazine. "I'm sorry to barge in like this, but I simply had to see Dave to tell him that—Dave—" she turned and began her account of the past 24 hours, but a little inhibited by the presence of the others. "So he's going to think it over and have a talk with you," she concluded. "Which I think we can safely say means that he'll help us."

"That's terrific!" Dave gave her the smile that had caught more unwilling donors of aid than Jo would ever have guessed. "Any idea when?"

"No, but I gave him your phone number and address. It should be soon, because he's going away."

"Hm, so am I, and I'd like to get it settled and all the ends tied up this month." Dave stroked his chin, apparently not noticing the start Jo gave.

"Did you say you were going away?" she exclaimed.

He nodded. "With Community."

"We thought you were another recruit," said Judith.

Jo hardly heard her. "Where?"

"Africa."

"Africa!" Jo echoed weakly. "But—but you never even— You never said a word."

"Didn't I?" Dave grinned. "But it was finally settled this week."

"When are you going?" Jo's voice betrayed the shock she felt.

"Oh, not for a few weeks." Dave went to the desk under the big dormer window and rummaged among the papers and books piled on it. "We're going to work on the new settlement scheme that's being co-ordinated with the Karhmi Delta irrigation project. Here," he found what he sought and turned back to her, a thick journal in his hands, "there's an article in there about it if you'd like to read about it."

"Thanks." Unseeingly she took it and held it without glancing at its cover. Dave going to Africa! She couldn't grasp it fully. She hadn't even known he had any connections with Community, the big, and now heavily sponsored, voluntary aid organization that was doing so much vital work where it was most needed. But Africa. . . .

Judith and Paul were moving toward the door. Paul said, "We're late. See you Monday, Dave," and gave a smiling nod to Jo, as did his sister. A moment later the door closed behind them, and Dave came back into the room.

"Well!" He ran one hand through his hair and looked quizzical. "Time for a coffee, I think. Have you?"

"If *I* make it," she said with a rueful nod of her head. "I will, for you."

"Good girl." He ruffled her hair affectionately on his way back to the desk. "I've a note to scribble. I can get it done while you make the coffee."

She went to the recess behind the partition where the kitchen fittings were housed and filled the electric kettle. Dave's breakfast things were still in the sink, unwashed. With a small sigh she began to wash them while she waited for the kettle to boil. Did he ever think of settling down, marrying, having a proper home instead of this tumbledown place in somebody else's house? She looked at the big, damp patch on the wall between the sink and the window, and the place where the crack had split the new washable paper Dave had put on only a few months ago.

A smile of reminiscence crossed her mouth. It had been fun doing the place up when he moved in. They'd scrubbed, painted, repaired, and gloriously stuck up with the new fast-setting plaster stuff one of the boys had brought to fill in the cracks. They'd had an impromptu housewarming almost before the paint was dry. It had gone on till three in the morning before they realized the time. . . .

The kettle hissed, and she made the two cups of coffee, found the cookies, and took them out into the main room.

Dave was still scribbling. As she pushed books aside to make room for the cups he threw down the pen and slid the note into an envelope. "Bless you—perfect timing."

"Oh, I have my moments," she said with very convincing airiness. "But I don't know what you're going to do without us."

"Neither do I. What else did Sir Sheridan say?" he asked abruptly.

"Oh, nothing much." She had almost forgotten him. "Dave . . . how long are you going to be there?"

"As long as I'm needed," he said quietly, looking straight at her.

"Months?"

"Probably."

She looked down into her cup. "Are Paul and Judith going?"

He nodded. "They're leaving next week, actually."

Jo was silent. Judith's small careless remark was only now registering. A recruit. The idea exploded in Jo's mind like a shooting star.

"Dave!" She set down her cup with a bang. "Do they want anybody else?"

He looked up sharply. "I should say they want all the help they can get. Why?"

"Take me. I'd love to go. No—I'm serious," she said quickly, seeing the surprise form on his face. "I mean it. I don't know why I never thought of doing anything like this. Something worthwhile, instead of money-grubbing. I hate my present job, anyway. It's a dead end, and there's no end product that's vital to humanity. Systems analysis," she interjected bitterly, "and public relations. It's all talk, plan, and spread over five years, or ten. But not much do. Not today. But all over the world people are hungry today, and children need medicine. Could you, Dave? Take me with the team? I'll do anything. It doesn't matter what as long as it's useful."

"Now wait!" Dave shook his head. "You're not serious, Jo?"

"I am!"

"Yes, I think you are. But have you the faintest notion of what it'll be like? To start with it's an area where typhus is endemic. Every so often it breaks out. And we're starting from scratch. There's nowhere to live."

"You can get immunized against practically everything. And if you can live in a tent I can. I'm not scared of discomfort."

He leaned back, his expression considering, and his whimsical features suddenly betraying the drawn lines of tiredness. But his eyes were gentle as they studied Jo's earnest face. At last he said slowly: "You never mentioned anything like this before."

"That's what I'm saying, Dave. I don't know why I didn't."

"How old are you, Jo?"

"Eighteen—so I don't have to have any permission, or do I?"

"What would your people say?"

"Nothing. You know I haven't any people now. Only my aunt in Devon, and my cousin in Edinburgh. I've been with Diane for nearly two years now, so I've learned my way around. No, I've no ties, Dave, nothing to stop me going wherever I want to."

"I think you should give a bit more thought to it," he said slowly. "Talk it over with Diane. She's pretty worldly, but she's sensible."

"She'd be appalled. Diane likes comfort. She'd write a check out, but that would be her limit."

"It takes both kinds, Jo." He fell silent, his eyes reflective as he picked up his cooling coffee. Jo watched him hopefully, her imagination already racing ahead, forming pictures, plans, trying to fill in what it would be like to be part of the Community project. . . .

"Of course you could join one of the youth volunteer schemes nearer to home," he said slowly. "Just to break you in, so to speak, before you tackled a tougher challenge."

She looked away. "I want to join this one."

"You know what you're saying, Jo, don't you?"

"Yes." Her mouth set stubbornly. "I know."

"No," he sighed and shook his head, "you have a dose of idealism, but it'll wear off."

"How do you know?"

He smiled wryly. "You'll hate me if I tell you."

"Dave! How could I hate you?" Indignant now, she stared at him, wide-eyed. "Why don't you just say it? You think I'm too soft. Well, how can you tell until I've had a chance to disprove it?"

He sighed. "I never said a word that suggested you

might be soft. Listen, Jo. If you were genuinely committed you'd go anywhere, do any job you were asked to, when you were asked. But you want to pick and choose. That's the wrong kind of idealism, Jo," he said gently.

She was silent, the instant ache of hurt swelling her throat even as she was honest enough to recognize the truth. But the truth behind the truth hurt even more. What if Dave had guessed the real reason? Supposing he laughed at her in secret. But Dave was too nice to laugh at her. He might be surprised, shocked, even embarrassed, but he would never laugh. She choked down the hurt and tried to appear casual. "I guess you're right," she said in a small voice. "I'm not brave enough to plunge in among strangers, not knowing where I'd be sent."

"I think you're brave enough all right," he said quickly, after a sidelong glance that was more perceptive than it seemed. "I think you haven't had enough time to think it over properly and decide what kind of job you'd do best. Meanwhile, somebody has to keep the Center going while I'm away."

She nodded, not yet willing to face another truth that lurked shamefacedly at the back of her conscience. That the Center would cease to be such a magnet once Dave had gone.

Diane, however, had no such sense of shame. When she heard the news she almost rejoiced.

"It's the best news I've heard for a long time," she said crisply. "Now you'll have to get over your stupid crush on him."

"I haven't a crush on him," Jo protested hotly. "You make it sound as though he were a rock star or something. Someone to pin up and admire from afar. It isn't like that at all."

"Isn't it?" Diane shook her head. "It's exactly the same. This thing you have for Dave is so—so sterile. It'll never come to anything, and the sooner you come out of these silly daydreams the sooner you'll find out what it's all about."

"What?" Jo flopped down despondently and stared at the blank television screen. "Is there anything decent on tonight?"

"No—I've some ironing to do. The last time we had the iron in the same plug as the fire and the TV, we blew the fuse, so you'll have to wait till I've finished." Diane stooped to switch on the power and leaned on the ironing board while she waited for the iron to heat. She studied Jo's woebegone face and said sharply: "For goodness' sake snap out of it. If you're like this now heaven help you when you *do* fall in love and it goes bust."

"But I *have* fallen in love. It never even started, so there's nothing to go bust," Jo said sadly.

"Love!" Diane laughed shortly. "You don't know the meaning of the word—yet."

"Really!" Jo sat up and glared. "And I suppose you do. Just because you're a mere four years older and think you know everything."

"I never said that." Diane laughed again and tested the iron. "But at least I am past the stage of juvenile crushes."

"Well," some of the pique died from Jo's face and was replaced by a certain thoughtfulness, "supposing you tell me exactly what is the meaning of the word *LOVE*!"

Diane glanced up sharply, amused by the heavy emphasis, and gave a small shake of her head before she resumed pressing her linen jacket. "It isn't defined as easily as that. No two people react in quite the same way."

"I thought the emotion was universal," Jo said dryly.

"The symptoms are," Diane told her in equally dry tones, "but the source isn't. The man who sets *your* adrenalin pumping would send *me* running in search of a real live man with fire in his veins instead of crystal morality." She bent over her task, frowning as she concentrated on a difficult collar detail. Jo watched her interestedly. Presently she went on, "This hero-worship nonsense makes me sick. Really, you should have grown out of it years ago."

"But I did," Jo protested. She regained a ghost of her sense of humor. "Didn't you know? This is what is known as unrequited love."

Diane made an unintelligible sound suggestive of disgust. "I bet if Dave ever came to earth long enough to notice that you were female, not a bad-looking kid, and made a pass at you, you'd be so horrified you'd faint or something."

"I wouldn't!" Jo leaned forward hopefully, a new light in her eyes. "Did you mean it, Di? Am I really not bad-looking?"

"Stop fishing, and keep off the chocolates, and you'll get by," Diane advised. She glanced at the clock and swooped on the iron plug, giving an exclamation of dismay. "I'm going to be late. Be an angel and tidy up a bit, just in case I fetch him back here later on."

Five minutes later she departed in her usual rush and a cloud of *Diorama*. Jo sniffed the lingering sweetness and felt utterly depressed. The dreariness of tidying the chaos of the little apartment did nothing to lift her depression, nor did obeying the unwritten rule of making herself scarce and leaving the sitting room free for Diane and the ravishing, young Nordic type with whom she landed back shortly after 11.

Jo went to bed. There wasn't much other choice and listened to Diane's light laughter and the deeper chuckles of the Nordic type, who seemed to be trying to start a course of Norwegian for Diane's benefit. It was nearly one when the little teach-in ended, and Diane came to bed. She sat on the edge and gazed dreamily at Jo's bunched-up form in the other bed.

"You asleep already?" she said softly.

"With you and the song of Norway forging international friendship till this time of morning?" Jo grumbled from under the pink chenille cover.

"Sorry, pet. Oh, he's a dream. He's divine." Diane gave a vast sigh and closed her eyes ecstatically. "I think I've fallen in love."

Jo heaved a different sort of sigh and pretended to be asleep.

CHAPTER THREE

The depression that had descended on Jo failed to lift over that weekend. The golden haze of bliss emanating from Diane only served to heighten the contrast of her own mournful mood. How did Diane manage to find the succession of gorgeous men whom she enslaved one after another? Admittedly Diane was a bit older, and it would be silly not to admit that Diane had a certain way with her. She never seemed lost for a bright remark; she was always self-assured and had made her own way of life for the past five years; that had taught her all the answers. But that apart, things happened to Diane. If she went to a concert it was more than likely she'd find herself sitting next to an attractive unattached male; Jo could go to the same concert and be parked next to a dear old lady up from the country for the day who would keep losing her program and tell Jo the story of her life during the interval. Children, old ladies, and stray dogs all took to Jo, but there was a time for everything. . . . Nothing exciting ever seemed to happen to her. . . .

The bad spell of weather seemed to be over too. The sun blazed down on London and encouraged picnics in the parks, and the sunbathing lunchers out onto the roofs of those offices fortunate enough to have roof-patio facilities. On the Tuesday morning Jo and her office friend, a plump 16-year-old with waist-length blonde hair that made Jo break the tenth commandment every time she saw Carol's crowning glory newly shampooed and rippling like wet silver-gilt, came prepared with sandwiches and a carton of milk. Carol even brought a tube of sun cream left from the previous year's summer holiday.

"We might get brown if it stays like this for the rest of the week," she said hopefully during their morning coffee break. "I'd love to start my holiday nicely browned instead of creeping down the beach the first day looking all pallid like an underdone rice pudding."

"You're going to Malta, aren't you?" said Jo.

Her friend nodded and turned back reluctantly to her typewriter. Jo felt despondency steal over her again. Carol was going to Malta; Diane was going to Greece. Yesterday she had made the booking for Mr. Thirle; he was going to Morocco. And *she* was going to stay with her aunt in Barnstaple. Worst of all, Dave was going away for a whole year—maybe two. It didn't bear thinking about. Why couldn't—

Her buzzer rang, and she hunted frantically for a sharp pencil before she hurried along to Mr. Thirle's office. But he was in the outer room of the suite. He stopped her, gesturing toward the phone and giving her a most peculiar look.

"Switch it back through when you've finished," he directed, then stalked back into his inner sanctum. She stared at the phone, heard him utter a sort of "Hrrmph!" and close the door sharply.

Somebody had made a mistake. Didn't she know the rules? No personal calls; and *never* on the boss's own line. She picked up the receiver and said in a wondering voice, "Hello?"

"Johanna Medway?" asked a voice crisp with impatience.

"Yes, but I think there's been some—"

"I was beginning to think they'd sent home for you," said the crisp voice that was somehow familiar yet not quite placeable. "Or is it simply that communications are not very efficient at your end?"

"Yes—no—that is—I'm terribly sorry, but who is it?" she stammered.

There was an exclamation. "Didn't they tell you? Communications *are* feeble. Leroy here. You recall our discussions last—"

"Oh, Sir Sheridan!" she cried, delight quickening her tone even as she mentally kicked herself for not recognizing that special voice at the very first syllable. "No, they didn't tell me. Have you some news already? I never expected—"

"I won't discuss it now," he cut in, "I have an appointment in two minute's time. Are you free at lunchtime?"

"Yes—I was just going to have sandwiches. Do you want me to come to your office?"

"No. I'll pick you up at noon, and we'll eat somewhere. All right?"

"Oh—" A long-drawn wail escaped her. "I can't, Sir Sheridan. My lunch hour isn't till one. I—" She stopped, thinking frantically. Would Mr. Thirle let her go at twelve-thirty? Oh, he *must*! She couldn't miss—

"I've already taken care of that," Sir Sheridan broke in smoothly. "At twelve, Miss Medway. Good—"

"No—wait!" she cried in the second before he could ring off. "You'll have to come all the way over here. Could I meet you and save you—?"

"You are a considerate child, after all." He sounded amused. "No, leave the arrangements as they are. Till noon."

This time he did hang up before Jo could say anything else. She looked at the white receiver before slowly replacing it and wondered what sort of looks she would get when Sir Sheridan rolled up in that great chariot of his to collect her. Something like the peculiar look Mr. Thirle had worn a few minutes ago. Sir Sheridan must have spoken to him first and fixed it for her to get away soon. All the same, better check. . . .

She tapped on Mr. Thirle's door, started her explanation, and was cut short.

Mr. Thirle said dryly: "Yes, I know. I suppose we'll see you back here about three o'clock."

"Oh no, sir." Jo looked shocked. "I won't take more than my hour."

He nodded, plainly not convinced, and Jo escaped to the cloakroom to make suitable beautifying preparations that took nearly half an hour and left so little time before noon that it wasn't worth going back to her desk. Surprisingly, no wrathful summonses descended on her head. Her guilty conscience prodded her until the first stroke of noon brought honorable release—in the shape of Sir Sheridan Leroy.

Jo was not sure whether to be thankful, or disappointed that he arrived in a taxi and had exchanged the formal city garb for much more acceptable gear. She took in the pale beige safari jacket, the very dark coffee-brown turtlenecked shirt, and the matching beige pants with immaculate creases. She knew a sudden hope that the supervisor was watching out of the window at that moment—and also Mr. Thirle. She also wished she'd had prior notice, so that she could have done a little more putting-on-the-style herself. However, she couldn't see any distaste in Sir Sheridan's eyes as he observed her blue and lilac paisley print and the end product of the half-hour's intense grooming.

He had dismissed the taxi, and after his greeting said casually, "I thought we might amble—I know a good eating spot about ten minutes from here."

She nodded, noticing happily that the London streets looked particularly inviting this day for walking. He added, "You've no objection to eating in a pub, I trust?"

"Oh no—one can relax better in a pub, I think," she assured him, quickening her steps a little to adjust to those long, deceptively slow strides.

"No one cares about elbows on the table," he agreed, lending a protective hand as they crossed the road. "Were you nagged to the brink of insanity as a child, young Johanna?"

"What about?" She stared up at the suave, cynical profile.

"Elbows on the table, feet wrapped around the chair legs, and a few dozen other meal-time failings that make eating more comfortable?"

She giggled. "And reading. My uncle always read the paper at breakfast, but my cousin and I never dared look at our comics."

"Newspapers—and adults—are exempt, didn't you know?" he said lightly. "And it all makes it so much more pleasant when one grows up and can break the rules."

She nodded, wondering when he was going to get around to the main business. Certainly he hadn't brought her out to lunch to discuss the horrors of childhood discipline, but something stopped her from blurting out her anxious questions. But he chose to wait until they were settled in a secluded alcove, the beef had been brought to their table and carved, and their meal was under way before he shed some of his casual, light-hearted air.

"I haven't the answer you're bursting to ask for," he said with a slight smile. "But I expect to have it in a few days," he added, seeing her surge of disappointment.

Her expression underwent a second speedy transformation. "You're hopeful?"

"Extremely."

"That's wonderful." She heaved a deep blissful sigh and leaned forward confidingly. "You see, Dave's going away with Overseas Community in a month or six weeks. It would be great if it was all settled before he went."

"Of course it may cost more," he said warningly. "If the new lease is granted you can hardly expect it on the nominal rent you're paying at present."

"Oh, will it be a terrible lot of money?" Jo's worried frown returned. "We're very poor."

He leaned back and a surprisingly understanding smile took away all the hardness of control and cynicism from his features. "We shall haggle and hope. I see no reason why some of these worthy gentlemen who support your cause shouldn't contribute something practical as well as their names and their interest." He smiled again, and Jo's heart melted with gratitude.

"Oh, you're wonderful!" she exclaimed impulsively.

His brows shot up. "Really? I fear you don't yet know me very well!"

"We'll never be able to thank you enough, anyway," she said. "The trouble is, there's nothing we can do in return. You have everything, and you can do everything," she added wistfully.

He laughed outright. "Everything? Not quite, I'm afraid. But actually, my quaint child, there *is* something you can do for me."

"Is there?" Jo sat bolt upright, transported instantly into a daydream in which she and the Youth Center rallied to a man in defense of Sir Sheridan and triumphantly helped him out of some frightful crisis. "What is it? You know we'll do anything we can."

"We?" One brow quirked. "I was referring to you yourself—not the others."

"Me?"

"Yes, you." A speculative glint had entered his eyes, and the slight curve of his mouth betrayed ironic amusement. "Hadn't you better hear what it is first, before you commit yourself so rashly?"

"Would it be rash?"

"That depends purely on personal viewpoint." He inclined his head. "Perhaps I should warn you that it's quite a committing favor I am about to demand in return for my services to you and yours."

"Demand?" She looked away, then back at him. "Do you always want paying back for helping people?"

He nodded, the ironic smile still lingering. "Haven't you yet learned, Miss Johanna Medway, that one rarely gets anything for nothing in this world?"

"I suppose so." Her voice was subdued, trying to hide disappointment. "Naturally you couldn't help every stranger. You'd very soon be bankrupt."

"True," he said gravely. "A fearful shadow ever present over worthy philanthropic types."

Jo's mouth set. She tried to assume worldly indifference and ignore the suspicion she might be venturing into deep waters. "What is it you want me to do?"

"I wish to engage your services for three weeks."

Her eyes rounded, then narrowed. "Me? How? Do you want me to go snooping around looking for evidence for one of your cases?"

He laughed softly and shook his head, then sobered at her outraged expression. "Nothing so clandestine or sinister, I'm afraid. No, you may remember my mentioning that Mellie, my secretary, had to go into hospital, and also that I was hoping to go on holiday."

Jo nodded, still a little indignant, and he went on, "Unfortunately I have a certain amount of work to take with me that with Mellie on hand would have been a fairly straightforward inconvenience, but without her is a damned nuisance."

"Oh, I *see*!" Jo's brow cleared and she grinned. "You want me as a part-time secretary and to help you clear up the arrears before you—"

Sir Sheridan was waving his hand, silencing her. "Not so fast. I want to take you in place of Mellie. To Corfu. On the 19th. We'll be there two weeks," he enunciated crisply.

Jo struggled with a welter of conflicting reactions, surprise, a wave of excitement, and then dismay. "I'd love to help you out, but it's impossible. I—"

"You can't alter your holiday arrangements?"

"No—it's not that." She grimaced disparingly. "Mine start on the 12th. I only have two weeks. They'd never hear of me altering the dates now, and as for having an extra week. . . . I'm terribly sorry, Sir Sheridan, but I shouldn't think you'll have much bother getting temporary help with a Mediterranean holiday thrown in," she ended wistfully.

"Mm," his nod was expressive, "that's why I thought of you. I take it, then, that you'd be willing to take on the job."

"Two weeks on Corfu? I'd work for nothing for the chance!"

"That won't be necessary. Naturally I shall pay your expenses and a proportionate salary." He leaned back and regarded her with some amusement. "I won't object if you wish to work in a bikini."

"Don't be funny," she said sadly. "Even if you're serious it's impossible."

"Actually, it's all arranged. I spoke to John Manning this morning. He was a trifle surprised but quite amenable."

"But he's one of our directors!"

Sir Sheridan nodded blandly. "We're acquainted, and he owes me a favor. I suggested that you have the next week as arranged. You may wish to shop, and I may need you to tie up a few ends before we leave."

But this latter part of Sir Sheridan's observation

passed over Jo's head. A disappointment she couldn't analyze logically brought a bitterness in its wake. He'd arranged it all; just like that. Leaving her the last one to be asked. Not even giving her the chance of trying to arrange it herself. Instead he'd just fallen back on that assurance and power he possessed in abundance. He'd merely. . . .

"It must be useful to be able to pull strings just like that," she said cynically.

"At times—yes. It saves time."

"If you're rich enough and powerful enough."

She had not intended to impart scorn in the assertion, but Sir Sheridan's calm expression tightened slightly. "I am not exactly rich, young lady, nor am I particularly powerful. I merely happen to possess a similar determination and driving power to that of yourself and your friends, plus the good fortune of being in the position in which to utilize those qualities. And may I remind you that your own motive in seeking me out was exactly that of which you accuse me? You sought someone who you considered would wield the necessary amount of influence. In your words: someone who might pull strings in your favor."

Jo was silenced and somewhat ashamed.

"And now," he added in cool tones, "I'll see you back to your office."

"Honestly, I don't understand him one little bit," she wailed to Diane that evening.

"I never try to understand a man. I try to keep him guessing about me."

"Yes, but this is different." Jo wandered into the bedroom, stared out of the window, and wandered back into the tiny lounge. "One minute he's being fun, the next minute he's way up, like a monarch on a monument. And he talks to me as if I were a kid, a not very bright kid," she grumbled.

Diane waited until she had coaxed her eyelashes into a perfect silken curve and studied the result before she looked through the mirror at Jo. "It's entirely your own fault," she said flatly.

"Mine? How?"

"Because you obviously treat him with awe and behave like a kid. I haven't had the pleasure of meeting the gentleman," Diane added, "but he looks as though he's a bighead."

"Oh, but he isn't. He has authority, but he isn't conceited," Jo said slowly. "And I don't think I defer to him. Sometimes I say quite awful things, and he just laughs. Until I put my foot in it today. He hardly said a word all the way back to the office," she added sadly.

"Which is just as well. It'll make it easier for you to turn down this ridiculous holiday job business," Diane said flatly. She looked into her bag, checked her appearance, and then took up her stand by the window to watch for her evening escort. "You didn't really take it all seriously, I hope."

"Going to Corfu with Sir Sheridan? Of course I take it seriously. Why should he ask me if he didn't mean it and go to the bother of asking Mr. Manning to let me have two extra weeks' leave?"

"Quite honestly, I don't know. I'm baffled."

"But it's simple. His own secretary's ill, and he can't get a temporary at such short notice."

"Rubbish. That's the whole idea of temporary help and two weeks in Corfu thrown in. . . ." Diane's mouth pursed. "Unless the man's a noted slave-driver any temporary should jump at it. What's he paying?"

"He didn't say."

"Well, you're not going, anyway, so it doesn't matter." Diane scanned the street below and tapped her foot impatiently—she hated being kept waiting, and seemed oblivious to the effect of her words.

"But I want to go. I've never been abroad, and I've always wanted to go to the Greek Islands. Why shouldn't I go?"

"Oh, for heaven's sake. . . ." Diane turned from the window. "You're such an infant, Jo. To start with, what are the office gossips going to think about it when it reaches the grapevine? You hardly know the man."

This aspect had never entered Jo's head, and she was horrified. She began to stutter an indignant denial, and at the sight of her shocked face Diane smiled cynically.

"No, my pet, I don't think so, either. The really sultry swingers will be more in his line when he's seeking amusement—not little sweet and innocence newly out of the nest. So," from under high arched brows she studied Jo with quizzical amusement, "we still don't know what made him pick on you."

"Does there have to be a reason?"

"There always has to be a reason where a man is concerned," Diane grinned, "and this one is particularly intriguing."

Jo was annoyed. She certainly did not consider herself a naïve country mouse, whatever Diane might think, nor did she read anything strange into Sir Sheridan's unexpected proposal. Jo was of an impulsive nature herself, so it rarely occurred to her to question the motives behind the impulses of others. On reflection, she had to admit that Sir Sheridan was the least likely candidate for imprudence, but he had probably thought of her because she happened to be in his vicinity at the time. His acquaintance with Mr. Manning would be a further prompting. He'd simply checked with Mr. Manning as to whether she was competent at her job before he mentioned the idea, thus saving himself the bother of contacting the agencies to find a suitable girl. Yes, that was all there was to it, she decided, and as for slave-driving . . . she didn't fear this unduly. After all, it was his own holiday as well—he had told her he didn't object to her working in a bikini.

The more Jo thought about the matter the more she became convinced that Diane was just being bossy. After all, Sir Sheridan's integrity was beyond reproach, so why should Diane worry? Most girls would jump at the chance, Jo decided. All expenses paid, plus a salary, for two weeks' temporary secretarial work in the sun on a Greek island. . . . It would be heavenly.

She said firmly, "I can't see why you're fussing. The reason's quite simple. In a way it's an emergency, and merely a way of returning what he's doing for the Center."

Diane smiled again, a smile that said a great deal, but before she could voice further objections the Nordic type came scorching around the corner in a low-slung streak of scarlet and chrome. Diane waved from the window and turned. "I'll probably be late, Jo. Be good."

She departed to the accompaniment of Jo's usual mutter of "depends what you mean by good," and Jo fell happily on a pile of holiday brochures. Diane had collected them some time previously when planning her own holiday. For a while she had dithered between Morocco and Madeira and had finally plumped for a two-center holiday at Rhodes and Athens; one which included skin-diving expeditions. A certain qualm caused Jo to seek the map and seek the proximity of her own destination and Diane's. However, Corfu seemed to be fairly well out of range of Rhodes and Athens, which was just as well. The beginning of Diane's holiday would now overlap her own. The idea of Diane perhaps taking it into her head to pay a friendly visit to Corfu was definitely off-putting.

The brochure pictures of Corfu were breathtaking. Jo pondered happily on the question of her wardrobe and that of Diane. Her roommate had just bought a divine shell pink creation to take with her for special evening occasions, and Jo wondered wistfully if she could persuade Diane to lend her the white crystal chiffon that Jo had admired ever since Diane bought it. The trouble was Diane was a couple of inches taller than Jo, and at least an inch more slender, Jo discovered as she surrendered to temptation and took the white crystal chiffon out to try on.

It was perfect everywhere, except under the high Empire-style bodice that was embroidered with silver thread and an intricate design of little crystal bugle beads. Wrist-length sleeves were full, floating and semi-transparent, and the skirt flowed, clung, and swirled in a truly romantic way when Jo essayed a series of experimental dance steps in front of the big mirror. If only Diane wasn't quite so skinny . . . *"Or I wasn't a digustingly fat size 12 . . ."* she groaned softly.

She twisted to look over her shoulder into the mirror, furious at the little vee shape between her shoulder blades where the zip wasn't closed. She dare not tug it right up in case she stretched the soft, fragile material. "If I starved right up to the day we left . . ." she murmured despairingly, and exclaimed as the door chimes tinkled through the apartment.

Dave's was the first name that came into her head, to be chased by the fear that he might go away if she stopped to remove the white dress and put on her own things. She scurried through the apartment and opened the door about three inches, peering through the aperture with full confidence that she would see Dave's cheerful face outside. Then her careless, "Hang on a sec—don't go away!" faded into the air and left her mouth parted in surprise.

"I beg your pardon?" said Sir Sheridan Leroy.

"Oh—er—yes." Jo recollected herself and furtively hitched one hand behind her back in case the zip chose to slide down. "I—I thought you were somebody else."

His brows went up. "You're going out?"

She knew he had noticed the dress and wished he'd chosen any other moment in which to arrive. "No, not tonight," she said awkwardly and stepped back, holding open the door in silent invitation.

"This will only take a few minutes," he said briskly as he stepped in. "The matter of the reservations and one or two—" He stopped, seeing Jo sidling with a curious backward gait across the room.

His slight stare vanished, and his expression became gravely impassive. "I'm most awfully sorry. I've chosen an awkward time to interrupt. Will you turn around and allow me to assist?"

It was quite obvious he knew all about zip difficulties, but she shook her head hastily and prayed he didn't know the particular reason for this case. "Thank you—but it doesn't matter. I was just trying it on when—"

He nodded, and she escaped thankfully into the bedroom where she threw off the white dress and hurriedly donned her slacks and a shirt. When she re-emerged Sir Sheridan was standing looking out of the window. He swung around, and she thought she detected a flicker of disappointment in his eyes.

"Doesn't it fit?" he asked carelessly.

"Of course it fits!" She looked at him coldly, stung by this casual little aside that was too near the truth for comfort. "You were saying . . . ?"

"Ah, yes. . . ." He gave no sign of having noticed her flash of pique and his expression remained solemn as he explained the dates and times of travel arrangements, putting one or two questions to Jo and inviting any queries that she in her turn might want to ask. It all seemed quite straightforward, except for one thing; they were not, as she had automatically assumed, going to stay at a hotel.

"I have a standing invitation to make myself at home at Professor Quayle's villa whenever I wish," Sir Sheridan explained smoothly. "And I'm sure you'll find it compares very favorably, comfortwise, with any hotel," he added dryly, as though assuming this to be the cause of her doubtful expression.

But it wasn't. Jo bit her lip and tried to stifle her doubts. It had to be all right; even though a villa seemed to suggest an infinitely less impersonal arrangement than a hotel. It was all Diane's fault, she thought crossly, putting ideas into her head where they had never existed. What on earth would he think if he knew? Probably howl with derision, she told herself bitterly, and that was another of Diane's sweet little aspersions. Sir Sheridan might suggest an assignation with any other girl but herself. Oh yes, that inference was all too clear; she wasn't in the high-flying class that would tempt a famous and handsome Q.C. to forget about little temporary secretaries and think about lighter pursuits in luxury villas on the shore of a Greek island. But one day she would show them, Jo vowed to herself. Did they think she was totally incapable of attracting a man? She looked up at Sir Sheridan and frowned. "Is it the famous Professor Quayle? The historian?"

Sir Sheridan nodded, a slight smile lingering about his well-shaped mouth. "You've met him?"

"No. I think I saw him on some program." Jo assumed a careless expression. "He looked frightfully forbidding."

The smile vanished. "Is that all that's worrying you? Actually he's one of the friendliest, most unassuming men I know, but I doubt if we'll see very much of him."

"He—he won't be there?"

"Oh yes, he'll be there—and so will several other members of his family and friends who have standing invitations to drop in any time."

"Oh." Jo did not know whether to feel relieved or disappointed. "So it'll be a kind of holiday party?"

"Something like that." He was studying her expression with quizzical eyes. "Did you fear that you might be alone at the mercy of my slave-driving?"

"Are you a slave-driver?"

"Occasionally—if my slaves dare to be lazy!" He was openly teasing her now. "But I never whip my feminine slaves."

"How grateful they must be." Jo wished she could respond with something more witty and resigned herself to the sad fact that she was one of those people who could always think of the clever retort half an hour later, never at the moment it would be most telling. How many willing slaves did he have, anyway? Mattie was one for sure, and Mellie seemed willing to die for him. And what about the beautiful redhead . . . ? She saw Sir Sheridan glance out of the window and became aware of her lack of manners. She said quickly: "I'm sorry—won't you sit down? Would you like some coffee?"

He swung to face her, his elegantly clad shoulders silhouetted against the dusty gold glare of the sunset. Suddenly he seemed out of place in the feminine untidiness of the little sitting room. He was going to refuse, she thought, and felt a flash of delight when he smiled and said, "Yes, I would, please."

She scurried into the tiny kitchenette and hunted frantically for an embroidered traycloth. When she took the carefully set tray back to the lounge she found Sir Sheridan immersed in the brochures she had left scattered all over the sofa and floor.

He glanced up. "Been doing a little homework?"

"Not really." She ignored the glint of humor in his eyes. "They're Diane's—she's going to Rhodes."

He nodded and accepted his coffee gravely.

"Besides," Jo went on, perching on the tapestry stool, "I realize I'm going to work."

"Oh, yes." He set down his cup. "That reminds me—your salary." He mentioned a sum that seemed inordinately generous and quirked inquiring brows. "Will that be satisfactory?"

"It's too much." She shook her head. "I mean, on top of the expenses."

"Not at all. And I propose to give you an advance on it now." He drew an envelope from his pocket and laid it on the coffee table. "You will need to buy clothes that probably you wouldn't otherwise have bought. There may be occasions when you'll want glad-rags, and the long list of trimmings that seem to be essential to complete each new outfit." He smiled at her surprised expression and nodded. "Oh, yes, even the make-up must match as well, if my sister is typical of the fashion-conscious young woman."

"You have a sister?"

"Margaret—you'll probably meet her." Abruptly he finished his coffee and stood up, obviously to depart. He added one or two reminders, informed her that he would contact her a couple of days before their departure, and then moved to the door.

Suddenly Jo didn't want him to leave. She sought for an excuse to keep him talking a little longer, unconsciously wanting to recall him to his teasing mood, and inspiration responded.

"What about a machine?" she asked.

"Machine?" One hand on the door handle, he frowned.

"A typewriter. I'll need one, and I don't have one of my own. But Diane has a portable," she added hurriedly. "I might be able to borrow that."

He appeared unperturbed by her concern. "Don't worry. That will be taken care of."

"And paper, carbon, and everything?"

"And everything." He smiled and tapped a crooked finger on the tip of her chin. "All you have to do, Jo, is be there when I want you. All right?"

That smile was quite irresistible. Jo nodded, and took the hand he held out.

The warmth of his solemn handshake stayed with Jo for quite a long time. She did not realize how dreamy her smile was as she stood at the window and watched him get into his car and drive away. Just be there when he wanted her . . . it seemed the nicest thing anyone had said to her for ages. . . .

CHAPTER FOUR

Diane was not the only one to question the wisdom of Jo's taking her new holiday job. Dave, after hardly listening to her when she told him about it, expressed doubt when he gave her a lift home from the Center a few nights later.

"Are you sure you should spend your holiday working, Jo? I mean because of this feeling of obligation to him?"

"I'd rather spend it working for him in Corfu than go to Aunt Ruth, or stay home on my own."

"Yes, but. . . ." Dave pulled at his lip and looked unusually worried. He gave her a level look. "You're such an infant, Jo. I'd hate to think of you getting into something you might regret."

"But what could I regret?" Jo started to giggle. "Really, Dave, you're as bad as Diane. She can't think of a logical answer to why she picked on me. Because she can't see that the simple answer is the truth she imagines every kind of intrigue instead."

"Well, a working holiday seems a bit odd to me," Dave said stubbornly, "and I wish you hadn't taken it on."

"Why ever not? You don't think Sir Sheridan has designs on me, surely?"

Dave's mouth went down at the corners. "When you've seen as much of life as I've seen, Tich, you're never surprised at anything."

"But if I'm such an infant . . ." she prompted slyly.

He sighed, and the amber light from the street lamp revealed an expression in his eyes she'd never seen before—for herself. "That's just it. When I first saw you a couple of years ago, young Jo, you were very much an infant, just out of school and eager to sample living. When you see a person almost every other day for a long time you tend not to notice any change in them. But I'm trying to see you now as though I hadn't seen you at all during that time. I can see those changes, small and subtle though they are, quite strongly marked in you. You're growing up, Jo."

If Dave had said this to her at any time up to the previous week Jo would almost have swooned with delight. Only a week ago she would have gazed back soulfully at him and whispered, "*Am I, Dave?*" believing that at last her prayer was being answered. But this reaction did not occur to her this particular night. She merely returned his concerned gaze quite calmly and said, "I'm glad you've noticed it at last," in such a dry little voice he burst out laughing. He opened the car door, reaching across her and then leaning back to wait until she got out, as he had always done.

"Away you go. Have a good time and don't flirt with the gods—I'd hate to have to climb Olympus to rescue you."

"Would you?" She stooped to look back into the car, but his face was in shadow.

"Would I? I might be tempted to come and join you." His laughing goodnight was lost in the closing of the door. She stood back to watch till the car disappeared around the corner of the street.

Suddenly she felt so happy she didn't know how she was going to get through the next two days before the departure. Life had never seemed so full of excitement. She fussed and fidgeted through those two days, almost completing her packing at least three times; then starting all over again to make sure everything was all right, and she hadn't forgotten anything. She still hugged herself with delight every time she considered the results of the shopping spree with the advance on her salary. Diane had gone with her. Together they had chosen a selection of gorgeous holiday clothes. Diane had a flair for fashion and matched separates with skill and style. Best of all, when Jo's packing was finally completed the white crystal chiffon reposed amid layers of snowy tissue in Jo's new cream Luxan case.

They were leaving on the Friday evening flight, and none of Jo's secret forebodings happened. There was no

fog, there were no major traffic jams, and nothing unfore-
seen cropped up to prevent her from being at the airport
well in advance of the appointed time. No doubt some of
the credit for this belonged to the unflappable Diane who
seemed to have forgotten her earlier doubts and decided
to become an ally instead. She went with Jo to the airport
and did not miss the taken-aback expression on Jo's face
when Sir Sheridan arrived accompanied by an extremely
attractive young woman and a small boy who looked
about five years old.

"Wife and child!" hissed Diane, giving Jo a sly nudge.
"Watch your step, my girl, with high-and-handsome
there."

Jo couldn't speak. She was watching the slender girl in
the brown and white trouser suit. She was carrying a
white jacket, and her dark hair was caught back in a gay
orange pirate kerchief. She looked absurdly young to be
the mother of the diminutive boy, but his small features
were a miniature replica of hers—apart from having an
uncanny likeness to Sir Sheridan's.

They reached Jo and Diane. The girl half smiled, waiting for Sir Sheridan to make the introductions. He
looked down at Jo, and her mouth felt stiff as she
responded to his greeting. It was only this moment that
she realized how much she had looked forward to the
journey. Now everything was different. She'd never
expected anyone else to be there, still less. . . . She tried to
check her thoughts, fiercely ashamed of them and caught
the sound of her own name, and the words "sister" and
"nephew." The girl was laughing and taking Jo's hand.
Suddenly Jo was smiling joyously while her bemused
thoughts clamored anew. *His sister!* His sister Margaret
and her little son, Ricky. Why hadn't he mentioned that
his sister and nephew would be traveling with him? But
why should he tell her? Anyway, what did it matter . . . ?

It was a happy flight. Margaret seemed to have a
warm, impulsive nature very like Jo's own, and was easy
to talk to. Soon she and Jo were on first-name terms and
chattering as though they'd known each other for ages.
Ricky was a little shy at first, but this soon wore off. As

the time passed it became obvious that he was fighting sleepiness.

"It's his first flight," Margaret explained, trying to restrain him from setting off on a second exploratory trip down the length of the cabin.

"But I want to see where the pilot is," he protested.

"Maybe, but does the pilot want to see you?" Margaret teased.

Ricky looked mutinous and tried to wriggle free of his mother's grasp. Sir Sheridan glanced up from the papers he was studying and frowned. So far he had more or less left the two girls to talk to one another, once everyone had settled down and immersed himself in a long, extremely legal-looking document. Now he returned it to his briefcase and addressed Ricky solemnly.

"Does this plane really have a pilot?"

Ricky forgot about walking down the cabin and looked as though he couldn't believe the stupidity of grown-ups. "The pilot flies it, Uncle Dane."

"Really?" The solemn expression did not flicker. "I thought someone pressed a button somewhere and it took off."

"No, that's an elevator." Ricky vaguely knew he was being teased, but in this case he had no objection to the teaser. He got up and leaned against Sir Sheridan's knees. "Uncle Dane . . . why don't we have parachute drill like you have life jacket drill on a ship?"

Margaret gave a shudder of pretended horror and relaxed back, obviously thankful to leave her brother to deal with the complications of small-boy questions. Jo was content to listen, touched by his grave patience with the child. She longed to ask if "Dane" was his first name, or the family's corruption of Sheridan, but naturally could not indulge this desire. The name suggested a blond Viking, rugged and tawny from the sea winds; the total opposite to the dark urbane attorney with his dry, sophisticated humor and unconsciously arrogant self-possession. And yet the taut little name suited him, Jo decided in the sleepy silence that had stolen over aircraft and passengers. It could be a name to evoke echoes of a dark, enigmatic personality. . . .

The plane came down through the soft darkness of the Mediterranean night and instantly dispelled the inertia induced by the flight. The scent of strangeness was in the velvety air. A promise of sweet magic discovery veiled by the midnight blue that kept Corfu a mystery not to be known until dawn stole in from the east.

A car was waiting at the airport to meet the party, and Ricky fell asleep almost the moment he clambered in, his small dark head tousled against Sir Sheridan's shoulder. None of them talked much during the journey. After some 15 minutes or so the car slowed to a standstill. Jo saw the outline of a white villa glowing like moon-silver against the indigo sky. A golden lantern hung above a high archway that framed scrolled iron gates, and the lacy web of their shadow parted as the chauffeur thrust them open. Sir Sheridan carried in the sleeping Ricky.

Jo had a confused glimpse of a curved terrace, and a cascade of blossoms over a huge urn. Then more light spilled in an amber rectangle across her path. A woman was framed in the open doorway. She hurried out, her strong brown features warm with the welcome of recognition for Sir Sheridan. But her fingers went to her lips as she gave an exclamation of tenderness for the sleepily stirring little boy.

"This is Kyra," said Sir Sheridan, putting Ricky down and keeping a steadying arm around the small shoulders. "Go with her while I see to the luggage."

He went outside to where the chauffeur was unloading the cases. Jo did not see him again until the following morning. Kyra had a cold supper waiting for them and soup simmering, but Margaret was anxious to get Ricky to bed, and none of them was hungry. Jo's room was next door to Margaret's. Finally, to please Kyra, they took a tray up to Margaret's room and shared milk, cookies, and little buttered rolls filled with chicken while Margaret got Ricky ready for bed. "He'll still be up at the crack of dawn, even though it's nearly two in the morning already," she said ruefully, "so I'm going to leave my unpacking until tomorrow and salvage what's left of the night for sleep. And if you're wise you'll do the same."

"I'm going exploring with Uncle Dane tomorrow,"

Ricky announced as his mother hustled him into the small room adjoining hers. "And when 'fessor Quayle comes back from Athens we're going in his boat."

Ricky had it all planned, Jo thought when she was in her own room and sorting out her night things. Silence lay over the villa, and yet she had never felt so wide awake as she turned back the beautifully embroidered cover and climbed between exquisitely cool linen sheets. She did not immediately switch off her bedside lamp, but let her gaze wander around the big airy white room and its comfortable furnishings. The fragrance of roses stole in through the open window. The rich glowing colors of an *ikon* that hung above an age-darkened carved wood chest caught her interest. It would be of St. Spiridion, the island's saint, she thought, and lay back contentedly, wondering if the soft sighing sounds she could hear faintly were those of the sea.

She fell into a happy daydream of hot sun and silver sand: the scent of orange groves and the chaste tree blossom, white spume over wet gleaming rocks, colored sails against the sapphire sea and a small boy gambolling in the water. Nebulous in the dream was a man called Dane, darkly handsome and carefree of gait, quite a different person from the cynical man of legal fame. . . . She heaved a sleepy, little sigh and groped for the lamp switch. The next two weeks were going to be terrific! As long as you remember you have a job to do, her conscience reminded her as she surrendered herself to that enticing little dream. It almost seemed too good to be true. . . .

Sir Sheridan, however, seemed in no great hurry to commence work. He was finishing breakfast when Jo, Margaret, and Ricky came down the next morning.

A table had been set on the wide curving terrace, and the view it overlooked temporarily banished all thought of food from Jo's head. It was even better than the brochures!

The villa itself was perched on a green shelf on the hillside. Above and behind rose woodland clad in the silver of olive and the black of cypress; below the terrace a lawn sloped gently down to a low, rough wall hewed out of the rock. Beyond this the garden dropped away steeply and was lost in the depths of a ravine that plunged down to a sparkling sapphire bay. A narrow beach curved around it like a silver-gilt sickle. The water was so clear that from where Jo stood she could see the dappled mauves, purples, and greens of the sea gardens under the blue crystal. So this is the incredibly brilliant light of Greece, she thought; the fabled clarity of color that artists raved about. It transformed the sense of seeing into an aesthetic and sensuous experience beyond definition.

"Don't say it," said a low voice just above her head.

"What?" She looked around sharply.

"That you wish you could paint it," said Sir Sheridan in the same little mocking voice.

"I wasn't," she returned equably. "But I can't help wondering how many artists have torn their hair in frustration because they couldn't capture that depth of color."

"Enough to set up a wig industry, I should imagine." Imperceptibly his tone had changed. "There's a path down to the beach, should you feel like exploring after breakfast, but I'd advise dark glasses and a restriction on the tanning time for the first day or so." Giving her a cool smile, he donned his own dark glasses and sauntered down toward the lichen-covered wall. Obviously he was bound for the beach this morning.

Ricky was itching with impatience to follow, gobbling down his buttered roll and fruit juice, but Margaret seemed rather tired and quiet this morning, Jo thought. After a moment or so she amended "tired" to "tense." There was a suppressed air of strain about the older girl and for the first time Jo wondered about her husband. Perhaps he couldn't get away from his work, or was planning to join his wife and son later. Or perhaps they were one of those couples who had modern ideas about spending holidays apart. Though that wouldn't be my idea! Jo decided, hurriedly finishing her coffee in response to Ricky's impatient promptings.

They collected beach gear and made their way down the steep narrow path to the beach. There, Ricky spotted the tall figure in the distance and loped along the sand. The man and the small boy turned and waved, then set off for the rocks beneath the headland.

"Thank heaven!" Margaret sat down on the big towel and started to apply suntan lotion liberally to her arms. "Peace for an hour or so—you'd better have some of this, or you'll burn."

"Thanks." Jo began the Mediterranean ritual of anointing, and idly watched the two figures far along the beach. Even from this distance it was possible to discern the perfect trust in the small face upturned to the man's. As though Margaret had guessed at her thought she said, "Dane's wonderful with Ricky, though you wouldn't think it to look at him."

"Why not?" Jo didn't move.

"Well, he has that case-hardened veneer about him. Half the time he never lets his left hand know what his right's doing," said Margaret with sisterly candor. "And he can be really ruthless when he feels like it. But he has a soft spot for Ricky, always has had." She paused, her eyes reflective, and reached for her wide-brimmed straw hat. "I wish he would get himself married and have a son of his own—as long as it isn't Celia Wincroft."

The name had a vaguely familiar ring, but for the moment Jo couldn't pin down where she heard it. She longed to prompt Margaret's confidences regarding her brother, but knew she must restrain her curiosity. She stayed silent, and a moment or so later was rewarded.

Margaret turned over and propped herself on her elbows. "Are you a good judge of character, Jo?"

"I—I don't know." Jo was surprised. "I've never given it much thought. I just go by whether I take to people or not."

"Instinct, it's the same thing, I think." Margaret's brow furrowed. "Have you ever met her?"

"Celia Wincroft?"

Margaret nodded.

"No, but I seem to know the name."

"You should. Her father's Aldo Wincroft, the property developer. He—"

Jo gave a sharp exclamation. Now she remembered. This was the man who wanted the site on which the Center stood.

"He started in a rented back room with borrowed money, and now he's a millionaire—good luck to him," Margaret went on, "but I wish he hadn't turned his only daughter into such a spoiled brat she thinks she has only to crook her finger and every man will come running."

Jo remembered something else. She said slowly, "Does she have red hair?"

"That's right!" Margaret nodded. "You have met her?"

Jo shook her head and on impulse decided to tell Margaret the whole story. When she had finished Margaret was giggling as much as Jo.

"I'd love to have seen his face when you popped up in the car that night, though I can picture it pretty well," she gurgled. "It's the sort of thing I'd like to do myself, but wouldn't have the nerve." She looked at Jo with unfeigned admiration and dissolved again into merriment. "What a pity my lady Celia wasn't in the car that night, or, better still, down at the cottage when he landed there with you."

"Was it?" said Jo dryly. "From what you tell me about her I might have been clawed to shreds."

Margaret made a face. "She's coming on the weekend—changed her mind at the last minute. And I told Dane he'd be every kind of a fool if he changed his plans and waited to travel with her. Oh, it makes me livid!" Margaret said furiously, all her merriment gone. "They had a fearful bust-up just before that weekend you did your stowaway act. I was so delighted I could hardly keep my face straight. And then she calls up and gets around him as though nothing had happened. Honestly, Jo, why are men such fools over the bitch-goddesses of this world?"

"I don't know." Jo shook her head. She too had taken

on a doleful expression. "Maybe she'll meet somebody else."

Margaret sighed. "I've been hoping for that ever since she met Dane."

The two girls lapsed into silence, their faces upturned to the sun, and succumbed to indolence. But Jo's thoughts continued to revolve around her new employer. When she was back at the villa and having a light salad and fruit lunch with the others she could not help studying Sir Sheridan under cover of the light-hearted table conversation. It was strange how he now possessed two co-existing personalities; the one she knew, and the one she glimpsed through his sister. She found it difficult to reconcile the imperturbable Sir Sheridan with the Dane who was Margaret's brother. She found it even more difficult to imagine him ever being a fool over a woman, no matter how gorgeous a bitch-goddess she happened to be. It was much easier to imagine women losing their hearts and their heads to him. And she didn't think Celia Wincroft was as irresistible as all that. After all, it was a darned sight easier to be glamorous on a millionaire dress allowance and no doors barred to the most exclusive beauty salons than to have to manage on a shoestring budget like countless no less attractive girls had to in less fortunate circumstances.

However, she temporarily forgot her curiosity about the red-haired enchantress. The Professor returned that day, and his nephew came in on the night flight from London.

Professor Quayle wasn't in the least like the somewhat terse and acid character Jo had imagined from the glimpses of him afforded by his television appearances. Erudite he certainly was, but dry, never. He possessed a droll sense of humor that sparked an immediate response in Jo. When Sir Sheridan, outrageously wicked, informed him that Jo had expected a dour, forbidding character he turned a sardonic eye to the attorney.

"You know, I've noticed the same thing in the way you come over—must be the make-up."

"Or real nature showing through," Margaret teased her brother.

Jo decided she liked the Professor very much. She also decided she liked his nephew, Alan Quayle. He was a quietly spoken, fair-haired man somewhere in his early 30s who didn't have a great deal of idle small talk, but when he did have something to say it was usually to the point. He was a research chemist with a small, independent pharmaceutical firm. An accident in childhood had left him with a limp. But he did not allow it to affect his activities any more than he could help, and he cheerfully indulged in the scampering and rough and tumble that Ricky adored. He also possessed an understanding that oddly touched Jo when they went down to the beach the following morning. She had already noticed that Ricky was very wary of deep water. He never ventured beyond knee-deep splashing distance of the water's edge. When Margaret or his uncle plunged in to swim he immediately came out and went solemnly about his own mysterious pursuit that involved a great pile of pebbles at the base of the cliff.

This morning, however, Ricky was anxious to investigate the sleek little white and blue painted motorboat belonging to the Professor. Their host was amiable; the boat was there whenever they felt inclined to take to the sea, but Sir Sheridan shook his head when Ricky looked expectantly at him.

"No boating for people who can't swim, I'm afraid."

Margaret said nothing, and Ricky's face fell. "It won't sink, Uncle Dane."

"No, but you might fall out, little 'un."

"I won't."

Alan said, "Well, you'd better learn to swim. Come on." He held out his hand, but Ricky turned away. His small face set mutinously.

Margaret sighed. "It's hopeless. He won't. I've given up trying. Some idiot threw him in last year, and he had a fright. So I decided just to wait until he's a little bit older."

There was a silence. Jo looked at the unhappy little boy, but before she could speak Alan had bent down and whispered something to him. Ricky fidgeted, still uncertain, and Alan said something else that none of the others could catch. Ricky ran to his mother.

"Is that true? Was my daddy a terrific swimmer?"

"He most certainly was," said Sir Sheridan before his sister could speak.

"And would he be sad if I never learned to swim like he did?"

Margaret nodded, and something that had puzzled Jo was now clear. The past tense in the child's words, and the glimpsed sadness clouding Margaret's eyes told their own heartbreak. Margaret was widowed.

Jo said abruptly, "I can't swim, either, Ricky, but I've always wanted to learn."

Ricky was wavering, and she jumped to her feet. "Anyone willing to give *me* a swimming lesson?"

"We'll all teach you!" three voices cried.

"And don't laugh at me," she enjoined as they closed around her, laughing.

As she had expected, Ricky followed the little group down to the sparkling ripples. He watched as she plunged in valiantly and threshed her way into deeper water, only to submerge and come up spluttering. Through the water in her ears she heard the distorted voice of Sir Sheridan.

"You two take Ricky between you. I'll see that Jo doesn't swim away with the dolphins."

"Dolphins! Are there dolphins?" cried Ricky.

It was a magic word, and it got him into the water, Alan and Margaret already indulging in a splashing match to gain his confidence. Meanwhile Sir Sheridan quirked humorous brows at Jo. "Can you swim at all? Even the dog paddle?"

"No." She fell into step with him as he began to walk along by the water's edge. "You see, I lived most of my childhood in a country village inland. There was no river nearby where one could swim safely. The nearest town with a swimming pool was 30 miles away." She shrugged wryly. "So it was sort of left out of my very small repertoire of achievements."

"And what didn't get left out?" he asked idly.

"Oh. . . ." She thought for a moment, looking down at the creamy ripples feathering over her toes. "Not very much, I'm afraid. I like lots of things—music and poetry and dancing—but I don't know enough about them to be able to express myself through their mediums," she admitted candidly. "I often wish there was something I was really expert at."

"Perhaps your talents lie in some less obvious field. Such as dealing with very difficult situations."

"Is that a talent?" she asked, laughing.

"It most certainly is." He stooped to pick up a particularly lustrous shell through which the timeless action of the sea had worn a smooth hollow. He held it up and squinted at the blue circle of sky it enclosed and said carelessly, "Some gimmick merchant would charge the earth for that—it's almost a natural ring."

"Oh, don't!" she exclaimed as he seemed about to toss it back into the sea.

"Do you want it?" He dropped it into her outstretched hand and sprang up onto a narrow ledge of rock along the base of the cliff. "Come on. Never mind about shell jewelry. There's a mooring ring along here that's about right for hanging onto."

Still interested in the pinky-blue mother-of-pearl in the shell that just fitted on her little finger, she followed him along the ledge, then looked down into pellucid water that seemed frighteningly deep. There was the thick old iron mooring ring trailing ferny green fronds just an inch or so above water level. Here it seemed was where her swimming tuition was to begin. He dived in and came up, treading water with the ease of one perfectly at home in the element.

"Well, come on."

"What, me?" She backed a step. "In there? It looks about a mile deep. Can't I start where it's shallow?"

"Presently. But I want you to get the buoyancy here

while you master the leg stroke," he explained patiently. "Then you can go in the shallows and try to co-ordinate both arm and leg movements."

He turned over and swam in a small neat circle below the surface; a sheer show-off that made scarcely a ripple and surfaced to tread water again. His hair glistened jet-dark now that it was soaked. His torso was unexpectedly muscular for a man whose occupation entailed spending a great deal of time in dry and musty courtrooms. He grinned a challenge. "Scared? I once passed a proficiency test in lifesaving, if that's any encouragement."

"I think you're trying to inveigle me into one of those difficult situations." With a sigh that audibly called on the fates not to desert her, she sat down on the ledge and slid awkwardly into the silken sea.

He proved an efficient teacher. Whether it was because he inspired confidence or that she had, as he told her, a natural aptitude, she found it wasn't nearly as difficult as she'd expected. Back in the shallows she tended to flounder during the first few attempts to harmonize arms and legs and remember everything he had told her, but she persisted again and again, until she felt the rhythm beginning to flow through her body

Ricky had arrived to watch. When she bumped aground and stood up laughing breathlessly he shook his head. "Uncle Dane ought to hold your chin like Mummy does. Watch."

He spreadeagled his little body in about nine inches of water and looked up expectantly at his mother. Indulgently she obeyed, and he set off in a comical little crab paddle that was entirely his own.

"Maybe he's right. One more try," said the deep, amused voice as Jo returned to her labors. A firm, warm hand cupped itself under Jo's chin. The tall figure stooped over her, drawing her gradually into deeper water. "Keep going—you're doing fine," he encouraged. "Feet together, smooth strokes. . . ."

Suddenly it felt marvelous. There was a joyous buoyancy and sense of freedom, as though she was going with the water and not against it. The sun was dancing across the ripples, as though it beckoned her on, and she opened her mouth to exclaim her joyous triumph. In the same moment she saw Sir Sheridan's head in front of her, almost level with her own. In the panic of realization that he also was swimming, her cry turned to a gasp as she swallowed what felt like a pint of the Ionian Sea. Suddenly she was floundering again, groping desperately with her toes for the sand bottom that wasn't there, and a voice said sharply, "Don't panic—I have you. Stay still."

Hands held her, and a dark head bobbed in front of her. He grinned at her scared face. "Look! You can swim!"

"How did I get here?" she gasped, seeing the shore a long way beyond the shimmering ripples. "I—I can't—can't—"

"Relax—I'll tow you in."

With the crisp command he gave an agile twist and put one arm under her shoulders. She saw a vast expanse of sky above, and with a vague idea of being helpful she started to kick. "Stop it," he said, "or I'll let you go."

She stopped, and the strong body beneath her resumed its smooth stroke. Suddenly she forgot the moments of panic when she realized how far out she had come. She was enjoying herself again. There was something rather satisfying about the hard arm hooked under her and across her throat . . . it would be pleasant to drift for hours in the warm turquoise silk under that immense blue sky. . . .

"Bravo!"

"Well saved!"

"Sure you weren't trying to drown her?"

Sir Sheridan left Jo sprawling in the wavelets and turned purposefully toward his sister. Her grin vanished, and she did not wait for his reply before she ran fleetly along the beach toward the cliff path. Ricky immediately joined in the chase, and Alan picked up his towel and held out a friendly hand to Jo.

They were all imbued now with the carefree abandon of holiday time as they made their way up the steep ascent to the villa. Jo's eyes sparkled as brightly as the little crystals of sea water that beaded her hair and clung to her sun-rosy shoulders. They had almost reached the bend near the top when she dropped back a little, obeying Ricky's command to look at some insect he had spotted on a leaf.

"I don't know what it is," she said. "Don't touch it in case it stings."

But Ricky's mercurial attention had already shifted elsewhere. "Who's that?" he asked, pointing.

"Where?" She straightened, looking around, and saw the stranger sitting on the low wall that edged the villa garden.

The man turned his head and looked toward them, but the glare of the sun prevented Jo seeing his face clearly. Then he stood up and held out his hands. A cry escaped Margaret. The next moment she was running the short distance that separated her from the newcomer. Their voices mingled with the loud squeal of recognition that Ricky gave.

"It's Uncle Neil!"

Jo gave a small exclamation as she saw the newcomer enfold Margaret in his arms. She was vaguely aware of Alan's sharp exclamation as he came to a halt beside her. Then she looked at the other tall figure that had now halted by the shallow steps up to the garden.

Sir Sheridan was watching the greeting with such angry eyes that Jo felt surprise. All his banter had gone, leaving sheer displeasure in every line of his grim expression; even the set of his shoulders seemed to echo his disapproval.

Margaret was turning to him, her eyes glowing and her hand still within that of the newcomer. Jo held her breath. Sir Sheridan looked as though he might hit somebody.

Then, unbelievably, he was smiling and making a casual greeting to the man that Margaret was calling Neil.

Jo heard her own name and found herself automatically shaking Neil's hand and meeting a pair of dark brown eyes that were frankly assessing. She withdrew her hand from a clasp that had lingered a trifle too long and looked again at Sir Sheridan.

His expression had re-formed into its more usual, enigmatic appearance. Jo blinked. He caught her puzzled look and raised one brow quizzically. She shook her head. She must have imagined it all.

But later she knew that she hadn't.

CHAPTER FIVE

Neil Clinton was the complete opposite of Alan. He was as dark as his cousin was fair, as flamboyant as the other was quiet, as blatantly sensuous as the older man was sensitive. He could no more help exerting his undoubted charm than Ricky could resist the lure of the gorgeous emerald-green Italian car in which Neil was planning to drive home across Europe.

"That's why I took so long to get here," he was explaining as they all turned involuntarily toward the big car. "I've just come off the ferry."

They gathered around it while he extolled the perfections of its design; the gadgets that did practically everything except read the map for the driver, and the sheer opulent comfort of its silver and white upholstery. Ricky was entranced, Margaret openly admiring, Alan appreciative in the way men are of other men's cars, and Sir Sheridan remarkably knowledgeable of the finer technical points that have a language quite their own. Only the Professor did not seem unduly impressed.

"How much did that set you back?" he said dourly.

Neil grinned. "Ssh—it's on the firm."

"And how do you think the firm'll stand it?" the Professor grunted and went indoors.

Neil pulled a face that did not convey as much respect for his stepfather as one might judge was due and said, "Well, who wants to be first to try her?" his glance was on Margaret's glowing face.

"Me!" Ricky cried.

Neil aimed a dig at him. "Sure. Anybody know if there's anything exciting to see on this island?"

"I have a guide book somewhere," Margaret said eagerly.

In the end only Jo, Ricky, and Margaret set off with Neil to explore the northern half of the island. After lunch Sir Sheridan announced that he had plans of his own, but at Jo's hesitation insisted that she join the outing. Alan said he didn't feel inclined to do any driving. Afterward, Jo wished she had cried off as well. Neil and Margaret obviously wanted to be together. Ricky grew restless sitting in the car after a very short time. When they returned that evening Jo retained only confused memories of where they'd gone. Neil was the restless kind of tourist who never stopped long enough in one place to absorb its quality. Consequently the succession of ever-changing vistas of mountains, valleys, villages and groves, and the intense blue of the sea, never missing for long, became difficult to pinpoint and identify when the time came for reminiscence over the leisurely evening meal at the villa.

Jo made up her mind later that night that she would suggest that Ricky spend the next day with her on their own beach: it would give Margaret a chance of being on her own with Neil, to whom she was plainly attracted. Jo's romantic imagination leaped ahead: Margaret couldn't be more than 23 or 24, which was terribly young to be left alone with a young child. It would be marvelous if she could fall in love again and make a second happy marriage. . . .

But Jo's tentative suggestion to Ricky next morning did not go unheard, nor did it appear to find any favor. Ricky was quite happy at the thought of a day on the beach, but it seemed that Sir Sheridan and Alan were now bitten with a desire to explore. So this time two cars set off on a day-long tour of the enchanting isle.

They lunched in a tiny fishing village and wandered through a sylvan grove where wild marsh orchids made dapples of mauve, and the silvery ferns rippled with each whisper of breeze, then they lazed, swam, and soaked up more sun and drove again. Evening found them dining and dancing in the more sophisticated surroundings of the Corfu Palace Hotel, from whence they idled their way back through the scented night to sleep like satyrs sated with the wine of the sun.

The day was to set the pattern for the rest of that week; a pattern of sheer indulgence in sybaritism that was all too easy to surrender to, Jo decided in one of her now rare moments alone. All the same, idyllic as the days had been, she was sure she wasn't imagining an undertone of ennui creeping into the party. Margaret had become rather quieter, and Neil was beginning to betray a hint of restlessness, as though he might decide to move on if the whim took him. It wasn't easy to tell what Alan was thinking, he was too equable in temperament. It was never possible to read personal motive or feeling in Sir Sheridan when he chose to be enigmatic, which was most of the time, Jo thought. He still appeared though to be in light-hearted holiday mood and sold on the theme of togetherness. Somehow it didn't ring true in him, she reflected, then wondered why she should have this impression. After all, why should she try to define his outward aspects of character? She certainly didn't know him well enough to judge with any accuracy. And what about work?

Jo frowned, conscious of a stab of guilt. For the past few days she'd almost forgotten that she was supposed to be here to work, but when she thought of her generous salary and travel expenses she felt like a fraud. She looked down at her bare arms where they rested indolently on the cool stone top of the terrace rail and could not help a sigh of satisfaction as she contemplated her deepening tan. In the amber glow of the overhead lamps her skin looked dark gold, and the crystal white of Diane's dress heightened the contrast. It was a dream of a dress to dance in, except that. . . . Her lashes shadowed her eyes, and she gave a tiny sigh as she let her thoughts range back to the night they'd all gone dancing. They'd met a group of young people who were on holiday at the hotel that week. Somehow she was drawn in with them, more than the others were. So she had danced only once with Neil, who was so expert and challenging a partner she found him difficult to keep up with, and only once with Sir Sheridan, who had been faultless to dance with but quite oblivious to the dress that seemed to do so much for her. And he hadn't offered any more swimming lessons, either. . . .

Abruptly she straightened and banished the silly little musings. Perhaps if she remembered the real reason for her presence here and reminded her employer—gently, of course—that time was slipping by and was it wise to leave everything to the last minute . . . ? She turned and looked back through the wide French windows into the brilliantly lit room. The Professor and Alan were quite near the open windows, and she guessed they were still engrossed in their argument over the theory that Corfu was the island of *The Tempest*. Neil was in the alcove where the miniature cocktail bar curved like a silver and amethyst half-moon, and he laughed as he wielded a cocktail shaker for the benefit of Margaret who was protesting. Neil and his efforts to invent a new Grecian cocktail! Jo's searching glance moved on, failing to find the object of her search. She was about to forget the impulse when a movement behind her made her spin around, giving a small exclamation as she did so.

"Hello—did I startle you?" said Sir Sheridan.

"Do you always creep up on people like that?"

"Creep?" His brows went up.

"Well, loom out of the darkness," she said defensively.

"I was merely having a breath of air, the same as you yourself are doing." He touched her shoulder, inclining his head toward the spill of light from the villa. "Come on, I'll mix you a drink to steady your nerves."

"No, thanks, I—"

"Of course, I tend to forget—you eschew the demon."

She tried to see his expression, but the shadows made its subtleties undefinable. "Don't laugh," she said with a tartness that surprised herself. "My nerves are perfectly steady, thank you."

"But I wasn't laughing," he assured her earnestly. "I actually envy the sturdy independence of people like yourself who have such strength of character."

She wasn't convinced and looked at him with a wide searching gaze in which doubt was more clear than she realized.

He moved, leaning back against the parapet, and the amber lamplight now fell directly onto his face. There wasn't a flicker of the amusement she had suspected, and she sighed and looked away.

"Are you enjoying yourself here?" he asked suddenly.

"Oh yes!" But her small features held such a seriousness as she faced him again that his brows quirked an instant querying response.

"Something concerns you?"

"Yes," she took a deep breath, "actually I was looking for you just now. I was wondering . . . Sir Sheridan, we've been here over a week now, and we haven't done any work. I mean, if there's a lot to do we don't want to be rushing at the last minute."

For a long moment he looked steadily at her, then he sighed. "I suppose you're right. Shall we have a serious talk about it?"

"If you can be serious about it," she said severely.

"So serious you may regret it," he said enigmatically and straightened. "Let's find a spot where we won't be interrupted."

Without waiting for her assent he led the way from the terrace, along to the black lacy web of the tall gate at the end. It clanged dully as he pushed it open and motioned her down the moon-silvered steps to the garden. The cypresses flanked the path like tall guardians in black velvet; a goddess ageless as time clasped her cool stone draperies about her smooth sculpted limbs. There was a small paved niche under the shadow of the cypresses, and an old fountain veiled in lichen. The great honey-colored moon cut a silvery stairway over the midnight sea. Sir Sheridan stopped and lounged against one of the vast ornamental urns that dotted the villa grounds. He regarded her thoughtfully.

"So you think it's time we toiled."

"You are paying me to toil," she said simply.

He smiled wryly. "What a conscientious child you are, Jo."

She experienced a flash of irritation. "What's wrong with being conscientious? And I'm not a child!"

"I wonder. . . ." His gaze was still thoughtful. "Then tell me, Jo, as a woman how would you react to a philanderer?"

"A philanderer?" she echoed. "But why? Who?" She took a step back, suspicion beginning to struggle with amazement at his totally unexpected question. "I don't understand. Not . . . not you?"

"Heavens, no!" he exclaimed, almost irritably. "It's quite simple. If you're not a child then you must be a woman, or consider yourself so. Do you know a philanderer when you meet one?"

"Well, yes," she said helplessly, wondering where on earth all this was leading. "But what does it have to do with all this?"

"Everything." He shifted his position and sought his cigarette case. "It's quite simple," he repeated. "Take a man, no one in particular, just a man. Attractive, well-dressed, amusing, a playboy type whose least worry is lack of funds. Supposing he pays attention to you. You feel attracted to him, but you know he's attractive to women and invariably successful with them. His reputation isn't exactly all that it should be. How would you react?"

"I—I don't know." She shook her head. "I've never met a handsome philanderer with pots of money. But how do I know he's as bad as people say?"

"That's the point, you don't—until somebody warns you." The trace of irritation sharpened his voice again. "But can't you tell? I mean, doesn't a woman's instinct warn her?"

"I think mine would." Jo was getting over her surprise. "I think I should run as fast as I could."

"I doubt it." He ground the cigarette under his toe and regarded her soberly. "As far as I can tell, a woman invariably seems blind to the fact that she's being—how shall I describe it?" he gestured. "Taken advantage of is such a Victorian-sounding expression."

"Used?" said Jo, tonelessly.

"Yes, used. Blunt but apt." His mouth compressed. "Perhaps you can throw some light on why they go like moths to the flame, then weep when their wings are singed."

There was a silence. He stared past her, at the mirror-like sea and the midnight curtain of the heavens that fell imperceptibly into the silvery dark rim of the far horizon.

Jo gazed at it, aware of the tendrils of breeze stirring her hair, cool on the nape of her neck. She smoothed back a wisp and said in a small voice, "I don't know, unless that's part of the attraction. But what's it to do with the job?"

"Nothing." He did not move. "But I might as well tell you now; I have no intention at all of spending my holiday toiling."

Jo's mouth parted and closed again. She looked up at his shadowed profile. "Then why did you bring me here?"

She heard his deeply indrawn breath and found she was tensing when he turned his head to face her. Then his faint smile came.

He said slowly, "Let's say it was a last minute inspiration that might, or might not, prove useful."

"Useful? I'm not sure I care for that word after. . . ." She looked up at him, unaware that her wide eyes pleaded for an explanation that wasn't going to destroy any illusions. She said steadily, "Before we came away you told me you just wanted me to be around when you needed me. Now it seems you don't. Wasn't it a rather expensive inspiration?"

"I think I'm the best judge of that," he said with just enough coolness in his tone to make her stiffen defensively. Then he said on an altered note, "You seem to have hit it off quite well with my sister."

"With Margaret? I like her very much. And Ricky too." Jo still betrayed puzzlement as she met his intent stare.

"Does she confide in you?" he asked abruptly.

Jo checked a small exclamation. She stared back, various things beginning to dovetail and make sense, even though she still couldn't fathom where she herself came in. She said warily, "It depends on what you mean by confiding."

His mouth hardened. "She's attracted to Neil Clinton, isn't she?"

"Well, a little bit, maybe," Jo said cautiously. "I think he's attracted to her as well."

"So you have noticed something."

Stung by the note of sarcasm, Jo said sharply, "Yes, I have. That's why I wondered at the way you planned things this week. I thought you might have. . . ." She saw the storm clouds in his dark gaze and faltered into silence.

"You thought I might give them every opportunity of being alone together, is that it?" he said angrily.

"Well, why not?" She gave a helpless little gesture. "Neil's good fun, and—and he seems to be very generous."

"Generous! That's exactly what I was trying to drive home to you five minutes ago. Can't you see what Neil Clinton is?"

"A bit of a playboy, I suppose," she said in a tone of doubt, "but I don't think Margaret will take him very seriously. After all, she's on holiday, and—"

"Neil Clinton is an out-and-out womanizer. I'll prevent her from having the chance to take him seriously, if it's the last thing I do," he gritted.

She was startled by the vehemence in his words, then a suspicion occurred. She turned away. "If you're going to ask me to spy on your sister—then the answer's no. I won't."

"I've no intention of asking you to spy on Margaret—it isn't necessary. I should have thought that was obvious," he added sarcastically.

Jo bit her lip. "Then what exactly are you going to ask me to do, Sir Sheridan?" she said quietly.

"I'm not really sure." The small negative movement of his head was wry. "But I *am* sure it's time you forgot the formal bit. My family and friends call me Dane, or hadn't you noticed?"

"I had, but then I could hardly regard myself as belonging to either of those categories," she returned gently. "After all, strictly speaking, you are my employer at present, even though the actual employment element seems to be missing up to now."

"Jo. . . ." Abruptly his tone changed, and he put one arm lightly around her shoulders, "I think we'll also dispense with that quibble. For one thing it's not really in keeping with the holiday spirit. For another it's already served it's purpose."

"Already?" Jo knew she was falling into the irritating habit of echoing his words, but she couldn't help it. "What do you mean?"

"It was the only pretext on which I could bring you here—though perhaps we may don our spectacles and city togs tomorrow and adjourn to the Professor's study for an hour, to allay any doubts that may occur," he said quickly, propelling her along toward an old stone bench in a manner that was distinctly confiding. "Let's sit down. I'll explain everything."

Warmth ebbed from her shoulders when his arm dropped away, and she could not repress a tiny shiver. Despite the darkness he did not miss this and checked his movement to sit down. "You're cold—I'll get your wrap."

"No—" she put out a hand "—don't. I'm quite warm, thank you." Unaccountably, her heart was beating a lot faster than usual as she sat down at one end of the bench and adjusted the folds of her dress carefully, so that they did not trail the ground. She composed her hands and looked at him expectantly.

"I don't know if Margaret told you," he began as he sat down. "She was widowed two years ago when Peter's car was in one of those expressway pile-ups during fog. She was completely bereft, declared she'd never marry again, that no man could ever take Peter's place. Naturally we respected her grief. We knew it was natural, even as we knew that time would eventually heal it and make her reconsider her avowal. She's young and very warm-hearted by nature. She needs love as much as young Ricky needs a father. It's quite unthinkable that she should go through the rest of her life alone."

Dane paused, the silver of the moon reflected in his thoughtful eyes. He went on: "Alan Quayle wants to marry her, and I can't think of a better choice. If only he's left to win her in his own way. Unfortunately, unless Margaret gives him a little encouragement I'm afraid he'll be too late in making a decisive move. He's conscious of his limp, I know. I'm just afraid that he thinks it might matter to her."

"I don't think so," Jo said. "If she loves him enough it won't make a scrap of difference."

"Meaning that you would support my theory?" Dane turned his head. "That what a man considers an infirmity holds no significance for a woman?"

"Not in the least. At least it wouldn't if she loved him."

Dane nodded, and his mouth curved with a hint of irony. "I've long suspected that the reverse is true. Where a man's instincts may evoke sympathy or pity, a woman's will evoke a fierce desire to love and protect from the rest of the world. But that's beside the point," he interjected more briskly. "I doubt if my sister knows her feelings regarding Alan, but now Clinton's on the scene she's less likely than ever to recognize them."

"Aren't you underrating her ability to judge people?"

"No. Because no woman—or man, for that matter—can judge impartially while they're infatuated with the object they would judge."

"Yes, but she may not be serious about him." Jo had an urge to supply comfort. "I'm sure she's very sensible, and whatever she does I'm sure she'll do what's best for Ricky's future as well."

"Not with Clinton." Dane leaned back and crossed his knees. "Neil Clinton is selfish, shallow, and basically incapable of being faithful to any woman. To start with, he's married. His wife left him three years ago. Since then he's had a succession of women. At first I never imagined he'd be attracted to Margaret; she isn't his type at all, but it seems I was mistaken. Now that I think it over it isn't so unusual after all. When he first met her about four months ago she was just beginning to emerge from her sadness. We could see the girl we'd always known coming back to life. But because she loved her husband very much there is still a subconscious feeling of guilt that it's disloyal to enjoy herself with another man. Alan understands this; he's prepared to give her time, but Clinton would plunge her headlong into an affair. It's only that sense of restraint that's stopped her falling into his arms. Every time I see her with him I see the danger signals."

Dane paused and took a deep breath. "I have to do something about it. I can't stand by and watch my sister waste herself on a man like Neil Clinton. Because I know exactly what would happen. She would have an affair with him and be deliriously happy for a few months, then he would ditch her. And she'd face heartache and disillusion. Worse, she'd feel guilty and disloyal every time she remembered Peter." Dane's mouth set grimly. "Somehow I have to stop her."

"But how can you?" Jo sat up very straight. "You can't very well forbid her to see him—she's not an irresponsible child. And you couldn't possibly keep tabs on her indefinitely."

"I know. Fortunately in this respect, she's not quite free to indulge in the round of night-life that Clinton's addicted to." Dane smiled sardonically. "Even you must realize that a child is a rein on one's personal freedom. Consequently Margaret can't drop everything and go when he decides to call. It's my guess that this could be part of the reason his interest has lasted so long. Particularly as he isn't quite the type to be a home-loving family man."

Jo nodded thoughtfully. There had been one or two incidents already that confirmed this. The previous day, for instance, when Ricky had had one of those flare-in-a-moment upsets very few young children escape. He'd been quite feverish in the night, and Margaret had been dubious about letting him get up. Whereupon Neil had concurred too readily that a day in bed was the most sensible answer, but that Kyra would care for him just as well as Margaret could. But Margaret had stubbornly refused to go out, so they had all lounged around all morning. By lunchtime Ricky was demanding to be up and so obviously recovered that everyone was too thankful to argue. And then he'd jumped off a rock, missed his footing and tumbled, gashing his knee. Neil had just looked on helplessly while Margaret tried to comfort him and haul him back to the villa for first aid. It had been Alan who had taken over without any fuss, dressed the knee, and actually had poor Ricky laughing—albeit a little wanly—before he had finished. Yes, Jo thought, he'd be a far better stepfather for Ricky, but would he be the right man for Margaret? No matter how kind and suitable he might be it was no use if Margaret didn't love him. . . .

"And you see," Dane was saying worriedly, "the circumstances here are infinitely more favorable. There's no shortage of baby-sitters in the villa if she did decide to seize some freedom."

"Yes." Jo sighed, a little touched that he should make her his confidante. She attempted a note of cheer. "But there's only two weeks to go—it's not very long. And didn't he say he was going to the States next month?"

Dane's mouth tightened. "That's true, but a lot can happen in two weeks. It's a hell of a long time to try to keep two people apart when the man's bent on conquest."

"But we're all here—it's not as if they were alone," Jo insisted. "And there's Ricky. That's why you've made sure we all went everywhere together, this week, isn't it?"

He nodded. "Originally I had planned to bring Mellie with me. She's very fond of Margaret and doesn't like the sound of Neil Clinton at all." His mouth curved ironically. "Mellie would have played gooseberry like an expert and relished the role. She's old enough and iron-willed enough to ignore Margaret's feelings and Clinton's annoyance if she thought it was for the best."

There was a silence, then Jo looked at him. "Don't you think you're being a little unfair to your sister?" she asked at last. "I mean, she may be fully aware of Neil's reputation, and—and—" she gestured helplessly, not sure how to frame what she wanted to say, "well, maybe just enjoying having Neil take notice of her."

Dane shook his head. "It isn't as simple as that." He turned and looked at Jo's earnest expression, and his own expression softened. "Perhaps I shouldn't talk in this way to you, Jo, but I want you to understand. Margaret isn't a young, unawakened girl hesitating on the brink of her first love affair, even though in years she's still very youthful. I don't want Neil Clinton to be the man who re-awakens her to love. Yet it's bound to happen. Once a woman has known love in its completeness the longing is very quickly aroused again. But when it happens to Margaret I want it to be the start of a permanent relationship with a man who will be husband, father, and partner as well as lover; not merely a transient physical affair that will leave her out on a limb when Neil tires of her, as he's tired of all the others."

Jo sighed. "It sounds awfully sad told that way."

"It's worrying as well as sad when it concerns a sister I happen to be very fond of," he said somewhat tartly.

"No, I didn't mean just Margaret in particular," she said slowly. "I meant how awful it must be to fall in love with someone, trust them, and then find they don't want you. What is it that makes two people fall in love and then end up hating each other?" she murmured wonderingly.

"If we knew the answer to that one it would wipe out at least half the heartbreak in today's world," he said flatly. "Perhaps eventually we'll solve it by computer analysis of a person's temperament and match lovers accordingly," he added dryly.

Jo could not check a small horrified exclamation. "How cold-blooded. Love by computer! It would take all the mystery, all the wonder—it wouldn't be love!"

"You think not?" He sounded amused.

"No, and neither do you, if you're honest," she cried. "You wouldn't be so worried about Margaret if you believed in that awful theory."

"I'm not sure I believe in love any longer," he said in dry tones. "And when you're a bit older you may change that starry-eyed idea of it too."

"But I want to believe in it." Her eyes took on a distant look, for the moment unguarded, as they sought the dark unfathomable reaches of the night. "If one doesn't begin by believing in love instead of hate, and goodness instead of evil, how *is* one to believe? In bitterness, selfishness?"

"I think you're going in a bit deeper there," he said, "and much farther than the man-woman relationship."

"No," she shook her head, "because it's part of it, one of the mainsprings. Shared love brings happiness. When people are happy they don't go around spreading their misery among other people."

"Simply put, but true," he nodded. "But is the price of failure worth the risk?"

"You don't have to think of it that way."

"Not even when you know that each failed relationship erodes a little more of one's trust and one's faith?"

"I think so," she said softly.

"It's very obvious that no one's yet really hurt you." His dark eyes were searching her small luminous features upturned to the silver moon. "You haven't the remotest idea of what it's like to have illusions destroyed, and, even worse, one's inherent trust gradually replaced by suspicion of human nature."

She was aware of his gaze, and suddenly, with a wave of unsteadiness, acutely aware of him. She wondered if he was thinking of Celia; if beneath that seemingly imperturbable façade of his he hid hurt and disillusion. Did he see in Neil Clinton the same qualities of attraction and the same destructive failings as he had found in Celia? Was he still desperately in love with her even as he knew she might use him as selfishly as he feared Neil Clinton might use his sister?

The thought filled Jo with a strong sense of depression, and again came that odd little desire to bring comfort. She looked up. "Sir Sher—I mean Dane—" A wave of confusion made her stammer and blush absurdly. "I—I think—"

"Yes, we seem to have digressed somewhat," he cut in with a return to his normal crispness. He slid back his cuff to peer at his watch and made as though to rise. "We'd better get back. Come on, young Jo. They'll think we're—"

The trite little "lost" ebbed into silence as Jo impulsively reached out a detaining hand. "Oh, no. Please . . . we must get this straight."

He sank down again. "Get what straight?"

"Well, this. Me." She gestured awkwardly. "All this salary you've paid me, and this holiday. I feel as though I'm here under false pretenses."

"Now, Jo, don't start that again," he warned. "I don't

usually commandeer people to suit my own plans without making some recompense."

"Yes, but it seems wrong," she protested. "And it's quite obvious you never had any intention of doing any work here."

"No," his brows went up, "I *do* actually have a couple of tapes to transcribe, and some case notes I should do. We'll have a go at them next week if it'll make you any happier."

"It would," she said firmly. "Then I wouldn't feel such a fraud."

"And of course there was the fact that I knew this party was going to be very unevenly balanced on the male-female ratio," he added, "apart from the vague notion I had of trying to keep Margaret and Clinton apart. I also felt certain that she would take to you. In nature you're not unlike her, when she was 17."

"Going on 19."

"Nearly 19—I apologize," he amended in amused tones.

Jo was silent. She was still a little puzzled and now disappointed. It seemed such a pointless thing to do, spending all that money to bring her here for two weeks, merely to help make up the number and with the vague idea that in a party of guests he might be able to stop his sister falling victim to Neil Clinton. Why hadn't he taken Margaret and Ricky off on a holiday somewhere else? Or. . . . To her chagrin, Jo found she couldn't think of any more answers on the spur of the moment. All the same, it wasn't exactly what she would have wished for herself. It made her feel more beholden to Sir Sheridan than ever. She hated feeling beholden to anyone, especially him, she decided in a sudden flash of discovery. She wished she. . . . She frowned, not quite able to define this either. But one thing was clear; she would have expected him to formulate a crisp plan of action without any of this difficulty. It just didn't seem to fit the picture she'd formed of him. . . .

"And so," he broke in musingly, "it's as I said; just one

of those irrational impulses I decided to act on. So I forbid you to have any more fraudulent feelings."

"I didn't think lawyers were subject to irrational impulses."

"Lawyers are human like anyone else." He looked amused again. "Believe it or not, we have our lighter moments. We have even been known to fall in love."

She did not smile, and he touched her arm. "It's getting late. . . ."

Obediently she rose, and silently he put a guiding hand under her elbow as they strolled back through the gardens. When they neared the steps to the terrace Jo paused, aware of a reluctance to go indoors. She looked at the black and silver patterns in the moonlit garden and said, almost to herself, "I wish there was something, all the same."

"Something?" His shoulder brushed her arm as he turned to her.

"Something I could do to help." She bit her lip. "I like your sister—I wouldn't like her to get hurt."

He sighed, as though he were weary of the problem. "We can't do anything more than keep the party together and hope Margaret doesn't rebel."

"Perhaps Neil will bump into somebody else," she said hopefully. "Did you notice that blonde girl at the hotel the other night?"

"The pink-sugar damsel?"

Jo giggled. "Her hair was a bit like pink candy-floss."

"Claws, Jo!"

"Well . . . anyway, pink sugar or not, she was definitely giving Neil interested looks."

"Hm," Dane flicked at a night insect that fluttered near his face, "I don't suppose you feel inclined to try your hand at playing the *femme fatale*?"

"What? Me?" She stared at him. "You mean try to attract Neil? *Me?*"

"Why not? You're not attracted to him, I gather, so you should have no difficulty in keeping it to a mild flirtation."

She got over her astonishment and giggled. "I couldn't possibly. I'm afraid I'm no *femme fatale!*"

"Every woman has a *femme fatale* hidden within her."

"Not me. Now if Diane had been here. . . ."

"But Diane isn't here, unfortunately."

"Anyway, Neil's hardly looked at me. He gave me the once-over the day he arrived and added it all up," she said frankly.

"Oh." Dane's mouth went down at the corners. "And what did it total?"

"That I'm a working girl. That I belong to a different world from his. I could never resemble one of the glamorous creatures he attracts."

"I don't agree."

She shrugged. "It's perfectly true."

Dane was intent now, and there was no trace of his former banter in the long considering gaze he turned on her. It was quite disconcerting. She felt herself beginning to color.

"Don't be so sure," he said at last. "I think you underestimate yourself, Miss Johanna Medway."

"Do you think so? Nobody else does." She was trying to be flippant, but the annoying warmth in her cheeks was persisting. She looked down and felt a cool, lean finger under her chin, lightly but firmly contesting the movement.

"That's exactly what I mean," he said dryly.

For a moment his warm touch stayed, then his hand fell away and his mouth quirked. "I can think of several attractive qualities you appear to be unaware you possess; one of them in particular quite vital," he went on calmly. "Besides youth and a certain gallant approach to life that I find extremely refreshing, you have that certain air that invariably intrigues a man's interest."

Jo's breath quivered in her throat. She had an absurd desire to preen mysteriously in appreciation of this masterly, if unexpected, analysis of her personality. Then she saw the quiver come again at the corners of his mouth, and something told her that he knew exactly how she felt.

"As yet, you are still not quite conscious of it," he went on in the crisp, unemotional voice she imagined he might use in the high court. "In fact, at the present moment you're not sure whether to giggle and fling back an inane flippancy at me, or summon up that mysterious air and invite me to embark on more of my foolish soliloquy."

"You'll have me believing it all if you do."

"Very neat—both alternatives combined. In more practical terms," he went on calmly, "the virginal air is still a potent challenge to most males, particularly the philandering types."

"Are you by any chance suggesting that I risk—?"

"Not at all!" he declared hastily at the shocked response. "I was merely stating a fact I thought you seemed in doubt about."

"Well, I wasn't. And I don't want to be seduced—not by that Lothario." Her eyes sparkled indignantly. "I'm not quite as dim as all that!"

"I never implied that you were."

"You'd better not," she said darkly, "I don't mind typing my nails to the quick for you, I'll do any work you care to ask me to, but leave me out of your schemes for scotching Neil Clinton's designs on your sister."

"Scared?"

"Not a bit. I—I just don't want to get involved with anything—anyone."

He looked at her, and the moonlight silvered the long lean line of his brow and cheek, lending a saturnine mystery to the shadowed side she couldn't see.

"Don't you want to fall in love—ever?"

She knew a wild need to express indifference. "Not particularly," she said.

"So you would flee the enchanter?"

She looked up at him, maintaining a show of insouciance she did not feel. "Have you been reading Greek legends, or something?"

"Or something—an old verse that springs to mind." He reached out those long, well-shaped fingers again, feather light on her face. "It seems to fit the moment. *The curved cheek of innocence, the flirting tress. . . . The thin*

*bright veil of desire's first entrancement, in mortal clash
with dull reason, lest the unruly heart, still fallow, awakes
and wings to the sweet spell of the enchanter. . . ."*

Gone now were the crisp, sardonic tones. The timbre of
his voice was rich and very clear. It made a strange,
compelling music of his words. There was a tautness in
the stillness of the night, one which she had not been
aware of until this moment. Uncertain if the cause lay in
herself she moved abruptly, free from the hand that still
lay lightly against the brown sweep of her hair.

"I think you do believe in the magic after all," she said
in tones not quite as light as she wished.

But they broke the spell. His brows went up. "In this
case, no. Merely in the association of ideas." He turned
away and looked at the luminous shape of the white villa
blurring away under the black shadows of the cypresses.
"That was a very silly suggestion of mine, regarding
yourself. Please forget it."

In the silence he escorted her indoors and bade her a
polite, enigmatic good night.

All the magic had fled.

In its place came an increasing sense of anger as she
brushed her hair with long fierce strokes. The more she
mulled over that provocative discussion the more ruffled
she became.

To start with he didn't seem to have much faith in girls'
common sense, at least where wolves were concerned. He
seemed to imagine that they wouldn't recognize the most
ferocious of wolves in the flimsiest of sheepskin disguises.
Perhaps Neil was a fast worker, but Margaret certainly
wasn't a guileless little ninny to be taken in as easily as
Sir Sheridan believed. She was as self-assured and
worldly as Diane, although not so hard and not so
cynical, Jo decided, mentally comparing the two of them.

But she does like Neil a lot, she thought, biting her lip
and resolutely keeping herself away from a line of
thought that was panting to be explored. No matter how
one reasoned, one had to admit that there was a certain
spark between Margaret and handsome playboy Neil.

How deep did it go with Margaret? And if anything went wrong would it have the traumatic effect Sir Sheridan feared? Perhaps he was right, after all. If the affair could be sidetracked quietly before Margaret became too deeply involved emotionally it might save her a lot of heartache later on.

Having conceded this point, Jo plunked down her hairbrush and got into bed, pillow-punching, heaving, and wriggling to settle herself comfortably. The moment she was lying still, and the big moonlit square of the window was casting its wide reflection on the ceiling her mind surrendered to invasion.

He really was the limit!

First of all he encouraged her to talk a lot of nonsense about love and all the rest of it. Then he told her he didn't believe in love; when she was older *she* wouldn't believe in it either, to say nothing of telling her she looked like a kid of 17. And then he had the nerve to start kidding her about playing the *femme fatale* for Neil Clinton's benefit.

He had almost convinced her that he meant it, too, she thought bitterly. All that business about underestimating herself, about that certain air. . . .

A whisper of breeze stirred the curtains and stole across Jo's brow. She raised one hand to a disturbed wisp curling across her cheek and seemed to feel the warm touch of other fingers. *Innocence . . . desire's first entrancement. . . .* How did that poem go? There had been something about his voice. . . . Jo stared wide-eyed at the ceiling, and that disturbing tautness began to steal through her body. *Awake and wing . . . to the sweet spell of the enchanter. . . .*

And then in the next breath he had told her to forget it all. Just a silly idea he'd had. Silly, because obviously he didn't believe she had the remotest chance of playing the enchantress to Neil Clinton—or any other man!

CHAPTER SIX

By the next morning Jo had almost succeeded in hardening her heart. If he didn't choose to work, well, it wasn't her fault. She was here, as asked, ready to keep her part of the bargain. After all, she hadn't asked for the job. How did she know that something wildly exciting mightn't have turned up if she'd kept to her original plan? So she might as well enjoy herself. There were 52 weeks looming ahead to be worked through before she had another holiday.

A little placated by this decision, she decided to lie in late that morning and spend a long luxurious hour in the bath and grooming her person, with the result that the dining room and terrace were both deserted when she finally went downstairs. No one appeared to have missed her, which was somewhat deflating. Rather belatedly she realized she had probably delayed Kyra's morning household schedule; not that the kindly housekeeper showed the slightest sign of this when Jo apologized.

The mail came while she was having her second cup of coffee. To her delight there was a card for her from Dave. It depicted the Tower of London and, typical of Dave, merely said, "Wish you were here," with a cryptic little question mark in brackets. She propped it against the coffee pot and studied it with bemused eyes, wondering how Dave's plans were working out. Would he keep his apartment, or vacate it? Someone would have to help him pack up his stuff if he did. And he would need some place to store it. I could store some of his books for him, Jo thought, and perhaps—

The sound of Ricky's excitable young voice broke into her musing. He was coming up the cliff path. A moment or so later he came into view, scrambling over the little wall and dragging long streamers of seaweed behind him. Presently Margaret followed a little breathless, and hailed Jo thankfully.

"Just what I need!" She flopped down and peered into the coffee pot. "Any left? Good! Ricky, run and ask Kyra for a cup, please. And leave your seaweed here!" She heaved a deep sigh as he scampered away and put her feet up on one of the other chairs. "I wish I knew where he gets his energy."

Jo smiled sympathetically, and Margaret said, "Have you seen the others?"

"No—I was going to ask you that."

"I think the Professor's taken Dane down to meet some fellow scribe at the literary club. I expect they've forgotten all sense of time by now. I'm not sure where Alan and Neil have gone to."

Ricky came running with the cup and saucer. Margaret paused to help herself to coffee. She raised the cup to her lips, then spotted Ricky's new caper and set down her coffee. Ricky stopped whirling seaweed around and backed away from his mother's warning hand.

"We don't want our faces slapped with seaweed, thank you. And not on the chair cushions, either." She sat down again and shook her head ruefully. "I'm afraid 'stop' and 'don't' are the two most overworked words in my vocabulary just now. Oh, Ricky!" she shook her fist at him, "you would choose to be playful just when I wanted to ask Jo a favor."

"Me?"

Margaret turned. "Yes, I was going to ask if you could possibly take him on for an hour or so this morning. I have a couple of chores to do, and—"

"But of course," Jo said instantly. "I'd love to."

"You're sure you've nothing arranged?"

Jo looked away. "I've nothing else to do," she said flatly.

"Bless you," said Margaret gratefully. "Just wait until I fill him with dire warnings to behave himself, then he's all yours."

However, her mock forbodings proved quite unnecessary. Ricky was as good as gold. He only wanted freedom to run, leap, ask endless questions, and work off his small-boy high spirits. Jo found her own spirits lightening in his company. You didn't have to pretend with a child, she thought thankfully, because they always knew instinctively if you were.

They went down to the village and wandered along the little harbor, watching the men repairing their nets and the sea birds hovering, eternally vigilant. The old men sat on stools outside cottage doors and gossiped of yesterday as they puffed at dark, gnarled old pipes. And now Jo could indulge her secret longing to explore the tiny narrow alleyways between the dazzling white houses, where open doors revealed glimpses of the true life of the island. Ricky was her passport, for a child may lead where an adult hesitates for fear of intrusion. Then she discovered she need not have feared, for the Greek is truly hospitable to the visitor, and she met only friendliness during her wanderings.

The hours flew. There was a pastry-shop that reminded Ricky that he was hungry. They sat on little wood stools, sharing green sherbet ices and rich honey and nut pastries that left fingers sticky and mouths coated with crumbs. Jo wiped honey off Ricky's chin and more furtively off her own. They set off again, in that happy mood that is ready to follow wherever chance might lead. When they finally returned to the villa only Alan was in to have lunch with them.

"Where's Mommy?" demanded Ricky.

"She isn't back yet," Alan told him, "but she said you could come aboard the boat with me this afternoon, if you wanted to."

Jo laughed at Alan's inquiring face. "Ask a silly question. . . ." she teased.

Ricky did want to—so much that he was ready to forgo lunch and set off that very instant. "Are you going right out to sea?"

"Well, I thought we might go along the coast as far as Mouse Island and perhaps do a little fishing when we come back."

Ricky's eyes glowed, and he tore into his *saltza*, so that he could look up from his empty plate and urge the grown-ups to get a move on.

"Shall we take Jo—if she hasn't anything better to do?"

Ricky nodded vehemently, and so the afternoon was planned. Certainly it was a heavenly day for taking to the water, Jo reflected when she and Ricky were settled in the *Miranda*. The sky was a brilliant, unfathomable blue unbroken by cloud. The wind was just cool enough to temper pleasantly the intense heat of the sun, and the *Miranda*, though she was no show-off in the motor-launch class, chugged briskly over the blue in a quite exhilarating way.

They did not go ashore at Mouse Island. As Alan said, the chapel and the island's legend were beyond a five-year-old's interest. It was more enjoyable when there was time to walk from Kanoni across the causeway to the other tiny island with the convent of Vlakherena. "The view is magnificent," Alan added.

Ricky made no comment while Alan recounted the story for Jo's benefit, except to ask why the island should be called after a mouse if it was supposed to have been Ulysses' boat turned into a rock by the angry Poseidon.

That question never occurred to me—it's probably another story," Alan said as he headed back in the direction of their own bay. "Remind me to look that one up, Jo."

She nodded, her gaze and mind distracted. The sun was lolling lazily across the island now, reminding her of how quickly the day had gone. It had been relaxing and undemanding, but a vague sense of unease had overtaken her. She could not explain it, but it crystallized into sharp little thuds of her heartbeats when the boat rounded the headland, and she saw the figure standing on the beach.

Even at that distance the figure was recognizable instantly as that of Sir Sheridan. Plainly he had spotted them, for he began to walk along the beach toward the landing stage.

She sat back, putting out a restraining hand to Ricky, who was bouncing up and down, and wondered if the sight of that tall, purposeful figure had anything to do with her inexplicable reluctance to reach the shore.

"Uncle Dane! Uncle Dane! Are you going to fish as well?"

"Nobody's going to fish, young man," said the two men almost simultaneously. "It's too near supper and your bedtime."

"But you promised!" wailed Ricky. "You said when we got back!"

"I said 'perhaps.' " Alan held the boat steady while Dane hoisted the protesting Ricky ashore. "Okay, Jo, up you get."

She stood rather unsteadily, the motion of the sea still affecting her senses, and waited until Alan scrambled up beside her. Dane had given her the briefest of nods. It had done nothing at all to assuage the feeling of unease.

He was walking on ahead at an apparently leisurely pace that nonetheless covered distance with a deceptive speed. She had to check herself from hurrying to catch up with him. She did not know that her unease and something very like hurt were mirrored clearly in her unwary young face as she stared after the tall imperious man, nor did she notice that Alan's features were shadowed. He was as silent as herself during the walk up to the villa. But when she saw the two on the terrace she knew the reason for Dane's displeasure.

Margaret was back. She was lounging in a chaise longue, one knee drawn up indolently. She looked extremely content and very lovely. Neil was sitting near her, a drink in his hand. His gaze was quite openly appreciating the long, lithe lines of her body in the pink swim suit. Jo could almost feel his reluctance to look up when she approached, and there was a distinct glint of triumph in his eyes as they switched to Alan.

"Had a good day?" Alan asked evenly.

Neil's brows went up. "Depends what you mean by good, old man. We nearly broke a spring on one of those infernal tracks, and we were lost twice, but we found a new eating place and had a superb meal. Margaret picked wild roses and maidenhair and lost her comb somewhere. I must have shot a few hundred feet of film."

"'And you were stung by a bee," Margaret said. "Is it still painful?"

Neil rubbed vaguely at his wrist. "A bit—the main thing is it wasn't you, my sweet." He stood up and looked down at her. "Like another?"

"Yes, please." Margaret gave him her empty glass, and their fingers intermingled as he took it. There was a slight smile on his handsome mouth and a something in Margaret's eyes as she returned his gaze that made Jo turn away.

As she did so she encountered Dane. He was standing by the opened French windows, and the shadow of the frame cut across him. This time there wasn't even a nod of recognition for her, merely a look of censure that no shadow could hide. Bitterness welled up in Jo's heart. She forgot her intention to draw out one of the terrace chairs and enjoy the last hour of sun. She brushed past him without speaking and went up to her room to while away the hour before dinner with her own dark thoughts.

By the time that hour passed she was feeling more angry and bitter than ever. Today had proved that the secret—if it had been a secret—was that no longer. The attraction between Neil and Margaret was openly acknowledged now for all the world to see. They spent the whole day together, uninhibited by the presence of a child. Only the most insensitive of observers could have failed to see the triumph in Neil Clinton's entire manner, the sheer possessiveness of him as he talked to her on the terrace, and that warm glowing response in Margaret's eyes.

And why shouldn't Margaret seek happiness? Jo whispered to herself. Dane had no right to try to manage his sister's life for her, even though he thought it was for the best. How could he know what brought a woman happiness? And he had no right to involve me in it, looking at me as though it was all my fault, she thought angrily. Just because he approves of Alan Quayle and disapproves of Neil Clinton. If Alan was so keen on her why did he stand by and let another man walk in? And certainly Neil was exciting, a good-looker, a man of the world. . . . But he wasn't free. . . .

Jo sighed and began a hasty tidying of her room before she went downstairs. Margaret knew that . . . maybe Neil would get his freedom. . . . But what if he didn't? What if Dane was right all the time. . . . Oh, to blazes with them all! she muttered under her breath. How could she help what people did?

Nevertheless, a small knot of guilt continued to constrict Jo's emotions. She knew that inadvertently she, and then Alan, had given Margaret her day of freedom. It did nothing to lessen her sense of guilt when Neil claimed Margaret immediately dinner was over and suggested a fling at the Casino. He had the car in motion and Margaret within before she had slipped a filmy scarf about her shoulders. A silence descended on the villa as the car sounds faded into the night. The Professor looked down at his half-finished coffee and pushed it aside, murmuring a brief excuse about seeing to something before he departed. Abruptly Dane stood up. He too made a brief, polite formality and went from the room, closing the door soundlessly behind him, and leaving Alan and Jo on their own.

She looked around the big lounge, at the after-dinner debris of coffee cups parked on side tables or floor beside empty chairs and wondered miserably what to do.

Alan was lounging in a deep armchair, his gaze abstracted, and he seemed unaware of her presence. She got up restlessly and wandered across the room. The windows still stood open to the warm soft night, and she stood there staring uncertainly across the dark gardens. It was too soon for moonrise and the mystery and the spell it could cast across the night. Enchantment—and the enchanter. . . . Abruptly she turned back and dropped despondently into a low chair.

"You don't have to stay here and take pity on me, you know," Alan said suddenly.

She started. "Oh, but I didn't—I mean—" She shook her head. "I wasn't thinking anything like that."

He smiled. "I know." He flexed his fingers and studied them reflectively, then he glanced up at her. "Don't look so worried, Jo. It wasn't your fault."

His glance was too perceptive for her to have any doubt about what he meant.

He said musingly: "It was bound to happen, anyway."

She stared. "But don't you mind? I mean, when you want—" She stopped, aghast. Supposing he didn't want to marry Margaret at all.

He smiled faintly. "Go on, say it, Jo. I know what you're thinking. You're wondering how I can sit back tamely and let another man try to captivate the woman I love."

Jo gave an exclamation of dismay, but he betrayed no sign of either embarrassment or discomfiture. He eyed her with ironic amusement. "I'm afraid I have to confess to eavesdropping. I overheard some of your conversation with Dane on the terrace last night."

Horror overcame her, and for a moment she struggled with the implication of what this might mean. How much had he overheard? And what? She felt her face going scarlet, and he said hastily, "It wasn't deliberate, I assure you. I'd gone out for a breath of air before turning in, and I was in that little sunken bit on the far side of the garden. I couldn't get back without passing you. I wandered away as far as I could get and surveyed the sea, then ambled back with the intention of giving you warning of my presence before I burst upon you." He paused, and his wry smile flashed. "But then I heard Margaret's name and have to admit I stayed still and listened. Dane has the true advocate's clarity of speech, you know. Even when he speaks in a quiet tone every syllable carries."

Jo relaxed slightly; thank heaven he hadn't heard all that little inquisition about her reactions to a philanderer. Or worse—what followed on the terrace before she went indoors. . . . She felt the scarlet rush into her cheeks again as she tried to recall exactly what Dane had said and what silliness she had said. She hardly heard Alan start to speak again until he stood up abruptly and moved toward the window.

"The time isn't right yet for asking Margaret to marry me," he said slowly. "She isn't ready to put another man in the place Peter held in her life. Dane is absolutely correct in his surmise that she will feel guilty about loving another man. She was totally in love with her husband,

and she was shattered when he died. It was nearly a year before she began to move back into social life and stop looking like a ghost of the girl we used to know."

Alan sighed and swung back to face Jo. "She's over it now, thank goodness, but I still think it'll be a long time before she's ready to admit another man fully into her life. And that's where Dane's utterly wrong about Clinton. She is young, vital and needs a man's love even while her loyalty to Peter's memory holds her back. She feels that guilt all right, but she'll expunge that guilt on Clinton. When the affair is over the guilt will die with it, then she'll be ready to make a new partnership. I hope it will be with me," he added quietly.

"So do I," Jo whispered, after a long pause. But she wasn't sure in her heart that both Alan and Dane were right in their approach to Margaret. Dane was obviously set on preventing her from having an affair with Neil Clinton, while Alan was prepared to stand back and watch, believing that she would come to realize Neil's instability and turn to a man who could give her the same secure, faithful love as her first marriage had brought.

It was a fair enough theory, she considered, except for the fact that neither of them seemed to have taken into consideration the sheer unpredictability of a woman's emotions. Supposing she fell utterly in love with Neil. She was halfway there already, Jo thought.

"But we shouldn't be loading you with our problems," Alan said abruptly. He came across to her and looked down at her with thoughtful eyes. "Seeing as everybody seems to have deserted us tonight we might as well amuse each other. Would you like to go out for a drive? See Corfu by moonlight?" He gestured broadly.

She knew he was only offering out of kindness, because he was that kind of person. She hesitated a second too long.

"Corfu by moonlight doesn't mean much at this particular moment, does it?" he said quietly.

She looked down, away from the perception that knew things almost before she knew them herself, and then tensed as firm footsteps sounded briskly along the terrace. She turned and saw the long shadow, then it was gone. The steps faded with the echoes of the iron gate swinging shut. She walked slowly out onto the terrace, hearing the slam of a car door, and the engine throbbing to life. For a brief moment the sweep of headlights outlined the tall gated aperture in the white wall and spilled a broad fan of light across the garden. The blackness afterward seemed more intense.

She knew it was Dane. The Professor never drove himself. Was he going down to the Casino, perhaps with the idea of chaperoning his sister whether she liked it or not? Or was he merely indulging a sudden whim to take a lonely drive into the night? He was such a remarkably self-sufficient individual. Many people seemed to need him, but he seemed immune to needs of his own. The thought was strangely depressing, and the bowing of her head more telling than she realized.

"He's going to the airport."

She whirled around. She hadn't heard Alan's approach to her side. Her first thought was the most instinctive one and raised an alarmed face to the older man. "He's not leaving?"

"Good heavens, no. He's going to meet Celia."

"Celia Wincroft?" Jo's voice had the edge of sharpness. She'd forgotten about Celia.

"Her plane gets in some time after 'midnight. Didn't you know?"

"Yes, I—I did hear she was coming after all," Jo said slowly. Her hands clenched and then opened slowly as she rested them on the broad parapet of the terrace rail. A cold, unreasoning hatred of Celia Wincroft was surging through her with an intensity that made her bite her lip till it hurt. That was the aspect she should have remembered. Hadn't Margaret told her? There was one weakness in that self-sufficient façade of his, and Celia Wincroft was that weakness. . . .

"You haven't worked with him for very long, have you?"

The quiet question broke in on her unhappy musing, and she shook her head numbly. "I—I don't really work for him at all," she said at last. "Just while Mellie's ill."

Beside her, Alan moved. He leaned forward and rested folded arms on the parapet and stared into the night. "Mind if I give you some advice, young Jo?"

"No—if you don't call me young Jo. Everybody does," she added sadly.

"Try not to get involved," he said.

"I think I'm involved already," she said flatly.

"Yes, I was afraid of that."

She took a deep breath. "Why do you say afraid?"

"Because you're different from the others, and I wouldn't like to see you get hurt."

She tensed, conscious of a desire to defend that new tender burgeoning she had scarcely had time to recognize herself and said unsteadily, "Why should I get hurt?"

His sigh sounded impatient, but his voice remained gentle. "Because you're on the way to it already, and because, as I said, you're different from the others."

"What others?"

"You know perfectly well." He straightened and gave her a direct look. "A great number of girls—and older women—have pursued Dane Leroy during the years I've known him. But with one exception he's remained completely impervious to them. Unavoidably, some of them were hurt. The others don't matter."

"But I'm not pursuing him."

"It amounts to the same thing, doesn't it?" he said softly.

She felt the warmth glowing in her cheeks and was grateful for the velvety shadows that veiled her.

"He can't help attracting women," Alan went on flatly, "any more than Neil Clinton can. But unlike Neil he makes no use of that power."

She was silent, pondering his words even as she knew they merely confirmed the truth of her instincts. She said suddenly, "Dave has that power too."

"Who's Dave?"

"Someone I know. He's quite different from Dane, but he has that same ability to make people want to do anything for him."

"It's a dangerous power if it's used selfishly."

"Dane isn't selfish," she said, instantly defensive for him.

"I didn't mean any specific person."

"I know, but he isn't. Neither is Dave." Her mouth curved reminiscently. "I used to think I was in love with him."

"Dave? Or Dane?"

"Dave." She sighed and turned away, upturning her face to the dark starlit heavens. "I know now that I wasn't."

"Perhaps you should pretend you are still a little bit in love with him," Alan said quietly.

"Do you believe one can fool the heart?" She tried to laugh, but there was no responding flippancy from this quiet man who had guessed her secret.

He looked down at her, and his eyes were gentle. "No, but sometimes one can fool pride."

His advice stayed in her mind long after she had switched off the light and settled down for the night; even as she tried to convince herself that there wasn't any need for advice, anyway: she hadn't really fallen in love with Sir Sheridan Leroy. He was attractive, charming, compelling. His voice was velvet, and his words could burn like acid if he chose to make them so. He could be utterly ruthless, and his smile could shatter all resistance. He was famous and arrogant. He had taught her to swim and confided his problem to her; he had talked to her about love, under a Grecian moon, and she wanted to whisper his name over and over again, because it was the most satisfying sound in the entire universe. Dane . . . Dane. . . .

She turned over feverishly and tried to shut out the other pictures that came to torment her, knowing there would be no sleep for her until the sounds of a car returning broke the stillness of the night.

Had she arrived?

In her imagination Jo haunted the airport reception lounge. Was he waiting impatiently . . . listening for the roar of the incoming flight? How was he greeting her? What were they saying to one another during that drive across the sleeping island? But imagination could not bear those disturbing pictures, and despairingly she switched on her bedside lamp and reached for a book. Somehow she had to escape this tormenting jealousy of Celia Wincroft. . . .

Despite the lateness of the hour when she eventually fell asleep over the open pages of the book she awakened with the feathery rose flush of dawn. The villa was utterly silent, and on impulse she decided to go down to the beach and bathe. A plunge might take away this jaded feeling that had resulted from lack of sleep and mental stress, she decided as she stopped to brush her teeth and don her swimsuit and beach jacket.

There was a beautiful silver film on the sea, almost as though some celestial artist had sprayed it with quick-silver and tinted the horizon with apricot and rose. The air was still and clear; the beach deserted except for herself and the sea birds wheeling overhead. The moment Jo felt the first cold swirl of the ripples over her toes an unutterable sense of loneliness possessed her. She almost turned back, looking up at the cliff and the villa drowsing under the lee of the hill behind. She shook her head impatiently. She might as well get it over with now she was here.

For a little while she bathed in the shallow stretch where it was flat and safe, half-heartedly practising her breast stroke and crawl, despising herself because all the attraction of swimming had fled. In retrospect, those mornings last week had been sheer joy, Jo decided, giving up her efforts and turning to wade ashore. But there wouldn't be any more delightful little sessions with her fascinating tutor. Celia Wincroft would see to that. He wouldn't—

"Oh!" She stopped short at the sight of her beach jacket flaunting its vivid scarlet folds from Dane Leroy's hands.

"Good morning, Jo." He wrapped the jacket around her. "Why this crack-of-dawn activity?"

"I—I didn't sleep very well." She was still startled by his appearance and wondering why not one of her senses had noticed his approach. "I woke up very early and decided I'd have a swim."

"Swim?" His brows arched expressively. "Is that what you were supposed to be doing?"

The mockery stung her. "Not really," she retorted. "I didn't expect an audience at this time of the morning."

"I too happened to awake very early." His steps were firm and measured on the steep cliff path. His immaculate appearance betrayed no indication of hurried grooming, or the somewhat jaded lethargy that Jo still felt despite her dip. "I also happen to be one of those unfortunates to whom sleep does not come easily after a late night. Invariably my problems line up to be solved when I feel least inclined to face them."

She hugged the jacket more closely to herself and gazed down at the scarlet and white toes of her sandals plodding into view alternately on the runnelled path. She said abruptly, "I couldn't help it yesterday—I just took Ricky down to the village. I didn't know she'd gone."

There was no reply, and she turned to look up at him. His set profile showed intent on where he was going, almost as though he hadn't heard her. She added in a pleading little rush, "I know you blamed me, but—but why did you go off for most of the day yourself if you—*Oh!*" She stopped as her unwary feet found a pothole. She stumbled, turning her ankle over.

"But I never said I blamed you." A steel-strong hand fastened around her arm and steadied her. "Where did you get that ridiculous little idea?"

"W-when we got back and saw them." Her face was drawn with the sharp burning pain a twisted ankle causes. Perhaps it also helped to make her sound pathetically childish as she added in a small voice, "I knew by the way you looked at me."

"I'm sure I don't recall anything of the kind," he said blandly. "Is that ankle damaged?"

"No—it's going away now."

"Sure?"

"Sure." She kept her face averted, dreading the sardonic light she was certain was in his eyes.

"Good." His grip slackened from her arm. "I shall require your services this morning—immediately after breakfast and until lunchtime."

This announcement effectively routed the discomfort of her ankle and her grievance at his bland denials. "But what about Ce—?" She bit back the name and the foolish impulse to blurt out her thoughts without thinking. "Yes, of course, Sir Sheridan. That's why I'm here," she said in a tight, formal voice.

"Slaving on your holiday, Miss Medway. How sad."

She averted her head and quickened her pace. If he wanted to laugh at her he could. It might teach her not to be so foolish in future, handing over her heart to a man to whom guile was second nature. So he couldn't help attracting women! They pursued him and were hurt, or rather the foolish ones did—the others didn't matter. If she had any sense, she vowed silently, she would take good care to make sure she never belonged to either category.

Imperceptibly his strides had lengthened. His shadow darkened over her; his hand shot out to seize her long damp hair in a thick, imprisoned bunch that effectively halted her progress.

"As prickly as ever," he observed in amused tones. "Stand still."

"I'm not—and I won't!"

He was looking down into her face; his glance enigmatic on the tell-tale brightness of eyes she could not turn away to hide. She tugged and winced. "That hurts!"

"I'm sorry!" He released his grasp and put his hands on her shoulders. "I warned you once, Jo, of the penalties of being a Crusader."

She saw the teasing quirks at the corners of his mouth, and she drew a deep angry breath. "Yes—I remember. But you forgot to warn me that my shield might get a bit buckled in the campaign," she exclaimed bitterly.

"I've worn out about four dozen," he said amusedly.

"Well, I don't happen to have such a good supply," she retorted and wrenched away out of his grasp.

She stumbled in her haste to escape a teasing that was

proving more than she could parry. Suddenly a warm arm came around her shoulders.

"What have I said?" he murmured down to her.

He was pulling her against him, making her bump awkwardly against him as they climbed. The new softened tone in his voice made her feel like an absurd child being offered sympathy. That was all he saw her as, anyway, she thought sadly; a child who seemed alternately to amuse and irritate him.

An obstinacy that was regrettably childish kept her silent, even as she was loath to surrender that warm nearness of him. A tiny sigh escaped her when they reached the top of the path and he released her.

He straightened and paused. "There's just one thing. . . ."

He had reverted to his normal cool, inscrutable manner, and she looked at him uncertainly.

"Celia arrived late last night," he said calmly. "You know that she's Aldo Wincroft's daughter, and Aldo is in the opposing camp as regards the future of your youth center?"

She nodded, a slight chill passing through her limbs.

"Try to keep off this tender subject while she's around—we don't want to jeopardize our negotiations."

"No—of course not," she said hurriedly. "I'll be very tactful."

He nodded. "Perhaps it's unfortunate that I have a personal stake in the matter."

Remote again, he moved toward the house, and the chill reached Jo's heart as she followed him.

CHAPTER SEVEN

They were halfway through breakfast when Celia walked out onto the terrace.

Jo's sole memory of her was a confused glimpse under a street lamp on a rainy night in London. From it she had formed a certain mental picture in which very few glamor flaws were present. Now, seeing reality clearly in the brilliant pure light of a Grecian morning, she discovered that for once her imagination had played no tricks. Celia Wincroft was gorgeous. No matter how one might dislike her, or try to detract from her beauty that fact was inescapable.

A sudden silence descended as she made her entrance.

No one could have accused her of seeking to impress fashionwise. She wore faded green denims rolled untidily to calf-length, a man's shirt of lemon poplin held closed by a single button and betraying that she wore precious little else beneath it, espadrilles on her small slender feet. Her hair hung free to her shoulders. Her make-up was limited to lipstick, her nails were innocent of lacquer, and she looked breathtaking.

The men stood up. She murmured a good morning that included everyone, smiled at Alan and the Professor, held out her hand to Dane and retained his with a small possessive gesture while she turned a light, inquiring gaze to Neil Clinton. "*I don't know you,*" it said. "*What are you going to do about it?*"

Dane made the introduction, and she gave Neil a cool nod that belied the message in her eyes, then, rather abruptly, he introduced Jo in a somewhat formal manner.

Jo took her cue from him, murmuring a polite greeting. Celia arched her brows charmingly. "I hope it isn't going to be Miss Wincroft and Miss Medway—I won't feel that I'm on holiday, poppet. May I sit here?"

With the words she moved to the place next to Jo, and four men drew the chair into place for her. Glancing across the table, Jo surprised a cynical little smile on Margaret's face. Then Ricky piped up, "Are you staying here for your holiday, Aunty Celia?"

"That was the general idea," Celia smiled at him.

"Oh. Uncle Dane said you weren't."

"Ricky! Get on with your breakfast." Margaret nudged him and whispered in a sharp undertone.

Ricky raised an indignant face. "But I only said what—"

"Don't be cross with him." Celia seemed amused. She leaned across the table and whispered confidingly to him, "You were quite right, darling. Your Uncle Dane and I had a little argument about where we should spend our holidays and he won."

"There! I—" Ricky's triumphant exclamation changed to dismay as he upset his glass of orange juice. Margaret gave a furious exclamation, Neil looked bored, and the others offered napkins and handkerchiefs. During the small diversion Celia turned to Jo.

"Is this your first visit here?"

Jo nodded, aware of being assessed, and knew her instinct hadn't played her false as Celia flashed that disarming smile.

"Forgive me—I know this sounds frightfully rude of me, but who do you belong to in this set-up? Just so that I don't put my foot in it."

"I don't belong to anyone in this set-up," Jo said clearly. "I'm taking Mellie's place."

The smile vanished from Celia's lips. She pushed back a heavy tress of red-gold hair and stared at Jo. "Mellie? You mean—?"

"I'm Sir Sheridan's secretary."

Hands and a shadow fell across her shoulders. "If you've finished breakfast, Jo . . . I've quite a bit to get through."

She saw Celia's surprised eyes look upward over her head. "But, Dane, you're not going to work? Now? It's my first day!"

"I'm sorry, but I can't alter my arrangements, Celia." His tone was equable but firm. "That's why I chose to come to the villa where I knew I'd have reasonable facilities to work in peace."

"But it's our holiday, darling!" she protested.

"Not exactly." The pressure of his hands seemed heavier on Jo's shoulders. "As far as I'm concerned it was here or not at all."

Celia compressed petulant lips, and Dane turned away. "The Professor's study, as soon as you're ready, Jo."

Jo stood up hastily, not daring to glance at Celia, and hurried after him. She could not help wondering why he had suddenly discovered this necessity to work; last week he'd just grinned lazily if it was suggested, and he'd practically admitted that bringing a secretary was merely a ruse. So why now? When his girl had arrived and the quarrel was over? Could it be that he was doing it deliberately to pay her back? But he couldn't, Jo decided. Even if Celia was spoiled and liked all her own way, paying her back in that way was petty. Dane wasn't petty. He was too generous for that.

The windows of the Professor's study faced out over the secluded side of the garden. Being tucked away as far as possible from kitchen and main living quarters it was utterly silent. Books lined the walls, and a casual untidiness of small furnishings lent a comfortable, relaxing atmosphere. A big, old-fashioned typewriter stood on a long table near the window. Jo went to it, ruefully prepared for misaligned keys and a threadbare ribbon, and discovered that it was in good working order. She also discovered that there was no pretense about work.

"I'll try to remember that you haven't our language at your fingertips, as Mellie has, and make allowances," he told her briskly, producing a disconcertingly hefty file of papers from his case.

Jo sat down obediently. As the morning passed she discovered that she wasn't in the least resentful of being kept indoors, knowing that the others were sunning, swimming, or otherwise enjoying themselves. Kyra brought coffee and little almond dainties still warm from the oven, and they shared the welcome "elevenses" in companionable silence while the bees drowsed softly outside the open windows. No one disturbed them. When it was time to join the others for lunch Jo discovered why it had been so quiet. The Professor had taken Ricky fishing and for a picnic lunch; and the other four had gone off together for the day.

"We have been deserted," Dane observed dryly. He betrayed no sign of annoyance, however, and after lunch was over he looked gravely at Jo. "I feel inclined to laziness this afternoon. Any bright ideas?"

She looked at the long elegant grace of him as he reclined on one of the loungers, legs crossed, and dark glasses shielding his eyes from the brilliant sun. Her own eyes held indulgence. But she feigned mockery.

"Don't mind me. Just sleep."

He shook his head. "Not a very bright idea. I have a better one. Have you the strength to drive into town?"

"If you have the strength to do the driving."

He stood up, all trace of indolence gone, and said, "Let's go."

It proved a delightful afternoon. When they reached the town Dane parked the Professor's car and hired a Victoria. Jo was enchanted. It was the first time she had ridden in a horse-drawn carriage, and the world seemed to take on an entirely new perspective from this unusual angle. She sat up very straight, her hands clasped in her lap, and felt as though she were driving back into time as the cabby urged their steed to brisker endeavor, and they bowled along the Esplanade.

The various influences superimposed by time on the island seemed more clearly sensed. Rome, Byzantium, Venice; all had come to the island, even the unmistakable hand of Georgian Brittania, imprinted on pompous bronze statues, the imposing Palace, the bandstand and the rotunda erected to the memory of Sir Thomas Maitland. There was even a cricket field. A word that Jo had heard several times in cafés and been puzzled by suddenly became so obvious when Dane explained: *tsinzinbera*—ginger beer!

Later, in the more orthodox mechanical transport, Dane drove her up to Kanoni, to the vantage point that afforded one of Corfu's most beautiful views of the mountain fringed sea and the two islets lying like gems in the sparkling turquoise mirror. When it was time to return to the villa Jo felt reluctant to leave the magic the day had become. Just before the villa came in sight she turned to Dane and thanked him shyly.

He seemed surprised. "You enjoyed it?"

"Oh, yes! It was the loveliest afternoon I've had for ages."

Perhaps her young voice betrayed a little more fervor than she knew, for the careless amusement went from his face. "I believe you mean that," he said with surprise.

"Oh, I do!"

For a moment he made no reply, then he said dryly, "I wonder how long you'll keep that joyous approach to unsophisticated pleasures."

"Always," she assured him.

"I doubt it." His tone was sceptical, and it brought Jo back to reality and awareness of her naïvety. This afternoon would be an unsophisticated pleasure to Sir Sheridan Leroy. Its amusement contained more in the observing of her delight than in the actual content of the outing, she thought with a flash of perception. His life had doubtless brought him many rich experiences and opened doors barred to the Johanna Medways of a workaday world. That was no reason why she should not admit a wholehearted enjoyment, even though she could never admit the true source of the magic ingredient that transformed pleasure into enchantment.

"You'd better make the most of it," he added as he swung the car into the villa driveway. "I shall be extracting my pound of flesh tomorrow morning."

"I don't mind," she said quietly.

"I believe you mean that as well," he said somewhat thoughtfully and turned to face her as he halted the car. Under the unexpected scrutiny she felt her face grow pinker. She moved restlessly.

"Why shouldn't I?" She tried to sound pert. "I'm the conscientious type, remember? The quaint child, the prickly one. You said so yourself."

"So I did." His glance was cool now, considering those pink cheeks. "What a good memory you have, Johanna Medway."

He switched off the ignition, and Jo sighed. She would never understand him and certainly would never predict his mood.

Celia annexed him that evening and made it crystal clear that it was to be strictly for two. But the next morning he made it plain that he wouldn't be free.

The atmosphere was distinctly chilly at breakfast. Neil had planned to take the party water-skiing and had made arrangements the previous day to hire a boat and gear. He made the announcement with complete confidence that everyone would instantly echo his own enthusiasm, but Celia was the only one who responded excitedly.

She looked at him with sparkling eyes and announced that she adored water-skiing. She thought it was a wonderful inspiration.

Neil looked gratified, and Ricky demanded to know what it was.

"Oh, somebody explain it to him," Celia said carelessly. "I remember the first time I tried it was when Daddy and I spent a month in Beirut a couple of years ago. It was the most fabulous holiday I've ever known—except for Bermuda, of course. But then that's different as we'll be living there when Daddy retires. He—" She stopped, perhaps aware of a certain quality in the silence, and flashed an ingenuous smile. "I'm sorry—I know I talk too much. It's a terrific idea, Neil."

"Count me out," said Margaret. "I know my limitations."

"I want to go, Mommy," cried Ricky.

"You'll have to want, I'm afraid," she responded so brusquely that Jo felt surprise. Margaret was usually very patient with him.

"And me too," Alan said. "Ricky and I have a fishing date today."

"Well then?" Celia turned a melting gaze on Dane. "We can go. Please, darling."

Jo waited, knowing the inviting gaze had bypassed herself, and felt her hands clench almost of their own accord. Slowly they relaxed as Dane shook his head. His eyes were enigmatic as he said coolly, "Each to his own."

It was now obvious that she and Neil would go alone. Jo was beginning to see Dane's intention. By his remaining aloof it made it a foregone conclusion that Neil and Celia would home to each other sooner or later. The similarities in their temperament became more obvious every day, and there was a flirtatious, challenging quality in Celia that evoked instant response in Neil's sensuality.

But what did Margaret feel about it? Jo wondered later that day when Neil and Celia failed to return for the evening meal. It was difficult to tell. She seemed to regain her normal friendly spirit when Alan and Ricky came back. They all wandered down to the beach to swim and laze in the sun, but by evening she was withdrawn. When the leisurely meal ended she did not linger downstairs very long, making the excuse of wanting to wash her hair.

The idea of an early night seemed to catch on, and Jo discovered that even doing nothing could induce weariness. Somewhat to her surprise she was in bed and asleep by ten o'clock, completely untroubled by the thought that Celia and Neil had not yet returned.

So she did not hear the car doors slam long after midnight, nor did she wake in time to overhear a cold little exchange on the terrace early the next morning. But Margaret did.

The older girl was finishing her breakfast when Jo came downstairs, guiltily aware that she had almost slept the clock around.

"Don't worry—it does you good to have a gorgeous long sleep occasionally," Margaret told her when she apologized. "Coffee or fruit juice first?"

"Fruit juice, please." Jo sat down and gazed around. "Where's everybody?"

"Gone," said Margaret in sepulchral tones. "Oh, they're around somewhere. Dane's gone for a stroll—he asked me to tell you he'd be back about 11, and he'd see you then."

"Oh." Jo bit her lip. "Was he mad?"

"With you? I don't think so." Margaret flicked at an insect that had lighted on her knee. "Jo, are you really working these mornings with Dane?"

Jo started. "Heavens! *Am I?* I didn't know the first thing about legal stuff until I started this lark. But Regina *v.* Domini has changed all that." She giggled. "I'm thinking of getting measured for my new wig next week."

But there was no answering smile from Margaret. "Did you say Regina *v.* Domini?" she exclaimed.

Jo nodded.

"Well, of all the—! I had a suspicion that my dear brother was up to something," she said grimly, "and now I know." She saw Jo's growing bewilderment and sighed. "That case is over. Weeks ago. Don't you see? He's been going over old notes, wasting your time as well as his own."

"But why?" Jo stared. "I'm sure he isn't. He's preparing new notes—that I'm not supposed to talk about," she interjected, "but as you're his sister. . . . I'm sure you're mistaken about that," she added, wondering whatever Margaret would say if she knew of her brother's determination to break up her affair with Neil Clinton.

"I'm not mistaken." Margaret's expression showed her annoyance. "I've known my devious brother too many years, and I know exactly how his mind works. He can't stand Neil, and he's determined to get us apart. Do you know, he never had any intention of coming here for his holiday? Until he discovered that Neil had suggested I spend mine here and bring Ricky, and he would join us for the second week. So dear Dane decides *he'll* change his plans and come here as well, no doubt with the intention of playing gooseberry. That was partly the reason for his quarrel with our dear Celia. She wasn't keen on the idea of a quiet holiday. She'd already made tentative arrangements for Dane and herself to join one of her jet-set cronies on his yacht. But Dane couldn't spare six weeks, even if he wanted to, which he didn't, so there was a spot of coolness over that. Then your youth club business came up. When she found that he'd changed sides and was gunning for dear Daddy the balloon really went up."

Margaret paused, but ignored Jo's exclamation and went on impatiently, "You see, that's the whole trouble with that brother of mine. I suppose it's that legal brain of his, but he seems to think that he can divorce all personal matters and emotion from business and professional life, and he can't. But it's hopeless trying to tell him otherwise. I mean," she gestured resignedly, "what's the use of him telling her that he has nothing personal against her father, or his desire to do a perfectly legitimate deal, but that he's simply fighting for a principle? The desire to uphold principles is in itself rooted in emotion, in something we care about. And so he really tears himself apart over this girl. He knows she plays him up, and yet he doesn't seem able to resist her when she puts on the old penitent act with that wheedling look of hers. It makes me sick," Margaret said disgustedly, "but it's hopeless trying to tell him that Celia Wincroft loves one person better than anybody else—herself."

Jo had stopped buttering her roll and was staring at Margaret with horrified eyes. "You mean they fell out because of me—and the youth center?"

"Oh, not entirely." Margaret gave an exasperated sigh. "It was just the last touch. They're completely incompatible. Dane's not really hard, you know. He has that outer shell that makes people think he's hard and cynical. I know he can be acid at times, but underneath he's a complete romantic, and idealistic. It's simply that his job has made him seem hard."

Jo nodded. There were things she wanted to say to Margaret, and she had forgotten about her breakfast, but she just wanted to go on listening to Margaret talking about Dane.

"I thought it was really over this time, and I was over the moon when I knew he was coming to the villa," Margaret went on. "And then she called up just before we left and said she wanted to come—if we would have her. If! I wish I'd answered the phone. But no. He takes her out to dinner that very same night and everything's on again. And now they're quarreling again. I have to admit I can see Celia's point of view this time."

"I thought he didn't look very happy yesterday," Jo said in a small voice.

"I eavesdropped this morning." Margaret lowered her voice. "They were out on the terrace, and she was putting on her sexy act. I heard Dane tell her he wondered if she was really in love with him. She pretends to be hurt and swears she is. Then he asks her why she goes out for the entire day and night with Neil. To which she says what else is she to do if he won't take her out." Margaret sighed. "I felt awful listening to them, but I couldn't help it. And then Celia told him quite bluntly that she was going to the Casino with Neil tonight, and what was he going to do about it? Then Ricky jammed the tap in the shower, and I had to rush there before he flooded the place. But I wish Dane would forget about me and Neil, and this stupid idea of letting Celia flirt with Neil so that I can see he's no good."

Jo sat bolt upright, her eyes wide. "You know?"

"Of course I know." Margaret's smile was humorless. "He disapproves of Neil as much as I disapprove of Celia. He's always telling me what a good chap Alan is, and how Alan should be married because he was born to be a family man. Honestly, he's as subtle as a sledgehammer on a tack. If Alan's so wonderful why doesn't he do something about getting himself a wife and family?" Margaret added tartly.

Jo picked up her roll and bit into it, studying the other girl. High color burned in Margaret's cheeks, her eyes were unusually bright with the fervor of her tirade. Jo chewed, then said indistinctly, "Yes, but you know how you feel about Celia. You don't want him to marry her in case she doesn't make him happy. Well, he feels exactly the same about you. He doesn't want you to get involved with Neil in case you get hurt."

"But I haven't the slightest intention of getting hurt by Neil. Oh, I'll admit he's terribly attractive, and I like him very much, but I'm not in love with him." Margaret's face softened, and she looked down at her hands. "I can't expect Dane to understand, and it's not very easy to explain, but I feel as though I'm starting a new life.

Losing the person who matters more than anyone else in the world is a traumatic experience. It's beyond description. You just feel as though your own life is over."

Jo nodded sympathetically, remembering sorrow in her own life, and the bewilderment of a child when a beloved mother is taken away forever. She said gently, "I know. But I'm sure Dane does understand."

"Maybe I am misjudging him. But I wish he wouldn't keep trying to push me toward Alan. I know everybody's being patient, giving me time to get over losing Peter, but they forget I'm a woman and lonely. It's over two years since Peter was killed, and the first year was hell. I didn't want anyone else, couldn't bear the thought of ever marrying again. But this past year gradually became better. I began to wonder what it would have been like if it had been me and not Peter. Would I have expected him to live out the rest of his life alone? I knew I couldn't have asked that, and I knew Peter wouldn't have asked it, either. I think it was then that I became a woman again instead of an empty shell. But everyone was waiting for me to give them a sign. Alan is waiting, and somehow I can't do that. I want him to come to me. And that's why I shall always have a certain feeling for Neil."

Abruptly she stood and put her hands on the terrace rail. "Neil made me feel like a woman again. Made me feel I was still attractive, desirable, and—oh! it was like coming back to life. I knew that my life wasn't over, that I would be able to love again. I shall always be grateful to Neil for that."

Watching her, Jo was silent. She wasn't entirely convinced about Margaret's denial of any deep feeling for Neil. Since Celia's arrival, and Neil's awakening interest in that direction there had been a tautness in Margaret's manner. But that could be pride, she thought suddenly. "What about Alan?" she asked slowly.

Margaret turned away. "Yes, what about Alan? Sometimes I think he likes Ricky better than me."

Jo hesitated, wondering if she had imagined bitterness in the other girl's tone. She said, "It's a shame that he has that limp."

"Limp?" Margaret's tone sharpened. "Good heavens, I forget that he has it. It's so slight it's hardly noticeable. You needn't feel sorry for him in that respect, Jo."

There was distinct annoyance in her face, and Jo said hastily, "I'm sorry. I didn't mean it like that. I—I just wondered if it mattered to you."

"Well, it doesn't. And it certainly wouldn't—" She stopped, and her tone changed. "Here's Dane. Oh, he's going straight into the house—and you've hardly eaten any breakfast while we talked," she added accusingly.

Margaret wore an automatic air of parental authority at times, Jo reflected wryly. *Not unlike that of her brother when I happen to be around.* She said aloud, "It doesn't matter—I'm not hungry. I'd better go now in case he wants me."

"Some holiday," commented Margaret ironically as Jo gulped down a mouthful of tepid coffee and hurried away.

However, Jo was not concerned with the holiday aspect as she went to the study. Her thoughts went back to Margaret's confidences, and the way they made some things fit. Should she divulge one certain fact to Dane? Only a moment's consideration made Jo decide that she must assure him that his fears regarding his sister were groundless. And she must tell him— Jo came to a halt at the door, and her heart began to beat with sudden tension. Instinct told her that this wouldn't be the right time for broaching personal matters. . . .

But the room was empty when she pushed the door open. She stood looking out of the window for several long minutes before she heard Dane's step at the doorway.

His greeting was perfunctory, no more than polite, and the set of his mouth was hard. He took a sheaf of papers out of his case and flipped them on the table. "I'll leave you to get on with those. When you've finished them will you shove them in the case and put it back in my room?"

Already he was moving away, taking for granted her assent, and she exclaimed softly, taking a step forward to detain him.

"Well?" He waited, and something in his expression told Jo that this wasn't going to be easy.

"Dane, I wanted to—" She hesitated, seeing nothing encouraging in his face, and rushed on, "I've been talking to Margaret. She—she isn't in love with Neil—it's all right. So we needn't bother with all this—this old work. I mean—"

"What old work?"

"Well, this." Jo gestured. "She said this case was over, and—"

"What did she say about Clinton?"

The tight little core of tension gathering again, Jo recounted in awkward little phrases what Margaret had told her. Fearing his lack of conviction, she added earnestly, "Honestly, you needn't worry about her. She's not getting seriously involved."

He paced to the window, and Jo felt the new familiar jolt to her heart that came whenever he approached. She looked steadily at the silver watch on his tanned wrist, knowing that if she looked at his profile, and he surprised her gaze she would be betrayed by a rush of color.

At last he said acidly, "You may inform my sister at the next gossip session that the Domini case is *not* over. There's to be an appeal."

"Oh, I didn't think of that. She mustn't have known," Jo said with a pathetic attempt at Margaret's defense.

"Then she should verify her facts before she makes statements," he said in the kind of way that evoked an instant image of the High Court. "And I'd be obliged if you would refrain from discussing confidential matters outside this room, even with my own sister," he added coldly.

"Oh, I wasn't—we weren't. It was just that I happened to mention the name, that was all."

He nodded, and she looked up at his face. There was bleakness in his expression, and she felt her own spirit chill in response. She turned away and stood by the table, her head downbent as she said slowly, "I've just found out about Celia's father and the youth center business. I didn't know that it was the cause of you and—I suppose it's natural that she resented your taking our side, but then of course I didn't know."

"You didn't know what?" he said in too-quiet tones.

Jo shuffled the papers together. "Well, that you and Celia were in love, and—" She whirled around impulsively. "I'm terribly sorry that it happened because of us. We never thought of it having any personal effect, or making you unhappy. If—"

"You and my little sister have enjoyed a cosy little heart-to-heart, haven't you? What else did she tell you?"

"Nothing!" Jo took a dismayed step back and bumped into the table. A book slid to the floor, adding to her confusion, and she stooped to grab it. "Your sister didn't say anything—it wasn't like that at all. It was—"

"In future," he took the book from her hands and threw it on the table, "I'd be grateful if my sister would leave my personal affairs out of her prattle with her girl friends. The same goes for you, Miss Johanna Medway."

He swung around and stalked angrily out of the room before Jo could recover her breath. She stared at the door he had slammed. Hurt choked in her throat. The attack had been totally unexpected—and she'd only tried to apologize for involving him in a lot of trouble. She took a step forward, obeying a sudden impulse to go after him and try to put things right, then stopped uncertainly. She might make things worse. . . . Sadly she turned back to the window, reflecting that this was the first time she had seen him lose that unruffled calm. It would have to be with her. . . . Sighing, she picked up the sheaf of notes, and then whirled as a peremptory knock came at the door.

Celia didn't wait for any response. She breezed in, and Dane's name checked on her lips as she saw that the room was empty except for Jo.

"Where is he?" she demanded.

"Gone."

"Gone?" Celia frowned. "Where?"

Jo shrugged. "Just a moment ago. Didn't you pass him?"

"No, I thought he—" She glanced at her watch and gave a small impatient exclamation. "Jo, be a darling and find him. Tell him we're all waiting—we're going down to the Yacht Club to meet some friends of the Professor. He has to come."

Jo wanted to say, *find him yourself*, but she went out wordlessly. He must have intended going with them; he'd left the papers for her to work on, alone. And why not? He's employing you. That's all it is—a business arrangement. The thought brought bitterness just the same as she glanced into the lounge and dining room and found them empty. Neil and Margaret were talking on the front terrace, and she could hear the Professor's voice mingling with Kyra's in the kitchen. Of Alan and Ricky there was no sign, and Dane appeared to have vanished. Her steps listless now, she walked down to the cliff edge and saw the solitary figure far below on the beach.

She began to run, stumbling on the rough steep path, and did not call out until she was halfway down. Perhaps the wind carried her voice away, or perhaps he did not choose to hear. He was almost to the little jetty at the end of the beach when she reached the foot of the path. She hurried, her steps soundless in the fine dry sand that impeded her haste and saw him climb down into the boat. She shouted again, and this time he looked toward her, but made no move in response.

Her heart was thudding wildly with fear that he was going to cast off before she reached him. Suddenly it had become the supreme objective to reach him in time. When she halted she was so breathless she could only stand and look down at him.

"Well?" His eyes were cold.

"They—they're waiting. For you. Celia sent me." Jo gulped for breath. "She says you have to come."

"Celia can go to the devil," he said distinctly and started the engine.

"But—but—" She gave a distressed little gesture toward him. "You can't go off like this. They're all waiting," she repeated helplessly.

"They'll have to wait, won't they?"

She stared at him, at a loss how to cope with this fit of male temperament, and knelt down on the edge of the jetty. "It'll only make things worse," she exclaimed. "Oh, please, Dane . . . I know it's my fault, but don't spoil things any more."

She had not realized that she had leaned forward and

rested one hand on the gunwale until the boat moved and she was caught off balance. She struggled desperately to regain her feet, seeing the deep swell under the jetty. She was seized and tipped unceremoniously into the well of the boat.

The engine kicked into a deep-throated roar, and sardonic eyes looked down at Jo. "Trying to get wet?"

She rubbed her elbow and struggled into a less inelegant position. The shore was receding rapidly, and the boat heading straight for the horizon. "Where are you going?" she faltered.

"Where I can escape people."

His tone was uncompromisingly brusque. She said, "What did you do that for?"

"Do what for?"

"Start before I got out again."

"It seemed the quickest way to end the argument."

Jo's lips parted, then closed again. He was at the wheel, obviously intent on the handling of the boat and equally oblivious to her presence now—if the outline of his back was anything to go by. Jo wriggled around on the stern seat, unobtrusively. She had the landlubber's fear of tipping the boat, because with the mood he was in anything she did was bound to be wrong and stared back at the little bay they were leaving behind. The villa looked tiny, white and red-roofed where it nestled amid the thick, dark green woodland clinging to the hillside. Now the headland of the bay beyond was coming into view. It seemed she was afloat whether she wanted to be or not.

Sighing, because there had been the inevitable trickle of bilge in the cockpit, and some of it was now drying out around the hem of her skirt, she tried to keep the wet patches from contact with her skin and stifle a not unnatural feeling of hurt. But it was not easy. She could find no magic in the lovely sweep of the island curving about the sparkling blue, and the green-clad mountains rising to the north. He seemed to be setting course for the northern strait, but what destination he had in mind she had no means of knowing. Nor did he seem to have any intention of enlightening her.

Almost an hour of silence elapsed before he spoke over

his shoulder. Then it was merely to inquire sardonically if she was feeling seasick. Jo replied in the negative as curtly as she could and hoped fervently the negative would remain true. He made no response, and a short while later he began to head inshore.

There didn't appear to be anything, except a pebble beach under the lee of the tall dark cones of the cypresses. The high ridge above that lay against the sky like the curving back of a sleeping cat. Then, as the boat nosed alongside the mole, she saw the mellowed red of a tiled roof nestling among the trees.

Dane moored the boat and turned to her. "Lunch," he said laconically.

She did not move, her uplifted face plainly betraying her uncertainty of him, and he said impatiently: "Oh, for heaven's sake, don't *you* start playing me up, Jo."

She stared. "But I'm not. I just. . . ." She shook her head, and he leaned down, stretching out his hand.

"Come on—you must be hungry by now."

"I'm not." Unsmilingly she took the outstretched hand and climbed up onto the narrow, weed-covered mole.

"You will be when you smell food."

Jo doubted it; she was still hurt by his brusqueness and concerned about the way in which he had deserted the villa party. But she seemed committed to picking her way along the primitive landing place and up the steep pebbled beach. She had no idea how far they had come or where they were, or if there was a village hidden in the folds of the cleft that ran down between the hills. But Dane appeared unconcerned as he strode along the pebbles, making for the low whitewashed building a little farther along.

A twisting green path led up to the inn and a couple of pink-washed cottages that lay beyond it. A small white goat with a black patch and inquisitive eyes looked up from its grazing, and she saw the blue amulet about its neck to ward off the evil eye. The Professor had told her that Corfu was the island of superstitions, and she repressed the impulse to remark on it to Dane. He was still in a brusque mood and doubtless quite capable of a scathing observation on the matter of superstition and folklore. Then she heard an unmistakable sound and forgot that neither she nor Dane were in exactly happy moods. "There's a waterfall somewhere," she exclaimed. "I can hear it."

"It's just behind the inn," he said. "You can see it later if you're interested."

His tone was uncaring, and she lapsed back into silence as they crossed the pebbled courtyard that fronted the inn.

It was a delightful spot with its myrtle tree, and its rustic well framed against the clumps of golden thistle on the hillside behind. A couple of old wine casks spilled blazing orange trails of nasturtiums. A white clematis rambled around the ancient, age-blackened door that stood open to the brilliant sunlight and revealed a darkly cool interior.

A young girl, slender and graceful in black, her long hair braided close to her head, came to the door and smiled a welcome. Her English proved meager, and Dane's Greek even more so, but understanding seemed to be reached without undue difficulty. It was a new experience for Jo to be invited into the kitchen, to sample the family's own cooking pot, or select fish that was displayed for her choice. Jo decided to leave it to Dane, who said, "*Langouste*," and was rewarded with a flashing smile from the girl's mother who was standing by.

Lunch took a long time. They were the only visitors, and while they waited for the *langouste* to be prepared they were shown into the parlor and brought wine and the traditional *mezé*. The girl was eager to talk, and the gesturing and guessing that contributed much of the conversation helped to disperse the chill from Dane's mood. When Jo commented on their being the only visitors he said, "This place hasn't yet been discovered. For me that's its main attraction—plus the lobster, of course!"

"That's all very well for you, but not for Clydia's business," Jo reminded him.

He had the grace to look rueful, and Clydia must have

grasped the gist of the remarks, for she shook her head, then nodded vehemently.

"No roadway—just boats. But come next spring." Her dark eyes glowed. "Road will be finished then, and many cars will come," she told them excitedly.

Dane nodded, but the news did not appear to inspire him greatly. "Nevertheless," he said gently, "that is very good news for you and your family, but promise me one thing, Clydia."

"And what is that?" the Greek girl asked, her white teeth flashing.

"Don't install a jukebox—please!"

"Jukebox? Oh—the music. Certainly not! We have our own music. We—"

Her mother summoned her at that point, and she went reluctantly toward the kitchen. Alone, Dane let the silence lengthen and stared at the vivid rectangle of sea and sky framed by the open doorway. His profile was clear-cut and remote in its unmoving expression. As she watched him Jo restrained a sad little sigh. He seemed acquainted with the inn and its owners. As he had spent several holidays with his old friend, Professor Quayle, she could not help wondering if he had brought Celia here to what was obviously one of his favorite haunts. It was a romantic spot—all of Corfu was romantic—but this was a secret place, a perfect rendezvous for lovers where they might lose themselves in its idyllic beauty. . . .

It was not a line of thought to induce any great joy; in Jo it only increased her sense of dejection and made her look up, to surprise Dane's direct gaze. Abruptly the faraway mist in her eyes vanished, to be replaced by the guarded look she was learning to acquire.

For a moment he studied her, until she turned her head away almost fiercely to evade that disturbing survey. Almost feverishly, she said, "We're going to be awfully late getting back."

"So what?" His voice was cool. "Unless you have some secret assignation tonight?"

Her mouth tightened at the mockery in his eyes. "You know perfectly well I haven't."

"But how should I know?" He lifted his shoulders

slightly. "The one thing I do know is never to be surprised at anything a woman does."

"Well, you know now," she returned flatly. "I haven't. And I've had few opportunities for making any."

"Of course, I forget. You take your duties so very seriously, Johanna Medway. How remiss of me." He flicked one dark brow upward and leaned back. "Some more wine?"

"No, thank you. I've had sufficient."

"One small glass?"

"We're not celebrating anything," she said, wondering what he meant by being remiss. "And I have that work to do that you brought down this morning."

"You'd better take the rest of the day off," he said flippantly and drained his glass. "Come on, I'll take you along to the waterfall."

It wasn't a very spectacular waterfall, only a sparkling stream tumbling over a narrow lip some ten feet up the cliff edge. But it splashed and trilled and rippled with a joyous abandon into a wide pool fringed with fern and yellow pimpernel. The restless chirruping of unseen cicadas added a strangely harmonious counterpoint to the music of the fall.

Jo stood silent. Perhaps she was becoming sated with Corcyrian beauty, but there was no enchantment here for her, none of the magic of that other afternoon spent with Dane. . . . She turned away, following his steps back to the beach and the boat. It wasn't fair. He seemed to be getting over his anger, assuaging it in the lovely deserted countryside and the endless fascination of riding the sea. He seemed to forget the effect his angry mood might have on others. He was talking now as though nothing had happened, pointing out one of the many small green and bronze inlets that stud the sea around the island's coast.

"I came here once," he said over his shoulder as he headed the boat toward the shore. "No one lives here now, but someone once did. There's a little ruined cottage and a tiny shrine to St. Spiridion. We came here, picnicked, and wondered who had put fresh flowers and herbs on the shrine."

"Weren't you trespassing?" she asked, when the

lengthening silence seemed to indicate she should make some response.

"Perhaps. But the islanders are generous to their visitors. The bounty of the island's beauty is freely given by nature for all to enjoy; they ask only that one does not abuse either that bounty or their trust."

She said nothing, pretending not to see the hand he held out to help her out of the boat. She could see the outline of the cottage through the trees. When she reached it she stared at its little white walls and sagging roof under the invading network of creeper. There was a lost, forlorn air about it, and an intense quality in the silence that hung over the little isle.

Dane thrust gently at the door that swung heavy on rusted hinges and looked inside. "It's exactly the same as two years ago," he said when he re-emerged.

"Is it?" She had found the ancient well, almost hidden now by encroaching bushes, and was kneeling on the moss-covered edge to peer into the dark depths.

He saw her and called sharply: "Look out—I should have remembered that."

"It's all right," she said mechanically, and he came across toward her, looking down into her shadowed face.

"What's the matter?" he said rather sharply.

"Nothing, except," she looked up, "I don't think I like your island very much."

There was a pause. "In that case, we'll leave it," he said lightly. "It's time we were getting back, anyway."

The sun was gilding the sea beyond the boat, turning it to bronze fire, and the mountains were deepening to a hazy purple against the skyline. Jo climbed down into the boat and wondered if they would get back before nightfall. It came so swiftly in the Mediterranean. One moment sea and island were bathed in the flame and gold of sunset, the next moment the purple veils had stolen down from the sky and suddenly it was dark.

She did not realize she gave a tiny sigh of relief as the first kick of the engine throbbed through the boat, or that it was really a sigh for what might have been—if the magic had come. She was stupid to weave romantic dreams about Dane, stupid to let herself be hurt by his moods, stupid to wonder if Celia Wincroft would make him happy. . . . When she returned home it would all be different, or rather, all the same as before. The island was the enchanter, not—

"Jo!"

She exclaimed aloud with shock at his peremptory shout. Her reverie shattered, she perceived the silence, the boat swaying free, and Dane thrusting the boat hook at her. "Fend her off—she's swinging in!"

Instinctively Jo obeyed as the swell carried the stern in. Dane secured bow and stern ropes cast off only moments ago, and once again the *Miranda* was moored.

"What happened?" Jo asked, judging it was now safe to ship the boathook.

"Engine trouble—don't ask me what till I've had a look."

"We're—we're not out of fuel?"

He cast a quelling glance over his shoulder as he opened the engine hatch. "That, my girl, has never been my favorite oversight when taking a girl out. You shock me, Jo."

"But I didn't mean. . . ." She subsided into silence as she watched him and wished she didn't feel such a helpless onlooker. "Is there anything I can do?" she said at last.

"You can scrounge around for a flashlight so that we're not hunting in the dark—this may take some time."

Glad that there was some measure of help she could contribute, she began to search through the lockers. The flashlight, when she eventually found it in the chart locker, didn't promise a very lasting illumination, but the stern locker yielded a battery lamp and a lantern.

Dane worked on, checking, seeking, while the sun dipped into a flame rippled sea. Oil permeated Dane's once immaculate white pants and coral silk shirt. His dark hair became more ruffled, and as Jo held the lamp and passed tools she glimpsed the more rugged personality underlying the polished façade of the attorney. Suddenly he straightened and shook his head wearily.

"I think the Professor is going to need a new engine."

CHAPTER EIGHT

The secondary implication of this statement did not instantly dawn on Jo. She moved aside as he straightened cramped limbs, and stumbled as she inadvertently stepped back on a ratchet. "Will it get us back?" she asked, stooping to pick up the offending tool and a couple of spanners.

"In its present state it won't—it's seized." He wiped his hands on a piece of waste. "At least we're lucky that it didn't wait until we were out in mid-channel."

Jo pictured them adrift, trying to do engine repairs in the dark, and nodded. Dismay had not yet disturbed her, and she moved to the hatch, to peer into the dark oily mystery of the works. "Will it take you very long to get it going?"

"I'm afraid I might not be able to get it going at all."

"What!" She whirled around. "But how are we going to get back? We can't stay here! We—"

"Don't panic," he said curtly. "That won't help."

His tone stabbed, and she stared back at him with hurt eyes. "Then tell me what will," she said bitterly.

"You can kneel down there and keep the lantern steady," he said calmly, "and you can listen and watch for a fishing boat. They put out at night. With a bit of luck we'll get taken aboard or in tow."

"But what if they don't see us?"

"They'll hear us. Sounds carry for miles on a still, clear night like this. Now don't chatter and do as I say," he told her. "I'm going to try and strip the engine down till I locate the cause of the trouble."

Obediently Jo took up her post beside him, silent now with the awareness of the deepening night and the murmuring sea crowding her senses. What if Dane couldn't repair the engine? What if no fishermen sailed this way? And what about Margaret and the others, worrying and wondering where they were. . . . Tense with the beginning of fear, she strained her eyes across the dark water in search of distant drifting lights.

It seemed hours later when Dane sighed and lit one of his rare cigarettes. She knew he hated to admit failure as much as she despaired of seeing the longed for glimmer of light. The lantern cast long shadows into the well of the boat, and the soft splashing sounds under the gunwales were ghostly little echoes of the wash against the shore's edge. She shivered, then saw Dane staring toward the main island.

She saw the lights, steady and unblinking, and felt a rush of hope. "Is it a boat?"

"No, I think it's the *taverna* where we had lunch."

Lunch! The very thought made Jo groan, aware of how hungry she was and how far away was food and drink.

Dane reached for the lamp. "It's worth a try. Somebody might notice it and come to investigate."

For a long time he sat immobile, his fingers depressing the lamp switch in a long patient signaling.

But there was no response, no sound or sign that any others than themselves were abroad that night. Then the *taverna* lights flickered and dimmed. There was only darkness.

Jo's shoulders drooped, and she could not repress a sigh. "What time is it?" she asked.

"Nearly 11." He stood up, and the boat swayed. "Are you cold?"

"No."

His hand touched her arm. "You are. Here, hold the lamp—and don't drop it."

She took the lamp, trying to suppress a shiver, and crouched down in the stern seat as he moved across the cockpit. He made a brief and brisk search, collecting several items, then turned back to her. "Time to find shelter."

She thought instantly of the lonely little islet and its one habitation, and did not move. "Not in that ruined cottage?"

He tucked the two cushions under his arm and said impatiently: "It'll be better than a day boat if the wind gets up. You'll be chilled by morning."

"I—I'd rather stay here," she said in a small voice.

"But I wouldn't. It's too cramped."

"Somebody might see our light, and we'd miss them."

"No," he shook his head, "we'd hear them."

She stayed unmoving, and he looked down at the small face upturned doubtfully to him. He said more gently, "There aren't any ghosts, you know, if that's what you're afraid of."

"It isn't. I—I just don't like strange places that are lonely at night. I'd rather stay here, or even on the beach," she said unhappily.

"All right—no ruins." He tossed the cushions and the tarpaulin bundle onto the rock ledge and climbed out. "Come on, up you come."

His hands were comfortingly warm, and his nearness reassuring. For the concern he showed they might have been strolling in the villa garden. She stayed close to him, almost brushing his arm with each step, and for once did not care if he noticed. The moon was not yet up, and the sun-bleached rocks loomed gaunt and skeletal out of the darkness. Dane's steps sounded unnaturally loud in a silence that was slightly unnerving. The rays of the lamp sent grotesque black shadows springing wildly ahead. Jo tried not to let her imagination translate them into scary shapes beckoning her on.

She was thankful when Dane chose a spot where beach and woodland met to form a small sheltered hollow. He opened the tarpaulin, threw down the two cushions, and said, "Curl yourself up in there and go to sleep if you can."

"Sleep?"

A slight smile touched his mouth at the incredulity in her voice. "Or count stars, or daydream, or whatever girls do when they suffer insomnia."

She looked down at the makeshift couch and back to the shadowy outline of him.

He gestured. "Please yourself. But it'll seem an awful long time until dawn if you sit and wait for it."

Slowly she sat down, crossing her arms and nursing her cold shoulders in her hands. Then she stiffened as she saw him turn away. "Where are you going?"

He paused, caught by the sharp note of her alarm. "Only to see if the water in that well is drinkable." He gestured with the baler. "We may get a little thirsty."

"I'm thirsty already, but I don't fancy that well." Abruptly she stood up. "I'll come and hold the lamp."

"Jo, I'm quite capable of carrying the lamp myself." He strode off, and she sat down disconsolately. The darkness and solitude seemed to rush around her, to taunt her with the truth she couldn't deny any longer. Her very first impressions of Sir Sheridan Leroy had been absolutely right. He was hard, arrogant, and uncaring, and that charm he assumed so effortlessly was exactly that: assumed. He was completely unconcerned about the others, that they would ˙be worrying, imagining an accident. He was sarcastic and impatient; he'd vented his temper on her, and it hadn't even occurred to him that she might feel hurt at such cavalier treatment. But then all she was to him was somebody who might be of use; whom he was prepared to pay well—as long as she was around when he wanted her. . . .

How foolish can one be? Jo asked herself bitterly as she stared across the indigo sea. It was not easy to face the truth—its shattering of her illusions brought too much pain. Her first meetings with Sir Sheridan had seemed such lighthearted frolics, and the prospect of taking his secretary's place during the holiday had seemed like an exciting dream come true. But the real picture was totally different, as was Dane from the picture her heart had painted of him. He was far from the romantic his sister imagined. Perhaps once, but not now. Any romanticism he possessed had long since been lost beneath the personality his career had made him. He used people and wielded a very potent charm to manipulate those people. And she had been foolish enough to fall victim to that charm. The enchanter. . . .

She was still sitting stiffly, her arms wrapped around her drawn-up knees, when Dane returned. She stayed unmoving, not looking up as his steps halted.

"Not asleep yet?"

"No." She steeled herself against the teasing note that

was dangerously irresistible and closed her eyes against a mental image of Celia that came suddenly and unbidden. Did he hurt Celia . . . ? Whatever Margaret thought of her, and however spoiled she might be, one had to admit the possibility that she didn't have things all her own way with Dane. He hadn't been particularly kind to her since she arrived; at times he had seemed quite indifferent to her wishes. Yet he was in love with her . . . Jo drew a shuddering sigh; heaven help his enemies!

"What's the matter?"

The softly spoken question forced her to acknowledge his presence. He had dropped down by her side, casual and relaxed, and she sensed his considering stare.

"Nothing." Her tone was flat. "Did you get any water?"

"No—the well was dry under all the leaves and stuff. Are you very thirsty?"

"Not really." She contrived to sound offhand. "Do you think anyone will notice the boat light?"

"They might. It depends if any of the locals has a favorite fishing patch around here—if patch is the right word," he added lightly.

"Ground," she said in the same flat tone.

"Ground," he acknowledged and lapsed into silence.

But he continued to study the small set profile that was faintly luminous in the shadows, until she moved almost fiercely to break that disturbing survey.

For a moment he gave no indication of having noticed the cold little withdrawal, then he put out one hand and brushed the back of it down her arm. "Didn't you bring a cardigan or something?"

Jo's mouth tightened. "I didn't have much chance to bring anything," she said bitterly. "Not even a comb or sunglasses. Not that they'd be much use now."

"Oh yes." His sigh was quite audible. "Once again I'm guilty of remission."

If only he cared! The glib little self-castigation came so smoothly from his lips, but it didn't mean a thing, she thought bitterly. She clasped her hands tightly and tried to ignore the tide of misery that rushed over her. Despite her attempts to convince herself she didn't care about anything except getting back to the villa and a semblance of normality, her mouth trembled ominously and her throat tightened.

He said softly, "I'm sorry, Jo."

She had to turn her head at that. "What for?" she said in a small disbelieving voice.

He smiled faintly. "For all this—for stranding you."

"Oh." She experienced a stab of disappointment. "It wasn't your fault—you didn't do it on purpose."

"I wasn't really meaning the boat's engine conking out on us," he said, after a perceptible hesitation.

She shrugged. "It's just one of those things."

"No, it isn't. I don't usually behave as boorishly as I did this morning," he said quietly.

She caught her breath on a tiny exclamation. The longing to believe in him was suddenly overwhelming, and the undoubted change in his mood almost as disconcerting. Feeling that some response was expected of her, she murmured in a choked little voice, "It's all right."

"Is it?" Suddenly his arm stole out and around her shoulders. "But I don't think it is, little Miss Medway. You must be both hungry and thirsty. If this choppy little breeze gets much stronger you're going to be quite chilly in that scrap of a dress."

"It's all right—I'm not cold," she said unsteadily, which suddenly was perfectly true. "This breeze would have been wonderful this afternoon, wouldn't it?"

"It certainly would." He showed no sign of taking away his warm, comforting arm. "But life rarely brings us exactly what we want at the moment we want it."

"No, it doesn't," she agreed. She could feel the warmth of him stealing through the two thin layers of the silk of his shirt and the cotton of her sundress. Tension was taut in her, born of the small conflict of longing to nestle within that sheltering arm, and guilt because she ought to draw away. Then a light on the sea distracted her, and she sat up sharply.

"Dane, what's that? It's like a searchlight! Are—do you think they're looking for us?"

But he was showing no sign of excitement when she looked back over her shoulder.

He shook his head and lay back, adjusting his cushion between his head and the somewhat gnarled bole of the tree against which he reclined.

"I noticed it before," he said, "when I came back along the beach. It's an Albanian patrol boat. Corfu is very close to the Albanian coast—parts of the northern coastline of the island are only a couple of miles or so distant. From some of the villages you can watch the searchlights playing across the strait all night, and their boats patrol the length of their coastline to prevent smuggling and illegal emigration," he added dryly.

"Oh." She watched the pencil of light travel northward until it dimmed from sight. Rescue was not yet at hand, and she was uncertain whether to lament or rejoice.

The situation which she found herself in was not unlike the substance of a certain favorite daydream she had cherished in secret during the early stages of adolescence. In this particular fantasy she was stranded on a desert island, aways with an adequate supply of food and beverages of course, and a quite superb wardrobe for the occasions when pagan beachwear of leaves or sarong was not suitable; naturally on an island possessing perfect climatic conditions. Her companion during these flights of fancy had varied, though. At the age of ten he had been a certain television newscaster; at the age of 12, inevitably the reigning rock idol of the year, and at 13 a certain French film actor of devastating charm. By the time she reached 14, however, she was searching for an ideal slightly less evanescent. Her choice fell on the English master, a hirsute gentleman of considerable literary attainment, but little idea of why one of his formerly less enthusiastic pupils should suddenly be possessed of such an insatiable thirst for English literature. Unfortunately, she discovered he was married with three children and instantly decided that any fantasy built around his unsuspecting person was highly improper. In any case, it was time to grow out of such childish fantasies. It was shortly after this that her aunt suffered a minor stroke, and she had to turn her hand to matters domestic instead of dreams about desert islands and the dream lover who would share her paradise.

Jo sighed deeply. Tonight she had her island, albeit a very small one, unfortunately minus anything remotely resembling nectar and ambrosia, despite its situation right at the heart of god and goddess land. But she did have the other vital ingredient, except that this time it was very real—a solid six-foot-plus of unpredictable male flesh and blood. She sighed again. She had the situation, but she wasn't at all sure how she was going to deal with it. . . .

"Jo. . . ."

She turned her head.

"Come here."

Slowly she took the three or four steps that took her back to him and stood there uncertainly, one hand to her brow to hold back the hair that the freshening breeze wanted to cloud about her face.

He stretched up one hand, and she could just discern the outline of his face. With its own involuntary movement her hand accepted the silent invitation. Quite gently he tugged, until she sank down into an awkwardly curled up position at his side. His clasp stayed warm around her fingers. "It's lonely down there," he said softly.

"Yes."

"What were you brooding about?"

She made a small, negative movement of her head. "Nothing special."

"You're not frightened, Jo?"

"What of?"

His thumb feathered across her wrist and stilled. "Of being marooned here, lost. You weren't imagining all kinds of frightful horrors, were you?"

"No." She sighed and looked down at the pale shape of their linked hands. "I was remembering . . . when I was a kid I used to imagine being stranded on a desert island. Silly, isn't it?"

"No more silly than many of the dreams children concoct—or adults, for that matter. We all have foolish dreams at times." He made the small feathering gesture again that was almost a caress. "I don't think dreams are foolish, as long as we recognize them as what they are and don't allow them to blind us to reality."

She was silent. Then she said slowly, "What should we recognize them as?"

"Isn't it obvious?" he sounded a little surprised. "A kind of seeking, and a reflection on our hidden character."

"Escapism," she said flatly. "An escape from what we are to what we would like to be."

"And sometimes to what we wish other people to be and do."

This observation was too near the truth for comfort, and she lapsed into silence again. Suddenly she wished she was different, that she was older, more self-assured—and loaded with the kind of sexual maturity Diane and Celia Wincroft possessed in abundance. No man or situation would defeat them. They possessed the ability to spark a man's interest—and keep it. Instead, all she had was this painful sense of inadequacy and an immaturity he had underlined all too clearly. A poor foil to a man of Dane Leroy's caliber.

She heard him laugh softly under his breath and saw him hold out his arm. "Come on, little Miss Medway—I got you into this pickle—the least I can do is offer you a shoulder."

"I—I don't want to weep."

"I should hope not! But I think perhaps this is one occasion when we might be permitted to dream."

She hung back, desperately wanting to succumb to the invitation of those arms, even though it was merely the invitation of protection and amused indulgence. "Dreams aren't much use now," she said sadly.

"Not of a luscious steak, heaped with mushrooms and crispy roast potatoes? Ham sandwiches? Potato chips? Oysters and champagne?"

"You're cruel."

He laughed suddenly and reached out. The next moment she was pulled firmly into his arms, and her head patted onto his shoulder.

"You will do as I say, Miss Johanna Medway," he said against her ear, "for one reason."

"And what's that?" She gave a deep sigh and surrendered.

"Because dreams are all we have at the moment," he said on the same note of laughter.

Contrary to Jo's romantic imaginings, curling up within the crook of a man's arm, with one's head on his shoulder, is as liable to induce cramp as any other position held static for a length of time. Once settled, he had no inclination for further conversation, or so it seemed to Jo when her tentative attempts at casual remarks met with unencouraging murmurs until the third one invoked no response at all. He seemed intent on seeking sleep, and apparently considered that he had met the requirements of conscience concerning herself in providing a shoulder and a sheltering arm instead of the hard earth.

After the first tense moments Jo decided that after all he mustn't be able to hear or feel the activity of her heart. It seemed incredible that he shouldn't—judging by the noisy shockwaves it was sending through all her pulses. She found she was holding her breath, but that only made it worse and caused her to give a long shuddering sigh as she relinquished the pent-up breath. She thought there was a response through the arm curved around her shoulders, then the deep even tenor of his breathing was resumed. Jo dared to relax; the soft silkiness of his shirt against her cheek, and the hard warmth of him pressing through the thin material was the most delightful sensation she had ever experienced. She had no desire to go to sleep, only to enjoy this new pleasure. Then the inconsequent thought came: she ought to be able to hear *his* heartbeat. . . .

But it took several moments of concentration before she detected the faint, steady beat somewhere just below

where her chin rested. She felt a pang of disappointment;
it was remarkably steady and even—not in the least bit
thuddy. Any effect she was having on him didn't appear
to be anything like the effect he was having on her!

She restrained another sigh and closed her eyes, trying
resolutely to ignore the beginning of cramp in the leg she
had unwisely curled underneath her. Even if she didn't
sleep it was hardly fair to stop him doing so. . . .

She must have succeeded, and despite herself fallen
into a doze. She was wide awake, her heart pounding and
every sense alert for the alien sounds and movements
hidden in the night. Something had startled her, yet Dane
had not moved.

He was looking down into her wide startled eyes, and
his clasp tightened a little, as though her tension
communicated itself to him, and he sought to dispel it.

She stirred. "I—I thought I heard something—I must
have dreamed it."

He shook his head. "*Be not afear'd: the isle is full of
noises. Sounds and sweet airs that give delight, and hurt
not,*" he quoted softly.

His voice filled her with calm and a flooding warmth of
reassurance. "Perhaps it was one of Caliban's 1000
twangling instruments. . . ." she said on a note of new
assurance.

"Perhaps. . . ." He bent his head and kissed her, one
brief sweet touch of his lips before she could perceive his
intention. As her mouth parted with surprise its small
involuntary movement was stilled again.

Jo's wide eyes saw the drifting cloud above, and the
first fall of radiance from the rising moon, then her lashes
fell. All senses ceased to record anything but the wild
sweet center of joy that was his mouth.

When he raised his head she was mute for long
moments, then the cloud was past, and the silvery light
was illuminating his features. It seemed to be etching
mockery in the quizzical face looking down into her own,
and Jo's whirling sense came to a full stop.

"What did you do that for?" she said shakily.

"Does there have to be a reason?"

His mouth was parted in a slight smile that seemed to challenge her. She looked away desperately, not knowing how to reply.

"Isn't the whole essence of a kiss in that it's a message without words?" he said softly.

But his message was like him—too enigmatic for her understanding. If only the message of her own senses were not so tumultuous—and transparent. A sudden fear lest she had betrayed herself made her move convulsively and scramble to her feet. But she forgot about cramped limbs and gave a small cry as her numbed legs refused to support her.

"Steady!" He caught her quickly as she stumbled. "Getting up so soon, my little one?"

"I—I have pins and needles—I didn't realize we'd slept so long."

"*You* slept so long," he amended dryly.

"Oh, I'm sorry—you must be cramped," she said wildly. "You—you should have wakened me."

"I did." He laughed softly. "I sneezed. Your hair was tickling my nose. It was my sneeze, not Caliban's ghost, that shook you awake."

"I—I'll speak severely to my hair about that," she said in a feverish attempt to match his mocking rebuke with a flippancy. "It won't happen again, I promise."

"No, I'm afraid it won't."

She noticed the changed note in his tone and leaped instantly to the conclusion that she'd failed him. But how? Had he taken a sudden notion to while away the long hours of the night by seducing her? Her heart plummeted like a piece of lead as he turned away from her and began to pace down toward the beach. Surely that hadn't been his intention. She watched him miserably, the brief wonderful memory of his kiss already turning to dross, tarnished by the bitterness of knowing how desperately she did want him to love her . . . but not lightly, not merely because there was nothing else to do. . . .

His dark form turned and retraced its steps. He came up to her and stared down at her averted face. "I thought I—what's the matter, Jo?"

"Nothing."

"Your stock answer." His warm hands closed over her shoulders, hard. "You're trembling."

Butterflies of panic whirled in her and suddenly the tall strength of him towering over her brought a frantic need to escape to a safe distance. Whether she did not trust him, or whether she did not trust herself, she did not think to define, but tore herself out of his grasp. "Can't I tremble if I want to?" she demanded. "Maybe it doesn't matter to you—you're a man. That makes a difference."

"What difference?"

The question was softly spoken, and to Jo it sounded dangerously so; as disquieting as his sensed presence behind her. Already beginning to feel foolish, she gestured vaguely and let her hands fall to her sides. "All this—here, and everything," she said hopelessly.

There was a long silence. She stared miserably at the moonsilver coating the sea and wondered if anything would ever be right again. Then she heard the soft scuff of his steps in the sand.

"I see," he said over his shoulder as he turned away. He halted a little distance in front of her, his hands thrust into his pockets and the set of his shoulders uncompromisingly straight. "So by some mysterious alchemy I do not feel any discomfort. I am immune to hunger pangs and thirst and weariness indefinitely, merely because I happen to be a man. Is that what you mean by difference?" he asked coldly.

"No!" she said in a choked whisper.

"Then what do you mean, pray?"

"Oh, I don't know." Her shoulders drooped sadly. "I'm sorry—I didn't mean it like that at all."

There was nothing about his stance, or the set line of his profile to suggest that he was mollified. He continued to stare across the luminous sea as he said coldly, "I was just congratulating myself on how cheerfully you were accepting the situation. It seems the thought was a trifle premature."

"Well, it wasn't!" she cried, stung by his curtness. "It was all right until you— *Until you spoiled everything*," she finished in an anguished whisper he was not intended to hear.

But she forgot the intense stillness of the night; a silence that could magnify the tiniest sound, and she also forgot his extremely keen ear.

He spun to face her, and even though his head was a dark silhouette against the moonlight she read impatience and cynicism in the deeply shadowed features.

"So that's it, after all!" he exclaimed. "I wouldn't have credited it in this day and age. Tell me," he took a step forward, "is this the way you react every time a man kisses you?"

She took an involuntary pace back, as though she could escape the pain of disillusion. But the instinct of pride prompted her to show anger. Her head was lifted proudly. "No," she said quietly. "Not if I know it's a kiss and not a pass."

"Pass!" he echoed, with a gesture that seemed to underline his derision. "Heavens, if that's the effect a kiss has on you I think you'd better go back to the nursery. I was under the impression you—" He stopped abruptly as she gave a stricken gasp, then flung out his hands impatiently. "Oh, for God's sake," he groaned, "don't start weeping about it."

"I'm not!" She fought the stupid tears that had betrayed her. She ran down to the water's edge, trying to dash them away without his seeing the despairing little movements.

"Jo. . . ."

She made no response, and for a moment there was silence, then she heard his soft footfalls. "Jo, this is crazy," he said in a softer tone. "What a baby you are . . . I believe you're scared of me."

"I'm not!"

"Then turn around."

"Why should I?"

"Why shouldn't you—if you're not scared?"

After a long hesitation she turned slowly and saw he was about four paces from her.

"Come here, Jo Medway," he said firmly.

Again she hesitated before she approached him warily. He looked down into the small set face and shook his head as though surprised. "Was all that because I kissed you?"

"No—it had nothing to do with it." She sighed helplessly. "I can't explain, you wouldn't understand. Oh, can't we forget about it?"

"You seem to be the one intent on remembering," he said dryly.

She looked down unhappily, aware of her total lack of experience in dealing with the opposite sex when it turned temperamental. When she did not reply for an instant he said coolly, "I suspect you are harboring at least two fallacies about me, young Jo. I take strong exception to both of them."

Her parted lips betrayed her bewilderment as she looked up at him. "I—I don't think so," she denied. "I—I've always respected you more than any other person I know, except Dave, perhaps."

"Ah, yes, Dave would never make a pass," he said sardonically. "No—" he checked her instinctive protest, "it's perfectly clear. You do not care to believe that an eminent, highly respectable attorney would stoop so low as to make passes at little girls stranded all night with him on an uninhabited speck in the sea."

A despairing sigh escaped her. "You'll never forget the silly, naïve things I've said to you, will you?" she said bitterly.

"Not as long as you harbor these silly, naïve ideas about me as well, Jo," he said flatly. "To begin with, I'm not in the habit of pursuing a pass where it's not wanted. On the other hand, to expect any man to hold a warm young female in his arms for two hours without feeling some response is asking a lot—if he *is* a man," he added dryly.

She was silent, and he laid one lean finger along the curve of her cheek. "You do nestle rather trustingly, young Jo."

"Yes," she looked away, "but I forgot something."

"And what was that lapse?" He seemed to be reverting to his normal imperturbable mien.

"The same one you forget," she said sadly. "You happen to belong to Celia."

His hand fell away. "Yes, Celia. You women have strange loyalties when it suits you." The enigmatic conclusion of his remark faded into the silence, and Jo saw that his gaze was now far away from her.

She said flatly, "There's nothing strange about loyalty or honor."

There was no reply. She looked up at his profile and felt sadness gather into a tight knot of despair in her heart. His profile was hard, remote; a plain indication of his total lack of interest. With a sigh for her foolish dreams she moved up the beach and was about to sink down despondently in the crumpled tarpaulin when Dane called, "You can gather the gear up."

"What?"

"Rescue is on the way—I think."

She sprang up and ran to his side, disbelief in her eyes as she scanned the wide, empty expanse.

"I can't see anything," she exclaimed.

"There's a boat around somewhere. Listen."

She held her breath, and above the sigh of the wind and the sea there came faintly but unmistakably the putt-putt of an outboard.

"I heard it before—or thought I did," he said. "I think it's on the south side. Come on."

He began to stride along the beach toward the landing place, and she hovered, irresolute. Go back first for the things, or. . . ? The things lost, and she hurried to catch up with Dane.

It took only a few minutes to reach the southern point and the outcrop of rock where they had left the boat moored. There, cutting across the swathe of silver on the strait, was a small dark shape.

"Got the flashlight?" Dane held out his hand expectantly.

"Oh, I didn't bring— Sorry! I'll go back for it." She turned with the jerky little utterances and scurried back. Dane cupped his hands to his mouth and sent a resonant hail across the water.

When Jo panted back with the flashlight there was no need for it. Clydia and a boy of about 12 and a young man were gathered around Dane, all talking at the same time.

The explanations were a little confused, but gradually, with a great deal of laughter, they became clear. As the boat chugged across the strait and down the coast to the *taverna* Clydia explained. Her young brother had gone out for squid with Spiro, the dark, slender youth whose boat it was, and noticed the light on the islet. The boy had wanted to investigate, but Spiro had refused, surmising that the visitors would be tourists.

"I think perhaps you are lovers!" called Spiro from the helm. "You not thank me! Yes?" His teeth gleamed very white as he grinned over his shoulder.

Jo was glad of the darkness to hide the mounting waves of color in her cheeks. She dared not look at Dane as he said lightly, "Rather hungry lovers, I'm afraid. All I can say is that Jo's feeling very thankful," he added dryly.

The boy said something in Greek. It sounded like an "*I told you so!*" kind of remark, and it induced an instant elder-sister snub from Clydia.

It wasn't until later, after a very welcome meal at the *taverna,* that Dane was able to explain that Clydia and Spiro were youthful lovers. It was due more to Spiro's eagerness to get back with the night's catch and his nightly tryst with Clydia rather than his discretionary regard for lovers' feelings. Usually Clydia stole out as soon as she had dispatched her young brother to bed, but this time the boy had not been so easily dispatched—and Clydia had remembered the English visitors at lunch time. And this time Spiro was quite eager to investigate—if Clydia came too! "Alas, little brother insisted on coming too," Dane concluded in an amused whisper, "or threatened to raise Grandmama!"

Clydia returned at that moment to say that she had heated water so that they could wash. They were to stay at the *taverna* for the remainder of the night. Dane was anxious to let his sister and the others know they were safe, but was forced to realize that little time if any could be gained by setting off immediately to return. To go by boat would take the night and much of the next day, and there was neither transport nor telephone within five miles. But Spiro had promised to borrow his cousin's bicycle and set off at first light for the nearest village where the *proedros* would telephone a message to Professor Quayle.

The family at the *taverna* could not have been kinder. Clydia loaned Jo an embroidered nightdress of stiff white cotton fragrantly scented with lavender and the cedarwood of the chest in which it had lain. Jo suspected that it might be part of Clydia's dowry, and that it was the Corfiote girl's own room that had been given up to her, but to have protested, no matter how well-meaning, would have risked giving offense. She settled down thankfully in the little white room high under the eaves, the soft sounds off the island night drifting through the tiny casement window, and knew that this night would be the one that would live longest of all her memories of the island.

Despite her troubled emotions she slept soundly and sweetly until long after the family were up and about their daily life. To her surprise her dress had been laundered and pressed for her. It smelled sun-fresh and sweet, unexpectedly pleasant against her skin when she donned it.

Her heart betrayed its unease when she went into the cool parlor for breakfast and knew she had to face Dane. But he had almost finished breakfast, and his mien was as imperturbable as ever.

"I asked them to let you sleep on," he said easily. "I thought you would be tired. Did I do right?"

She nodded. He stood up, excusing himself, and wandered outside. Jo watched him till he passed from sight and could not help wondering if she had dreamed the interlude on the islet. But if she had it would remain a dream so vivid she would never forget it—even if it were only a kiss. A kiss without reason . . . to him!

The Professor arrived just as Jo finished breakfast.

He pretended a certain terseness at the inaccessibility of the spot that they had chosen to be stranded in and the resultant effect on his car springs, but Jo guessed it covered a deep thankfulness at finding them safe.

He had brought Ricky and Margaret with him. After Margaret's first rather poignant little embrace of Dane she lapsed into a silence. Only Jo appeared to notice she seemed somewhat worried.

However, there was a great deal of explaining to be done, mainly in the exchange of technical theory between Dane and the Professor on the subject of the boat's trouble. Ricky joined in enthusiastically, between asking Jo innumerable questions as to what it was like being marooned in the dark. Margaret's silence passed unnoticed except by Jo. It wasn't until they reached the villa that the point which had nagged at Jo appeared to register with Dane.

He got out of the car and stared at the deserted terrace. "Where's everybody?" he asked.

The Professor seemed not to have heard, and Margaret glanced at Jo before she turned to her brother.

"Alan had a cable yesterday," she said in a curiously controlled voice. "It was from his firm, asking to cut short his holiday and return as soon as he could. Some emergency."

"Hard luck." Dane's brows went up. "He would go on the morning flight, I expect."

Margaret nodded and took a deep breath as he moved forward. "Celia went with him."

Dane halted. "She's *gone*?"

Margaret moved to his side. "She—she was worried about you when you didn't get back last night—we all were. But when the message came through this morning, she announced she'd decided to leave as well. She might as well travel with Alan as there were vacancies on the flight."

At that moment Ricky spotted the villa cat and made a rush for it. The sounds of his pursuit sounded strangely loud in the silence that followed Margaret's announcement. Dane did not move. Watching his bleak expression Jo wished she was anywhere except on that exact spot halfway along the path leading to the terrace steps. But she found she could not move to pass Dane, and a sick little pain coiled around her heart as he exclaimed:

"Is that *all*?"

"No." Margaret sighed and looked up at him. There was impatience in her eyes. "She told me to tell you she'd see you as usual on Tuesday—at the Caprice. She also said she'd heard from her father. He'll be in touch with you. He's pulling out of the Marcombe Road development business. So that's good news for Jo."

Dane did not answer. He turned his head toward Jo, but she could see no recognition in his eyes. They simply seemed to register that she was there before he moved slowly on toward the house.

As he reached the end of the terrace Neil Clinton appeared at the open French window. He gave a loud cry of mock surprise and made a broad gesture of welcome.

"So you're back, you two—and you didn't have to swim for it, after all. Hi, Jo—you'd better come with me next time, girl—I'm a better mechanic!"

Jo tried to smile, but her mouth felt stiff. She had never felt less like smiling.

Abruptly Dane brushed past the younger man. "We're all leaving tomorrow, in any case," he said coldly and went indoors.

CHAPTER NINE

They spent their last evening at the Akhillion, the great ornate villa Elizabeth of Austria had built for the brief spells when she could escape to her "magic isle." Set against the hillside, its lights sparkling like crystal necklaces in the velvet night, the pale gleam of marble statuary reflecting their glow along the terraces, it provided a romantic setting for the more imaginatively inclined. To Jo that night it brought only a sense of unreality. She felt as though she had strayed into a film setting where she had no right to be.

Neil had booked a table at the restaurant, and afterward they spent an hour in the Casino, where Jo, implicitly following Neil's instructions, astonished no one more than herself by winning 500 drachmas. It brought a momentary lightening of her spirits as she acknowledged credit for her luck to Neil.

"It's all a mystery to me," she said as they turned away from the table.

"And see that it remains a mystery," Dane said shortly.

His tone and expression banished the brief exhilaration. She was almost thankful when it was time to wind up the evening's farewell to holiday time, return to the villa, and packing in preparation for the departure next morning.

The journey home was uneventful. Of the four of them, only Ricky could be said to look as though a thoroughly happy holiday lay behind him. He chattered nonstop practically all through the flight, and the car journey at the end of it. Dane collected his car and drove Jo home to the apartment before taking Margaret to her home in Kensington.

"I'll call you," Margaret promised when the goodbyes were said, "and you must come over some weekend."

"I'd love to." Jo thanked her and summoned a smile

for Ricky. "We'll go swimming one Saturday, shall we?"

Ricky agreed and showed signs of curiosity concerning where Jo lived, and Margaret promptly drew him away. "We haven't time today—we have to get home and Jo will be busy." She flashed a harassed mother's smile at Jo and took her young son firmly back to the car.

Dane put Jo's case down in the little hallway and turned to her. "I'll be in touch, Jo, as soon as I have any news."

She nodded wanly, and he turned away instantly. She stood still, listening to his steps echoing along the long tiled outer hall and the slam of the car door before she shut her apartment door.

The apartment felt chill and lonely. Diane wouldn't be back for another week; there'd be nothing in the fridge. Before she even looked in the bedroom she knew that Diane would have left it looking as though a cyclone had swept through it. There wasn't even any nice mail, only a bill, a circular offering her a free set of non-stick pans if she purchased a super-de-luxe dishwasher before the end of the month, and her own postcard to Diane.

It must have taken nearly a week to come and missed Diane, she thought dully as she stared at the brilliant colors of the view from Kanoni. If she closed her eyes she could remember the morning she had sat in the blazing sun and penned the message on this very card. If she stretched out her hand across the café table she could touch Dane . . . hear the little click of his ballpoint pen as he dutifully started on his own quota of cards. . . .

Abruptly she tossed the card on the table and tried to close her mind to sentiment. She had to face reality; the stores and stocking-up the kitchen, the apartment needed cleaning from top to bottom. It was back to work on Monday. . . .

It was the dreariest week Jo had had in years, and Tuesday was the worst day of all. She lived for the phone ringing, sure that Dane would keep his promise; unable to believe that there was nothing left, that once the youth center business was over the one slender link between herself and Sir Sheridan Leroy was severed.

But what was there? she asked herself fiercely during the desolate hours of the Tuesday night as she imagined his reunion with Celia. They would make it up again, that was certain. Because there was no doubt that he loved her. The memory of his face that morning when he found she was gone. . . . And how could any man resist her? Jo wondered despairingly. She was irresistible and would always win, no matter how a man might try to arm himself against her.

And why should you care? she adjured herself. *He doesn't!* She imagined his astonishment and his amusement if he knew her thoughts and dreams woven around himself. He'd never made any secret of the fact that she amused him, or that in his eyes she was still an immature youngster. *A quaint child. . . .*

For once she couldn't even raise any enthusiasm for the youth center. She went along on the Wednesday evening because that was pow-wow night. She knew she should be present, and then wished she hadn't bothered. Dave wasn't there and had left no message for her, and judging by the careless greeting, "What! You back already!" nobody seemed to have realized she'd been away.

Roy seemed to have taken charge in Dave's absence. When she joined the little group around the table he picked up a page of notes and leaned forward self-importantly.

"I'll recap for Jo's benefit—okay?"

They nodded, and he went on: "So we're agreed on that. It's no good waiting for the ax to fall. This is an occasion when it's shortsighted to be hopeful. We have to prepare for the worst. And that means planning out a complete course of action in advance."

There was a murmur of agreement around the table. Jo stayed silent. Already a suspicion had occurred to her, but she waited to hear Roy out.

"Right." Roy consulted his notes. "So I've drawn up this list as we planned last Wednesday, and I vote we approach these people. There're five possibles here—two of them very promising." He then read out the names of five firms or premises in the Marcombe Road area, all of whom had one thing in common: a small section of property either semi-derelict, or not being fully utilized for some reason or other.

"Holleys would be the best," Muriel broke in. "Since they built their new cafeteria the old one's just been closed and various old stuff stored in it. It would be great because it's got all the public utilities."

Roy nodded. "Actually, I've already been in touch with their sales manager—I happen to know his daughter," he interjected with a slight heightening of his color. "He's promised to make discreet inquiries about what plans the firm have for it—if any—but he did say it might be a heftier rent than we'd be able to meet. However, that's one bridge we won't cross till we come to it. In the meantime there's the old primary school in Bridge Lane. My father says there's no development or closing order on it, as far as he knows, but he's going to investigate. So we—"

"Just a minute!" Jo couldn't stay silent any longer. "You're thinking of these as alternative quarters for us? For the Center? But we're going to fight to stay here, surely?"

There was a silence, then Roy shook his head. "We've decided it isn't worth it. My father says he doubts if we'd have it for more than a couple of years, even if we did succeed in getting Mrs. Jackson to renew the lease."

"Yes, but surely Mrs. Jackson can let us have a longer lease than that!" Jo protested. "It's her property and her land. And now that—" She stopped, suddenly wondering if they had heard the news about Aldo Wincroft. "There won't be any difficulty," she cried. "Didn't you know? Aldo Wincroft changed his mind. He doesn't want it after all."

"So you've heard that." Roy gave her a sharp look. "I didn't think it had come onto the grapevine yet. But it still doesn't make any difference. She'll have to sell in any case."

"I don't think so. We should ask her before we start looking around elsewhere," Jo persisted. She looked around the circle of intent young faces and back to Roy's rather superior smile. Suddenly she liked him less than ever, even as her conscience admitted the unfairness of a purely personal reaction. He was working for the sake of the Center, as they all were. But all the same. . . . "What does Dave think about it?" she asked hotly.

Roy leaned forward and rested his chin on interlaced fingers as he looked directly at her. "Dave's leaving."

"Yes, I know. But. . . ." In a flash of dismay she knew, even before Roy spoke.

"Dave's handed over to me."

Jo could hardly restrain a small exclamation.

"We put it to the kids last Friday, and they all agreed," Muriel said gently.

"And I think we have to be ready to build a new Center," Roy said firmly.

The meeting had done nothing toward lightening Jo's heart when she made her way home that night. Usually she was happy when she had been to the Center, but the more she thought about Roy taking Dave's place as leader the more miserable she felt. The moment she reached home she went straight to the phone and dialled Dave's number.

Long moments later she put the receiver back and listlessly took off her jacket. She had to get used to the idea of Dave not being around. Perhaps he might be in by the time she'd had something to eat. . . .

Half-heartedly she made herself a snack that she ate in her armchair while she looked unseeingly at the TV. The movie finished at half-past ten; she would sit it out and by then Dave must be home.

But he wasn't, or if he was he wasn't answering his phone. She looked at the dishes in the sink and sniffed her disfavor, then made herself wash them and set out her breakfast things. It was now ten to eleven. She'd try Dave's number once more. She had to talk to *somebody* before she went to bed. . . .

When the burr-burr repeated its unmistakable message she experienced an almost fatalistic sense of relief. No one would be foolish enough to persist any further.

She did not replace the receiver. Almost of its own

volition her free hand depressed the stops and reached for the directory. It seemed like a beckoning portent that part three, L to R, should be on top; that when she opened it at random it should be to the exact page. . . . She ran her finger down the column. L . . . Le . . . Leroy . . . and penciled a bold ring around the number.

She began to dial quickly, before she could repent on the impulse. Her heart was drumming so loudly she could hear her hammering pulses. As the last digit spun back she nearly clamped down the receiver before the number could ring. She shouldn't do this. She should wait for him to keep his promise. She was being foolish and weak. But she so desperately wanted to hear his voice again . . . and it was important that he should know the latest development. He wouldn't thank her for letting him waste his time if they'd changed their plan. Dave was out of it now so. . . .

"Hello! Leroy here—speak up!"

Suddenly her fingers were nerveless around the receiver. She stammered, "Hello, Sir Sheridan . . . I'm sorry to—"

"Is that Jo?" he said sharply.

"Oh, yes, I'm sorry to bother you so late, but I—I had to speak to you. It—it's about the Center."

"Yes, I'm sorry I didn't let you know sooner," he cut in before she could continue. "So you've heard about it."

A frown puckered her brow; how did he know? Then it cleared; one of them must have phoned him. But why hadn't they—? They might have told her! She said, "I just found out tonight. I think it's awful. I—I felt I had to call you because I thought it was awful after all you've done. It seems such a waste of your time."

"Don't worry too much about that," he said quickly. "It's unfortunate, but I'm afraid this is one occasion where we have to admit defeat."

The little frown chased over Jo's brow again and suddenly settled. "Yes, but I'm still against it, and I'm sure that Dave wouldn't have agreed if he'd been staying on."

"I don't think he'd have much choice." Dane sounded

rather surprised. "Even though I'm aware he possesses almost superhuman powers—in your opinion."

She noticed the sarcasm and countered quickly, "He'd never have done it without consulting you. Without waiting to hear from you. They decided on this last week. But we—you were still away."

There was a long pause. Then Dane said, "I think we're talking at cross purposes, Jo. Tell me; who decided on what last week? This policy you're convinced Dave would have vetoed?"

"About finding a new Center—I thought somebody must have told you," she said with some bewilderment. "I just found out tonight. You know that Dave's going to Africa? Well, Roy is taking over—his father's a councillor, and he's terribly bossy. He's persuaded the others that it would be best to give up. Not bother about trying for a new lease, and look for a new place. He's got a short list already, and he—"

"Not so fast! We have been at cross purposes. This new leader of yours must have heard a whisper from his father. There's a new by-pass on the board, Jo. Still officially secret, but not for long now, I'd say. It will cut right through the middle of your club premises and Mrs. Jackson's land."

For a moment Jo was speechless. If Roy had known he had certainly kept his own counsel. Certainly none of them had foreseen this happening, even though they had guessed that redevelopment must take place eventually in the Marcombe Road area. Then she forgot the Center and themselves.

"But what about Mrs. Jackson? Does this mean they're going to take her land off her?"

"I'm afraid so." He sounded gentler. "But she'll be compensated."

"But not as much as Aldo Wincroft would have given her. So this is why he changed his mind."

"Yes." Dane sighed. "He heard about it and dropped the idea like a hot cake. Incidentally, I went to see Mrs. Jackson this morning. If it's any consolation to you your efforts on behalf of the Center have indirectly helped her."

"How?" Jo cradled the receiver and tried to "see" Dane as he talked.

"Before I went on holiday I instructed a surveyor to inspect the site and the property, make a full report, and assess its value as a current market proposition. I also acquainted Mrs. Jackson's lawyer with certain facts and suggested he approach the Council for outline planning permission for light industry. Until this was done Mrs. Jackson was *not* to accept Aldo Wincroft's offer. I gather he was horrified," Dane said in a lower, more confiding tone that made Jo hug the phone more closely. "I also kept Dave informed, and he agreed entirely with me that Mrs. Jackson's interests must be protected."

"You never told me," Jo said softly.

"I was waiting until matters were a little more definite—you have this consuming impatience of the young for instant everything," he said in amused tones.

"I don't!"

"In any case, you never asked me."

"Because I didn't want to be a nuisance, pestering you. I was giving you time—instead of expecting instant everything," she retorted.

She thought he chuckled, but his voice was grave again as he went on, "The inquiries we made turned up these various proposals for redevelopment, and this proposed new road. I'm afraid that even if we'd been successful your days in your present premises would have been numbered."

"Yes." She sighed. "I think we knew in our hearts that we couldn't go on imposing on Mrs. Jackson's kind heart. She needs the money badly—I hope the Council gives her the full value."

"I intend to do everything *I* can to see that she gets fair compensation."

There was a silence. It seemed that the conversation was ready for conclusion. Jo frantically tried to select something from all the things she wanted to say, anything to postpone the evil moment of saying goodby. The trouble was that most of the things she wanted to say to him would have to remain locked secretly forever in her heart. A point that hadn't yet occurred suddenly did so. She said wistfully, "So it wouldn't have made much difference anyway, even if this hadn't happened."

"Even if what hadn't happened?" he said idly.

"Once you had established Mrs. Jackson's rights about the place, and even if Mr. Wincroft hadn't withdrawn his offer, I think you would've tried to talk us out of asking her for a new lease."

He paused before he replied. When he did his tone was crisp, almost impersonal. "There isn't any point in speculating over that now. I think what you really mean, Jo, is that I wouldn't have been acting in your interest."

Although Jo's surmise had been very near this statement she hadn't thought of it in that way at all. "I didn't!" she denied hotly. "I never meant that."

"Not intentionally," he said coolly, "but the subconscious thought was there. You haven't yet learned to isolate your personal feelings from business affairs."

There was another pause while he left her to make what she could of that. Then he said suddenly, "Is Diane back?"

"No—not till Saturday."

"Hm, so you've been on your own all week."

"Yes." She could not restrain the wistful sigh.

"Lonely?"

"No—not terribly," she said, summoning pride.

"Not nervous?"

"Not very."

She could almost see the sardonic tilt of his brows during the dry little exchange.

"You haven't heard from Margaret since—" He stopped abruptly. Jo thought she heard a muffled sound at the other end of the line. An instant later she knew she hadn't imagined it as a soft sweet voice said, "Darling, who do you have there?"

Then the sound was blanked by a simple device Jo recognized easily. She had closed her hand over the mouthpiece too often herself at the office.

The silence lengthened, then abruptly Dane's voice came through, coolly impersonal again. "Sorry—I was interrupted. Is there anything else?"

"No," she said in a small voice.

"Goodnight, Jo."

"Goodnight," she whispered numbly and put down the receiver with a trembling hand.

Celia!

Somehow the week dragged to its close. Diane arrived home in style, escorted by the Norwegian heart-throb and two of his compatriots who had met Diane at the airport. Two more Scandinavians—girls—and one of Diane's ex-boyfriends arrived shortly afterward. They whooped it up in fine style until the small hours. And on the following Tuesday the Center held its farewell party for Dave.

He was leaving very early the next morning, so all the goodbyes and good wishes had to be said at the end of the celebration. For the first time ever Dave took Jo in his arms and hugged her tightly.

"'Bye, Tich. Thanks for being such a willing and wonderful aide." He took her face between his hands and kissed her lightly on the mouth. "See you in two years—God bless."

It was warm and wonderful, something she had often longed to experience, but now it meant nothing except the pleasure of genuine affection. Dave's lips were just the lips of a friend. . . . How could the heart change so completely? She could almost laugh at herself when she remembered her foolish adolescent passion, if only it didn't begin a train of very frightening thought. . . .

It was impossible to hide anything from Diane. She was too observant and too experienced. Before many days had passed Jo's secret was a secret no longer, and Diane was as forthright and dismissing as ever. And with chilling authority she succeeded in underlining the fear Jo didn't want to admit.

"You're *not* in love with him," Diane said. "It's just another crush. And unless you want to make an idiot of yourself you'd better forget it right away."

"It isn't." Jo sighed hopelessly. How could she make Diane understand that she didn't want to forget it? She wanted to love Dane for as long as she lived. Even if he never knew, never saw her again, she could never forget him. "It's different!" she wailed.

Diane gave her an exasperated look. "It always is—until the next time. Listen, Jo. The trouble with you is that you're a late developer. I'd lost count of my affairs by the time I was 19—and lost all my illusions as well," she added dryly. "But in that respect you are different. For heaven's sake, try to be logical about it, because it's so simple I thought they learned it in the nursery these days. You'll go on having these crushes," she gestured, "these fixations on various men who take your interest until eventually you have your first real affair, or get married. And by affair I don't mean gentle necking before he kisses you good night. I mean an in-at-the-deep-end affair," Diane added impatiently. "Do I make myself clear?"

"Perfectly," said Jo in tragic tones. "You don't have to explain about the birds and the bees, Diane. I'm not quite so backward that I haven't heard of the sex drive."

Diane reached for a cigarette and flopped into her chair. "I wouldn't have guessed," she said sarcastically.

"We've had all this before," Jo said wearily. "We're different, and that's all there is to it. I want to be in love completely. I want to share everything, laughter, interest, and plans for the future. And I want the kind of understanding that only comes from a relationship in which I know I'm special to one man only and he's special to me."

"No wonder you haven't found many boyfriends," Diane said flatly. "If you talk like that to them they'll run a mile."

Jo turned away. "I don't. It won't be necessary to put it into words. With the right person I'll know. And he'll know."

"Romantic little idiot!" Diane watched the younger girl start to pile the supper things on the tray. Her expression softened. "Leave those for a minute and listen."

"I think I've listened enough." Nevertheless, Jo stood still, her hands resting on the tray ends.

"Don't think I don't approve of your choice," Diane said dryly. "I can quite understand how he's had this effect on you. I wouldn't say no to a whirl with him myself. But men like that don't get caught, my sweet. Worse luck. So the best thing you can do is not waste any more time yearning. Okay," Diane waved her cigarette around in search of an ash tray, "so you had a decent holiday—though his current love light being there must have taken the gilt off for you. You didn't do badly financially out of it, but it's time to come back to reality. Miracles don't happen that way, Jo."

Jo's mouth compressed. She had never expected much sympathy from Diane, not the sentimental kind anyhow, but her harsh assessment made Jo wince. Silently she carried the tray into the kitchen and began the mundane chores of the final clearing up for the night. Maybe there weren't any miracles; Diane had probably forgotten her existence already. But Margaret might remember her promise. . . .

The workaday routine gradually reformed; the rush each morning, the sandwich lunches, the frantic crush getting home, Mr. Thirle's sledge hammer humor at everyone's expense, and the brave pretense that she was a happy, successful career girl. The Center was settling down under Roy's leadership, but something of the old atmosphere had gone. The slow grinding mill of bureaucracy left the fate of Marcombe Road in a limbo that could last years. The compulsory purchase order hung over Mrs. Jackson's head; she could not sell her property, so the Center stayed there, at her request. Someone might as well benefit for as long as possible, she told them when a group of them went to see her to discuss the matter.

When three weeks had gone by Jo relinquished her last hope of keeping a link with Dane. She should have dismissed Margaret's lightly made suggestion for what it was—a careless invitation intended quite sincerely at the moment, but doomed in the way of countless similar invitations. "*We must get together some time. . . . Drop in any time. . . .*" Some time. Any time. *Never. . . .*

Exactly four weeks to the day after the evening she had last talked to Dane she resigned herself to the sad fact that Diane was right; it was time to forget dreaming. That afternoon she received an unexpected summons to Mr. Thirle's office.

Wondering as ever what she had done wrong this time, she presented herself and received the first of two shocks at being bidden in avuncular tones to sit in the chair usually reserved for the clients.

Mr. Thirle didn't proscrastinate. He spoke briskly and concisely for several minutes. When he concluded he looked at her astonished face for a moment or so, smiling slightly at the effect of his proposition.

"Think about it, Miss Medway," he said kindly. "But we must have your decision by Friday morning."

"Yes, Mr. Thirle." Dazedly she got through the door he held open for her and hardly saw Carol staring at her in the corridor outside.

"Whatever's happened?" Carol bent close to her. "He—he hasn't— You've not been fired?"

"No," Jo recovered from her speechlessness. "He wants me to go to Newcastle. He wants me to go to the new branch."

"I don't believe it! You!"

"Yes. Me. I can't believe it, either."

It took a little while for the surprise to wear off. Although Jo had known for some time that the firm was opening a new branch in the north of England it had never occurred to her to imagine herself as part of it. And certainly not with promotion, a raise, and her hotel expenses for the first couple of weeks until she'd had time to look around for suitable accommodation.

"Congratulations," said Diane. "It's the best thing that could have happened."

Jo stared. There was a certain satisfaction in Diane's expression that wasn't exactly joy for an opportunity of advancement. "What do you mean?" she asked.

"It'll give you something else to think about. At the time you most need it. You're getting too mopey, Jo."

Jo said nothing. She wandered around the room and stopped by the window. "It's starting to get dark sooner," she said, drawing the curtains slowly against the dusk.

"It's nearing fall. When do you go?"

"I don't know yet if I'm going."

"You don't know! You mean you— Didn't you grab it?"

"I have to let them know by Friday."

"There can't be any doubt. It's a marvelous chance." Diane gave her a sharp look. "Jo, you're not going to be silly about this, I hope."

"I don't want to go. I'm going to turn it down."

There was finality in Jo's young voice, and Diane exclaimed her shock. "You little idiot! What on earth for?"

"Because I want to stay here. I don't know anybody up there."

"You mean you want to stay and mope over a man who isn't remotely interested in you. A man you've made into a fantasy figure with all this hero-worship. And because of that you'd turn down a chance like this. I think you're—"

She checked the outspoken opinion. Jo's shoulders had trembled, and the stiff, averted angle of her head told its tale. Diane bit her lip and crossed swiftly to Jo's side. She put her arm around her and said softly, "That's why, honey. Honestly, it would be for the best. And there's nothing binding about it. You're a free person, you know," she went on persuasively. "You can come back if it proves too grim. Give it a trial for three months, or till Christmas, say. Then ask to be transferred back. If they refuse," Diane shrugged, "then there's only one answer. You look for something else. A good secretary can always find something if she's prepared to work hard."

"Do you think so?"

"I know. Give it a trial, please," Diane urged.

Jo raised wide doubtful eyes. "Do you really think I should? Leave London?"

"Yes. I think you'll be glad eventually if you do."

"You won't take another girl in here? Not unless. . . ."

"I won't, I promise." Diane hugged her gently. "I think I can pay the rent alone until the end of the year. By then you'll know. All right?"

"All right," said Jo after a long, agonized struggle within herself. "But there's one thing, Diane," she caught at the other girl's hand. "If—if he rings, you'll tell me instantly. You'll call me up that very minute—I'll refund the call—but promise, please?"

For a long moment Diane looked at the imploring young face and compassion softened her rather hard eyes. She nodded. "I promise."

But it was a forlorn hope.

CHAPTER TEN

The days passed quickly after that. Mr. Thirle wanted her to leave the following week. He was going up to the new branch himself to stay for the first few days and interview new personnel. Jo found her promotion started from the moment she gave him her decision. His secretary was brisk and helpful. She crammed a great deal of lore into Jo during the short time left before the transfer, and on the last day whispered wryly, "Now for goodness' sake try to keep him happy and laugh at his morning jokes even if it kills you. Remember I have to see him all the time when he comes back."

Jo promised. She had glimpsed something of what Diane had meant. Jan—Mr. Thirle's secretary—would virtually carry on for him while he was away. She would placate the clients, make minor decisions, keep things ticking and report to him on his return. She was like Mellie; unobtrusive but almost indispensable.

Jo tried to shut her mind to the thought of Mellie—just the name opened the gate to everything she was trying to forget. The temptation to call him was almost overwhelming, just a brief casual call to tell him she was going away. But somehow she resisted it. The following Thursday when the Tyne-Tees Pullman train drew out of Kings Cross she was on it, with the knowledge that pride had won—and that pride could prove a bitter victor.

However, she had to admit that in a sense Diane had been wise. There was so much to do she had little time to spare for brooding. The new offices were in a tall block north of the city, not far from the university. Mr. Thirle was not entirely pleased. The paint was scarcely dry, the heating was too fierce, but when the windows were opened the boisterous northeast wind swept into the building and set off a chain reaction of slamming doors.

"Obviously we fry in summer, freeze or suffocate in winter, and take the rest of the year to recuperate," Mr.

Thirle said sourly. "Get those heating engineers back, Johanna."

She recalled the engineers, chased up a consignment of stationery that had failed to arrive, began to organize the filing system and layout as near that of the London office as possible. Mr. Thirle interviewed office staff and told her that Mr. Laidler, from Manchester branch, would be arriving the following week to take charge. Suddenly the various departments seemed filled with staff, all wary, all set to jostle for supremacy. It had hardly yet dawned on Jo that she was now a junior executive and was expected to know the answers when asked the questions.

Mr. Thirle surprised her by taking her out to dinner one night and complimenting her on her efforts. She was surprised and pleased, especially when he said expansively, "Know why I picked you, Johanna?" (he hadn't unbent quite as far as calling her Jo).

"No, Mr. Thirle," she said politely.

"Because you're conscientious and not forever on the phone in the firm's time, or wanting to be away soon on some pretext or other."

She felt a little self-conscious and must have betrayed it, for he patted her hand and said, "You'll be all right. Have you found somewhere to live yet?"

She shook her head. "No, but Molly—the new junior typist, the one with red hair—says she knows of a nice apartment. It's part of an old detached house that overlooks the Town Moor. She says it's very nice. Unfortunately it won't be vacant for three weeks. The girl in it is getting married."

"Hm." Mr. Thirle stroked his chin and caught the waiter's eye. When his second brandy was on the way he leaned back and surveyed her. "Three weeks. I think we could stretch the budget and help you out with your hotel expenses until then."

"Oh, no!" Jo looked shocked at the thought of such extravagance. "I have it fixed. Molly says I can stay with her until the apartment's free. She says she would have liked to let me have a room permanently with her family, but her young brother and sister are getting too big to share a room, so they won't have a spare room any more. But she says I'm very welcome if I don't mind sharing with her. It's not for very long."

Mr. Thirle frowned, and she said impulsively, "They're terribly kind here. I mean, Molly hardly knows me, but as soon as she knew I hadn't found anywhere she made inquiries about this apartment and offered to take me in for the time being. I'm invited out to her home on Sunday," she added.

"Yes, Northerners are very warmhearted," he agreed. "All the same, I'd prefer you not to form such intimate alliances right away. Keep a bit of reserve until we're running smoothly. Stay where you are for the next three weeks. I'll arrange to lose it on the expense account."

At that moment Jo suffered her first twinge of guilt. When she remembered her secret intention to pack it in if she was too homesick she knew it was disloyalty. And in a way she could have been happy if things had been different. The city was a friendly one and its people kindly, even if the cold northeast wind tended to cool the hottest of days, and some of the Tynesiders spoke a dialect almost incomprehensible to her untutored ear. There were moments when she experienced an almost painful nostalgia for the metropolis, for the incomparable London stores, the colorful, ever-changing scene, even the cavernous smell of the Underground railway. . . . But the job was a challenge, the salary increase made her feel unexpectedly affluent, and the old gray city on the Tyne had its own individual atmosphere that took strangers to its heart.

Jo told herself she must give it a chance and not lapse into foolish longing again. Diane had written twice and phoned once. There had been no answer to the unspoken question Jo did not need to voice. She went to Molly's home for tea one Sunday and met the homey little family who had offered such kindness. Gradually the new branch settled down under the managership of Mr. Laidler, who was fair if firm, and understanding as well as efficient. The day came at last when Jo held the key of the apartment in her hand. Then her evenings were filled for some time to come with transforming it from a forlorn, deserted habitation into an individual apartment that was home.

By the end of two months she was almost convinced that Diane had been right. It was going to work. She was never going to fall in love again, but she might become a dedicated career woman. And some day she might succeed in forgetting a tall, dark man who wasn't quite real . . . whose spell had been potent, but not quite potent enough to resist a human enchantress who didn't have to work for her living, who could beckon and know a man would follow. . . .

And then Mr. Laidler became ill.

On a gray October morning he collapsed. The hastily summoned doctor diagnosed a serious virus infection, and Mr. Laidler was rushed into hospital. Jo informed Mr. Thirle, who promised to send his new deputy manager—"His baptism of fire sooner than he expected!"—and reminded her to be sure to see that Mr. Laidler had anything he needed during his illness, let his family know, and not forget to keep himself informed.

The same day there was a letter waiting for Jo when she returned home that evening. It was from Diane, and it made her so angry and unhappy she wept. Diane wrote: "*I don't know how to explain about this—you're going to hate me! The enclosed came for you about a couple of weeks ago. I re-addressed it and slipped it in the pocket of my white jacket to mail on my way to the office. Somehow I forgot, and unfortunately I didn't wear it again until today. I hope it isn't anything frightfully important. Forgive me? Love, Diane.*"

Jo studied the unfamiliar handwriting, knew it wasn't Dane's, and felt the stiffness of the missive within before she ripped it open. A silver-embossed card slipped out; it was an invitation to a wedding.

Margaret and Alan were being married—*today*.

The full implication of what might have been struck her and her eyes filled with tears of bitterness. If only Diane hadn't . . . if only she'd sent it a day sooner . . . *I could have gone down on the night sleeper*. To have seen Dane once more. . . .

She was wan and miserable when she faced the new day

next morning. All thought of the new man had fled. She sat down at her desk and turned pages unseeingly. Her cup of coffee was cooling undrunk when the door flew open and the newcomer paused on the threshold and stared at her.

Jo looked up, half rose to her feet, and sank back because she thought she was going to faint. The man standing there was the double of Sir Sheridan Leroy.

Jo struggled to dispel the mists swirling in front of her eyes as the newcomer stepped forward. From behind him Molly brushed past and said anxiously, "Jo, this is Mr. Anstey. He's just arrived."

"Yes—thank you, Molly." She turned to that incredible likeness. "Would you like some coffee, Mr. Anstey?"

"I'd love some coffee—and you're Jo?" he said easily.

She took a shaky breath. "Make some more coffee, please, Molly. I'll show you your office—at least, where Mr. Laidler worked." She was moving past him as she spoke. "We've moved Mr. Laidler's personal things over to that table for the time being. These are the current systems, and this is the Ibrox file—it's our most important contract at the moment." She bent over the desk and opened a book. "These are his appointments. I cancelled today's. I—I didn't know what time you were expecting to arrive."

"That's fine. I think I'll wait for that coffee first." He sat down in the desk chair and swiveled gently from side to side, not taking his glance from her still pale face. "Relax, Jo. Do I alarm you so much?"

"No, of course not, sir." She groped for a return to formality. "I didn't know you'd arrived."

"I like surprising people." He flashed a challenging grin and leaned back indolently. "Actually I arrived on the late train last night, so I don't think there was much point in forewarning you this morning."

She nodded, finding it difficult not to study his dark, handsome features. Now the first startled impression had faded she could see the differences. His dark hair was thick and fell away from the same left parting as Dane's. He had the same broad forehead, the same long line from high cheekbone to chin, and the same tilting quirks that suggested dry humor at the corners of the well-shaped mouth. He even had Dane's trick of elevating one dark brow. But the line of his jaw was slacker and betrayed a tendency to fullness. In years to come his chinline would run to fat and his mouth would coarsen. His eyes were brown, with a trace of boldness as he assessed Jo's taut young form.

"I think we'd better have lunch together today," he said at last. "You can give me a run-down on everything then. Okay?"

She inclined her head and withdrew. When she returned to her own office and sat down she discovered she was trembling. Somehow she had to get a grip on her nerves. If he was going to have this effect on her every time she came into contact with him she'd be a wreck in no time. But he isn't really like Dane, she tried to assure herself.

Unfortunately, the uncanny resemblance continued to send a shock through her every time he came into the office. In working hours he wore the dark-hued, immaculately tailored suits that Dane tended to choose. This all helped to heighten the illusion as he broke upon her vision. It was also unfortunate, however, that Jo did not realize that a sense of this emotion was bound to communicate itself to him sooner or later.

Molly thought he was divine. She made no secret of her envy when the first lunch date with Jo was followed by another early the next week. Certainly he called on her working capacity more than was really necessary. Jo changed his hotel booking when he decided that the Five Bridges was too far away from the office to suit him. Jo had to escort him to the hospital to see Mr. Laidler; and he could have arranged his own car hire. Yet he possessed a beguiling charm, one that was not easy to resist when he chose to exert it. Before the second week was out she was on first-name terms with Philip Anstey and accepting his invitation to spend the Saturday with him.

"If it's fine we'll go exploring," he suggested. "If it isn't we'll dodge the showers in town and do a show."

Jo's hope that the sun would shine was fulfilled. When

he called just after ten to collect her it was one of those fine, crisp fall mornings with the sharp snap of winter's harbinger in the wind.

"Where shall we go?" he asked. "I'm a foreigner here."

"So am I, if it comes to that," she returned. "Shall we go to the coast?"

"A bit chilly, I think. Let's try the country."

"Let's go and see the famous Wall," she said suddenly.

"Let's go to Scotland and hunt for haggis," he said fatuously. "Here's the map. Stick a pin in it."

He put an automobile club's book on her knee and uncapped his pen. "Here, close your eyes and plunge."

Laughing, she obeyed, and the point descended somewhere in the heart of the Northumberland moors. "At least five miles from the nearest track," Philip said, switching on the engine. "Come on, let's go and find it."

In that mood they started off. Philip drove fast and confidently. Jo was not surprised to see the road signs for Jedburgh and Edinburgh flying past. The colors of Northumbria were wild and beautiful; red and gold and bronze stretching into the dry, peaty brown of the moorland and the purple billows of the Cheviots. Inside the car it was warm, but the leaves pattered down and whirled along the ditches like yellow and brown snowflakes in the play of the wind. By the time the car rushed over the worn border line that marked Carters Bar and Philip cried, "Sassenach!" Jo was beginning to respond with an animation she had almost forgotten she possessed.

"Sassenach yourself!" she retorted, and he chuckled out loud.

It did not occur to her to define the exact reason for this excitement he had unexpectedly evoked in her. She shied from the subconscious knowledge that he filled a kind of wishful substitution role at a time of emotional unhappiness, but had she probed farther into her reasoning she would have realized that Philip Anstey was the first older and experienced man to treat her as an adult.

From the first time she had ever considered the oppo-

site sex in relation to herself it had always been a mature
man she had pictured herself responding to, never a boy
of her own age. With boys of her own age group she
invariably felt awkward or immeasurably older; unfortunately, the few older men who had taken any notice of
her had tended, apart from one old lecher who had sent
her running like the proverbial scalded cat, to treat her
with humorous indulgence that did little to increase her
confidence. But with Philip she felt like the way Diane
appeared to her; self-possessed, a girl of the world. Philip
seemed to take it for granted that her youthfulness was
her own particular little feminine act and that she knew
her way through the jungle of intersexual relationships.
She had no illusions about the end of the day's joyride;
Philip would "try" her, and depending on the outcome it
was quite likely that this would be her last date with him.

She was wise enough to remain sitting in the car when
he pulled up outside the darkened house. She knew
enough of the rules for that. Instinct warned that Philip
might not be content to bid her good night on the doorstep.

For a moment he looked at her, a hint of a smile touching the corners of his mouth. "You still have moorland
roses in your cheeks, my sweet."

His hand came to curve the soft oval of her face as he
spoke, uptilting it to him till his eyes could make their
warm, more intimate search. His left arm slid along the
back of the seat. The predictable moves of experience,
thought Jo, knowing that the claiming of her mouth
would come any moment. She had a strange feeling of
detachment, almost as though part of her stood back and
watched dispassionately. Then he bent his head and the
thread of detachment snapped. She wanted to thrust him
away, as though it was disloyal even to think of giving
herself into the embrace of another man. He was totally
different. How had she ever imagined that he was like
Dane?

Then Philip said softly, "If I didn't know otherwise
I'd say those roses were blushing . . . I believe you're
shy. . . ."

The soft whisper of challenge came against her mouth, and Jo's emotions underwent another rapid change. The memory of another kiss and the message of a man who had obviously even forgotten she was still alive brought a surge of defiance. "It helps keep those roses in order," she said coolly and let her lashes fall as he claimed her mouth.

The kiss had little effect on her. Whether or not he had guessed instantly that his guess had been too accurate she could not tell. But he made no demur when she made it quite clear that a goodnight kiss was all she was prepared to offer. His eyes were thoughtful as he released her. She reached into the glove compartment for her scarf and purse.

She turned to him. "Thank you for today," she said sincerely.

"Thank *you* for being such charming company," he responded, then touched his fingertips to his own mouth and lightly pressed them to hers. "I have to play golf and have lunch with Mr. Carstairs tomorrow, which amounts to a royal command almost, but will you come out for a meal with me in the evening?"

She hesitated, and he said quickly, "If you don't there'll be nothing for me except to do the Scotswood Road crawl."

"I've never heard of it." She saw the glint of devilry in his eyes and could not help waiting for his response, as he had known very well.

"Carstairs was telling me about it the other day," he grinned. "It was a Tyneside challenge in the old days—to have a pint at every bar on Scotswood Road and still be standing up at the end of it."

"Oh." Her raised brows showed distaste. "Would you really?"

"On the strength of the local beer—I doubt it. But apparently it's a very long road. There was a bar at nearly every corner. Carstairs couldn't remember how many—but it's been rebuilt since then and most of them have vanished."

"Just as well. You need a clear head for Monday morning," she said primly.

He laughed. "I'll pick you up about half-past seven. Okay?"

Her steps were light as she let herself into the apartment. The day had flown. It was difficult to believe it was now nearing midnight, and she'd spent the entire day in Philip's company. If nothing else, her morale had received a badly needed boost.

The rich meal she'd had earlier in the evening had left her thirsty. She lit the gas under the kettle, promising herself a cup of tea to drink in bed, and went through into the bedroom. It felt cool and rather lonely. Despite herself she felt weariness begin to depress her spirit. She studied herself in the dressing table mirror as she unfastened the gilt chain of her pendant watch. It was true; as well as feeling older she looked older. Her eyes held a depth left by sadness, and her face was definitely thinner. At least it made her look more interesting. She had always longed to have those thin, high-cheekboned contours like models had.

The reflected mouth smiled wistfully at the thought, then sobered abruptly as she opened the lacquer box in which she kept her few treasured pieces of jewelry. The gilt chain had curled into a little crinkly heap where she had dropped it. Under the gilt was the soft luster of pinkish mother-of-pearl.

Slowly she picked up the shell and was unprepared for the wave of sheer anguish that caught her and carried her back in time. She felt the hot Corfu sun and the warm sand under her feet. She saw Dane's eyes crease at the corners as his tanned hand held up a hollowed shell like a spyglass. The echoes of his voice whispered again, and her own foolish protest when he would have tossed the shell back into the sea.

She closed her eyes and tried to blot out the memories. It all seemed an age ago, unreal as though it had never happened. How long before she made herself forget?

She heard the shrill sound of the kettle whistle and turned away impatiently. Then she felt the hardness of the shell that unconsciously she had slipped onto her little finger.

Fiercely she wrenched it off and winced as the broken

edge cut into her skin. A silly stupid shell with a hole in it! Why couldn't she sling it in the wastepaper basket?

Despising her weakness, she dropped it into the lacquer box and closed the lid sharply. Not yet, soon perhaps, but not until she could look at it and hold it without remembering. . . .

CHAPTER ELEVEN

Sunday dawned with a cold gray mist that did nothing to restore Jo's spirits. She went to the window and rubbed a clear patch in the clouded pane, to stare bleakly at the flat gray-green stretch of the Moor. The city's lung, they called it, or so Molly's brother had told her. In mid-summer it was the scene of the annual Race Week Fair; once claimed to be the greatest gathering in the country of traveling fairground shows. But the old people said the fair wasn't what it used to be in their young day. . . .

Jo shivered and went to feed the gas meter. It had a voracious appetite, or was it that she was extravagant with the fire? She would have to remember to collect some more change before tonight. She sighed; it was quite a spacious apartment, larger than the one she shared with Diane. She'd made it quite attractive with new drapes and a row of bright posters along the main wall. It was marvelous to have space to spread herself, but she missed Diane, missed the heart-to-heart chats at night when they switched out the light and recounted what the day had brought them. . . .

Impatiently she snapped out of nostalgia. If she was going out with Philip tonight she would have to get her weekly home chores done and tidy the place up. And she had to write to Margaret. . . . Once again she repressed the surge of bitterness that the thought engendered. It was useless to blame Diane; she hadn't done it on purpose—Jo herself couldn't honestly say she'd never stuck a letter in her pocket and forgotten to mail it. It was one of those things. If she honestly believed that even if she had been able to go to Margaret's wedding it would have made any difference she was selling herself the biggest pipe dream ever. It would only have started the yearning all over again, she told herself flatly.

As long as she kept herself busy it was easier not to

brood. Imperceptibly the morning slipped by as she rinsed underwear and tidied the apartment. She had planned to devote the afternoon to a bath and hairdo, but after lunch the mist dispersed and the sun tempted her out of doors. If she returned by five she would still have ample time: three full hours. She wouldn't want much to eat if she was dining out—Philip believed in luxury dining, that was all very well on an expense account, she reflected, but without rancor. So she'd allow half an hour to bathe, an hour and a half for shampoo and set, half an hour to dress and make-up. She'd still have a good half hour to spare, she reckoned as she scuffed her toes in the leaves carpeting the tree-lined road.

There was nothing wrong with her timetable. She returned promptly at five, glowing and pink-cheeked, her hair in considerable disorder from the sportive breeze that had sprung up during the afternoon. Unfortunately she had failed to predict the element in her hair dryer deciding to give up at five to six. Swearing, she shook it, peered into it, wondered how long the cold air current would take to dry her set. Five very cold wet minutes later the door bell pealed.

"Bother!" she said aloud. It was probably the woman in the apartment across the hall wanting to borrow coffee again. It was a temptation to wait, hoping the borrower would decide she was out and go away to try elsewhere. But the bell rang again, imperiously. Sighing she clutched her robe closer before she opened the door a couple of inches and peered out from behind it.

Her mouth opened with dismay.

Philip stood there, an expectant look on his face and a huge bunch of bronze chrysanthemums in his hand. He saw her and his smile wavered.

"It's only six o'clock!" she exclaimed.

"Ten past," he said mildly.

"Yes, but you said. . . ." she trailed into the silence of dismay. What on earth did she do now? She couldn't ask him to wait, not in the state she was in. That damned hair dryer. . . . "I'm not ready," she said helplessly.

"I can see that." He looked whimsically at her over the

flowers. "I'm sorry, honey girl, it's my fault. But I found I'd time to kill, so I decided to come along on the chance of finding you at home. However," he grinned and held out the flowers, quite unabashed, "I know when I'm not welcome, so I'll push off until the appointed hour."

"Oh dear, it's not that." She dabbed a trickle making its way down her neck and looked down at the flowers. "They're gorgeous—thank you—but my hair dryer's gone 'phut.' I might be a bit late."

"Is that the cause of that worried little frown! Maybe I can mend it. May I?"

"Could you?" Rather doubtfully she stood back and let him enter.

He picked up the hair dryer, tested it and frowned. "The element's broken, otherwise it seems okay. I might be able to join it temporarily, but you'll have to have it repaired properly before you use it again. Safety first," he eyed her sternly. "Got a small screwdriver?"

"No."

"Nail file, then? These screws are so tiny a point might turn them."

She sorted out every implement that might help and went to hunt for something to put her flowers in. In the way of most furnished places, only the barest essentials were there, and not all of those. Jo still missed the fridge, a kitchen fitting she considered as essential as the stove. If she was going to stay here for any length of time she was going to have to budget more stringently in order to indulge in a few more home comforts. The rather noisome little cupboard under the sink smelled of mice and gas pipes, but yielded a couple of dusty jam jars that would hold the flowers left over from the one vase the flat boasted. The result was decidedly top-heavy—the chrysanthemums were big hothouse blooms—but they would be safe on the broad windowsill. The vase would take pride of place on the table. She carried them carefully into the sitting room and looked hopefully at Philip.

He turned from the window and made a rueful gesture of failure. "Sorry, darling, I can't get the damned thing apart. Anyone nearby who might have a midget screwdriver?"

She thought of the house owner who had the big first floor apartment, and remembered he'd gone off for the weekend. "I don't think so. The tenants are all women, older than me. If anything goes wrong the landlord usually mends it—he's very good. But he's out."

Philip frowned. "Can't you rub it with a towel, or something?"

She smiled faintly. "You wouldn't want to be seen with me tonight if I did. I have to let it dry pinned up like this or it doesn't hold my style when I brush it out."

He put the hair dryer down and came toward her. "But it's positively soaking, darling girl." He reached out and touched the wet pincurls set close to her head. "Your ears are like little frozen snowflakes trying to thaw out. Whatever time are we going to get out to eat?" he added teasingly, bending his face close to hers as it was captive between his hands.

"I'm sorry. I—" She bit her lips and drew away rather jerkily, suddenly conscious of his warm gaze and her state of undress under her cerise robe. Until now she had been worried only about looking her worst, but now she felt acutely perturbed and wished with all her heart she was fully dressed. If only she'd done all this during the afternoon, instead of. . . . She might have known her lousy luck! The impulse to retreat into the bedroom was very strong, but a deeper instinct stopped her. The partition that divided one large room into two smaller ones was extremely flimsy. It did not even reach the ceiling, and she did not trust Philip Anstey to stay on the other side of it while she dressed. For the first time in her life the thought of the simple actions of donning clothes was charged with an atmosphere of intimacy that started a troublesome quiver of unease in her. And yet it had to be done. She said despairingly, "I—I'll have to dry it in front of the fire, and if it's a mess you'll just have to go without me."

"What unpredictable creatures you girls are!"

He followed her to the fireside and sat down in the

armchair while she knelt on the rug and tilted her head toward the heat. "If I'd known it was going to be like this I'd have brought a hamper and a bottle of wine," he said after a brief silence.

She said nothing, aware of the slight sounds of him lighting a cigarette as she turned her head the other way. Then he stood up, and she tensed. But all he said was, "Where do your ash trays live, darling?"

"There's a glass dish on the windowsill." She wished he would stop calling her darling. It didn't mean anything, except a casual emphasis of the intimate atmosphere he had brought into the apartment. She listened for his footfalls returning across the carpet. The heat of the gas-fire had already become unbearable on her face, but she wanted to wait until he sat down again before she straightened and let her burning face cool. She had solved the problem of dressing while he was here; she would take her things along to the bathroom. It seemed so simple a solution she rose to her feet without thinking and put her hands to her scarlet face.

He was standing behind her and suddenly he put his arms around her and his mouth against her ear. "I had no idea how girls suffered in the pursuit of beauty. Is it essential to turn yourself into a delectable little piece of toast?"

Her hands went defensively to the strong ones locked across her midriff. "Yes, if you're determined to be sitting down to your *filet mignon* by eight o'clock."

"I prefer toast at the moment."

She stiffened. The hands beneath her own seemed disinclined to respond to prising. They stayed firmly locked around her and the evasive tactics of her head merely left her throat undefended. "Phil, please. . . ." she tried appeal, "I have to change and—"

"Not another little act, Jo."

"What?" Startled by the accusation and suddenly finding herself free, she spun around to face him.

His mouth was cynical and his eyes amused. "You're not going to start now denying that I attract you."

Her lips rounded. "When did I give you that impression?"

"Darling!" he shrugged elaborately, "surely we're not going through all the dreary old hard-to-get ritual."

She gasped again, shocked by the derision in his tone.

"I don't know how you can deny it," he went on mockingly. "Something sparked between us the moment I first walked into the office. In fact, I got a distinct impression that I lit quite a fire in you." He paused. "Don't tell me it's gone cold already."

"I—I—there was never any spark!" she gasped. "Not like—"

He caught her slender, petrified form before she could move and buried his mouth in her neck. "We'll have to do something about that," he said in a muffled voice, then found her lips.

"No—!" She fought to get her hands against his chest and push him away and felt blind panic at the strength of the arms holding her fast. Her struggle seemed to inflame him as she strove to back away from the hard pressure of his body against her own. Her wrap was slipping off one shoulder. She cried out as his mouth burned into her shoulder. "Let me go! Phil—the bell! There's somebody there."

"Let them go away again." He looked down into her distraught face. She sensed the flare of desire in his quickened breathing.

"Phil—*please!*" she tried to repel him with wide eyes.

"Please what?" he said in a dangerous whisper.

In a final desperate evasion she bowed her head toward his chest and tried to wrench free. She did not see the door swing open, or hear the astounded ejaculation from the man who stood there.

The pinioning arms fell away from her, and Philip cried,

"Who the devil—! How did you—?"

Jo took a trembling step forward and every vestige of color drained from her face. She stared unbelieving across the room. Her mouth shaped the name, but no sound passed her lips.

"I beg your pardon," said Dane icily.

She saw the chill mask of disgust his features had become, saw him turn away, stretch out a hand to draw the door shut, and life rushed back into her petrified limbs.

"No!" she screamed. "Dane! Don't go! Don't—" Her voice choked on a sob of anguish, and she flew to him. She seized his hand, beyond caring what his reactions might be, and held it with all her strength.

For a moment of agony she thought he was going to thrust her aside. Then her despair seemed to get through to him. He looked at her, almost as though he were reluctant to do so. Sick revulsion gathered in the pit of her stomach. She saw herself and Philip Anstey as though through Dane's eyes, and hated what she saw.

"Please stay—this is a wonderful surprise—I never dreamed. . . ." A high babbling voice that didn't seem to belong to her at all sounded a long way away, and she was holding his arm as though it was a lifeline. She did not know why or how he was here. Even if he were real. . . . It just seemed like a miracle when she had given up praying for one.

"Who the devil's this?" Phil asked harshly. He glared at Dane. Discomfort was plain in his handsome rakish features.

Jo gulped. "Dane, this is Philip Anstey, my boss. Phil," again she swallowed hard, "this is Sir Sheridan Leroy—the Q.C. He—"

"Ye gods! You fly high, darling, don't you?" Phil's mouth twisted. "Is he coming to dinner as well?"

She felt the surge of anger in Dane and made a desperate little lunge to plant herself in front of him. They were glaring at each other like a couple of angry dogs ready to snarl at each other's throats. Panic flared in her. "No, Dane!" she exclaimed under her breath, "please. . . ." Praying he wouldn't move or speak, she broke away and ran to Philip. "Phil, I'm sorry—this is all my fault. I never meant you to think that I—"

"You might have told me you were spoken for, darling." His mouth curled. "I don't like being made a fool of."

"That's not true, and you know it!" she flashed.

Suddenly she didn't care if he sacked her, if she lost her job altogether—in fact it would be the best thing that ever happened to her. The only thing she cared about was getting rid of him and trying to obliterate the ruinous picture she must have made in Dane's eyes.

Tears choked in her throat as she said, "It wouldn't have happened if you hadn't come so soon. I hadn't washed my hair." She tried to control her trembling mouth and looked steadily at him. "I'm sorry, I can't go out now. Will you forgive me—I can't help it."

For a moment she was afraid he was going to argue. Then he glanced over her shoulder at the grim-faced man at the door and took a deep breath. "You don't need to spell it in capitals, my sweet. And I certainly don't need to stay where I'm not welcome."

He snatched up his sheepskin jacket and shouldered past Dane without another word. The slamming of the outer door trembled through the apartment, and then there was silence. A silence so tense it threatened to suffocate Jo.

Then Dane closed the room door and leaned back against it. "How long has that been going on?" he asked disgustedly.

"What?"

"How long have you been having an affair with him?"

"But I haven't—except yesterday," she choked.

His disbelieving gaze ranged coldly over her still wet hair, the disarranged robe, the bare feet in blue mandarin slippers, and the distraught young face. His mouth tightened. "Anstey appeared to consider you'd made a fool of him; don't try the same trick on *me*, Jo."

"But I'm not!" She stared at him from tear-filled eyes. "He said he was coming at seven-thirty, and he came at six. I'd just come out of the bath and washed my hair. My hair dryer broke, and my hair wouldn't dry, and—and—" she was weeping now, "it wouldn't have set in time. Then he came with those flowers. And he tried to mend it, and then—and then—" Sobs overcame her, and she turned away, dabbing hopelessly at her swimming eyes.

"And then?" he said coldly.

She sniffed. "He started to make love to me and wouldn't let me go, and—"

"What did you expect? Can't you see yourself?"

"You don't understand!" she cried. "He accused me of inviting him to. He said he knew I was attracted to him, but I wasn't. It was all a horrible misunderstanding," she went on, now beyond all caring or pretense. She pressed her hands to her face. "It was because he was like you!" she whispered.

Dane walked into the center of the room. He looked at her bowed head and trembling shoulders for a long moment, then pulled a chair near to the fire.

"Sit down," he ordered in an expressionless voice, "and get that ironmongery out of your hair."

Sheer surprise stilled her grief. "W-what?" she faltered.

"Loosen your hair," he said in the same flat tone.

Slowly she fumbled with the pins that held the curls. The wet tendrils began to flop over her face, and dimly she heard him moving around. Then he stood behind the chair, and the folds of a towel descended over her head. He began to rub her hair with hard, rough movements.

"How long have you been north?"

"Two months." She was still shaky and wary.

"Is it a permanent transfer?"

"I—I think the firm intends it to be."

"And Philip Anstey's in charge?"

She hesitated. "At the present—yes. But only till Mr. Laidler gets back. He became ill two weeks ago, but he's out of hospital now and may be back next week. Then Mr. Anstey will be going back to London."

If Dane noticed the return to a formal reference he gave no sign. The toweling activity ceased for a moment. She tensed as his hand ran through her hair. He resumed drying and said coolly, "Do you want to stay here?"

"I—I don't know. I— No, I don't," she said flatly.

There was a pause. "So you didn't make Margaret's wedding."

"No. Oh, but I wanted to. I was furious when Diane. . . ." She went on to explain as steadily as she could, trying to keep emotion out of her voice. "I wrote to

Margaret today, to explain. I hope she'll understand. And—and perhaps you could suggest something for a wedding present. I want to get her something this week."

"As long as it isn't another set of fish-knives. She had four." The towel fell away from her head. "I think it's dry enough now."

She stood up and took her comb off the mantelpiece. Slowly she combed out the tangles, taking a long time because she had not yet regained enough courage to face him. Then she remembered something. "How did you get in?"

"Here? The door was open. When nobody answered, and I heard your voice I decided to come in and knock at the inner door—don't stand so near the fire!" he broke in sharply. "Those old-fashioned overmantel mirrors are a menace."

Philip mustn't have latched the door—thank heaven.

Without speaking the thought she stepped back a small pace, drawing the belt of her robe tighter as she did so. She resumed combing, until her hair fell in two long soft lustrous veils against her cheeks. A shadow fell across the light, and she saw his reflection behind her own.

He said, "What did you mean by saying it was because he was like me?"

She tensed. "I—I— Did I say that?"

"You did."

Her heart began a long increasing crescendo. She raised the comb to her hair and felt it taken out of her hand. He put his hands on her shoulders and turned her to face him.

"It was a strange remark." He regarded her with a calm, unwavering gaze. "It seems to require defining."

The crescendo was racing in her breast now. She gave a tiny shake of her head. "I—I don't know why I said it. He—he isn't in the least like you."

"I should hope not."

His gaze held her now, and unhurriedly he drew her close to him. "Isn't it time you discovered the reason?" he said and bent to her mouth.

The sweet fire of love's alchemy raced through her

veins. Only one particular man's mouth could make the magic. Jo was helpless under its spell.

At last he relinquished her lips, and a tremor sighed through her.

"Well?" One brow quirked with the soft query. "Found it?"

There was a tiny smile on his parted lips, almost of triumph. Jo took a deep quivering breath. He looked as though he was going to kiss her again, and she summoned a vestige of pride, enough to avert her face. "No—I remember you were the one who said a kiss didn't have to have a reason."

"But I'm not talking about kisses."

"It's the same thing." She avoided his gaze, trying desperately to resist the enchantment.

"Still frightened of a kiss?"

"No." She bowed her head. "I just don't want to be kissed unless—" She stopped with a small, defiant shake of her head.

"Unless what?"

His quiet insistence would not be denied. She looked up. "Unless it means something."

"Yes, I feel exactly the same way about—our kisses."

She stared at him, wanting with all her heart to believe what she thought he meant by those words. She faltered, "You mean. . . ?"

"I mean I'm in love with you, Jo."

For a moment she could not speak, echoing his words over and over in her brain to convince herself she had really heard them. Then she uttered his name like a cry of ecstasy and flung herself into his arms.

He murmured her name, and his arms closed fiercely around her, curving her against him and caressing the long slender line of her back. They exchanged lovers' whispered endearments and incoherencies between ardent kisses. Until gradually they were silent. Even words ceased to have any place within this new passionate sphere of ecstasy. And then Jo felt a strange note of tension and a new urgency in the hands caressing her. Their sensuous warmth through the thin, cerise silk of her housecoat made her aware of the new, dangerous yielding sensation that throbbed through her body.

Dane broke the kiss and clamped his hands to her shoulders, almost thrusting her away. His darkened eyes looked down at the parted robe. He groaned softly under his breath.

"Jo—for God's sake. . . ." A muscle moved along his jaw. "Will you get some clothes on—unless you're hell-bent on my seducing you this very minute."

He released her and turned away. For an instant she could not move, so great was the weakness that had made her limbs feel like water. With trembling fingers she drew the silky lapels closer to her throat and tightened the sash. She took a step forward, stood behind him.

"Dane. . . ?"

"Didn't you hear me?"

"Yes . . . Dane. . . . You won't go away?"

He swung around, and the dark hunger in his features as he looked at her gave her the answer. He said gruffly, "And you wonder why Anstey made a pass at you."

"I hated it. But I love you!" Suddenly she laughed aloud for the sheer joy of loving him.

His mouth stayed unsmiling. "Johanna Medway, are you going to get dressed? Or. . . ?"

Possessed by the glorious sense of the effect she was having on him, she gave him a prim look from under her lashes. "Don't dare go away—you promised."

When she emerged a few breathless minutes later after the quickest transformation ever he was nowhere to be seen. Sounds from the kitchen led her there on flying feet to find him making coffee. He looked at her glowing cheeks, the gay, scarlet dress that enhanced her sparkling eyes and lustrous brown hair.

His lips formed a kiss, a sweet silent tribute that said a great deal. She ran forward to tilt up her face for a real kiss. She carried the tray into the sitting room and drew the little coffee table up to the sofa. Settled in the curve of his arm with her head on his shoulder, she said at last, "I still can't believe it's all true. That you love me. That you're here, now. I thought I wasn't going to see you again, ever."

He sighed softly. "I must be honest with you, my darling, I did try to stay away from you. When we got back from the island I was so unsettled I couldn't even work. I knew I was attracted to you that night we were stranded, but the way things happened I didn't want to admit it to myself."

"Was that why you were so awful to me?"

"Was I so awful?" He caressed her cheek and tangled his fingers in her hair. "I didn't mean to be, but to start with I'd had a bit of a shock at the feeling you aroused in me. I tried to tell myself it was simply nature, having you asleep in my arms, but I knew I was kidding myself. And I knew it was unfair to make love to you, even if you'd shown any signs of wanting me to. Then when you made such a fuss I was thankful I didn't."

"I thought you were crazy over Celia."

He sighed deeply. "Margaret told you about that, didn't she?"

Jo nodded, still unable to repress the painful stab of jealousy that Celia's name could cause.

"I had a kind of madness over Celia when I first met her. She's that kind of girl. But all the time I knew in my saner intellect that it wasn't the kind of madness to bring happiness. I knew it would be fatal to marry her. Yet I couldn't bring myself to end the affair, even though there were plenty of opportunities during the many quarrels we had. And yet I wanted to marry. That is, I wanted to share my life completely with someone. But somehow I could never imagine it happening with Celia, no matter how hard I tried to convince myself. There are disadvantages to all professions," he interposed wryly. "In mine it is that the use of logic becomes second nature, even to the extent when it can override one's more personal emotions."

He paused, his mouth sensitive and tender despite this statement. "And then you came on the scene. I'd never known a girl who was so frank about her feelings toward me. So different from the usual feminine attitude of evasion. There was one instance in particular—that first time we had lunch. You suddenly said: '*Oh, you're wonderful!*' And really meant it."

"But you are," she whispered. "And I still mean it."

He caught her to him and touched his lips to her hair. "That's what *I* mean. No one ever said that to me before, not the way you did, with such complete sincerity. I was aghast when you didn't turn up at the wedding. I was banking on it."

"And I could have killed Diane," she confessed, sighing against his shoulder. "I knew you'd be there. Even if I could only look at you again. But it would have been torture if you'd been with Celia."

"My poor darling!" He tilted her face up and searched it with dark eyes for a moment before he effectively dispelled the small shadow of the memory. A little while later he said quietly, "That night you phoned me, when you heard Celia's voice. That was the night I knew I'd never been in love with her, nor she with me; not in the way I'd rediscovered ideals I'd almost forgotten. That was the night I knew I wanted to marry you; it was also the night I discovered certain truths about myself. Truths I didn't much like. That I was becoming cynical, self-centered, and shallow. I'd seen too much of what people do to themselves and each other. I'd lost too many illusions in the process."

"You're not selfish or shallow," she said vehemently. "Margaret told me you were an idealist."

He smiled faintly. "She also told me I was a fool to let you slip away. But I wanted to wait until the wedding, until. . . . You see, I knew you had this gratitude thing toward me because I'd tried to help with the Center business. I was also conscious of your youth against my 36 years. So I made myself wait until the wedding. By then the Center's fate was settled, and the holiday in Corfu just a memory. I thought I would gauge things by your reaction and take it from there. I knew you would betray yourself if you'd missed me, but if you didn't. . . ." He sighed again and his arm tightened. "I'm afraid I didn't want to admit that possiblity to myself."

"If only I'd known!" Her eyes were wistful for the lost weeks of love. "Diane made me take this job. She said . . .

but never mind what she said. . . ." Jo took a deep breath and decided that the truth must be told. "That's why Philip was here, really. It's quite true. He did remind me of you. And in that way of mine you seem to like so much," she added ruefully, "I couldn't hide it."

"Yes—and you'll hand in your resignation tomorrow," he said sharply. "I want you back in London."

She stared dreamily at the glow of the fire. She was so utterly happy she wanted time to stay still forever. "Tell me about Margaret and Alan."

"Oh," Dane smiled, "Alan suddenly decided he'd been patient long enough. I think Neil's arrival in London shook him. We'd only been back a few days when Neil landed. Alan practically abducted Margaret and carried her off to his cottage in Cornwall. He told her he'd compromise her so thoroughly she'd have to marry him. That's why she didn't get in touch with you. She was fully involved. But I've no doubt she'll tell you all when she sees you."

Jo nodded. He didn't seem to want to talk about anything else, and there were lots of questions she wanted to ask. Some of them could wait, but. . . . "Did you come here especially to find me?" she asked, still not sure it was all true.

He nodded. "When you didn't turn up at the wedding I had to."

"Can you stay a while?" she asked shyly.

"For this week, then I'll have to go back, alas."

"A whole week!" She gazed at him with ecstatic eyes.

"A whole week." He returned her ardent look, then stood up and drew her to her feet. "Time to eat. Shall we go to my hotel?"

"Anywhere." Her love was unhidden now, and abruptly he pulled her into his arms.

"Love me?"

"Desperately." She felt his heart thudding against her breast, and she remembered the island. "I fell in love with you that night in the villa garden. When you quoted those lines and touched my cheek. . . ."

"And you told me you didn't want to fall in love, ever," he reminded her. "You'll never try to run from me again, promise?"

"I promise." She gave him her lips and knew that indeed her heart had taken wing to the sweetest spell of all. *This* enchanter she would never flee. . . .

WHEN BIRDS DO SING

When Birds
Do Sing

Flora Kidd

"You're either blind or being deliberately naive," Scott said. "I may as well be frank with you. I invited you to come here today for one reason—to get you away from Alex and let someone else have a chance."

Lindsay was bewildered. From his first forced entry into her mother's house to his cryptic remarks about Alex, she had found Scott Nicolson a rude and thoroughly impossible man. But also devastatingly attractive.

Convincing herself that she was postponing her return to Canada in order to help her widowed mother sort out her problems, Lindsay took a position as nurse in the quaint Scottish village and found she had problems of her own!

CHAPTER ONE

The north-bound train clattered over the points and whistled a warning. Going home, going home, going home. The words kept time with the swinging rhythm of the express. It was approaching the town of Kendal, gateway to the English Lake District, and soon the rhythm would change as it slowed down for the long haul over Shap Mountain.

Looking out at the crisp winter's day, across hilly fields and leafless hedges to the frost-rimed distant brown fells, Lindsay Bell felt a lift of spirits as she recognized familiar contours and realized that now she was amongst the high land of north-west England she was almost home.

Well, not quite almost. But after Shap the going would be downhill all the way to the border, as her father used to say. And once across the border she would be safely home in Scotland.

It was strange to be glad to be going home when three years ago all she had wanted most was to leave the set ways of the old country and to travel, to work in a new country; to see new faces and places. It was strange to want to feel safe.

The opportunity to leave Scotland had come when she had met Joan Parker, a fellow nurse at the Glasgow hospital where she had been training. Joan had also possessed the same urge for adventure and had also wished to try her luck in distant places. They had schemed and saved, and eventually they had flown to Canada to stay with Lindsay's elder sister Beth, who was married and lived in Toronto. Beth had assured them that once they were there they would have no difficulty finding work in the local hospitals, and that once they had passed certain examinations they would be accepted as qualified nurses.

And so it had happened. In the freedom of their new surroundings both girls had flourished and were soon independent of Beth's sponsorship. They had joined fully in the pleasant social life. It was not long before Joan had decided to marry a Canadian and to make her home in Toronto.

Lindsay, who was enjoying her work as well as her play, remained free, although her way of life was interrupted for three weeks when she and Beth had had to fly back to Scotland for the funeral of their father. His death had been a great shock, because he had been only in his late 50's. Both Lindsay and Beth had thought he would have lived long enough to retire from his work as head of the English Department at Duncraig High School and to enjoy many years in the old house in the village of Cairness that he had loved so much.

At the time of the funeral Lindsay had offered to stay with her mother, but Ruth Bell would not hear of it.

"No. You have your life to live, and I still have a lot of mine," she had said. "Enjoy yourself while you can. I have many friends here and many interests, so I won't feel lonely. As long as you and Beth write to me regularly, I'll feel you are near me. Later, when I can see my way more clearly, I'll fly out to see you both."

Lindsay had returned to her friends and her hospital in Toronto. She had written regularly and her mother had written back, perhaps not as regularly, but certainly with vigor and humor. Although Mrs. Bell had not fulfilled her promise to fly out to see them, there seemed no reason to worry about her. Consequently when summer arrived Lindsay had gone with three of her friends by car, on a tour of the west, driving across the prairies through the Rockies to Vancouver. On that trip she had met Maurice Vedell and had fallen in love for the first time in her life.

The train was slowing down. Gone was the lilting rhythm; the joy of going home. Lindsay stared out at the gray-green of the mountains as they closed in around the train and remembered other mountains soaring high, cutting the blue sky with sharp white peaks; the Rockies, where she had met Maurice.

She gnawed at her lower lip and frowned. If she had not fallen in love with Maurice, if she had not discovered one heartbreaking day 12 months after their first meeting that he was already married and had merely been using her as a convenient and pleasant companion when he visited Toronto on business, she might not have been so ready to agree to Beth's suggestion that she should fly home at Christmas time to see Mrs. Bell.

"I'm worried about Mother," Beth had said in her forthright way, one day in the middle of December. "You've been so immersed in what the romantics would call 'your private grief' that maybe you haven't noticed the change in her letters recently."

"I haven't heard from her since the end of September," replied Lindsay. "She always writes more often to you than to me . . . just as she has always talked to you more than to me. Something to do with you being so much older, I expect."

"Thanks, dear. I suppose seven years' difference amounts to a generation gap these days."

"What's the matter with her?" Lindsay had questioned quickly before her sister was carried away on her favorite topic. "Is she ill?"

"I don't know. She doesn't say as much, but there's a distinct change of manner. Usually her letters are full of little stories about her friends and neighbors. Recently there have been fewer, and this last letter is definitely strange, as if she's living under some kind of strain."

"How can you tell?"

"She keeps mentioning a man, but she doesn't name him. All she says is 'He came back today.' and 'Next time he comes I'll not open the door.' Here, see for yourself."

Lindsay glanced through the two-page letter across which her mother's rather disjointed handwriting sprawled. The sentences were stilted and carefully phrased as if her mother had not known what to write.

"Why don't you write and ask her who the man is? There's probably some simple explanation," she had suggested.

"I think it would be better if you went home and found out. I think she needs one of us and won't ask. It will have to be you, because I can't leave Gregor and the kids right now. Also it will do you good. It will help you to forget that snake in the grass."

"Maurice isn't a snake!"

Beth had grinned unrepentantly, "Oh, yes, he is."

"You've never liked him."

"No, I haven't. I've always thought there was something two-faced about him."

"Then why didn't you say so?"

"What good would saying do? You were so smitten by his big brown eyes and his smooth manners that you wouldn't have believed me. Anyway, I suppose it's an experience you won't forget. You'll be more careful next time."

"There won't be a next time."

"Oh, come off it! There will be," Beth had scoffed, but the expression in her eyes had been anxious.

"No," Lindsay had been adamant, "no love and no marriage for me. I'm not getting involved with anyone again. It's too painful."

"Not with the right person, it isn't," Beth had countered.

"And how do you know who is the right person?"

"Oh, I don't know. You just do. It's a feeling of . . . of responsibility."

"Sounds dull," Lindsay had commented. "Is that all you feel for Gregor? I always thought you were different, and that you both found the love of your life when you found each other."

"So we did, but that doesn't make us different. There are many like us, in spite of what you read these days; happy normal people, loving each other and feeling responsible for each other. In a way Maurice has never felt, neither for you nor for his wife."

Mrs. Bell had not written again, so Beth made a transatlantic telephone call one Sunday. Their mother had answered and had chatted happily, never mentioning once the man who had visited her. She had been delighted when Lindsay told her she intended to go home for Christmas and New Year.

"Then come as soon as you can, dear," she had said. "I keep the beds aired all the time. Will you fly to Prestwick? If so I'll ask Frank Crosbie to drive up and meet you."

"I'll write and let you know."

In the end Lindsay had not flown to Prestwick because all the flights to Scotland had been fully booked for the week before Christmas. She had been able, however, to get a booking on a plane flying to London on the day before Christmas Eve. As a result she was sitting in the corner of a crowded second-class compartment on the express train from St. Pancras.

The train pulled itself pantingly up the mountain. It seemed as if it would not make the last few yards to the top of the pass. Groaning and straining, it crawled forward. A small white signpost at the side of the track announced modestly that it was Shap Summit, 1000 feet, and then the train stopped groaning, its pace quickened and soon it was rolling steadily downhill toward the dust of Shap granite works.

At Dumfries, Lindsay left the train. She had to wait for the bus to Castle Douglas, so she put in her time in the snack-bar drinking tea, listening to, and watching the people who came and went. Everything was so much smaller than she had remembered, and there was an absence of haste that at one time she would have found frustrating, but which she now found soothing. For a while it would be good to stay in a place where nothing had changed drastically for many years.

By the time the bus left the station it was dark. Lindsay looked with lively interest as it passed through the center of Dumfries and then went down Buccleuch Street, across the river Nith and along the road to the west. Once out of the town limits she had to guess at the scenery through which it passed, recalling the many times she had traveled the same road in the past. Yellow lights twinkled from the scattered farmhouses and cottages, or provided a welcoming glow in the small villages that the bus trundled through.

At last it entered the outskirts of Duncraig; the small

country town where Lindsay had attended school. It passed the council house estate and the park, turned left over a bridge and rumbled down the main street past familiar shops and stopped in a small square by the war memorial.

On asking at the gas station in the square which was the only place open at that hour, Lindsay discovered that a bus no longer went to Cairness in the evening. Shivering a little in the damp air, she stood under one of the street lamps and waited, hoping that Commander Crosbie, R.N. (Retired) would recognize her when he saw her. She was thinking of inquiring about a taxi when a small black car raced into the square coming from the direction of Cairness. It circled the memorial and stopped beside her. The far door opened, and a tall thin man got out.

"So there you are, Lindsay Bell, turning up like a bad penny!"

His face was composed of sharp angles and under his prominent forehead his eyes twinkled merrily. He was not Commander Crosbie.

"Alex Wilson!" exclaimed Lindsay. "What are you doing here?'

"Practising medicine. I'm in partnership with McDonnell. This is your lucky day, Lindsay. I've just been down to Cairness to visit your mother. She said you'd be arriving on the Castle Douglas bus, and that there was no one to meet you because Commander Crosbie has gone down with flu, so I offered to take you down there."

"Is Mother ill?" questioned Lindsay as she entered the car beside him having seen her luggage safely put in the trunk of the car.

"She's had flu and is supposed to be recovering, but she's having a hard time of it. I'd have been down earlier to see her, but I've been rushed off my feet today."

The road they drove along went due south toward the coast. At first it was bordered by old terraced cottages and then by neat modern bungalows, and was lit by street lamps. There were no people about, and each house glowed with light. Then the houses and the street lamps ended abruptly; their places were taken by drystone dykes edging dim fields, and by the reflectors down the middle of the road known as "cats' eyes" that twinkled warningly when the car lights lit them up.

For the first few minutes Alex and Lindsay were busy with questions and answers. They had known each other when they had both worked in a Glasgow hospital. Alex was a native of Castle Douglas and had often given Lindsay a lift home in his little sports car when both of them had had a free weekend. Good-natured and possessing a lively sense of humor, he had always treated her in a brotherly manner, often teasing her about her urge to travel. So it was easy to fall into that familiar relationship, and she answered his questions about Canada readily.

"You make it sound so marvelous I'm wondering why you have bothered to return to this underdeveloped neck of the woods," he teased.

"Beth and I were worried about Mother," she replied, watching the road. It was wide and straight-edged on both sides by shadowy trees. She could not think why it was different.

"About her health?" queried Alex. "You shouldn't be worried about that. She's sound in wind and limb, although I think she became run down during the fall. She's having trouble shaking off the effects of flu. She'll soon recover now that you're here."

Lindsay made no comment, as she was still puzzled by the road.

"We are going to Cairness, aren't we?" she asked at last.

"As far as I know we are. There's only one road there and only one road back, and this is it."

"But it's different."

"Oh, so you've noticed that a few of the twists have been taken out of it. Remember what it was like here? That awful corner on the gradient? Look at it now—a smooth wide sweep up and over. Unfortunately it isn't like this all the way. But it will be."

She could not agree with him that it was unfortunate that the road was not wide and straight all the way to

Cairness. One of her memories of her home that she held most dear was of this road: twisting and turning its way to the village on the estuary of the river Cairn; clear and uncluttered in places and offering wonderful views of the rolling countryside; dark in others where it tunneled under arching beeches. Someone had changed it, and the change in a place that she had thought would never alter disturbed her.

"I'm not sure I believe in your reasons for returning," said Alex, ignoring her silence.

"But it's true. What other reasons should there be?"

"Let me see. What other reason could there be?" he remarked jocularly. "You're either on the run from some fantastically wealthy man who wants you to be his third wife, or you're suffering from unrequited love and have come home to lick your wounds."

He changed gear as the straight road came to an end, and he had to negotiate a sharp bend. The cats' eyes had ended, too, and the road had narrowed. It was once more the familiar slow road home.

"Am I right?" challenged Alex.

How had he guessed? She supposed during the time she had known him at the hospital he had come to understand her quite well, so she did not bother to fence with him.

"The last," she admitted. "Unrequited love."

"And you're hoping that he'll miss you and will write beseeching letters asking you to return to the prairies to grow corn?"

"Wheat," corrected Lindsay.

"All right, wheat . . . or to return to his ranch to ride horses and feed the cattle?"

"You are a fool! Not all of Canada is prairie or ranch land. I lived in Toronto, which is a big city. And he won't be writing any letters, because he's married."

"Oh, bad luck. Then you've come to the right place to recover, and perhaps you and I can hold each other's hands, because I'm suffering from the unrequited sort myself."

"Who is she? Anyone I know?"

"Moira Innes."

Lindsay whistled softly. The wealthy Innes family belonged to Glasgow and were well-known biscuit manufacturers. They owned a house in Barrcliffe, the village next to Cairness. It was the family holiday home that they visited in the summer, at Christmas and New Year's and in the spring. Moira was the only daughter, a tall dark beauty who had been hopelessly spoiled by her father.

"You've been flying high," she said to Alex.

The road curved to the right, and they descended a hill toward the estuary. Lindsay's heart beat a little faster. Only another half-mile to go.

"Not as high as the fellow who's cutting me out," muttered Alex.

"And he is?" she prompted.

"Scott Nicolson. He's been straightening this road. You must know him."

The name was slightly familiar, but Lindsay could not put a face or figure to it. It was just a name that she had heard perhaps twice in her life, and to which she had attached no significance.

"I can't place him, but now I have two reasons for disliking him," she said.

"What are they?"

A building jutted out into the road ahead, creating a bad corner. Square patches of light glowed rosily in its bulk. Alex swung the car over to the right of the road close to the merse or marsh that bordered the estuary. Then twisting the steering wheel he turned sharply left and into the driveway beside the building. Gravel crunched under the wheels, and the car stopped in front of a door paneled with panes of glass, so that it also served as a window. It was the front door of Merse Cottage, the home of the Bell family for over 70 years.

"He's spoiled the road I like best," said Lindsay, answering Alex's question before she left the car, "and he's come between you and Moira. Why is he straightening the roads? I thought Tom Henderson was district road surveyor."

"He is. But he's been ill. Scott is his assistant. I think Tom is going to retire and then Scott will take over his job. Do you mean to tell me you don't know who he is?"

"Should I?"

"Maybe not. His family might have moved into Duncraig by the time you were old enough to notice. He used to live in the old gatehouse on the laird's land. We've just passed it. They had to move when the old laird died because the estate had to be sold, and the purchaser didn't want a sitting tenant."

Merse Cottage had originally been the toll house on the road that started at Cairness and went over the hill to Barrcliffe and along the coast of the Solway. Lindsay's grandfather had bought it and made it into a comfortable house to live in when he retired. When his father had died John Bell, Lindsay's father, had inherited it and had decided that he would live in it permanently and travel every day to the high school in Duncraig where he taught. So Lindsay had moved there when she was two and had no memory of any other home.

Whenever she had returned, she had always felt pleasure in seeing how little it had changed. Now after being away from it for three years except for the short time when her father had died, it seemed very small and incredibly old. Inside, the glass paneled door opened into a small hallway which was at the end of the house farthest away from the road. From the hallway steps led down through an arch to the living room-cum-dining room. It was long and low. Original beams crossed the ceiling. In the wide granite fireplace, a bright fire flickered. In front of it sat Mrs. Bell, her fair, almost white hair looped back in an elegant French roll at the back of her head. She wore a beautifully crocheted shawl of many colors around her shoulders. She was reading the newspaper. Sitting there quietly, she added to the sense of permanence.

On hearing the door close she looked up.

"Lindsay, at last! No, I won't kiss you—I'm full of cold. It's lovely to see you. Poor Frank couldn't dash up to meet you after all, but Dr. Wilson kindly offered."

The thought of anyone as staid as Commander Crosbie dashing anywhere made Lindsay smile as she took off her coat and flung it down on the chintz-covered sofa and went over to her mother.

"I was thinking of getting a taxi when Alex came, like an angel in disguise. Thanks, Alex," she said.

"You're welcome. I'll be asking you to do me a favor one day, so don't think you're getting off lightly."

"Would you like to stay and have supper with us?" invited Mrs. Bell, who obviously approved of the young doctor.

"I'd like to, but I'm afraid I can't. I have to go home to Castle Douglas tonight. Now don't forget what I told you earlier, Mrs. Bell. With Lindsay here you'll have no difficulty in carrying out my instructions. She still has a temperature, Lindsay, and by rights should be in bed. Keep her there tomorrow."

When he had gone Lindsay made a light supper for herself and her mother. They ate before the fire while she talked about Beth and her children and relayed their many messages.

"I wish they could be with us for Christmas and New Year's," sighed Mrs. Bell. "I feel I'll never know my grandchildren."

"Then you should have made the effort to fly over and stay with them," scolded Lindsay gently.

She could see a change in her mother. Apart from the drawn, pale appearance given to her finely sculptured features by the flu, there was a strained look around her eyes that was not normally there. No doubt she would soon learn the reason for the strain, because Mrs. Bell did not like being worried about anything. The daughter of a wealthy industrialist from the North of England, she had been protected from the difficulties of life first by a masterful father and later by a kind and loving husband. Consequently, whenever she had had a worry she had always unloaded it onto her husband. By doing so she would think she had rid herself of the responsibility of the problem. In other words she was spoiled, thought Lindsay whimsically, and yet none of them could ever help spoiling her because she was so lovely and elegant.

"I know I should, dear. But with one thing and another I haven't been able to plan a trip. It's all been very confusing for the last few weeks."

A faint frown wrinkled the fine skin of her forehead.

Lindsay waited. Now perhaps she would learn what the problem was and who the unknown man was.

But instead of confiding, Mrs. Bell put a long-fingered hand to her head and moaned slightly, "Oh, my poor head! You won't mind if I go to bed now? Such a pity on your first night home . . . and Christmas Eve too! I intended to have all the decorations done, and the mince pies made. . . ."

"Never mind, Mother. I'm here and we're together, and that's all that matters. In a few days you'll be feeling better. Then you can tell me all the news. Did you switch your electric blanket on?"

"Aggie did that before she left. She's been very good, but I'm glad I have one of my own here to look after me."

For the next few days Lindsay looked after her mother. The days had a pattern. Except for Christmas Day when she stayed in all the time, she walked to the village store after taking her mother's temperature and coaxing her to eat a little breakfast. At the store she bought the newspaper and some sundries, then walked back the length of the village staring at the familiar view of the mudbanks, marsh, and the farmland of the opposite shore. Beyond the farms the rounded curves of a small range of mountains varied in color from day to day, sometimes smoky blue, sometimes black, or violet and green according to the mood of the weather. Every day Lindsay thought how small and neat everything seemed, how limited in extent as she compared it with the wide expanse of Ontario countryside which she had become familiar with during her stay in Canada.

As she slowly adjusted to the quiet unhurried life of the village, she often found herself wishing she was back in Toronto attending one of the many parties that would be taking place at this festive season of the year. And then she would remember Maurice and would be glad she was in a place where there was no chance of him appearing.

At this time of the year the village had a deserted air, although many of its residents were there. The hotel, which she noticed had had some additions made to it since she had left home, was closed. Next to it the yacht clubhouse had a similar deserted appearance. On the slip in front of the yacht club, the small yachts and racing dinghies that sailed on the estuary were mastless, shrouded in canvas tarpaulins. Yet the life of the village continued. New boats were being built in the sheds belonging to Ian Prentiss. A new house was being built on the hill at the back of the village.

But what was most distressing to Lindsay was that the road which went through the village was obviously going to be widened at the cost of the long gardens stretching in front of the Victorian villas that formed the main part of the village.

One afternoon as she hurried home after an extra walk when she had mailed a letter to Beth, she noticed that the road-builders equipment was already parked on the grass that bordered the shore of the estuary. In the rapidly deteriorating light of the afternoon, men were unloading drainage pipes.

She did not linger long to watch because the dark clouds sweeping down from the north were bringing snow. The hills on the other side of the river had already disappeared behind a veil of stealthily falling flakes.

When she reached the cottage she found her mother peering out of one of the windows.

"Not very nice weather," she commented. "You came in just in time. I hope it won't be a blizzard. The radio forecasts heavy snow in hilly regions. . . . Oh dear, he's here again, Lindsay. You must send him away. Tell him I'm ill and that I can't see him."

Before Lindsay could ask who had arrived in the car that had just crunched over the gravel, her mother had disappeared up the stairs to her room. The door bell was ringing. Grabbing her white nursing overall from the closet in the hall where she had put her coat, she pulled it on and buttoned it. The door bell rang again imperiously demanding to be answered.

Wishing that she had asked her mother to explain the vague references in her letter, she opened the glass door to see a broad back clothed in a sheepskin jacket and a head of dark hair on which snowflakes alighted gently, only to melt.

On hearing the door open, the man turned to look at her. Surprise flickered across his lean weather-beaten face and made his clear hazel eyes widen slightly.

"Good afternoon," said Lindsay in her crispest nursing voice. She tilted her chin and drooped her eyelashes in imitation of her mother's haughtiest glance.

He did not speak. The clear eyes with greenish depths surveyed her curiously from head to foot. Just as curiously Lindsay stared back. He was tall and broad. Apart from his eyes his coloring was the sort she associated with the gypsies who at one time had camped in the old quarry. But he was no gypsy. He was well-dressed, and his whole attitude spelt authority.

"Good afternoon," he said pleasantly, and his voice had a depth which made the rolled "r" and sing-song intonation pleasant to hear. "I'd like to speak to Mrs. Bell, please."

"I'm afraid that isn't possible. She's had flu and isn't very well. She's gone to lie down."

"When she saw me coming, I've no doubt," was the slightly cynical rejoinder.

Inwardly shaken by his quick reply, Lindsay was pleased that she did not blink an eyelid.

"Not at all. She went to bed because I told her to," she said coldly. "I'm her nurse."

The calm speculative hazel eyes inspected her again.

"You may be her nurse, but you're also a Bell, to judge by your frozen manner and fair hair. The younger daughter, is my guess. It's as well you've come home. I'll talk to you instead," he announced arrogantly.

"I'm sorry, Mr. . . . . er . . . ." Lindsay allowed her voice to trail away disdainfully.

"Nicolson," he supplied. "Scott Nicolson, assistant district road surveyor."

"I'm sorry, Mr. Nicolson, I haven't time today. Come back when my mother is well. Good-bye."

She swung the door to shut it, but it could not close because there was something in the way. She looked down and saw a foot shod in a brogue of brown punched leather set between the edge of the door and the jamb. Astonishment that anyone could be so insolent, caused her to relax her hand on the door momentarily. Immediately it was pushed open. He stepped inside and closed it behind him.

"How dare you!" she snapped. "Get out!"

His glance made her feel feeble and inadequate.

"I dare because I must. This matter is most important. Hasn't your mother told you anything? She's been sent letters about it which she hasn't replied to. She's been telephoned, but every time she has hung up. In the end I decided to call on her, but since the first time she hasn't bothered to answer the door, although I've known she was in."

"I'm not surprised she hasn't answered the door if your manners have always been as uncouth as they are today," retorted Lindsay, wishing once more that she had persuaded her mother to confide in her. If she had known, she would not have experienced this strange feeling of having to fight this man in the dark.

He smiled and the flash of his teeth against the swarthiness of his coloring roused a vague tantalizing memory.

"I wouldn't use such tactics with her," he admitted.

"Will you please leave?" insisted Lindsay. If Beth had been here instead of her she would have known the reason for his being here, having coaxed the confidence from her mother. She would never have let him in.

"Not until I've told you why I'm here. And while we're on the subject of manners it would be polite if you would ask me to remove my coat and to sit down."

Lindsay stood hesitant; uncertain what to do. Her brave show of defiance was over. She was not normally cold or hard and had only recently developed an armor to cover her natural warmth and friendliness. He spoke with such authority, she was beginning to think that perhaps her mother had done something wrong.

There was no hesitancy on his part. Removing his sheepskin jacket, he tossed it on the hall chair. He was wearing a dark brown checked tweed jacket, dark slacks, and a green shirt. Brown and green, like his eyes, thought Lindsay inconsequently.

He went down the shallow steps into the living room as if he owned the house.

"In here?" he asked, half turning to see if she was following.

"Yes," she snapped.

In the glow of the fire, the room with its old gold carpet and yellow and orange chintzes looked warm and welcoming on that dreary day. Lindsay discovered she was nervous, and to cover her confusion she took a cigarette from the box on the coffee table and lit it with the table lighter. Then she sat on the sofa.

He stood in the middle of the room and looked around. He put up a hand and touched one of the beams. He walked over to the hearth and examined the granite. Then he walked back and stood on the other side of the coffee table to examine her. She drew on the cigarette too quickly. The smoke tickled her throat and she choked. He smiled.

"Put it out. You're not a smoker," he suggested, and she did as he told her, at the same time hating him for noticing.

"I've never been in this house before," he said. "It's very interesting."

"But I thought you said you'd been to see Mother once."

"I talked to her, on the doorstep."

His wide mouth twisted a little, and she had the impression that he derived a certain amount of amusement from her mother's ability to keep him standing on the doorstep.

Lindsay looked at the window. Pale flakes fluttered against it. A log fell in the hearth, and the noise underlined the silence. Scott moved around the table, and to her surprise, sat down beside her. "You aren't like Beth," he said.

Lindsay looked at him with wide gray eyes. "You know her?" she asked.

"I used to know her. I lived in the old gatehouse up the brae. But I don't suppose you remember. You were only a wee bairn. I can't even recall your name."

"Lindsay," she replied involuntarily, the answer surprised out of her by his sudden personal interest.

"Linten Lindsay."

"Linten?" she queried.

"Your hair." His glance moved over her fine, long, blonde hair. She realized, with a little shock of alarm, that by sitting beside her and directing the conversation into personal channels he had almost disarmed her.

Annoyed to think that her newly acquired armor had slipped already, Lindsay sat up straight and said coldly, "I haven't all afternoon to spend waiting for you to come to the point. Having forced your way in here I think you should tell me your business and leave."

Her freezing tactics had little result. He raised his eyebrows and his smile was regretful. "Now that's a pity, because I do have all afternoon. The men had to go off early because of the weather. I thought that since I was down here I could spend the rest of the time seeing your mother. And I hoped that as it's the season of goodwill, tomorrow being New Year's Eve that a little hospitality might be forthcoming. But I can see that you have a heart of stone like the other members of your family and that I won't be offered anything."

He was mocking her and his mockery was based on knowledge which she did not possess; knowledge of her family and its relationship with him. Although she could not remember when he lived at the gatehouse she had discovered two other memories.

One was of a long summer evening when there had been a dinghy race. Beth had been in a triumphant mood, having crewed in the winning boat. They had watched the last dinghy cross the finishing line, and Beth had called out tauntingly to its helmsman as he had come up the slipway, "Last again, Scott? But what can you expect in a homemade dinghy? It sails like a bathtub!"

And the young man had turned away from her, a red flush staining his dark-browed face.

The other memory was of a similar evening about three years later. She had been walking with her father and Beth. As they had passed the hotel a group of young men and women had come out of the bar and had stood in the narrow roadway, blocking the way. Her father had stopped and had waited. One of the young men, tall and as dark as a gypsy, whose white teeth had flashed when he smiled, had noticed the waiting group of Bells. His eyes had glinted with malice as he had called out, "Good evening, Mr. Bell. It's a fine night. Stand back, everyone and let Mr. Bell and his daughters pass. He'll have you in court if you don't!"

The young men and women had moved with a few embarrassed giggles, but the dark young man had not been embarrassed. He was not embarrassed now ten years later, as he sat waiting patiently for her to come out of her daydream.

"Why do you think the Bells have hearts of stone?" she asked curiously.

"If you don't know, I'm not telling you," he said, evading the question coolly. "Since you're not going to offer me afternoon tea I may as well come to the point, as you suggest."

He put a hand in his inside pocket of his jacket, pulled out a long buff envelope, and tossed it into her lap.

"That's a copy of a letter that has been sent three times to your mother. I brought a copy in case she's lost the others. Read it."

Before she could open the letter the telephone rang. She put the envelope on the coffee table, excused herself, and went into the little hall to answer the phone.

"Hello, Lindsay, Alex here. I've been meaning to call you, but I haven't had time until now. How's your mother?"

Lindsay replied cautiously, conscious that the man in the living room would be able to hear her.

"A wee bit better," she said.

"Is she well enough for you to leave her tomorrow evening for a few hours?"

"Yes."

"You sound very distant. Would you like to come to a party with me?"

"Yes, please."

"Good. I'll pick you up about nine. Be prepared to stay and let the New Year in. See you tomorrow. Bye."

When she returned to the living room there was no sign of Scott. Panic spread through Lindsay. Supposing he had gone upstairs without her noticing him? He had nerve enough if he wanted to see her mother.

An awful screech came from the direction of the kitchen, followed by the low mutter of a man's voice. The door at the far end of the living room swung back, and Scott appeared.

"I trod on your cat," he explained. "I hope you don't mind me going in there. I was curious to see what was beyond this door. I suppose the kitchen is the original office where the toll-keeper sat. It's a most unusual house. It's a pity it has to go."

He stood in the middle of the room. Lindsay had an impression of strength both physical and mental. What he wanted he would get. He might not be too particular as to the means he used. The thought chilled Lindsay, and she disliked him even more.

"What do you mean, it has to go?" she asked.

He pointed at the brown envelope. "Expropriation," he said. "That letter is from the Council to your mother telling her that they require the land on which this house stands in order to widen the road. She's never answered it, so they haven't been able to value the property to say how much they'll offer her. You may have noticed that work on the road widening is about to begin. I should like to know when she'll be ready to vacate the house so that it can be demolished."

Lindsay had the oddest feeling that the house was already crashing down about her.

"But why?" she stammered.

"It's a danger to traffic because it creates a blind corner," he explained patiently.

"But it's my mother's home! You can't do this . . . the Council can't! There must be some way of widening the road without destroying the house. Can't you take land from the other side?"

"That will happen in any case, but there isn't much land available because of the river estuary. That land is really only marsh and is likely to flood. No, I'm afraid Merse Cottage has to go."

"We shall fight the compulsory purchase in court," announced Lindsay scornfully, although she felt very unconfident.

"It will cost you money, and I think you've left it too late to appeal. Even if it isn't, you won't win unless you can provide a sound alternative to the plan already adopted by the committee. So your mother didn't tell you?"

"No. Although Beth and I guessed there was something wrong, because her letters referred to a visit by a man. She didn't give his name or the purpose of his visit, but I gather it was you."

"I came because I thought I might be able to help. I knew she was on her own, and that she must have received a shock. But she wouldn't listen to me. She seemed to have some preconceived idea that I'd come to gloat over the fact that she would have to move. I came back several times. She wouldn't answer the door."

"Do you have to widen the road? It's a lovely road, and you've spoiled part of it already."

"Spoiled?" He was annoyed. "The new part is a particularly good piece of planning and construction, as any driver will tell you."

"Maybe, but in widening it you've taken away much of the charm and character of the drive from Duncraig to here. If you remove this cottage you'll destroy some of the character of Cairness."

He drew his breath in sharply as if his patience was wearing thin. "This part of Galloway is very attractive to tourists," he said, "and tourism happens to be one of its main industries. If we're to keep people coming here we have to make some improvements, mostly to the roads and, I hope, at little cost to the natural beauty of the place. It may interest you to know, Miss Bell," he placed wicked emphasis on the words Miss Bell as if he did not think her worthy of being addressed in such a way, "that no one loves this part of Scotland more than I do. That's why I stay here and work here."

That was another nasty crack at herself . . . and possibly at Beth, thought Lindsay. The man certainly had no hesitation in speaking his mind and did not care if you disliked him for it.

"It may also interest you to know that you're not in the minority. There are many who would prevent any improvements because they would like to keep the place to themselves. Last summer there were three bad accidents on this road. The fatal one occurred outside this cottage. In the past, as you must know, there have been others. It depends on what you value most; human life or the old-world character of a house."

"I value my mother's peace of mind," she retorted. "She's not accustomed to having to make difficult decisions. My father always dealt with this sort of problem."

"But she has a lawyer, and as far as we can make out she hasn't informed him of the problem at all. It's as well you have come home to help her. Maybe you can persuade her to see sense soon."

"But where will she live?" exclaimed Lindsay.

"Oh come, she isn't exactly a pauper. It isn't as if she hasn't an income. I believe the Council have offered alternative accommodation in a Council bungalow in Duncraig."

"My mother would never agree to live in one of those places," said Lindsay indignantly.

"Some people have no choice," he remarked gently.

Incensed by his rebuke which she realized uncomfortably was merited, Lindsay plunged on recklessly, "If it was your home would you let it go without a fight?"

His eyes glinted with interest and a slow smile curved his mouth. "No. I like a fight, even if I'm proved wrong in the end," he replied.

"Then why do you expect me to be any different?" she challenged.

He did not answer. It was growing dark. Snow still flitted stealthily against the window pane. The glow from the fire burnished the faces of the two people who stood facing each other in the middle of the room.

"I'm glad you're not any different," murmured Scott. "Perhaps now we'll have some action. It seems to me that your mother has stayed quiet for a remarkably long time this afternoon. I hope she's enjoyed listening to our conversation. Please give her my regards and tell her I'm sorry not to have seen her."

He walked past her and up the steps into the hall. Not sure what to make of his last speech, Lindsay followed him, the letter in her hand, and watched him pull on his jacket.

"What shall I do with this?" she asked, surprising herself by consulting him.

"Read it. Show it to your mother. Then show it to her lawyer and tell him what you want to do. I think you're too late to appeal against it, but you're entitled to try."

He opened the door. Cool air and a few powdery flakes of snow rushed in. Without another word, he walked out into the dark and closed the door after him.

"I can't understand why you didn't tell us," said Lindsay to her mother. Mrs. Bell had appeared several minutes after Scott had left and had asked immediately whether he had been about the expropriation. "Of course he told me about it. That's why he came. They're going to start widening the road and wanted to know when you would be vacating the house."

Mrs. Bell shuddered delicately and huddled nearer to the fire. "I thought I'd told you and Beth. Surely I mentioned I'd had a visit from the dreadful man?"

"You said that a man had called, but you didn't tell us his name, and you didn't tell us his reason for calling," said Lindsay. "Nor did you tell us about the Council wanting to purchase the property."

"Didn't I?" answered Mrs. Bell vaguely. "Well, it was all so difficult to explain in a letter. I thought that if I ignored their letter they wouldn't be able to do anything. After all, it is my house."

Lindsay sighed. If only Beth had come instead of herself. She understood their mother much better. Being so much younger, Lindsay had always accepted without questioning the authority of her parents and consequently was unused to arguing or setting her will against her mother's.

"Yes, it is your house," she agreed. "But these days a Council has power of compulsory purchase if it requires land for improvement of a public utility. If you didn't want them to destroy this cottage you should have appealed against the order, or you should have had Cuthbert Murray to appeal for you."

"Him!" Mrs. Bell was scornful. "He's no use at all. I showed him the letter, and he said I would be wise to comply with their request. He said I should let them buy the house, and he would look for another place for me to live in. He even suggested that I take up their offer of one of those bungalows built especially for elderly people by the Council. As if I could live in Duncraig!"

"You realize, of course, that by not answering the letters and by doing nothing you might have left it too late to appeal?"

"Who told you that?" Mrs. Bell looked surprised and dismayed.

"Scott Nicolson."

"I'm surprised you let him set foot in this house," replied Mrs. Bell haughtily.

"I had no option," said Lindsay dryly. "He was in before I could stop him."

"Forced his way in, no doubt. How typical!"

"He seemed quite sincere, though, when he said he was sorry about the house, and that he'd called several times to see you because he was concerned. He knew that both Beth and I were away and thought he might be able to help you."

"As if I would accept help from that . . . that gypsy!"

Lindsay looked at her mother's tilted chin and tightened mouth and sighed again. It was so difficult trying to find out what lay behind her mother's attitude.

"He isn't a gypsy. He's a qualified engineer in a position of authority," she said.

"Oh, I know that. But his grandmother, Annie Robertson, was a gypsy, or at least she was descended from them on her mother's side," asserted Mrs. Bell.

Lindsay knew this could be true. Once there had been a gypsy kingdom amongst the hills of Galloway, and the small amount of gypsy blood could account for Scott's dark coloring and individuality.

"But that's no reason for disliking him," she objected, completely ignoring the fact that she disliked him herself.

"You don't dislike a person because of his rather distant origins," she added, thinking of the friends she had made in Toronto who had all come from widely different ethnic backgrounds, and whom she had learned to value for their differences.

Mrs. Bell, who strangely enough was beginning to look better, possibly because her annoyance had brought color to her cheeks, smiled indulgently at her younger daughter. "Of course, I'm forgetting. How can you know anything about him and his family? It was Beth who knew him. You were only five when he and his mother moved away from here."

"They must have been your nearest neighbors. Why did they move?"

"The laird died and there was no successor to the estate, so it was sold. The Nicolsons were given notice to quit because the purchaser didn't want a sitting tenant. The day after the notice was served, Grant Nicolson died suddenly of a heart attack. He hadn't been in very good health since he had returned from the war. I can't say we were sorry to see Ann Nicolson and her son go."

"Why? What was wrong with them?"

"Grant was a very clever man, an engineer and an inventor. But he was rather eccentric and married an extremely unconventional woman. Neither of them had any control over their son, who ran wild and was always trespassing on our property and tormenting Beth. I tried to be a good neighbor, but Ann was secretive and withdrawn. When I remonstrated with her about Scott, she would just look at me and smile. Once John threatened to take them to court because we caught Scott taking apples from our tree. Scott, who was very outspoken even then, was very rude to your father."

"Didn't Scott used to come down to Cairness when he was older, though? I seem to remember him sailing."

"Yes. He came back during his holidays. Needless to

say he was the center of any mischief that went on down at the sailing club. The tales Beth used to tell me."

Lindsay could see that she had come up against a wall of prejudice in her mother that both astonished and upset her. Yet she had a feeling that her mother had not told her the whole story. The reason for the feud between the Bells and the Nicolsons must be deeper and more fundamental than mere irritation because a mischievous boy had trespassed on their ground.

"Well, this won't help us solve this problem of expropriation," she said. "What are we going to do? The letter says they need 75 feet for the widening. That means the whole house and most of the remaining land. There would be nothing left for us to build on," she said.

"It would cost a lot of money to build," said Mrs. Bell rather diffidently, "and the sum they offer for the property is only nominal, not nearly enough to build a house."

"Haven't you enough savings to afford to build another house?" asked Lindsay, groping backward in her mind trying to remember the exact amount her father had left her mother, as well as the considerable sum she had inherited when her own father had died.

"I've had many expenses recently," replied Mrs. Bell coolly, as if she resented the question.

"What sort of expenses?" persisted Lindsay. Surely her mother realized that if she was going to help her she must know everything? "I know you've had the house redecorated and you've been away on holiday."

Mrs. Bell looked guilty.

"I loaned some money to my cousin Marcus," she admitted reluctantly.

"Oh, Mother, loaned? You might as well say you've given it to him. You'll never get it back. How much?"

The amount was enough to pay for the buying of a piece of land and the building of a small house.

"Does Mr. Murray know this?" asked Lindsay, feeling thoroughly defeated. So much for her fighting words to Scott.

"Yes."

"I suppose that's why he wanted you to comply with

the Council's request. He knows you can't afford to fight the order."

"Yes. I can't. Oh, Lindsay, I don't know what to do. If only your father were here!" wailed Mrs. Bell helplessly.

For the first time Lindsay was touched by her mother's distress and realized that an appeal was being made for her help. She knelt beside her and put her arms around her, to comfort her.

"Never mind. I'm here. We'll work something out," she murmured.

The discovery that Mrs. Bell was short of money gave Lindsay plenty to think about. Although it went against the grain to give in to the compulsory purchase order without a fight, the more she thought about it the more she came to the conclusion that the order might be a blessing in disguise.

Much as she was attached to Merse Cottage she realized that it was for sentimental reasons and not for practical ones. There had always been problems associated with its construction and its position. As time went on these problems were going to tax her mother's small income more and more. Would it not be better, she argued, if her mother sold it to the Council and moved into something more modern for which someone else had the responsibility of upkeep? With herself and Beth so far away and unable to help their mother very much, this seemed a logical suggestion. But how to persuade her mother to agree was another problem.

The preparation for the party that she was to attend with Alex gave her a welcome distraction from her thoughts, and she dressed with care. She coiled her long blonde hair into a bunch of ringlets on top of her head and made up her face carefully. She put on a dress of sugar pink with a low neckline that was deceptive in its simplicity. Over it she wore a short white furry coat she had treated herself to in Toronto just before Christmas. Her appearance in the mirror was exactly as she had wanted it to be. She looked assured and a little sophisticated, not a person you would take advantage of.

It was the first time she had been out in the evening

since she had returned to Cairness and was surprised to find how much she was looking forward to the party. With Alex, an old friend, she would be able to relax. He would not be expecting anything from her, and his company would protect her from others.

"Where is the party?" she asked him as they drove right through the village along the road to Barrcliffe.

"At the Innes' house. Moira and her father live there permanently now because he retired last June. She invited me and asked me to bring a friend. I thought for once it would be a good idea to show her that I have a friend and a very pretty one too. I'm tired of attending her parties and finding competition there in the form of Scott Nicolson.

"Will he be there tonight?" A little of Lindsay's excitement at going to the party was dimmed.

"He's sure to be."

"He came to see us yesterday afternoon. Did you know that the County Council have decided to tear the cottage down in order to widen the road?"

"No, I did not. I'm not surprised, though. It's a deadly corner. So that's what's been worrying your mother. It'll mean finding somewhere else for her to live."

"Preferably somewhere to rent. She can't afford to build or buy."

"No funds?"

"Not enough. It would help if I could find some work to do while I'm here. I had hoped to go back at the end of January, but I'm beginning to think I'll have to stay longer to help Mother. Do you know if they'd take me on at one of the hospitals near here, on a temporary basis?"

"I'm sure they would. But I have a better plan. Why not work for Doctors McDonnell and Wilson?"

"Not really?"

"Yes, really. We've been thinking we need a nurse to carry out all those little jobs such as weighing people, taking blood pressure, and bandaging wounds. You'd be ideal. When could you start?"

Lindsay laughed out loud. This offer sounded too good to be true.

"It would be temporary, remember," she warned. "As

soon as Mother is settled again, I shall be off to Canada again."

"Fair enough. By then we'll know whether employing you is a good idea. You can start on Monday as soon as the New Year holiday is over. It's long this year because New Year's Day is on a Friday. Report to our consulting rooms at eight-forty-five a.m. How will you get to town?"

"By bus, I expect, unless mother lets me use her Mini."

"That's fixed, then. Now tell me what you thought of Scott."

Lindsay thought back to the previous afternoon and tried to clarify her impression of the man who had invaded Merse Cottage.

"He's unscrupulous," she said distinctly.

"Oops! That's a strong word. What did he do to deserve such a damning assessment?"

Lindsay described how Scott had forced his way into the house. Alex chuckled appreciatively.

"Sounds like him. Having made your assessment how would you deal with such a person if you found he was a rival?"

"Be unscrupulous too."

"Rather a tall order if you're not so inclined, like me. Ah well, perhaps the sight of you in my company will do the trick and pique Moira, because I know she can't stand competition. Having drawn her attention to me, you could then distract the unscrupulous Scott and keep him away from her side," said Alex facetiously.

Lindsay laughed. "Sounds very complicated to me," she said. "Supposing Moira is so taken up with Scott she doesn't notice you have another interest?"

Alex sighed with exaggerated melancholy.

"Then I shall give up and let the better man win."

"He isn't better," said Lindsay sharply. "He's . . . he's . . . he's. . . ."

"Go on. He's what? Don't tell me you're feeling that fatal magnetism already?"

"No, of course I'm not. I'm immune to the deadly disease," said Lindsay impatiently. "He's just more determined about getting what he wants, whereas you tend to give up easily when you think there's opposition."

"Yes, I'm afraid you're right," agreed Alex with a ruefulness that possessed a certain charm. "I need encouragement all the time."

CHAPTER TWO

Cliffe House was situated in the village of Barrcliffe. It lay to the east of Cairness on the other side of the long snout or ness of land, that divided the estuary of the River Cairn from Barrcliffe Bay. With its wide sandy beach the village had always been a popular holiday resort for couples with young families who wanted nothing more than smooth yellow sand, shallow water for bathing, and a southern aspect.

When Cameron Innes, flour miller and biscuit manufacturer, had bought Cliffe House and had renovated it as a holiday home for his family, the village had suddenly become a center of interest for other company directors and business men. Two adjacent cottages on the waterfront had been snatched up at bargain prices and had been miraculously transformed into a beautiful holiday house complete with all modern conveniences, picture windows and sun balcony. A year later a similar fate had overtaken three more of the cottages. Gradually the whole front row of cottages was changed into a few select residences which were nicknamed "the Palaces", by the local people. The wealthy owners of these houses appeared occasionally to participate briefly in the life of the parish during the summer, or on the long holiday weekends in spring and fall.

Cliffe House itself was set back from the road and was approached along a wide driveway. As Lindsay and Alex drove near to it they were welcomed by the warm light gleaming from every window. After leaving Lindsay at the porticoed doorway, Alex had to drive back down the drive to leave the car near the gates because there was no space close to the house for him to park.

Waiting for him on the doorstep, Lindsay could hear the sound of voices and laughter coming from the house and was stricken with shyness. She wished she was not going to the party. It was not the first time she had experienced this shrinking feeling, and she knew it was the result of the loss of confidence she had suffered since she had learned of Maurice's deceit.

In an attempt to overcome the feeling she tried to remember Moira Innes and managed to conjure up an image of dark, glossy hair, a trim figure, a haughty profile, and an arrogant manner. But although she could remember Moira's appearance she could not remember ever having spoken to her. Moira was slightly older . . . nearer Beth's age . . . and had tended to mix mostly with the wealthier group of summer visitors. Beth had once referred to her as a snob of the first degree, and Lindsay had accepted her sister's assessment. That was why it was strange to associate Moira with Scott Nicolson, who was so obviously a local.

Alex came into view, squelching across the pools left by the melted snow on the drive.

"Standing under that porch light in your beautiful Canadian coat you look rather ethereal . . . strangely insubstantial," he commented. "It must be the combination of light shining, fair hair, and white fur."

He raised his hand to press the doorbell, and Lindsay seized it suddenly and whispered, "Do we have to go in?"

He was surprised and puzzled. "What's the matter?"

"I . . . I'm not sure. I feel nervous, like I used to feel before taking an exam."

"Butterflies?" he asked sympathetically.

"Yes."

"You'll feel all right once we're inside. Moira is expecting you. She said she remembered you and Beth. You'll find her and her father easy to get on with, and there are bound to be some other people you know." He gave her a quick, searching glance and added, "Don't take what I said about playing up to Scott seriously if that's what's worrying you. I was only joking. Anyway his car isn't here, so he can't have come."

The feeling of relief that surged through her was as unexpected as it was strong. Had it been a subconscious desire not to meet the domineering Scott Nicolson again that had caused the attack of nerves, and not shyness?

She smiled at Alex. "I'm all right now. You can ring the bell. And I promise I'll melt into the crowd and leave you with Moira at the earliest opportunity."

When Lindsay came down the stairs from the bedroom where she had left her coat, Moira was standing in the hall talking to Alex. Tall, with the dark glossy hair Lindsay had remembered, she had a long high-cheek-boned face and a flawless pink and white complexion. Fine sparkling blue eyes surveyed Lindsay speculatively before Moira smiled, revealing large white teeth.

"You're as blonde as ever, I see. How do you do it? Most blondes go mousy eventually," she murmured. "This is the first time we've actually met, although I know you and your sister very well by sight. Come and meet my father."

She linked one arm through one of Lindsay's and the other through one of Alex's and guided them into the big lounge that was full of people, sitting and standing laughing and talking. She took them up to a tall thin man with graying hair. He had a gentle, lined face which lit up with a cheerful smile when he heard Lindsay's name.

"Lindsay Bell, eh? Och, it's a beautiful name ye have," he said in a soft voice. "Now tell me, how is your mother? I haven't seen her lately.

"She's recovering from flu. But I didn't realize you knew her," replied Lindsay as she accepted a glass of sherry offered to her by Alex.

"Och, yes. Many's the time I used to go sailing with her and Grant Nicolson when I was a boy. Those were the great days before the place became known. Not many people owned cars then, and we were able to keep it to ourselves. It was all ours . . . the river, the islands, the Firth. The days were long and seemingly cloudless. Have you ever noticed, Lindsay, how the days of your youth always seem to be sunny and fine? But what am I thinking of? They'll still seem like that to you."

Grant Nicolson, father of Scott Nicolson. Lindsay had never heard the name until the previous afternoon when her mother had mentioned it. And now she was hearing it again in connection with her mother.

"Was Grant Nicolson a friend of yours?" she asked.

"We were summer friends. I used to see him when my parents brought me here for the holidays. We used to rent a cottage next door to the one his parents rented. Then your mother used to stay with her people in a house on the cliff. But ye'll know all about that. Your mother will have told you. I'm sorry she's been ill. Tell her I was asking after her, will ye?"

He introduced her to a man in his late 50's called Bill Pearson who revealed that he worked for the Innes biscuit company and was in Barrcliffe especially for the New Year's Eve party. After talking to them for a while, she and Alex moved on to another group of young local people. Lindsay particularly noticed a girl slightly younger than herself. Plump and smiling with dark hair and merry brown eyes, she seemed on good terms with Alex. He introduced her as Janet McMorrow from Glenfoot Farm on the other side of the estuary from Cairness.

There were many people she knew, and Lindsay soon forgot her attack of nerves as she talked and listened. Alex stayed by her side and they went together to the dining room when Moira announced that supper was served.

"Are you enjoying yourself?" asked Alex, as they helped themselves to cold meat and salads from the big table in the center of the room.

"Yes. I didn't think there would be so many people I know here. As you said, Mr. Innes is very easy-going. I didn't think he would be like that. I thought he would be big and bossy. How are you making out with Moira?"

"That's one of your Canadian expressions," he commented. "I'm not sure I'm making out anything with her. She doesn't stay in one place long enough . . . and she's abstracted. Scott was expected, but he hasn't turned up and she's anxious."

Alex sighed and looked melancholy. They went over to a small side table and sat down at it. Looking around, Lindsay noticed Janet McMorrow watching them from the other side of the room with a rather wistful expression on her face, but before she could analyze the cause of the wistfulness she saw Moira bearing down on them from the direction of the door. An imp of mischief made her lean forward and place a hand possessively on Alex's arm and looked deep into his eyes.

For a fraction of a second he was surprised, and then understanding dawned in his eyes. Placing his hand over hers he leaned forward and whispered, "Is she coming?"

Lindsay nodded, and he leaned across the table toward her so that to anyone watching they looked as if they were having a very intimate conversation.

"I hope you helped yourself to everything you want, Lindsay." Moira's voice seemed a little sharper than usual, or was that wishful thinking?

"Scott has just phoned, Alex. He says he was unavoidably detained by an unexpected visitor, but he'll come and let the New Year in for us. What a good thing he's dark, isn't it?"

"Yes, it is," replied Alex, who was still gazing at Lindsay.

"I think I'll have some dessert with you," announced Moira. She sounded slightly exasperated, and Lindsay longed to look up to see the expression on her face. Moira moved away to the big table, and Alex turned to watch her go.

"It's unkind to behave like this," said Lindsay as she tried to stifle her giggles.

"Not if it has the right effect, it isn't. And I'm rather enjoying it, aren't you?"

Moira returned and continued to sit with them before Lindsay could reply while they drank their coffee. She chatted brightly, talking mostly to Lindsay about Beth, about Canada, and eventually about Lindsay's future plans.

"Lindsay is coming to work for me while she's here," answered Alex.

"Oh, really? How nice," said Moira. "I didn't know you were a nurse. Wouldn't you prefer to work in a hospital? They're awfully short-staffed."

"No, she wouldn't," put in Alex. "She's booked to smooth the path for Doctors McDonnell and Wilson. I keep thinking how pleasant it will be to walk into the office and to see you sitting there all serene and smiling. Roll on, Monday."

"I'm looking forward to it myself," said Lindsay, sending what she hoped was an intimate glance in his direction.

Moira stood up quickly. "I hope it's a wise arrangement. Don't you think that being such good friends might distract you both from work? We're having a little entertainment before the old year goes, and I must go and arrange the seating in the lounge before everyone returns to it. Would you mind if I borrow Alex for a few minutes, Lindsay?"

Lindsay looked up and met a challenging glance from eyes that were very blue. It gave her an odd feeling to realize that Moira did not like her.

"No, not at all," she answered.

Alex's attempt to appear reluctant to leave with Moira almost destroyed Lindsay's coolness. She longed to laugh and wished she had someone to share the joke with. Once more she noticed the pretty, dark girl staring at her—Janet McMorrow. The name was familiar, and she remembered that Janet had been two years behind her at school. She was just thinking of going across the room to talk to her when Janet stood and hurried out of the room, leaving Lindsay with the distinct feeling that she had been the reason for Janet's abrupt departure. Janet had deliberately avoided her.

The entertainment turned out to be unique. A young friend of the Innes family called Gay Smythe was an accomplished violinist and was studying at Brussels Conservatory. She was home on holiday and staying with the Inneses. Moira had asked her to play for her guests. She was accompanied at the piano by a young man called Colin Martin. They played a Beethoven sonata and then two short pieces by Mozart. Looking around at the absorbed faces of the guests, at the elegant decorations and furnishings of the room, Lindsay thought what a perfect setting it was for that kind of entertainment. It was not difficult to imagine that similar entertainment had been offered in the same room when the house had been built at the beginning of the 19th century. Only someone with the self-assurance and initiative possessed by Moira could have arranged it and carried it through. Lindsay glanced at her graceful hostess with admiration; glad that she did not have to compete seriously with her.

The classical music was followed appropriately by renderings of old Scottish ballads that they all sang. As the last note of the last song died away, the grandfather clock began to strike midnight. Immediately Mr. Innes and Moira appeared with trays of drinks for the toast to the New Year. The last chime had hardly finished when there was a hammering at the front door, and inconsequently Lindsay discovered that her heart was hammering too.

But Alex was there, bending to kiss her and wish her a Happy New Year, and there were other hands to shake and other cheeks to kiss, so she did not see Scott's arrival; only heard the laughter which greeted him. Then there was more singing this time of "Auld Lang Syne" and more shaking of hands and kissing. Lindsay found herself on her own in a corner by a window, half hidden by a tall indoor plant, watching Scott shaking hands with the Morrisons. He was wearing a dark gray suit and a sparkling white shirt that emphasized the darkness of his hair. Hand in his pants pocket, he looked very much at ease as he talked with the Morrisons.

Lindsay longed to move out of her corner before he noticed her, but she saw Alex with Moira, looking happy. She remembered his joking suggestion that she should distract Scott's attention, and the same imp of mischief that had motivated her earlier in the dining room now prompted her to take action.

She moved forward and accidentally knocked against the plant. It quivered and then to her consternation began to tilt over. Scott saw it tilting and moved quickly to prevent it from falling. He righted it, said a few words to the Morrisons, then turned slowly to look at Lindsay. Hand outstretched, he approached her. Reluctantly she placed hers in it.

"I thought I'd wished everyone here a Happy New

Year," he said. His clear gaze observed everything from the bunch of silver gilt ringlets on the top of her head to the silver gilt of her shoes.

With a quiver of alarm she felt him pulling her gently toward him and tried to withdraw her hand. She did not want to be kissed by him. He bent his head and whispered, "You can't refuse at Hogmanay, with everyone watching."

Was everyone watching? She couldn't see, but his suggestion was enough to stop her resisting. It wouldn't do to make a scene before her mother's neighbors. So she presented her cheek to him. To her annoyance he put his other hand against her averted cheek, turned her face and kissed her soundly on the mouth.

"That wasn't fair!" she hissed, as he released her. He smiled.

"And now we'll tak' a cup o' kindness, Lindsay, for auld lang syne," he murmured. He was still holding her hand. She looked around to see if anyone was watching them. But everyone seemed too engrossed in conversation. She could see Alex sitting on a sofa with Moira and some other people. She looked up at Scott and smiled back.

"All right," she agreed.

"Stay here," he ordered and walked away.

She sat down quickly on the elegant rosewood and tapestry sofa against the wall beside the window that was partially hidden from sight by the plant. She had to sit down because her knees were trembling. No one had ever had this effect on her before, and she was at a loss to account for her reaction.

Scott returned with two glasses of whisky and water. He handed one to her and then sat down beside her as he had done the previous afternoon. There was less space on the small antique sofa, and his arm brushed against hers as he leaned back. Nervousness pushed Lindsay into talking.

"There's really no reason why you and I should remember auld lang syne," she said. "We didn't meet until yesterday and you didn't know my name."

"We used to be neighbors, that's reason enough," he

replied, "and although I couldn't recall your name I remembered you." Lindsay sipped at her drink. His self-assurance was destroying her façade of composure and was beginning to wish she had not given in to the prompt-ings of mischief.

"Do you really remember me?" she asked eventually in order to break a silence that had lasted too long. He gazed deliberately at her hair, then at her face, and finally his gaze wandered downward to linger on her neck and her small slight breasts outlined by the fitted bodice of her dress. His deliberate manner made her want to slap him but when he glanced up again and she saw the twinkle in his eyes, the desire melted.

"Not as you are now," he said, "but I remember a roly-poly of about four years old who once fell off the end of the slipway into the mud when the tide was out at Cairness and who squealed like a pig until she was rescued."

Lindsay had only a vague memory of the muddy incident, and the fact that he apparently remembered it clearly and accurately confused her.

"How d'you know?" she asked.

"I rescued you." He raised his glass to her. "A guid New Year to you, Lindsay. 'Here's tae us, whae's like us, damn few, they're all deid.' " He drank, and Lindsay laughed spontaneously.

"I haven't heard that toast for a long time. Happy New Year to you. I didn't know it was you who pulled me out of the mud. Is it too late to say thank you?"

"No. I had little thanks for my trouble at the time. Your mother gave me a tongue-lashing as usual. I think she believed I'd pushed you in."

"I suppose you were capable of that, too," said Lindsay.

"Och, yes. I once pushed Beth into the mud because she called my mother a gypsy. But I wouldn't have pushed a wee bairn, as you were then." His gaze flicked over her again. "You don't remember me at all, do you?"

"I can't remember when you lived at the gatehouse, but now that I've met you I realize I've seen you twice before.

I saw you come last in a sailing race. Beth made fun of you."

"I remember that, too."

He sat silently looking down at his drink. Lindsay wondered if it was the end of their conversation and racked her brains for another subject with which to hold his attention. Looking through the leaves of the plant, she could see that there were not so many people in the room, and she assumed that most of the older couples had gone home. Someone had produced the inevitable guitar and was strumming it softly. Alex and Moira were still sitting together, and she recognized the dark curly hair of Janet McMorrow and the square-set shoulders of Bill Pearson amongst the group of people around them.

"When I was a boy and we lived in Cairness, I wanted nothing more than to own a dinghy and to take part in the races," said Scott suddenly, musingly. "I didn't manage it until I was 19. I'd worked all winter on that boat. I knew nothing about sailing, so I was bound to be last. Being made fun of by Beth made me all the more determined to win one day. Three years later I did . . . in the same boat."

"And that was the second time I saw you. You came out of the hotel with some friends. Beth and I were out walking with my father. You blocked the roadway, and we couldn't pass. You were rude to my father."

He glanced at her sharply. "You hold that against me?"

"No, but my mother does. She says you were often rude to him, particularly on the day your father died and Dad went to offer to help your mother."

He was silent again and the expression on his face was somber as he swirled the remains of liquor around in his glass and then drank it. She must make more effort than this to hold his attention, thought Lindsay. Reference to death was hardly the way to attract a man sufficiently for him to want to stay with her.

"When you're young and hurt, as I was that day, you tend to lash out at the first person who comes along," he said, to her surprise. "I knew your parents were glad we had to move, and somehow it seemed to me then that it was hypocritical of him to come and offer help."

"He wasn't a hypocrite. He was a very kind man," flared Lindsay.

"How was I to know that? None of the Bell family had ever shown kindness to me," he replied quietly. "Did you know that your mother was once in love with my father and was engaged to him?"

Lindsay shook her head dumbly, her gray eyes wide.

"I do believe I've shocked you," he remarked. "They all used to come here for their summer holidays, your parents, my father and Moira's parents . . . much as we all come today. They played together, went sailing, hunting, fishing or played golf, grew up and fell in and out of love with each other. My mother was the interloper, the stranger, even though she had lived locally all her life. It was she who broke the group up. Your father had met her at some village dance and invited her to come here to some event. She met my father. It was a case of immediate magnetic attraction. They ran away together, and when they returned a year later just before the war started they were married and I was on the way. Now you know why your mother never liked us and resented us when she discovered we were her neighbors."

Lindsay felt stunned. She did not doubt the truth of the story. It bore out what she had sensed the previous evening; that her mother had a deeper reason for disliking the Nicolsons than the one she had given.

"How do you know all this?" she asked.

"My mother told me, the day I was rude to your father when he came to offer help. She thought it would help me to understand your parents' attitude better. And now your mother thinks that I'm enjoying getting my own back because I'm responsible for widening the road that will destroy her home. Doesn't she?"

His voice had hardened, and he looked at her directly.

"Aren't you?" she countered.

"No. I'm doing my job, that's all. It would be easier to do if I didn't know the people involved and if there hadn't been a certain amount of feuding between us in the past. But I'm certainly not doing it out of revenge. In fact, as I've told you, I'd like to help."

"Surely you realize that my mother wouldn't accept help from you?"

"Just because I'm the son of the man she hoped to marry once, because I'm Ann Robertson's son, because I was rude once or twice to her husband?" he jibed. "I learned to forget and forgive, can't she?"

Lindsay looked away across the room through the leaves of the plant. Moira was glancing curiously in the direction of the corner where she was half hidden with Scott. In a few minutes she would be over to break up the apparently intimate conversation. Alex was now sitting with Janet, who was talking animatedly to him. Why was he wasting precious time with her instead of talking to Moira?

"How could you help?" she asked Scott.

"By offering your mother a house in which to live in Cairness?"

"Which one?"

"Glendoon. I bought it last spring. It's the only house in Cairness, or Barrcliffe for that matter, that is available, and if your mother doesn't want to move away from her friends she would be wise to rent it."

Lindsay's head was whirling. She was learning too much too rapidly. Now he was trying to push her into making a quick decision. His offer seemed genuine enough, but she could not forget the impression that he was unscrupulous; the first one she had formed about him. He could see a way of turning her mother's plight to his advantage by renting a house to her.

"Thank you for the offer," she replied as coolly as she could, "but at the moment we have made no plans. Mother's lawyer will be looking after her interests, and I expect he'll find her somewhere to live." He gave her a sidelong sardonic glance.

"How well you do it," he observed.

"Do what?"

"Set me at a distance . . . push me back to my side of the fence. You remind me of someone."

She was quite unprepared for the change in his manner. Off-guard, she asked curiously, "Who?"

"Whom," he corrected absently. He stared at her with narrowed eyes and she moved uneasily, feeling that he was assessing her and finding her wanting. It was strange to feel that perhaps she did not measure up to this man's standards.

He snapped his fingers triumphantly.

"I know, *La Belle Dame Sans Merci*— 'Full beautiful, a faery's child'. I wonder if I'm going to awake and find myself alone, 'On the cold hillside.' "

Remembering Keats' poem about the lovely cold temptress who had lured men on to love her only to reject them, Lindsay was not sure whether she was pleased or annoyed by the comparison.

"Did you come here by yourself?" asked Scott.

"No . . . no . . . er . . . I came with Alex Wilson."

To her relief the hazel eyes flickered away from her and looked across the room.

"He looks busy and not exactly 'alone and palely loitering,' " he commented dryly. "I'll take you home."

Lindsay gulped. This was going farther than she had anticipated, but if it meant that Alex would be able to stay with Moira longer without the company of Scott the risk would be worth it. What risk? She pulled her thoughts up short. Whatever was she thinking about?

"Yes. It's time I was leaving," she agreed sweetly. "Mother hasn't been well, as you know, and I promised her I wouldn't be too late."

He stood up as if the matter was settled.

"Then go and get your coat while I tell Moira we're leaving." He was going too fast for her, hustling her, and she wondered why he was in such a hurry.

"No. I'm not ready. I must speak to Alex first. After all, I did come with him."

She walked across the room. Alex looked up and winked at her over the top of Janet's head.

"Alex, I think I'd better go now," she began.

Disappointment clouded his face, but he stood up obediently.

"Of course."

"Oh, what a shame," said Moira. "We were having such a happy time. Why not come back after you've taken Lindsay home, Alex?"

"Yes, I suppose I could do that," he agreed.

"Don't disturb yourself," put in Scott smoothly, from behind Lindsay. "I'm leaving now, so I can easily take Lindsay home."

Alex's face brightened immediately. Janet who had turned away when Lindsay had approached looked up straight at Scott and smiled warmly.

"Could you? Is that all right with you, Lindsay?"

"Yes, if you don't mind."

"But, Scott, I've hardly seen anything of you," complained Moira.

"There'll be other times, Moira," he said easily. "I promised I'd go duck-shooting this morning with Dougie at Southerness and I want to go home and change. I'm meeting him at four-thirty."

Immediately there was a chorus of interested questions about the duck-shooting expedition. Lindsay knew that the excuse was probably valid, because she remembered her father once going out on New Year's morning before dawn in order to go shooting on the marshes.

"I'm so glad you were able to come, Lindsay," Moira was saying politely. "We must meet again. Perhaps you would like to come over for tea one Sunday with your mother. I'm sure Father would like that. They could talk over old times together. I'll come and show you where your coat is."

"Don't forget that starting on Monday you're working for me, Lindsay," Alex called after her as she went toward the door. "I'll call you tomorrow or the day after about it."

The early morning sky was blue-black and star-sprinkled; bushes and rocks were dark shapes looming up at the side of the road that twisted over the hill to Cairness. Below in the estuary, water gleamed faintly, and from the far side of Glenfoot Island an intermittent beam of light shone as the automatic beacon revolved, sending its message of warning across the Firth.

It was the first day of the New Year, and she had spent the first hour and a half with a man whom she scarcely knew. She hoped that her agreement to allow him to take her home was of assistance to Alex. The feeling of nervousness that she had experienced earlier had returned. She could put up with it only if she thought she had been of use.

She told herself that it was silly to feel nervous. He had not spoken to her since they had left Cliffe House, nor had she spoken to him. There was no need now to put on an act, to pretend interest in what he was saying in order to keep him by her side and away from Moira. But then had she had to pretend interest back there in the corner of the lounge? Not really, because it was he who had held her attention; subtly spinning a web in which to catch her with his recollections of her as a child, his strange story about her mother and his father, with his unusual personal comment. And it was no use denying that for a while she had been caught in the web.

Lindsay sat up sharply. The drive home was not yet over, and it was possible that he was still spinning.

"Have you forgotten something?" he asked idly. They were over the hill, and the road was descending in a series of bends down to Cairness.

"No. Why do you ask?"

"For a while you relaxed, then you sat bolt upright like a startled rabbit. You needn't be afraid. I intend to take you straight home."

"Thank you," replied Lindsay, weakly, and he laughed.

"I believe you thought my intentions were dishonorable," he scoffed.

"Well, you were rather determined to remove me from the party," she countered. "I wonder why?"

"Let's say I was acting on behalf of a good friend of mine and leave it at that. I noticed that you didn't show much reluctance to leave," he replied coldly. "Do you have to go and work for Wilson?"

"I can't live on air while I'm staying here, and my mother's income isn't sufficient to keep us both."

"But why pick him?"

"I didn't. He picked me. He offered me the job on the way to the party."

"He's a fool," was the caustic comment as they turned into the driveway at Merse Cottage.

Lindsay drew a deep breath as the best way of keeping her temper and then spoke carefully.

"Mr. Nicolson, I realize you're entitled to have opinions about people and that you're also entitled to express them, but I can't understand why you think that Alex is a fool because he has offered to employ me as a nurse when he and his partner need a nurse and I happen to be one. It seems to be remarkably sensible to me."

She wished that she had left the car and gone into the house instead of reacting to his remark, because he leaned toward her, stretching one arm along the back of the seat behind her. When he spoke she felt his breath on her cheek.

"I'm not questioning the sense that lies behind his hiring of a nurse. I can understand that he and McDonnell require one to make their practice more efficient. But I do think he's a fool to employ you in particular."

Indignation made Lindsay turn to look at him. Then she wished she had not done so, because he was very, very near.

"Why? What's wrong with me?" she demanded.

"If you don't know, look in the mirror some time."

He moved away and resting his hands on the steering wheel, he continued in a bland conversational tone, "Think about my offer of Glendoon, and if your mother would like to rent it let me know. You can reach me at the Council offices, or you may see me down here when I'm watching the progress of the work."

He revved the engine of the car as if he was impatient to be gone, and she got out of the car as fast as she could. The car had backed into the road and had departed in the direction of Duncraig long before she was able to unlock the front door. Her hands were shaking so much she had difficulty in fitting the key into the lock.

The morning was sunny and mild. The remains of the snow were melting rapidly. The sound of running water was everywhere as it trickled down the roof, from the downspouts, and along the gutters of the road. Although she had gone to sleep quickly, Lindsay had not slept long and had wakened at seven.

She lay in bed thinking about the party. So much had happened in so short a time. She had been offered a job. She had met Moira and Cameron Innes. She had met Scott Nicolson for the second time that week. She had learned much about her parents that she had not known before.

It was incredible to think of her mother being in love with anyone other than her father. As she remembered them together they had represented a perfect partnership; a perfect example of stable marriage to their daughters that Beth had been able to emulate, and that she had once hoped to follow herself. Now, of course, she would never marry because she would never be able to love a man enough to want to live with him for the rest of her life. As she had told Alex last night, she was immune to the deadly disease.

She yawned and turned over on her side. No wonder her mother had not liked Ann Nicolson if the strange woman had enticed Grant Nicolson away from her. Inconsequently she wondered which of his parents Scott favored. His darkness suggested that it must be his mother with her small dash of gypsy blood. And yet his eyes, the color of hazel nuts when they were ripening, clear brown shading into green, were they like his father's?

Lindsay sat up in the same way she had sat upright in Scott's car on the way home. What was she doing mooning about a man's eyes at this time of day? What did the color of his eyes matter to her? Nothing. Nothing at all.

She caught sight of herself in the dressing table mirror. "Look in the mirror some time." The words echoed in her mind, and she stared at her reflection. She saw a thin, fine-boned face lit by wide, luminous, gray eyes and framed in a tangle of fine blonde hair.

Thoroughly awake by now, she bounded out of bed, thrust her feet into her slippers, and flung on her quilted nylon dressing gown tying the belt tightly around her slim waist. She padded down the stairs into the sunlit living room and went straight through into the kitchen. There she filled the kettle and switched it on, then turned on the grill of the electric stove. She found bacon and eggs in the small refrigerator, and from a cupboard above the stove took down the necessary pans.

Tiger, Mrs. Bell's marmalade cat, roused from its early morning nap, mewed to be let out, so Lindsay opened the door that led into the small garden. The dampness of the air made her shiver, and she closed the door quickly, wondering how long it would take her to become acclimatized once more to her native land.

She switched on a small transistor radio. The sound of Scottish country dance music filled the room. That was better. Nothing like gay music and practical work to drive away daydreams. She broke eggs into a bowl and whipped them, put the bacon under the grill and placed sliced bread in the toaster.

She would take the breakfast up to her mother's room. They would eat together while she talked about the party and about Moira's suggestion that they should go to tea at Cliffe House one Sunday. Later she would call Alex and find out how he managed after she had left the party. Judging by the way Moira stayed near him, it was possible that their little scheme to separate her and Scott had worked.

But why had Scott reacted so strangely? Why had he taken her away from the party? Who was the good friend on whose behalf he had said he was acting? And what had lain behind his suggestion that Alex was a fool to employ her?

There was a smell of burning. Lindsay snatched the grill pan from under the grill. Drat the man! Now he had come between her and the breakfast.

Looking at the blackened mess of bacon, she decided

not to cook any more and concentrated on scrambling eggs, buttering toast and making tea, all the time humming the lilting familiar tunes that came from the radio. She set a tray, arranged the plates of food and cups and saucers on it, and set off through the living room to the stairs. But on the way she caught sight of herself in the big mirror over the mantelpiece. With a smothered exclamation she set the tray down on a coffee table, went to the bookcase, and drew out a small, thin, blue book. Thumbing through it quickly, she found the page she wanted and read rapidly. Phrases leapt out at her; phrases that she imagined were being spoken by a deep taunting voice.

"Full beautiful, a faery's child:
   Her hair was long, her foot was light
   And her eyes were wild."

She found herself fingering her hair and glancing at her outhrust foot, stopped doing both with another disgusted exclamation, and read on:

"And there I shut her wild, wild eyes
   With kisses four . . .
   And I awoke and found me here
   On the cold hillside."

Shuddering a little, Lindsay closed the book with a bang, put it in its place, and picked up the tray. So that was why Scott thought Alex was a fool to employ her. He regarded her as *La Belle Dame Sans Merci*, who had held all men in her thrall and then had starved them of love. The devil! How dared he come to conclusions about her character just because she resembled the woman described in the poem? And why should he be concerned for Alex? She made her way upstairs hurriedly realizing that the breakfast was growing cold.

Although Mrs. Bell seemed recovered from her bout of flu, Lindsay could see that she had lost much of her former vitality, and that the year and a half since her husband's death had been a great strain for her. It would not be fair to let her live alone again for a while. Lindsay had decided she might as well say goodbye to any plans she might have had for returning to Canada at the end of January. She would stay and see her mother through the agonizing problem of parting with the cottage, where she had spent so many years with John Bell, and would help her to find somewhere else to live where she could be happy and contented.

The pleasure which lit Mrs. Bell's face when Lindsay announced her decision to stay at least until the end of April showed that she had done the right thing.

"And Alex has offered me a job . . . to be a nurse for him and Dr. McDonnell. I start on Monday."

"Oh, I'm so glad. It will be a great relief to have one of you here. But I wanted the decision to be yours. I didn't want to be a burden to you." Tears of weakness filled Mrs. Bell's eyes.

"You could of course come to Canada with me and live with us out there," suggested Lindsay tentatively.

"No, that wouldn't do. I'd rather be here with my friends. I may come with you for a holiday when you return, but not to stay."

"Then that's settled," said Lindsay, "so you can stop worrying."

"Dr. Wilson is such a pleasant young man," mused her mother. "You could do worse."

"I suppose I could . . . but I'll reserve judgment on Alex as an employer until I've worked for him a few weeks."

"Wouldn't it be nice if he asked you to marry him?" went on Mrs. Bell.

Lindsay controlled the impatience she felt with her mother's attitude to life and said teasingly, "You're worse than any 18th-century matchmaking mama. I'm taking this job so that I can stay here with you for a while, not so that I can marry. I'm not interested in marriage."

"Why not?" Mrs. Bell sounded unusually severe. "What's wrong with marriage? Now don't tell me that a daughter of mine is following this new trend I've read about in the newspapers, all the nonsense about women not having to marry any more, and having the same freedoms as men. I hope not, because that isn't the way you and Beth have been brought up."

Lindsay sighed. Already her mother was jumping to conclusions.

"I'm not following any trend. I'm not a conformist. I do as I wish. I'm not interested in marriage because the man I love is married already. I've no desire to break his marriage up."

To her surprise Mrs. Bell smiled indulgently and leaned forward to pat her hand that rested on the bed.

"I'm glad you didn't do that, dear. But you mustn't think that you'll never love again. I had a feeling you were unhappy. Why didn't you tell me about it?"

Lindsay searched her mind for a reason. She was only just beginning to realize that she had not confided in her mother because confidences had never been encouraged by either of her parents. They in their turn had never confided in her. She thought of Scott saying that his mother had told him all about the relationship between his father and her mother, and was suddenly possessed by envy of the relationship he must have had with his mother at quite an early age.

"I suppose I haven't told you for the same reason you didn't tell me about the Council wanting to tear down the house. I didn't want to worry you," she excused herself.

"You thought I wouldn't understand?" asked Mrs. Bell shrewdly.

"Yes," admitted Lindsay.

"But I do . . . I can. I felt like you do, once. Yet I learned to love someone else and was very happy."

"Even when you discovered you were living next door to the Nicolsons?" Lindsay queried quietly.

Mrs. Bell's eyes widened. "How do you know? Who told you? Cameron Innes? Surely not. He's too much of a gentleman. He would never gossip."

"No, he didn't. He only mentioned that he used to go sailing with you and Grant Nicolson . . . which I must admit made me start to think. It was Scott who told me that you had once long ago been engaged to his father."

Mrs. Bell gasped and leaned back against her pillows, her eyes closed as if she was in pain. She opened them slowly to look accusingly at Lindsay.

"You discussed me with that . . . that . . ."

"That gypsy?" supplied Lindsay with a smile. "Yes, we talked about you. He was explaining why he wanted to help you, and why you detested his family so much. He told me because he thought it would help me to understand your attitude to him."

"But how did he know?"

"His mother told him."

"There, isn't that typical again? She told that boy everything. There wasn't a thing he didn't know. He was never innocent."

"Perhaps she believed in keeping the doors of communication open," suggested Lindsay.

"Whatever do you mean by that?"

"I mean that if you had told me more, I'd have understood more, not only about the Nicolsons but also about myself. Maybe I wouldn't have felt so badly when I found out about Maurice. Already I feel better because you say it's possible to recover and to love again."

"I still can't understand why Ann had to tell him about Grant and me."

"She wanted him to understand why you disliked them so much. She wanted him to learn to forgive and forget the way in which you had treated them. . . ."

"You make it sound as if we were deliberately cruel to the Nicolsons," objected Mrs. Bell. "We expected them to keep to their side of the fence, that's all, and to leave us alone."

"I can imagine the effect that would have on a lively boy," murmured Lindsay. "Mother, Scott was trying to convince me that his offer to help you is quite genuine, and that he isn't enjoying having to destroy this house. Now you have to admit you thought he'd come to gloat, and that you wouldn't listen to him because you were prejudiced against him."

"It seems to me you've gone right over to his side,"

said Mrs. Bell indignantly. "What else could I think? Oh, it's been so difficult since your father died. I haven't known whom to trust, Cuthbert has been absolutely no use. . . ."

"I haven't gone over to anyone's side. I'm trying to see everything in a reasonable light," said Lindsay gently. "You think Cuthbert is no use because he hasn't been able to solve your problem the way you want it solved. I think we'd better ask him to come and talk about it, don't you? Then we can ask him what he thinks of Scott's offer to help."

Mrs. Bell pleated the bedcover between two fingers. Her face was drawn and tired-looking as she considered Lindsay's suggestion. At last she said, "You've grown up. You're no longer the girl who used to dream of traveling to far distant places searching for what you used to call your fate," she commented. "Very well, we shall ask Cuthbert to come and see us tomorrow. But you haven't told me how Scott Nicolson can help us."

"He owns a house in Cairness—Glendoon, and he's willing to rent it to us. That way you could stay in the village and be near your friends."

Mrs. Bell was silent as she still pleated the bedcover between nervous fingers.

"It's a good house," she said. "But to be dependent on a Nicolson. . . ."

"We wouldn't be dependent on him. We would pay him rent, and from what I've learned about him he won't scruple to exact a good rent from us. It will be all legal. Cuthbert would make sure we had a contract so that we couldn't be turned out at a moment's notice."

"But to live in a house belonging to that man," muttered Mrs. Bell. "It would be very difficult."

"Yes, I know. We would have to sink our pride. But think of the alternative; having to move away from Cairness," persisted Lindsay. She picked up the breakfast tray and moved toward the door. "I wonder why he bought a house like that," she mused out loud.

"I seem to remember Aggie having something to say about it, but not liking gossip I didn't listen very well. I believe he bought it because he was going to get married and thought of living here, but the girl jilted him."

"Then that makes two of us," murmured Lindsay as she went out of the room.

CHAPTER THREE

There was no telephone call from Alex. When eventually Lindsay phoned his home she was informed that he was out. Lindsay hoped that he was with Moira. This hope was destroyed, however, when Moira herself telephoned to invite Lindsay and Mrs. Bell to tea at Cliffe House on the following Sunday afternoon.

"I'd have asked you to come tomorrow, but we shall still have our guests here. I know Daddy would prefer to have you to himself."

Lindsay accepted the invitation provisionally, saying that the visit would depend entirely on the state of her mother's health. She was about to say goodbye and hang up when Moira said, "I hope you arrived home safely this morning and that Scott behaved himself."

Lindsay was almost tempted to say that he had not behaved himself to find out what Moira's reaction would be, but she controlled the mischievous urge and replied coolly, "I arrived home quite safely, thank you. We came straight here and made good time. Mr. Nicolson left immediately."

Moira laughed, rather apologetically. "Now I've offended you. I'm sorry, I'm afraid I expressed myself rather badly. I meant that I hoped Scott wasn't unpleasant or unkind to you," she said placatingly.

"Why should he be?"

"Well, he's a bit of a misogynist . . . but of course you won't know the story. He was going to marry, and the woman jilted him for someone else."

"Almost sounds like history repeating itself," murmured Lindsay facetiously.

"I beg your pardon? I'm afraid I didn't quite catch what you said," said Moira sharply.

"I said he didn't give me the impression last night of being a misogynist," replied Lindsay, the mischievous urge getting the better of her.

"Oh, really?" This time Moira sounded extremely distant. "I can assure you it's true though. Of course he isn't like that with me, because I've been able to help him over a very difficult patch in his life. We're very good friends. I'd like you to realize that."

Lindsay stiffened. She was being warned off. It could not have been put more plainly. But she found the suggestion that the self-sufficient Scott had required help and had accepted it from a person like Moira quite incredible. And it was beginning to look as if Alex had been mistaken when he said that Scott had come between himself and Moira. Here was Moira admitting her interest in Scott and making it quite clear she did not want anyone interfering in her friendship with him.

At the moment there was only one thing she could do and that was try to help Alex's cause, so she said, "I hope you haven't been wasting your time and your sympathy. Misogynists are notoriously hard nuts to crack."

"Why do you say that?" Moira sounded alarmed.

"I was thinking that while you've been looking in a certain direction you may have lost a more valuable friendship with someone who isn't suffering from a built-in hate of women. Thank you once again for the invitation. Mother and I shall look forward to seeing you. Goodbye."

Lindsay hung up and smiled benignly at the black instrument. She had done her good deed for the day. She had planted a seed of doubt in Moira's mind. Would the woman have the sense to look around and realize that the valuable someone she had almost lost was Alex? Lindsay hoped so.

Next morning Cuthbert Murray, the family lawyer, came in answer to Lindsay's invitation. He arrived early so that he and Lindsay could talk before Mrs. Bell was up and dressed. A short, portly man in his mid-40's with a head of remarkably curly hair sat on the edge of the sofa in the living room and looked at the letter from the Council containing the final offer for the property.

"Well, Lindsay, I told your mother that there wasn't a

hope of the Council allowing the house to remain standing, and she wouldn't listen to me. In fact she has been extremely difficult to deal with for the past 12 months."

"Then why didn't you write to us and tell us?"

"Och, I thought I could handle her myself. I thought she'd come out of it. It seems as if all her common sense deserted her with the death of your father. That cousin came to see her, and she loaned him money she couldn't afford. I had to tell her she had acted foolishly and was shown the door."

"Yes, I can imagine," murmured Lindsay.

"Then this compulsory purchase order came through and she behaved in the same way. Ostrich mentality. Don't do anything . . . pretend the problem doesn't exist and it will go away. I happened to meet Scott Nicolson in town one day and told him the situation. He said he'd come and try to talk to her. But he had no luck either. Thank heaven you've come. Imagine what it would have been like if we'd had to knock on the door one day and say to her 'The house is going to be demolished today. You'd better leave!' "

"We can't stop the demolition, then?"

"No. Too late. Not a chance. The Council have been watching this corner for years. They just didn't have the money available before. You could ask them to pay more money, though. I think we could make out a good case for that . . . about your mother being on a fixed income and you not being here all the time. Have you decided where you would go and live, by the way?"

"We've been offered a house in Cairness."

"Take it, take it. Anyone I know? I thought all the places were rented."

"Glendoon."

"Uhum—Nicolson's place. And your mother agrees?"

"Not yet. But I'm trying to persuade her. She isn't very well. I think I should have stayed with her when Father died, but she was so insistent that I should return to Canada."

"Aye, a very stubborn woman is your mother, and when you're young it is difficult to set yourself against an authority that you have always obeyed. But sometimes it's necessary. I'm glad you're seeing sense. You've no prejudices against the Nicolson lad, I gather?"

It was rather odd to hear such a mature person as Scott referred to as a lad, and Lindsay had to hide a smile.

"Not any that would prevent me from paying him rent for a house."

"Good. That's fine. I'll fix up the legal side for you."

The interview with Mrs. Bell passed off much better than Lindsay had anticipated, and to her surprise her mother introduced the subject of Glendoon herself.

"Lindsay has found me a place to live, Cuthbert. I haven't seen it yet, but I think it might do," she announced calmly.

"May I ask where it is?"

She told him without mentioning the name of the owner.

"Aye. A good house," he observed with a surreptitious wink at Lindsay. "It used to belong to Miss Edwards. Grand position—better than this. Fine views of the estuary and the Firth. You'll need a gardener, though. There's a fair amount of land. Maybe we could make sure that the owner takes the responsibility for that."

"But I like gardening," protested Mrs. Bell.

"No doubt you do, when you've only a pocket handkerchief-sized one like you have here. Yon's a third of an acre."

It seemed more than a third of an acre to Lindsay's inexperienced eyes as she inspected the garden of Glendoon that afternoon. Her own interest and her mother's promptings had caused her to walk through the village and up the lower part of the road to Barrcliffe to see the house.

It was a mild, damp day. All the snow had gone from the village and the hill behind it. There were still patches of white on the slopes of the hills on the opposite side of the estuary, making a stark contrast to the dark green of the conifers that crowded together in the glens. A watery, yellow sun shone fitfully, glinting on the smooth mudbanks of the estuary that were exposed by the out-going tide.

The house was built of granite blocks. It was a simple,

gable-ended, house with a slate roof from which three dormer windows protruded; two at the front and one at the back. Downstairs there was a plain front door set between two bay windows. The only addition that had been made to the house since it had been built was a garage.

Lindsay noticed that the driveway was asphalted and in good repair as she walked up it toward the house. She went to one of the bay windows and tried to see inside. Shading her eyes with her hand and leaning against the windowpane, she could see that the room was empty and had been completely renovated. It extended the full depth of the house. She could see through to the backyard and the garden beyond it.

After peering through the other bay window at another renovated room, she walked around to the back of the house and surveyed the garden. It sloped upward toward a little wood of rowan, dogwood, and elder. Part of the garden had been screened off by a hedge of hawthorn. Peering curiously behind the hedge, Lindsay was surprised to see Brussels sprouts and winter cabbage apparently flourishing.

Turning back to the house, she guessed which window belonged to the kitchen. It was higher from the ground than the front windows were, and even if she stood on tiptoe she could not see into the room. She looked around to see if there was anything in the yard which she could stand on, but there was nothing. Everything was neat and tidy. There was a wooden, garden shed, so she tried the door thinking that there might be a ladder in it. The door was locked.

Refusing to be put off, Lindsay put her hands on the windowsill, and scrabbling with her toes on the granite blocks of the wall managed to get a purchase on the sill with her elbows, so that she could lean on them and look through the window. It was an uncomfortable and ungainly position, but at least her curiosity would be satisfied.

"Are you looking for someone? Me, perhaps?"

The voice she recognized immediately as Scott's surprised her, and she lost her precarious grip and fell backward. The height which she fell from was not great, but one of her legs buckled beneath her and she sat down in the gravel of the small yard at his feet.

"It's usual when wishing to see the inside of a house to inform the owner first, and so avoid all possibility of being accused of trespassing," said Scott coldly. "It's also probable that the owner would allow you to enter so that you would receive a better impression than the one received from pressing your nose against a window-pane."

Was he laughing at her? She could not be sure, but annoyance at being found peering at his property prodded her into attack.

"If you were a gentleman you wouldn't have crept up behind me and spoken so suddenly. You startled me. And you might show some manners now and help me up!"

She flung back her head and looked up at him. Her gray eyes challenged his calm speculative gaze.

"But I've never claimed to be a gentleman, nor to have any manners," he returned smoothly, and she realized with a shock that he did not like her any more than she liked him.

At that moment a boy of about 12 years of age careered around the side of the house. He came to a dead stop when he saw her and Scott.

"Who's she? What's she doing here?" he exclaimed, staring at Lindsay. Accepting the fact that she was going to receive no help at all, she struggled to her feet and tried to brush the mud and gravel from her raincoat.

She noticed that the boy had black hair, a dusky complexion, and that he resembled Scott closely; so closely that he could have been his son, she thought with a strange lurch of her stomach. But how could Scott, who wasn't married, have a son?"

"She's a trespasser," said Scott severely.

"Och, is she really? Are you going to prosecute her, as it says on the notice?" asked the boy.

"That all depends," said Scott slowly. He put his hands in the pockets of his raincoat and rocked back and forth on his heels. "It depends on what she offers as a forfeit."

Now she was convinced he was laughing at her.

"Och, forfeits," said the boy disgustedly. "A girl's game. Aren't you going to ask her name?"

His eyes were smoky black, not hazel, and Lindsay was conscious of a feeling of relief.

"I know her name," said Scott. "It's Lindsay Bell. Lindsay, meet my brother Coll."

Brother! Lindsay's wide, gray glance upward expressed her amazement.

He smiled slightly and added, "My mother married again."

The relief she felt at this piece of information was enormous and quite incomprehensible.

She smiled at the boy and held out her hand. "Hello, Coll."

He smiled back shyly and took her hand. "Hello, Lindsay. What are you going to pay as a forfeit? In the game the girls play, they usually make us kiss them if we haven't anything to give."

"What a good idea," commented Scott. "But I don't think we'll insist on sticking to the rules of the game today. Lindsay has been embarrassed enough. Do you want to see the inside of the house?"

Although she had managed not to blush, Lindsay met his gaze with difficulty. "Yes, please," she said stiffly.

"Why?"

The question disconcerted her. Coll was watching them with bright, observant eyes so she pulled herself together and replied.

"I heard that it's for rent, and we . . . my mother and I are looking for somewhere to live."

He raised his eyebrows slightly, and she saw amusement glint in his eyes.

"Then you may as well see it while I'm here," he answered. "It will save me a journey."

He produced a key from his pocket, inserted it in the lock of the back door, opened it, and then all went inside.

Scott did not show Lindsay around the house. After they had entered the bright kitchen that was equipped with two stainless steel sinks, numerous cupboards, and working surfaces, he waved a hand toward a doorway leading to another room and said brusquely, "Go ahead. Look around. Please excuse me. I came to do a few necessary jobs. Coll," he called, turning away from Lindsay as if he had lost interest in her reason for being there, "never mind sloping off to see Ian Prentiss. Here's the key to the shed. Go and bring that box of tools."

Feeling like an unwelcome guest, Lindsay wandered through the door into what had once been the living room of the house. It had been extended to include the entrance hall and stairway. The extension gave the room light and space that must have been missing previously. Although there was a fireplace, she noticed that an up-to-date system of hot air heating had been installed because the room was pleasantly warm after the dampness of the air outdoors. The walls had been painted pale green, and the woodwork around the doors and windows was white. As she stood in the middle of the empty room, she tried to visualize her mother's furniture in it and came to the conclusion that it would all fit in.

Beyond the staircase there was a door opening into the room that extended the depth of the house. It was also light and airy and had been painted in pale green with a white trim.

Pleased with the downstairs rooms she had seen, Lindsay mounted the stairs. She could hear Scott talking to Coll in the kitchen and wondered whether he had renovated the house himself. The thought that he might have done gave him an entirely new dimension. She noticed how the more attractive parts of the house such as the original plaster mouldings on the cornices of the ceiling had been preserved and had been carefully repainted. Under her hand the wood of the banisters had been scraped clean of varnish to reveal the lovely pale gold of the pine.

In the three bedrooms built-in closets had been added, and the bathroom had been completely gutted, and a new modern suite had been fitted.

Looking out of the window of one of the bedrooms at the view of hills, river and sea, Lindsay thought about Scott preparing this house for the woman he had wanted to marry. Had that woman helped to choose the house? Had she contributed to the change in the interior design? Or had it all been his own work, an offering of love which had been rejected?

Remembering the turmoil of emotion she had experienced when she had learned that Maurice was married the bitterness and dejection that had followed, Lindsay realized she had something in common with Scott besides having once been his neighbor. Like her, he had taken an emotional beating, yet she had a suspicion that he had recovered from his more rapidly than she had from hers, possibly because he was older and was more accustomed to being hurt. Moira had hinted that he had taken it badly and as a result had developed into a woman-hater, although she had been quick to point out that she was not amongst those whom he hated.

But Lindsay was not so sure that she agreed with Moira's evaluation of Scott. From what she had learned about him to date, she could imagine him accepting being jilted stoically. He had perhaps retired from the lists temporarily, but he would return, possibly with not very much respect for the opposite sex as his treatment of herself showed, but certainly with renewed vigor.

She inspected the rest of the upstairs again, taking careful note of the views from different windows, so that she could describe them accurately to her mother later. Then she went downstairs and looked at the two entertaining rooms again. In the living room she stood by the window and regarded the trim, front yard that consisted of a lawn guarded from the roadway by a sturdy stone wall. In front there was a shrubbery of laurel bushes.

The house was clean, wholesome, and airy. It would be easy to run. It was not far from the bus stop and the village store. It commanded beautiful views. She could imagine her mother sitting at this window and watching all that went on down by the river and never finding it dull. In fact the house was perfect. All she needed to know was the rent, and after that she would have to persuade her mother into seeing it and renting it.

Her decision made, she returned to the kitchen. All that could be seen of Scott was a pair of legs protruding from a cupboard under the sink. There was no sign of Coll. Lindsay cleared her throat. Immediately the legs moved toward her, and Scott shuffled out of the cupboard and sat up. In one hand he held a plumber's wrench.

"Have you seen everything?" he asked.

"Almost. I'd like to see where the furnace is for the central heating, please."

He jerked his head toward the door on the right.

"Through there. You'll also find an extra bathroom complete with shower, and another entrance, useful for people who go sailing and come back soaking wet," he said. "Go and look, while I finish fixing the waste pipe. Unfortunately the joint wasn't tightened properly, and last time I used the sink in here there was a small flood."

He disappeared into the cupboard again, and Lindsay went to examine the furnace room and the extra bathroom. The furnace was a green monster cowering in a small room next to the bathroom that possessed two shower compartments and racks for clothes. Lindsay, who had known in the past what it was like to come back from a dinghy race sopping wet, could appreciate what an asset the extra entrance and showers would be to a sailing family.

When she went back into the kitchen, Scott's voice addressed her from the depths of the cupboard.

"Turn on a tap and let it run, will you, please? I want to see if I've stopped the leak."

She did as he asked. After a few seconds he told her to turn the tap off.

"No leak," he announced. "Put the kettle on. . . . It's already full of water. You'll find tea, mugs, and some sugar in a cupboard to the left of the window."

Lindsay hesitated. She had intended to leave immediately as she did not want to be caught up in any conversation with Scott. All arrangements about the house would have to be made through Cuthbert Murray, so there was really nothing she had to discuss with the owner of Glendoon. She felt that it would be better that way.

"Having a cup of tea with me won't commit you to anything," remarked the voice from the cupboard. At once she walked over to the kettle, plugged it in and switched on. Opening the cupboard, she took down a tin tea caddy and two blue mugs. There was no tea-pot.

"What shall I make the tea in?" she asked the legs.

Scott came out of the cupboard bringing with him the tools he had been using. He stood up and placed the tools in a box.

"Tinker's brew . . . in the mugs," he said laconically. "Only these days we're very refined and use tea-bags, one in each mug."

Picking up the tool box, he went outside, presumably to the shed. When he returned, the kettle had boiled, and Lindsay was pouring water into the mugs. He rinsed his hands under the tap and dried them on a towel hanging on a rail behind the door. Lindsay put the mugs on the breakfast counter and set out the glass jars of sugar and the two teaspoons she had found. She pulled out one of the stools pushed under the counter and sat down. Scott leaned against the counter on the other side and helped himself to sugar.

For a while there was silence. Lindsay wanted to tell him how much she liked the house, but she could not find a way in which to approach the subject naturally. She was suddenly very much aware of being alone with Scott. It was the same nervousness that had attacked her at their first meeting at Merse Cottage and that had alarmed her during the return drive home from Moira's party.

Being alone with him had a peculiar effect on her physically. She developed the feeling in her stomach described by Alex as "collywobbles"; her heart beat too fast and she became breathless. She found she could not look at him directly. Instead she had to stare at his bare forearms. He had rolled back the sleeves of the checked, woollen shirt he was wearing. They were muscular forearms and were covered by dark hairs.

"I didn't think I'd see you again so soon," he said, and the sound of his voice made her jump for the second time that afternoon. In order to cover her nervousness, she picked up her teaspoon and stirred her tea slowly.

"Well, I certainly didn't set out this afternoon with the intention of meeting you," she retorted, and he grinned.

"Then we were both surprised," he said. "Do you find the house suitable?"

"Yes, I do. But Mother isn't yet fully persuaded that she could live here; in a house owned by you."

She was able to look at him at last and met a very clear direct glance.

"Is that all that's stopping her from considering it?" he asked.

"Yes."

His face darkened and tautened. She had a brief glimpse of a formidable temper that she realized would be better not to test too severely. He struck the formica top of the counter with the fist of one hand.

"But why should it? I'm an honest, respectable citizen. I've done nothing to harm her . . . apart from stealing a few apples from a tree at Merse Cottage and pushing her abominable daughter into the mud."

"Beth isn't abominable!"

"She used to be," he muttered. Then more quietly and rather bitterly, "Och, I know that those aren't the reasons. It's because I'm Annie Robertson's grandson, and my grandmother happened to have some gypsy blood in her veins . . . and because my mother ran away with my father, isn't it?"

Lindsay agreed reluctantly. "Yes. But if I think that the house is all right and that the rent isn't too high, she'll get over her dislike and prejudice. And as long as everything can be arranged through lawyers and doesn't have to meet you. . . ."

His glance was scornful.

"That can be arranged," he replied coldly. "So you've decided not to fight the compulsory purchase order?"

"I talked to Mr. Murray today, and he agreed with you that there isn't much point in fighting. The Council will take it anyway. He suggested that we should ask for more money."

"You'll probably get more, especially if you don't want the alternative accommodation they've offered," he said briskly. "I shall want 12 pounds a week for this house."

"Isn't that rather high?" queried Lindsay, thinking that she must not appear to give in too easily to him.

"I could get more quite easily . . . and double in the summer season. I'm not a philanthropist. I can't afford to be, but I'm offering the house to your mother at a reduced rent to help her."

Although he spoke in a businesslike fashion there was no doubting his sincerity. Lindsay wished that her mother was there to hear him say what he had said.

"I . . . I . . . appreciate your offer," she said shyly.

He shrugged her thanks aside.

"The house is worth the rent. I've spent a lot on it, and since your mother can't bear the sight of me I'll have to hire someone to look after the yard. You won't have time, and she hasn't the strength to look after it."

Now she knew who was responsible for growing the healthy-looking winter vegetables. He was full of surprises.

"Did you renovate the house yourself?" she asked curiously.

"Most of it. It's a spare-time occupation which I enjoy. Tim Prentiss from the boatyard helped with the carpentry and of course I had to have the furnace put in professionally." He frowned slightly, impatiently. "It's all taken longer than I had hoped, but I think it's ready for occupation now."

"You must feel very disappointed. . . ." Lindsay stopped abruptly—too late. The words were spoken, and he had noticed. He put down the mug and stared at her.

"Why should I feel disappointed?"

In for a penny, in for a pound, thought Lindsay whimsically. There was no going back now.

"Because you're not going to live in it yourself, because you're not getting married and bringing your wife to live here," she answered honestly.

The blankness in his eyes was rather frightening. He seemed to be looking right through her. She had an urge to turn and look behind her to see what he was seeing.

"Who told you?" he asked quietly.

"Mother. She said she'd heard that you'd been jilted ... and Moira told me the same story yesterday."

His eyes focused properly, and now their expression was not pleasant.

"You've been busy since Hogmanay," he jibed.

The implication that she had been prying into his private life roused her.

"If you think I've been going around trying to find out all about you, you're more conceited than even I had thought," she sniped. "I merely said to Mother that it seemed strange for you to own a house and not want to live in it ... and she told me what she'd heard. Moira volunteered the information herself when she telephoned me yesterday. She was rather concerned about how you might have behaved when you took me home from the party. She seems to think that your experience has made you a woman-hater, and that you might want to work out your spite on other women. Although apparently she regards herself as an exception."

Lindsay stopped talking again because after looking incredulous, then puzzled, he was now looking thoroughly amused.

"I wonder where she learned about Lorna," he said. His query seemed inconsequential, but it pricked Lindsay's curiosity, and she asked involuntarily, "Who is Lorna?"

"A woman I used to know," he replied with deliberate vagueness.

"The girl you were going to marry, and for whom you bought this house?" she asked.

The unpleasant expression was back in his eyes.

"Is this a court of inquiry?"

"I'm sorry," hating him as well as herself. Why had she allowed herself to become involved in this conversation?

"I'd no idea my actions were of such interest to the community," he said sarcastically. "Next time I buy a house I shall have to hand out printed leaflets beforehand to explain why I'm buying it."

The back door burst open, and Coll rushed in.

"Ian's taking a boat up to Glencross now. He said I could go with him if you agree. You will, won't you, Scott? You could pick me up there on the way to Glenfoot," said the boy breathlessly.

"It's not the time of year I'd want to go up river in a boat, but I suppose you can go. How long will it take? About an hour and a half?"

"Yes, with the flood tide under us. Thanks, Scott. 'Bye, miss." He went as quickly as he had arrived, banging the door after him.

Lindsay finished her tea. She supposed she would never know now whether Scott had really intended to marry and had been jilted. He had made it clear that he disliked discussing his personal affairs. It was obvious that he had never discussed them with Moira either, so how had she known he was getting over "a bad patch" as she had called his reaction to being jilted?

To show that she had lost interest in the matter she said conversationally, "Coll is very like you."

Again his eyes glinted with amusement.

"And you thought he was my son, didn't you? You're not the first to think so."

"You must find it irritating to have to explain who he is all the time, since you don't like giving information about yourself," she replied, annoyed that he had noticed her expression in the yard when Coll had appeared.

He grinned mischievously.

"If I don't feel like explaining who he is, I don't. Anyway, most people around here know who he is."

She picked up the two empty mugs and walked over to the sink to rinse them out. Fencing with Scott made her feel confused. He did not bother to disguise the fact that, although he was willing to help her mother, he had little or no respect for herself and any other member of the Bell family. She should have known better. She should not have let herself be tempted into discussing anything else other than the renting of the house. She dried her fingers on the towel behind the door, conscious that he was leaning against the counter watching her.

"Thank you for letting me see the house. I was going to make arrangements to see it anyway."

"Through Cuthbert Murray, of course," he commented dryly. "I suppose I'll hear from him whether you're going to rent it or not?"

"Yes. I'd like Mother to see it first. Perhaps you would let Mr. Murray have a key."

"And arrange not to be around here on that particular day? Yes, I think that could be managed. So as not to upset your mother."

"Oh, stop jibing!" flared Lindsay. "I thought you said you'd learned to forgive and forget."

"And I thought I had. I'd forgotten that prejudice exists. Supposing it was a more serious situation? Supposing you and I wanted to marry, and your mother. . . ."

"That is a totally unrealistic supposition," interrupted Lindsay sharply.

"How right you are," he agreed smoothly. "Because you promise but never give, which is no use to any man. And I . . . well, I need only quote Moira . . . I am a misogynist." Amusement glinted briefly again. "I use the hypothesis only to point out how uncomfortable prejudice can be."

"I must go," muttered Lindsay, seeking escape.

"Yes, you must. Tim Prentiss will be here soon to finish some carpentry, and if he found you here alone with me—och, we'd spend the rest of our lives explaining. Goodbye, linten Lindsay. Don't trespass again, or I shall be forced to demand a forfeit."

CHAPTER FOUR

Hands in the pockets of her raincoat, Lindsay walked home fast. The tide was coming in down in the estuary, flooding the mudbanks with swirling brown water. In the middle of the channel a small open fishing boat of a type long used in the district was chugging upstream helped forward by the strong current. A man stood at the tiller of the boat, and beside him Lindsay could make out a smaller figure. That would be Coll, Scott Nicolson's half-brother.

The sight of him made Lindsay think of Scott's mocking remark that Coll was often mistaken for his son and of the cynical amusement he derived from letting people continue to be mistaken. Her mouth tightened. He had made several cutting remarks in the kitchen, and as a result Lindsay was smarting from a new experience—the experience of knowing she was disliked. Never before had she had such an experience. Always people of both sexes had seemed to like her. No one had shown such obvious contempt for her until this afternoon. And he disliked her not because she was a woman, which in view of his own experience might have been understandable; not because she was a Bell, which again might have been reasonable. He disliked her because she was herself; because she was the person called Lindsay Bell.

"It doesn't matter," she said to herself defiantly, trying to ignore the bewilderment that the knowledge caused, "because I don't like him either. I don't like him because he's big and bold, because he makes me quiver and quake, because he doesn't care what I think of him." The more she thought up reasons for disliking him the more the last one took on importance until she admitted to herself that she wanted him to be concerned about her opinion of him. She wanted to matter in his life, but she didn't, so she disliked him.

Troubled by her thoughts, Lindsay was glad to see

Alex's car parked in the driveway of Merse Cottage. A short time in the company of pleasant undemanding Alex would soon help her to forget the tough treatment handed out by the owner of Glendoon.

Alex was sitting by the fire with her mother, chatting comfortably, and when she entered the living room he stood up politely.

"Where have you been?" asked Mrs. Bell. "I told Dr. Wilson you wouldn't be long . . . and he's been waiting over an hour to see you."

"Oh, I'm sorry, Alex. You should have phoned and let me know you were coming."

"Not to worry," he said with a smile. "I'm off duty this weekend, so I thought I'd come down to talk about the job. By the way, Jim McDonnell would like us both to go to dinner tomorrow night at his house. He wants to meet you before Monday."

"If you're going to talk about work you'll want to be by yourselves," said Mrs. Bell, rising to her feet. "I'll go upstairs and lie down for a while. It's been so nice talking to you, Dr. Wilson."

"Have you come to any conclusion about this place?" asked Alex once Mrs. Bell was out of earshot.

"Yes. We're going to let the Council have it."

"Good, because the sooner your mother gets out of here the better. It's preying on her nerves."

"You don't have to tell me that. The problem is finding somewhere else to live. I've just been looking at Glendoon."

"Where's that?" he asked.

"The house at the end of the village. Scott Nicolson owns it, and he's offered to rent it to us. If only I can get Mother to agree to take it."

"If the house is suitable, ignore any dislike she may have for him and rent the house. Once the move is made she'll be fine. It's this havering about and having to make decisions that's tearing her to shreds," asserted Alex.

Lindsay laughed with relief.

"Oh, Alex, you're just the person I need most," she said. "You're in her good books at the moment and can do no wrong, so I think she would do anything you suggested. Tell her that you think it would improve her health if she moved. Tell her this house is too damp, and that she needs to live at a higher elevation. She'll believe you, and she'll agree to take the house."

"I'll certainly do that if you think it will help," he agreed. "But why doesn't she like Scott? Is it because he's responsible for widening the road?"

"Not really. There are many other reasons that are actually rather petty, and she should have got over them years ago. But you see she's been rather spoiled, shielded from reality first by her father and then by my father."

"And now you're doing the same for her?"

"I suppose so. Anyway the story is a long one, and it shouldn't be allowed to influence her now . . . more than 30 years later."

"All right, I'll take your word for it and do my bit," he said equably. "I called to say thank you for coming to the party the other night."

"Did my presence there do any good?"

He grimaced lugubriously and shook his head.

"I don't think so. Certainly the fact that you were there with me roused Moira's interest . . . but on the other hand she was very put out because Scott took you home and didn't return to the party. I didn't stay long after you'd gone because Moira organized me into taking Janet McMorrow home, and after driving all that way, it was too late for me to do anything but go home to bed."

Lindsay had a vague idea that the McMorrow farm was at Glenfoot, the other side of the estuary.

"Have you seen Moira since?"

He looked melancholy again.

"No. I was on call yesterday. I knew it was no use trying to see her today because she had guests staying. It was like this last summer. She was always entertaining, or playing golf with someone."

"Scott?"

"No. Golf isn't one of his vices. It's usually with her father, or with one of his business associates. She was always entertaining in the evenings too. I don't have much free time, as you must realize."

"Well, why didn't you play golf?"

"You haven't seen me play, have you?" he asked miserably.

Lindsay quelled a desire to laugh at his air of comical despair.

"No. Is it bad?"

"It's terrible. I can't drive straight, so I'm always losing the ball. And if I do manage to reach the green the stupid thing always keeps by-passing the hole. I'm much better on a horse."

"Then go riding with her."

"The Innes family own the only horses within miles. I have to wait until I'm invited. I can hardly phone up and say, 'Look, Moira I'd like to ride your bay this afternoon,' can I?"

"Scott would," murmured Lindsay, thinking that a little thing such as lack of an invitation would not stop Scott from going where he wanted to go.

"Maybe he would. But he doesn't have to. He's invited," said Alex mournfully.

"Weren't you invited once?"

"Before he came on the scene, yes. I knew Moira in Glasgow, but I didn't realize how attractive she was until she came to live here permanently when her father retired. I was doing pretty well until Scott put his oar in . . . at least I like to think I was."

Lindsay recalled New Year's Eve and Moira's complaint that she had scarcely seen Scott all evening. Then she remembered Moira's admission over the phone that she had helped Scott and her veiled warning to Lindsay to keep off.

"You won't like what I'm going to say, Alex," she warned, "but I think you're wrong in thinking that Scott has been cutting you out. Moira has been doing a lot of the running herself. He has crossed her path, a new and interesting personality, with a past."

"What past?"

"He was going to marry, and the woman jilted him."

"I've heard about that," he told her. "Difficult to imagine that happening to a character like Scott. But if what you say about Moira is true, I might as well throw in the sponge now."

Lindsay looked at him impatiently. It was quite obvious he was going to make no effort to help himself.

"Alex Wilson, I'm surprised at you! If you really loved Moira you wouldn't let anyone come between you and her. And if I thought there was no hope I wouldn't be prepared to go on helping you."

"How can you help?"

"I can teach you how to improve on your golf . . . and shake you out of that low opinion you have of yourself."

His face brightened immediately, and he looked interested. "How? It's not the time of year for golfing."

"I know it isn't, but there's nothing to stop us having a few rounds on the old parish golf course, is there?"

"No, I suppose not. We'll have to be careful of the laird's sheep, though. He uses it for extra grazing."

"Well, let's start tomorrow afternoon, if it's fine. I'll look for some clubs for myself. I presume you have some?"

"What a great idea," said Alex enthusiastically. "Yes, I have some clubs."

The next day was fine. Fluffy white clouds sailed slowly across a blue sky, and sunshine slanted across the wide satin smooth Firth. A few birds twittered amongst the leafless birches that edged the old golf course, giving the impression that spring was on the way, although anyone who was knowledgeable about weather in that part of the country would recognize the day as being a lull in the usual series of storms that marked the winter time.

Alex had not been unduly modest when he had described his game as terrible. It was, and it was not helped by the fact that his clubs were so old as to be a vintage variety.

"You might have provided yourself with better ones than these," Lindsay scolded. "They must have come out of the Ark. Look at this driver. The string is about to unwind at any minute. Where did you get them?"

"They're some my father handed on to me when I went to University. Not being very interested in the game I thought there was no point in buying new ones. You think new ones would help?"

"Yes. But you have to concentrate too. It's no use letting your attention be distracted from the ball by a bird in a tree."

"It's not only the bird in a tree which distracts me, it's you," replied Alex, looking at her admiringly. "How anyone as fairy-like and as fragile-looking as you manages to drive a ball so hard and straight beats me."

"I keep my head down, that's all. If you did the same you'd drive straight too."

They were about to drive off from the third tee on the old countrified golf course that stretched over the hillside between Cairness and Barrcliffe. They were on a ridge, and the third green lay below them. Lindsay drove off first, then went to the edge of the ridge to see where her ball had landed. Two people were strolling across the course, apparently out for a walk. They were moving slowly, and she did not think they would be in any danger, so she told Alex to drive off.

Alex fiddled around for a while, took several practice swings, and drove off. The head of the ancient driver came off and sailed through the air with yards of string unraveling behind it. Ball and head were going in the same direction. Lindsay glanced with alarm toward the green. Just beyond it the two people she had noticed before were passing by.

"Fore!" she shouted at the top of her voice.

They both looked up and dodged out of the way of the missiles which landed with separate thuds in the rough grass where they had just been walking.

Lindsay stared at them, dismay taking place of alarm. Moira and Scott were the last persons she had expected to meet in that place on that afternoon.

Alex, who had come to stand beside her, covered his

face with his hands. She could not be sure whether it was to hide his laughter or his dismay.

"Oh lord," he groaned at last. "I'd better go and apologize. See what happens when I try to make an impression?"

Winding the string around the shaft of his golf club, he went down the path toward the other couple. Lindsay picked up both bags of clubs and followed him, secretly wishing that she was far, far away.

"Hello, Moira, Scott. Lovely day." Alex sounded far too jovial. "I'm terribly sorry about that. These old clubs, you know. I think I'll have to conform and buy some of those new steel ones."

Lindsay arrived at his side and put the bags down. She looked at the other two, trying to ignore their cold impersonal stare and smiled cheerfully.

"Hello. We thought we'd have the course to ourselves at this time of the year. Alex wanted to practise."

"I didn't know you played golf, Lindsay," said Moira, making an obvious effort to appear interested. "We often walk this way. Climax enjoys it."

Lindsay assumed that Climax was the golden Labrador dog which appeared out of the trees, its nose to the ground. Approaching her, it sniffed around her until ordered to sit by Moira.

"Lindsay's a great player," enthused Alex. "You wouldn't think that anyone so small and dainty could hit so hard, would you?"

Moira, tall and slim, was dressed in smart navy blue pants and windbreaker with a red, white, and blue scarf at her throat to set off her pink and white complexion and blue eyes. She eyed Lindsay up and down.

"No, I wouldn't," she concurred.

"She's a good sport, too," continued Alex, still enthusiastically, making Lindsay wish that he would not praise her so much in front of the silent, observant Scott. But he continued in the same way.

"She doesn't get annoyed either, when I make a mess of my drive and lose the ball."

"Which you undoubtedly did that time."

The caustic comment came from Scott. It was spoken unpleasantly with the suspicion of a sneer, and it caused Alex to look at the speaker sharply. Lindsay also shot a swift glance at him. It was intended to wither him for being unpleasant to Alex, but it wavered when she discovered that Scott was watching her with narrowed eyes.

"Then you're very fortunate to have found an amenable partner," Moira was saying smoothly to Alex, apparently oblivious to the sudden tension. "It helps tremendously when you have someone sympathetic to practise with. Don't you think so, Scott?"

He shrugged his shoulders indifferently. "I don't know. I don't play golf," he replied coldly. "It's time I went back to Duncraig. Are you going to help to look for the ball? I'm sure Climax would love to help and would be of great assistance."

Without another word to either Lindsay or Alex he started to walk back in the direction of Cairness, leaving Moira standing beside them looking rather nonplussed.

"I'd better go too," she said hurriedly. "I hope you find the ball. Goodbye."

With Climax at her heels she strode swiftly after Scott. Lindsay and Alex stood silently watching the retreating figures. When he was sure they were out of earshot, Alex groaned and threw down the beheaded golf shaft in a violent gesture which expressed his disgust.

"You're right, she is doing the running. I might as well stop deceiving myself," he muttered. Then he grinned at Lindsay. "Thanks for the golf lesson. It was worth a try. But I don't see much point in continuing with it. I'll never play with Moira, so I'll stick to sailing."

"You do give up easily," observed Lindsay.

"No, I just recognize when the odds are against me and retire gracefully," he replied and glanced again at the distant walking couple. "Scott was pretty wild about something," he added.

"How do you know?"

"He's not usually so abrupt and rude . . . not to me, anyway. We usually get on fine together."

"He was like that because he doesn't like me," suggested Lindsay.

"And what have you done to him?"

"Nothing. I'm just me, that's all, and he doesn't like me."

Alex regarded her; a puzzled expression on his face.

"I don't think I understand," he said slowly. "But if it's any help I think he's nuts for not liking you."

Lindsay laughed at his attempt to bolster her ego, and they began to look for the ball. By the time they had found it, the winter dusk was closing in and a few stars were glittering in the sky. They walked back to Merse Cottage in happy companionship and had afternoon tea with Mrs. Bell.

CHAPTER FIVE

Lindsay had no time to wonder about Alex's sudden decision to give up trying to impress Moira. On the day after the golfing fiasco she was plunged into work, and it took her the rest of that week to orientate to her new job. In the big city hospitals in which she had always worked, the atmosphere had been exciting but impersonal. In the consulting rooms of the two country town doctors it was mundane, but very personal. Many of the patients knew her, or had known her father, and as a result were very interested to find her there. Many of them also took a lively interest in the doctors. Both had grown up locally, so there was always plenty of conversation going on in the small office where Lindsay dressed scalds, bandaged wounds, looked after the filing system, and sterilized instruments.

Meanwhile Mrs. Bell had taken a new lease on life. As Lindsay had expected, her mother had been quite ready to accept Alex's suggestion that she should move from the cottage for the good of her health. She contacted Cuthbert Murray herself and asked him to arrange for her to see Glendoon. After seeing the house, she gave him permission to negotiate a contract to rent it from Scott. Then she signed an agreement to let the Council buy Merse Cottage from her for the purpose of demolition.

Consequently when the Bells went to tea with Moira and her father on the following Sunday, they had plenty to tell the Innes as they sat in the pleasant lounge which overlooked an ornamental garden. Lindsay was, however, conscious of a certain amount of constraint in Moira's manner when they told her they were going to live at Glendoon. She was not surprised when Moira questioned her about it while Mrs. Bell and Cameron Innes were discussing another matter of great interest to them both.

"I find it strange that Scott didn't tell me last Sunday about renting Glendoon to you," Moira said quietly, moving to sit closer to Lindsay, so that their conversation would not be heard by the others.

"Perhaps he thought you wouldn't be interested," murmured Lindsay.

Moira's blue eyes flashed as she took exception to the remark.

"How can you know what he thinks about me?" she said shortly. "Why, without my interest and support he would never have finished renovating the house. He would have given up when that woman jilted him. I've been a constant visitor at the house. I was over there last Sunday before we took Climax for a walk on the golf course."

Lindsay had nothing to say. Moira had been the woman who had contributed to the re-design of Glendoon, and not the woman called Lorna. For some reason the information was displeasing. Then she recalled Scott's surprise when she had mentioned that Moira had told her the story of him being jilted, and she asked curiously, "How do you know he was jilted? Did he tell you?"

Moira blinked and looked puzzled.

"Everyone in the village and Duncraig knew. She was with him when he looked at the house before he bought it. Then she came several times to see it. She had red hair, so she was easy to recognize. Then she stopped coming, and Scott became rather morose and remote. We all assumed the worst had happened."

"Haven't you ever asked him about her?"

An expression of distaste crossed Moira's face, and she looked down her nose.

"No. I considered the matter too delicate." The expression changed to one of smugness, and she added, "I think that's why Scott likes having me as a companion. I don't ask questions."

"And that puts you in your place, Lindsay Bell," thought Lindsay whimsically. She could imagine Moira being the "good friend" who stood by helpfully in times of stress. Scott could be as unpleasant as he liked, and she would take it; would not be hurt, or answer back. And one day he would decide that such unstimulating companionship was preferable to none at all and would ask Moira to marry him.

On the whole, though, the visit to Cliffe House was pleasant, especially for Mrs. Bell and Mr. Innes, who could have talked all night about old times and acquaintances. Before they parted they had arranged with each other to visit some mutual friends who lived in Kirkcudbright after the move to Glendoon had taken place.

The move was planned for the first of February, and for the rest of January Mrs. Bell spent her time clearing out the accumulated rubbish that had been hidden in the loft and various cupboards in the house over a period of 20 years.

Lindsay helped her during her spare time, and they were often given assistance by Alex who would call in on a Saturday or Sunday afternoon. His visit sometimes ended with him staying for a meal. Sometimes he would invite Lindsay to go to Dumfries or Castle Douglas with him for a meal. His visits and invitations relieved the routine of living with her mother. Lindsay was finding it rather irksome to have to inform Mrs. Bell where she was going, what time she would be back, and in whose company she would be, after so many months of freedom from that sort of supervision.

Occupied and entertained, she had almost forgotten about her meetings with Scott. It was not until the day before the move that she thought about him consciously as she stood in the empty kitchen at Glendoon. She had walked over to the house to make sure it was clean and ready for the furniture.

She discovered he had been there all the time, at the back of her mind, as she opened the cupboard near the sink and found his kettle, mugs, and tea-caddy. She wondered whether he would be thinking about her and her mother moving into his house tomorrow, and whether he had any regrets about renting it to them. Of course he woudn't. He would be busy with some other project and was not the sort of person who would have regrets; not even about a woman called Lorna, in spite of what Moira had said about him.

Why had Lorna of the red hair jilted him? Had he done

something she had not liked, and had her love not stood the test? Or had she been prejudiced too? Had she been unable to accept the reality that Scott's mother was descended from gypsies? Yes, that might have been the reason. He had said in this room when they had been discussing her mother's prejudice, "Supposing it was a more serious situation? Supposing you and I wanted to marry?"

That was it. He had lost his love through prejudice. The hypothesis he had presented to her had been convenient because it had been uppermost in his mind. It was not unrealistic at all. Then why had she reacted so violently against it? Lindsay retreated in haste from the direction in which her thoughts were leading her, closed the cupboard door firmly, and leaving the kitchen continued her inspection of the house.

It was all ready for occupation. As she closed the back door and turned the key in the lock, she felt a little leap of excitement at the thought of moving into it. Naturally she would be sorry to say goodbye to Merse Cottage and to see it demolished, but the change would be good for Mrs. Bell. Lindsay was sure that her mother would regain her old liveliness of spirit in a different house. The past was precious, but the present and the future had their value too.

The move went off without a hitch and had an astonishing effect on Mrs. Bell. The arrangement of her beloved pieces of furniture in a new setting; the fitting of carpets and curtains to different rooms filled her days and most of her conversation. For the first two weeks in the house she did nothing else, and yet she did not become tired or depressed. Merse Cottage was forgotten with an ease that Lindsay would have considered impossible at Christmas time.

She began to wonder how long the period of activity would last. What would her mother do when there was no more sewing to do? She suggested that Mrs. Bell slow down and spread the work over the months.

"But I must get it fixed so that I can invite my friends

to see it," stated Mrs. Bell firmly. "I want to have a housewarming. I haven't entertained like that since John died. We shall ask the Inneses too, and Alex, of course. I must find my best recipes and think about the best way in which to arrange everything."

Lindsay relaxed, ceased to worry, and wrote a long letter to Beth describing her mother's activities. She had kept her sister informed of all that had occurred since she had returned to Cairness. Beth had replied in letters addressed to both her mother and her sister in which she had approved of the selling of Merse Cottage and the removal to Glendoon. In only one letter had there been anything personal for Lindsay, and that had been a note about Scott Nicolson in which she had referred to him as a handsome devil who had tormented not only her, but other girls as well; and whom, she had thought, had received his just deserts when he had been jilted.

After the first fine day of February, the month was rain-sodden and stormy. Squalls swept in from the Firth, and the swollen river, enlarged by high tides, slopped over the wall that edged the village road and flooded it. It was already a mess of potholes and mud churned up by the equipment being used to widen it. The villagers had plenty to grumble about, but the work of widening went on steadily, if more slowly than the Council would have liked.

The corner by Merse Cottage was flooded several times, and Lindsay could see why the house had to come down. She was able to appreciate the danger of the corner much more since she had been driving to Duncraig and back. The necessity to drive to work had arisen when she realized she could not get a bus back to Cairness after the two late surgeries the doctors held every Tuesday and Thursday evenings. At first Alex had taken her home after both, but Lindsay did not wish to be too dependent on him. She felt she was seeing enough of him as it was, since hardly a weekend passed without him calling on her. So Mrs. Bell had agreed to let her use the little red Mini twice a week.

One Thursday night in late February the rain was

particularly heavy. The number of people wishing to see Dr. McDonnell was reduced by the bad weather, and he decided to call it a day soon after seven. After he had gone Lindsay stayed to tidy up in preparation for the next day. As she worked she thought about Alex. She was beginning to feel a little uneasy about the number of times she had seen him lately out of working hours. Could it be that he was in the process of transferring his affection from Moira to herself? She hoped not, because she did not want to hurt his feelings.

Her work done, she took off her white overall, unclipped her hair from the French roll, and shook it free. She felt strangely restless and wished she was going out somewhere, preferably with a pleasant escort who would not demand anything from her. Not that there was anywhere much to go in Duncraig on a wet February evening. How much longer would she be able to stay here? How much longer could she stand the quiet uneventful way of life?

The shrill sound of the doorbell made her jump. For a moment she did not move as she wondered whether to answer it or not. Then she pulled herself together. It must be an emergency. She went through the waiting room which the front door of the consulting rooms opened into. Outlined against the glass panel she could make out a masculine figure. Perhaps it was Alex returning for something he had left in his room.

She opened the door. Scott Nicolson stood on the step. He was holding his left hand, wrapped in a white handkerchief, in his right hand. From the controlled set of his mouth and the narrowness of his eyes Lindsay guessed that he was in pain.

"Come in," she said quickly. "What's the matter?"

He stepped in, and she closed the door. He held up his left hand. She could see that the handkerchief was spotted with blood.

"I tried to split my second finger in two with a chisel, but I didn't quite manage it," he replied.

He unwound the makeshift bandage to show her the wound. Lindsay looked at the red, torn mess of flesh and everything blurred before her. She swayed forward and came into contact with a slightly damp tweed jacket. An arm closed around her waist and held her.

"You're not supposed to do that. You're a nurse," scoffed Scott, laughter chasing surprise from his voice.

She shook her head and pulled away from him. She blinked, and everything came into focus again. She had almost fainted at the sight of blood, something which she had never done before. How ridiculous!

"Come in here, and let me clean it up," she said crisply, walking into her little office. He followed her.

"Are you all right? You're very pale," he said gently.

The gentleness was so unusual that she was afraid it might defeat her, and cause her to collapse again.

"Of course I'm all right," she snapped coldly. "Please sit down."

He remained standing. "Isn't McDonnell here? Perhaps he'd better look at it," he said.

"He isn't here. We finished early, and he's gone home. I'm perfectly capable of examining it. But first you must sit down."

He glanced at her curiously, then sat down and held out his hand. It was wide-palmed and very capable looking. She held it in hers and wiped away the clotted blood. The wound was nasty. The chisel had cut right through the nail and through the flesh underneath. Blood began to well again, and she swabbed it quickly and wrapped a bandage around it.

"The nail will have to be removed. It might need stitches, and I think it should be X-rayed," she said, wishing that the collywobbles in her stomach would stop.

"I thought so."

"I'll drive you to the hospital. They'll do it in the emergency ward."

"I can drive myself," he answered stubbornly.

"With a hand like that? Did you drive here?"

"No, I walked. I live up the street."

Lindsay put on her suit jacket, grabbed her handbag and raincoat.

"If you don't mind riding in a Mini, we'll go at once," she said.

"I don't like putting you to so much trouble."

"Think of it as being part of my job," she replied coolly, following him to the front door. He turned and grinned at her.

"I see. You would do this for anyone. Do you also faint at the sight of anyone's blood?"

She might have known he would not stay gentle for long. He was himself again, calm, cool, and tantalizing. Ignoring the insinuation, she flicked off the lightswitch and opened the door.

"Wait here, and I'll bring the car around."

Recognizing the stubborn nature of the man, she half expected him to have gone when she brought the little car around to the front door, but he was waiting at the curbside in the pouring rain, his wounded hand held against his chest. By the time he was seated beside her there was not much room in the front of the car. To avoid knocking her with his arm while she was driving, he sat sideways and rested his right arm along the back of her seat.

The little car nipped smartly through the dimly lit main street, hopped over the bridge, and turned right along the road to Dumfries. Once they were clear of the town Lindsay put her foot down on the accelerator and went as fast as she dared considering the slippery conditions of the surface.

After a while she realized how silent her passenger was and wondered whether he was suffering much pain. In order to take his mind off it she decided to talk, even if it was only to ask questions that he would probably object to answering.

"What were you doing with the chisel when it slipped?"

"I'm finishing a dinghy that I've been making for Coll's birthday. It's a secret, so don't tell him if you see him."

"I'm not really likely to see him."

"You might. Alex is the family doctor, so Coll might come in some day with an injury for you to bandage. Or you might see him in Cairness. He haunts the boatyard."

"Why don't you buy him a dinghy instead of making one?"

"Because I like making things . . . anything. I suppose

at heart I'm a frustrated inventor like my father was. I've designed the dinghy myself, and I'm interested to see whether it sails well."

"But isn't it difficult for you to keep it a secret from Coll if you live in the same house?"

"We don't live in the same house. Coll lives at Glenfoot Farm. My mother married Dougie McMorrow. Don't tell me someone has neglected to give you that important piece of information."

He was being sarcastic, obviously referring to their last meeting when she had revealed that she had learned about him being jilted.

"Then where do you live?" she asked. Janet McMorrow must be Dougie's daughter by his first marriage, she thought.

He chuckled. "I can see I have you completely puzzled. I live by myself in my grandmother's old house, or at least in part of it. I've rented the other part. She left it to me when she died. It had been in the Robertson family for years."

"Then why did you buy Glendoon, if you already owned a house?"

"She died after I had bought Glendoon," he explained. "And the next question is 'Why didn't you sell one or the other when you found you had two houses?' And the answer is 'I like renovating old houses and renting them for a profit.' Curiosity satisfied?"

"I'm sorry if I seem nosy," replied Lindsay.

"Don't apologize. I'm merely surprised by your ignorance. I'd have thought that whoever informed you about my unsuccessful attempt to get married would have told you everything else about me too. But don't let me put you off. It's more likely to be the truth that way," he said dryly. "Take the right fork here, and we'll go over the other bridge to the hospital."

They had reached the outskirts of Dumfries, and Lindsay did as she was instructed. She asked no more questions, and he offered no more topics for conversation, so they crossed the Nith in silence. Once they were over the river Scott gave her a few more terse instructions on how to reach the hospital and then relapsed into silence as they went down the street on which it was situated.

The silence was tense because he was so near in the dark confines of the car. She knew he was looking at her, taking advantage of her having to watch the road. His nearness made her nervous again, and she snatched at the gears when she had to change down to turn through the hospital gates. There was a horrible and embarrassing grating noise.

It was too much to hope that he would not notice.

"Don't take it out on the poor car," he mocked, then followed that with a remark that both startled and puzzled her. "You must realize that it's as bad for me as it is for you."

What did he mean? She was so confused that she put her foot on the brake too sharply. The car screeched to a stop, and they were both jerked forward.

"I suppose I should be glad that we have both arrived safely," he said as he removed his arm from behind her shoulders and opened the door beside him using his right hand. "Maybe I'd better drive back."

"You won't be fit after that gash has been stitched. And I wouldn't be surprised if they keep you in for the night," she retorted.

"That was said with a relish which only a woman who delights in seeing the stronger sex brought low could give it," he replied. "I wonder why you dislike me and why you want to see them 'so haggard and so woebegone' . . . to quote Keats again."

"I don't want to," she flashed back.

"Then why don't you leave Alex alone?"

With that retort he got out of the car and slammed the door shut. Lindsay, who was seething with indignation, scrambled out on her side, ready with a stinging reply. But he was already making for the entrance to the casualty ward, and she had to bottle up her fury.

She could see by the bright light in the entrance hall that he was very pale and that his eyes looked strained. The fury evaporated as the warmer emotion of compassion took its place.

"Is it bad?" she whispered.

He looked down at her; his glance softened as it met hers.

> " 'She looked at me as she did love,
>   And made sweet moan,' "

he murmured. "From the same poem . . . as if you didn't know." His mouth hardened, and his eyes went blank. "I've known worse pain," he added cryptically and turned away to the registration desk.

He was whisked away by a brisk, efficient nurse who smiled with professional sweetness at Lindsay and told her to wait in the waiting room.

At first Lindsay was interested in watching the comings and goings. The smell of antiseptic brought back memories of the hospital in which she had worked, and she experienced a longing to return. But the interest and the nostalgia did not last long. She thumbed through a magazine, not seeing the pictures because she was thinking about Scott; discovering again that his physical presence had a shattering impact upon her. The sound of his voice, the glance of his clear eyes, the feel, although he had not actually touched her, of his arm behind her shoulders in the car had all roused her senses to the pitch where they acknowledged his attraction while her mind was closed to it. Unless she simmered down going back to Duncraig, returning was going to be worse than coming had been.

He came at last, paler than before. His hand was neatly bandaged, and a guard had been put over the finger. The same nurse issued instructions about how it should be cared for and, with another bright smile, walked away.

"Who drives?" asked Lindsay challengingly.

"You do. I capitulate. Do you think we could go to the nearest hotel so that I can have a good strong whisky . . . and you can have a soft drink, since you're driving?" he asked with a grin. The grin widened as she shook her head and he commented, "I can see you don't approve of the idea."

"No, I don't. You must go straight home to bed."

"Now what makes you think that I'm going to bed at

this time of night?" he said as they went out into the damp air.

"An injury like that is very exhausting, and when the anesthetic wears off you're going to be in pain. Did the nurse give you something to take to help you to sleep, because if she didn't we can stop at the surgery. I'll get you something."

"She gave me enough dope to keep me asleep for a week. I won't take any of it," he stated firmly.

"Why not?"

"I can manage without it."

"You accepted the anesthetic, so your attitude is inconsistent."

"I accepted it because if I hadn't the surgeon would have had problems stitching the wound. He couldn't have done it if he had thought he was hurting me. But I don't have to take the sleeping pills. Any sleeplessness I suffer from won't hurt anyone, since at the moment I sleep alone."

They had reached the car and stepped into it. He sat as before, his arm behind her shoulders. This time Lindsay was not concerned about the effect he had on her. That was forgotten as she grappled with his unusual attitude to pain. For a person who had sustained a painful, self-inflicted injury he had been remarkably patient. Even his reaction to her bad driving had been humorous rather than irritated. He had not complained once. He was not just stubborn, he was thrawn—the old Scots word to describe someone who resisted, or opposed authority. She guessed that this characteristic was inherited rather than acquired and began to feel curious about his mother and wished she could meet her. To do so, she felt sure, would enable her to understand Scott better.

"How are you liking Glendoon?" he asked, breaking the silence. She had forgotten that he was the landlord and would have an interest, so she answered fully, chattering away telling him how her mother had furnished the rooms, knowing instinctively that he wanted to know how the house looked.

When she paused he murmured, "I'm glad you find it comfortable, and that your mother is content. I'm thinking of buying another house."

"What on earth for?"

"To renovate it and rent it. Did you know that Glenfoot Island is for sale?"

"No. What happened to Old Mr. Curry?"

"He grew old like everyone else does and had to leave the island. He's living with his daughter in Dumfries. Last year the family rented the cottage on the island to holidaymakers, but now they've decided to sell it because they can't be bothered with the upkeep. It is just opposite to my stepfather's land. He would like it for extra grazing land for sheep. We thought we'd buy it between us."

He talked naturally, easily, assuming her interest, showing no sign of the dislike she had sensed at Glendoon and later on the golf course. And Lindsay responded, forgetful of the tension which had existed earlier in the evening.

"I used to love visiting the island," she said. "We used to go out in Bob Walker's boat. We'd stay for the day and picnic. Once it rained heavily, and Mr. Curry asked us into the cottage to shelter."

They were approaching Duncraig, passing the high school where her father had taught and which she and Scott had both attended when younger.

"I'm going out to the island on Sunday, if the weather permits. You could come with me," he said casually.

The invitation was so surprising that Lindsay had no reply ready. They passed over the bridge and went down the main street past the ghostly store windows.

"You can drop me at the end of Gower Street," suggested Scot. "I can walk from there."

Rain was still falling, slanting through the lamplight like shining slivers of steel.

"I'll take you to your house, if you'll tell me where it is," replied Lindsay.

"The end of the street will do fine," he answered firmly, and she did not argue but slowed the car down and guided it into the curb at the end of Gower Street. The narrow street sloped up a hill and was lined with big solid-looking houses.

"Do you always have to have your own way?" she asked tartly, feeling annoyed because he would not allow her to take him home.

"Most of the time," he answered equably. "Although I'd be willing to give as well as take with the right person. Will you come on Sunday?"

At one time she would have welcomed the invitation, but with him she was extra-cautious. She was not really looking for ways to spend several hours alone with him. That pathway looked decidedly dangerous. He noticed her hesitancy and said gently, "You don't have to decide now. I'll leave the invitation open. I shall be leaving Glenfoot Farm at two o'clock on Sunday afternoon. If you're not there at that time I shall know you aren't coming. If you do decide to come be prompt, because I won't wait. Thank you for taking me to the hospital, Florence Nightingale. Goodnight."

As he withdrew his arm from behind her, she felt his fingers touch the back of her neck. She was not sure whether the gesture was deliberate or not, but it set up a tingling sensation down her spine, and when she replied "Goodnight," her voice trembled.

CHAPTER SIX

Lindsay reported Scott's injury to Alex the next morning. She explained the action she had taken and received a curious glance, but all Alex said was, "Did he have much pain?"

"He wouldn't admit it."

"Hmm. Sounds like Scott. He's a thrawn beggar. Did you tell him to call in and show it to me today?"

"No. But the nurse at the hospital told him to report to you. I can't help wondering what sort of a night he had. You must know what it's like to have a pain in any extremity. It throbs . . . and there's no relief."

"Don't I just!" replied Alex, with a grin. "I was called out in the middle of the night a few months ago, and in my haste I opened the bedroom door over my big toe. The pain was awful, but I didn't receive an atom of sympathy from anyone. You gave Scott something to help him sleep?"

"He was given something at the hospital, but he told me he wasn't going to take it. He said he could manage without."

Alex nodded his head knowledgeably. "Ah yes, I remember now. The whole family refuses to take drugs. It's the old grandmother's doing. She passed on the attitude to Scott's mother who has passed it on to her children . . . and even to Jan, that's Janet MacMorrow, Dougie's daughter. You remember her?"

"Yes. She was at Moira's party, and I knew her at school. But she avoided me at the party . . . and I've often wondered why."

"She's a nice girl. She teaches here in the elementary school, and she's crewed for me in races at Cairness," said Alex casually. "By the way, the hospital report on Mrs. Anderson is back. You'd better call, and ask her if she can come and see me this evening."

The morning took its usual course. At lunch time,

tempted by the almost springlike sunshine outside, Lindsay went for a walk. She crossed the main street and walked up Gower Street. It was entirely residential. The houses were all detached, double-fronted edifices built at the beginning of the 20th century and fronting right on the sidewalk.

She walked up one side to the top of the street. It ended abruptly at the wall that went around a school playing field. Most of the doors she had passed had small name plates on them; not one of them bore the name Nicolson. It was not until she was halfway down the other side of the street that she found a house with two name plates on its door revealing that the house was divided into two apartments. One of the names was Nicolson. The door was new, panelled in squares and painted Wedgwood blue, as were the window frames of the house. The light blue contrasted pleasantly with the gray of the granite blocks, and distinguished it from the other houses, most of which were painted conventionally with dark green or black.

Lindsay walked on, hoping that no one had seen her staring at the house. Back in her office she began to prepare for the ante-natal clinic that Alex was holding that afternoon. While she checked through the patients' cards her mind kept wandering to Scott's invitation. Should she go with him to the island? If the weather was like today it would be a pleasant trip. She had a longing to feel the movement of a motorboat as it bounced over the water and to feel the sting of spray in her face.

She was tempted, there was no doubt about that; tempted as much by the off-hand way in which the invitation had been issued as by anything else. Scott had sounded as if he would like her company and yet had been diffident about urging her to go with him, so he had left it open. If she turned up, he would be glad to see her. If she didn't then he would not be offended. In her present state of mind the casualness of his approach appealed to Lindsay; while at the same time she felt pleased because he had asked her, not Moira.

But if she decided to go would she be able to tell her

mother where she was going? After the little scene which had happened the previous night when she had returned to Glendoon she was quite sure her mother would object. Quite naturally Mrs. Bell had been rather anxious because Lindsay had been late. Without thinking Lindsay had explained that she had taken Scott to the hospital.

"I think that was quite unnecessary," Mrs. Bell had snapped. "He could have gone in a taxi, or had someone else drive him."

Exasperated at being taken to task for being late and used to not having to account to anyone, Lindsay had protested.

"He might not have gone if I'd left him to do that," she had said.

"That would have been his lookout. You had no right to make a convenience of yourself for him. We may live in his house, but that doesn't mean he can make use of us."

"That has nothing to do with it. He was badly hurt . . . and I am a nurse. It's my job to help people who are hurt. I did the obvious . . . I took him to hospital. Please try to understand."

"Oh, very well. If that was the case then of course you had to do your duty. But I wish you wouldn't become involved with him."

Going to the island will be becoming involved, argued Lindsay with herself, so it's safer not to go. But she wanted to go. The more she warned herself against going the more she wanted to go. It was an overwhelming urge, a rather frightening urge, that she had never experienced before, not even when she had been in love with Maurice.

But had she ever been in love with Maurice? The question shocked her. She stopped sorting through the cards in the filing cabinet and stared at a painting on the wall above it. It was one that Alex had chosen and was similar in style to the others he had used to decorate the walls of his consulting room. It was a smudge of yellow, green and white; if you stared at it long enough it resolved itself into a waterfall cascading over rocks.

She tried to remember Maurice, but no matter how

hard she tried his image would not impose itself on the blur of color. She had forgotten what he looked like. Apart from the fact that he had been tall and slim, she could remember nothing. That he had not loved her had been proved by the way in which he had behaved, but she had been sure she had loved him until today; until she had realized that his physical presence had never affected her at all.

Lindsay shut the filing cabinet with a clang that resounded through the room. She was thinking nonsense. Didn't she know that love was not entirely physical? That physical attraction was only a part of the state of loving? But it is a part, insisted a small recalcitrant voice in her mind, and she had not experienced it when she had known Maurice.

A door opened, and Alex came into the room.

"Hello. What's wrong with you?" he asked. "You look rather wild-eyed. Lost a card?"

"No . . . No. Alex, do you know if Moira and Scott are still seeing each other?" The question came out of its own accord. She was sure she had not intended to say that.

"As a matter of fact I've not been in the least concerned whether they have or not. I haven't seen Moira. I'm beginning to think that all I felt was temporary infatuation," he said with a shamefaced grin. "Which reminds me, how would you like to go to the sailing club's fitting-out dinner with me on March 27?"

"I . . . I'll let you know," stammered Lindsay.

"Something else to do?" he asked.

"No. I'd just like to think about it."

"Fair enough. Then how would you like to come with me on Sunday to Ayr, if it's a fine day? I promised I'd go and visit my sister. I'd like you to meet her."

"I'm sorry, I've made other arrangements to go out already," she replied vaguely.

"Oh." His disappointment was disturbing, but there was nothing she could say to help.

The sound of the street door opening and closing and the squeak of shoes on the linoleum flooring of the waiting room warned them that a patient had arrived for the clinic. An expression of impatience crossed Alex's face.

"I must talk to you," he muttered urgently. "We'll go somewhere tomorrow night."

"No, I can't. I'm taking Mother to Dumfries to shop in the afternoon, and we'll be staying there to have supper with Aunt Margaret."

"Damn!" he whispered and went through the door into the consulting room.

Perturbed by his behavior, Lindsay gathered up the clinic cards and drew a deep breath. She felt as if she had just had an escape.

"He's a fool to employ you in particular. Why don't you leave Alex alone?"

Scott's forthright criticisms returned to haunt her. Was this the situation he had anticipated? Alex becoming possessive about her? Then she was glad she had said she could not go out on Sunday. It would remind Alex that she would not always be available as a companion, and that it was not her intention to be taken seriously by him, or by any other man for that matter.

She accompanied her mother in and out of the stores in the Vennel, Dumfries, the old narrow street of stores that linked Whitesands, a wide strip of level land beside the river Nith, to the busy High Street. Lindsay tried to solve the problem of how to tell her mother where and with whom she would be going the next day. She did not want Mrs. Bell to assume that she would be going with Alex, and yet she knew there would be a violent reaction if she said she would be going to the island with Scott.

By the time they had finished shopping she had decided to give up the idea of going with Scott. She did so with regret while acknowledging that her decision was wise. Folly to be wise, folly to be wise. The well-known phrase taunted her for the rest of the day. Why was it folly not to tread a path that she had already considered as dangerous? What would she miss by not going? She could find no answer to the questions.

They arrived back at Glendoon soon after eight-thirty. Mrs. Bell did not like staying out too late because she did not like being driven a long distance at night. They had hardly entered the house when the telephone rang. The caller was Cameron Innes, and he wished to speak to Mrs. Bell. When the conversation was over she came into the kitchen where Lindsay was preparing a hot drink. Her gray eyes were shining, and her face was slightly flushed.

"You remember Cameron asking me if I would like to go and see Lizzie and Robert Fines in Kirkcudbright?" she asked. "Well, we're going tomorrow after church. I'll be so pleased to see them again. They were unable to come to John's funeral because Robert was unwell at the time. We should be back soon after eight. You won't mind if I'm not here to have dinner and tea with you, will you, dear?"

"No. Is Moira going?"

"Just the two of us. I believe she has gone away for the weekend. Now what shall I wear?"

"The new hat we bought today," suggested Lindsay, feeling rather guilty about the wonderful swinging sensation of relief that suddenly possessed her.

Sunday was the third day of March. It was mild and lamblike. In the estuary the mudbanks gleamed like gold-shot brown silk, and the narrow river reflected the blue sky. All morning the sun shone on the hills behind Glenfoot, making the whole area on the opposite side of the estuary appear tempting. Occasionally a cloud would dim the sunlight and a dark shadow would pass over the land, but the darkness did not stay for long.

After waving goodby to Mrs. Bell as she departed in Cameron Innes's car Lindsay stood outside the house, contemplated the placid day with its hint of warmth and promise of spring, and felt a sudden surge of gaiety. It was a giddy feeling; a sense of freedom. The unhappiness associated with autumn, the anxiety of the winter weeks, were behind her. She could look forward to new adventures. Although she still had a few doubts about going to the island with Scott, she decided impulsively to reverse her decision of the previous day. After all, she had all the afternoon to do as she pleased, the Mini at her disposal, and her mother would not be back until past eight o'clock, well after she herself had returned to the house.

As she drove along the western side of the estuary toward Glenfoot Farm she could not help but compare her feelings with the nervousness she had experienced when going to Moira's New Year party. Then she had lacked confidence and had been afraid of meeting Scott for the second time. Now she was going to meet him willingly. If she was wise she should avoid the meeting. But it was folly to be wise, and she was young. There was a feeling of spring in the air, even the birds were beginning to sing. She wanted to go across the water in an open boat, smell the tang of sea air, and feel the sting of the spray. And, she had to admit it, she wanted the added spice of Scott's company.

She glanced at her watch, put her foot down, and drove a little faster. It was five minutes to two. She must hurry because he had said he would not wait for her, and she had no reason to think he would change his mind.

He was sitting on the dry stone wall at the end of the rough road leading up to the white farmhouse that nestled amongst the tall trees. As she approached he slid to his feet and waved to her to stop. He opened the car door, sat down beside her, and closed the door.

"The boat is at the fishery at the point, so we'll drive down there. There's space for you to park the car."

Dressed in a navy blue fisherman's jersey, blue denim pants and a short, yellow, oilskin jacket he seemed bigger and seemed to take up more room. He sat in his usual position with his right arm along the back of her seat.

Quelling a feeling of disappointment that she was not going to see his mother or the farmhouse, Lindsay engaged second gear and the car glided down the road. Now that he was with her she was stricken with shyness. As she changed gear again, the noise was agonizing as she forgot to put her foot on the clutch.

Scott clucked his tongue mockingly. "It's a good thing you don't often have me as a passenger," he said.

Her shyness fled. "How like you to think that you have such a devastating effect on every woman you ride with!" she retorted spiritedly.

"Now I never thought of that. It isn't just for my

benefit, then. You drive like this all the time? Isn't it expensive?"

"Oh!" The exclamation came out in an outraged gasp. She glanced at him sideways, caught sight of his smile, and burst out laughing. Scott laughed with her. Somehow the sun seemed to shine more brightly, the water in the new estuary seemed bluer. The humpbacked island that came into sight around the headland seemed like a green paradise that beckoned enticingly.

"How is your finger?" inquired Lindsay.

"Fairly well, thank you."

"You didn't come to see Alex on Friday."

"I didn't have time."

"It should have a new dressing put on it."

"Yes, nurse," he agreed with suspicious meekness. "My mother changed the dressing this morning. Coll wanted to come with us, but Mother insisted that he should go visiting relatives with her and Dougie. Stop here."

They had reached a small bay. A breakwater running out from the southern arm of land gave protection from any swell that might set in from the Firth. Three sturdy open fishing boats were moored behind it.

Leaving the car parked under some trees, Lindsay followed Scott to where some dinghies lay upside down on the turf that bordered the shore. He turned one of them over and began to push it toward the water. Once it was afloat he told her to climb into it and to sit in the stern. When she was in he pushed off. Wading into the water he climbed into the boat and sat on the center thwart. Taking the oars from the bottom of the dinghy, he began to row with swift short strokes toward one of the moored motorboats.

"I'm glad to see you've dressed for the part," he remarked. "I forgot to warn you on Thursday night. Although the weather has been good up to now, I think we're in for more rain and perhaps a gale."

Lindsay looked down at her blue waterproof ski jacket, relic of her stay in Canada, her gabardine pants, and the pair of rubber boots she was wearing.

"Have you forgotten that I spent most of my life living

at Cairness and messing about in boats? I found these boots in a cupboard at Merse Cottage. I think they must have been Beth's."

"I suppose you've told her about renting Glendoon. Does she approve?" he asked idly.

"Yes, she does. She's glad Mother is feeling better and is more settled."

"Did you tell your mother you were going to the island with me today?"

This time the question was not so idle, and he gazed at her steadily waiting for an answer. She wished she could have said yes, and that she could have added that her mother had accepted the news without one of her flare-ups of prejudice.

"No, I didn't," she replied, avoiding his eyes.

"I suppose she thinks you're with Alex," he said coldly. "You've been going out with him on Sunday afternoons pretty regularly recently."

How did he know? Where had he seen them?

"I don't know," she replied stiffly. The easy relationship that had been between them at the start of the outing had gone. "She was so taken up with her own affairs for today that she didn't seem interested in knowing where I might be going, so I didn't bother to upset her. She's gone to Kirkcudbright with Cameron Innes."

His only reaction was to raise a surprised eyebrow. They had reached the nearest fishing boat, and the dinghy bumped against its side. Scott shipped the oars and caught hold of the side of the bigger boat.

Standing up quickly and lightly, Lindsay pulled herself over the gunwale of the motorboat and into its cockpit. Scott handed her the painter and the rowlocks from the dinghy and followed her. Then he walked up to the bow of the motorboat where the small mooring buoy rested on foredeck and attached the painter to the buoy.

Refusing to allow his sudden coolness to dampen her spirits, Lindsay sat down on one of the cockpit seats and looked around. The boat was about 20 feet in length, and apart from the small foredeck at the bow it was completely open. In the middle of the cockpit was the engine that was covered with a wooden casing. A bulkhead or thick beam of wood divided the boat roughly into half and beyond the division there were more bench seats like those in the cockpit. Attached to the bulkhead was a canvas shelter or dodger with a metal frame. At present it was folded down, but in rough weather it would be raised to give shelter to anyone sitting in the cockpit. The boat was, she recognized the usual sturdy, open, fishing boat that had been built in Cairness for years and that could be used for pleasure purposes if necessary, or for carrying goods and even animals.

Scott came back into the cockpit and started the engine, then he went forward quickly to cast off the mooring buoy, came back again and took the tiller to steer the boat toward the mouth of the estuary. Seagulls wheeled about above them, and looking up, Lindsay noticed that there were many more flying higher, coming in from the sea. Toward the west, cloud was building up, and it looked as if Scott's prophecy of rain and wind was right. However, the sun was still shining. There was time to go to the island, look around, and return before the bad weather came.

As the boat cleared the end of the breakwater, it met rougher water and began to roll slightly and to pitch its bow into the waves. Lindsay stood up and went to stand beside Scott.

"Whose boat?" she shouted above the noise of the engine.

"Dougie's."

"Does he fish as well as farm?"

"Dougie does everything," he replied with a grin. "Look over there." Lindsay looked in the direction in which he was pointing. Another point of land jutted into the estuary dividing it into two. Close to it she could see the stakes or poles to which nets could be attached. At low tide the fishermen who owned them would go out to the nets and gather the catch of sole, plaice, or cod and sometimes a good salmon.

"Did you ever live at the farm?" asked the curious Lindsay.

"Not much. I stayed with my grandmother because it

was much easier for me to go to school from her house."

He seemed disinclined to talk to her, and some of the lightness of heart that she had known earlier in the day was dimmed. They were near the island, and she could see the seagulls on the small rock-strewn shore below the cottage perched on a ridge of ground at the protected northern end of the island.

Scott guided the boat close to the shore and took it alongside a small jetty. Slowing the engine, he ordered Lindsay ashore to catch the bow rope he threw to her. He told her to tie it to a large ring set in the jetty. That done, he cut the engine and joined her on the jetty. The boat, tied by its bow, drifted away from the stone wall to ride gently in its shelter.

Without speaking Scott set off toward the cottage, following the narrow path that wound up the hillside. Lindsay went after him, feeling the wind lift her hair, hearing the seagulls crying plaintively as they circled above hoping to return to their resting place on the shore.

The cottage was small and rather decrepit. It was a one-story gable-ended building; its slate roof was in need of repair. Beside it there were two other buildings, one of which was obviously a barn.

Scott produced a key, opened the front door, and went in. Lindsay followed. The door led straight into a large empty room with an old-fashioned fireplace complete with oven and a tank for heating water on either side of it. At the back of the room were two porcelain sinks without taps. There was a big floor-to-ceiling closet beside them. Scott opened a door and went into the other room which was also empty except for an old plush-covered armchair.

Lindsay walked over to the window and looked out at the small yard, that was protected from the wind by a stone dyke.

"Is this all there is?" she asked.

"Yes." He was examining the wall closely, looking for damp.

"It's rather dreary. I thought you said it had been used as a holiday cottage."

"It has."

"Without furniture in it?"

"The Currys took the furniture out of it when they decided to sell." He went back into the other room, and after a rather discouraged glance around the big room, she followed him to find that he had gone outside and was already striding toward the barn. She went after him, noticing that the wind had increased and the sun was not shining so brightly.

The barn looked dim and dank.

"What do you think of it?" she asked.

"Hm? What?" He looked down at her as if surprised to find her there.

"What do you think of the cottage?"

"It has possibilities," he replied reservedly. "I'll go and shut the door, and we'll take a quick walk to the other side of the island. Then we must go before the weather gets too bad."

They followed the grass track that skirted the higher ground and went around the eastern point of the island. Across the water the "palaces" of Barrcliffe were still glittering in the sunshine peeping at them from out of the side of a big cloud. As they rounded the point they could see that the distant mountains of the English Lake District across the Firth were already shrouded in cloud.

The grass track ended at the automatic lighthouse, and from there they had to pick their way across the grass to the edge of the cliffs that formed the western end of the island. They stopped to look at the view down the Firth. Dark headlands jutted out into the shimmering, perpetually moving water.

"There are caves in the cliffs," said Lindsay. "I remember walking around the shore once to see them."

"Want to look at them now?" asked Scott. He sounded totally disinterested.

"No. No, thank you," she said, retreating in the face of such coolness.

She looked at him, and Beth's description came to mind. "He was a handsome devil," she had written, "and he knew it." He was still handsome and could be charming when he chose. But in this detached, disinterested mood he could hurt far more than he could possibly know. She preferred it when he showed dislike.

She braked her thoughts sharply. Hurt? Who was hurt? She wasn't. A person only had power to hurt you when you loved them, when you expected more from them than they were prepared to give, and that was not the situation between her and Scott.

She was suffering from a case of anticipation being better than realization, that was all. She had looked forward to this outing. It was not turning out to be as pleasant as she had hoped. That was nothing new, and there was only one thing she could do about it—pretend that it was pleasant.

"This is a lovely island," she announced cheerfully. "So quiet and peaceful. I'm glad I came today."

She had said it, now she would feel like that, and she had at last captured his attention because he turned to look at her his eyebrows raised in surprise.

"Are you? I wonder why?" he asked.

"I've told you. It's a lovely place."

"Wouldn't you prefer to be practising golf with Alex?"

"No. If I wanted to be with him I wouldn't be here. He asked me to go out with him today, and I refused."

"How did he take your refusal?" he asked with a shrewdness that disconcerted her.

"Not very well, I'm afraid. I think he's growing rather fond of me."

Scott's crack of laughter was scornful, and it aggravated her.

"Fond?" he repeated. "You're either blind, or being deliberately naïve. I may as well be frank with you. I invited you to come here today for one reason . . . to get you away from Alex to give someone else a chance."

Bewilderment and something else, a vague ache that was just beginning and that she was unwilling to acknowledge yet, made Lindsay silent. She had thought that she preferred his open dislike of her to the detached attitude he had shown since they had arrived on the island, but now that the dislike was evident again she was not so sure.

"But how did you know I would accept your invitation?" she stammered.

"I didn't know. It was a gamble I took based on what I learned about you on Thursday night."

That brought her head up. Wide-eyed, she looked at him, trying to read the expression in his eyes. They were the same as usual, calm and speculative. What had he learned about her on Thursday night? That his presence in her car affected her driving? She felt suddenly vulnerable and had a desire to run away and hide. The sun had gone behind the thin, spreading, gray, nimbus cloud. The surface of the water was disturbed by dark flurries.

"I hope your gamble paid off," she managed to say in a choked voice, and turning, began to run back to the lighthouse, along the grass track to the cottage. The day that had promised so much was really spoiled now. She had been foolish to come. She could not understand why she, who had been so determined not to be hurt by a man again, had left herself wide open to this hurt. As she approached the cottage she slowed down, out of breath, and answered her own question. She had come because she had hoped that Scott had overcome his dislike of her and had wanted her company.

When she rounded the corner of the island and walked down the track to the cottage, the wind that had been growing stronger flung a few drops of rain in her face. She looked down at the narrow strait of water separating the island from the nearest headland. It was dark gray and swirled dangerously. The voyage back was going to be uncomfortable because the boat would roll, but it would not take long. They would soon be in the shelter of Glenfoot Bay.

Lindsay stopped walking as she noticed something white being tossed about on the waves. She looked at the jetty. There was no boat tied to it. The rustle of an oilskin jacket told her that Scott had caught up with her. He was breathing heavily as if he too had been running.

"The boat's drifted away," she said dully and pointed to where it cavorted on the water.

He stared incredulously. Then he turned on her, and she felt the full force of his anger.

"I thought you said you'd spent most of your life messing about in boats?" he barked. "What sort of knot did you use to tie that line to the ring?"

"A half-hitch on a bite," she answered. Her knees trembled, but she held her head high and looked him in the eye.

"And tied it carelessly, so that it worked loose when the wind started to push the boat farther away from the jetty. You should have used a clove hitch."

"I'm sorry," she muttered.

He looked down at her, and some of the anger faded from his face.

"It's as much my fault as yours," he admitted. "I should have checked the knot and perhaps attached another line. I . . . I . . . was thinking of something else."

A sudden vicious squall hit the island, tossing a few stunted trees that huddled around the cottage and rattling the loose slates on the roof. The boat that was being pushed one way by the ebbing tide, and the other way by the wind, twirled around. Lindsay turned her back to the wind and felt cold rain strike through her hair, some of which had been pulled out of the tortoiseshell barrette which held it at the back of her neck.

Scott gripped her arm firmly and said, "No point in standing here to discuss what we should do next. We'll shelter in the cottage."

Together, pushed by the wind, they ran through the yard. Scott found the key, opened the door, thrust Lindsay inside, and followed her just as another squall whirled by.

In the kitchen Lindsay undid her barrette and smoothed back the wet hair. Then clipping all the hair within, she fastened it. Scott leaned against the door and watched her with interest.

"You realize, I hope, that we'll probably have to spend the night here," he said quietly.

Lindsay absorbed the meaning of his words slowly. Then as the implication attached to the situation became clear she exclaimed, "Oh no, we can't! We mustn't. I must get home."

"And how do you intend to get home? By swimming,

perhaps?" he asked her, with an ironic twist to his mouth.

"Surely someone—Dougie, perhaps—will come out for us when we don't return," she said.

"I doubt it. Dougie and my mother have gone visiting, as I told you. They won't be back until dark. There's only Eddie Thom at the farm. He's there to milk the cows, and he won't be watching the clock for my return."

"But when Dougie comes back won't he go down to the fishery to make sure the boats are safe?" persisted Lindsay. "He'll see the Mini."

"Maybe he will. But maybe it will be one of the other fishermen who'll go and check the boats. He won't know where we've gone, and he'll have to wait until Dougie returns to find out if it is an emergency or not."

"We could light a fire to attract attention," persevered Lindsay.

"Have you any matches?" he asked.

She shook her head miserably, unable to find any way out of the dilemma. He moved away from the door, came toward her, and looked down at her. Lindsay stared back wondering why he was subjecting her to such a close scrutiny. Suddenly he smiled and brought a hand out of his jacket pocket in which there was a box of matches.

"Fortunately I have," he said. "We could light a fire outside later when it starts to go dark and when the squalls have stopped. But for the time being any fire we light will be in that fireplace to keep us warm. Look in the old press there by the sink and see if there's any old paper while I go and get some wood from the shed. If there isn't any paper, rip some of the stuff off the walls. No one is going to miss it."

When he opened the door, the wind whipped it out of his hand and slammed the door open against the inside wall. Lindsay went and closed it, then through the window she watched Scott struggling, head bowed against the wind, toward the shed.

In the press she found one sheet of yellowed newspaper that had been used to cover a shelf. Automatically she rolled and twisted it into a triangle as she did at home when she used a paper to light a fire. Going over to the fireplace, she set the triangle in it behind the black bars. It looked ineffective, so she went into the other room where she found some more paper in another cupboard. Pleased with her find, she crumpled it up and set it around her triangle just as Scott kicked at the front door.

When she opened the door he came in with his arms full of wood and logs.

"It isn't very dry," he said as he set the lot down by the fireplace. "There's an ax in the shed, so I'll break up some boxes which are in there. Then I'll collect some grass and whin for banking later. Is that all the paper?"

"Yes."

"Then it will have to be a first time job. Don't do anything until I return."

"After the episode of the boat he will never trust me again to do anything," she thought. But then neither would she trust him again, and the likelihood of them ever doing anything together again was extremely remote.

The faint ache started again, only this time it was stronger. It wasn't physical. It was in her mind. She had thought at first that it was disappointment, but now it felt suspiciously like regret.

A violent kicking at the door roused her from her reverie, and she ran to the door and opened it. Loaded again with logs and firewood, Scott walked straight to the fireplace and dropped the wood on the floor, then squatted in front of the hearth. Lindsay knelt beside him and watched him as he arranged the wood on the paper. He struck a match and muttered, "It's now or never."

The paper was very dry and thin. It soon lit, and bright orange flames licked around the kindling wood. They both stared at the flames waiting for the crackling sound that would mean that the wood was going to burn.

"How are we going to light the fire on the hill?" asked Lindsay.

He turned to look at her, and she realized how close to him she had knelt and shifted a little way back.

"I don't know. Everything is going to be soaked out there. We'll not try to cross that bridge until we come to it," he said softly. He was looking at her closely again. She nodded, and her glance slid away from his. She wished now that she had not thought about him while he had been out getting the wood. Thinking about him had made her doubly sensitive to every word he uttered and every action he made.

The flames took hold on the sticks that crackled and spat, sending sparks up the chimney. Scott stood up and went into the other room, to reappear with one chair; the red plush armchair whose springs had gone and from which the stuffing was sticking out.

He heaved it across the room and set it down before the fireplace.

"There, sit down. Might as well be comfortable."

"In that?" queried Lindsay.

"It's better than the cold hillside that would have been your lot if we hadn't had the key to the cottage," he replied.

"If you hadn't been coming to look at the cottage we wouldn't have come to the island at all," retorted Lindsay as she sat on the sagging seat of the old chair.

"How do you know?" he countered, as he placed more wood on the fire. "We could have come to explore the caves. Island was the magic word. It enticed you. You probably thought, 'I'll go with him to the island because there we shall be alone. I'll be able to lull him into a sense of false security, and when he awakes he'll find he's in my thrall. . . .'"

He was laughing at her; teasing her, making reference once more to the poem by Keats about the beautiful merciless woman.

"You have that poem on the brain," she retaliated.

He grinned tantalizingly. "Only when I'm with you. I know other poems too, such as: 'Sweet is revenge, especially to women.'"

Lindsay was quick to answer: "That's by Byron . . . from *Don Juan*."

"It's obvious that we've both been influenced by the same English teacher," he commented. "And you have to admit that both Byron and Don Juan had considerable knowledge of women."

"But I'm not like that," she objected. "I don't want to make men fall in love with me and then reject them."

"Are your intentions toward Alex honorable, then? Do you want to marry him?"

"No, of course not."

"Then why have you made a dead run at him?"

"I haven't." Lindsay sat up straight and glared indignantly at him. "All I've done is to go to a party with him because he wanted to show Moira he had a woman friend and. . . ."

"And show him how to play golf, and go out to dinners with him, and take rides in the country with him," he put in wickedly. "What had Moira to do with all that activity?"

"I . . . I . . . Oh, he was tired of you cutting him out," she gasped.

"Cutting him out of what?"

"Coming between him and Moira. They were more than friends before she began to take an interest in you, and you'll not deny she's interested in you. She told me herself she had helped you over a bad patch after. . . ."

"She told you . . . what?" he interrupted, astonishment mingling with amusement on his face.

"She said you had a difficult time after the woman you were going to marry jilted you."

"I had a feeling we'd get back to that. Since we're dealing in plain talk, I couldn't be jilted, because I've never asked anyone to marry me."

Lindsay stared incredulously. Laughter-lit hazel eyes stared back at her.

"But Glendoon . . . and the woman with red hair . . . Lorna," she said.

"Glendoon is one of several houses which I and Dougie have bought to renovate and to rent as holiday houses. Galloway is becoming increasingly popular as a holiday resort. To own and rent a house is a good proposition. Dougie and I are in partnership. We started by doing up the cottages on his land and renting them. Then we bought others scattered amongst the seaside villages that have been going for a song because they need so much done to them before they could be rented. As for Lorna, how can I describe her?"

A faint, enigmatic smile curved his mouth as he poked at the fire with one of the pieces of wood. Flames shot up the chimney.

"I suppose you could say she was an old flame," he said whimsically. "I met her in Glasgow, years ago. Then she turned up in Dumfries, and we picked up where we'd left off. She's moved now, to the Midlands. She's a nurse too . . . and she wasn't interested in staying in one place."

Lindsay continued to stare as she tried to sort out the implications of what he was saying. He was implying that he had had an affair with the red-haired woman, but he had not asked her to marry him because she had not wanted to stay in Galloway.

"Alex isn't in love with Moira now," he said grimly. He stood up, looked down at her, and added nastily, "He's besotted with you."

"He isn't. He can't be," she replied, hating him for the unpleasant emphasis that he put on the word "besotted".

"Then why has he ignored every other woman in the vicinity for nearly two months? Why has he refused invitations?"

"Moira hasn't invited him. He told me so."

"She hasn't . . . but someone else has, someone of whom he was apparently very fond before Moira and her father came to live here permanently at the end of last summer."

"Who?" whispered Lindsay.

"Jan . . . my stepsister."

The image of a shyly-smiling, curly-haired girl who had deliberately avoided her at Moira's party flashed into Lindsay's mind.

"I didn't know," she said lamely.

"No, you wouldn't know. You didn't even care to see," he jibed. "Now perhaps you can understand why I'm concerned. First Moira came and dazzled Alex. I saw what was happening and decided to attract her attention . . . with success. Then you had to come back."

He squatted in front of the fire again. This time he put a log on top of the merrily burning wood, and the glow that had filled the room was dimmed slightly as the log spat and hissed in reaction to the heat curling around it.

Outside wind and rain still besieged the house. Lindsay stared at the streaming window pane and remembered the disappointment on Janet McMorrow's face when she herself had approached Alex and had said she wanted to go home.

"That was why you took me home from the party, and she is the good friend you were acting on behalf of," she murmured. Everything was becoming clear now, especially Scott's dislike of her.

"Yes . . . but I could do nothing about you going to work for him," he replied. "There seemed to be no way of drawing your attention away from him as I had drawn Moira's because you were naturally suspicious of me owing to your mother's attitude. All I could do was watch Alex become infatuated again. I tried to persuade Jan to give him up, but she said she was sure that he meant nothing to you and that if she could only get him to herself, all would be well again. But it was difficult to achieve because he wouldn't accept any invitation to tea at the farm. He was always going somewhere else, and she guessed he was with you. I knew he was with you because several times when passing Glendoon I saw his car outside the house. Moira told me several times she had seen you together. Then last Thursday night gave me an opportunity to ask you to come out with me. I didn't push the invitation too hard because I thought you might not accept if I seemed too pressing."

"And did Jan ask him to tea again?" asked Lindsay.

"She did when I told her what I'd done. She called him yesterday and although he said he wasn't going out today, he refused because he told her that he was thinking seriously of asking you to marry him."

So that was why Scott had been waiting confidently for her. He had guessed she was coming because he had known she was not going out with Alex.

"It seems strange that Alex should tell Jan that he would like to marry me before he's told me," she said coldly.

Scott shrugged his shoulders and did not reply. He was still squatting easily before the fire; a position which seemed to come naturally to him as if he had squatted that way before many camp fires. His handsome profile: straight, high forehead under a drooping lock of damp black hair, well-marked eyebrows, straight chiselled nose, firm mouth and jutting chin, was silhouetted against the new flames that spurted from under the log.

Lindsay thought of the unscrupulous way in which he had inveigled her into coming today. How well he had read her! As he had said, he had not been too urgent. He had been off-hand enough to entice her. His gamble had paid off.

Another feeling of hate surged through her. She hated him because he had known what to say to make her come. She had a longing to strike at him in some way.

"It's all your fault," she seethed. "If you hadn't interfered between Moira and Alex in the first place, he would never have asked me to go to the party, nor asked me to work for him, and then he wouldn't have . . . have. . . ." She paused because she did not want to say that Alex had fallen in love with her because she did not believe that he had. "He wouldn't have become infatuated with me."

He half-turned to look at her, and his mouth curled cynically.

"You think not?" he murmured. He laid down his makeshift poker and stood up. He walked over to her, and Lindsay stared up at him, involuntarily bracing herself. He sat down on the arm of the old chair, and she leaned back against the other arm as far away from him as possible.

"Did you ever look in the mirror, that night, as I suggested?" he asked.

Surprised by the question, she answered without thinking.

"No. I looked the next morning."

He seemed to consider her reply thoughtfully, then smiled and shook his head.

"That wouldn't be quite the same . . . although I've no doubt it was interesting."

"I can't see what your question has to do with Alex and me," she said impatiently.

"I'm trying to show you that he was attracted to you before he ever thought of inviting you to the party. You possess a fragile grace that would tempt most men. Alex used the party as an excuse to ask you to go out with him, and he suggested that you showed an interest in him to pique Moira in order to keep you with him."

"Oh, you're so clever," she jeered. "What you don't know, also, is that he asked me to use my wiles to keep you away from Moira!"

He stared at her in perplexity for a moment. Then his frown dispersed, and he put back his head and laughed heartily.

"I can't see anything to laugh at," said Lindsay.

"You will when I tell you . . . at least I hope you will," he gasped. "You and I were doing the same thing at that party. You were keeping me away from Moira and I was keeping you away from Alex. Och, I know you'd like to think the blame is all mine, but you're just as much to blame for this muddle you've landed in."

Maybe she would see the funny side later, but at the moment all she wanted to do was push him off the arm of the chair where he balanced precariously as a punishment for his complacency and his laughter. Instead she said, "Since you're so superior and detached, like a Greek god, perhaps you can see a way out of the muddle. Or perhaps you have the ability to read the future like other gypsies. Look in your crystal ball and tell me what you can see so that I can avoid making another mistake."

His glance was pure scorn, and he slid off the chair and went over to the window to look out. Left in the chair,

Lindsay closed her eyes. Her surge of hate turned against herself. Why had she spoken so nastily? She wasn't normally caustic, but Scott had a disastrous effect on her, and she could understand why. She remembered that he had once pushed Beth into the mud for calling his mother a gypsy. What would he do to her now for suggesting that he had powers that were attributed to gypsies?

She couldn't let it stand. She had to apologize. He was probably proud of the fact that he was descended from the band of gypsies who had once had a kingdom in Galloway. She seemed to be spending her time apologizing to him today; today, the lovely day that he begun so well, and from which she had obviously expected too much.

She walked over to the window and looked out. The scene that met her eyes made her spirits sink lower. The wind was whipping the water, and spindrift was creating a haze through which the mainland appeared intermittently as a vague shape. The chances of lighting a fire on the hillside in such weather was very small. Probably if they managed to light one it would not be seen. And even if it was seen, who was going to risk their life to fetch two people off an island where they were perfectly safe?

She touched Scott on the arm and said quietly, "That was a nasty remark. I take it back."

His eyes were blank when he looked at her, and she realized his thoughts had been far away. Then slowly understanding dawned. He smiled, a warm smile which had the most unusual effect on her.

"Forget that you made it," he replied softly. "Remarks like that are water off this duck's back. I've been thinking."

"I had noticed," she commented dryly. Now that she had apologized, now that she knew what had caused his dislike of her, she felt more at ease with him.

His smile widened. "Was I so far away?" he asked calmly. "I've been thinking that the muddle you're in with regard to Alex is nothing compared to the one which you're going to find yourself in when everyone in Cairness and Duncraig learns that you spent the night on a deserted island alone with me. You can see for yourself that no one is coming to rescue us in this weather."

"I suppose not," she agreed glumly. "My mother is going to be terribly upset when I don't return home, and when she can't find out where I am."

"Serves you right for not telling her you were coming with me. And on top of all that anxiety she'll have to put up with the gossip which is bound to arise as a result of your inability to tie the right knot."

His humorous reference to her tying up of the boat was an attempt to soften the blow, she realized. Gossip was something which she had not thought about. Living as she had been doing in a city where people did not concern themselves about their neighbors' affairs, she had forgotten that Duncraig and the surrounding district was a small parochial community where the conventions were still strictly observed, and where any departure from them by anyone was discussed in full. There would be many repercussions after this episode, and she knew that her sensitive and highly conventional mother would suffer severely as a result. Past history of the Bells and the Nicolsons would be dragged out and mulled over, there would be arched eyebrows and knowledgeable smirks, and Mrs. Bell would feel humiliated. All the good done by the move to Glendoon would be undone.

Lindsay stared desperately at the flattened grass in the garden as it flinched under the onslaught of the gale. Beyond the garden the storm-tossed water flung itself over the jetty. She felt as if she was imprisoned.

"What can we do?" she groaned.

"We could always say we're engaged," suggested Scott lightly. "That's a sure way of stopping malicious gossip."

"But would anyone believe us?" she replied seriously.

"Probably more easily than they're going to believe that we stayed on this island together for a whole night without anticipating marriage," he answered smoothly, his gaze bright and direct.

Delicate color stained Lindsay's cheeks as she caught the implication of his words.

"Is that the sort of reputation you have?" she asked hesitantly, thinking of the woman called Lorna.

"Possibly. You see, I'm my father's son, and people have a way of thinking in a situation such as this . . . like father, like son."

And his mother had run away with his father. Lindsay's eyes avoided the bright, questing gaze of his. The atmosphere seemed to be charged with all kinds of dangerous currents.

"But I don't want to marry," she said weakly, voicing the only coherent thought that occurred to her out of the confusion his statements had created in her mind. "I want to return to nurse in Canada at the end of April."

"Then don't worry about it." He spoke coolly yet soothingly. "I was merely pointing out that that could be a solution to this problem. I can imagine your mother wishing she could say when someone asks her a particularly awkward question about us and our night here, 'Oh, but it was perfectly all right. They're engaged, you know.' "

He mimicked her mother's gracious way of dealing with unpleasantness so accurately that Lindsay could not help smiling.

"That's better," he commented gently. "When you smile you look less tragic. And this isn't a tragedy. After all, we're safe and we have shelter . . . and we should be able to keep warm. But we shall need more fuel if we're to keep the fire going all night."

He moved away to the fire and put another log on it. Lindsay continued to stare out of the window bemusedly. Gradually the tension eased. He was accepting the situation calmly, with a touch of humor, and she felt the effect of his attitude. It was no use worrying, as he had said, and at least they were warm and dry.

The rustle of oilskin told her that he was putting on his jacket in readiness to go out again. As he approached the door she stepped in front of him and said appealingly, "Can we light a fire on the hillside, please? I feel we should make some effort to get back. And have you thought of how hungry we're going to be?"

"I'll see what the weather is like. If the rain has eased

off we can try a fire. I doubt very much if anyone will come for us, but someone might see the fire and will guess that we're safe and not adrift in the boat. I can't do much about hunger except offer to share this with you." He brought a battered packet of chocolate out of his pocket and gave it to her. "And we won't be thirsty. The waterbarrel is overflowing."

As he looked down at her the expression in his alert eyes changed. He put his hands on her shoulders in a comforting gesture. Their warmth and strength made her feel secure.

"Today has turned out rather differently from what you expected, hasn't it?" he asked softly.

"Yes, it has," she admitted. "I was foolish and expected too much."

His eyes narrowed with puzzlement, but he did not ask any more questions. All he said was, "It's been different for me, too."

His fingers tightened on her shoulders, and for a wild moment she thought he was going to kiss her. If he did she would be unable to resist, she thought crazily. Then all the gossip that would result from this escapade would be based on the truth, and unconsciously she stiffened. His hands slid from her shoulders and he murmured, "I must get more fuel."

And walking around her he opened the door and strode out into the wind and the rain.

Lindsay went back to the chair and sat down. Leaning forward, she hugged her knees and gazed at the fire. Being marooned on the island with Scott was fraught with dangerous problems, she realized, not least amongst them being the physical attraction between them. Now she understood what he had meant when he had said the night she had taken him to the hospital; that it was as bad for him as it was for her; now she understood why he had disliked her on Jan's account, and why he had said once that she promised much but did not give, like La Belle Dame Sans Merci. He was attracted to her, and he did not want to be. She could say the same was true for herself.

Her thoughts meandered to Alex. In her efforts to help

him she had apparently changed the course of true love instead of furthering it. But how could she have known about Jan? Alex had mentioned her very casually and had seemed to think of her only as a girl who crewed for him when he raced. How scornful Scott had been about Alex's infatuation for Moira and then for herself, as if he regarded himself superior to such wayward behavior. And she could see now that it was wayward. Alex's affections veered as easily as a weathercock's. He needed someone strong and placid to keep him pointed in one direction. Someone like Jan.

Scott returned, his arms laden with logs and gorse. He dropped his load and turned back to the door, saying over his shoulder, "I found another chair in the woodshed. I'll go and get it."

When he returned with a wooden kitchen chair, Lindsay was sitting curled up in the old armchair eating chocolate. Half the bar of chocolate lay on the arm of the chair.

Scott picked it up, broke some off, and ate it.

"Would you like some water?" he asked.

"Yes please, I would. I found an old mug in the cupboard." She pointed to the mantelpiece where she had put the old enamel mug she had found. But he did not look in the direction she was pointing. He went on staring at her. She moved uneasily under his gaze, wondering what was wrong. She guessed she must look a mess with her hair uncombed and scarcely any make-up. In the end she had to speak to break a silence that was becoming increasingly uncomfortable.

"Is something wrong?" she asked.

"You have chocolate stains all around your mouth," he told her.

"Oh!" She fumbled in her slacks pocket for a handkerchief and scrubbed at her mouth with it.

"And you look as if you've decided to stop struggling against fate and to accept the situation in which we find ourselves," he added.

His observation disconcerted her. Very little passed unnoticed by those alert hazel eyes.

"Yes, I have," she admitted. "How do you know?"

"You've relaxed. Do you still want to light a fire outside?" The room was growing dark except where the glow of the fire reached. Nightfall was approaching fast.

"What's the weather like?" she queried.

"Still blowing, but the rain has stopped. I haven't any idea of how to get a fire started out there without some kindling. I've built a fireplace of sorts out of stone. If we could carry some of this fire out there it would help, but I can't find a container."

Lindsay jumped to her feet, willing to be of use.

"There's an old bucket in the cupboard."

She groped in the cupboard and brought out the old, galvanized pail and took it to him.

"Just the thing. Now put your jacket on and bring some of the sticks while I carry some fire in the bucket."

Using the iron shovel that lay in the hearth to lift some of the fire, he tipped it into the bucket.

"Open the door," he ordered. She did so and he ran out, through the garden and up the path onto the hill. Her head bowed to the onslaught of the wind, Lindsay followed him.

He set the bucket in front of a square hearth he had made out of loose stones he had found.

"Put some sticks in the bucket, or the fire will go out," he ordered.

She placed some small dry sticks on the flames in the bucket, and they began to crackle.

"Do you think anyone will be able to see it from the mainland?" she asked.

"No."

"Then why did you bring the fire out here?"

"Because you wanted to try . . . and because it gives us something to do," he replied. Suddenly he kicked the bucket over toward the makeshift hearth. There was a sizzling sound as the hot sticks touched the wet stones. A pall of gray smoke rose in the air. "Put some sticks on it, quickly," said Scott.

The sticks revived the fire a little, and it flickered merrily, but it was very small. Lindsay realized that there was very little possibility of it being seen from the fishery. Even if it was seen from Barrcliffe it was unlikely that anyone there would understand its significance.

She noticed that Scott had disappeared and wondered where he had gone. The wind was cold and pulled at her hair. Darkness was closing up the sky, and soon there would be no daylight left. She pushed her hands into her jacket pockets to keep them warm and wished that she had never suggested that they should light a fire on the hillside.

Scott reappeared with more wood that he began to feed the fire with.

"I had to mend the other fire," he explained. "We don't want to lose it. Will you go back and watch it, please? It'll be warmer for you than standing about out here."

"What will you do?"

"I'll tend this one for a while."

She was reluctant to leave him, but she could see the sense of his suggestion, so she trudged back to the cottage. She took the mug from the mantelpiece and blundered her way outside to the waterbarrel. It caught rain water from the spout which collected it from the roof. She drank some water, then filled the mug again, and took it back into the cottage with her.

She sat down by the fire and let the warmth seep through her before taking off her jacket. Darkness hid the dreary emptiness of the room; the glow from the fire gave it an appearance of coziness. She thought of Scott out in the wind and the cold tending the other fire. She was lucky she was stranded here with him and not with Alex; whom she could imagine being no practical use whatsoever in a situation like this. And as for Maurice—well, strangely enough Maurice didn't matter any more.

CHAPTER SEVEN

She must have dozed off, because the fire had gone low without her noticing. Hastily she grabbed some gorse and pushed it onto the embers and then placed more sticks on top of it. By the light of the flames that sprang up she looked at her watch. It was half past nine.

She looked around. The wooden kitchen chair on the other side of the fireplace was empty. There was no sign of Scott. Hurriedly she crossed to the window. It was raining again. Outside it was pitch dark, and she could hear the wind howling. She had an odd impression that there was nothing beyond the window pane, and the cold fingers of panic clutched at her.

What had happened to Scott? Over two and a half hours had passed by since she had left him. Had he come in while she had been dozing? Unfortunately she had no idea what time she had fallen asleep, so she could not tell for how long she had slept. It could have been for an hour, or it could have been for ten minutes.

When the latch of the door lifted and it opened, relief flooded through her. Scott stepped inside and closed the door behind him. His oilskin jacket glistened wetly in the fireglow. He took the jacket off and draped it over the pile of logs beside the fire.

"Well, that's that. No more fire outside," he said. "And no one is coming to take us off, so we may as well settle down for the night."

He crouched in front of the fire and held his hands out to its warmth. His wet pants and rubber-boots steamed. Lindsay wished she could have made him a hot drink to show how grateful she was for his presence. She wished she had the right to put her arms around him and hug him to show how glad she was to see him. Instead she said shyly as she sat down in the armchair again, "Thank you for trying."

He cocked an eyebrow at her and replied, "You're

welcome. I don't do that sort of thing for every woman I know."

"I don't suppose you do," she rallied, "but then not every woman would tie a boat up wrongly, so that it would drift away."

He grinned his appreciation.

"I knew you were in a class all by yourself when we met for the first time at Merse Cottage," he mocked, "but little did I realize then what I was letting myself in for."

He stood up and removed his boots and placed them beside the fire. Then he sat down on the kitchen chair, sliding down so that his back was fully supported and his long legs were stretched in front of him. He folded his arms across his chest and observed, "Here we are like Darby and Joan, one on either side of the fire discussing the past . . . or would you prefer to discuss the future?"

Although she was glad he was back, she was aware of how very much alone they were, completely cut off from the rest of the world.

"Would you like to sit here?" she offered. "It's more comfortable?"

"I doubt if there's room for two, though," he answered derisively.

"I didn't mean we should share the chair," she retorted, feeling her cheeks burn, glad of the dim light. "I meant I would change chairs with you, so you could sleep if you wanted."

"That's considerate of you, but you stay there. When I want to sleep I'll use the floor."

Lindsay glanced at the rough floorboards. They did not look very comfortable. Then she looked back at him. He was staring at the fire. His face was wind-burned, and it glowed red in the light from the fire. As she watched him his eyelids drooped wearily. Eventually his eyes closed.

The fire crackled, and long shadows danced on the walls of the room. The wind shook the door and the windows. Lindsay felt glad that no one had ventured out to fetch them off the island. There would be a great deal of explaining to do tomorrow; not only to her own mother but to Dougie McMorrow about his boat, and also to that person who loomed so formidably in her mind, Ann

McMorrow, Scott's mother. She wondered whether Mrs. McMorrow knew that her son had brought Lindsay Bell to the island and if she did, what she thought of his association with the daughter of her former neighbor. And what would she think when she knew they had been here all night?

She leaned forward to put more wood on the fire. Her movement disturbed Scott who stood up and placed another log on top of the wood. For a moment he stood watching the flames.

"Watching a fire is always fascinating," said Lindsay.

He leaned one shoulder against the mantelpiece and half-turned to look at her. She could not see his face properly, only burnished angles, surfaces, and shadowed hollows.

"And so is playing with fire, as you must know. You've been doing it ever since you came back to Scotland," he answered.

"In what way?" she challenged, covering her uneasiness at the manner in which he had picked up her idle comment and had twisted the conversation into personal channels.

"Alex. And now being marooned here with me tonight."

"You say that as if you think I'd tied the boat with the wrong knot deliberately," she said indignantly.

"Didn't you?"

"You know very well I didn't!"

"What a blow to my self-esteem," he murmured in self-mockery. For a few moments the silence was broken only by the crackling of the wood in the fire. Then Scott said, "I can't understand why you don't want to marry. You don't seem to be a hard-headed career woman unwilling to give up her much-vaunted independence, so I have to assume that some unpleasant experience has led you to take such an important decision."

This time the mockery was directed at her, and it taunted and flicked.

"Don't mock. I can assure you it was a very unhappy experience," she replied in a low voice.

"I see. Did you put some poor man on a pedestal where

he didn't belong and worship him? And when he didn't live up to your expectations, did you vow never to love again and to take your revenge on other unsuspecting males by causing them to fall in love with you?"

He was baiting her, for some reason, and the only way to stop him was to tell him the truth.

"That's not true!" she burst out. "I loved Maurice, and I thought he loved me. I hoped we might marry some day. Then I discovered he was married already."

"And you let that stop you?" His surprise had a sneering quality that made her furious.

"Yes, I did. His wife wouldn't give him a divorce, and I wasn't prepared to go on seeing him under the circumstances. I felt I didn't want to love again if it caused so much pain. But I didn't plan revenge as you keep suggesting."

The shadows danced on the wall. The wind howled outside. Lindsay was suddenly aware of the intimacy of the conversation. No one had ever spoken to her as critically as Scott had done; no one had ever tried to break through her reserve.

"You may not have planned it, but it's happened. And it will happen again, because although you may not want to love again you can't stop a man from loving you," he said quietly. "And you get your revenge by not returning his love."

The beating of her heart was extremely loud in her ears. He had not moved, and it was impossible to see his face clearly. What did he mean? Could he possibly mean that he was in love with her? No. She dismissed the idea quickly. He was referring to Alex again and criticizing her. She remembered the first verse of the poem he was always quoting:

> "O what can ail thee, knight at arms,
>   Alone and palely loitering?
>   The sedge is wither'd from the lake,
>   And no birds sing."

Was that how Alex appeared to Scott? How could she convince him that she hadn't planned it all?

Scott moved, and she tensed immediately. He stood in front of her, and now she could see his face quite clearly. It was grimy with smoke from the fire. He sat down on the arm of the chair and surveyed her seriously.

"You're all on edge again . . . and it's my fault," he said gently, surprisingly. "Relax, Lindsay, and go to sleep, because that is exactly what I'm going to do, now that I've found out what I wanted to know. I'll bank up the fire with grass and gorse. Will you be warm enough, do you think?"

He was sitting so near to her that she could feel the warmth of his body. She had a longing to snuggle up to that warmth.

"Yes. I'll put my jacket over me. But will you be able to sleep on the floor?"

"Och, yes. The way I feel now, I could sleep anywhere."

He picked up her jacket, placed it over her, and tucked it around her. The homely, considerate action disturbed her more than any other would have done, and the curious ache started again.

She watched him attend to the fire. Then he made a pillow of his boots, placed his oilskin on the floor, and lay down on it. He shuffled about for a while, trying to find the best position. When he was settled he murmured, "Good night, Belle Dame. Sleep well."

"Good night, knight at arms," she replied softly.

Soon his deeper breathing informed her that he was asleep. she sat wondering what he had wanted to know, what had lain behind his seemingly simple question "Why don't you want to marry?" Well, he had learned all about her and Maurice as a result. Was that what he wanted to know?

On impulse she sat up and looked down at him where he lay fast asleep. She got up quietly and placed her jacket over him. Then creeping back to her chair, she curled up, closed her eyes, and willed herself to sleep.

"Aye, I can see it's a fine, wee house. We'll make an offer for the island this week, then. Meet me in town on Tuesday. We'll go and see Plaidy about it."

The singsong voice awakened Lindsay from a dream in which she was explaining to a judge how to tie a clove hitch. She opened her eyes. The wan light of a dismal, gray morning filtered through the dusty panes of the window.

"Aye, we could do that."

That was Scott agreeing. Lindsay moved stiffly and looked around. He was leaning against the wall behind her talking to a short stocky man whose thick black curly hair was sprinkled with gray. The man was wearing the blue denim overalls over a thick, woollen shirt she always associated with farmers, and a long oilskin coat. As she stood up he looked at her, and his shrewd, brown eyes twinkled as he smiled at her.

"So you're awake at last, lassie. Did ye have a fine sleep?"

"Yes, thank you."

"Lindsay, this is Dougie McMorrow, my stepfather," said Scott. "He came over at the crack of dawn, but I must warn you that he's more worried about his boat than about us."

"I'm sorry about the boat, Mr. McMorrow," said Lindsay earnestly. "It's entirely my fault that it drifted away. I didn't use the right knots."

"Just so, just so," he nodded. "But I'd like to know what Scott was doin'. It's not like you, lad, to be so careless. Why didn't ye check the knots?"

"I don't know. I wasn't thinking very straight yesterday," Scott excused himself. "I had a moment of mental aberration."

Dougie chuckled and winked at Lindsay.

"Aye, now I've seen Lindsay I can believe that . . . although I'm thinkin' it wasn't so much an aberration as deliberation. Intentional, ye might say. Y're not the first who's used a trick like that to get a lassie to himself for a night."

Startled by this innuendo, Lindsay flashed an accusing glance at Scott. He shook his head slowly from side to side, obviously denying that he had left the boat carelessly tied up intentionally. But she could see that

Dougie's implication amused him, because his mouth quirked at the corner, and his eyes gleamed with laughter.

"Dinna fash yeself about the boat, now, lass," went on Dougie. "It's safe enough. I had a call from a fisherman down the Firth. He said it had come ashore on the high tide during the night."

"I'm so glad. When did you realize it was missing?" asked Lindsay.

"Not until I walked down to the fishery after we had come back from Moniaive last night. I saw the wee red car there too. I went straight back to tell Ann. She came with me to the fishery, and while we were there we saw the fire ye'd lit on the hillside here. 'They're safe, Dougie. They're on the island. Although I knew it before I saw the fire,' she said."

"But how would she know?" asked Lindsay.

"Och, Ann always knows whether her loved ones are safe or not," said Dougie matter-of-factly. "It's the gypsy blood, ye ken. Anyway we decided it was best to leave ye here than to risk sending anyone out in the storm to rescue ye. Ann kenned ye'd be all right with Scott to look after ye. But she made me take her over to tell your mother where ye were."

Thinking of how her mother might react to a visit from Ann McMorrow, Lindsay gasped.

"Was she all right? What did they say to each other?"

"I canna say. I didna go in, ye ken. I waited in the car. But she told me she'd put your mother's mind at rest, and that she was glad she'd gone over. Are ye ready to leave now, Scott, or are ye thinkin' of setting up house here, at once?"

The twinkle was back as Dougie looked knowledgeably first at Lindsay and then at Scott.

Lindsay put on her jacket, which she just realized had been covering her again when she had awakened.

"I'm ready," she said. "And I'm very hungry. I have to be at work by nine o'clock."

"Ann will have a good breakfast ready for ye when ye get to the farm," replied Dougie as he escorted her to the door. "I'll go ahead and start the engine. This one is a wee bit sluggish this morning. Needs coaxin', ye ken."

He swung down the path, his oilskin flapping around his legs. Scott locked the door of the cottage and fell into step beside Lindsay. Gray light gleamed wanly on the pale sea that was no longer raging, but was flat and still, seemingly exhausted by the fury of the night. The morning air was raw, and Lindsay shivered. To her surprise Scott put an arm around her and held her close against him as they walked down the path. She made no attempt to pull away.

"Cold?" he asked. "I haven't had a chance to ask you what sort of a night you had. Did you sleep well?"

"I think so, although I woke up once to put some more fuel on the fire."

"A good thing you did, because I didn't waken until Dougie hammered on the door. You'll have noticed that it's begun already. He assumes that once we knew we were stranded here for the night, we put the opportunity to good use, as of course any country lad with his lass would have done, knowing that he was going to marry her anyway."

"But surely he knows that you and I . . . surely your mother will have told him that we're not . . ." stammered Lindsay. She was too cold and hungry to deal with complications.

"Not going to get married," he finished for her. "I don't know. My mother goes her own way, as you will have realized from her decision to go over and see your mother. I wonder what they said to each other after all those years."

They had reached the boat, and he helped her over the gunwale into the cockpit. He undid the warps and came aboard with them, then sat down beside her. On the water she felt colder than ever and could not control the shivering that she guessed was caused as much by reaction and nervous apprehension as it was by the damp air that seemed to penetrate right through her clothing to her skin.

Scott put his arm around her again and pulled her

against him. The warmth of his body offered shelter, and involuntarily she turned toward him in search of more comfort. She felt his unshaven chin rasp against her face as he bent his head and whispered, "Not long now, then you'll be able to have a good hot bath, followed by porridge . . . and you'll be ready to face the questions and deal with them."

The sound of the engine changed as the boat stopped reversing away from the jetty and went ahead. Scott shouted something to Dougie, and Lindsay turned to look at the other man who was standing by the tiller. He was looking at her curiously, and as their eyes met he smiled kindly and called out, "Ye've found a good warm place, I see, lass. I should stay there if I were you. You'll come to no harm."

Listening to the steady beat of Scott's heart beneath her ear, feeling the strength of his arm about her, she knew that Dougie was right. She had come to no harm last night. With the limited means at his disposal Scott had kept her warm and fairly comfortable. He had shown the same patience and mental stamina she had noticed when she had taken him to the hospital, and yet not once had he made her feel helpless or a burden.

Now that she could see yesterday in a more objective light she realized that in turning out differently from what she had expected the day had given her more than she had ever hoped. It had given her knowledge about Scott, and insight into his character that she might never had had otherwise.

Once they reached the mainland, they left Dougie at the fishery and drove up to the white farmhouse. Coll met them at the kitchen door, his dark eyes flashing with interest and excitement.

"Some people have all the luck," he complained. "I wish Mom had let me come with you, then I could have been stranded with you."

"And maybe it would have been better for everyone concerned if I had let you go," said a soft voice behind him. "Come away in, Lindsay Bell. It's glad I am to see the two of you, none the worse for your adventure. Away with you, Scott, to the phone. Mr. McBean from the Council offices called you a few minutes ago. Och, 'tis a lot of questions you'll be having to answer for last night's mischief, but I can guess you have all the answers ready at the end of your smooth tongue. Now, Coll, go and brush your teeth. It's almost time for the bus. Tell Jan to hurry too."

The owner of the voice was tall and full-breasted. She had an oval, olive-skinned face, fine black eyes set under winged dark eyebrows and graying dark hair wound in two braids around her head. She went up to Scott, and for a moment the two dark heads were close together as she kissed him. She whispered something in his ear, and he grinned and went off through the door. Lindsay heard the click as he lifted a telephone receiver, then his voice as he asked for a number.

Then she became aware that she was being studied closely by the black eyes. The calm gaze reminded her of the way Scott had studied her at Moira's party when she had thought he had found her wanting. Maybe Ann McMorrow, his mother, felt the same way about her, thought Lindsay, so she lifted her chin and stared back.

The tall woman smiled faintly. The smile had an enigmatic Mona Lisa quality.

"You remind me of your mother when she was about the same age," she said. "You are so slender and so fair. I haven't seen you since you were a wee, plump bairn. I can understand now why poor Jan has been feeling unhappy. But you'll not want to stand there listening to me blether. Come, I'll show you where the bathroom is. There's plenty of hot water, so don't be afraid to use it."

"I . . . I'd like to telephone my mother, if I may," said Lindsay as she followed the other woman through the door past the telephoning Scott.

"After you've bathed," replied Mrs. McMorrow firmly. "She's fine. I went to see her last night, and we had a wee chat. She was very anxious about you because you hadn't told her where you were going, which was naughty of you, but then bairns are often naughty. I explained about you and Scott, or at least as much as I knew. I told her you were safe, and she calmed down."

By this time they had mounted the wide staircase and were in the enormous high-ceilinged bathroom that was obviously a converted bedroom. Mrs. McMorrow turned on the bath taps.

"There are towels, soap, bath oil, and everything else you need. Scott will be finished on the phone by the time you're bathed, so you'll be able to use it then."

The hot water, good soap, and scented bath oil gave Lindsay a feeling of luxury. She wished she had time to wallow, but the need for food made her hurry.

As soon as she was dressed, and her hair was brushed and tied back neatly she went down the stairs to the telephone that was on a table in the cavernous entrance hall of the old house. It was not long before she was speaking to her mother.

"Where are you now?" asked Mrs. Bell.

"At Glenfoot Farm. I'm going to have breakfast, then I'll come home to change before going to work."

"I'm glad you're all right. But why didn't you tell me about you and Scott? I'd have understood, or at least I'd have tried to understand."

Lindsay bit her lips. What had Mrs. McMorrow told her mother?

"There isn't time to discuss it now, Mother. Later, when I come home," she said.

After a few more words she hung up and went into the warm kitchen. Scott was sitting at the table eating. He had shaved, but he was still wearing the same clothes he had worn on the island. He stood up when she came in and went over to the big stove, poured some porridge into a dish and placed it on the table.

"Sit down and eat," he ordered brusquely. "Mother has gone to see Jan and Coll onto the bus. She always has a feeling that Coll is going to skip school one day and go down to the fishery instead."

"I suppose she learned the hard way . . . with you," said Lindsay as she helped herself to cream.

"Yes, she did. Poor Coll, he doesn't have a chance."

There was a newspaper on the table beside him folded

open to the lists of houses for sale; he turned his attention to it, and there was silence. Lindsay ate several mouthfuls of the porridge. Except for the strangeness of her surroundings she felt as if the episode on the island had never happened, as if she and Scott had never shared the experience of spending the night together in a ramshackle cottage on a deserted island. He had withdrawn from her and was apparently far more interested in what was offered for sale in the newspaper than he was in her.

It was foolish to feel resentment because he had withdrawn, but she could not help it and was trying to find some topic of conversation to attract his attention when Mrs. McMorrow returned to the kitchen.

"Did Scott pour some tea for you, Lindsay?" she asked. "Och, isn't he forgetful!"

She poured tea from an enormous, brown, earthenware teapot into a large willow-patterned teacup and set it down beside Lindsay's dish. She poured more for Scott and some for herself, then sat down at the end of the table.

"What did you tell Mrs. Bell last night, mother?" Scott asked, pushing his paper aside.

Mrs. McMorrow put sugar in her tea and stirred it before replying. Her oval-shaped face was calm and meditative as she watched the spoon go around the cup.

"It would have helped if you hadn't been so secretive about Lindsay," she said. "I knew so little . . . and when I found that Ruth knew even less I didn't know what to say. I had to tell her that Lindsay was with you, and I anticipated that she wouldn't be pleased. What I did not anticipate was her immediate assumption that you'd taken Lindsay off to the island to seduce her."

She picked up her teacup and sipped from it. Lindsay laid down her porridge spoon and stared in consternation at Scott. His face was expressionless, but she was sure he was trying not to laugh. He glanced at her and murmured, "You see? It's as I told you it would be."

"I see," she replied.

"I know why Ruth was thinking like that," continued

Mrs. McMorrow. "She was remembering when Grant and I ran away together. She has always believed that I seduced Grant, and now she believes that Scott has inherited my supposed lack of morals. Anyway, in an attempt to defend you both I suggested that you had been seeing each other without telling her because you thought she would be upset if she knew. Immediately she announced in her most dignified manner that if you like each other enough to marry, she will never come between you. From then on she warmed to the theme, and by the time I left her she was almost planning the wedding."

"Oh no!" gasped Lindsay, while Scott could contain his mirth no longer and burst out laughing.

Mrs. McMorrow looked from him to Lindsay and back again with a puzzled expression on her face.

"I must say I find your reactions extraordinary. I thought you'd be relieved to know that Ruth has enough sense not to allow prejudice to affect her attitude when it comes to something important as the marriage of one of her daughters."

Scott had stopped laughing and was watching his mother narrowly.

"Mrs. Bell's change of attitude finds favor with you, doesn't it?" he asked.

"Yes, it does, especially now that I've met Lindsay." Mrs. McMorrow turned and smiled warmly at Lindsay. "I have to admit that when I learned you were working for Dr. Wilson, and when I saw Jan was so unhappy, I was as much prejudiced against you as your mother has been against Scott. But now I know that Jan has nothing to fear from you."

Again Lindsay looked inquiringly at Scott. How much had he told his mother? He looked back at her with clear candid eyes.

"I've told Mother nothing about you," he explained in answer to her unspoken question. "She's guessing. She does it to try and find out the truth." A trick he had learned from the tall, dark, mysterious woman, thought Lindsay, remembering the way he had baited her the previous night to find out about Maurice.

Now he was saying to Mrs. McMorrow. "So you've arranged everything with Mrs. Bell, have you?"

She smiled at him, the same enigmatic smile Lindsay had noticed before, and said nothing. Standing up, she took Lindsay's empty dish, placed it in the sink, and went across to the stove.

Taking advantage of her hostess's turned back, Lindsay leaned across the table and whispered, "What are we going to do?"

"Nothing . . . yet," Scott whispered back, then held a finger to his mouth, warning her to silence.

"There, eat it up," said Mrs. McMorrow as she returned to the table and set a plate of bacon and egg in front of Lindsay. "Then both of you must be off. It would be kind and polite of you to go to Cairness with Lindsay, Scott, to explain to her mother."

Scott stood up.

"Not now," he said crisply. "Now I have to go to Duncraig to change, then I must go to work. The road across the moors had been practically washed away by last night's weather. I must go and inspect it. I'll see you later, Lindsay. I'll be calling in to show this to Alex." He wagged his injured finger at her.

Mrs. McMorrow went with Scott when he left the kitchen. Alone, Lindsay began to eat hurriedly. Now that he had gone she felt lonely and vulnerable. Mrs. McMorrow was even more formidable than she had imagined. How, for instance, had she guessed that Jan had nothing to fear from Lindsay's association with Alex? And why was she in agreement with Lindsay's mother's attitude to the island escapade?

Apparently Mrs. McMorrow herself was aware that Lindsay was puzzled, because as soon as she sat down at the table again she said, "I hope you understand why your mother thinks the way she does about what happened last night?"

"No, not really. Nor can I understand why you're concerned," said Lindsay. "Whatever Scott and I did or did not do is entirely our business. We're both adults and have no need to account to other people for our actions."

The slow Mona Lisa smiled appeared as midnight-dark eyes studied her.

"At one time . . . how long ago it seems now . . . I thought exactly as you do, only I was younger than you are now. Experience proved me wrong. I discovered in a very distressing way that all our actions have repercussions, sometimes unpleasant ones . . . on ourselves, on our families, and on our children."

"But this situation is different," objected Lindsay. "Scott and I spent the night on the island as the result of an accident. You and his father ran away together because you were in love."

"Does being in love give anyone the excuse to be inconsiderate of the feelings of others?" asked Mrs. McMorrow, and went on to answer her own question. "I know now that it doesn't. Grant and I were not in love . . . we were infatuated with each other, although we learned to love each other later. Neither of our parents approved of our association with each other, and because we were both stubborn, we went away together. In a way our parents were a little to blame because they didn't take the trouble to sit down and talk to us to explain their point of view. If they had maybe we would have done the thing properly and would not have hurt anyone. Love does not exist where there's no sense of responsibility, Lindsay." She sighed deeply. "Well, I've had my say. But I think you should be warned that your mother is very worried about what her neighbors are going to think."

"Thank you for telling me," replied Lindsay gently, realizing that Mrs. McMorrow had gone out of her way to explain why she felt as she did. "Scott thought she might be."

"Did he suggest any way in which you might combat the gossip?"

"Not seriously. He said we could pretend we're engaged, but he meant it as a joke." It was suddenly much easier to talk to the older woman now that she knew more about her feelings, so Lindsay added quietly,

"There's no reason why Scott and I should consider marriage. We're not in love with each other, and he didn't seduce me."

Did she imagine it, or was that an expression of relief that flickered in the dark eyes?

"Nor you him," murmured Mrs. McMorrow. She reached out a hand and patted Lindsay's. "Thank you for being honest, Lindsay. You may think that parents fuss needlessly about something that is unimportant to you, but it's because we love our children and because through our own experience we know the pitfalls. I'm very fond of Scott, but he's extremely independent and has always gone his own way. There was a woman. . . ."

"Lorna?" asked Lindsay and immediately received a sharp shrewd glance.

"Did he tell you about her?" asked Mrs. McMorrow, looking surprised.

"A little, very little."

Disappointment chased the hopeful surprise from Mrs. McMorrow's face.

"It's the only subject which he hasn't talked to me about," she said sorrowfully. "And I thought I had done well to keep the doors of communication open between us."

"Perhaps there was nothing much to tell," offered Lindsay comfortingly.

"Perhaps not. Well, I must not keep you any longer. Ruth and the doctors will be wondering where you are. We shall meet again soon, Lindsay."

CHAPTER EIGHT

Lindsay drove to Cairness as fast as she could, around the top of the estuary, crossing the river at the little port of Glencross, then following a narrow secondary road beside the river bank. The road was full of potholes and was flooded in some places, but it saved her having to go through Duncraig. In Cairness the main road was a mess. She found herself not envying Scott his job. Road damage must have been widespread after the storm.

As she hurried into Glendoon, she heard her mother talking. The end of a sentence came quite clearly to her.

"And I've been expecting them to announce their engagement for some days. Oh, here she is now, Alex. I'll tell her you're busy this morning, and that you're expecting her. Goodbye."

Lindsay walked into the kitchen where her mother was just placing the receiver on its stand.

"Mother, what are you saying? What are you doing?" she exclaimed. "You've no right to tell Alex. There's no engagement! Scott and I are not. . . ."

"Hello, dear," interrupted Mrs. Bell blandly. "You must be tired and a little overwrought. It's a pity you have to go to work after such an experience, but Alex expects you. He sounded rather taken aback when I told him why you hadn't arrived at work. He didn't know you were seeing Scott . . . but then none of us knew. Lindsay, you should have told me."

The gently scolding tone and the affectionate knowing glance were lost on Lindsay. No matter how much it upset her mother she would have to put a stop to this nonsense about an engagement.

"You must listen to me," she persisted. "Forget what Mrs. McMorrow said. Yesterday was the first time I've ever been anywhere with Scott Nicolson."

"Oh no, it isn't. You took him to the hospital when he hurt his hand. I remember thinking at the time that it was a rather unusual action for you to take, but you said it was because it was your duty as a nurse. Then you met him a few times before, at that New Year's party and at Glendoon. Sometimes it happens that way . . . a few brief meetings and then click!"

Lindsay stared in astonishment at Mrs. Bell. She was learning more about her mother every day.

"What happens?" she asked.

"Love."

"Mother, I haven't time to talk about it now, but you must *not* tell anyone else that Scott and I are engaged, because it's untrue."

"Not tell anyone? But, Lindsay, I must say something when people ask me. I can't have everyone thinking that you and he spent the whole night together, and that you're not going to be married. . . ."

Lindsay was suddenly reminded of Beth holding forth about the generation gap. Here was a prime example of it. How could she convince her mother that these days no one worried about who spent the night with whom?

"Why not? Oh, Mother, you're being an ostrich again. You think you can gloss over the incident in this way, but there's no need to. The fact that Scott and I spent the night on the island doesn't mean that we . . . er . . . we. . . ."

"That you anticipated marriage, or that you didn't think marriage necessary," put in Mrs. Bell smoothly. "I know that, dear, but you must remember you're not living amongst sophisticated people here. These are country folk, Lindsay."

"I can't talk about it now," reiterated Lindsay and ran upstairs to her bedroom. She changed quickly. Her mind was in absolute confusion. She had thought it would be so easy to present her mother with the facts and talk her out of her insistence on an engagement. But as Mrs. McMorrow had said it was going to be difficult. And now there was the added complication of Alex having been told.

There was no time to discuss personal issues with Alex. The waiting room was full of patients, and when she looked into his consulting room to show that she had arrived he gave her a cold glance, or as cold as gentle Alex could manage, thought Lindsay with a smile.

The morning rushed by. At lunchtime Lindsay had a sandwich and a cup of coffee at the café in the main street. She was just leaving when she walked into Moira, who was about to enter the café.

"Hello, Lindsay. How are you? I haven't seen you for a long time, and only this morning I was hearing all about you."

Moira was smiling, but there was something cold and insinuating about her smile and her words. Lindsay was immediately alert.

"Oh. What have you been hearing?"

"Have you time for another cup of coffee? I'm waiting for Father. He's talking to his lawyer."

"I have a few minutes."

They went into the café and sat down at a table. Moira gave the order to a waitress.

"I was hearing about your adventure on Glenfoot Island. It must have been very wild out there last night, but I daresay Scott looked after you."

Hard blue eyes stared at her directly. No matter how she tried, Lindsay could not prevent herself from blushing at the mention of Scott's name even while she derided herself for behaving like an innocent adolescent.

"But how do you know?" she managed to ask at last.

"Your mother called us last night just after I'd returned from Glasgow. She was worried because you weren't at home. She had called Alex's home, but you weren't with him, and she didn't know where you had gone. Naturally I could give her no information. Then this morning Mrs. Rowan, who is our housekeeper, heard from the mailman that you and Scott had been on the island all night."

"How did the mailman know?" asked Lindsay, her spirits sinking as she realized that the gossip had started already.

"He delivers over the other side of the estuary too. Eddie Thom who works for the McMorrows had told him that Dougie had brought you and Scott back from the island early this morning. You can guess that the story is all over the parish by now."

"Yes, I can guess," said Lindsay glumly.

"Anyway, Daddy was very concerned about your mother's reaction to such a tale, and he phoned to see how she was and to get the truth. Imagine his surprise when she told him that you and Scott are engaged."

Lindsay's spirits touched rock bottom. She looked at the other people in the café. They were like so many puppets who grimaced and gesticulated silently. From far away she could hear a voice saying, "Lindsay, is anything wrong?"

Moira was looking at her, a worried expression on her face.

"No, no." Lindsay tried a smile, and surprisingly it came quite easily. "No, I'm all right. It's just that it's taking me a while to get used to the idea of being engaged."

That wasn't what she wanted to say at all. She wanted to tell Moira that there was no engagement, that the whole idea was a fabrication on the part of her mother. But the image of Mrs. Bell's hurt expression at being found out in a deliberate untruth stopped her.

"I'm sure it is, because it all happened rather suddenly, didn't it?" Moira's voice was as smooth as honey. "I'm surprised at Scott allowing himself to be caught by such an old-fashioned trick."

Caught? Trick? Lindsay's face felt cold and pinched. An urgent desire to deny the engagement, to free herself from the taint of Moira's suggestion that she had set out deliberately to trick Scott into becoming engaged to her almost overwhelmed her decision to stand by her mother. Again the thought of the hurt that she would deal out to Mrs. Bell stopped her.

"There was no trick," she said coolly. "Why don't you ask Scott?"

Moira raised her eyebrows haughtily.

"Maybe I will. I suspect it's only from him that I shall hear the real truth."

She beckoned to the waitress and began to draw on her gloves. When the waitress moved away after giving Moira the bill, Moira said blandly, "This has been an interesting chat. May I give you a word of warning? You may think you've netted Scott for good, but mere physical attraction won't be enough to hold him. Scott likes to communicate at all levels, and I hardly think you can reach him on any other. I'll pay for the coffee. Goodbye."

She walked away, leaving Lindsay at the table feeling limp. Moira was jealous. There could be no other reason for her spiteful remarks. She had helped Scott through a difficult period when Lorna had moved away, and now she regarded him as her special property. Mrs. McMorrow had pointed out only that morning how one's actions had repercussions beyond one's imagination. Lindsay had just witnessed another resulting this time from her own mother's reaction to last night's episode. Moira was hurt.

She swallowed her lukewarm coffee and hurried out of the café. Outside she looked up and down the street, but there was no sign of Moira's tall, elegant figure. The town hall clock chimed two, and the sound sent Lindsay running in the direction of the doctors' offices. There was no time to search for Moira and to explain.

She let herself into the offices, took off her coat, flung on her white overall, and began to check through the cards for the afternoon appointments. The first for Alex was at four o'clock, and after that there was one every half hour until six o'clock. Four hours before Scott would arrive to have his finger examined. Four hours before she could tell him about the terrible muddle she was in, and that he was in too. Would he laugh and say it was all her fault? Or would he be angry? She found that she did not care what his reaction would be, she wanted to see him, to talk to him. Remembering the comfort of his arm around her in Dougie's boat this morning, she wanted to feel that comfort again. Lindsay closed her eyes as the longing for him made her dizzy. Impatiently she shook her head as she tried to shake the feeling away. But it stayed with her all afternoon; the same ache she had experienced on the island and that she now realized was much deeper and more intense than mere disappointment.

Alex came in a few minutes before four o'clock and looked through the patient cards. Lindsay, who was feeling exhausted, sighed heavily, and he glanced at her.

"Why are you sighing?" he asked.

"I'm tired, that's all."

"Oh yes, I'd forgotten. You spent the night on the island. Quite a strenuous experience, I expect."

She looked at him sharply. Was the usually good-natured Alex being sarcastic?

"Why didn't you tell me you were seeing Scott?" he asked, rather diffidently.

"It didn't seem necessary. Would it have made a difference if you had known?"

He looked puzzled as if he was having trouble in sorting out his thoughts.

"I'm not sure," he murmured. "Your mother told me this morning that you and Scott are getting engaged. I'd like to wish you every happiness, if that's what you want, Lindsay. I'm glad you weren't immune after all."

"Immune?"

"Yes—don't you remember when I suggested that you might draw his attention away from Moira? You said you were immune to love after your experience in Canada."

"Yes, I remember."

Alex fiddled around with the cards. She watched him. He did not seem unduly disappointed at the news of her engagement, and she wondered whether Scott had been right when he had said that Alex was besotted with her. But then Jan McMorrow had told Scott that Alex had told her he was seriously considering asking Lindsay to marry him.

"Well, I expect you'll be going to the sailing club's dinner with Scott, so it's no use my repeating my invitation," said Alex, banging the cards together.

"Why don't you invite Jan McMorrow to go with you?" she suggested.

He appeared to consider her suggestion thoughtfully,

then shrugged, "Maybe I will ask Jan. At least I know I can depend on her."

He went into his consulting room, and Lindsay drew a deep breath of relief. There was one good result of last night's episode. Alex had been prevented from proposing to her. Although he was puzzled by what had happened, he had accepted the fact that she was engaged to Scott without one objection. It was just possible that his unprofitable pursuit of Moira and then of herself had made him realize Jan's worth.

As she had expected Scott was the last patient to arrive that afternoon. He went in to see Alex, who brought him through into Lindsay's office to have the finger rebandaged.

"It's mending nicely," said Alex to Lindsay. "Come back next Monday, Scott, and I'll take the stitches out. That's all for today, so I'll be on my way. Good night."

Lindsay had almost finished dressing the finger before either of them spoke. She was waiting until she heard the outer door close after the two doctors as they left, and then she would know she and Scott were alone and could talk without any possibility of being overheard.

At last she heard it close, just as she was putting the leather guard over the finger. Quite suddenly she was conscious of Scott's nearness. Her legs shook and her fingers trembled, so that she could not tie the strings of the guard.

"Now what's wrong?" he asked and she felt his breath stir her hair. "There's no blood this time."

"Nothing's wrong," she snapped, trying to control herself. "I'm tired, that's all."

She finished tying the strings, then began to tidy the desk.

"Alex has just congratulated me on my engagement to you," said Scott slowly. "I hope I didn't look too surprised. We can't talk about it here, so I suggest you come and have supper with me when you've finished."

"Where?"

"At my home . . . 62 Gower Street."

"I'll have to phone Mother."

The corner of his mouth lifted in an appreciative smile.

"Do that. I expect she'll be delighted to know you're with me, for once. Don't hurry. It'll take me a while to get organized."

Although she did not hurry he was not organized when she arrived at the big, granite house. He lived in the lower half and took her through to the big, modernized kitchen to help him prepare the meal. It was not until they were sitting at a table under the kitchen window that he brought up the subject of their engagement.

"Any idea on how you are going to disentangle yourself from this muddle?" he asked.

Having enjoyed herself up to that particular moment, Lindsay was reluctant to face up to reality. She did not want to spoil the close companionship that they had known for the past hour while they had cooked together.

"The obvious way . . . denying that we're engaged doesn't seem to work," she said with a sigh. "I told Mother that we had no reason to want to be married, and she wouldn't listen. She's told Alex and Cameron Innes. You can assume that they've told others. Goodness knows how many more people she's told since I left home this morning. I met Moira at dinner time. She was very upset. She thinks I've deliberately tricked you into having to propose to me."

"Why didn't you tell her you haven't?"

"I couldn't. I mean I told her that I hadn't tricked you, but I couldn't tell her that I wasn't engaged to you, no more than I could tell Alex. I kept on thinking of the spot in which it would place Mother."

She could not tell whether he was annoyed or not. His dark-browed face was impassive, and his hazel eyes were blank as he stared at her.

"How did Alex take the news?" he asked eventually.

"He was puzzled, but he showed no objection. It stopped him from proposing to me. I'm hoping that as a result of knowing I'm engaged to you, he'll invite Jan to the sailing club dinner instead of me."

"In that case we might say our night on the island has done good to someone."

"I hope so. But what good is the fact that everyone thinks you and I are engaged going to do us?"

She had an impression that he was wholly detached, indifferent to the problem, and as on the island his attitude hurt. The ache started again. He was not saying what she wanted him to say, or reacting in the way she wanted him to react. She wished he would show some emotion.

"It will protect your good name," he said.

"What rot! As if I cared whether people think you seduced me or not."

"You may not care, but I do."

Reaction at last, but it was cold, icy, as if he was disgusted with her. For a while, late last night, early this morning, and as recently as this evening, she had thought that he had overcome his dislike of her. Now, facing his cold gaze across the table, she was not so sure.

"Maybe I put it wrongly," he continued quietly. "I should have said it will protect *my* good name. It may seem odd to you, but I have no wish to figure as a seducer in the eyes of the local people. My parents, both my mother and my fater, suffered too much from that sort of prejudice."

Lindsay swallowed hard. She had not looked at the situation from his point of view before. She had thought he would disregard any smears on his name. He had not seemed to mind when people had gossiped about his affair with Lorna. But then everyone had assumed that he was going to marry Lorna.

"You want everyone to think we're going to be married?" she asked hesitantly.

"I see no harm in the idea."

"But we're not in love," she objected.

He frowned and glanced at her with narrowed speculative eyes. Her description of him as being unscrupulous came to her mind, and she prepared to fight any suggestion he might make. Seeing the stubborn stiffening of her face, he laughed suddenly.

"Don't worry, I'm not going to drag you off to be married against your will. Those days are really over. But

I'll strike a bargain with you," he offered. "Are you interested?"

As once before, the offhand way of presentation enticed her. She nodded in agreement.

"To get ourselves out of this muddle which your mother has placed both of us in I suggest that we fall in with her plan . . . for a while. The gossip about our stay on the island will die a natural death, Alex will recover rapidly from his infatuation with you, and eventually you'll be able to return to Canada, from where you will write, breaking the engagement." His mouth twitched with amusement. "I'm sure Moira will be only too glad to help me over another bad patch."

He was calm, slightly amused. She had never seen him other than calm except on two occasions; once at Glendoon when he had been angry about her mother's prejudice, and once yesterday when he had been furious because she had not tied the boat up properly. But there had never been any other signs of passion. She wondered how he would behave if he really wanted to marry her, if he were in love with her.

The thought made the blood creep into her cheeks. She put her elbows on the table and her hands over her cheeks to hide the tell-tale color.

"Keep your mind on the subject under discussion," he mocked softly.

"I am," she replied, trying to emulate his calm. "But if we pretend to be engaged we'll have to go around together, be seen together. . . ."

"That won't be difficult," he observed dryly. "Already my neighbors will have noticed that your car has been parked outside this house for more than an hour and will be surmising. We can go to the sailing club dinner together with Jan and Alex. I can visit you at Glendoon, and you can visit Glenfoot Farm, where I can assure you you will be very welcome. And after spending a night on Glenfoot Island together you can scarcely say we find each other's company unpleasant, can you?" His eyes challenged her.

"No," she muttered. She could not explain why the

idea of pretending to be engaged to him frightened her. She could not tell him that she was afraid that too close an association with him might cause her to fall in love with him. It was very evident from his detached attitude that he was completely uninvolved emotionally in the same way that he had been on the island. If he had been emotionally involved he would have made love to her in the cottage, not with words but with actions. And maybe there would have been no need for pretense. . . .

Her thoughts were going off at a tangent again. Lindsay hauled them back desperately and forced herself to concentrate.

"What about Moira?" she asked. "When she wouldn't believe that I hadn't tricked you I told her to ask you herself."

"I'll deal with Moira. She'll understand when I've talked to her," he replied confidently. "Do you accept the bargain?"

It was a simple way out of the muddle. No denials would be necessary. The only explanation would be the one Scott would have to make to Moira. And it would not be for long; four weeks of March and the whole of April. Would it be cowardly to accept? Facing the challenge in Scott's eyes, Lindsay decided that it would be more cowardly to refuse.

"I accept, but I want to make it quite clear that I'm doing it to prevent Mother from being upset," she said. "And also. . . ."

She was not sure how to put into words her fear without revealing the troubled state of her emotions.

"And also?" he queried. "Have you another stipulation to make?"

"Yes. You mustn't think because you have your own way again that you can take advantage of us pretending to be engaged." It came out in a rush, and she was not sure whether she had made her point at all.

"From that rather muddled statement I gather that you don't want me to make love to you. Am I right?" he asked blandly.

Yes.” To her mortification she could feel her cheeks turning pink again.

He considered her thoughtfully, and there was no sign of mockery in his face.

“I refuse to make promises that I might break,” he replied coolly. “And now I think we’d better go and see your mother.”

Exhausted by the events of the day, Lindsay slept well that night. When she went downstairs next morning she was surprised to find Mrs. Bell already in the kitchen preparing the breakfast.

“Good morning, dear,” she greeted Lindsay brightly. “Did you sleep well? You were worn out last night after all the excitement. How do you feel now?”

“Better, thank you. How about you?”

“I feel better too, much better than I did yesterday morning,” replied Mrs. Bell as she brought the food to the breakfast counter. She poured tea. Lindsay found herself comparing her with Mrs. McMorrow with whom she had eaten breakfast the previous morning. How totally different they were in manner, and yet how alike in their concern about their respective children.

“It was nice of Scott to come down and see me last night,” said Mrs. Bell. “He’s very different from my preconception of him.”

Lindsay stared wide-eyed at her mother. She could hardly believe she had heard correctly. This was her mother admitting that she had had preconceptions about a person, and above all, admitting that she had been wrong.

“In what way is he different?”

“He’s much more considerate than I ever thought he would be. I realize now that it was silly of me not to let him in when he came to see me about the cottage. But my memories were of a wild, mischievous boy who could be very rude. He’s much more mature than Grant ever was.”

“But when you knew Grant he was much younger than Scott is now.”

“I knew him when he was our neighbor, remember, when he came back from the war. I don’t think he was always the best of husbands. Ann is very fond of Scott and wants him to be happy. I suppose she was as worried as I was the other night in case he was making the same mistake that she and Grant made. She called me up yesterday to tell me that her mind was easier now that she had met you. Now I can do the same, now I know more about Scott."

"Three cheers for the telephone," murmured Lindsay.

"What did you say, dear?"

Lindsay grinned affectionately at her mother.

"I was thinking aloud. What a marvelous thing communication is. What a pity we don't use it more often. I must hurry, or Alex will be calling again to see why I'm late."

She kissed her mother's puzzled face.

"You say the strangest things. What has communication to do with what we were discussing? I'm always talking to people," complained Mrs. Bell.

"Yes, I know you are, but not always so that they'll understand you. It works both ways, Mother, so don't be down-hearted about it."

By the end of the week Lindsay had received so many congratulatory messages on her engagement to Scott that she was quite accustomed to the idea. She did not see much of him, however, because he seemed to be busy not only during the daytime but in the evenings as well. She tried not to feel neglected, telling herself that it was better if she did not see him because of the disturbing effect he had upon her. But she could not help wondering what he found to do during the evenings, and whenever she left the surgery she would glance up Gower Street hoping that she might catch a glimpse of him as he returned to his house.

On Friday evening she cleared up after the last appointment, thankful that the next day was Saturday and that she would work only in the morning. When she went out of the door into the street she noticed that it was still light, the pale, uncertain twilight of mid-March that gave promise of spring.

A tall figure came toward her across the road, and her heart leaped.

"Coming for supper?" asked Scott.

"Again?"

"Why not?" His voice was sharp as if he resented the question.

"Isn't it too soon after Monday?" she asked uncertainly, not wanting to reveal that she feared being alone with him in his own house.

"You can relax," he murmured and put a hand under her arm to guide her across the street. "We're going to Glenfoot . . . at Mother's request. Your mother is going with us. She's over there in my car. I tried to phone you earlier to tell you about this command performance, but the number was engaged."

"I suppose it's all right for me to say yes, then," she said.

He laughed and squeezed her arm.

"Yes. It's all very conventional and above board . . . a tea party complete with aunts and uncles," he conceded flippantly.

Three months ago Lindsay would never have thought it possible that her mother and Scott's mother would have discovered that they both possessed a passion for playing whist. But during the course of the meal that had been attended by various members of the McMorrow family as well as the Nicolson family, the mutual liking for playing cards had come to light. As soon as the dishes had been cleared away, washed up and dried by Mrs. McMorrow and Jan with help from Lindsay, Coll had been sent to bed, Lindsay and Scott had been banished to the sitting room, and the card tables had been set up in the living room.

The sitting room had a musty, unused smell and was furnished with large Victorian pieces, hard horsehair armchairs, an enormous buffet, and a huge sofa that faced an ornate fireplace where a good fire flickered. Lindsay wandered around the room and gazed at the old-fashioned, murky engravings on the walls that seemed to consist mostly of women dressed in classical robes holding urns upon their heads, or of soulful-looking Highland cattle.

Aware that Scott was very quiet and that he was not paying any attention to her, she turned to look at him. He was sitting in a corner of the big sofa. On his knees was an open pad of paper which he was sketching on.

Slightly piqued by his lack of interest in her, she sat down beside him and peered at the pad.

"What are you drawing?" she asked.

"Plans for altering the cottage on the island. Our offer for it has been accepted," he replied absently. His pencil did not falter, and he was quite obviously undisturbed by her nearness.

"When will you work on it?"

"On weekends when the weather improves . . . and I'll take my vacation early, probably in May to try and finish it for renting in the summer."

Vacation in May. By then their bargain would be finished, and she would be back in Toronto. Somehow the thought did not excite her as much as it should.

Laughter came from the next room together with the sound of good-natured argument.

"I can hardly believe that your mother and mine are sitting in there playing cards together," commented Lindsay.

"It's highly probable that Mother is telling fortunes too," murmured Scott. "So we can say that something else good has come out of our Sunday night experience. We've patched up the family feud, for the time being. I suppose you realize we've been sent in here to do our courting?"

"Yes, I do."

"You're not making a very good job of it," he mocked.

"I'm sitting beside you on the sofa, isn't that enough?" she retorted.

He laughed and continued to sketch. She watched a plan of the cottage growing on the pad and had a sudden desire to whip the pencil out of his hand and fling it across the room, to see how he would react. Did any emotions at all lie sleeping beneath his calm exterior? The temptation to find out created a new ache; the ache of frustration.

"What would you have done tonight if you hadn't been invited to come here?" he asked casually.

"I was going to wash my hair," she replied.

"I suppose you have to wash it often, with it being so fair," he observed.

He was making conversation, uttering polite platitudes, behaving in an un-Scott-like way. He was doing it to keep her happy, so that she would not think he was ignoring her, treating her as if she was some young acquaintance in whom he had no interest whatsoever, and whom his mother had told him to entertain for an hour or so.

This time Lindsay made no attempt to resist the temptation to twist the sleeping panther's tail. She snatched the pencil from his hand and flung it as hard as she could toward the fire. It sailed over the brass rail of the big fireguard and fell into the flames.

"You don't have to entertain me with trite talk!" she flared, and her voice shook. "No conversation at all would be better than trivialities."

She sat on the edge of the sofa, taut and tense, waiting for his reaction. He did not move, but remained leaning back out of her line of vision.

"I haven't another pencil," he said at last. He spoke quietly, too quietly. "Conversation has just been banned. To fall asleep would no doubt be considered rude at this time of the evening. I can only think of one other form of entertainment."

There was no mistaking the threat in his voice. Alarmed, Lindsay turned to look at him. Immediately she was seized by the shoulders. His fingers bit deeply into her flesh. His eyes had lost their usual clarity and were opaque between narrowed lids. Lindsay's triumph at having roused him at last was tempered with fear, but there was no escape. His weight pushed her backward down onto the soft cushions of the sofa seat behind her.

She heard him say, "It's time you paid your forfeit for trespassing."

And then his mouth was on hers in a bruising kiss that was meant to punish and did.

CHAPTER NINE

After a while Lindsay gave up trying to struggle free. Crushed and breathless, she was incapable of moving.

But the punishment, although painful, was brief, and when Scott sat up she had a foolish desire to cry because it had not lasted longer. Instead she sat up too and slapped him across the face. To her astonishment he retaliated, slapping her back with a light stinging blow.

"Now that we've both got that out of our systems, what do you suggest we do next by way of entertainment?" he asked caustically.

Anger made him a different person. It thinned his mouth, flared his nostrils, and darkened his eyes, giving his face a touch of wildness that frightened her.

"Nothing," she replied shakily. "Because I'm not staying in this room with you any longer."

Before he could detain her she stood up quickly and went out into the hallway. There she hesitated, wondering where to go. More laughter came from the card-players. She decided to go to the kitchen, and as she passed the door of the living room Mrs. McMorrow saw her and called out, "Can I get you anything, Lindsay?"

"No, thank you. I just want a glass of water. I can help myself."

The water was cool and refreshing against her hot bruised mouth, but her hand shook so much that she spilled some onto the frill of her blouse. She dabbed at the drips with a towel and tried to control the recurring desire to cry.

A black and white sheepdog that had been lying in a corner of the warm kitchen padded up to her and sniffed at her hand, then padded back to its corner and lay down again.

Perhaps Scott would follow her and apologize. She listened for the sound of his footsteps in the hall. But when footsteps came they were light and feminine. Hastily Lindsay turned on the tap and rinsed the glass she had used. Why should Scott apologize? It had been her fault. She had behaved badly because, because. . . . She squeezed her eyes closed to prevent tears from falling, because she could not bear it when he ignored her.

"Scott thinks it's time you were away home and he's probably right. I forgot that you have to work on Saturday morning." It was Ann McMorrow, her dark eyes missing nothing as they roved over Lindsay's face. "Would you like to put the kettle on? We'll have a cup of tea before you leave."

If Mrs. McMorrow noticed anything unusual she was not going to comment. Lindsay felt a sudden rush of affection for her, as she helped her to put out cups and saucers on a tray and to cut and butter slices of fruit bread. While they worked Mrs. McMorrow talked about the game of whist she had just been playing.

"The cards were very interesting tonight," she observed finally.

"Can you really foretell the future with them?" asked Lindsay.

The other woman smiled her mysterious smile.

"I suspect that like Scott you're very dubious about such things. I like to think I can. Some of the happenings I've foretold have come true after a fashion. My mother was much better than I am. I read teacups too, so maybe I'll have a look at yours when you've drunk your tea."

When they went into the living room Scott was already there talking to Dougie. He had his sketch with him and did not look up when Lindsay placed a cup of tea on the card table in front of him, but continued to explain his plans for the cottage.

"Ann says she can see a double wedding in the cards," said Mrs. Bell cheerfully to Lindsay.

"And a man in your mother's life, a tall thin man," added Jan McMorrow softly.

"Sounds like Cameron Innes," said Lindsay with a teasing glance in her mother's direction as she tried to behave normally. If only Scott would look at her she would know everything was all right. But he didn't, and the awful ache was starting again. "What does she foretell for you, Jan?" she asked, smiling at the dark, plump girl.

"A social evening that will be a great success," replied Jan with a rueful grin. "That's vague enough to cover anything from the school's spring concert to the sailing club's fitting-out dinner."

Lindsay drank her tea. As soon as she had finished, Mrs. McMorrow seized her cup and turned it upside down on the saucer to allow the small amount of liquid remaining in the bottom to drain away. It left behind the tea leaves in a pattern that she could "read."

"Mmm, I can see tears, a tall woman with long hair, and what's this?" A worried frown creased the fortune-teller's high forehead. "A car, a very small car . . . in an accident."

She put the cup down quickly after glancing rather guiltily at Scott, who had looked up at the mention of an accident, and held out her hand for the cup being used by Dougie McMorrow's sister.

"I think you've had enough glimpses into the future for one night," said Scott firmly, rising to his feet, taking the new cup from his mother's hand, and putting it on a table. "It's time we were going. I'll be down tomorrow, and if the weather is good we'll go out to the island," he said to Dougie.

"You'll bring Lindsay with you?" asked Mrs. McMorrow brightly.

"He looked at Lindsay then, a cold, indifferent glance.

"I don't think so," he said. "I learned last Sunday that it's better not to mix business with pleasure."

"Never mind," said Mrs. McMorrow consolingly, as she turned to Lindsay, who was feeling as if she had just received another slap across the face. "Come another day. There's such a lot to see on the farm in the spring time. New lambs and baby chicks. . . ."

They talked about the coming spring while they put on coats. Soon Lindsay was sitting in the back of Scott's car where she had sat on the way to Glenfoot, leaving her mother to have the comfort of the front seat. She could tell Mrs. Bell had enjoyed her evening out because she chattered about the card games to Scott. Her chatter covered up his silence. Lindsay occasionally encouraged her mother to continue talking by asking a question, or by making a brief comment.

But all the time she was thinking, if it's going to be like that until the end of April, it's going to be hell for the two of us. Better that we two had never met, "Never met . . . or never parted, We had ne'er been brokenhearted. . . ." The words from Burns' poem *Ae Fond Kiss* jangled in her mind. One fond kiss! It had not been fond. It had been shattering, and unlike the couple in the poem she and Scott had not loved kindly or blindly, and so they would scarcely be brokenhearted when they parted.

Then why did she suffer from this dreadful ache? Why did she long to put out her hand, touch him on the shoulder, and say "Please forgive me for behaving badly, but I can't bear it when you ignore me?"

Scott took them to Duncraig where they transferred to the Mini. He said good night rather curtly and disappeared up Gower Street. Fortunately Mrs. Bell was too taken up with the enjoyable time she had had to notice that he had left them without a word about his next meeting with Lindsay.

He made no attempt to contact her during the weekend, and she spent two empty wretched days. The signs of spring, the purple and yellow spears of the crocuses thrusting through the grass in the front lawn, the sound of bird song in the morning were small instruments of torture. Spring, the season for lovers, was on its way.

"When birds do sing, hey ding-a-ding-ding:
    Sweet lovers love the spring."

There were times, thought Lindsay impatiently, that it didn't help at all to have had a father who had loved poetry and had persisted in quoting it at every suitable opportunity. Here she was, the birds were singing, and she had no sweet lover.

When Scott did not turn up to see Alex about his finger

on the following Monday she began to worry. Sinking her pride, she went to his house and rang the bell. She rang it a second time, but the door remained closed. He was not in. Disappointment was flamelike, searing her spirits all evening as she tried to concentrate on helping her mother with her sewing.

Next morning, however, there was a note addressed to her lying on the mat behind the front door of the surgery. It had been delivered by hand and was from Scott. It was very brief.

"I shall be working late all week. See you next Sunday at Glendoon." It was silly to feel so happy just because she had received a terse un-loverlike note. But she did, and although she did not see him she was not allowed to forget she was engaged to him. At the ante-natal clinic she was teased by two of her old school friends who were expecting their first babies and predicted she would be in their shoes by next spring if she married in the summer. She found herself wishing that there was a basis of truth for their innuendoes and jokes at her expense. She began to wish that she was going to marry in the summer.

What had happened to her? Where was her avowed intention never to marry? Why had she lost the cool sophisticated attitude to life that she had adopted when she had discovered Maurice's deception? The pendulum of her emotions was swinging high and then low, but refusing to face the truth, she continued to blame the coming of spring.

Sunday came. The air was clear and balmy. The sunny morning brought frustrated sailors down to Cairness to remove the canvas covers from their boats and to stand around talking about . . . boats, of course.

From her bedroom window Lindsay had a good view of the slipway, and she was pleased to see that Alex was accompanied by a small, dark girl as he peered and prodded at his dinghy.

Sunday's midday dinner was over, and she was helping her mother with the dishes, wondering how she was going to conceal her disappointment at the non-appearance of Scott, when she heard the sound of a car in the driveway. A few seconds later the front doorbell rang.

She opened it and for a minute, or so it seemed, they stared in silence at each other. Then Scott began to smile.

"Can I come in?" he asked with uncharacteristic diffidence.

Lindsay started guiltily.

"Oh . . . er . . . yes, of course," she stammered.

He stepped past her into the hall.

"I thought for a moment that you were going to keep me standing on the doorstep," he commented dryly. "You seem surprised to see me. Have you forgotten we're engaged?"

"No. But I thought you had," she retorted lightly.

"As usual you have to have the last word," he scoffed. "I thought we might go for a walk."

"Where shall we go?" she asked, hoping that her eagerness to go with him was not too obvious.

"It's a clear day, and I fancy climbing Griffel."

Griffel! Lindsay was surprised. Griffel was a hill near Dumfries. It was almost 2000 feet high. She had once climbed it with her father, and she knew that the views of the Firth and of the surrounding countryside were magnificent on a clear day.

"Don't tell me that your life in the city has made you incapable of climbing it," he jibed, immediately aware of her hesitation, and as usual Lindsay responded to the challenge.

"No, I'd like to come. Go and talk to Mother while I change."

To reach Griffel they had to drive through Duncraig and along the road to Dalbeattie. From there they followed the main road to Dumfries. Halfway between Dalbeattie and Dumfries they turned off the road onto a country road that went south toward the coast and the village of New Abbey.

They passed through the Sunday quiet of the village street that was overshadowed by the ruins of the Abbey from which the place took its name. It had been built in 1273 by the Lady Devorgilla of Dumfries over the tomb of her husband John Balliol. He had founded Balliol College at Oxford University and had been the father of the

Scottish puppet King at the time of Bruce, and Edward the First of England.

All that remained of the building, familiarly and affectionately known as Sweetheart Abbey, was a gable end. There was a fine example of a circular window typical of the geometrical designs carved in the stone of ecclesiastical buildings erected at the end of the 13th century; and a simple square buttressed tower pierced by single oblong windows.

As they turned out of the village onto the coast road Lindsay gazed up at the Abbey, entranced as always by the prettiness of the pink sandstone glowing in the sunlight.

"She must have thought a lot of him to have built a memorial like that," commented Scott. "Women don't seem to have the same sort of respect for men these days."

"Can you blame them?" countered Lindsay spiritedly.

"You said that with feeling," he replied with a grin. "I'm sorry I slapped you last time we met."

He made his apology calmly and without embarrassment. It dispersed completely the last vestiges of constraint that had existed between them since they had set out.

"I'm sorry too, that I slapped you and that I threw the pencil in the fire," replied Lindsay happily. Amends had been made, and she could be at ease with him at last.

"Then we're friends again?" he asked, and once again there was that uncharacteristic touch of diffidence as if he hadn't been sure. The idea that he considered they could be friends disarmed Lindsay, and she had difficulty in replying because her throat seemed to have closed up. She swallowed and said huskily, "Yes. But that doesn't mean I'm going to build an abbey to your memory when you die."

He had guided the car into the side of the road and had stopped it while she had been speaking. He responded to her attempt at humor with a laugh, put an arm around her shoulders, and kissed her roughly on the cheek.

"That's more like you . . . linten Lindsay. I like you better when you fight back."

He removed his arm, and they both got out of the car. To the left of them was the blue, dimpling water of the Firth. To the right was the curved shoulder of the hill, a patchwork of green and brown, seeming to move against the thin blue of the sky.

They locked the car, climbed the dyke, and made their way across a meadow to the edge of a thick, conifer forest that sloped away up the side of the hill. Keeping the forest to the right, they followed a well-worn stony path. Soon they cleared the forest and were out on the moorland. The going was fairly easy over the tufty grass and clumps of reeds, but gradually the gradient grew steeper. Lindsay found herself becoming short of breath, so they rested for a while against a large boulder. The climbing seemed to affect Scott very little, although he had removed his windbreaker and carried it slung over one shoulder as they set off again following the narrow sheep tracks that zigzagged back and forth across the hill, winding amongst the fallen rocks.

The ground was marshy in parts because of the numerous trickling streams of water. Once or twice Lindsay had to squelch her way out of muddy places. Scott made no effort to help her over the difficult places, leaving her to scrabble up as best she might. While she scrabbled she reviled him silently for leaving her, but once she had surmounted the obstacle she was glad that he had not helped her because she experienced such a sense of achievement.

At last she reached the top, a ridge of rock on which there was a small pile of stone known locally as the Douglas Cairn. Scott cheered her as she walked toward him. He was leaning against the cairn and put an arm out and drew her against him. For a while she was content to lean back against him and to look at the view.

Below to the east lay the flat land adjacent to the shining water of the river Nith. The day was so clear she could see it widening northward to Dumfries. Directly in front was the shimmering Solway and beyond it the flat foreshore of the English coast; beyond that the gray-blue mountains of the Lake District. Excited by the sight of the mountains, Lindsay had a brief argument with Scott about their names, insisting that she could see the distant peak of Scafell Pike as well as the nearer, more easily recognizable shapes of Skiddaw, Helvellyn and Saddleback.

To the west the land fell away to the valley of the Urr, and beyond it was another small range of mountains. Behind, to the north, the brown moorland of Cuil hill stretched away to meet the blue sky.

"It's beautiful," murmured Lindsay.

"I think so," agreed Scott. "And whoever takes me on will have to be willing to stay in this part of the country."

He must mean whoever married him, and immediately Lindsay thought of Lorna, the woman with red hair, who had moved on. It had not been prejudice that had prevented her from marrying Scott after all. She had been unwilling to make her home in a small country town, and Scott in his wisdom had not proposed to her and had let her go. If it had hurt him at the time there was no visible scar now. He had been resilient. He had recovered.

"Will you expect whoever takes you on to climb mountains too?" she asked lightly.

He grinned down at her and then blew softly at the tendrils of hair that lay on her forehead.

"Not all the time," he replied, then bent his head and kissed her. It was different from when he had kissed her at Glenfoot Farm. He was not punishing her this time, at least not deliberately.

She pulled away from him.

"Now you've spoiled the afternoon!" she complained shakily.

" 'Gin a body, kiss a body, need a body cry,' " he mocked gently. "Why should my kissing you spoil the afternoon?"

"Because you're taking advantage of the circumstances."

"Of course I am. I'd be a cold-blooded sort of man if I didn't. I didn't promise not to kiss you, if you remember."

"But you didn't take advantage on the island."

"The situation then was very different," he said rather vaguely. "All right, we'll ban kissing together with sketching and talking trivialities. But how are we going to put in time together until the end of April?"

"We managed quite well before we had to become engaged," she said, feeling unusually prim.

He removed his arm from her shoulder slowly, and she felt his fingers caress the back of her neck before he moved away from her.

"Did we?" he queried. He looked past her, and the expression on his face changed. "We have company," he murmured.

Lindsay whirled around and then laughed with relief. A small, dark-gray pony was watching them with sloe-black, unwinking eyes. It was short, dumpy, and judging by the white hairs around its mouth and nostrils, it was quite old.

Glad of the interruption, Lindsay went toward it, her fist outstretched. It sniffed at it delicately and then tried to bite it. She bent nearer to the pony and blew gently in its face in much the same way that Scott had blown at her hair. The pony stopped trying to bite her hand and blew back.

Lindsay turned in triumph to Scott.

"It works!" she exclaimed.

"What does?"

"Blowing gently on an animal's nose. It assures it that you're friendly and mean no harm. Ouch!"

She was pushed from behind by the pony and landed against Scott, who put both arms around her to hold her upright while he burst out laughing.

"How well it works!" he jeered.

They went down the hill much faster than they had climbed up it, and when they reached the lower slopes they ran and slid on the grass in a race to the bottom. Instead of going back through the village of New Abbey they returned by way of the coast road, passing through the neat, white village of Kirkbean, birthplace of John Paul Jones, one-time rebel and founder of the American revolutionary Navy.

When they reached Southwick they turned right along a road to Dalbeattie. From there it did not take long to return to Duncraig and then to Cairness where people were still walking about enjoying the warm sunshine.

At Glendoon Scott made no move to get out of the car.

"Won't you come and have some tea?" asked Lindsay, looking back at him through the open door."

"Considering the circumstances and the limitations that you set there doesn't seem much point," he replied with a wicked glint in his eyes.

"Oh very well," said Lindsay stiffly, trying not to show disappointment. "It isn't really necessary for you to come in."

The glint faded, and the expression in his eyes softened and he said more seriously, "I must get on with Coll's dinghy. I've not been able to do much this week. The damaged finger doesn't help much. It makes working slow."

"Perhaps I could help," she offered eagerly. Here at last was a chance to show friendship.

He looked surprised.

"Perhaps you could," he replied slowly. "I'll see you tomorrow when I call to see Alex. I'll let you know then."

Lindsay could not help noticing the difference in Alex when she arrived at work the next day. He swept into her little office whistling cheerfully.

"Hello, Lindsay. It's a grand morning. Did you enjoy your climb yesterday."

"How do you know I went climbing?"

"I don't actually know. Jan and I could only assume you were on Griffel. We saw his car parked by the side of the road. Was the view worth the effort?"

"Yes. It was perfect. Did you have a good day too?"

"We looked at the Abbey and then went back to the farm for tea. Sweetheart Abbey is a good place for people like us at this time of the year. Spring, and all that. I'm sure someone has said it better than I have. Unfortunately poetry was not my best subject at school."

" 'In the spring a young man's fancy
  Lightly turns to thoughts of love',"

suggested Lindsay with a grin. "Tennyson."

"That's it exactly," he answered seriously. "The feeling hasn't changed at all since his time. The cleverness lies in recognizing it these days when there are so many other distractions. I had no wish to come to work today. I wanted to play truant and go walking across the fields with Jan."

" 'When birds do sing, hey-ding-a-ding-ding,
Sweet lovers love the spring,' "

carolled Lindsay mockingly and added mischievously, "Shakespeare."

"Wonderful," said Alex admiringly. "You've caught my meaning precisely . . . perhaps because you're feeling like that yourself. Now who had that first appointment today?"

Pleased that Alex's good humor was restored and that Jan was the cause of his happiness, Lindsay felt light-hearted all day. The springlike feeling was infectious and toward the end of the afternoon she began to look forward to Scott's arrival.

When Alex brought Scott into the office to show his finger to Lindsay, he stayed to talk and to make arrangements with them about going to the sailing club's fitting-out dinner. From then on the conversation was concerned with the preparation of dinghies for the coming sailing season.

"I was looking at mine on Sunday. It's in fine shape," said Alex complacently. "Fiberglass is all that it's recommended to be. Hardly any upkeep."

"You're right," agreed Scott. "I'm beginning to wish I'd bought a fiberglass hull and finished it for Coll, but I had some old-fashioned notion that he should start his sailing career in a wooden boat."

"I prefer wooden boats," asserted Lindsay, who was finding it rather difficult to meet his calm gaze. She was afraid she might show how much his presence in the room excited her.

"Coming to help me tonight?" he asked. "I promise to feed you first."

Her heart was loud in her ears, but she managed to sound off-hand as she replied, "I'll come."

"But not before you've finished here, nurse," put in Alex sternly. "Spring fever has come between you and work enough as it is. She's been very absent-minded," he explained to Scott.

"Look who's talking!" retorted Lindsay. At last she looked up, directly at Scott. She pointed at Alex. "*He* mixed up his serums."

Scott smiled faintly, but made no comment. The intensity of his gaze unnerved her, and she glanced away and stammered, "Should I dress the finger?"

"If he's going to do woodwork, yes," commanded Alex. "Come back on Friday, Scott, and I'll have another look at it."

He went out of the room and left silence behind him. Silence continued as Lindsay dressed Scott's finger. As always when she had to be close to him her knees began to shake. This time she was clumsy and she hurt him accidentally. He jumped and withdrew his finger from her grasp.

"I'm sorry," she muttered desperately, and her knees shook more than ever as his pain became hers. His grin was rather twisted.

"At least that's made you look at me. I was beginning to think you had developed an aversion to my appearance," he said mockingly. "I saw Jan last night. She's feeling more hopeful."

"I'm glad that everything is sorting itself out at last."

"So am I. Soon you'll be gone, and then we'll all be back to normal. I'll see you later."

Soon you'll be gone. There had been neither regret nor gladness in his voice. He had merely been making a statement of fact. In a few weeks she would take off from Prestwick and would wing her way over the wide Atlantic, Toronto bound. She would go back to the brightness of the Canadian sun, back to the sudden swiftness of the Ontario spring, back to the hurry and bustle of a big hospital.

After supper in Scott's kitchen she went out with him to the workshed in the small yard at the back of the house. He showed her the 12-foot dinghy that he had built for Coll. She admired the design and workmanship and was told that he required help with attaching of fittings to the sidedecks, foredeck, and transom stern. Although she was good at anticipating which tool he wanted and was quick in handing it to him, Lindsay soon discovered that she needed patience too, because Scott was a perfectionist. Each fitting had to be placed in position many times before she was asked to hold it steady while he marked the places for the screw holes before drilling the holes in the wood. Then she had to hold each fitting while he screwed the screws in.

While he worked Scott said little. Lindsay, who was unable to stay quiet for long and feeling a great need to communicate with him, told him about the boat that Beth and Gregor owned and which they sailed on Lake Ontario. Then in answer to a specific question from Scott she went on to talk more generally about her life in Canada.

He was screwing the last fitting into place when she eventually dried up as she noticed he had been very quiet for a long time. In the harsh light cast by two unshaded lamps hanging from the ceiling of the shed, his face looked rather weary and drawn. She wondered what thoughts made him look like that and caused him to be silent. Did his finger hurt? Or had he had a difficult time at work today? She longed to ask, but guessed that her inquiry would be brushed aside. She sighed at the thought, and he glanced up quickly, his eyes alert.

"I expect you're longing for the day when you'll be able to return to Toronto," he said.

"It will be nice to see Beth and all my friends again," she admitted cautiously.

"Now that your mother is settled again there's nothing to keep you here."

Was that a question or a statement? She couldn't be sure. He had finished screwing and was leaning back against the work bench, watching her with narrowed eyes.

It should have been easy to agree, to say lightly, "No, I haven't anything to keep me here." But it wasn't. The words stuck in her throat, and she was unable to say anything.

"Possibly you find this place rather confining," he continued in the same dry statement-issuing voice. "You obviously enjoy your independence and freedom."

She had a feeling he was doing what he had accused his mother of doing; he was making statements in order to surprise her into telling him the truth. It was a tactic he had used on the island too when he had needled her into telling him about Maurice.

"Why should I find it confining?" she countered.

"Having to live with your mother must impose certain restrictions, exact certain commitments. And then, as you must have realized recently, the concept of marriage and of family is very strong here . . . and that could be limiting for you since you don't intend to marry."

Was he jibing her? She wanted to retort that she did want to marry and have a family. Then she realized that it would contradict her statement on the island, and it would admit that she had reversed her attitude. She had changed.

The discovery was disconcerting. She had thought she was so set in her attitude, in her determination to remain free from emotional entanglement; to have men friends, yes, but not to be involved with any of them.

Now she wanted to be involved with Scott. She wanted to know why he looked tired. She wanted to have the right to offer comfort and consolation to him. She wanted above all to share more experiences with him.

"It's half-past ten," he murmured, "and you haven't spoken for almost five minutes. Thanks for the help."

He moved away from the bench and walked to the door. He opened it, switched off the lights, and Lindsay walked past him into the moonlit yard.

"I could come again," she offered, turning toward him as he locked the door, "if you like."

They stood close together on the moon-dappled grass. Scott bent his head, and Lindsay did not retreat. This time when he kissed her she would not slap him, or pull away.

"Time you went home, Lindsay," he said gruffly and walked past her to the back door of the house.

CHAPTER TEN

It was foolish to feel disappointed because he had not kissed her, especially since she had asked him not to, thought Lindsay as she sat beside Scott in his car on the way home to Cairness. But foolish or not the ache was back and it was worse; a hollow desperate feeling that had almost reduced her to tears. No almost about it. It had reduced her to tears because the windscreen was blurred, and there was no rain.

Impatiently she brushed the tears from her cheeks with the back of her hand. A sidelong glance at Scott informed her that he was not noticing. He was watching the road, and she would never know what he was thinking about. It was time she took herself in hand. Soon she would be far away, and Scott would be a memory just as Maurice was, only . . . the tears welled again, drat them . . . only she had shared more with Scott than she had ever shared with Maurice. She would have liked to have gone on sharing.

He left her at Glendoon with a curt good night, reversing out into the road and driving away before she had opened the front door, reminding her of that night three months ago when he had taken her back to Merse Cottage.

She went to bed and spent a hopeless, restless night trying to find an excuse for returning to Toronto sooner than she had intended and succeeding only in talking herself out of every excuse for ever going back to Canada.

When the alarm clock sounded she dragged herself wretchedly out of the deep escapist sleep which she had eventually fallen into and went to the bathroom. Her reflection in the mirror told her that her usually shining eyes were dull, their expression unhappy, and that her hair was tangled and was lacking its normal luster.

"Whatever happened to *La Belle Dame Sans Merci*?" she muttered to herself. "I'm the one who is 'palely loitering' and who is 'so haggard and so woebegone.' Oh Scott, is this what you intended to do to me?"

In contrast to her own depressed spirits Mrs. Bell's were soaring. She was going on an outing to Edinburgh with the Women's Rural Institute. The next day she was going with Cameron Innes to Ayr to visit some more mutual friends.

"He and Moira called in last evening. They'd walked over from Barrcliffe. They had a guest with them . . . a Mr. Pearson. We had a pleasant talk, although I thought Moira was a little on edge. You know, Lindsay, I have more visitors here than I ever had at Merse Cottage."

"It's not so draughty and has central heating," suggested Lindsay.

"You can think that if you like, but I think it's to do with you being here, and your engagement to Scott. Everyone has taken such an interest. Must you go back to Toronto? Can't you get Beth to deal with the unfinished business you left behind?"

"No, I can't. Has the mail come yet? There should be a letter from her for me."

"Yes, there is. Before I forget, dear, I must tell you I've decided to invite all the McMorrows, Scott and Alex over on Sunday to tea . . . and cards later. Ann is so clever at reading the cards. It looks as if she was right about the double wedding, doesn't it?"

"Does it? Why?"

"Well, you and Scott and possibly Alex and Jan. Whoever would have thought it was going to turn out this way when you came home at Christmas?"

"Yes, whoever would have thought?" murmured Lindsay dryly.

"You *are* in a bad mood this morning, dear . . . and I can guess why. You went to bed too late last night. I'll have to have a word with Scott about it. Plenty of time for making love after you're married without burning the candle at both ends now. Heavens, is that the time? I must go and get ready, as I want you to drop me off at Jean Gammell's house on your way to work. We're all meeting there to get the bus."

She went out of the room. Lindsay closed her eyes and leaned her head on one hand. "If only you knew, Mother, I'm worse when he doesn't kiss me than when he does," she thought.

Opening her eyes with a sigh, she picked up Beth's letter. In her own last letter to her sister, Lindsay had explained in full the real reason for her engagement to Scott, and why she had to have a good excuse to return to Toronto at the end of April.

Beth's reply began uncompromisingly, going straight to the point.

Have you gone crazy? Stay where you are. If what you've written about Scott's behavior on the island is true he must be in love with you. For Scott Nicolson to spend a night on a deserted island alone with a girl and not make love to her is news indeed. Since when has he had such an over-developed sense of responsibility . . . since he met you, I'll bet. And think of the lamblike way in which he's been willing to go along with a mock engagement! You must be blind if you can't see the devious way in which his mind is working. But they say love is blind.

If you must have an escape route, think up your own. Greg and I are having nothing to do with it. We're looking forward to Mom's next letter when we hope she will announce the date of your wedding, and then we can start making arrangements to fly over.

Our best wishes and congratulations to you and Scott, dear Lin,

Love,
Beth.

"Dear sister Beth, it's you who are crazy. Love is blind, indeed! I'm not in love with Scott nor he with me. We're attracted to each other, it's true, particularly on the physical level, although we communicate on all levels," thought Lindsay as she replied mentally to the letter. It was strange how both Beth and her mother had changed their tune about Scott since they had realized that he might become one of the family.

Well, there was no help forthcoming from Beth, so she would have to think up her own excuse for returning to Toronto. She could always say that the hospital had given her leave only until she had settled her mother's affairs, and that the management expected her back on May first.

But Beth's comments stayed with her all day. Had it really been a sense of responsibility that had made Scott behave himself on the island when there had been ample opportunity for him to make love to her? Lindsay did not think so. He had still disliked her when they had been in the cottage, and now that she knew him better nothing would make her believe that he would make love to a person he disliked just for the sake of making love. She was convinced that he was not that sort of person.

The last appointment in the book that day was for Miss Innes. Smallpox vaccination. Moira must be thinking of traveling. When she was sure that Moira had arrived, Lindsay opened the door into the waiting room and went in. Moira was there, alone. She was dressed in a suit of soft blue wool, and her hair was smooth and glossy. When the door opened she looked up from the magazine she was reading. Her face was a smooth social mask that hid all true feeling.

"Hello," said Lindsay politely. "The doctor won't be long."

"I'm in no hurry," replied Moira coolly. "I'm going up to see Scott after I've had the vaccination. He won't be home until after six-thirty."

The answer jolted Lindsay badly. She had forgotten that Scott probably continued his friendship with Moira. Why shouldn't he? He had said he would explain his engagement to Moira so that she would understand. The realization that Moira knew all about it made Lindsay feel rather forlorn. Scott shared not only with herself but with Moira too, and he probably shared laughter with her about the peculiar situation in which he had been placed. Lindsay scowled at her thoughts and rearranged the waiting room chair with unnecessary clatter.

"Are you going abroad?" she asked in an effort to make conversation.

"Not until May. But I need re-vaccinating. I thought I'd get it done early because I was very ill the last time I had it done. We're thinking of going to Spain, but we haven't made the final arrangements yet."

Moira must be referring to her father when she referred to "we", Lindsay decided. But the next moment all her complacency was shattered.

"It's quite silly," said Moira with a coy little laugh. "We're having difficulty in booking a double room in the hotel where we want to stay."

Double room. May. Scott had said he would take his vacation in May. He had said he might renovate the cottage on the island. But Moira could have persuaded him to change his mind.

"I believe you're leaving us and returning to Toronto at the end of April," Moira was saying smoothly.

Leaving us. Scott must have told her when his "engagement" would be at an end, otherwise how could Moira know that she was leaving?

"I'm not sure. I might," Lindsay answered and had the satisfaction of seeing Moira look surprised. The door of the consulting room opened and the previous patient came out. Alex appeared and beckoned to Moira, who rose to her feet and followed him into his room.

It was almost eight o'clock when Lindsay finished work. Curiosity made her drive up Gower Street before she went home. The small black car that Moira drove was parked outside Scott's house.

There was not much pleasure to be derived from satisfying curiosity after all, thought Lindsay as she drove down the next street back to the main road. Moira was with Scott, and the knowledge was disturbing. She hoped she was not going to have another sleepless night.

At Glendoon she found her mother still in high spirits after her outing to Edinburgh.

"It was a delightful trip," she said enthusiastically. "I'll never tire of going around the Castle and Holyrood Palace. Do you remember the time we took you when you were a little girl? You refused to go into the room where Rizzio was murdered in front of Mary, Queen of Scots, because you said his ghost was there. Well, the place is just the same . . . with that strange, cold, clammy atmosphere. Lindsay, whatever is the matter with you? You're prowling around like Tiger does when he wants to go out, and I won't let him."

Lindsay laughed at her mother's comparison and sat down.

"I'm sorry I'm so restless, Mother. I've been trying to make up my mind . . . and now I think I have. I've decided to fly back to Toronto on Saturday. Beth can't do what I asked her to do, and . . . and I'm beginning to think that Scott and I aren't suited to each other after all."

"But you've only been engaged for three weeks," complained Mrs. Bell. Then her face, which had sagged into lines of distress, brightened again. "You've had a quarrel . . . last night. That's why you looked so dreary this morning . . . and he hasn't been to see you today. Now don't act rashly, dear. I know how you feel, but it will pass. Tomorrow you can see him and tell him about the teaparty I've planned for Sunday. It will give you an excuse to see him. I think you'll find he wants to make it up as much as you do."

"But, Mother—" remonstrated Lindsay.

"Try, dear, for my sake. I'll have such a difficult time explaining if you fly off to Toronto in a huff."

Lindsay bit her lower lip. Disentangling herself from this engagement to Scott was going to be more difficult than either he or she had thought. But she must do it. It was only fair to Scott and to Moira. While she stayed Scott felt he was under an obligation to stand by the bargain he had made with her; a bargain he must now be regretting. She would remove herself from the scene, and he and Moira would be free to continue their friendship. She was beginning to realize she had disrupted it from the time of the New Year's party. She would not tell Scott she was leaving, however. She would write from Toronto explaining why she had broken their mock engagement.

After all, she was only anticipating by a few weeks what would have happened anyway.

The biggest problem as usual was her mother. If only she could take her to Toronto too. Her mind leaped at the thought, and when she phoned the travel agents next morning she reserved two seats on the plane leaving Prestwick on Saturday for Montreal and Toronto. Confronted with a reservation, Mrs. Bell would have difficulty in refusing to go. She would worry about having to cancel her teaparty and about not having the right clothes, but Lindsay was sure she could overcome such objections. Then once her mother was away from Cairness it would be possible to tell her the truth.

As it was Wednesday, Lindsay was able to leave her work at five o'clock. Having made her decision she was eager to get home early and to start packing. It was raining, a slow steady drizzle, that was filling the gutters of the roadway with fast-flowing streams of water. She was glad she had the Mini in which to ride home, because that meant she would not have to put in time waiting for the bus.

As she left the surgery and closed the door behind her she caught sight of a gray car sliding to a stop across the street. Scott had come home early. It was too late to go back into the surgery, because he had seen her and was striding across the road toward her. She turned quickly and ran down the narrow side street where she always parked the Mini.

"Lindsay, wait, I want to talk to you!" he called after her, having no qualms about disturbing the people who lived in the street.

She ignored his shout and on reaching the car unlocked the door and got into the driving seat. She started the engine, released the handbrake and crashed into first gear just as his hand touched the handle of the nearside door. The car glided away. She changed gear rapidly and accelerated, sped down the road, turned left at the end, then left again in order to return to the main road. She glanced in the rear view mirror, but the gray car was still stationary. Apparently he had decided not to follow her.

Driving along at a steady 50, grateful for the first time since she had returned to the district for the new wide road, she tried to analyze her reasons for avoiding Scott. She had avoided him because she dared not be with him, because she could no longer duck the truth about herself. She was in love with him and had been in the process of falling in love with him ever since he had walked into Merse Cottage one snowy afternoon. He had walked in and love had walked in with him, unnoticed by her.

No wonder she had been so restless recently; no wonder her emotions had been erratic. She had succumbed to the deadly disease which she had thought she was immune to forever. And knowing that she loved him and guessing that her love was not returned, she could not stay, not even to keep the bargain they had made.

The drizzle was heavy, a dense gray rain reinforced by a sea mist. But Lindsay did not reduce speed. She wanted to put as many miles as possible between her and Scott. He might follow her, and if he did, she intended to be safely behind a locked door at Glendoon which she would refuse to open when he rang the doorbell.

She was so intent on her purpose that she did not glance in the rearview mirror until she was approaching the corner where Merse Cottage had once stood and where the road-making equipment was parked.

She looked in the mirror and saw the gray car creeping up on her like a stealthy cat. She put her foot on the accelerator just as the Mini passed over a greasy patch of road close to the marsh. The car skidded across the road and back again out of control straight onto the marsh, where it stopped at the edge of a deep creek. The wheels sank halfway into the soft mud, then touched the harder resistant layer beneath and stopped sinking. The car tilted forward toward the creek where water was already swirling as the tide came in.

Trembling with shock, Lindsay managed to open the door of the little car. The tilt caused the door to swing open sharply, and she was able to step out. She sank at once into mud, almost up to her knees.

"Ooh!" she cried as the cold slippery stuff seeped through her shoes and stockings. "Help!"

She glanced around wildly. With a mixture of dismay and relief, she saw Scott making his way carefully across the marsh in her direction. When he reached the edge of firm land he called out, "Walk toward me!"

"How can I? I'll only sink again," she wailed.

"Better than standing here all night!" he yelled back tauntingly. Once, years ago, he had waded into the mud to rescue her, but apparently his days of knight-errantry were over. Reviling him under her breath for being inconsiderate and ungentlemanly, she managed with great effort to pull one leg out of the sucking mud. Her foot, she noticed miserably, was without its shoe.

The effort unbalanced her, and she had to put her foot down quickly. As a result she fell over.

"Try again," came the hateful taunting voice. "It isn't far."

She was on her hands and knees, plastered with mud. There didn't seem much point in standing up, so on all fours she struggled to the edge of the marsh where he was waiting. He bent, put his hands under her armpits, and hauled her to her feet.

Muddy from head to foot and dizzy with shock, she leaned gratefully against him.

"I was going to punish you for running away from me when I wanted to talk to you," he said gently, "but now there's no need."

He lifted her in his arms and carried her to his car. Lindsay was dimly aware of a passing car stopping and the driver speaking to Scott. It was Commander Crosbie. What a tale he would have to tell the whole of Cairness, thought Lindsay.

Scott put her in the front seat of the car, got into the driver's seat, and drove to Glendoon.

"Mother is out," mumbled Lindsay as they stopped in the driveway.

"Perhaps it's just as well she is," replied Scott dryly. "Have you a front door key?"

"No. It's in the Mini. Oh, and I've left my purse too."

"I haven't a key either. I'll get in through a window at the back." He walked around the house. Lindsay sat numbly waiting for him to reappear at the front door. In a short while it opened, and he came out of the house and opened the car door for her.

"Think you can walk?" he asked.

"I'll try, but I feel dizzy."

She swung her legs out, stood up, and swayed. Scott put an arm around her.

"Come on, Lindsay, you're tougher than that," he rallied her.

"I'm not tough at all," she cried and burst into tears. She was still sobbing when they reached the hall. He pushed her down onto the hall chair, shut the front door, knelt before her, and began to peel off her muddy stockings.

"We should have used the entrance for soaked sailors," sobbed Lindsay.

He looked up and smiled at her.

"I suppose we should. Stand up now, and take off that coat and skirt. Then you can go upstairs, have a bath, and change while I make some tea."

Still feeling slightly weak, Lindsay was warmer and not so weepy when she went downstairs again. She had bathed and had changed into gray, green and white checked pants, a white round-necked sweater, and had tied her hair into a ponytail.

Scott was sitting on a stool at the breakfast counter in the kitchen reading the advertisement section of the local newspaper. The teapot and cups and saucers were set out on the formica top of the counter. Lindsay sat on another stool opposite to him, and he looked up. When he saw her he blinked in surprise.

"You look as if you were 15 instead of 23 with your hair like that," he observed. "Any damage?"

"Bruised ribs only. The steering wheel, I suppose," she answered briefly, watching him pour tea.

He pushed her cup across and passed the sugar. Then he took a pencil out of the inside of his jacket pocket and circled something in the paper.

"At last," he murmured. "Ness Farm is up for sale."

Lindsay knew that Ness Farm covered all the land on the long snout that stretched out into the sea beyond Cairness, and that it had always been considered one of the best farms in the district.

"Are you interested in it?" she asked.

"I'm going to buy it. I've been waiting for it to come on the market."

"But why? Not for building purposes, surely. Oh Scott, you couldn't!" she exclaimed anxiously.

He raised his eyebrows slightly.

"And you're so concerned," he commented. "I thought you wouldn't care one way or the other about what happened here."

"Of course I care. I'd hate to see anywhere around this district spoiled. Your roads are bad enough."

"You can say that after you skidded on that bad bend?" he rebuked her. "No, I won't build. I shall farm it. I've been thinking for some time that I would like to farm. It's just been a case of waiting for the right one to be available. My grandmother left me a considerable sum of money that I've been saving for such a purpose."

"But what about your job as a road surveyor?" asked Lindsay. At the back of her mind she was thinking that Moira would prefer to be the wife of a well-to-do farmer, especially if the farm was big enough and carried the prestige in the county that Ness Farm did.

"I'll resign from that. That's no problem," he replied carelessly and continued to read the paper.

He was more interested in his plans for the future than he was in her bruised ribs, thought Lindsay miserably.

"What happened at the corner?" she asked. "What did I do wrong?"

"You accelerated at a bad place. You were already going too fast for the state of the road."

"Oh yes, I remember. It was because I saw you. You gave me a fright. Why did you follow me?"

He folded the paper deliberately slowly.

"I wanted to talk to you," he said coldly. "Why have you decided to fly to Toronto on Staurday?"

"H . . . how do you know?" she exclaimed. "I haven't told anyone yet. I only made the reservations this morning."

His eyes narrowed, and his mouth tightened.

"Then you've decided to go?"

"You didn't know!" she whispered, realizing he had tricked her into telling him.

"No, I didn't know," he admitted. "I only knew you were thinking about it. Your mother phoned my mother about it this morning, and my mother phoned me. Why are you in such a hurry to leave? Can't you wait until the end of April?"

Lindsay looked down at the newspaper. The print blurred as the desire to weep again overcame her.

"I thought that by going away I would release you from that stupid bargain we made," she muttered. "After talking to Moira yesterday I began to see what a nuisance it is to you, so I decided to leave sooner."

"Without telling me?" The question seemed to crackle about her ears like a whiplash.

"Yes."

"Why? Surely as a party to the bargain I should be told of your intention?"

His calm was shattered. He was angry, more furious than he had been when the boat had drifted away.

"Yes," she quavered.

"And you persuaded yourself that you were acting in my interest when actually you were acting in your own," he said scathingly. "You found you couldn't keep the bargain because the idea of being engaged to me . . . even on a temporary basis was abhorrent to you . . . you dislike me so much."

"That's not true. I don't dislike you. I would have kept the bargain, but Moira said she was going away on holiday in May and that you'd had difficulty in booking a double room in the hotel where you wanted to stay in Spain, so I knew she wasn't going away with her father."

Puzzlement chased the anger from his face.

"She said *I* was having difficulty? Did she mention my name?" he asked.

"No, but she kept talking about 'we.' I knew she wouldn't want a double room to share with her father, and she was going to see you. I knew you were very good friends before . . . before I. . . ."

Now he was laughing at her. Not out loud, but she knew he was laughing because his hand was in front of his mouth, and above it his eyes were bright with mirth. It was the last straw.

"Oh, stop laughing! You're always laughing at me. I expect you've laughed at me with Moira. Go away. You've found out what you wanted to know. I'm flying to Toronto on Saturday, and our engagement is over!"

She leaped to her feet and ran out of the room, up the stairs to her bedroom. She slammed the door shut and leaned against it, hands to her cheeks that were wet with tears. When the tumultuous beating of her heart had subsided a little she went over to the window and looked out. The day was crying too. Raindrops glittered on the roof of Scott's car that was still parked in the driveway. Globules of water balanced delicately on the thick, dark green leaves of the laurel bushes in the shrubbery before they slid off to the dark brown earth. Beyond the yard wall the brown river was swelling in size as the tide continued to swirl upstream.

Drip, drip, drip. Water was dripping everywhere. Tears gathered in her eyes and slid down her cheeks as she waited for Scott to appear on his way to the car.

Five minutes passed. He did not appear. What was he doing? Going around the house perhaps making sure that it was in good order, and that his tenants were looking after it properly? If she remembered the unscrupulous side of his character she could pretend she did not like him. It was easier that way. She sniffed, dried her cheeks, and sat down on the bed to wait until he had gone.

The handle of the door rattled. She gazed at it in disbelief as it turned and the door opened. Scott walked in without being asked.

"Have you recovered yet?" he asked smoothly.

"Go away!"

"No. I can't go until I've sorted out this business of Moira going to Spain with me. Moira isn't going anywhere with me, and I've never discussed you with her . . . except to tell her I was engaged to you when she doubted the truth of your story."

"But she was going to see you. Her car was still outside your house when I went home at eight o'clock."

This time he did not try to hide his amusement. He laughed openly.

"Och, Lindsay, you should have come to the house. You'd have found me all alone, struggling with the dinghy, wishing you were there to help me, wishing I'd had the courage to accept the offer to come again which you'd made the night before."

The edge of the bed sank downwards as he sat beside her.

"Why didn't you accept?" she asked.

"I was afraid to be near you, to be with you too often. After Moira had called in to tell me that she and Bill Pearson have decided to get married in May, she went on to visit a friend of hers who lives next door. Do you still want me to release you from that stupid bargain? If you do there'll be no Moira to help me over that bad patch I'm bound to hit when you jilt me."

Lorna had moved on and left him. Could she do the same? The strange tumult of noise was in her ears again. She turned and found him close to her. She leaned toward him and their mouths touched, gently at first, and then with more seeking, passionate intensity.

"I can see I've been very foolish," said Lindsay breathlessly when they had finished kissing. "I don't know what's been the matter with me."

Scott laughed outright again, then pulled her into his arms.

"If you don't know how do you expect me to know? Och, it's your foolishness that has given me hope, that has made me realize eventually that you're no hard-hearted calculating woman, but a silly, stubborn, wholly lovable girl. I'm assuming that your recent demonstration of affection means that your answer to my question is no, and that you're prepared to keep the bargain until the end of April as we arranged."

All her hopes came clattering down about her. The

ache started again, the terrible ache that grew worse with every meeting with Scott.

"Only until the end of April?" she whispered.

"We can't get married much sooner than that . . . or aren't you sure yet? Would you prefer to continue the engagement a little longer? Yes, perhaps we should do that. I'd forgotten your aversion to marriage." Lindsay cried and hiccupped all at once.

"Whatever is the matter now?" demanded Scott.

"I thought you . . . I didn't know that . . . Scott, do you love me?" she gasped.

"I wouldn't want to marry you if I didn't, would I? My biggest problem has been trying to find out if you love me. It's very difficult when a girl won't let you kiss her. But I think I know now."

"But you seemed to dislike me so much. . . ."

"Of course I disliked you. Just when I'd recovered from one emotional involvement and had decided to keep my freedom, you came back. I was attracted at once, and what was more infuriating, so was Alex, to such an extent that he ignored Jan again. Then on the island I found that I didn't merely want you . . . I found I cared when you were worried. I wanted to protect you, and I wasn't joking when I suggested that we should become engaged to be married. I thought that an old-fashioned engagement had its uses; that it would be a good way to find out whether I love you enough to want to live with you for the rest of my life. When your mother jumped the gun and began to tell the whole parish we were engaged, I was ready to fall in with her plan."

"But if you thought that you loved me, why didn't you make love to me on the island?"

"I've told you. I found I cared too much, and I didn't want to hurt you. Believe me, it wasn't easy. Why do you think I stayed out in the wind and the rain tending a fire that wouldn't burn? It was to get too dog-tired to do anything but sleep."

Beth had been right after all, thought Lindsay happily. Oh heavens! The end of April! Would Beth and Gregor be able to come to a wedding then?

"Would you mind if we delayed the wedding for two

weeks until the second week in May? I'd like Beth to be here," she said.

Scott groaned facetiously, "I'd forgotten I'd have to have her as a sister-in-law!"

Lindsay put a finger on his mouth and scolded gently, "Shush . . . that's prejudice!"

He bit her finger and was about to kiss her again when they both heard the sound of the front door opening followed by the sound of Mrs. Bell's high light voice and Cameron Innes's deeper tones.

"They must be somewhere in the house," said Mrs. Bell, her voice floating up the stairs quite clearly. "Lindsay, where are you? I'm home."

"What will they think?" Lindsay asked Scott.

"They'll think we must be married soon at all costs," whispered Scott flippantly and began to kiss her again.

"Lindsay! Are you upstairs?" called Mrs. Bell. "Come down, dear. I've some news for you . . . about Moira."

Lindsay broke away from Scott and straightened her sweater. She stood up and walked out onto the landing and called down, "Coming, Mother! Scott's here. He's been looking at the crack in the bedroom ceiling."

"Prevaricator!" murmured Scott in her ear as they walked to the top of the stairs. They walked down one behind the other. Mrs. Bell smiled up at them.

"There, what did I tell you, Lindsay? I knew Scott would come to make it up with you. May is such a lovely month for weddings, don't you think, Cameron?"

"Certainly seems popular with the young people this year," agreed Mr. Innes as he followed her into the living room.

"You can't escape now," observed Scott to Lindsay as they reached the hallway. "Your mother has our wedding all arranged for May—in front of a witness too."

"I don't want to escape any more," replied Lindsay, smiling up at him.

He smiled back and put his arm round her protectingly and said, "I'm glad to hear it, because you wouldn't get far if you tried. Hunting is something that I do rather well."

Lindsay could not help challenging him.

"You mean you'd leave your beloved Galloway to follow me?"

His eyes darkened, and his arm tightened around her.

"I'd even do that," he answered, and despite the lightness of his voice Lindsay knew he was perfectly serious. She felt suddenly giddy with happiness. He loved her more than he had loved Lorna.

"And now," he was saying, "there's the small problem of the Mini in the mud. I think it would be better if I tell your mother. She's sure to think I was responsible anyway!"

BRIGHT WILDERNESS

BRIGHT WILDERNESS

Gwen Westwood

CRAIG

The letter expressly stated that a *man* was needed to preserve Aunt Nan's South African farm after her husband's death.

With only a city girl's meager knowledge of farming but with a fierce desire to help her aunt maintain the farm, Bronwen flew from London. She found Lewis Galbraith, author of the letter and Aunt Nan's arrogant neighbor, far too free with his advice urging her aunt to sell the farm—preferably to himself.

Bronwen resented Lewis. "I think you are high-handed, domineering and quite impossible," she told him. "You seem to think you can make anybody do anything."

Unfortunately, her heart didn't quite follow the dictates of her head!

CHAPTER ONE

There was a wonderful view from the top of the kopje, thought Bronwen, but she had not had time to notice it before. Their neighbor's farmlands stretched for miles over grassy country, golden now in the early morning light. Groups of low thorn trees with their deep tap roots were the only trees that could successfully weather the long periods of drought in this frequently rain-starved part of Southern Africa.

With hands bruised from her attempts at replacing the rough stones, she sat with her back against the wall that had given her so much trouble and watched the two servants still struggling to fill the gap.

"Sit down," she advised them, handing them each one of her meat sandwiches.

They smiled shyly, accepting the food with two hands cupped and a gracious gesture of the head, then retired to a place a few yards away in the grass. Bronwen's fair curls clung damply to her forehead. Gratefully she felt a small cool breeze blowing at the collar of her shabby open-necked shirt. She was glad she had put on her blue shorts even if Nan did say that fall was here already.

When she had picked a couple of late roses this morning for Nan's breakfast tray, there had been a sparkling chill, like iced champagne, in the air, and the sun had glittered upon the huge spiders' webs hanging from the silver thorns of the acacia trees. But now the sun was hotter than she had ever known it in London. Not that she had had to mend stone walls in London, she pondered ruefully. The life she had led for the last three months was a far cry from her usual secretarial work.

Nan was Bronwen's mother's sister. When her vital, impetuous husband had died tragically and suddenly from a heart attack, Mrs. Hughes had urged her sister to come to England for a long rest.

"Goodness knows how she will run this farm on her own," she had said to Bronwen. "It's not, mind you, as if they were well set up there, and no wonder, for that Irish husband of Nan's was always thinking up some crazy scheme, indeed. This time it was oil. He wasn't interested, you understand, in running the farm as a farm. No, he must go pouring the money he had into boring for oil, when a school child could tell you from his geography lessons that there's little oil in that part of Africa."

"But, Mom, she seems to have loved him very dearly," said Bronwen, thinking of the heartbroken letter that she had been allowed to read.

"She did indeed. More's the pity. She's a beautiful, peaceful, vague creature. Not a bit like me," added Bron's practical, bustling little mother. "She's tall and slender . . . elegant, fine bones. She's never happier than when she's drawing flowers, or studies of animals and birds. She's very good at that, mind. But never a thought has she for practical things. Followed her husband all over the world, she did, saying yes to all his wildcat schemes for making a fortune."

"Do you think she will come to us for a holiday?"

"I have my doubts. She says she can't leave the farm. I should have thought she could employ a manager for a while."

"Perhaps she can't afford to pay one."

"Very likely," sighed Mrs. Hughes.

While they were still awaiting a reply from Nan, they were surprised to receive a letter with the South African postmark, but not in Nan's writing.

"There is extravagance to use such heavy paper for the air mail," said Mrs. Hughes, becoming more Welsh in her speech as she did when anything excited her in spite of all the years she had spent living in London. "Beautiful, it is, though. Who can be writing to us now? I hope there's nothing wrong."

"Lion's Rest," Bronwen read the address that was embossed in Gothic lettering upon the letterhead. The writing was in clear, black, thick strokes, looking very emphatic against its background of heavy, gray paper.

Dear Mrs. Hughes,

I am your sister's nearest neighbor and have

decided I must write to you, because, although hitherto I have tried to help her, I will be absent in South America for the next three months.

Last week Nan broke her leg while upon a rather ill-advised expedition to photograph Bushman paintings upon a krantz in the district. From all points of view, my own included, it would be best if she were to give up the farm, but like most women, she will not listen to reason. Is it possible that you could send some *male* relative here to guide her to a decision?

Yours faithfully,
Lewis Galbraith

"What an abrupt letter. He certainly doesn't sound as if he has much opinion of women!" exclaimed Bronwen. "Just look at the way has has emphasized the word 'male.'"

There were three thick strokes under the qualifying word.

"But kind he is to be concerned about Nan," murmured Mrs. Hughes, who liked to find the best qualities in people.

"I wonder. Reading between the lines, it sounds as if he wants to buy the farm for himself."

"Don't be so suspicious, Bron," chided Mrs. Hughes. "You know nothing about the man. Working in that business office makes you too eager to suspect double motives."

Bronwen smiled at her mother's rebuke. The kindly accountant she worked for could hardly be classed as a business tycoon.

"Anyhow, Mr. Lewis Galbraith sounds unbearably self-righteous, and his writing is far too sure of itself."

Mrs. Hughes laughed. "He's probably a tiny little man who disguises a meek personality with strong black writing and tough handshakes. Maybe you will find out for yourself what he is like, if you stay long enough."

"You mean. . . ."

"I can't leave your father, and he would not be able to go. I think you must go and see what you can do to help

Nan, since we haven't any male relative who is free, three stroked or otherwise."

And so, three months later, here she was sitting on top of a hill trying to supervise the repair of a stone wall, instead of spending her days typing in a small, dark office.

Certainly the last months had not been easy. Nan, frail and elegant in a wheel chair, had been pathetically grateful to see her and had trustingly turned over all the affairs of the farm to her young niece.

Worn out by her hectic, fevered existence with her Irish husband, shattered to the heart by his sudden death, and now temporarily confined to a wheel chair by the accident she had suffered, she did not seem to realize the true position of the farm. Her husband had poured money away upon the costly drilling for oil and had neglected the more practical aspects of farm life. During the last months Nan had tried to economize by cutting down upon the number of farm workers, and consequently she had been left with one aged maid, who, while devoted to her, tyrannized over her gentle mistress and refused to take orders from anyone else.

There were no grown African men to help. The labor force consisted of a few *quedines*, young boys not yet initiated into manhood. All those who were grown up found it more profitable to go to a recruiting office and join the Bombella train, which took them to Johannesburg, the city of gold. In their opinion, a spell in the mines proved their manhood.

Nan's attorney spoke seriously to Bronwen. "It would be better if your aunt were to sell the farm now, even if she doesn't make much profit. The way it is going, she will end in bankruptcy."

But there was a stubborn streak in Nan's gentle make-up.

"Darling Bronwen, you are being an angel," she protested gratefully. "But selling the farm is not the way I see my future life. When this wretched leg of mine is properly better, we will plan together how we can improve the farm. I don't want to give it up and start wandering again. I've had so much of that. Besides it was my last home with Patrick, and I love it here. What could I do, stuck in a city? I've grown so fond of this country—dry, strange, bright wilderness that it is."

Looking down into their neighbor's valley, Bronwen thought sympathetically of Nan's passion for this hot, beautiful land with its very atmosphere so different from the soft, pearly air of a Northern climate. Across the valley, mountains were clear cut, deep purple in the crystalline blue sky; but on the surrounding slopes near at hand, the queer-shaped rock outcrops were a dusty rose. No green growth disturbed the harmony of dry, golden grass sweeping downward into the valley, but the sheep, gray as old lichen, still seemed to be able to find nourishment from small plants amongst the rock outcrops.

The neighboring farm, Lion's Rest, lay in the deep shadow of early morning, its white buildings outlined, beautiful and precise as a careful etching. From the white gables, fantail pigeons rose up to grasp the first rays of the sun. In the clear air, Bronwen heard the harsh cry of a peacock echoing from the flagged terrace.

This gracious house, built by his ancestors, seemed a strange setting for such a man, for, by all accounts, Lewis Galbraith had a character in keeping with the strong strokes of his handwriting. He was coming home, accompanied by his 17-year-old ward, Sarah, any day now, from his trip to South America. Lately Bronwen had become quite tired of hearing about this paragon who lived on the next farm.

It seemed that the whole valley, the farmers, the market gardeners, and the small storekeepers in the little sunlit town, with its one main street, could talk of nothing else.

"I understand he's bringing a bull home with him that is worth twenty thousand rand," an acquaintance of Bronwen's informed her when they met in the Post Office. "And a Palomino filly too."

"You haven't met him yet, have you, Miss Hughes?" asked the postmistress, a spinster who was old enough to learn to restrain that silly giggle, thought Bronwen, a little crossly.

"He's so tall, so good-looking," went on the post-mistress. "There have been lots of women quite crazy about him, but he doesn't seem to need a wife yet."

"Gets his fun elsewhere, I dare say," said Mrs. Tremayne, an acidulated widow who spent much of her time serving on local committees.

"Well," said Miss Dudley the postmistress, charitably, "you can't blame a man for having a bit of a flutter when he's so attractive. But it's my belief he's waiting for Miss Sarah to grow up. Though I'm not sure that would be a good idea, for when it comes to recklessness, they are two of a kind."

"Sarah's a sweet child underneath all the brashness," said the Rector's wife who had entered just in time to hear the end of the conversation.

The other women, looking a little disappointed that their gossip would now have to be curtailed, hastened to agree.

"It was just as well Mr. Galbraith took her away for a while. She was seeing too much of that young Watson. I think that's why they went away for three months. But mark my words, he'll end by marrying her himself," said Miss Dudley.

"Oh come, Milly, she is barely 17, and he must be all of 36."

"Well, we'll see. Maybe he has met someone in South America. I understand the girls there are beautiful and rich."

"I hear nothing but talk of Lewis Galbraith and his ward, Sarah," grumbled Bronwen when she returned to Nan. "I hate the sound of the man before I have even met him. The way people talk anyone would think he was the uncrowned king of the district."

"Well, in a way, I suppose he is," laughed Nan, carefully scrutinizing a flame-colored cactus flower she was painting upon a board fixed across her wheel chair. "His family came to settle here when it was still a wilderness, and the Africans were still raiding the pioneers' farms. He has a very distinctive personality. Anyone a little larger than life is bound to rouse gossip in a small community like ours. I like him. Come to think of it, I've never met any woman who doesn't. He can be courageous and careful, reckless and discreet, cruel and kind . . . but underneath all his flamboyance, he's an absolute honey."

Quietly Bronwen decided that she would make up her own mind about Lewis Galbraith when she met this peerless wonder.

"It's odd," she pondered, "how offputting it is when you hear a person overpraised. But in any case, Nan and I lead a very quiet life, and he is obviously an important personage around here. He won't have much time for two lone women, who are struggling to make a go of a small farm."

"How is it that he has a ward?" she asked, remembering the rest of the gossip.

"Sarah? She's the daughter of a friend of his who was his senior by a few years. He and his wife were killed while flying their small plane. Lewis found he had been made ward to a 10-year-old girl. I suppose they had named him as executor of their estate never really envisaging they would die together."

"Sarah has been very spoiled in some ways, but brought up in a Spartan way in others. She has masses of long, bright, silky, red hair and a temperament that goes with it. She isn't over lady-like—no finishing school manners for young Sarah. She is often brusque and rude, and she likes having her own way, but I must confess I find something attractive about her."

"Why did he take her to South America? Has she left school?"

"She had a succession of governesses, but I'm afraid she proved a bit too tough for most of them. She seems to have scratched up a certain amount of education. Of course she has traveled extensively with Lewis. She is a superb horsewoman and just lives for horses."

"In her own way she adores Lewis. Lately, however, she and Lewis have been at loggerheads over a young boy she showed an interest in. He was a bit of a ne'er-do-well from a bad family. Or so Lewis thought. Sarah has a highly developed protective instinct, and the young man seemed to appeal to this.

"Lewis, of course, thinks no one is good enough for her, and in any case she is scarcely grown up. He whisked her away as soon as he scented trouble and set the young man up in some job a few 100 miles away, somewhere along the coast."

"He sounds very domineering. They implied at the Post Office that he was interested in Sarah himself."

Nan looked startled and thoughtful at the same time.

"Really! Such a thing has never entered my mind. People will say anything to create a sensation."

She applied herself assiduously to her painting, and Bronwen felt slightly rebuked for listening to gossip.

Nan's flock of eland antelope, the cause of their trouble with the stone boundary wall, were grazing some way below on Lion's Rest ground. They had no right to be there, of course.

"I had better try to drive them back," Bronwen thought.

She knew it was hopeless to ask the *quedines* to do it on their own. They were used to driving cattle, but such methods would not suffice with the gentle, highly strung eland. This herd of large antelopes was another relic of Patrick O'Hara's unusual schemes. The customary livestock upon a farm, he theorized, needed too much care and attention. But if one stocked one's grazing lands with a wild animal, gentle enough to be domesticated, yet tough enough to withstand the rigors of the climate and the chances of disease, it could be profitably sold for meat.

But the whole point of the experiment had been lost because Nan simply could not bear to send any of the beautiful creatures to the butcher. One could hardly blame her, thought Bronwen, as she tentatively approached the trespassing animals. Although they were very heavy, they were far from clumsy. With their cream and taupe hides gleaming in the sunlight, their gracefully twisted horns and noble stance, they seemed like creatures out of a book of fairy tales.

"I will have to get them back before we mend the wall any farther," thought Bronwen and she summoned Kim, the old sheepdog, who, at her signal, ran around the herd and flattened himself in the golden grass, squirming along toward them like a seasoned commando raider. Meanwhile Bronwen walked quietly toward them trying to drive them to the gap without startling them into a stampede.

They were a few yards away from the broken wall when they suddenly lifted their heads and maddeningly ran down the slope, then stood a few hundred yards away, gazing at Bronwen with mild curiosity but losing all the ground she had so painstakingly gained.

She looked around to find out what had startled the shy animals and saw a chestnut horse with a white blaze galloping surefootedly up the hillside track from the direction of the farmhouse. From this distance man and animal looked like one creature; a centaur in keeping with the fabulous appearance of the eland. As they drew nearer, Bronwen saw the man's close-cropped hair was of the same gleaming chestnut as the horse. He had the square-cut features, the firm, broad jawline that Bronwen had come to think of as typically South African.

His likeness to a mythical figure of ancient Greece was increased by the fact that above a pair of dark, denim jeans, the expanse of broad shoulder and deep chest gleamed a uniform golden brown. The ferocity of the hawklike nose was softened by a pair of blue eyes, startlingly vivid.

When he reined his horse and dropped to the ground beside Bronwen, he still towered head and shoulders above her. She had never before found herself near to anyone so overwhelmingly masculine. Her usual secure self-confidence was badly shaken.

"Having trouble with the eland?" he asked abruptly.

"I was managing them quite well until you disturbed them," snapped Bronwen and then felt aghast at her own discourtesy. But this disconcerting man seemed to have a most devastating effect upon her normally civilized behavior.

"You need a few more helpers," he said. "You can't

possibly manage all these animals with just a couple of piccanins."

He put his fingers to his mouth and let forth an ear-shaking deep whistle that had the effect of summoning half a dozen farm workers, who seemed literally to have sprung out of the earth below them.

"I suppose you are Nan O'Hara's niece," he said. "I'm Lewis Galbraith, as I expect you know."

Bronwen's attempt at a polite response to this abrupt introduction was drowned by his next words.

"It's absurd to keep on this herd."

He watched his minions driving the huge animals through the gap in the wall.

"I'm sure it can't be worthwhile. What does the butcher pay for them?"

Bronwen looked at the soft dun-coloured flanks of the great beasts. "I suppose to a man like him," she thought, "they are just so many thousands of pounds' weight of venison."

She was furious with herself for blushing as she stammered, trying to meet the hard, blue eyes with an equally determined look, "I don't know—that is—Nan won't sell them."

"Won't sell them? But what's the point in keeping them then? They are using up the grazing that your cattle need. Incidentally you will be short of grazing in a couple of months' time. Have you planted your winter feed yet?"

"We will soon," said Bronwen hastily. She dared not admit that Nan had never thought of it. Dear Nan; if she was painting nature studies she was happy. Her mind did not embrace things like winter feed. And she herself was still groping hazily to grasp the elementary facts of farming in this dry countryside.

"You are from London, aren't you?" said Lewis, frowning. "I don't suppose you know much about conditions in this country. I'd better come to see you soon to discuss your future program."

Bronwen looked at him doubtfully. How exasperating it was that she would have to rely on this arrogant man's advice. But her own ignorance was such that for Nan's sake she could hardly refuse. She watched, half-relieved, half-resentful, as he instructed the Africans to put back the stones that the eland had displaced. She and the two youths had struggled for over an hour to move the heavy natural rocks, but, with this additional labor force of strong grown-up men, it was finished in a very short while.

"Did you really believe you could complete this job with a couple of youths?" asked Lewis.

"I—I'm quite strong," Bronwen replied. He turned to inspect her, his blue eyes surprised. For the first time he seemed to take in her appearance; the tangled mop of fair curls, her face streaked with dirty marks, the old shirt that could not disguise the gentle curves of her breasts, the delicate column of her throat, and the strong golden legs revealed beneath the dusty, creased shorts.

"You don't mean to say you were lifting those stones yourself?" he demanded.

She turned away, very conscious of his analytical gaze.

"They would have taken all day," she said softly. "I had to give some help. We have so little labor."

"Absurd!" he snapped. "A woman can't do an artisans work in a climate like this one. I'll speak to Nan."

"Please don't," she pleaded. "Nan doesn't know how difficult everything is."

She was alarmed to feel that her eyes were filled with tears. For three months she had labored and no one had even realized how strange and difficult the farm life was to her. Nan lived in a dream. Bronwen had been too busy, too isolated to become intimate with their far-flung neighbors.

Without warning he seized her hands in his own large ones. His were surprisingly long and slender for such an outdoor type of person, she thought, cool and comforting to her bruised fingers.

"Just look at you," he chided, smiling at her as if she were a small, disobedient child. He took the drinking flask from his horse's saddle and bathed her poor, battered hands with cool water, taking no notice of her embarrassed protests.

"There, that's better," he said, patting them gently with a large, spotless handkerchief.

The wall was completed now, the eland peacefully grazing upon the farther side.

"What you really need here is a jackal-proofed fence," said Lewis.

"But Nan . . . we both like this wall. It's much more picturesque than a diamond-meshed fence."

Lewis laughed. "Picturesque—a wall that breaks down at the slightest puff of wind? You have to be practical to be a farmer these days. I'll come to see you soon, and we can discuss your problems," he added. "Tell Nan not to hesitate to ask for help. My farmhands are not overworked. I can easily spare them."

Bronwen thanked him a bit reluctantly, knowing that Nan, vague as she was, was still too proud to accept help from her rich neighbor.

Without warning, he seized her by the waist and swung her over the wall. Then jumping astride the chestnut horse, with a wave of his arm, he was away down the hill.

She watched him go, feeling deeply disturbed. The touch of his hands upon her body was still there.

"Don't be ridiculous, Bronwen," she admonished herself. "You're not a teenager to be carried away by any physically attractive man. It's absurd. He knows that women like him. He's far too handsome, far too sure of himself. Well, in short, he isn't your type at all, and you know it. So don't forget it."

CHAPTER TWO

Sunday was a day of comparative rest for Bronwen. At least it usually started off well enough, but the afternoon was often disastrous because the youths whose duty it was to come back for milking often conveniently forgot about their duties, and the brunt of the tasks fell upon Bronwen. So by Sunday evening, she fell into bed as exhausted as she was upon every other day of the week.

But she would not think about the evening yet, she decided, as she dressed herself for the morning church service. After days of wearing shorts and jeans, she felt feminine and pretty in last year's mist-blue jersey suit and the small beret that matched her eyes.

"How nice you look," commented Nan. She was coming too, for at last she could manage to hobble around with the aid of a stick, and Bronwen would drive the station wagon into the small town. "You always look so fragrant, clean, and healthy."

"You make me sound like an advertisement for soap. I'd rather look beautiful like you," protested Bronwen.

Even at 40, Nan had an effortless elegance that was a matter of fine bones and did not depend upon the clothes she wore.

"It's so good to be out and about again," said Nan, "even if I am a bit dotty and carry a cane. It was hardly summer when I had my accident and now, look, there down by the river, you can see it's fall."

The leaves fell like gold sovereigns from the tall poplars, and the willow trees tossed their branches that were lemon yellow in the light wind.

"It's so dry here," said Nan. "The leaves fall almost as soon as they have turned in color. A few people grow Canadian maple in the town. I must get a branch to paint while they have their full color."

In the gardens on the outskirts of the little town, there were bushes of bright yellow blossom.

"Cassia," said Nan. "But if we get an early frost it nips the blossom in this part of the world."

"I can't imagine frost here," said Bronwen. "It seems as if this gorgeous sunshine must last forever."

"So it does," said Nan. "We have sunshine all through the winter, beautiful sparkling days; but the moment the sun goes down you feel you've been plunged into a fridge. That's when you need a fireplace. The nights are very cold, and sometimes we have snow, usually unexpected and sometimes disastrous to the sheep."

The small church was not old by English standards. It had stood for scarcely 100 years, but in this new country, it had achieved an air of timelessness with its simple design of hewn gray stones and the blue slate roof that had replaced the original thatch. The deep windowsills each had a vase of yellow and bronze chrysanthemums interspread with orange berries of cotoneaster. Shining brass tablets commemorated early settlers, or those who had fallen in different wars. Some of the bright, stained glass windows portrayed scenes from early settlers' history.

A white-haired Verger greeted them warmly, helping Nan to sit comfortably near the back of the church, so that she would not have to walk far. It was good, thought Bronwen, to sit in peace far away from the laborious grind that made her working day. The words of the service flowed over her, familiar and comforting.

But, disturbingly, there was a stir of excitement, a rustle like the sound of the whispering willow leaves, and then silence. Looking up, Bronwen saw Lewis striding from his seat near the front to take his place at the lectern that was shaped like a bronze eagle. She felt a quiver of excitement. How astonishingly different he looked from the mythical centaur of their previous encounter, this tall, distinguished stranger in the dark suit and immaculate white shirt that showed off the bronze face and long, brown, well-shaped hands. Only the chestnut waves of his hair displayed some reluctance to follow this conventional portrait of a well-known townsman reading the lesson.

It was the first chapter from the Book of Ruth. "Entreat me not to leave thee . . . for whither thou goest, I will go . . . thy people shall be my people . . . nought but death shall part thee and me."

The beautifully modulated tones of his voice would have done credit to an actor.

"And he is an actor," thought Bronwen, fighting against the spell that seemed to drown all her senses. "He is playing a part. His real self was that wild creature upon the hillside who criticized everything I did because he doesn't like women. No, that's not right. He may not approve of women, but they said he had been interested in quite a few."

She tried to give her attention to the service, and in the hushed atmosphere something of her earlier peace returned. But against her will, her eyes kept straying to the front of the church where she could see the square-shaped chestnut head and the strong brown neck above the rim of white collar. Beside him she caught a glimpse of a flowing mane of silky red hair. It was of that vital, pure auburn that seems to have a life of its own. Against the gray pillared background, it glowed with startling, vibrant beauty.

There was quite a press of people in the small church-yard, all waiting to greet the returned travelers. Bronwen could hear Lewis's deep tones and Sarah's excited chatter as she was embraced and kissed by old friends. She herself settled Nan upon a bench in the shade of the porch and went to bring the station wagon nearer to the lych gate. There were very many cars parked in the avenue that was lined with golden-leaved plane trees. It took Bronwen some time to negotiate all the traffic and the little groups of chatting people.

When she returned to Nan, she found that Lewis and Sarah were with her. Sarah, a vivid figure in a pleated green skirt, soft suede coat and velvet beret, seemed to be doing all the talking. She was not exactly beautiful, Bronwen thought. The features were too irregular, the nose a bit *retroussé*, the mouth wide with the prominent teeth that make for an attractive smile. But her large, pure gray eyes with dark brows and lashes were a startling contrast to the tossing fall of bright hair.

"It was fabulous, Nan, quite fabulous," Sarah was

saying with an engaging mixture of childishness and sophistication. "Huge ranches, gorgeous parties . . . and the women were so beautiful and glamorous. Lewis had a grand time."

"Don't give away secrets, young lady," laughed Lewis, tweaking one of the red locks of hair hanging below the green velvet beret. Bronwen ventured a glance at him.

"They both seem larger than life," she thought. "No wonder they create a stir in the neighborhood."

Absorbed in her study of Lewis's craggy features, she was suddenly conscious that Sarah was gazing thoughtfully in her direction. There was a slight smile on her face as if she was used to women taking an interest in Lewis. Bronwen hastily looked away and turned to Nan.

"You mustn't get too tired, Nan. We had better take you to the car now."

"I'll help her," said Lewis, and very gently for so large a man, he steered Nan toward the car. Sarah lingered beside Bronwen.

"Can I come to see Nan soon?" she asked. "Is she well enough to have visitors?"

"Yes, of course. She would love to see you."

"I'll bring my photographs of the trip. Can I come next week?"

"Any time," said Bronwen.

"It's so flat and boring here now. All my friends seem to have gone away."

"It usually seems so after an exciting trip."

"Lewis wants me to go to a finishing school in Switzerland." She laughed, head flung back, beautiful white teeth gleaming. "Imagine me being finished! I told Lewis I haven't even begun yet."

They reached Lewis who was standing beside the station wagon.

"I was just saying to Nan that I think you need to employ more help on the farm. I will visit next week some time to discuss your winter program."

"We would love to see you, Lewis darling," said Nan. "But it's difficult to take your advice about extra help. Labor costs money these days as you must know. However, do come. We would like your advice even if we don't intend to take it."

"Well, there's a thing. . . . What do you say, Miss Hughes—will you take my advice? Will you be glad to see me?"

He was looking quizzically at Bronwen, his blue eyes alight with teasing laughter. Whatever she said would sound foolish in her own ears.

"Of course, we . . . we . . . will be pleased to see you," she stammered. How stupid that he could make her feel so self-conscious.

"This niece of yours looks quite delightful in blue, doesn't she, Nan?"

"She's a honey," said Nan.

To cut off any further conversation, Bronwen climbed into the driver's seat and started the engine.

"We'll see you soon," shouted Sarah, waving heartily.

"She is half-child, half-woman," commented Nan, as they drove away. "A difficult stage in a girl's life for a bachelor to supervise, especially one as attractive as Lewis."

"I'm tired of everyone telling me how attractive he is," snapped Bronwen, crashing the gears.

"My darling," said Nan, astonished, "that's not like you."

But whether she meant her bad temper or the car's ill-treatment, Bron could not decide.

"Sorry, Nan," she said.

"But now that you have met him, you must admit that he is rather nice," Nan persisted.

"I hardly know him. I can hardly express an opinion upon such short acquaintance," said Bronwen repressively. How could she say to Nan that, although she had only met him twice and that very briefly, the sight of him set her heart pounding and seemed to make her lose all her well-hoarded common sense? "What has happened to me?" she asked herself desperately. "I must gather my wits together and resist this crazy emotion. There would be just as much sense in it if I fell in love with some rock star. I must put him out of my mind."

"Be a darling and tell Tabitha she must do some baking this week," begged Nan, when Bronwen took her her breakfast tray next morning. "We must have something to offer them if Lewis and Sarah come for tea. It's quite shameful for a farmer's wife to have empty tins."

Bronwen thought the orders would have come better from Nan, but she suspected that Nan was a little timid about giving the old African servant instructions to do extra work. So after breakfast she ventured into the kitchen, which, as she had soon realized, was Tabitha's own domain.

It was a far cry from the neat yellow and white kitchen over which Bronwen's mother reigned. It was quite extraordinary, thought Bronwen, that such a place could exist in the 20th century. The floor was stoneflagged. A black metal range, like a statue of some heathen god, occupied the whole of one wall. Every so often Tabitha seized a metal rod, opened a hole in the top and thrust wood into the black monster's inside.

The heat was overpowering. Large pots and pans over the whole of the top of the stove seemed to need constant shifting. A coffee pot stood permanently on one side. Kitchen utensils seemed to consist of a scrubbing brush and several brooms made of grass. For all household cleaning, Tabitha was content with bars of blue mottled soap. Modern detergents had no place in her scheme of things.

A small child stood at the porcelain sink rubbing at the piled up greasy dishes with a small mop. Nan turned a blind eye to Tabitha's methods. It was the only way to keep peace. Bronwen dreaded to think how she would manage in this kitchen if Tabitha were ever ill.

"*Molo*, Tabitha," she said placatingly to this dark keeper of the household goods.

"Good morning, Miss Blon," Tabitha replied.

Bronwen wished she would smile a little. It was so easy to get on with the delightful African herdboys who seemed charmed by her attempts to learn their language. Tabitha was a one-woman servant, devoted to Nan, but suspicious and scornful of all Bronwen's attempts to friendliness. Bronwen supposed that she was as strange to Tabitha as Tabitha was to her. But it was very difficult to ignore the dour silences and the disapproval of one's attempt at housekeeping.

Madam would like you to bake some cookies and cakes this week," she said. "Some people may come to tea."

"People?" asked Tabitha.

"Mr. Galbraith and Miss Sarah."

"Baas Lewis? Ja, I know Baas Lewis well. It is good he has come back. Baas Lewis very good man, nice and fat, very strong."

Tabitha's old face crinkled into an unaccustomed smile until it looked like an old prune. Bronwen experienced a pang of jealousy. Why could Lewis's charm work upon an old servant like Tabitha, when all she could get from her was disapproval?"

"What kind cakes?" asked Tabitha, bringing her back to the present problem.

"I—I don't know. What kind can you bake?"

Tabitha looked at her with infuriating superiority.

"All kind: Dundee, Madeira, meringues, shortbread," (the familiar words sounded strange pronounced by the rich African voice). "But can't make them today."

"Why not?" asked Bronwen bravely.

"No flour, no castor sugar, no raisins, no cherries, no icing sugar, no baking powder."

Bronwen sighed. "But Tabitha, I have asked you before; why can't you tell Madam when supplies are running short?"

"That Madam's business," replied Tabitha, mulishly.

Nan trusted the old servant to look after all the groceries and would not have dreamed of locking anything away. However it was maddening the way Tabitha would let supplies run short until they were completely finished before telling them what was needed. It was a slipshod way of housekeeping, but Bronwen dared not interfere. They relied so much upon the old woman's help, so they must put up with her slowness and irritating ways.

Bronwen had intended to set the youths to clearing a

mealie field for planting winter oats, but she would have to set them some other tasks and leave them without supervision while she went into town for supplies. What a waste of gas! Nan was happily painting a spray of yellow cassia in a green glass jar. She declined the offer of an excursion into town, merely asking Bronwen to buy some more drawing paper.

Going through the garden, Bronwen pinned a late rose to her pink linen dress, slipping it through the pin of the gold cameo brooch she had inherited from her grandmother. She could not explain why she did this, but it seemed to give a lift to her spirits. Adjusting the rose in front of the mirror in the station wagon, she contemplated her appearance thoughtfully. The healthy glow of her skin was reflected by the pink dress and the pink rose, the fair curls shone in the sunlight. In the strong light her eyes were almost violet. She looked very different from the pale girl who had worked in the dark London office.

"Wholesome, that's me," she sighed. And she remembered how a man who had shown some interest in her at one time had said, "No one would ever notice you in a crowd, thank heaven!"

It had been a dry summer, and the usual fall rains had not arrived yet. As she drove along the farm track, a cloud of dust rose behind the station wagon. Fortunately the wind was blowing away from her so the dust did not seep into the car as it often did.

The farm gate was opened by a bunch of children dawdling along on their way to school. The conventional navy uniforms and white blouses looked strange yet becoming to the shining brown skin and large eyes. Bronwen was touched by the way they walked with their shoes slung around their necks to save shoe leather. In their hands they carried old-fashioned slates. They smiled and called shy greetings as she drove past.

The cobs of Indian corn had been harvested from their tall stems, and cattle were wandering in the lands, grazing amongst the brittle yellow remains of the plants. When she first arrived they had been bright green with tightly closed green cobs silkily tasseled.

Tall gum trees lined the side of the road. The trunks were like silver except where large pieces of bark had peeled from the tree. Soon Bronwen reached the low red-roofed houses of the little town, each one set in its extensive yard. There was no shortage of land. The houses spread themselves around their large plots in single storeys. Ample garages and servants' quarters were necessities here. A life spent in a small South African town could be a very happy one, thought Bronwen, as long as you had moderately good means. A little narrow perhaps; a trifle smug. The women had leisure that had become a thing of the past in most other places in the world. They played tennis, swam in each other's swimming pools, played bridge, in the certain knowledge that when they came home Mary would have set the table and prepared meals; Jim would polish the floors and mow the lawns.

How long could it last, thought Bronwen, this complacent, almost feudal life? To the north, it had broken up already, but here people lived as if it would go on forever. But she had enough problems of her own without worrying about the future. Nan's income was alarmingly small, and Bronwen felt tied to helping with the farm until Nan could be persuaded to make a decision.

There was no difficulty about parking here. If you wanted to go to the grocer's, you parked in front of the grocer's, and if you wanted to go to the bank, you parked in front of that too.

When you made your purchases, hands were waiting to carry your parcels out to the car. She had opened the large back door of the station wagon and was stretching into the recess, loading groceries, while the assistant handed them to her. A voice in her ear made her start and almost drop Tabitha's flour.

"Bronwen, my little herdgirl! This is a pleasant surprise. Come have tea with me. We must talk about the farm."

In cream-colored safari jacket and shorts, Lewis looked more deeply sun-tanned than ever. His brown shoes shone like new chestnuts. The long, dark green socks were presumably a concession to his urban surroundings.

"Tea!" said Bronwen, astonished at such a domesticated invitation. He grinned in that maddening, teasing way.

"Too early for gin, love. Sun hasn't reached the yard-arm yet. Besides, haven't you learned yet that everything stops for morning tea in South Africa?"

He took her arm and led her into the small local tea-room. Heads turned as they sat at a wicker table. What a humdrum place to produce such a feeling of happiness, thought Bronwen. It was typical of hundreds of refreshment places up and down the length and breadth of Southern Africa. The front section had a counter with an infinite variety of candies and chocolates in a glass case. In another glass case, cooled by refrigeration, were sausages, cheese, butter, bacon. On the shelves at the back of the counter were mounds of bread; above them every variety of cigarettes and sparkling bottles of colored drinks.

Wherever there was a blank wall space, the proprietor, a fat, merry Portuguese, had plastered large posters, depicting glamorous girls in bikinis or girls in cars with dogs advertising varieties of cigarettes and cool drinks.

Now the Portuguese left the counter to his numerous sons and daughters and came rushing to Lewis's table.

"Mr. Galbraith, welcome home! How nice to see you! And how was South America?"

"Hello, José. Their girls were beautiful, but their paella not as good as yours."

José looked pleased. "Is that so, *meneer*? Just give me the command, and you shall have it next time you come into town."

"You must try it," Lewis told Bronwen. "It's out of this world."

"Is not bad," nodded José, "though crayfish is frozen, mussels and clams out of cans. Only chicken has been running till the day before. Bring the young lady. We will make it very special for her."

Bronwen was caught up into a confusion of mixed emotion by this fat little man's assumption that Lewis was interested in her. On the one hand she felt happy and relaxed by the friendly atmosphere, but she was embarrassed that Lewis might be forced to issue an unintended invitation. But she should have known better. Lewis passed it off casually.

"I'll do that," he said. "I'll let you know, José."

He made no further reference to it when the little man had departed after taking his order for tea and pastries.

"Of course he didn't mean it," Bronwen assured herself. "He was just being polite. Goodness knows, I would hate him to be forced into taking me out to dinner. I'm just being stupid again. I must get this man off my mind."

"It would be better if you were to concentrate on sheep," said Lewis.

"Sheep?" she asked, startled, then burst out laughing, realizing that she had not been listening to his previous remarks. He looked a little astonished, wondering what the joke was, and she hastily pulled herself together.

"Oh yes, sheep," she said.

"You know, those animated hearthrugs with a stupid face at one end and a leg at each corner. Don't you have sheep where you come from?"

"Not many," admitted Bronwen.

"Nan could run more sheep than she has on her ground. With so little labor available, you can hardly go in for crops. Did she get rid of that stalk borer?"

Bronwen stared, then stammered, "I think so."

"Nan needs a manager, but I suppose she can't pay one."

"No," said Bronwen, reluctant to disclose Nan's true position to this man who seemed suddenly to have become very brusque and technical.

"How long do you intend to stay here?"

"I don't know much about farming as I suppose you realize, but I will stay as long as Nan needs me."

"That will be forever. You should persuade her that it's

hopeless. You can't run a farm without capital. I've told her I'm quite willing to buy it. She will get a better price from me than anyone else."

"You don't understand, Mr. Galbraith."

"Lewis," he insisted.

"You don't understand, Lewis," Bronwen repeated obediently, feeling rather shy. "Nan loves the farm. She wants to stay there."

"Nonsense! The way things are going she's just throwing good money after bad. I'll have to come and see her. If she won't have a manager, I will have to stand in for one."

Suddenly Bronwen felt humiliated and furious that she was in the position of having to accept favors from this man. He seemed to her to be too confident, too knowledgeable, too maddeningly sure of himself.

"We are managing quite well," she said. "Once Nan's leg is properly better, she will be able to help me."

"You think so? Let me tell you you haven't a hope. Nan's a darling, but she is too romantically minded for practical farm life. Take my advice and persuade her to give it up. Just because her husband was a fool, there's no need for her to still suffer for his blunders."

"I suppose it's beyond your comprehension," said Bronwen, "but Nan loved Patrick. She adored him. This fixation on the farm hasn't anything to do with material considerations. She wants to stay here because wherever she looks she can imagine Patrick; riding over the lands, Patrick, with his plans and schemes. Maybe he was foolish, but he had a zest for life that no one could forget, least of all Nan. She wants to stay there where she was happy with him."

"Quite a psychologist, aren't you, little Bronwen? Did you know that when you are cross, your eyes go a beautiful color of dark violet? Most impressive phenomenon. But tell me, why do you consider that love is beyond my comprehension?"

She looked at the teasing grin; the laughing blue eyes.

"Your idea of love is not the kind that Patrick and Nan had."

"What is it then?"

He leaned across the table and casually took her hand, examining it as if it could yield up some important secret. Bronwen fought back the wave of tenderness that seemed at his touch to dissolve all feeling of hostility.

"It's a light, flirtatious, philandering kind of love, if you can call it that. I don't think you could be capable of deep feeling. You would never let yourself get too involved. If you felt yourself becoming enmeshed you would laugh it off."

Lewis laughed now. "Becoming enmeshed! Like a poor fish in a net. You are a delightful, surprising girl, Bronwen. A bit serious perhaps in your ideas. You must tell me more about love one day. Give me a practical demonstration perhaps."

Bronwen was saved from replying to this by a pair of women who rushed up to the table and greeted Lewis with enthusiasm. He kissed them both heartily, and there was much teasing laughter and badinage.

"Sorry I didn't introduce them," he said to Bronwen as they walked out of the tea-room. "I can't for the moment recall their names."

It was Bronwen's turn to laugh. "You are impossible," she said.

He accompanied her back to the station wagon, and when she was already seated, he stood looking down at the top of her fair, curly head.

"Think over my advice about persuading Nan to sell the farm, even if I do make you cross," he said.

She looked up at him, smiling a little pensively. Without warning, he cupped her chin in his hand, turning her face up toward him. For a wild moment she thought he intended to kiss her. She fought down the panic this idea caused, feeling her face flush pink.

"Dearest," he said.

Her dark blue eyes widened.

"Your rose, I mean," he grinned. "That's the name of the rose you are wearing, didn't you know? It's one of my favorites; pretty but modest, lasts much longer than its more spectacular sisters, generous in its blossom. A good rose for a young girl in a pink dress with violet eyes and a most delicious blush."

He let go of her chin and smiled engagingly as she started the car.

Driving back to the farm, she tried to think sensibly of Lewis. When she had heard all the gossip about him before he came, she had never for a moment thought that she would become so swiftly involved with him. He liked women's company, that was obvious. Women were attracted to him, but he had reached the age of 36 without marrying. Bronwen admitted to herself that she had never before felt so deeply attracted to any man. But she knew the attraction was hopeless if not downright stupid.

"I must try to keep out of his way," she thought. "It would be too humiliating if he guessed my feelings. And where women are concerned he seems most astute. Probably because he has had lots of experience," she thought sadly. "I can't leave here. I can't let Nan down. If he stands in as manager as he said he would I'll see him far too often. If only we could afford to employ a manager, then I could just ignore him, and this foolish emotion could die a natural death."

Absorbed in her thoughts, she was almost abreast of him before she saw a young man at the side of the road waving his hand in her direction. Nan had warned her not to pick up hitchhikers, but it was broad daylight and she was only a few miles from the farm. The man looked young and harmless. With a squealing of brakes, she pulled up.

"I'm not going far," she said. "Only to the next turn-off."

"That will be better than nothing. I've been waiting here for over an hour, and only one car has passed. If I get a few miles farther on, I'll perhaps be able to get a lift at the branch of the main road."

He was fair and slight with a rather apologetic expression, but his voice was educated, his manner pleasant.

"Have you come far?" asked Bronwen.

He named a coastal town.

"But I'm tired of the city. I was born in the country, not far from here, as a matter of fact. I've been working in a garage. I'm good with mechanical things, but when you have lived in the country all your life, town takes a bit of getting used to. What I'd really like would be to work on a farm. But I'd have to be apprenticed or something because I don't know a great deal about it. I haven't the money to pay a farmer to teach me. I came back here hoping to borrow some money from my dad to take some kind of agriculture course, but he's broke too."

Bronwen drove some way without speaking. But her brain was racing madly. "Why not?" she thought. If the young man wanted to work on a farm perhaps he would consider coming to them. Goodness knows there was very little she could teach him, but it would be another pair of hands and experience for him. Most of their food was homegrown, so they could cater for a healthy appetite.

"If you are really keen to work on a farm," she said, "you could come and stay with us."

The young man turned to her, his face alight with enthusiasm.

"But that's fabulous!" he exclaimed, looking quite transformed by his excitement.

"Don't be too carried away until I tell you the circumstances," Bronwen cautioned him. And she explained about Nan.

"We could hardly pay you anything. It would only be for your keep with enough for a little pocket money, but you might learn a little while you were with us. You could try it for a few weeks if you like. Then later when you know more about it, you might get a job as a farm manager and save for that course. It would tide us over a difficult patch."

"It sounds wonderful. I won't let you down, I promise. Where is your farm?"

"Around the next bend. It's called Bushman's Fountain."

"Bushman's Fountain!" the young man looked startled.

"Do you know it?"

"No, but . . . oh, well, it couldn't be better. I'm very grateful to you, Miss. . . ."

"Hughes," said Bronwen.

"And my name's Douglas Watson," said the young man.

CHAPTER THREE

If Douglas Watson went on as he had started he would be worth his weight in gold, thought Bronwen. It made a tremendous difference to have someone on hand with whom to discuss what needed to be done. He was pleasant and very interested in the work. It was like having a young brother.

He regarded Bronwen as his equal if not superior. It was good to work with him feeling none of that maddening superiority she had sensed in Lewis's attitude to her farming. Nan had fallen in with Bronwen's plan to employ Douglas without protest

"He seems a nice boy," she agreed. "It's astounding that he is willing to work for so little, but young people do please themselves these days, don't they? Rather nice, really, when they are not materially minded."

She thoroughly approved of Douglas's interest in living in the country. He could speak the local African language, which was a great help. With his coming, Bronwen began to feel that a little of her burden had lifted.

This morning he was in the shed trying to put an old plough into working order, so that they could prepare the lands for planting winter oats. He was whistling away merrily. His young flushed face was streaked with grease; his fair hair eclipsed by the dust that, disturbed by their movements, fell from the long neglected beams of the old barn. The barn was a miniature junkyard for all kinds of broken down machinery.

"Ever noticed this old car, here?" he asked Bronwen. "I believe it's an old Model-T Ford. Poor old car. They were highly thought of in their day."

"It doesn't look worth much now," said Bronwen. It was a high open car, obviously a very old model. The folded hood was torn, the seats grimy and covered with bird droppings, the brasswork on headlamps and radiator badly tarnished.

"Would you mind if I worked on it at night?" asked Douglas. "It might be fun to get it going again."

"Not at all," said Bronwen. "I'm sure Nan would consent."

"It might give him an interest, keep him amused and occupied," she thought to herself.

She and Nan had both feared that his enthusiasm for the farm would wane because he lacked young company here.

"Can you imagine how this car looked in its heyday with its gleaming brass headlamps and radiator, the large wheels with their narrow tires, the shining bosses instead of hubcaps?"

He refused Bronwen's offer of tea.

"I'm too hot and dusty," he said.

"I'll bring some out here for you."

"I can't let you wait on me. Ring the bell when it's ready, and I'll come to collect it from the stoep."

Whatever work Bronwen was doing on the farm, she always tried to join Nan for morning tea. They very seldom had visitors, so this morning she was startled to see a small bright red Mini in the driveway near to the house.

Shady in summer, the stoep was delightfully warm in winter. They usually sat out there in the balmy sunshine, so different from the burning rays of midsummer. As Bronwen came up the steps she easily recognized the vibrant, young voice of Sarah talking to Nan.

"Bronwen seems a dear, but I thought she would be much more glamorous than she is, Nan, being your niece," she was saying.

"She's an absolute honey," said Nan. "I don't know what on earth I'd do without her."

"Oh, I know that, dear. I'm not complaining. I'm quite relieved really. Beautiful women make life with Lewis so complicated. You should just have seen them in South America. . . ." She broke off as Bronwen arrived. "Hello, Bronwen, you see I've come at last, though Nan doesn't approve of the way I came."

"No, I don't," said Nan. "You know Lewis would never consent to your driving a car on the main road."

Nan sounded quite strict.

"I'm too young to have a license yet. You can't get one until you are 18, but I've been driving around the farm tracks since I was about 10. Don't worry, darling Nan. I have a wonderful red-haired angel who works overtime looking after me."

"And you certainly need one," commented Nan. "Poor angel. I wouldn't exchange jobs with her."

"It's a him," said Sarah, grinning. "I don't go much for women, only you, darling Nan."

"And Bronwen, I insist you go for Bronwen," said Nan, laughing.

"We'll see. I tell you what, I will vow to like both of you so long as neither of you gets dopey about Lewis. I've been fending away females for years."

"Poor Lewis, no wonder he hasn't married if he has such a fierce watchdog," said Nan.

They were interrupted by Tabitha arriving with the tea trolley.

"Darling Tabitha, your special cheese scones!" Sarah exclaimed. "Aren't you pleased to see me?" She relieved her of the tea things, then jigged her around in a semblance of an African dance. Bronwen was amazed to see Tabitha smiling.

"Eheu, Miss Sarah, too much strong for old mama like Tabitha. Where your husband? You tell Tabitha you go to this far country to find husband."

"Ay, Tabitha, nobody would have me. No one would give Baas Lewis enough lobola for me. How many cows am I worth, Tabby, 50 . . . 100?"

"Oh yes, husband will have to pay much lobola for Miss Sarah."

She went off back to the kitchen, singing and doing a little jig.

"You should come more often, Sarah. I've never seen Tabitha so merry," said Bronwen wistfully.

"Tabitha's all right, but she has to know you for a

million years before she gets really matey. She looked after me for a while when I first came here, before she came to Nan, but Lewis decided I needed someone younger to keep up with me."

They poured tea, enjoying the crisp golden-topped scones light as air, dripping with butter and the sugar-topped rock cakes tasting of lemon rind, full of plump raisins and currants.

"Tell us about South America," asked Nan.

"I have some photographs here," said Sarah, carefully wiping her buttery fingers and finally running to wash them under the yard tap.

Her photographs were not very professional, and she had not wasted much time upon the countryside, buildings, or statues. Obviously her interest had been in the people she met and the animals. There were pictures of beautiful horses, magnificent bulls.

"Here's Lewis with the Palomino he has bought. We hope it will be coming next week."

Bronwen looked at the tall figure in magnificent embroidered riding habit beside the beautiful cream horse with its darker, golden brown mane.

"That habit was a present from our host. It was gorgeous. It made Lewis look like a prince. Here's the ranch where we stayed."

It looked more like a Moorish palace to Bronwen. Its white castellated buildings seemed to be constructed around a central quadrangle.

"And this is Carlotta, one of Lewis's girl friends there—the most successful one I should say. Awfully glamorous. Quite beautiful in fact."

Carlotta was laughing: a glass of champagne in her hand, her head tilted with sleek dark hair piled high in an elaborate style, lovely shoulders bare, two tiny jeweled straps holding the black chiffon evening dress, the neck-line of which plunged deeply between the perfect breasts. She was like one of those beautiful Spanish dolls; her features perfect as if moulded from fine wax, her eyes large and dark with long, curling lashes. There was a provocative air of innocence and allure about her that

Bronwen imagined could have a most devastating effect upon any man. Beside her in the photograph stood Lewis, his eyes alight with admiration.

"She's lovely," said Nan. "Like a tropical flower, hibiscus or something."

"More like magnolia," agreed Sarah. "Her skin is like white velvet. Wish mine was. Lewis will never believe I'm grown up while I still have these wretched freckles."

She produced a picture of herself in a simple white evening dress beside a young, handsome, dark man who was regarding her with a very dashing air.

"This is Carlotta's brother, Ramon. We had a great time at their place. They may be coming here one of these days. They have some scheme for a sea voyage quite soon. Nan darling, I'm thirsty. I've done too much talking. Do you think I could have some more tea?"

"Oh good heavens!" said Bronwen, springing up. "I'd forgotten all about tea for Douglas. I said I'd ring the bell, and he could come."

"Douglas?" said Sarah.

"He's a young man Bron picked up along the road, a would-be farmer. He's proving enormously useful, though we don't know how long it can last."

"What's his other name?" asked Sarah.

For the first time Bronwen noticed the despised freckles, for they seemed to stand out vividly against her white skin.

"Watson," she replied. "Douglas Watson," and rang the bell. Douglas came up the steps wiping his hands.

"Good morning, Mrs. O'Hara," he said. "I'm not fit for decent company, I'm afraid. I'll just take my cup of tea standing and go."

"Hello, Douglas," Sarah said quietly.

The cup shot out of his hand and shattered upon the stone flags of the stoep.

"Sorry, Nan, I made him break your cup," laughed Sarah. She seized his oil-stained hands in her own.

"It's gorgeous seeing you again after all this time. Whatever are you doing here? I thought Lewis had banished you forever."

A closed-in look that Bronwen had never seen before marred Douglas's usually frank expression.

"I couldn't take it, Sarah. I had to come back."

Sarah's eyes were brilliant.

"I'm glad, glad, glad! But Lewis is going to be raging mad when he knows you are here. Oh boy, I can't wait to see his face when he finds out."

"Well, you won't have long to wait," said Nan, dryly. She and Bronwen had been giving each other desperate looks during this conversation. "For here he comes."

Lewis's sleek Aston Martin could be seen coming along the farm road. But at this sudden turn of events, Sarah's defiant attitude evidently petered out.

"The gates will delay him," she said. "Quick, Douglas, go back to the barn."

"What do you think I am? I'm not skulking around there as if I'm scared of him."

"Go. Go quickly," said Sarah frantically. "He's probably come after me because he's missed the Mini. He'll be mad at me anyway. Oh go!" she commanded imperiously, gray eyes flashing, red hair flung back like a banner as he still hesitated. "If you can't consider me, think of Nan and Bronwen."

"Very well, but I don't like it."

He disappeared reluctantly in the direction of the barn.

"Here's a pretty how do you do!" exclaimed Nan.

"Oh, Nan darling, I do adore your Victorian sayings," said Sarah, her momentary panic forgotten.

"Never to worry, I've been coping with Lewis for nearly seven years. He has overplayed the stern, old-fashioned father figure in this business over Douglas. Just because Douglas happened to be the only available young man in the neighborhood at that time, I went around with him. You don't have to be desperately in love to enjoy a chap's company. But Lewis behaved as if Douglas intended to seduce me at any moment."

"There's no need to try to shock us, Sarah," Nan said firmly. "I'm not easily shocked even if I do use Victorian phrases. You have made your point. But if there wasn't anything on your side, there must have been more feeling on his. Otherwise why has he come back?"

"Shh . . . here comes Lewis," cautioned Sarah. "Oh boy, just see that scowl!"

She was like a naughty child, thrilled and yet scared by her own daring, thought Bronwen, as the car door slammed shut and Lewis strode onto the stoep. His mouth had a very determined set to it, but in spite of his obvious ill temper he was carefully courteous to Sarah's hostesses.

"Sorry to barge in on you like this, Nan," he said after he had greeted them. "But I couldn't allow Sarah to drive back, once I had discovered she had taken the Mini."

Sarah stretched up her arms to place them on his shoulders, smiling persuasively.

"Lewis darling, you know I can drive quite well. I only drove on a teeny stretch of main road."

"And if you had had an accident on that teeny stretch, what then? No, Sarah, it's no good wheedling. I've told you before, you mustn't drive until you are old enough to have a license. Say goodbye to Nan and Bronwen; you have wasted enough of my time already."

His expression was very stern. Bronwen experienced a frisson of alarm when she thought that Douglas was so near to the homestead. It would be the worst possible time for him to find out that the boy was back while he was in his present mood. The sooner Lewis and Sarah departed the better. But Nan seemed to have forgotten about Douglas.

"You can't go straight away," she said. "Bronwen, ask Tabitha to make some fresh tea."

"No, sorry, Nan, we must go. Get into the car, Sarah."

"But what are you going to do about the Mini?" asked Sarah, her lips drooping. "You should have brought one of the men to drive it if you didn't trust me to bring it back."

"They are all far too busy this morning," said Lewis, shortly. "I wondered if Bronwen could bring it over when it suits her. I will drive her back."

Bronwen's foolish heart betrayed her common sense by thumping madly at the idea of spending some time with Lewis, but she answered calmly, "Yes, certainly, I can bring it over tomorrow afternoon."

"We'll expect you then," said Lewis, an unexpected, charming smile lightening his grave expression, and with a wave of their hands they were on their way.

"Next time I come I'll ride over," shouted Sarah, whose high spirits evidently could not be repressed for long. "Thank goodness nobody needs a license to ride a horse."

Bronwen suspected that Lewis would have more to say about her misdemeanor when they were alone in the car. She felt sorry for Sarah. She herself would not like to face Lewis's anger. With a qualm she remembered that very soon she might have to . . . what a muddle it seemed that she had employed the very young man whom Lewis had disapproved of so much. Nan, of course, had not registered his name because at the time she had been too involved in Patrick's death to take any notice of local gossip.

What could they do about it now? Douglas was invaluable around the farm. He was such a help to Nan and herself. Sarah did not seem wildly in love with him. It had seemed such a good solution to their own problems. Why should they lose a good worker because of Lewis's prejudices?

She went into the barn where Douglas was still working at the plough, his face moody. As she came in, he flung aside his spanner and turned to face her.

"I'm sorry, Miss Hughes. You must be furious with me. I didn't want to deceive you. You have been so kind to me. But I was just so desperate to get back."

"What exactly is the position, Douglas?" asked Bronwen. "I gather Lewis disapproves of your friendship with Sarah?"

"Yes, he does, but, Miss Hughes, he would disapprove of anyone who so much as looked at Sarah. He thinks she is still a child. And I suppose she is in lots of ways. But he set too much importance on the whole thing.

"It's true I care a lot for Sarah. She's the most wonderful girl I've ever met. But I have sense. I know she's too young yet to know her own mind and that I'm nobody. But in a few years' time, who knows? That's why I'm so keen to go to some college and make a success of myself, but Lewis wouldn't see that. He wouldn't even listen to me.

"I kept Sarah out too late one night. It was because I had a breakdown. My car was so old, I suppose I shouldn't have risked taking her out in it, but she made me. Mr. Galbraith just about blew his top. It was after that that he insisted on getting this job for me, and my dad was scared to refuse. He has lived all his life here and thinks the Galbraith family are royalty.

"Between them they bundled me off to this garage job in the town. I gave in because I thought it was hopeless to hold out, but after a while I knew if I stayed in town, it would be a case of one dead-end job after another. I would never get any nearer to my aim of doing farming one day.

"I'd rather work here with you, try to learn a bit more; help to work the farm up a bit. If I get results, maybe Mrs. O'Hara will be able to pay me a bit more, and I can try for a scholarship at the Agriculture College. But I didn't think ahead enough. I can see now that once Lewis knows I'm back it will be the same old story over again."

He looked so disconsolate in his greasy overalls with his fair lock of hair loose over his brow and his worried gray eyes that Bronwen felt very compassionate. Why should Lewis always get his own way just because he was rich and had influence?

"You can stay here," she said impulsively. "What does it matter to Nan or me what Mr. Galbraith thinks? It is our business if we employ you."

A grin split Douglas's face like sunshine after rain.

"Gee, Miss Hughes, that's wonderful. I'll work hard for you, I promise, if only you can see your way to letting me stay."

CHAPTER FOUR

As Bronwen drove the small red Mini back toward Lion's Rest, her spirits lifted. It was a perfect afternoon. Late fall in the Southern Hemisphere was like the weather must have been in the garden of the Hesperides, she thought. A golden shimmer lay over the land; a clear, glittering compound of blue sky, distant blue mountains, waves of grass turning from gold to silver as the wind swept through it.

Here and there agave plants thrust out their yellow blooms like glowing candelabra. On every kopje the smaller candles of aloes glowed pale orange above their harsh leaves. By June, Nan had said, the flowers would be spikes of bright orange-red, looking as if Africans in their dark ochre blankets were marching perpetually upon the hillside tracks.

The pale turquoise sweater she was wearing with her cream skirt enhanced the golden glow that all the outdoor work had given to her fair skin. "This niece of yours looks quite delightful in blue," she had remembered Lewis's words as she exchanged her working slacks for a more becoming dress and had discarded the newer red sweater she had intended to wear.

The gates of Lion's Rest were not the usual farm gates, not even the more elaborate wagon-wheel gates that Bronwen had often seen in the district, but were made of wrought iron in an exquisite filigree pattern. The supporting stone pillars on each side were surmounted by a snarling lion.

But within the gates, the resemblance to an old country estate was subordinated to the efficiency of a scientifically managed farm. Bronwen could not help feeling pangs of envy as she realized the difference between the results of her own feeble efforts with Nan's farm and this seemingly perfectly run place.

The fences were uniform, surrounding the green spears

of winter oats with military precision. The flocks of sheep were heavy with lamb, the cattle sleek and doe-eyed, obediently lining up to take their turn at the troughs where the fodder was scientifically fed from neat towers. In the paddocks near the house, young horses pranced nimbly as if they felt the call of spring instead of the crisp greeting of approaching winter.

Some ancestor of Lewis's must have admired the houses he saw in the vineyards of the Cape, for the old house was built in the early Cape Dutch style, not indigenous to this part of South Africa, but still such an early imitation that now it looked ancient in its own right.

There was a wide shady stoep in front of a palisade of white curving gables; the windows oblong with small frames. The long, large building had a spacious welcoming air. In front were green lawns with spreading old oak trees. Tall blue cranes, gray birds with the mincing walk of mannequins, stalked upon the terrace. A peacock sunned itself on the low wall.

As Bronwen braked the car, a beautiful golden labrador, a cream and brown setter, and a soft-eared spaniel lifted their heads from their snooze on the warm flags, alert to the familiar sound of the car. As they ran toward it, she saw Lewis stride out from a small French door. Through the window she caught a glimpse of a rolltop desk and office equipment.

"Bronwen," he said and seized her hands in his. "Good of you to bring the car back. I'll ring for some tea."

Once he had let go of her hands, Bronwen felt better able to combat this sensation of drowning. She looked all around, carefully observing the house, and trying to avoid looking at the man whose presence defeated all her good resolutions to fight this senseless attraction. Then she bent to caress the dogs who were nosing her curiously.

"Would you like to look around the house while we are waiting?" Lewis asked, when he had ordered tea. "It probably doesn't seem very old to English eyes, but by our standards it's positively Elizabethan.

"Actually it was built about 100 years ago. The first farmhouse here was a homebuilt affair of wattle and daub with a roughly thatched roof. Here it is. A great-great-grandmother painted a watercolor of it."

In place of honor above the study fireplace, there was a faint attractive painting of a small building surrounded by aloes, thorn trees and a stone kraal, encircled by an outer wall of thorns.

"There really were lions here in those days," said Lewis, when she commented upon this extra protection for the cattle. "They had hard work to keep their few animals safe from wild beasts and marauding natives."

He showed her into the flagged hall that was enlivened by Khelim rugs in glowing orange, blue and cream. It led through to the large dining room with its huge stone fireplace and dark wood paneling. This was evidently used as a living room too, for there were many comfortable, brightly patterned chairs. A huge log box of gleaming copper stood before the fire that was laid ready for lighting.

The round table was of Georgian design. The natural grain of some huge mahogany tree had made a kind of ostrich feather design tapering in perfect formation toward the center. Portraits of Lewis's ancestors revealed the chestnut hair and the devil-may-care expression that was not to be disguised by sober clothes or spade-shaped beards.

The drawing room was beautiful, but evidently little used. The Aubusson carpet in faded pinks and blues; the delicately shaped brocaded chairs in pastel colors; the gilded ormolu display cabinets; the crystal chandeliers; all displayed the feminine taste of some previous chatelaine, which seemed to accord ill with the masculinity of their present owner.

"We seldom use this room except when we have a party," said Lewis. "Then we clear away all this junk and use it for a ballroom."

"Junk?" laughed Bronwen. "But, Lewis, it is exquisite."

"Do you think so? Yes, I suppose it is. I suppose it was some Galbraith woman's answer to her husband's masculine pursuits; a feminine retreat from the realities of farm life."

He led her toward the staircase that swept above the hall in a generous curve. The passage at the top of the stairs seemed wide enough to drive a coach along it. Sarah's room was a characteristic mixture of childish hobbies and growing sophistication. The blue walls held pictures of horses; the striped blue and white curtains were looped back across a windowsill filled with Royal Worcester figures of ponies and dogs; but the white painted furniture with the ruffled spread was girlish and feminine.

The furniture in the other rooms was covered with dust sheets except for the large room above the drawing room. Bronwen was surprised to find that this was where Lewis slept. Somehow she had imagined he would have a small masculine cell with little comfort; a place that was quite spartan and rough as if in a barracks. But she was mistaken.

The room was luxurious in a very masculine way. The walls and woodwork were painted white and made a foil to the large glowing Persian carpet that was woven with strange beasts amongst a design of exotic foliage. Drawers and closets were of gleaming rosewood. There were deep crimson leather chairs in front of the Adam fireplace. An enormous bed, lacquered in red and gold, had oriental carvings of dragons supporting the brocaded canopy.

"What an astonishing bed," said Bronwen. "I'd feel quite scared to sleep in it."

"Would you, little one?" said Lewis, laughing. "I'm very attached to this bed. Galbraiths have been born and have died in it for the last 100 years. It gives one a feeling of continuity, doesn't it? I warn you, Bronwen, whoever takes me must take the ancestral bed as well."

He was joking, but Bronwen sensed a seriousness behind his manner. She had imagined he would have some narrow Spartan couch, but now she had seen this, it seemed much more characteristic. Sleeping here would satisfy his pride in his family.

"Incidentally this is known as the Bridal Chamber, not awfully suitable for a bachelor, is it? But I've altered the furnishings to my own taste. Couldn't put up with all those frilly curtains and covers in my own room, could I?"

"No, I suppose not," said Bronwen, laughing. She was conscious of Lewis's eyes upon her.

"You look very sweet when you laugh like that, Bronwen. You are such an unself-conscious person."

This remark immediately had the effect of making Bronwen self-conscious, a state of mind increased when Lewis carelessly put his arm around her to guide her down the stairs.

"I hope you don't mind having tea in my study," he said. "Sarah has gone to tennis, but in any case we seldom use the drawing room these days . . . too formal."

He led her into the small, comfortable room where she had seen the rolltop desk, a beautiful old specimen with red, tooled leather top. There was a brown leather sofa with a table nearby upon which tea was laid. Bronwen had to sit in close proximity to Lewis as she poured the tea. He seemed content to regard her profile with a quizzical gaze, not even speaking.

"Do you usually stay indoors in the afternoon?" she asked desperately trying to think of something to say.

"Not at this time of year, though in summer I try to finish the field work during the morning, then do a spot of paper work in the heat of the afternoon."

She had a sudden vision of him astride the horse on top of the mountain, wearing only blue denim jeans.

"What is amusing you?" he asked, regarding her intently.

"It's just . . . you didn't look as if you were used to doing office work the first time I saw you."

"Oh, that . . . sometimes the mood takes me, and I want to do nothing but maybe ride to the end of the world. Then I realize that I'm a farmer with various responsibilities and people depending on me."

"A feudal lord, in fact," said Bronwen.

"Well, there's a lot to be said for the early days, the Viking times or the Middle Ages, when a man was Lord of his Manor, dashing off to fight the occasional war, then coming back to look after his own."

"And his wife . . . what was she doing when he was gallivanting off to the wars?" asked Bronwen, laughing.

"Having children, of course," said Lewis. "Caring for the house and everyone in it. Even now, you know, the Xhosa word for mistress of the house literally means a basket of food; she who gives out the food."

"Poor wife," said Bronwen. "What if she felt the urge to dash off somewhere as well . . . ride to the end of the world?"

"She would need someone with her," said Lewis, adamantly.

"You like women to be dependent, I can see that," scoffed Bronwen.

"I like my women to be women," said Lewis.

Bronwen felt as if a cloud had passed before the sun. Her high spirits drooped. She thought of her struggles with the farm, and his first sight of her in shabby shorts struggling to mend a wall. Lewis probably thought her unfeminine as well as foolish. The photograph of Carlotta arose vividly in her mind. That was the kind of woman who would attract Lewis. She rose to go.

"I'm wasting your time," she said.

He did not make any polite demur, but stood up as well.

"How is the farm going? I'll come over to see you soon," he promised, but he made no effort to keep her there.

"No, please don't. We are managing quite well," said Bronwen hastily.

"Have you got the winter feed in yet?"

"We will have soon. The plough has been out of commission but. . . ." Bronwen broke off as she had a swift vision of Douglas's grease-streaked moody face.

"For heaven's sake, why didn't you tell me before. I'll phone down to my manager."

He picked up the phone before she could object.

"Hello, MacDonald. What are you doing? Mm, we'd better get the vet to have a look at her. Look, can you spare a plough? We've just about finished, haven't we? I want to lend it to Mrs. O'Hara. Their plough has broken down. Yes, I know I mentioned it before, but I thought you had forgotten. What?"

Bronwen saw the sudden change of expression in his rugged, mobile face. A cold shiver began in the pit of her stomach and traveled slowly over her body.

"You say you did offer, but young Watson said he was fixing their own plough. Young Watson? You don't mean Douglas Watson . . . what's he doing here?"

There was more explanation from the other end of the phone while Bronwen sat feeling her courage ebbing away at this unexpected turn of events.

"You thought I knew. No . . . no, I didn't know. Nobody bothered to tell me. Yes . . . yes . . . I can't talk about other business now. I'll see you later."

He slammed down the phone and turned to look at Bronwen, his eyes like blue flames.

"So . . . you didn't care to accept the help I offered you, but you preferred to employ a young inexperienced boy, so unreliable that he quit the job I found for him without even giving notice."

Bronwen's heart was pounding, her eyes wide and dark emphasizing the extreme pallor of her heart-shaped face, but she tried to speak calmly.

"I didn't know he was the boy you disapproved of when I employed him."

"You employed him! Where was Nan in all this? I was under the impression that it was her farm. For someone completely ignorant of farm work, you seem to be taking a lot upon yourself."

"Nan wasn't there when I met him but she thoroughly approved of my decision."

"And where, may I ask, did you meet him? I hadn't even heard he was in the district."

"I . . . I picked him up. He was hitch-hiking."

Lewis seemed even more angry at this information.

"Bronwen, how could you be so foolish?" He was talking to her almost as if she were Sarah. "I know you aren't used to this country, but such behavior is the height of folly . . . for a woman on her own to pick up a hitch-hiker."

"Oh, I know, but he was only a young boy and looked perfectly respectable. Anyhow he has been a marvelous help to us ever since he came. I don't know how we could manage without him now."

"Well, I'm afraid you're going to have to, because I must request you and Nan to get rid of the boy as soon as possible. I had enough of his hanging around Sarah before, and I thought I had solved that problem. I'm certainly not prepared to let it start all over again. I will come and see him. I'll soon get him moving."

By now Bronwen had got over the first shock of his discovery. His high-handed manner had made her as angry as he appeared to be.

"Just who do you think you are, Lewis Galbraith, to move people around the country and think you can control their lives, just because you don't like them? Douglas is working splendidly for us. He's a perfectly sensible young man. If you would take the trouble to make his acquaintance, you would find this out for yourself, instead of thinking you're feudal lord of all you survey. Sarah could go a lot farther and fare worse than falling in love with Douglas, but I don't for a moment think she is in love with him yet."

Lewis smiled without humor.

"He seems to have made a deep impression upon you, certainly. Perhaps you yourself are attracted to him. That would be a solution to my difficulty over Sarah, wouldn't it?"

In all her civilized life, Bronwen had seldom experienced this primitive urge to violence. But now if she could have slapped the calm, handsome face, or hit the mouth that was so blandly making these outrageous suggestions, it would have given her enormous satisfaction.

She turned away and faced the window, trying to control her fury and digging her nails into her hands.

"I think you are high-handed, domineering, and quite impossible," she said. "I could no more be attracted to Douglas than I could be attracted to you."

It was not a lie, for at that moment her feelings toward him were completely antagonistic.

"Really?" said Lewis. "So I'm terribly unattractive to you? We must try to remedy that."

Before she knew what he intended, he had turned her around and was kissing her with practised skill. In vain she fought down the impulse to respond with the warmth and passion she really felt. For a few moments she let herself drift in the exquisite tide of emotion that was bearing her away.

With a great effort of will she managed to jerk herself away from him.

"You really are the most arrogant man I've ever met. You think, don't you, that all women are completely bowled over by you? Well, let me tell you here is one that is not!"

He relinquished his hold, but his vivid blue eyes were on her face. He had the wicked half-smile she had seen in old pictures of fauns.

"You know, you kiss very satisfactorily for a girl who is not in the least attracted to me," he grinned. He put his arm around her squeezing her in almost a brotherly fashion. "Sorry, Bronwen, I shouldn't have teased you, but I just couldn't resist it. It must have been those angry, dark violet eyes."

So it was his idea of a joke. It had not meant anything at all to him.

"I would like to make it quite clear to you, Lewis, that I am not used . . . I mean . . . I am not as available as you seem to think. . . ." she broke off, confused.

"You mean that I am wicked, insufferable, and I must never do such a thing again. Can't promise, you know. I'm not very good at keeping promises. Besides it was most enjoyable. Now, about young Watson. . . ."

How could he turn so matter-of-factly to the business in hand when her heart was beating so wildly she was afraid he would hear it?

"If you get rid of him, Bronwen, I promise I will supply you with plenty of help. I'll come over and talk to Nan about it. She will accept it, I know, when she knows you are doing me a favor by getting rid of this young man."

If this happened, she thought, she would become still more deeply involved in this fatal enchantment.

"But why should we?" she protested. "He isn't a pawn to be shifted around just because you want it. There's his life to consider too. You seem to think you can do anything to anybody. And now, really, Lewis, I would like to go, if anyone is available to drive me home."

"You mean you don't want me to do so."

"No," said Bronwen.

He rang for a servant and gave instructions.

When she was sitting in the car, he regarded her stony profile almost anxiously.

"I'm sorry if I offended you, but Bronwen, please get rid of Douglas. I mean that."

"And I mean to keep him as long as he wants to work for us," said Bronwen.

"Even if I beg you, tell you I really want you to do this for me?"

"I can't consider your desires, Lewis. I must think of Nan's interests first."

CHAPTER FIVE

Bronwen told Nan she had spent a pleasant afternoon. She thought it was no good worrying her at this stage with an account of her quarrel with Lewis. As long as they could keep Douglas, she thought, they should do so. With his supervision, the lands had been cleared, ploughed and planted with winter crops. He had organized the young Africans into a routine of duties that Bronwen herself, with her lack of knowledge of the African language and way of thinking, had found well nigh impossible.

He had asked Nan's permission to work upon the old Ford, and this occupied him during most evenings. He had found various spare parts among the rubbish in the loft of the barn. Privately Bronwen did not believe he could possibly make a car out of the sorry wreck, but he seemed so keen on the project that she had not the heart to discourage him.

The afternoons were becoming short now. By five o'clock the sun had set, and there was a wintry look about the sky, glowing gold where the sun had gone behind the hill. In the east streamers of pink and azure blue gave a fleeting radiance to the darkening air.

A stray hen attracted her attention. The *quedine* must have missed it when he came to lock them up. She had better go after it. Passing the barn, she was surprised to hear voices and found that Sarah was in there with Douglas. The shed was already dark; the glow from the lamp made an incandescent curtain of her hair. Her low, eager voice went on and on with an occasional gruff rejoinder from Douglas.

They looked very absorbed and happy, but it gave Bronwen a pang of conscience when she thought how she had defied Lewis upon this very problem. From Lewis's point of view, she supposed Douglas was not a very good focus for Sarah's interest. Young people's feelings could be so intense. Bronwen had a flicker of uneasiness over whether her defiance of Lewis's wishes could lead to trouble. Then she smiled. The pair of them looked very far from being involved in a desperate passion. Sarah was holding a greasy piece of engine. She looked up and smiled as Bronwen approached.

"Hi, Bron. What do you know? I'm mobile now."

She indicated a moped bike standing near the barn door.

"I nagged at Lewis until he let me buy one. It's all above board. I've got a license and everything. He wasn't too keen, but I wore him down. He made me promise I'd wear a crash helmet all the time."

She was dressed in a very smart outfit of white overalls. A bright red crash helmet rested on the seat of the bike.

"Look, Douglas, see my snappy overalls. I bought them specially for working on the car."

"A lot of use they will be when we get going—or must I do all the dirty work?" asked Douglas, taking the greasy engine part away from her. But he was grinning happily.

"He looks at her as if she is the most wonderful girl in the world to him," thought Bronwen. "She is so young and yet a man's wholehearted adoration seems a most natural thing to her." A sharp, unhappy pang struck like a sword into her heart. She smiled wryly to herself. "Lewis could never give himself up to another person so utterly."

"I don't want to drive you away, Sarah," she said. "But it's almost dark. Surely Lewis would not want you to travel these roads alone at night."

"It's all fixed, Bronwen. Douglas will come with me. He doesn't mind walking home. He can come over the hill. He's used to walking."

"I know every pathway over the hill, Miss Hughes," said Douglas. "I should do . . . I used to poach guinea fowl and hares when I was a youngster."

He did not mind the long walk back, feeling himself amply rewarded if he could spend a little longer with Sarah. Obviously Lewis would not be told what company she was keeping. Or would he? Surely he would demand to know where Sarah had spent the evening. As if in answer to Bronwen's thoughts, Sarah said, "Lewis has a Show Committee meeting this evening. He will be late. They always talk for hours."

Ought she to leave them together? Sarah would think her very old-fashioned if she should suggest she needed a chaperon. Douglas had a rondavel, a small round, thatched hut, a little way from the house, where he usually took his meals. Bronwen felt responsible for the quicksilver Sarah.

"Would you like to join us for supper?" she asked.

"No thanks, Bronwen. I brought a whole lot of stuff, sausages, bread rolls, tomatoes, and a flask of coffee. We are going to picnic here, so we can get on with the car."

"I haven't told you, Miss Hughes," said Douglas. "Sarah says there is to be a *Concours d'Elegance,* a competition for the best vetern car at the Show. An oil company is offering a prize of 1000 rand, 500 pounds. If we could win it with this car it would help me go to college. Once I was there, I'm sure I could win a scholarship."

"Wouldn't it be fabulous?" said Sarah.

Looking at the old wreck, covered with bird droppings, the stuffing showing through the rents in the leather seats, Bronwen felt this was all a bit optimistic.

"Well, I suppose it's worth trying," she said.

"You haven't been here for a Show. It's usually earlier than this, but this year it's the Centenary. Show Week is absolutely super, isn't it, Douglas?"

"Smashing," he agreed.

"Lewis and I enter for the equestrian events. We show all our prize stock. And there's a huge ball in the Assembly Rooms. Everyone has a new dress. I'm wearing . . . no, I won't tell you. I want to keep it a secret from Douglas."

Bronwen noticed that Douglas was looking a bit depressed, but Sarah babbled on enthusiastically. It sounded as if she expected to go to the ball with Douglas. But how was that to be accomplished, Bronwen wondered, in the face of Lewis's disapproval?

She continued on her way toward the house. Through the window she could see firelight flickering on the ceiling of the living room.

"A fire already?" she exclaimed. "Nan, you really have become a South African!"

"Turn the other lamp up, Bronwen dear. I've worked long enough at these drawings in the half light. Yes, when Tabitha brought in the logs from that old apple tree, I couldn't resist lighting a fire. There is a hint of frost in the air tonight, don't you feel it?"

Bronwen laughed. "I hadn't noticed, but the logs look and smell lovely."

The fire gave the shabby room a comfortable, homely, English look. The faded chintzes of the deep armchairs blended in with the glowing yet subdued colors of the rugs that Nan had collected years ago during their travels in India. On the sturdy oak table, a green glass vase held sprays of japonica; the colors of the delicate blossom graduating from deepest pink to almost white. A copper bowl of yellow chrysanthemums illuminated the darkest corner of the room.

Nan was more mobile now. She had been sitting at her desk in the bay window, creating meticulous paintings copied from photographs of Bushman art found in caves in the district.

"How do you like these?" she asked.

"They are fascinating," said Bronwen, examining them. The tiny stick-like figures had a surprisingly vivid life of their own, small elf-like little yellow men pursuing brown and cream antelope.

"I think I will have these ready for the Show," said Nan. "If only I hadn't had that stupid fall before I was able to take the photographs, or make any sketches of those new ones I found that day. That accident was such a disaster in more ways than one. I was hoping to do a complete portfolio of drawings for the Show. I said so to Lewis this afternoon."

"Lewis?" asked Bronwen. "Was he here?" She was dismayed at the sinking sense of disappointment she felt when she thought she had missed the chance of seeing him.

"How stupid can I be?" she admonished herself. "I refused his help and antagonized him over Douglas because I didn't want to see him too often. Now I feel disappointed when I miss him."

"No, I phoned him about the paintings. He knows a lot about them. He is very interested in the early history of the country. He's very keen I should make a complete record of the paintings and of the flora too."

"Did he . . . did he say anything about Douglas?" asked Bronwen. She had not told Nan how bitterly Lewis disapproved of their keeping Douglas on the farm.

"Douglas? No, why should he? Are you still worrying about that? What does it matter? Sarah doesn't seem to be very interested in him now."

"No? Sarah is in the barn helping Douglas with the car at this moment."

"Really? What hope has Douglas of making anything out of that old wreck? But it may not mean anything that Sarah has come here. After all there are very few young people left here for Sarah to meet. It's only natural she should turn to Douglas. Anyway there's no chance of their getting too deeply involved yet. Douglas has sense and ambition. Lewis intends to send Sarah away quite soon."

"I hope you are right," said Bronwen, recollecting the adoring look on the boy's face. "But I don't think Lewis would approve of her being here."

"Lewis is not such an ogre, Bronwen, although it seems you have taken a bit of a dislike to him. He really is rather a pet. I'm surprised you are not more aware of his charm. I hope you aren't going to mind terribly but I decided you needed to get to know him a bit better, so when he phoned just now, I seized the opportunity. I know you are going to enjoy it."

"Enjoy what?" asked Bronwen, surprised that Nan had taken so much notice of her apparent reaction to Lewis.

"Oh, Bronwen darling, you think I don't notice anything, but I know you have had quite a difficult time since you came here, with very little time for any recreation. So when Lewis mentioned he was going to Seahaven for the day tomorrow to take delivery of his new filly, I asked him if he would take you too."

Bronwen was appalled.

"What . . . what did he say?" she stammered out.

"Well, of course, he said he'd be delighted."

He didn't have much choice, thought Bronwen ruefully. Dear Nan, thinking she was giving her a treat! How was she to know that she and Lewis had parted on bad terms the last time they met?

"He is calling for you at six a.m., so you will have a nice long day there," Nan informed her, smiling cheerfully.

"However am I going to get through the whole day with him, when I know he didn't really want my company in the first place?" thought Bronwen.

But next morning, when she woke, even before she opened her eyes, she experienced the glow of pleasure one feels as a child on a special day. The sky was still red in the east with the blue shadows of darkness gradually lifting away. Then as the sun rose a little higher, shafts of light silvered the grass, where a light sprinkling of frost promised that winter was imminent.

In this kind of weather it was difficult to know what to wear for a day in town. By midday the sun would be hot, but after four all warmth would have gone. Bronwen dressed in a trim, gray flannel skirt with a matching jacket and gay, striped cotton sweater. If the weather became hot toward the middle of the day, she could discard her coat.

She had half hoped that Sarah would decide to come too, but Lewis arrived promptly driving a truck with a single horsebox and accompanied only by his stable boy.

"What a little person you are," he said as he took her elbows and hoisted her onto the high steps of the truck, grinning down at her with no sign of disapproval. One would have thought the idea of taking her to Seahaven was entirely his own. Bronwen's spirits rose for she had been tied to the farm for so long that this unexpected day's excursion seemed a rare and delightful treat.

The long, tarred road stretched ahead through brown,

undulating countryside that looked clean and swept by the dry winds of autumn. Sometimes amongst the farmlands were African huts, round beehive-shaped single roomed dwellings constructed of hardened mud walls and conical thatched roofs. Red aloes bloomed around the square cattle kraals. Occasionally goats or fat black pigs that had strayed through the fences wandered perilously in front of the truck.

Now and again they would come to a village; a place that existed only to supply goods to the farmers and to the Africans who sat on the verandas of the stores, their draped blankets leaving a permanent stain of red ochre against the walls.

Lewis hardly spoke, and Bronwen was content to have it so. Almost she wished that the journey need never end, that she could go on driving through this windswept countryside at Lewis's side forever. Imperceptibly the landscape changed. Great stones, natural dikes stood out like giant's teeth in the grass; a ridge of mountains planted with conifers refreshed eyes used to rolling grasslands.

"This is the mist belt," Lewis informed her. "Even in winter you are liable to encounter bad driving conditions here."

Bronwen noticed the small "cat's eyes" on the side and middle of the road, put there to help the night traveler.

"But we will be home long before dark, I hope, so you needn't worry," he added.

"Of course I wouldn't worry," Bronwen protested. "I've driven in far worse things overseas than a little mist."

"Sorry, ma'am," Lewis wore his teasing grin. "I forgot you are a tough farm girl."

Did he know, Bronwen thought, that she had worked in a city office before she came here? Did he realize what a struggle it was to attempt to keep the farm going? She hardly thought he could understand her difficulties; he who had been born to farm life and his ancestors before him. Almost as if reading her thoughts, he said, "I often think of how extraordinary it must have been for women, used to a comparatively easy life in England, to have found themselves in this barren wilderness.

"For that is what it was in the 1820's when they came. And, although they were unaware of it at first, they had been brought out to act as a buffer against the African tribes on the wild border of the colony."

He was absorbed in his spoken thoughts, and Bronwen was able to observe him properly; a large, handsome man, sure of himself, utterly relaxed, his capable hands guiding the steering wheel, his profile clearcut, his eyes thoughtful and mouth unusually serious.

"After months on sailing ships, they were brought from the coast, left without transport and very few worldly goods, to live or die where they stood. Crop after crop failed because they did not know the country. When at last they began to make some settled life for themselves, the tribal Africans raided their farms, taking their cattle, burning their homes, killing those who opposed them. And still they stayed and rebuilt their homes, making a prosperous cultured way of life for themselves.

"They were not only farmers, but poets and writers. From the early English settlers came the institution of a free press. And the missionaries amongst them organized education for those very Africans whose fathers had fought with them. Those are the kind of people you have come to live amongst, Bronwen."

"The women must have been very brave," she said.

"Yes, especially when you consider that they were cultured, educated people, not used to hardship. One woman settler who came here called it a 'dark, bright land.' I've always thought that a good description."

"I remember Nan calling it a 'Bright Wilderness' once."

Lewis smiled, glancing at her, his face lively and animated again, the brooding, thoughtful look gone.

"That's a good name too. Look, there's the sea at last."

There were white houses in the distance cradling a cup of blue water, and soon they were driving through the neat little town, with steep streets of whitewashed red-roofed houses. A long windswept promenade led to a rocky foreshore and precipitous sand dunes that looked as if they might lead away into the desert, but were really a screen to the grassy parklands and modern villas behind them.

Bronwen noticed that the flaunting red hibiscus, which would have been at home on some tropical island, was trained and tamed here to grow in neat hedges along sedate suburban streets.

"We will go down to the harbor first. I'm anxious to see how Cara Mia has weathered the journey. When we have her into the horsebox, we will leave her with Amos and take a taxi to town to find ourselves some lunch."

The harbor was a small one formed by the estuary of the river mouth, but it had the eternal fascination of a place given over to departures and arrivals of ships from all corners of the world. Stevedores worked amongst the cargoes that were being loaded and unloaded. Yellow grain cascaded into the hold of one ship, while on the quayside, great bales of wool were seized by giraffe-necked cranes and plunged down into the depths.

"Careful, little one," said Lewis, putting his arm around Bronwen and drawing her aside from a swaying crane. He kept his arm there while he guided her to a cargo boat flying a South American flag.

They had left the horsebox a little way off. Lewis could not bring it nearer because the quay was narrow and interlaced with railway tracks upon which were shunting trucks. The horse had to be lowered in a sling with Lewis supervising every move, until at last the beautiful cream-colored Palomino stood trembling upon the quay. Obviously shaken by her experience, she stood tossing her golden mane, her dark eyes wild, her whole body poised for flight.

Bronwen watched, amazed, as another gentler Lewis emerged. As he approached to release the horse from the sling, she reared, pulling at the thongs that bound her and showing her teeth as she whinnied frantically. But Lewis spoke to her in the low voice of a lover. Involuntarily

Bronwen trembled as she heard the husky tones directed toward the startled animal.

"Cara Mia, my lovely, the long journey is over now. You have come home, my sweetheart, my dearest."

Beneath his soothing hands, the shuddering mare grew quiet, the flashing eyes softened as she regarded her master. The regal head bowed to receive his caresses. She allowed herself to be led toward the horsebox. The Africans who had been watching the scene and waiting in case there should be any difficulty, murmured in amazement over the fact that Lewis had so quickly tamed the frightened filly.

"Hau, hau!" they exclaimed, nudging each other. "She knows her master, this one. She knows that he is truly *indoda. Indoda . . . a man!*"

"And now for lunch," suggested Lewis, after the docile Cara Mia had been comfortably settled into the horsebox and left in the care of Amos. "Shall we take a taxi, or would you prefer to walk? It's not very far along the esplanade. You might like to see something of the town."

"Let's walk," said Bronwen.

A southeast wind had risen and was blowing strong and free, gusting along the empty promenade and plucking the waves skyward into dancing white caps. There were few holiday people at this time of the year. Those who were there had retired into cafés and hotels away from the whipping wind.

But the cold blustering breeze could not take away Bronwen's pleasure. She tried hard to match her steps to Lewis's long stride, but every now and again she had to give a little skip to catch up with him. This amused him and eventually he put his arm around her to steady her. Then, having reached the end of the promenade, they stood leaning against the old, corroded rails as Lewis pointed out the landmarks on the long, open beach where sand dunes retreated into the distance in an opalescent haze.

A large notice warned bathers against sharks if the temperature of the water should reach a certain degree of warmth.

"No sharks today, that's for sure," laughed Lewis, as they regarded the glass green waves. "I'm sorry, Bronwen, I'm afraid this wind has spoiled our day. It seemed so calm when we set off this morning."

Nothing could spoil her day, thought Bronwen, for she had given herself over to happiness. It was impossible to deny to herself that she was desperately attracted to this man who was so different from any other man she had ever met during her life in the city. He was strong, virile, handsome, eminently suited to the harsh, shining, beautiful country in which he lived; his moods and character as unpredictable and passionate as the sunlit and storm-tossed days of his bright wilderness.

"My day's not spoiled. I'm enjoying it," she assured him. He took her chin in his hand and turned her face toward him.

"You are very sweet," he said. "I'm sorry if I offended you last time we met. Can we forget it and be friends again?"

Enclosed in his warm arms with his mobile, smiling mouth so very close, it was impossible to deny him. Beyond the quivering of her senses, she only vaguely remembered that the quarrel had been about Douglas and that the problem still had to be resolved. She nodded, feeling rather breathless.

"I hope we can be friends," she agreed.

"Thank you, little one," he smiled and kissed her lightly.

"Though friendship is certainly not exactly what I want," thought Bronwen wryly.

"And now for the lunch I promised you," said Lewis. "We will go to the most luxurious place in town, where you can forget you are a farm girl just for this once."

CHAPTER SIX

"You must be mad," she admonished her reflection as she washed in the powder room of the hotel with its mushroom pink carpet and gilded fittings. "You aren't his type at all. He likes feminine, glamorous, beautiful girls." The dark blue eyes looked back at her, bright and lively. Her face glowed vividly from the walk beside the sea. She combed through the short tumbled curls, applying a light dusting of powder to her thin, clear skin and wielding a pink lipstick.

"This lovely day is half over," she thought regretfully. "But I still have lunch to look forward to, and then the long drive home."

She had been so absorbed in her own thoughts that she had hardly noticed another person enter. Behind her there was a swish of silk and a whirl of movement. At the same time a glorious fragrance, flower-like yet exotic, pervaded the small mirrored room.

Then, reflected beside her own, appeared the most beautiful face she had ever seen. The creamy skin, the dark, perfectly shaped brows, made the large dark shining eyes seem even lovelier. The vision wore a perfectly tailored black suit, made feminine by its trimming of jet beads and pleated black ribbon; the small hat revealed a halo of shining dark hair.

Bronwen felt suddenly dissatisfied with her radiant pink cheeks, her schoolgirlish gray suit. She felt gauche and countrified and began to worry that she would not look suitably dressed in this grand hotel. But when she saw Lewis waiting in the foyer, again she experienced a lifting of the heart.

Even if she did not quite live up to this grand hotel, he was obviously the most handsome man there. The head waiter rushed forward to greet him and to give him the best table in a window alcove. Soon he was ordering what sounded like a fabulous meal from the large menus that had been presented to them.

"Do you like seafood?" he asked Bronwen.

"Love it," she replied.

"Then let's not be conventional, but concentrate on fish. We will have a large prawn cocktail, followed by Sole Belle Meunière. How does that suit you?"

"It sounds wonderful."

"And a white wine is indicated, I think." He glanced at her teasingly. "We'll have Blue Nun, shall we? The name suits my companion's demure looks. A mild wine that grows more fascinating the longer one tastes it. Isn't that so, Kelly?" he appealed to the waiter.

"Yes, sir," agreed the waiter as he glanced curiously at Bronwen.

She at once wondered if Lewis often brought his women friends here. But she determined not to think of it. They looked out from the bay window at the wind-whipped sea.

"Look," exclaimed Bronwen. "What are those dark things in the water? They could be rocks but they seem to be moving."

"Dolphins," said Lewis. "They often play in the waves, quite close inshore."

To Bronwen, who had only seen pictures of the gentle smiling mammal, they had always seemed a symbol of happiness. She watched fascinated as the creatures with their black curving backs gamboled just beyond the foaming line of surf, performing a curiously graceful kind of ballet. Seeing these half-magical animals seemed to round off her joyous day.

With a flourish, the waiter set the prawn cocktails in front of them. They were set in a crystal sphere upon a large container that held a bed of ice. The small prawns covered with a delicious pink tabasco-flavored sauce were placed in a nest of thin shredded pale green lettuce.

"Good?" asked Lewis.

"Delicious," nodded Bronwen, sampling her first one.

The Sole Belle Meunière arrived upon large silver platters. Fried in butter to a delicate gold, it was covered by a sauce of mushrooms flavored with lemon. The wine in tall tulip-shaped glasses was smooth and gentle to the palate.

"I like a girl who appreciates good food," said Lewis, when Bronwen expressed her admiration of the food and wine.

"Perhaps I should be more subtle with him, more *blasé*," thought Bronwen. "But how can I take this delicious meal and this happy day for granted after all the weeks of depressing difficulty on the farm?"

After they had sampled the soft, creamy Camembert upon small biscuits with the last of their wine, Lewis suggested they should have coffee elsewhere. For some strange reason, Bronwen felt reluctant to leave the intimacy of the table in the round window, but she obediently rose. Lewis directed her to the place where cane chairs with striped cushions gave a gay outdoor appearance to the enclosed veranda overlooking the churning sea.

No sooner had they sat down however when there was a flurry of silk, a waft of perfume. The girl Bronwen had seen previously stood before them. Lewis sprang to his feet, seizing both her hands.

"Carlotta, by all that's wonderful! What are you doing here? Why didn't you let me know you were coming?"

With her beautiful face flung back, she embraced Lewis warmly, not kissing him but placing that lovely velvety skin against his brown cheek for a fleeting tantalizing moment. Clasped in Lewis's arms, she cast a puzzled, sideways glance at his companion. In the swift analytical look that took in her simple appearance, her adequate but inelegant clothes, Bronwen seemed to sense the dismissal of any idea of her as a rival. She shrank back embarrassed into her chair.

"Lewis, my dear, I thought you knew. We arrived last week. So you didn't get my letter. Oh, this South American mail system is too dreadful. I said to Ramon, we must somehow have missed your reply."

"Ramon is here too?"

Carlotta dimpled. "Well, of course, Ramon is here.

You could not think, dear Lewis, that I would be permitted to travel alone, especially when I was hoping to visit you in your bachelor establishment. No, my brother is here too. This is a business trip he is making, but I seized the opportunity to come with him. Ramon is looking forward so much to meeting you and your family again."

"Well, of course," said Lewis. "You must come to us straight away. Sarah will be delighted to see you both again."

They sat down at the table, but to Lewis's murmured introduction, Carlotta hardly responded. The beautiful, wide, dark eyes were concentrated entirely upon Lewis, a white hand with pearly, pink, almond-shaped nails rested delicately upon his sleeve. The lovely, full, bee-sting mouth, a little open, revealed a small, pink tongue clenched between perfect white teeth in a child-like but alluring gesture, as she regarded Lewis, head on one side.

"Let me look at you. Oh, I am so pleased to see you, Lewis. We are in such tr-rouble. I tried to phone you this morning, but they told me you had come here. I asked the customs official which is the hotel where a man of the world is likely to dine. He directed me here."

"That was sensible of him. But what's wrong, Carlotta, what's the trouble?"

The large brown eyes widened, filling with tears that spilled over onto the lacy white jabot. Bronwen thought she had never seen anyone cry so becomingly. How heart-breakingly lovely and helpless the girl looked! Even Bronwen felt the urge to console this beautiful doll-like creature, but glancing at Lewis's concerned face, she decided any comforting must be left to him. "We were hoping to come to visit you very soon. Ramon bought a beautiful car, but now he finds that his papers are not in order. He is not allowed to drive it. There was some little trouble with the police in Johannesburg. Your police are very officious, Lewis dar-ling. They would not even listen to me!"

The beautiful mouth was drooping now; the dark eyes enormous. Miraculously the tears had dried, leaving not the slightest stain, only a dewy look which made her lovelier than ever.

"Is that all?" said Lewis, smiling. "We will soon solve that problem for you, sweetheart. Leave it to me. We'll soon get you to Lion's Rest."

Carlotta's face sparkled. It was like seeing a rainbow after a shower.

"Oh, Lewis, I knew you could help. It would be marvelous if we could come to you for a while. I am tired of all Ramon's business affairs. I should like a calm peaceful time on your so beautiful farm."

Lewis grinned.

"Since when did you want life to be calm and peaceful, Carlotta? Is this the girl who could dance the samba with me the whole night through?"

Carlotta smiled roguishly.

"Naughty Lewis. You made me behave . . . how you say . . . so people talk too much."

She gave him a teasing intimate glance.

"Would you be willing to come home with us this afternoon?" asked Lewis eagerly.

Carlotta flung out her arms. "Oh yes, indeed. How ravishing! I am sure that is what Ramon would like and me . . . most of all, I would like to be with you, Lewis, in your beautiful country."

Lewis turned to Bronwen. He seemed suddenly to have awakened to the fact that she was still there.

"Bronwen, you saw the road this morning. Do you think you could drive the horsebox back for me?"

Her heart gave a great lurch of disappointment.

"Why did we have to meet her?" she thought rebelliously. But she agreed quietly that she thought she was capable of driving the vehicle.

"You can follow us. We won't be far away. I'll take the car back to the farm with Ramon and Carlotta. We can sort out the business of Ramon's license in our own town."

Lewis found that the car needed some minor adjustments before it was ready for the road. By the time they had arranged this it was late in the afternoon.

Bronwen would have preferred to start driving while there was still hope of daylight, but she did not get a chance to express her wishes for Lewis seemed to be totally absorbed in his friends' affairs. They met Ramon at the hotel at four o'clock, a dark young man as masculine in his Spanish good looks as his sister was feminine.

He insisted upon buying a bottle of champagne to celebrate their meeting. Bronwen hardly touched hers, but nobody seemed to notice. She would need alert senses if she was to negotiate the winding part of the road through the forested mountain area.

Ramon shrugged his shoulders over his trouble with the police.

"They said I was driving too fast. Maybe I was. Who knows? Certainly I am used to driving fast cars. It was unfortunate that they caught me. But perhaps when we come to your home, Lewis, the police may be kinder to me, no? Meanwhile Carlotta and I are looking forward so much to your hospitality. We are panting to see this farm with the curious name, 'Lion's Rest.' "

"You are the lion, Lewis, no?" said Carlotta. With a delicious mock shiver, she shrugged herself deeper into the short, dark, sable jacket she was wearing. "A fierce, handsome, tawny lion who eats small gazelles whole."

It was true there was something of the antelope about Carlotta, thought Bronwen: the soft, brown, yielding eyes utterly feminine, the slim graceful limbs—just the kind of woman Lewis would like.

"Another bottle?" asked Ramon, looking around. "Miss—er—Hughes—you haven't had much of your champagne!" He looked closely at her for the first time. What he saw, the fresh skin, the dark violet eyes, the fair curly hair, seemed to please him. "What a pity you must drive alone, Miss Hughes. Lewis, can I not accompany her?"

"Certainly, Ramon, if she will have you. It might be better, Bronwen, if you have company."

He is longing to be alone with Carlotta, thought Bronwen.

"Very well," she agreed. "That might be a good idea." But she was alarmed to see the ardent interest of a born philanderer upon Ramon's face, and a knowing glance pass between brother and sister. However it was difficult to draw back now.

The almost rapturous happiness that Bronwen had felt during the whole of this unexpectedly glorious day had fallen about her like a badly-put-up tent that had now collapsed leaving her exposed to the elements. Well, it had been stupid, she thought, to put any value upon Lewis's kindness toward her during this excursion. It was his nature to try to charm any woman with whom he had to spend some time. In fact he did not even have to try. It was as natural to him as breathing. To be fair, when they had walked along the esplanade, he had offered her friendship, nothing else. And what else could she expect, she thought, remembering Carlotta's allure.

"What a beautiful girl your sister is," she remarked to Ramon, as they drove behind the sleek, black car out of the dock gates and away from the town. Lewis had given Cara Mia a tranquilizing injection. The groom was installed in the horse box with her, so he had assured Bronwen she need not worry about her. But it was not the care of the filly that was troubling Bronwen. It was Ramon's appraising stare, his lingering grasp as he helped her up the high steps.

"Yes, she is beautiful. All our family are good-looking. We are from a Spanish family, very old, very historic."

Bronwen glanced at him. There was an enormous contrast between his good looks and Lewis's. Lewis resembled a Viking, a man who spent his whole life in the open air, but Ramon was as sleek and sophisticated as his choice in cars. His face was that of a Spanish nobleman; the kind that looks out from a painting by Velasquez or Goya: dark hair, slender, proud features, a cruel mouth.

But his appearance was contradicted by his way of life. He talked entertainingly to Bronwen about his playboy wanderings around the world. It seemed his father ran the great cattle ranch, and Ramon was allowed the freedom of the carefree bachelor. Looking after some of his father's interests, he and his sister had decided to come on this trip, half business, half pleasure.

"This Lewis . . . I am interested to see his farm. He is a striking personality . . . yes?"

Bronwen agreed without further comment.

"It seems he has made a great impression on Carlotta. He is a man, that one. She insisted upon coming with me. My father liked Lewis very much. He cannot deny anything to Carlotta. She looks soft as silk, but she has character. She is very determined. When she wants anything, she usually gets it."

The black car seemed to have gone ahead more quickly than Bronwen had expected. At first Lewis had slowed down frequently to allow Bronwen to catch up with him. When she was within a few yards of him, she could see the lovely dark head very close to Lewis and white hands gesticulating as if Carlotta were engaged in very animated conversation.

But for a long time the road had been empty of traffic. Bronwen supposed that Carlotta's conversation must have engaged Lewis's attention to the exclusion of everything else. Well, it did not really matter. She could not miss the main road. It was getting dark now, but she did not mind. In fact she would be glad when the confusing half light had gone. The sunset seemed to linger in a red glow upon the rock cuttings which the road led through, and in this confusing light distances were hard to judge.

But there was little traffic. Far ahead they could see the tail-light of a truck about the same size as theirs. Probably Lewis had thought this was their horsebox. Very occasionally they passed an African riding a bicycle. Sometimes a rabbit, hypnotized by the headlights, escaped death by inches.

They had started to climb now. Bronwen remembered that this was the part that Lewis had described as "the mist belt," but the stars were shining and there seemed no reason to worry. She negotiated a sudden rise successfully, then all at once without warning they were in thick mist. It was like a soggy, white blanket. They slowed down to a crawl.

"*Madre Dios!*" exclaimed Ramon. "Should we not stop?"

But before she could carry out this intention, it had happened. A young ox loomed up out of the mist looking to Bronwen about the size of an elephant. As she braked to avoid the beast, the truck skidded to the side of the road and sank into the soft earth.

"Fortunately we have a peon in the back," said Ramon, when she had unsuccessfully tried with the engine to get the truck out of the sand. She looked at his slender white hands as he lit a small cigar and settled down to enjoy it. Certainly she could expect little help from him.

She jumped down and went around to the back of the truck. Cara Mia was still under the effects of the drug, so she need to not worry about that. The "peon" was sleeping soundly, undisturbed by the fact that they were stuck. With difficulty she aroused him and made him understand what had happened. They tried at first to pit the tires against the branches of trees, but it was no good.

Amos, Lewis's groom, understood English.

"Ma'am, I will go find people in huts," he said. "They will push us. Don't cry, ma'am, for this thing. I will come back soon."

Bronwen felt very far from crying. She was thoroughly exasperated with herself for getting into this difficulty, and she was anxious about the horse and the truck. The mist had turned to heavy rain. How was Amos, the groom, ever to find huts and rouse the inhabitants to come out in this weather?

There was nothing to be done but await his return. She was so tired from the strain of the long drive in the unfamiliar truck. She would have liked to stay in the back of the truck and lie with her face against the warm flank of the gentle cream filly, but Ramon rapped upon the small window of the cab and beckoned to her to return.

"He will think it odd if I don't go back," she thought, and emerging once more into the rain, she climbed back into the cab. Ramon had seen the African depart and did not believe in missing an opportunity when left alone with a girl, who, although not exactly his type, was not unattractive.

He regarded Bronwen by the light of the dashboard. Her damp hair in fair curly tendrils and the large blue eyes made her look like some angel in an Italian church, but that was nothing to go by. English girls, he had found during his travels, often pretended to be like angels, but were surprisingly amorous if given the chance. While he smoked the remainder of his cigar, he spoke reassuringly to Bronwen, telling her that he was sure help would come soon. She was not to worry.

After a while, he flung the cigar in a glowing arc through the wet darkness. The steady drip of rain on the roof of the cab was the only sound.

"Come across here," he said. "That wheel looks so uncomfortable. There is plenty of room for two where I am sitting."

The seat next to the wheel was cramping. It seemed churlish to be suspicious of Ramon just because he was a handsome foreigner, so she edged a little nearer, still leaving plenty of seat between them. It was too humid in the cab to shut the window entirely, and the mist and rain were drifting in through the crack she had left open. She was certainly not dressed for these weather conditions and involuntarily she shivered. It was the opportunity Ramon had been waiting for. He swiftly slid across the seat and put his arm around her.

"Poor child, are you cold? Let Ramon keep you warm then." And he caressed her tenderly on the pretext of making her more comfortable.

"Please-don't, Ramon. After all, I hardly know you," said Bronwen.

She was embarrassed and angry, but tried to control her feelings because she did not want to quarrel openly with one of Lewis's guests.

"That is something that will be remedied with the passing of time," said Ramon, meaningly. "I find you most charming, little Bronwen." A thought struck him. "You are attached to Lewis, yes?"

"No," said Bronwen emphatically. "Not in the least."

"Then what is there to hinder us? Here we are alone,

the night is cold, but we can keep each other warm in the most delightful way, don't you agree?"

"No, I don't," said Bronwen, but Ramon thought this a huge joke. He was intent on showing her how gallant he could be, so bent and kissed her hands. Then, as she protested, he took her face in his hands and silenced her with a very experienced kiss.

The door of the cab was flung open, and a torch flashed upon their faces.

"Sorry, I seem to be interrupting something," drawled Lewis. His hair was plastered to his forehead, his clothes drenched. He smiled good humoredly at Ramon, but did not look at Bronwen. She could sense that in spite of the smile he was furious.

"When I realized you were missing, I left Carlotta at a roadside hotel and came back to look for you. Fortunately I met Amos along the road. We have brought men and ropes to tow you out. It should be easy. You don't look as if you are very badly stuck. How's Cara Mia?"

"He finds me in this embarrassing position, and it was all his fault. Then he asks after his horse!" thought Bronwen, feeling furious.

"She is still sleeping peacefully. I'm so sorry, Lewis, about this, but I don't think there is any harm done to the horsebox."

"That's fortunate anyway. I should have known better than to trust a woman to drive such a large truck," said Lewis shortly.

"I would have been perfectly all right if I had not met that ox," said Bronwen.

"Oh, is that what caused it? Well, that was a piece of good luck for Ramon at any rate, wasn't it?"

Ramon, on Lewis's appearance, had started to make some show of supervising the Africans as they tied ropes to the truck, so he was out of earshot.

"But not for me!" declared Bronwen.

"Really?" Lewis's expression was quite maddening, she thought. "You certainly seemed to be enjoying Ramon's company when I opened the cab door. I felt quite embarrassed to interrupt you, in fact."

The truck gave a sudden lurch, and Lewis hastened to

assist Cara Mia, before Bronwen could think of anything sufficiently scathing to say to him.

"I will drop you at the hotel. You can drive the car the rest of the way," said Lewis, when the truck was back on the road. "It may be safer."

Carlotta did not look very pleased when she was told of the change in arrangements. They found her comfortably settled at the hotel. Without much difficulty she had persuaded the manager to light a fire. She was sitting in the most comfortable chair in the lounge, sipping a sweet vermouth on the rocks in front of its blaze, while the local inhabitants gazed with great interest at this vivid beauty who had suddenly been dropped from the skies into their midst.

Nevertheless she spoke very sweetly when Lewis explained his plan.

"How clever Bronwen is to be able to drive these large vehicles," she said. "But she looks so str-r-rong. Me . . . I am not good at these things. I prefer to leave them to the men." And she directed a melting glance at Lewis.

"Yes," said Lewis, a little abruptly. For once Bronwen thought he seemed a little tired. "Well, we will see you later. Drive to Lion's Rest, Bronwen. Perhaps you had better stay the night there. We can phone Nan later."

Bronwen was determined not to stay, but thought she could argue about that when the time came. She felt tired and depressed; shaken by the mishap to the truck, the scene with Ramon, and Lewis's subsequent anger.

Yet in spite of his ill temper over the truck, he apparently took it for granted that she should drive a strange, powerful car for the rest of the way home.

"Next time I live," she thought, "I must remember to be born a little more feminine, a wee bit helpless."

She was still muddy and dishevelled; the sight of Carlotta still exquisitely groomed did nothing to make her feel better.

Carlotta pouted as Lewis helped her into the car. "Oh, Lewis, why can't I go with you and Cara Mia?"

"You will be more comfortable with Bronwen, Carlotta. It's not far from Lion's Rest now."

Carlotta smiled bewitchingly. "I do not care about the comfort when I have your company, Lewis. You should know that."

But Lewis was adamant. Could it be that he wanted to separate herself and Ramon, thought Bronwen. She could hardly believe he cared one way or the other. His anger over the kiss had been more on account of the whole situation, the truck in the ditch, worry over Cara Mia, and the belief that they were indulging in lovemaking instead of trying to repair the damage.

"What do I care?" thought Bronwen wearily.

The car was easy to drive . . . no changes of gear . . . it almost drove itself. But she was bone tired. After the emotions of the day, followed by the strain of the drive and the mishap to the truck, she longed to be by herself, or peacefully sitting with Nan.

But Carlotta chatted vivaciously, asking her all kinds of questions about Lewis and Lewis's house. She seemed not to have any idea of Bronwen as a rival for his affections, but she cross-examined her to make the position clear.

"Do you know Lewis well?"

"Not very well," said Bronwen. "I've known him only for a short while since he returned from South America."

It was really amazing, she thought to herself, how few times she had met him, and what havoc he had wrought in her senses. But now she really must pull herself together and forget that the mere sight of that laughing craggy face across the room, or the glimpse of a chestnut head and whipcord body at one with the horse he was riding below in the valley, could set her heart pounding.

"He is attractive man, yes?" said Carlotta. "He has many girl friends here?"

"I—I don't really know."

"I have many boy friends."

Carlotta stated the fact simply like a child. "Men always fall in love with me. I have, how you call it, much charm. Many, many men want to be affianced to me, but my father, he is very strict. Until Lewis came. He like Lewis, but my father not want to lose me. I had to cry many tears before he would let me come here. One must be clever with men . . . with fathers too."

There was something confiding and very attractive about Carlotta. Even a woman could not help feeling her charm. Sweetly childish, apparently entirely self-centered she was completely certain of her own doll-like fascination. She was like a half-grown kitten; graceful and beautiful, deliciously playful and desirous of being stroked.

"No one could be more feminine," thought Bronwen and thought of Lewis's dictum about liking women to be women. Carlotta would appeal strongly to his extremely masculine temperament.

"Now I will sleep," the girl announced, and closing her eyes, in about five seconds was asleep. Bronwen really needed someone to talk to her to keep her going over this last stretch of the road. She had to force herself to keep alert while Carlotta breathed gently beside her looking like a young, sleeping Madonna.

"I can't face watching her charming Lewis," thought Bronwen. "When we get there I will borrow the Mini again and drive home. Anyway, Lewis couldn't care less what I do. But I wish Nan had never suggested he should take me to Seahaven. My beautiful day certainly collapsed about me very successfully. It was like a glimpse of Paradise suddenly snatched away.

And she laughed at her own foolishness.

CHAPTER SEVEN

"Now we know what Mr. Galbraith was doing on that South American trip," said the postmistress, as she handed Bronwen her letter. "My dear, did you ever see such beautiful clothes! They positively shout Paris."

"Oh, go on with you, Milly, what do you know about Paris, I'd like to know!"

"Well, I may not know much about that, granted, but I do know a pretty face when I see one. She's absolutely gorgeous. Don't you think so, Miss Hughes?"

"Yes, she is very attractive," Bronwen agreed.

"I really think he has met his match now. She seems dead set on him. Good luck to her, I say. It's time Mr. Galbraith settled down. It doesn't look as if she would come to him penniless either. I see there's a letter from your mother, Miss Hughes. She must be missing you. How much longer are you thinking of staying?"

"As long as my aunt needs me," answered Bronwen.

"But I wish I could go tomorrow," she thought as she stepped into the village street and made her way toward Mr. Prothero, the attorney's, office. "It's sheer madness to be eating my heart out for a man who has never even thought of me in that way and now seems to be in love with someone else."

"I must come out to visit Nan," said Mr. Prothero. "Quite frankly, Miss Hughes, her position is gradually deteriorating. There's very little coming in. Even with your small expenditure . . . and I think you yourself have done wonders, you can't hope to keep your heads above water for very much longer. This Douglas Watson now, you can't really afford to pay him even though his salary is very low.

"But I do agree he seems to be a great help. The position seems to be that you can't afford him, and you can't afford to do without him. So what's to be done? I can only repeat that the sensible thing would be to sell the farm now."

"I know it would be best," Bronwen agreed. "But Nan shows no interest in living anywhere else."

"Poor soul, she is still recovering from the shock of Patrick's sudden death. It takes quite a while. But she must see sense soon. I wonder . . . would she take advice from Lewis Galbraith? He's a wise man and kind too. He knows to some extent what a battle you are having, but would you and Nan mind if I told him what the true position is?"

"Oh no, please don't," said Bronwen. "Not yet anyway. Even Nan does not realize how poor we are. But I will talk to her, I promise. Only can't it wait until after the Show? Nan is so happy preparing her paintings. I hate to worry her now."

"Well, I suppose the position can't get much worse, so a few weeks here or there can't make much difference. Things are fairly quiet now on the farms, but soon you will be faced with lambing. It's hard work, you know. How will you manage about that?"

"I think we will be all right," said Bronwen. "Douglas is there to help, and I've bought a book about it."

An amused smile flitted across Mr. Prothero's face.

"I'll say this for you, you have plenty of grit," he said.

Bronwen's own small savings had dwindled to practically nothing. The few clothes that she had brought with her were becoming increasingly shabby. Tabitha's violent ministrations in the way of laundry did not help. Fortunately she spent most of the time in slacks and an old leather lumber jacket that had belonged to Patrick, but the weather was getting colder every day. She would have loved to buy a couple of bright wool sweaters to wear in the evenings, or a plain wool dress, but it seemed as if she would have to do without new clothes in her present position.

While driving home, she decided that she must curtail visits to the town as much as possible. Even the small amount of gas used increased their expenses. If only she could get some type of part-time secretarial work. She would be much more efficient at that than at farming, but it was difficult to find part-time work to do in such a small community.

Nan came hobbling to meet her. She looked so frail, Bronwen thought with a pang. She was really much better than she had been although it would take a while before she was absolutely fit again. She seemed livelier now. The interest in doing the paintings for the Show was slowly taking her mind from her grief for Patrick.

"But after that, what?" thought Bronwen. "Will she relapse back into the trough of despair she was suffering from when I first came? It's true, it is a bit morbid for her to stay here, but she seems so set on it."

"Lovely news! We've been asked to a party," said Nan.

"Where? Where?" exclaimed Bronwen, trying to respond to Nan's unusual gaiety, but having quick feminine thoughts about her wardrobe or lack of it.

"Lewis wants us to go to a welcoming party for his South American friends. Won't it be fun? I'm really most intrigued to meet them after your vivid descriptions."

"I . . . I don't think I can go. I haven't really anything suitable to wear to an evening function."

"You needn't worry about that. It's a *braaivleis*. Lewis wants to show them how South Africans entertain."

"Is it like a barbecue?" asked Bronwen.

"Yes, that's it. You need only wear slacks and a shirt. Your oldest clothes will do."

Bronwen privately doubted the last statement. Next afternoon she pressed her best navy slacks, wearing them with a freshly laundered white blouse and a deep blue cardigan, that, though fluffy from numerous washings, still reflected the color of her eyes.

Nan, as usual, had a kind of timeless, unobtrusive elegance in an old gray tweed skirt with a pale cyclamen sweater.

Douglas, who had not been asked to go to the party, said he would keep an eye on the farm during the evening, while working on the old Ford. Lately he had had a quiet, depressed air. The old exuberance and enthusiasm seemed lacking. Bronwen felt a little worried about this, but put it down to the fact that Sarah had not visited Bushman's Fountain lately.

She was probably absorbed in the novelty of having South American visitors, but it seemed a little hard on

Douglas. But Lewis, at any rate, would approve of her absence. Bronwen was torn between relief that the problem seemed to be solving itself and pity for Douglas's wasted devotion.

The party at Lion's Rest was to be held in a big barn a little way from the house. Lanterns swung from the ancient beams, and a few astonished hens clucked anxiously from the leaping shadows. Outside bales of hay were arranged in a huge circle surrounding a trench that contained glowing coals. Above these sizzled great grids of chops, steak and sausages, bringing to the guests what must, Bronwen thought, be one of the most delicious smells in the world: the fragrance of thornwood smoke combined with that of roasting meat.

It was true as Nan had predicted that people were not elaborately dressed. The men wore denim jeans or casual slacks and open-necked sports shirts, bright or sober as their taste dictated. Lewis's dark green shirt and slacks, eminently practical for supervising the cooking, made him look like some latter day Robin Hood.

In vain Bronwen tried to quell her delight as she saw him wholly absorbed in his task; chestnut hair glossy in the firelight, the handsome craggy features almost of Red Indian hue. He was laughing in so carefree a way that Bronwen felt a swift stab of hurt that he could look so happy when he had given her so much heartbreak.

"Don't be so foolish," she admonished herself. "You have only yourself to blame."

He waved a careless greeting across the glowing trough of flame. "Glad to see you people. I think you know practically everyone here. I'll be with you in a moment. As you can see, I'm working very hard here."

He called to one of the servants, who was making the rounds with a tray of glasses of lager and cider. As they were taking a drink, Sarah came bouncing up to them. She looked very young and gay in a bright plaid slacks suit with a jabot of frilly lace and silver-buckled black pumps.

"Isn't this terrific?" she cried. "I'm so glad to see you. Haven't been around for ages, I know, but we've been showing our visitors this little bit of Africa."

"Hello, Bronwen . . . how you say it, this so difficult name?" asked Carlotta.

Bronwen looked at her as Sarah introduced Nan. It was difficult to keep one's eyes from the creamy skin, the shadowy hair, the perfect features. No masculine slacks for Carlotta! She was wearing a dark green velvet suit, the pants and jacket moulded to the round curves of her small Tanagra Venus figure. A frilly white blouse was fastened at the neck by an oval brooch of Inca gold. She and Sarah, one vigorous and Titian-haired, the other sweetly curved with magnolia coloring, presented a perfect contrast.

"Do you like our outfits? We found them at the little boutique in town. At least Carlotta did, and she altered them to look more stylish. Isn't she clever?"

"I have, how you say, the nose for *le Style*, even in a small place such as this," said Carlotta.

She looked at Bronwen's navy slacks and faded jersey. "This boutique is not bad, not bad at all, Bronwen. You should make visit there. You have very nice eyes, pretty skin. You could look well with more stylish dress. I will come with you. I would like to help you. You could look smashing smart."

They all laughed. The offer was very well meant. Carlotta was kittenish and very feminine, but not malicious. Nan came to the rescue.

"I like Bronwen just as she is," she declared. "Please don't make her smashing smart, Carlotta. She isn't the type. She looks sweet in her own simple clothes."

"I do not understand the English," Carlotta deplored. "It is natural for a girl to make most of herself, no? I not like this how they say in English Vogue, 'understated style.'"

Looking at Carlotta's glowing beauty, Bronwen felt inclined to agree with her. She felt very "understated" at the moment. It must be heavenly to look in a mirror and see that hauntingly lovely face, knowing it was your own; to be able to afford gorgeous clothes even for a simple party like this *braaivleis*, and to know without doubt that one had charm enough and allure to attract any man one chose.

"Why are you girls hiding away like this? Can't you hear the music?" demanded two young farmers, appearing on the scene. Taking Carlotta and Sarah by their hands they danced them away to the barn. Bronwen and Nan were not alone for long however. In a little while Ramon found them and was introduced to Nan.

His gray silk shirt and perfectly tailored pale blue slacks looked a little elaborate when contrasted with the South African men's attire, but without doubt he had a unique type of handsomeness far removed from the pleasing yet rugged features of the local men.

The episode in the cab of the horse-truck seemed never to have taken place as far as he was concerned.

"I suppose it was just a snatched opportunity, best forgotten," thought Bronwen, but all the same she felt humiliated to have been used like that.

Ramon was charming to Nan; his manners quite impeccable. She was obviously gaining a very good impression of him. Through the wide open door of the barn, they could see the couples whirling by in a kaleidoscope of color; bright slacks and shirts, green, red, purple, gold, as they gyrated to the beat of the small band, the throbbing guitars, mingling with the lower beat of the drums. They saw Sarah laughing up into her partner's face, the long swinging red hair like a sheet of burnished gold.

"How nice for Sarah to meet more young people," said Nan. "She has had very little opportunity up to now. Lewis has always kept a very tight rein on her."

"What is this 'ward'?" asked Ramon. "What does it mean?"

"It means that Lewis is in charge of her, in the place of a father," explained Nan.

"A father?" asked Ramon, smiling. "He is a little young, no, to be father to an attractive young girl?"

"He was a family friend, and there were no other relatives. She will inherit a considerable fortune when she comes of age. So Lewis has had to be strict with her. He has tried to bring her up sensibly as best he can."

"Indeed?" said Ramon, looking thoughtful. "Can I get you something, Mrs. O'Hara, a little wine perhaps?"

"No thank you, not just now," said Nan. "Please don't worry about me. Why don't you two dance?"

"Certainly," said Ramon obediently and bowed to Bronwen.

But when they came into the barn, they found it was a version of dancing "Musical Chairs"—a kind of elimination dance in which one changed partners when the music stopped. Several minor tussles seemed to be going on around Carlotta, and Ramon managed to steer himself and Bronwen near to Sarah. Partners were exchanged, and she found herself dancing with several strange young men who responded with monosyllables to her conversational efforts.

"Back so quickly?" asked Nan, when finally she was eliminated from the contest. "What has happened to the charming South American?"

He was still dancing with Sarah. Goodness knows how they had managed that, thought Bronwen.

"How radiant Sarah looks. It's lovely to see her enjoying herself so much," said Nan. "Lewis is inclined to be too strick with her, there's no doubt about it."

"Who's talking about me?" asked a laughing voice. Bronwen's slight depression over the rather unsuccessful dance vanished at the sight of Lewis, who was followed by a servant with a large tray of succulent steaks, chops, and *boerewors* or farm sausage.

"You two must taste some of my cooking. I can vouch for it. You have never tasted better."

He chose what he considered especially good chops for them and sat down at their side, motioning to the men to go on serving the crowd.

"Mm, they are good," said Nan. "Who would be a vegetarian? Though it does make me feel very guilty."

They ate the meat with their fingers. Hot rolls and jugs of beer and cider completed the feast.

"My guests seem to have taken to South African entertainment," said Lewis.

Bronwen followed Lewis's glance to where Carlotta was sitting as if enthroned upon a couch of hay bales, surrounded by half a dozen young men who were plying her with pieces of sausage on a fork to the accompaniment of much giggling.

Although the dance was over, Ramon was still talking to Sarah, Bronwen noticed. They seemed to have a lot to say to each other. The meat was growing cold, untouched upon their plates.

"A lovely party, Lewis," said Nan, wiping her hands on the large, bright, red paper napkins provided. "I love the informality of a get-together like this. I'm afraid Bronwen has had rather a poor time with me since she came here. We are not able to be very sociable."

"Nonsense, Nan. You know I've been very happy with you," Bronwen assured her. "I've been so busy since I came, I wouldn't have had time to meet people in any case."

"Let's do something about it now, shall we?" said Lewis. "I must go and mingle with my guests. Can I take Bronwen away from you, Nan? Here's your old friend, Mr. Prothero, coming to see you."

Nan's attorney was advancing with smiling face. Bronwen hoped he would not choose this evening to be depressing about Nan's affairs. It was hardly likely. To her surprise, Lewis took her by the arm and led her amongst the various groups of people, stopping to chat and introduce her at the same time. He could not have been more charming. And when the band struck up again, he led her onto the floor.

"I haven't had a chance to test the band up to now. Let's try, shall we, little one?"

It was all very informal. Dust brought in on the feet of the dancers rose in a mist above the floor. The band played a *vastrap*, the jigging persistent rhythm of a swinging country dance, to which there had to be impromptu steps, invented to fit the lively beat.

Carlotta was demonstrating more intricate steps to an admiring young man, and Bronwen noticed that Sarah and Ramon were still sitting in close conversation. But

Lewis did not seem to notice. When the music stopped he swung Bronwen around in his arms.

"Whew . . . let's look for some fresh air," he said. Putting his arm around her, he drew her outside. The air had a touch of frost now; a tangy tall smell mingled with the scent of wood smoke. The moon was rising clear and silver over the stable clock; the stars looked very far away above the distant kopjes.

"I must go to the stables to see Cara Mia. She seemed a shade off color today. Will you come with me?"

"I'd love to see her again," said Bronwen.

"Yes, she's a grand girl."

The stable buildings were a little distance from the barn, but the moonlight made the way clear. It was like being on a seesaw, thought Bronwen, being in love with Lewis. One moment she was cast down in a deep pit of despair, then up again, swinging into the sky, breathless and exhilarated by his very presence.

"I have never thanked you for coping that night, when we brought Cara Mia home. I'm sorry there was so much confusion. I hope you didn't find Ramon too impetuous. He's a good chap, but apt to be carried away when he finds himself alone with an attractive woman."

The last two words were the only ones that seemed to be of any importance to Bronwen.

"I didn't take it any more seriously than. . . ." said Bronwen and then stopped, biting her lips. How to explain to him without being too self-revealing that she found his own slight gestures of affection much more disturbing. Yet she knew that to him they had hardly any meaning.

"Give him the slightest encouragement, and he will take it for an open invitation," said Lewis.

"I didn't encourage him."

"No? Ah well, we must blame those huge violet eyes of yours. They must have wrought the havoc in our young South American's sensitive soul."

They had reached the stable. It was strange to move along the quiet stalls at night, hearing only the soft sounds of horses at rest, and smelling the sweet, clean odor of hay, horses, and some kind of disinfectant. They seemed so far away from the dancing and the throbbing distant sound of guitars.

"Here she is," said Lewis, hanging his lantern upon a hook. "How are you, girl? She seems much better now."

"She is lovely," said Bronwen. She put out her hand to stroke the creamy head, and the large dark eyes gazed wisely into her own. She submitted politely to Bronwen's caresses, but it was really Lewis she wanted. When his hands curved over her reassuringly, she turned her head and gazed adoringly at this man to whom she seemed to have swiftly given all her affection.

"You will be all right in the morning, girl. Right as rain, my darling one. Don't forget we have a date, the Show Ring, in a few weeks' time."

"That's a relief," said Lewis as they left the stable. "There's nothing much wrong with her. It's all part of settling down. I guess everyone finds it difficult at first. Did you, Bronwen?"

"Why yes, but that was different. She has a secure home, while I. . . ."

"What is happening, Bronwen? Are things difficult at the farm?"

He would know soon enough if things went on the way they were going. She did not want to spoil this lovely moonlit evening by giving Lewis a recital of her troubles.

"I hear you still have young Watson with you?" he said.

"Yes."

"Wouldn't think he's much use. Fellow at the garage was telling me he spends all his time fixing this veteran car."

"He's very keen on it. It would mean a lot to him if he could win this contest."

"And so you let him waste the time he should be giving to you. Come, Bronwen, you and Nan shouldn't be so soft with him."

"It's his own time. He can't work the whole day and night. It's a harmless occupation doing up the car. He and Sarah have had a lot of fun out of it. . . ."

She could have bitten off her tongue.

"Oh, so Sarah is in on this too? Of course, I would be the last to know."

"I shouldn't have said that. She has hardly been to us since your visitors arrived."

"And I will see to it that she doesn't! Really, Bronwen, I thought I could trust you. You know how I feel about Douglas. He can't be much use to you. Why must you be so obstinate about him?"

"I'm not obstinate. But he is very useful. I just don't see any reason to dispose of our only good worker just because you are hopelessly prejudiced against him."

"This attitude of yours infuriates me. I offered you help, but you ignored it. Yet you deliberately encourage this boy to stay here and associate with Sarah. It's almost as if you were going out of your way to annoy me."

"That is ridiculous, Lewis. I'm only thinking of running the farm for Nan as well as I can. It has nothing to do with you that I find Douglas's help indispensable."

"But you won't accept mine! What have you against me, Bronwen? Why at times do you appear to hate me?"

She looked at him, astonished.

"I—I—" No, she could not deny his accusation for if she did she would burst into tears.

"Show me you don't hate me by getting rid of Douglas," he demanded.

"I can't do that," she said.

"So I'm right. You are risking Sarah's happiness because you have some prejudice against me. Well, let me warn you, Bronwen, I am a hard man to cross."

She was back again in the deep pit, far away from the brilliant stars. Returning her to Nan, he bowed formally and went in search of Carlotta. Bronwen saw him whirl the South American girl away from her crowding admirers.

He asked the band to play a samba. The guests crowded around the dance floor while he and Carlotta performed an intricate exotic solo.

"Let's go home, Bronwen, you look tired and cold," Nan said. "We can slip away. Lewis won't notice, and we'll phone him tomorrow.

Bronwen stood up obediantly. As she negotiated the

car down the driveway, the headlights showed two figures in a secluded seat in the garden. She noticed a waterfall of bright hair leaning toward Ramon's dark face. But Lewis would not notice Sarah's absence from the dance. He was too absorbed with the sweet charms of Carlotta.

CHAPTER EIGHT

A few days later, Bronwen came in to find Nan engrossed in her painting, but with a secretive, pleased smile on her face and a twinkle in her usually grave, gray eyes. Bronwen picked up her folio to admire the delicate paintings, while Nan wiped her paintbrushes, stretched herself, and lit a cigarette.

"What are you looking so pleased about, Nan?" asked Bronwen. "Are you thrilled with the way your paintings are going?"

"That, of course. I am pleased with the way they are turning out. This stage of painting is always heavenly; when you have almost finished and are pleased with your work. You feel very triumphantly and victorious when you have just completed it. You always feel it's the best thing you have ever done. It's only afterward that the doubts begin to creep in."

"So that's why you are smiling like a cat who has been given a saucer of cream?"

"No, no. I wasn't thinking of the painting when you came in. I had a bright idea this afternoon. I acted on it quickly before I could begin to hesitate."

"What was that?"

"I thought it was time we did some entertaining. You lead such a dull life here, and we owe the people at Lion's Rest an invitation after that gorgeous *braaivleis*. We should be hospitable to Lewis's South American guests. So I phoned and asked them to dinner. They are coming a week on Saturday. Won't that be fun?"

"But—but what will we give them to eat?"

"Don't worry about that. Tabitha will cope. Her cooking is quite good, you know."

Nan was so pleased with her idea and so convinced that she was giving Bronwen a special treat that Bronwen did not have the heart to argue with her. In any case it was done now. The invitation was issued, and they could hardly draw back. When Nan was absorbed in her painting she hardly noticed food. Tabitha's plain cooking, mutton stew, mashed pumpkin and mealie rice, while perfectly edible to Bronwen and Douglas who had spent the whole day in the open air, was hardly suitable for a dinner party. They could hardly give the guests cakes for an evening meal.

"We must buy some sherry and a few bottles of dinner wine. Do you think we should run to champagne? There's a delicatessen store in town . . . José's . . . that stocks Camembert and Brie. We had better get the imported kind, don't you think?"

She had been foolish not to let Nan know how very poor they were, thought Bronwen. She had thought while Nan was happy and absorbed in her painting, she would not worry her until after the Show. But even a small dinner party such as this with a few extra luxurious items would make dangerous inroads into their remaining available money. She would have to try to manage without much expenditure, but without worrying Nan.

"If you will break the news to Tabitha, I will take over the cooking for the dinner," she offered. "Leave it to me, Nan. You know I love doing anything like that. I haven't done any fancy cooking for ages."

"Oh, but lovey, I didn't want to give you extra work," Nan protested. "I wanted you to have fun. You do like Lewis better than you did at first, don't you?"

"Yes, I like him," said Bronwen.

"That's good. I'm a bit disappointed that he seems so keen on Carlotta. She's not really his type."

"I would have thought she was," said Bronwen, thinking how strange it was that one could feel an actual physical stab in response to an emotional reaction. "She's very beautiful, very feminine, very attractive."

"Mm," said Nan. "A bit too much like Turkish delight for my taste. Lewis is such a lamb. I'd like to see him married to someone who was gold all the way through, not just a lot of glitter on the surface. Pity you don't seem to take to him very much, because it seems to me your type of person would make an ideal wife for him."

"Me?" gasped Bronwen. "Whatever gave you that idea?"

"Why not?" said Nan. "Let me tell you, Bronwen, you are too modest. Anyone who gets you for a wife could count himself very lucky. But I'd hate to lose you yet, Bron dear, so perhaps it's just as well Lewis goes for all that curvaceous allure. Because if he tried his charms on you, even you would succumb. I wonder if they will announce their engagement before our dinner party. That would be fun, wouldn't it?"

Bronwen tried to nod. She turned over Nan's folio of drawings blindly fighting back the tears that pricked hurtfully at the back of her eyes, for she must not shed them or let Nan know how the few careless words had hurt her.

At the same time she felt a great longing to get away, to go somewhere where she could be alone and sort out her ideas and emotions, so that she could face the sight of Lewis and Carlotta together at the dinner party. The small, black, stick-like figures and red, running antelope danced in front of her eyes.

"Didn't you say, Nan, that you would like a photograph of the scene you were trying to take when you had your accident? Would you like me to go and get it for you tomorrow? I can go by myself, if you give me instructions and draw a little map. I'm sure I will be able to find the way."

"Oh darling, that would be marvelous. It's just what I need to complete the series. But won't you take Douglas with you? It's pretty rough country, and we don't want a repetition of my mishap."

"No, Douglas is needed here. Really, Nan, I will be quite safe. You don't have to worry. I'm pretty experienced at negotiating this countryside now."

"It isn't farmland. It's on the borders of our African Reserve, but it will be interesting for you. I wish I could come with you, but this stupid leg of mine isn't up to it yet. I will stay at home and plan a wonderful menu for our dinner party."

"Yes, do that," said Bronwen, relieved that she had succeeded in her determination to be alone.

As she set out early next morning, there was rime on the grass at the side of the road, the spiky branches of the thorn trees were outlined in sparkling silver. The road climbed upward until she passed the town reservoir, nestling like a Scottish loch in its circle of hills. There was a thin edge of ice around the edge, and the brown Nile geese flapped their wings displaying a lining of bright green feathers and shouted harsh recriminatory greetings at each other, while gawky waders with fantastic feet sought their food along the muddy shore.

The road climbed higher between great cuttings of red sandstone. Occasionally Bronwen passed small groups of Africans who were walking into town to do their shopping. They were the "Pagan" kind, the red blanketed Africans, who even now, after all these years of living near settlements, had not embraced the Christian faith but adhered to the ancient beliefs of Africa.

The women were dressed in swirling, beautifully draped skirts made from blankets that had been dyed in red ochre to a beautiful shade; the orange red of the candelabra aloes upon the hillsides. These skirts swung like kilts as the women walked, and the graceful movement was emphasized by the deep rows of black braid around the edge.

Legs and arms were festooned with copper bangles; necks deeply encrusted with beadwork collars. Upon their heads rested black berets, the size and style a status symbol for increasing age, so that the more wrinkled an old African woman was, the larger would be her headgear.

They walked behind their husbands, carrying their belongings upon their heads. The men strode in front, their ochre blankets draped like Roman togas, woollen caps on their heads, carved sticks in their hands, a long pipe and a beaded tobacco pouch their only burdens.

As Nan had instructed, Bronwen stopped the car on a flat piece of ground at the top of the valley. She was at the head of the pass now. From here there was an astonishing drop to the land on the other side. The ground fell away into a deep vale crowded with beehive-shaped African huts. In the clear still cold air, smoke rose vertically from the cooking fires, and voices from below sounded clearly calling over a great distance.

Near at hand was a formation of red rocks in fantastic shapes; great overhanging stones and deep niches that formed a kind of lookout over the valley below. Hawks wheeled in hovering circles at eye level.

"This is it," thought Bronwen, as she walked across the level tablelike top toward the edge. How different this wild country was from the pleasant grassy meadows she had thought of as "country" in England. At her feet were bare ground and rocks. As she looked closer, she was intrigued to see all kinds of odd plants, small aloes, cacti, and tiny succulent plants fighting for their existence in every crevice of the rock; stone-like plants, hiding amongst the pebbles, so similar that it took a quick eye to detect them. It was winter, and the insect world was partly stilled, but a solitary purple and brown butterfly fluttered over the red flower of an aloe.

Nan had said the cave was down below, beyond that steep *krantz*; a large hollow with a great overhang of rock that had helped to preserve the paintings. She could see from the small map exactly where it must be. It would be best to take the photographs now while the light seemed suitable, and she would eat later.

She began to descend. It was more difficult than it looked. Child's play, no doubt, to a Bushman or a goat; it was very steep and precipitous to an ordinary person. No wonder Nan had fallen. But it had not happened on this descent. It had happened later when she was coming back. Nan had assured her that it was due to her own stupidity in trying to take a photograph of the valley, while she was perched on a rock, that the accident had happened.

She had lost her camera too in the valley below. A little reasonable precaution was all that was needed, Nan said. Scrambling over the rocks, clinging to any likely hand-hold, reaching tentatively for footholds that seemed to crumble away upon the slightest touch, Bronwen eventually managed to arrive upon the ledge that held the Bushman's Cave.

Exhausted as she was, she still realized that this was the

most fantastic sight she had yet enjoyed in Africa. Below her the bowl-like valley stretched away to distant blue hills. No wonder that long ago the Bushmen had chosen this place for their home. From this level plateau, they must have been able to see the whole valley. Any approaching enemy could not remain hidden for long. In those days game would have roamed over the whole area.

She tried to visualize Africa as it must have been in those days: a golden country, teeming with great herds of antelope, buffalo, and giraffe. There had even been lions and elephant in these parts then, and the leopard that in the old days they had called "tigers." "Here be tigers," she thought and turned to regard the Bushman's pictures she had come to photograph.

Yes, in those days, the little apricot-colored man with the slanting golden eyes had been monarch of his wild kingdom. It was only later that the white settlers had come to claim his waterholes and forbid his shooting with poisoned arrows. And the Africans too had come from the North and enslaved him, so that, at last, he had withdrawn farther into the desert, where only he, with his fantastic knowledge of wild life, could survive.

And so the bright wilderness of Africa knew him no more. But here was his memorial, almost as clear as upon the day they were painted: the animals and little figures running joyously over the walls of the cave.

Bronwen photographed them from every angle. Then sat for a long time on the ledge, eating the sandwiches she had brought and feeling more at peace than she had felt for a long time.

She must get away soon, she decided and forget the crazy passion she had developed for a man who could never care for her. She must stop drifting. After the Show she must tell Nan that they could not hope to carry on with the farm and that they must both go home to England. Yes, that would be the best thing to do: to put as much distance as possible between herself and the large, unsuitable, charming farmer who had so deeply impressed his rugged personality upon her innermost being.

The earth was soft and warm inside the cave, and when she had been sitting there for an hour or so, brooding over her problems, the heat of the sun against the rocks lulled her to sleep, lying with her head upon her haversack. The cave caught the warm rays of winter sun all day at this time of the year as it traveled in a wide arc, low across the sky.

When she woke at last, she did not know how long she had been sleeping and hardly noticed the blue shadows lengthening across the lovely valley. She only roused herself when on the track far below she heard the *quedines* driving home their longhorned cattle. She saw the women going home, burdened with enormous bundles of firewood, or buckets of water held upon their heads by one hand as they trotted along to cook the evening meal.

She felt reluctant to leave the Bushman cave where she had spent this peaceful solitary day. Yet now she had made a decision to return to England soon and get away from her infatuation, she felt strangely calm. The sun had gone down, and over the valley the lilac and rose light was giving way to darkness. In the valley she could see the pin-prick lights of cooking fires far, far below.

She had left her return later than she had intended, but it was only a little way up to the road, she thought. She loaded the camera equipment in her haversack and started the steep climb upward. But in the fading light she mistook the track and found herself up against a huge boulder impossible to circumnavigate. It took her a while to get back, and then she found it even more difficult to climb up by the direct path. She had not realized during her descent that it was quite so steep.

When stones, dislodged by her searching feet, fell, they crashed with terrifying, bumping sounds into the *krantz* below. At last she found herself unable to progress any farther over the crumbling, slippery rocks. In the swiftly gathering darkness, she realized that the safest thing she could do would be to descend to the ledge and wait until daylight.

She was not so much scared as exasperated and annoyed with herself at first. If she did not get back Nan would worry. It was going to be very cold and uncomfortable spending the night upon the ledge. But she had matches and a certain amount of food. Fortunately she had brought her duffle coat that was lined with lamb's wool.

"How could I have been so stupid? But I'll survive," she told herself.

She ate the remainder of her food and drank the coffee that was still quite hot in its flask. Then somewhat cheered she set herself to light a small fire from the scanty materials she could find near at hand. There was a dried dead bush at the mouth of the cave, and she used this together with dried cattle dung she found upon the rocks. They must be very agile cattle to get up here, she thought, but then African cattle were like goats. You saw them perched upon seemingly impossible rocky faces for the herdboys liked to drive them up the hills and away from the fields of crops.

When the fire had died down to a steady glow, and she felt a little warmer, she lay down upon the soft earth and tried to sleep. The Bushmen had known what they were doing when they made their home here. The cave was dry, warm and untroubled by the night wind. But there were all kinds of queer noises; little rustlings, squeakings, the occasional patter of small feet. Once she saw an owl like a white phantom swooping toward its intended victim. Near at hand a nightjar called loudly, startling her with it almost human shout.

"Thank goodness the snakes hibernate in winter," she thought. "At least, I hope they do."

Of course, once she had started to think of a snake, slithering its cold curves over the dry sand of the cave and curling against her for comfort, she could not get the idea out of her mind, but after a long time weariness overcame her, and she slept.

Some while later, she started wide awake, aware that something unusual had aroused her. Far away she heard a weird, unearthly clamor. Again it came, a dreadful wailing, howling noise like a spirit mourning at a wake.

"Oh please, let the night pass," she implored the stars with a little sob. "I'm tired of pretending to be brave."

Beneath the huge canopy of the sky, she felt very tiny, very insignificant.

"I'm tired of this queer, strange country. Why did I ever come here?" she thought desperately.

Her spirits were at a very low ebb; her nerves jangled by the unearthly sounds and the wild strangeness of the place where she had been forced to spend the night. "Let the dawn come soon," she prayed, but when she had fed a few twigs to the embers of her fire she found to her despair that it was only one-thirty.

In this place, where, in the valley below, Africans practised the same pagan rites that they had had for centuries, it seemed to Bronwen's heightened imagination that one could believe quite easily in witchcraft and all its accompanying evils. The peaceful harmony of her thoughts upon the Bushmen's way of life had left her. She thought now of conversations she had heard about African customs; the sacrifice of cattle to ancestors, the fact that illness was believed to be caused by a wizard casting a spell; the custom of smelling out witches; and the belief that at night the witch rode abroad upon a hyena.

Again she heard the weird, snuffling, unearthly howls, half-animal, half-human, but this time they seemed to be nearer. At the same time she saw flashing beams and heard something that sounded like approaching footsteps. Her loneliness, the weirdness of her surroundings, the atavistic terror of darkness, the feeling of a primitive African community so near at hand; all combined to rob her of any recourse to reason, and she screamed out, at the same time realizing that she was giving her hiding place away to whoever was scrambling across the rocks.

Instinctively she called upon the man she loved, "Lewis, Lewis!" the echo of her voice sounding high and terror-stricken against the walls of the high cliff.

"Bronwen," his voice answered, quite nearby, anxious,

but warm and infinitely reassuring, making nonsense of all her silly fears.

"Are you in the cave? I'm coming down."

"Do be careful, Lewis, the rock is very crumbly."

"I have a flashlight. Are you hurt?"

"No . . . it's just . . . I couldn't get back."

"H'm." The grunt might have expressed relief, or on the other hand, disapproval, disgust, and a curse upon all stupid females who attempted more than they could do. And now the flashlight caught Bronwen in its beams. Her eyes were wide and dark blue from her recent terror. Seeing Lewis looking so big and comforting in the mouth of the cave, she lost all her usual restraint and flung herself sobbing against him.

His arms went around her, and he kissed her dirty, tear-stained face, soothing her gently and murmuring soft endearments as if consoling a terrified child. But soon the gentle caresses changed to fiercer passion, and his kisses became ardent, demanding a response that she found too easy to give.

At the back of her mind she knew this was madness, caused by the provocative situation of finding her in the isolated cave below the starlit heavens, and that her quick surrender to his caresses was a natural sequence to the black, lonely hours she had suffered that night.

"Let me stay a little longer in his arms," she implored the sparkling sky, but it was he who drew back, holding her by the shoulders and shaking her with a gesture that was anything but gentle.

"What in the name of heaven possessed you to come here alone?" he demanded. "You frightened Nan and me nearly out of our wits."

"I wanted to be alone, but I'm sorry about Nan," she responded.

"But not about me, is that it? I suppose you think I like haring all over the countryside in the dark looking for stray girls stupid enough to do a Garbo in the middle of the African *bundu*? Well, let me tell you it's not a form of pastime I appreciate."

"You are exaggerating, as usual. Nan knew exactly

where I was, and in any case I didn't want you to come looking for me. I would have been quite safe here until morning. I stayed here too long. Darkness came before I realized it would."

"But why?" asked Lewis in an exasperated voice. "Surely you could see the sun was near setting, and it was time to come home?"

"I . . . I fell asleep. I was tired."

His mouth softened a little.

"It's all the fault of this silly obstinacy about keeping the farm going. You get far too exhausted to engage in an expedition like this. Any woman would."

Bronwen had a sudden vision of Carlotta: her lovely face and white helpless hands that were useful only for twining themselves around a man's heartstrings. She gave an angry shrug.

"You always speak as if women shouldn't do anything. I suppose you think they should sit on a cushion and sew a fine seam?"

"No, I don't, but it was sheer madness to come alone to a dangerous place like this. I appreciate courage in women as well as men, but you knew there had been one accident here. Why did you do it? Even your friend Douglas would have been better than no escort. Oh yes, you wanted to be alone. But why?"

"I . . . I wanted to think," said Bronwen, furious at his harsh interrogation and the bitter contrast between his first affectionate greeting and his grim attitude now.

"Think?" said Lewis. There was a frown in his voice though she could not see his expression.

"Even women are capable of thinking, you know," said Bronwen. "And sometimes they like to get away on their own. They are not completely dependent on men's company, believe it or not."

"It seems to me you were glad of my company when I first arrived," said Lewis. "Are you sure you hadn't been the least bit afraid all on your own here?"

"Not in the least," lied Bronwen. "I was just settling down to sleep until the dawn when you disturbed me. . . . Oh Lewis, what's that?"

The last question was uttered in an entirely different tone of voice from her previous attempt at dignity. The ghostly ululation of sound that had terrified her before sounded, it seemed, just at their feet. Without wishing to, she sought his protecting arms again, much to his amusement and her shame.

"It's only a little jackal. Poor little one, didn't you know that?"

He laughed and laughed while he rocked her in his arms. Suffering from extreme nervous reaction, she would have liked to do something childish; stamp her feet, or scream in a tantrum.

Angrily she dragged herself away from him.

"You really are the most infuriating man I've ever come across," she declared. "And, in future, Lewis, I'd be glad if you would keep your casual lovemaking for your girlfriends. I certainly don't consider myself to be one of them."

His laughter vanished, and his voice sounded flat and tired as he answered her.

"No, you have always made it quite clear that you have a pretty low opinion of me, Bronwen. I'm sorry if my touch offends you. You will have to put up with it for a little while longer until we get up to the road."

With the help of the flashlight, they negotiated the steep path without much difficulty. Over the steep places he held her firmly, but now it was entirely impersonal. In the dim light his expression looked as if he had been carved from the rock itself.

They locked her car. Lewis promised he would send a servant to fetch it tomorrow. He had brought a flask of brandy with him and insisted on her taking a few sips. The harsh spirit made her cough, but she was grateful for the warm glow that spread itself through her tired body. It did nothing however for the frozen feeling in her heart and mind.

CHAPTER NINE

"Would you like to come and have a look at the car, Bron?" asked Douglas a few days later when they had been discussing some farming matter together. Since Sarah's defection he had worn a forlorn look, something like Nan's spaniel when he had been scolded. Bronwen felt sorry for him and a little guilty.

He worked so hard for so little return, and now he did not even have the joy of Sarah's company. She followed him into the shed, determined to praise his work on the car even if she could not see any improvement. But when she saw it, she was amazed at the transformation. The old Ford looked beautiful; painted a bright yellow with black mudguards, its brass fittings shining brilliantly in the sunlight.

"Good heavens, Douglas, I can't believe it!"

He grinned happily, the sad expression vanishing in his delight at her enthusiasm.

"I knew she would turn out a beauty," he said, patting the car affectionately. "Surprising what a difference a little make-up and a new dress can make to a car, or a woman, isn't it, Bronwen?"

"I should say it is. I can't get over how beautiful she looks. It really will be glorious, Douglas, if you can win the prize."

"There's lots of competition, I'm afraid. Some of these people who are keen on veteran cars have lots of "bread" to spend on them. However we'll see. I have lots of faith in her."

"So have I now I've seen her," Bronwen agreed.

"Wonder what Sarah would say if she could see her now," said Douglas, a trifle dourly.

"Hasn't she seen the car lately?" asked Bronwen, a little curious to know what the position was between the two now. "She seemed so interested at first."

"Yes, she was dead keen, but since this South

American chap arrived, she hasn't had time for anything but him."

"Ramon? I would be sorry if I thought that was true. He is too old and sophisticated for a young girl like Sarah."

"You would think so, but girls like that type, don't they? They tell me in the village that she spends all her time with him. I don't know whether Lewis knows about it though. Ramon would be pretty careful not to offend his host, I guess. Lewis is like a cat with one kitten over Sarah. But they say Ramon's sister is keeping Lewis pretty occupied, so maybe he hasn't noticed."

"Do they think he is in love with Carlotta, then?" asked Bronwen, despising herself for listening to gossip, but not able to resist the temptation.

"Sure thing. It's not surprising. I've only seen her in town but she looked pretty dishy to me. A girl like that would increase any man's adrenalin output, if you get me. She's kind of cuddly, like a kitten. Yet you feel she knows all the answers. I can see how Lewis might react, and I can't blame him, though she's not my type. I go for girls with a bit of character like—oh, well, forget it."

"Isn't it charming of Lewis?" said Nan, a few days later. "He phoned to ask if he could send us some wine for our dinner. It seems a friend of his from the Cape sent him a case, and he would like us to try it. Sarah is riding over to bring it this afternoon."

Bronwen's first reaction was one of indignation. How dare he patronize them with gifts of wine?

"I suppose he was afraid he might not get any if he didn't supply it," she murmured aloud. Nan looked surprised.

"It isn't like you to make such a waspish remark. Bronwen, don't be like that about Lewis. I can't understand why you still seem to dislike him. I thought you were getting over it."

"I'm sorry, Nan. Yes, I'm getting over it, I hope."

But it was not dislike she had in mind when she said this.

Sarah rode over during the afternoon, looking brilliantly attractive in her well-fitting jodhpurs and an emerald green turtle necked sweater that made her flaming hair look even more like a sheet of burnished copper.

She was tremendously vivacious. Bronwen seemed to detect echoes of Carlotta's mannerisms in the tone of her conversation. But of course anyone as young and pliable as Sarah would inevitably be influenced by someone she admired.

"I've been having a fabulous time," she declared. "Ramon has been helping me to prepare Lady Pearl for the Show. He's awfully clever with horses. He has taught me all kinds of new ways to handle her."

"Not only clever with horses," thought Bronwen, looking at her glowing face.

"Douglas has done a wonderful job on the car," she couldn't resist saying. "It's all ready for the Show."

"Has he? I must go and see it," said Sarah, somewhat indifferently. "Poor Douglas, I'm afraid I've been a bit of a broken reed about helping him, but the days just fly past since Ramon and Carlotta came. There seems so much to do all the time."

"Which reminds me," said Nan, who had come to greet Sarah, "I must get back to work, Sarah. I'm trying to finish the last Bushman painting in time for the Show. It's the one Bronwen photographed for me last week."

Sarah giggled. "What did you do to Lewis when he had to rescue you, Bron? He was like a grizzly bear for days afterward. He kept bringing down curses on all obstinate women. You sure managed to drive him wild. It took all our womanly charms to soothe him. But Carlotta seems to be able to manage him when he's in a bad mood. I guess she could manage any man. I wish I had half her charm."

"Just go on as you are, Sarah darling," said Nan. "Two Carlottas would be too much for even Lewis to handle. I'll see you later." And she left to continue her painting.

"Goody," said Sarah. "I wanted to talk to you alone, Bron."

Bronwen regarded the serious, pure gray eyes with their fringe of dark lashes.

"What is coming now?" she thought.

The wide mouth held a touch of mischief.

"Don't you think Ramon's terrific, Bron?" asked Sarah.

"He seems a well-mannered enough young man," Bronwen replied reservedly.

Sarah exploded into rather unseemly mirth.

"You sound like a maiden aunt, Bron. Golly, you must be getting really old if you don't feel his charm!

"Anyhow," she added thoughtfully, "it's just as well for my idea if I know you are nice and safe."

"Safe?" echoed Bronwen, puzzled. She found it difficult to follow the trend of the conversation, but winced somewhat at the reference to her great age. She supposed the difference of seven years between herself and Sarah seemed enormous to the young girl.

"It's this way. I've had a brilliant idea, only I need your co-operation. Bron, I'm quite bonkers about Ramon."

"Bonkers?"

"Crazy, sent, wild about him, and all that jazz. I never knew I could feel like this."

"What does Lewis think about it?" asked Bronwen, her thoughts flying straight toward him like homing birds.

"He doesn't know, and I don't want him to know yet. He's quite capable of turning Ramon out of the house if anything should go wrong. You know what he's like about me . . . I'm too young and nobody's good enough. I must go to this boring finishing school and learn more of the Great Big World. Good grief!"

"That sounds sensible," said Bronwen.

"Sensible, of course it's sensible . . . and horribly dull too. Oh, Bronwen have you ever been in love?"

"Yes," said Bronwen.

Sarah looked somewhat surprised, but seized on this admission for her own purpose. "Really? Then you know what it feels like. If Ramon speaks to Lewis, there will be all that jazz about waiting until I'm 21. And I can't wait. Why, it's four whole years, an absolute lifetime!"

"The thing is," said Sarah, shaking back her mane of

hair, "we don't want Lewis to find out about us until we have decided what to do. This is where my brilliant idea comes in. I thought if Ramon could appear to be making a play for you it would put Lewis off the scent. He's getting a bit suspicious of us, but if Ramon pays you attention at this dinner on Saturday, it might do the trick. Don't you think that's a rather wizard idea?"

"No, I don't," declared Bronwen. "I don't want any part in deceiving Lewis. It's a foolish notion, and Ramon would never be attracted to me anyway. I'm not his type."

"Oh, Bronwen, please be a dear. It's only for a little while until Ramon can be sure of Lewis's favor. And it can hardly matter to you what Lewis thinks of you because everyone knows Nan will have to sell. One of these days you will be going home again, and all this will be forgotten."

"So people are saying these things before we have even decided on a plan of action ourselves," thought Bronwen despairingly.

"Do as you please," she said, suddenly tired of the whole sorry business. "But warn Ramon that he mustn't behave too realistically in this wild attraction he is to acquire for me."

Sarah giggled. "Oh, Bron, you are a yell. If he does, I'll scratch his eyes out and yours too. You are a darling, Bron. We intended to do this anyway. Ramon said I shouldn't tell you, but I thought it best in case you should think Ramon was really serious about you."

"Very kind of you to warn me," said Bronwen.

Sarah seemed to realize she had gone too far and turned to her with interest, changing the subject away from Ramon.

"I didn't mean that you couldn't be attractive to anybody, Bron. Who were you in love with? Was it a long time ago? Why didn't you marry him?"

"Ages ago," lied Bronwen. "And I didn't marry him because he was completely unsuitable. Anyway he never asked me."

"How disappointing. You should get some hints from

Carlotta. She has some great theories about how you should treat men. I must try to think of someone who would do for you."

It seemed that Sarah, having discovered love, was eager to pass it on to her friends.

"What about Douglas?" she said.

"Douglas? I thought he was one of your boyfriends?"

"He's very sweet, and I wouldn't mind a bit if he fell for you, Bronwen, now I have Ramon. It was just a boy and girl affair," said Sarah from the height of her new-found maturity.

"I think maybe he's a little bit too young for me," said Bronwen.

"Perhaps you are right. But, don't despair. I'm sure to think of someone soon. What are you wearing at your dinner party? I warn you Carlotta and I have decided we will be 'smashing smart.' Carlotta doesn't have much chance to show off her pretty dresses here."

Tabitha came to clear the tea things.

"Hello, Tab, how goes it? Are you cooking us a fabulous dinner on Saturday night?"

Tabitha's face, that had broken into a beaming smile at sight of Sarah, closed up like a nutcracker.

"Miss Bronwen will cook. Tabitha's cooking not good enough for big baas's friends, Miss Sarah."

Sarah realized she had said the wrong thing and shrugged apologetically at Bronwen as she watched the old African shuffle out.

"Whee, did I drop a clanger? Tab's really crabby these days, isn't she? Must be getting old. I'd better go before I do anything else wrong."

"You should try to see Douglas's car. I'm sure he would be delighted to show it to you. I'll call him if you like."

"No, don't bother. I haven't really any more time to spare. I promised I'd meet Ramon before it gets dark to put Lady Pearl through her paces. I'm sure to see the car at the show."

"But I thought—" said Bronwen and then stopped. She frowned as she watched the slim figure galloping away.

The silky hair and the silky mane swayed up and down in graceful unison. She knew that Douglas had been hoping Sarah would be his passenger in the *Concours d'Elegance*, but evidently Sarah had forgotten all about her promise made just a short while ago.

"What shall I wear on Saturday . . . my blue velvet dress, or my blue velvet dress?" she asked Nan.

Nan laughed. "It may seem shabby to you, but you have hardly worn it here. Your eyes look beautiful in that color. You can borrow my lapis-lazuli necklace and earrings. I'm sorry Tabitha's a bit sulky about dinner. I'm afraid we made a mistake in offending her about the cooking. Now she doesn't seem prepared to do anything."

It was true that a sulking Tabitha was more of a hindrance than a help. The day before the party she scorched the old lace tablecloth that Nan had produced from amongst her treasures and left the silver smeared with white powder, so that Bronwen had to clean it all over again in the evening when she had left the kitchen.

She had decided upon a simple meal. Chicken casserole with bacon, tiny onions and herbs was to be accompanied by yellow rice and small green peas. This was to be followed by a crême caramel, made with real cream and eggs, covered by a brittle caramel top, accompanied by some of Nan's brandied peaches.

"I would like to serve a first course," she said. "But soup is a bit too dull or too filling, and things suitable for hors d'oeuvres are so expensive," she grumbled to Douglas who was a sympathetic listener though not very well informed on haute cuisine. "Things like shrimps, prawns, anchovies, and olives cost such a lot."

"I suppose you couldn't do anything with mushrooms?" asked Douglas.

"Where would I get mushrooms?"

"They grow in that far pasture near the stream. It seems to be damper there than anywhere else."

"Are you sure they are safe?"

"I've been having them every morning with bacon for breakfast."

"That's guarantee enough. You look quite healthy. Champignons à la Grecque!" said Bronwen.

"Come again?" said Douglas.

"They are mushrooms stewed in oil and wine with bay leaf, and onion and tomato puree. They're wonderful. Will you show me where to get them tomorrow morning?"

"Sure thing. I'll meet you at six-thirty. It's hardly light before then at this time of year."

There had been a heavy dew upon the grass during the night, and this had been silvered over by a slight frost. A huge, red sun sent its first rays to make drops of moisture glitter on every thorn like the jewels of an empress.

"Good mushrooming weather," laughed Douglas. His slight, medium height figure was made unusually bulky by an old suede duffle coat, his fair skin reddened by the cold morning air, and his blond hair hung untidily over his good-humored gray eyes. He had a slightly forlorn look.

"He is really rather a dear," thought Bronwen. "I'm sure if Lewis knew him better he would like him. There I go again. I must stop thinking about Lewis. But if it were Lewis walking at my side in this radiant light, I would be so stupidly happy, as if we were going to search for treasure instead of mushrooms."

She resolved to make Douglas feel she was enjoying his company, for he had had a thin time lately worrying about Sarah. She sensed under his youthful bravado a lack of confidence in himself that would only be cured by some achievement, and by the feeling that people liked him.

So she set herself to interest him, and they chatted companionably as they walked through the pasturelands.

"It's so different here from England," she said.

"In what way?" he asked.

"For one thing the ground seems so dry and the grass so sparse. I know it's a good sheep country, but I'm always astonished because it seems all little rocks, thorn trees, and dry grass."

"I thought England was all built up anyway."

"Most of it is, of course. But when you see grass it is really green. The color just hits you. When I first came here everyone said the *kopje* looked very green after the summer rains. But it looked almost brown to me. It's a sort of yellow green here instead of blue green."

"Don't forget that the sunshine is very fierce and more or less permanently with us. It scorches the young grass before it has a chance to show. If we have three days of cloudy weather here people say what ghastly weather we are having."

"Oh, I know, it's wonderful here; the dry air, the clear light. At first you think it's colorless, then you realize that everything glows; even in the winter you have all these shades of sepia and hazy blue."

They came to the place near the stream where mushrooms grew. They were large white ones with pink gills underneath, standing amongst the dry grass like small sunshades. After they had picked enough, they sat on a log to rest, and Bronwen lifted the basket to her nose. The evocative smell was somehow secret, exciting, and reminded her of childhood expeditions in her mother's native Wales, when the search for creamy mushrooms in the emerald grass brought a sense of magic to an early morning walk.

"It was such fun looking for mushrooms when we were children," she said to Douglas. "I miss that green grass."

"I suppose you will be glad to go back one day. Or are you going to go on struggling with the farm, Bronwen?"

"I don't know yet, Douglas. We will see when the Show is over. Things don't look too good, as I suppose you realize."

"Yes. I'm sorry. You have worked so desperately hard, and I have tried to pull my weight, but I guess I'm not good enough. I am not sufficiently experienced to make a go of it."

His good-humored face was frowning and worried as he looked at her. She felt the need to reassure him with some definite gesture, so she took his hand and pressed it with her own.

"Don't think that, Douglas. You have really been marvelous. I don't know what we could have done without you. I hope with all my heart that you get that prize and you are able to go to Agriculture College."

"Do you, Bron?" he said, turning to her, his eyes serious. "I find it hard to talk sometimes, but I want you to know that I am really grateful for this break I've had here. You have been pretty wonderful to me too. I never had a sister, but if I had I'd want her to be just as nice as you."

He put his arm around her as they sat on the log and gave her a gentle kiss.

"That's to say 'Thank you for everything,'" he said.

Bronwen was touched but thinking there had been enough emotion for one morning she rose to go.

"I think we both need breakfast, and I have a lot to do today. It's lovely here, but we had better start on our way back."

Just then a liver and white setter splashed across the stream and came bounding toward them waving its silky tail. It was Lewis's dog. Of course, the stream marked one of the boundaries of his land. She caressed the silky head, careless of the large fringed wet paws unceremoniously placed against her slacks.

There was a sharp whistle from the other side of the stream, and a horse and rider came into view. The low rays of the sun struck copper lights from his hair. The dog, at his master's call, impatiently abandoned Bronwen's caresses and splashed back across the water. Lewis lifted his whip and called some greeting, but it was lost in the noise of the shallow stream running across the rocks. They waved back and continued on their way.

Bronwen was annoyed by the bitter, regretful emotion she felt at this brief encounter.

"Did he see Douglas's affectionate kiss?" she thought. "But if he did, what on earth difference can it make?" And at the back of her mind was the vain thought, "If only Douglas had not been with me!"

Douglas was having more practical thoughts.

"I'm sorry to drag you away from your dinner preparations, but I'm afraid I will have to ask you to help me dose the sheep this morning. It can't wait."

"What could be more romantic?" thought Bronwen, laughing to herself.

CHAPTER TEN

The sheep dosing took up the whole morning. In any case Bronwen had decided that it would be better to make her preparations for the dinner after lunch when Tabitha had cleaned up the kitchen. She could not face working in the muddle that the old servant left during the whole morning.

It was her method to clean the rest of the house first in her own slow deliberate fashion and leave the breakfast dishes piled up in the sink until the lunch plates had joined them. Her granddaughter, Tombi, would come back from her school session and give some help.

In the afternoon, the fire was banked down and the kitchen looked comparatively clean and tidy. Bronwen looked forward to a peaceful period of cooking, free from Tabitha's awkward presence.

However, when she returned from helping Douglas, Nan was looking very pleased with herself.

"I've done the flower vases," she said.

"They look glorious," marveled Bronwen.

The living room and hall were transformed by great copper bowls and jugs filled with tawny chrysanthemums, dried leaves, and red berries. Nan had prepared a strange dried arrangement for the center of the oak table, a fascinating mixute of fungi and queer dried plants in a harmonizing mixture of gold and brown shades.

"And Bron, you'll be glad to know that I screwed up my courage and spoke to Tabitha. I said she must help you as much as she can with the dinner."

"That was brave of you. And what did she say?"

"She was a bit sulky at first—you know how she is, but I told her you had said you just could not manage without her, and that made her get over her bad mood."

"But the thing that made the most impression was that I told her the dinner was very important because Lewis was bringing the girl he might marry. She thinks the world of Lewis, so that did the trick. She's wild with curiosity now to see Lewis's future bride. You don't think I've been a bit too premature, do you?"

"No, I don't suppose it matters," said Bronwen. "Everyone talks as if they intend to announce their engagement at any moment."

"Of course, I'd never dream of saying anything to Lewis before they announce it, but it was a good way to sweeten Tabitha, don't you agree?"

Bronwen nodded, scarcely trusting herself to speak. How silly to feel so cold and depressed just because Nan had stated in plain woods just what everyone else was thinking.

"I asked Tabitha to joint the chickens for you, so it would save you time this afternoon. She needn't be in your way. She can clean the rest of the silver in the pantry. We will use the silver candlesticks—I haven't used them for years. Or do you think the copper ones might look better with this arrangement? Tombi can help with any little things you need to have done . . . I'm worse than useless at cooking so I won't interfere, but I'll just be responsible for the table arrangement and so on."

After lunch when she went to the kitchen, she could not believe her eyes when Tabitha actually smiled at her. She had been used to the old servant's dour manner for so long that she found her newly found benevolence quite embarrassing.

"Madam say dinner must be special smart for Baas Lewis's young lady," she informed Bronwen. "Miss Bron, you must cook it nice."

"I'll try," said Bronwen, trying to respond with a smile to Tabitha's enthusiasm.

"Lady who please Baas Lewis must look nice. Is she fat?"

"Not exactly," said Bronwen.

"Never mind. She will get nice and fat when she has children. Baas Lewis will get many sons."

It was ironical, thought Bronwen, that she had longed for Tabitha's approval and conversation, and that now the erstwhile, silent, old African should blossom out with the gossip that was as painful as it could be for her.

"Madam said she asked you to joint the chickens,

Tabitha," she said, trying to change the subject. "Are they ready?"

"Yes, Miss Bron, I cut them all up, very nice."

"That was good of you. It will save me a lot of time."

Then she gazed startled at the big platter Tabitha had brought from the refrigerator. Instead of being jointed into legs, wings, and large pieces that could be fried in butter and placed in the casserole without fear of disintegration, Tabitha had cut the chicken into such minute pieces that it was practically shredded.

Bronwen experienced a few moments of utter panic. "What can I do? There isn't anything else. We haven't killed a sheep this week, and it's too late to kill other chickens. Besides I can't waste all this."

She had to smile and thank Tabitha, while her brain was whirling around seeking a solution to the problem. She dared not offend the old servant by any reproach, risking a return of the sulks. What would be the use anyway? The damage was done.

"I will have to cook it with a cream sauce," she decided. "It will look a bit left-overish, but it will taste good. I will make a Bechamel sauce with nutmeg, cream, and some of the white wine, and we can serve it with rice. Thank goodness we have those small lettuces and tomatoes. I can make a green salad to add a bit of color.

"But then if I serve creme caramel after that, it will be too similar, made with eggs, cream and milk."

She bitterly regretted the Coq au Vin she had intended to serve in a large brown casserole; a hearty meal for a man, that she thought Lewis would have enjoyed. With its green peppers and tomatoes it would be pleasing to the palates of the South American guests.

"It can't be helped. I will make up for the rather invalidish chicken dish by serving shortcake filled with Nan's bottled strawberries and ice cream."

And she set herself to work, cheerfully trying to ignore the fact that a helpful Tabitha seemed to be more of a hindrance than a dour one had been.

When at last her preparations were complete, she lay for a while luxuriating in a warm bath and using up a little of her carefully hoarded perfumed bath salts. It was fun to dress up a little, even though it was only her old blue velvet dress. She had lost weight since she came here and the low neck showed up the frail outline of her collarbone and the whiteness of the expanse of skin beneath the golden-tanned throat. But there was nothing that could be done about that. The lapis-lazuli necklace and earrings looked exquisite, emphasizing the dark blue of her eyes.

Her face was pink from her exertions in the kitchen, so she applied very little make-up and brushed her hair up into a more sophisticated style. On the whole she was pleased with the result, and Nan assured her she looked lovely. Nan was very elegant in a draped gray jersey dress. She wore the opal jewellery she had inherited from Patrick's mother, and her earrings and brooch flashed fire from their milky depths as she lit the candles. The table gleamed with her old lace tablecloth, her crystal wine glasses, and antique candelabra.

"I hope the dinner tastes as good as the table looks," said Bronwen, a little nervously.

The log fire was enlivening the faded chintz and old Indian rugs with cheerful light. They both felt festive and pleased with the results of their labors.

"What fun this is," said Nan. "It's worth the effort. We should do it more often."

Bronwen, placing sprigs of parsley on her "Champignons à le Grecque" felt inclined to agree. "These mushrooms don't look awfully glamorous, I'm afraid, Nan, but they taste gorgeous. At least, I think so."

"They smell very good," Nan agreed.

"Here they come," she said, a few minutes later. "I can see the car lights."

An involuntary trembling caught Bronwen unawares when she saw Lewis enter the room. Apart from that one time in church, she had not seen him dressed in a dark suit before. At first he seemed like a handsome stranger, and the velvet dress evidently made the same kind of impression upon him.

A strange guarded expression, that she could not interpret, seemed to disguise emotion as he took her hand. She thought this must be because he was still annoyed with her, but for Nan's sake must try to be polite.

Carlotta and Sarah, as they had promised, were "smashing smart." Carlotta's dark beauty was emphasized by a dress of fine oatmeal wool, the neck cut low to reveal the uniform creamy olive of neck and breasts. It was trimmed with a heavy border of gleaming, dark, ranch mink at neck and hem. Gold earrings swung almost to her shoulders, and again she wore the beautiful Inca gold brooch and bracelet.

Bronwen felt a little pang of disappointment when she looked at Sarah. But it was a very natural stage of her development, she supposed, when a girl tried to look older than she really was. She was wearing a lurex dress with long sleeves in gleaming silver and green like the body of an iridescent dragonfly. Her bright Titian hair was piled up high upon her head in a most sophisticated fashion. She looked very different from the young horsewoman with hair streaming in the wind, who was usually dressed in turtle-necked sweater and jodhpurs.

Ramon, the last member of the party, looked very correct, the dark suit and white linen emphasizing his slender Spanish good looks. After greeting his hostess in like fashion, he lingered somewhat longer than necessary over kissing Bronwen's hand, giving her a significant look.

Up to the moment, she had quite forgotten about her conversation with Sarah and the crazy plan that Ramon should seem to be flirting with her. For that matter she had not taken it very seriously. Now the recollection came rushing back.

"Oh no," she thought. "I had hoped to enjoy this evening!"

Carlotta exclaimed politely over the flower arrangements.

"Dear Nan, you will teach me, yes? I do not understand so well the flowers here, but I think a girl should know the art of flower décor. In Japan one learns from very early age to do these womanly things to please husband. I like to do flower arrangement, embroidery, all those kinds of things."

"And how is your cooking, sweetheart?" asked Lewis, smiling down at the doll-like figure beside him. She put her arm through his and pouted, fluttering the incredibly long lashes.

"In my country, is no need for lady of house to cook. Nor in this country either. It is true, no? A husband who loved me would not want me to spoil my hands by cooking," she said, dimpling.

"Then your country wouldn't do for Bronwen. She's a marvelous cook," said Nan.

Bronwen glanced at her own hands. Several livid blotches showed where the old, heathen monument of a wood stove had defeated her during the afternoon. She noticed Lewis looking at them as he took the decanter from her to pour the sherry. But he made no comment.

"He can't help noticing the contrast between my hands and Carlotta's slender white fingers," she thought. But she was glad he did not question her. She did not want him to know the dinner had given her quite a lot of hard work.

Carlotta was talking to her hostess. Evidently she had a jackdaw's eye for jewellery for she commented very admiringly on Nan's opals. "But most of all I love diamonds," she said. "Though emeralds are very nice too."

She was like a child stating a preference for certain sweets. Now Ramon came to Bronwen's side ostensibly to take the tray of glasses. While he waited, he slipped his arm around her and grinned mischievously at Lewis.

"This dark blue suits Bronwen's coloring, does it not, Lewis? Is she not charming in this pretty dress?"

"I like her just as well in shorts and an old shirt," said Lewis gruffly.

"Well, of course, Lewis. It is always enjoyable to see pretty legs, I agree."

Lewis frowned and turned aside. Bronwen, feeling embarrassed and uncomfortable over this exhange, tried to get away by taking the tray, but Ramon with a bow insisted on seizing it from her, leaving her standing with Lewis beside the wine cabinet.

"Ramon is not the first man to find you attractive today," commented Lewis.

"What do you mean?"

"From the view I had across the river, it seems young Watson is getting amorous ideas about you too. I should have thought you would have more sense than to encourage someone so young. If you want my opinion for what it's worth, even Ramon would be a better proposition. He's nearer your age. However I don't know that there's much to choose between them. Ramon is nearer your age and has more money, I guess, but he spends it like water."

She turned toward him, so that her face was hidden from the company. They were some distance away from the others who were grouped around the fire.

"Why do you always have to be so horrible? It's no concern of yours who interests me!"

She had intended to deny interest in either Douglas or Ramon, but his tone goaded her to say rash things that she did not mean.

"I know, I know. You made that plain enough the last time we met. I've learned my lesson. Nothing you do is any concern of mine. All the same I'm fond of Nan, and I don't like to see her niece making a fool of herself."

"Really, Lewis! When I need your advice I'll ask for it."

She was so furious that she took her glass of sherry and crossed over to Ramon, smiling at him and pretending a vivacity that she was very far from feeling. He, with a glance at Sarah, responded by appearing to find her very charming. That is how Bronwen interpreted it, but actually Ramon was enjoying himself. From the first he had found the little Welsh girl intriguing, but his courtship of Sarah seemed more promising, for with his expensive tastes it was essential that he should marry for money. However now that Sarah had encouraged him to pay Bronwen some attention, he was far from reluctant to engage in a flirtation.

He had hardly noticed before how lovely she was. Her dark violet eyes blazed, and her color was high and brilliant. Nor had he realized before that she had so much character. With her eyes flashing fire, she looked almost Spanish in temperament. As instructed by Sarah, he set himself with a will to charm and encourage her.

Sarah was determined not to feel jealous. After all it had been her idea. But she did have one or two qualms of doubt when she saw how well Ramon and Bronwen were creating an impression of mutual attraction. She herself was wildly in love with Ramon. She was so young that she scarcely understood and was thrilled and yet afraid of the passionate feelings he aroused in her.

If only Lewis was not so strict and forbidding. To her this first love was so precious, she was afraid of the whole thing being shattered by too premature a revelation.

Now she hoped that her idea had not been all a waste of time, for Lewis seemed to be ignoring Ramon and his flattering conversation with Bronwen. Carlotta was talking to him, to the exclusion of everyone else. The golden earrings flashed in the firelight as she chattered vivaciously. Her voice was low and caressing. Every now and again a silvery peal of laughter rang out.

Sarah talked to Nan about Lewis's plans for sending her to Switzerland, but she scarcely knew what she was saying for she neither wished nor expected to go there. Vaguely and quite impractically, she envisaged herself and Ramon in a kind of Young Lochinvar episode; the two of them riding away to get married, her bridal veil streaming behind her.

Nan pulled together the scattered threads of her dinner party by asking Bronwen if she thought dinner would be ready. Bronwen sprang to her feet, as if she had forgotten such a thing as food existed, raced to the kitchen, then came back a few minutes later to announce that everything was in order.

The mushroom hors d'oeuvres met with loud acclaim. Carlotta was the only one who picked at it a trifle dubiously. Ramon smiled across at Bronwen, proclaiming that she was a wonderful chef as well as a very pretty girl.

But it was Lewis who sprang up to help her serve the wine, and again she was painfully aware of his nearness as they both attempted to dislodge the foil. She found refuge in the kitchen where Tabitha, magnificent in black satin turban, navy cotton dress sprigged with small white flowers, and covered by a dazzling white apron, was dishing up the creamy chicken mixture and fluffy rice.

She followed Bronwen into the living room, placing the tray on a side table and giving quick curious glances at the assembled company, then greeted them formally, making some remarks to Lewis in her own language that made him laugh.

"What did she say?" they wanted to know, after she had gone.

"No, no. It's difficult to tell you. It will lose in translation," he assured them.

"What did it mean, Sarah?" asked Ramon. "You know the language."

She started as if from a dream. "I . . . I didn't hear. I'm afraid I wasn't listening."

But Bronwen blushed as Lewis's amused gaze rested on her. Her association with Douglas and his speech with Africans had made her able to follow Xhosa to a certain extent. She could not rely on her own translation and did not dare to ask Lewis about it, but she thought that Tabitha had said that Carlotta was a little fragile and that she, Bronwen, would make a more fruitful wife. Tabitha had supported this claim by various anatomical reasons that Bronwen preferred not to consider too closely.

Nan was careful to keep conversation general, but Carlotta was obviously absorbed in just one person at the dinner table. She flirted delicately and brilliantly with Lewis. Bronwen found it difficult to keep her eyes from the lovely, flushed face with its perfect profile turned so archly toward him.

In a way it was a good thing, thought Bronwen, that Carlotta should claim all Lewis's attention, for Sarah was being far from discreet. "She may have told Ramon to pay attention to me," she mused, "but really when she looks at him her whole soul is in her eyes. Thank goodness, I'm not as young as that . . . at least I can disguise my feelings a little."

She glanced away from the sight of Lewis and Carlotta and saw Nan eyeing her speculatively. "I wonder . . . Nan is so deep but she can't have guessed what I feel for Lewis, she is probably just wondering when we should serve the dessert."

With this she brought her thoughts down to more mundane levels and helped Tabitha clear the table in preparation for serving the strawberry shortcake.

"This is absolutely wonderful, Bron," said Sarah, whose lovesickness did not seem to have affected her appetite.

"I must congratulate you, Bronwen," said Lewis. "If you ever want a testimonial as a cook, you can apply to me."

"You do this as a profession, yes?" asked Carlotta, wide-eyed.

"Lewis is only joking," explained Nan kindly. "Are you going to be here for the Show, Carlotta?"

"Yes, we hope so, if Lewis will so kindly up with us put."

When the laughter had died down, Nan asked her, "Have you thought of entering for the Show Queen Contest? It's not restricted to local girls."

"What is this Show Queen? Lewis, you did not tell me."

Lewis was frowning.

"I did not think you would want to make a spectacle of yourself, Carlotta."

"I do not understand. What is this spectacle? One has to wear glasses?"

"Lewis means," explained Nan, "that perhaps you would not like to appear in front of a huge crowd of people. But, Lewis, it is quite respectable. The girls don't have to appear in bikinis. It's not only beauty that counts, but charm as well. I'm sure Carlotta has plenty of that."

"What does this Queen have to do?" asked Carlotta.

"She appears at the Show and is the most important person at the Show Ball. She opens it by dancing with her partner in front of the other guests."

"Lewis, why you not tell me of this before? Me, I love to be Queen in front of crowd. What is the harm? And if I had to open dance, you would be my first partner. I do not think then you would mind about spectacle. It is that you are a little jealous, no?"

She smiled enchantingly, and Lewis could not but smile back.

"No man could resist her," thought Bronwen.

"I am sorry for Lewis. Carlotta seems rather a stupid girl," Nan said to Bronwen, when she had followed her into the kitchen to help bring the coffee.

"She doesn't need a single brain in her head with beauty like that," Bronwen assured her.

"I think Lewis deserves better," said Nan. "Someone who will bring him real happiness."

Sarah had asked if she could bring her recorder on which she had taped some South American tunes. After coffee they rolled away the rugs and proposed to start dancing. Lewis asked his hostess to dance first, but she protested that her dancing was too rusty. Having made this guesture of politeness, he swept Carlotta into his arms, and they embarked upon a passionate Spanish form of dance.

Bronwen, her heart aching, had to admit it was a joy to watch. Carlotta's brain power might be poor, as Nan said, but what need was there for a mind, when she could speak with her body, interpreting all the joys of courtship and love, leading her partner into a crescendo of passion? Bronwen found she could not bear to watch any longer and slipped out through the French door onto the stoep.

The grass glittered with frost and the cold, after the warm atmosphere of the living room, was breathtaking. The stars seemed very near; the Southern Cross hanging low above its two pointer stars. She strolled down the path of Nan's garden. The roses had all gone now, and the thorny stumps of branches that had been cut back looked as if they could never bloom again. It was so quiet here, she might have been 100 miles from the passionate dancing. She felt lonely, sad, and defeated. How much longer must she stay here, seeing Lewis, adoring him, but knowing that he cared for someone else?

In the black shade of an acacia tree, she seemed to sense a darker shadow. "Is anyone there?" she called, but there was no reply. When she reached the place she concluded that it must have been her imagination, for there was no sign of a living person. Standing under the tree and looking back she realized that from here there was a perfect view of the living room. It was as if it were on a television screen. Lewis and Carlotta were still dancing, but now they were in each other's arms and Carlotta's carefully arranged hair had become loosened until it resembled a cascade of dark silk.

Nan and Sarah were talking but she could not see Ramon. She had better go back. Nan would think it strange if she stayed away too long. As she turned to go, a dark figure loomed in front of her, causing her to start violently.

"Don't be fright, Bronwen," said Ramon's voice. "It is I. It is cold out here, no?" and he attempted to take her in his arms.

"You need not pretend here, Ramon," Bronwen said sharply. "Sarah had told me you intended to pretend to flirt with me in order to distract Lewis's attention."

"No pretend," declared Ramon. "I find you ver' charming, dear Bronwen. From first time we met, you remember, is it not so?"

Although compared to Lewis, Ramon was slight, there was a whipcord strength in him. When she tried to disengage herself from those encircling arms, it was like trying to get free from pliable steel. The dark head descended above her blotting out the stars, and she felt herself caught up in a seeking, experienced kiss that utterly revolted her. With a great effort, she managed to wrench her face away, but still he kept her in the vice-like grip.

"Sarah . . ." she gasped, hoping to remind him of his commitment to Lewis's ward.

"Do not think of Sarah, Bronwen dar-r-ling. She is charming, but young girl, inexperienced, whereas you have traveled, you are woman of the world—we understand each other, yes?"

"No," said Bronwen. "And I have no wish to understand you, Ramon. Now please let me go."

But the more she struggled, the more persistant he became.

"I like women to resist," said Ramon. "It is amusing, no? Who would have thought such small person could be little wild tiger cat?"

Deliberately he kissed her once more. Her resistance seemed to excite him, and one hand groped upward to her throat, bared by the low sweep of the blue velvet dress. She was feeling quite desperate now. She had hoped she could manage him without calling for help, but her strength was ebbing, and he refused to let her go.

But suddenly she felt herself grasped and thrust aside. In an instant some other person was between herself and her too persistent suitor.

"Are you all right, Bron?" said Douglas's voice. "Just a moment while I deal with lover boy here."

She heard the sound of a blow and a thud as a body hit the ground. Ramon had been taken by surprise, otherwise she did not think that Douglas could have floored him. He sprang up again. Now they were both fighting, fairly evenly matched and both unwilling to give way.

By now the noise of the fight had attracted the attention of the people in the house, and Lewis came striding down the path, closely followed by Nan with a flashlight.

"Good God, what on earth is going on here?" he exclaimed.

At the sound of his voice, the two of them seemed to come to their senses and stopped fighting.

"Oh, it's you, is it?" Lewis grunted when he saw Douglas. "I might have known it."

The first blow had closed Ramon's eye, and he looked as if he had had the worst of the encounter. Nan was horrified that a guest in her house should have come to harm.

"How could you, Douglas?" she said, as if deeply grieved. It was obvious that the tone of her voice made Douglas feel very guilty indeed.

"I'm so sorry, Mrs. O'Hara," he said. "He annoyed me. . . ." then he stopped. Whatever he said would make it worse. He had leaped in to protect Bronwen, but he would be the first to admit that he would not have hit Ramon so hard if he had not been carrying a great deal of suppressed resentment over Sarah's infatuation for the sleek, handsome South American.

Ramon on the other hand dared not to tell the true reason for the fight without arousing Sarah's jealousy, so he kept quiet too. Nan led him into the house where she and Sarah administered first aid to him with tender sympathy. Sarah had not heard of Bronwen's part in the scene, so thought they had been fighting over her. She was thrilled and elated that her dream lover should have acted in such a virile and story-book fashion.

Bronwen stayed behind hoping to get an opportunity to thank Douglas, but Lewis seemed determined not to leave her alone with him.

"It was my fault. . . ." Bronwen started to say, but Douglas shook his head at her firmly. "I'll be going," he said. "I'm sorry about this scene, but I couldn't help it."

"That's your opinion, of course," said Lewis. "It seems disgraceful to me that a young man of your age can't have better control of his feelings."

"Oh, Lewis. . . ."

"Kindly keep out of this, Bronwen. Don't think I don't realize why these two suitors of yours fought. You are obviously at the bottom of this."

"Why, you—" said Douglas, looking as if he were prepared to start another fight.

"Please go, Douglas," said Bronwen, quietly. "I will see you tomorrow."

With a dubious glance at Lewis, Douglas left.

"I wish you wouldn't think so badly of Douglas, Lewis. He was only trying to help me."

"Why?" The monosyllable sounded flat and angry. She tried to read his expression, but all she could see was a craggy profile silhouetted against the dark blue night sky.

"Ramon was . . . well, he was trying to make love to me."

Lewis laughed cynically.

"What on earth did you expect? You have been encouraging him madly all evening. Then you come out alone into the garden with him, on a cold night when there isn't even the slightest excuse to come out and are shocked and outraged because he tried to make love to you.

"And where does Douglas come in all this? It's quite legitimate, I suppose, to play one man against the other, but, if you behave like that, don't be shocked if you run into an ugly scene like this fight tonight.

"Remember this, Bronwen, you can't rouse the primitive in a man and always get away with it. You are not a child. If you don't know how a man reacts when he feels desire for you, then it's time you did."

And he strode back into the lighted room to where Carlotta was waiting for him, infinitely sweet and yielding. He could hardly complain that Carlotta did not know how to treat men, thought Bronwen in despair.

CHAPTER ELEVEN

As Show time approached, the tempo of the little town quickened. It was the great week of the year for the farming community: the time when they laid aside their worries and came into town to show their animals in friendly rivalry; to look at the newest agricultural equipment; to buy the prettiest clothes they could afford for wives and daughters; to see people they seldom had the time to meet during the course of the year.

The talk in the Post Office was all of the Show. Lewis and his romance seemed to be temporarily forgotten, except for one or two comments from mothers of daughters when it was learned that Carlotta was to enter for the Show Queen Contest.

The Rector's wife did her best to be charitable.

"It's true there's no rule it must be a local girl, and in any case. . . ." She left the sentence unfinished in her usual vague way as she left the shop without her stamps.

"Run after her, there's a good lad," said the postmistress to a young boy who was waiting to be served, when they had finished their chat. "I suppose she's right. The young lady is going to belong to the district in the long run, I suppose."

"Not so much of the long run, Milly. Lewis Galbraith won't want to wait all that long for something he's set his heart on, will he, Miss Hughes?"

"What . . . oh, yes . . . I mean, no," said Bronwen.

"Aren't you going to have a bash at the Show Queen contest?" asked the postmistress kindly.

"Good heavens, no. I wouldn't be suitable for that kind of thing."

"Oh, I don't know. You have a sweet face, Miss Hughes, and that lovely English complexion. It's not gorgeous looks that count all the time, you know. They judge you on personality as well."

"So they say," said one of the customers. "If you ask

me, it's nice legs and a good figure the judges look for, being mostly men."

"Oh, well," said Milly, philosophically, "we can't all be beauty queens, can we? Someone said you had had a bit of nursing training, Miss Hughes. They are short of helpers in the Voluntary Ambulance Unit for the Show days. Do you think you could help out on a couple of days?"

"Yes, willingly," said Bronwen. She had done some voluntary nursing work before. At one time she had thought of making nursing her career.

"It's not hard work. You just have to look after anyone who feels faint and be on duty when they have the horse events in case anyone breaks their neck."

"You make it sound dead easy," laughed Bronwen. "All right, you can tell the Chief Officer that I will come when he wants me."

Douglas had finished his work upon the Ford. It looked beautiful with bright yellow paintwork shining in the sun and the brass fittings glittering.

"Will you ride with me, Bron?" he asked. "I need a woman passenger to create the right impression."

"What about . . ." asked Bronwen tentatively.

"Sarah? Forget it. These days, she only has time for Ramon. She used to have such sense. I never thought she would go overboard for a guy like that. She's crazy about him. But she had learned one lesson from going around with me. This time she's clever enough to keep it from Lewis."

"She's young, Douglas. He can't stay here forever. She will forget him when he has gone."

"I hope so. But if Lewis marries Carlotta, I suppose he might be glad to have Sarah marry his wife's brother. I don't know. Anyhow if I can only go to college, I will be well out of it, even though I will miss you people and this farm."

"We know you can't stay with us much longer, Douglas. In any case, after the Show, we will have to decide on our future plans, you know."

"Yes, let's forget it all and enjoy the Show. How about it? Are you going to ride in Lizzie?"

"I'll be honored to, Douglas."

So Bronwen borrowed an Edwardian dress from one of Nan's friends who had a collection of old dresses. It had been someone's "going away" dress and was made of fine yellow cashmere, tucked and braided with brown velvet.

The day before the Show opened, she drove Nan to the Show ground with her precious folio of paintings that were to be shown in the Homecraft and Hobbies section of the exhibition. It took a long time to set them up in accordance with Nan's perfectionist standards, but Bronwen was not too busy to appreciate the tremendous activity going on all around her.

It did not seem possible that a small community like this could have so many hobbies. Collections of shells and stamps jostled with fine needlework, knitting and cobweb lacework. Bottles of preserved fruit flashed jewellike with their golden peaches, ruby plums, nectarines, cherries, and pineapple.

Outside the hall, in the long sheds divided off into sections, cattle and sheep were being groomed like film stars for their public appearance. The cows especially looked as if they had been rubbed with boot polish, and the ewes had the aristocratic appearance of dowager duchesses.

"Oh, there you are!" said Sarah, bouncing up to them, looking a child again in her jodhpurs and emerald sweater. "Lewis said you would probably be here, and that I must ask you to come and have a tea-break in the Members' Enclosure.

All morning, Bronwen had been conscious that they might meet Lewis. She longed to see him and yet dreaded the encounter. She had not seen him since the disastrous night of the dinner. In fact Nan had remarked on his prolonged absence. It was for Nan's sake, Bronwen supposed, that he had sent this invitation now.

As she walked across to the Members' Enclosure, carefully avoiding the milling crowd of grooms leading horses, of small herdboys persuading reluctant pigs to their new lodgings, of trusted servants leading huge bulls by the nose, she tried to quiet the excited breathless exhilaration that seized her whenever she was to meet this fascinating, exasperating man. As he sprang up to greet them, and she met his penetrating blue gaze, she had the sensation of drowning, so that she was glad to take the chair he offered and to look away, pretending a false interest in the antics of a small bull calf as it was led past the picket fence.

The Members' Enclosure was a rather grand name for a strip of lawn surrounded by a low fence and dotted with small tables surmounted by sunshades.

"Your guests are not with you?" asked Nan, a little surprised.

"No, Ramon was expecting a business call from the Transvaal so stayed at the farm, and Carlotta is at the beautician's gilding the lily in preparation for the Show Queen contest tomorrow."

He raised his eyebrows quizzically and looked at Bronwen, who was immediately conscious of her ruffled curls and face devoid of make-up.

"As a matter of fact she wanted to phone you, Bronwen, to ask your opinion of the hairdresser, but I told her I thought you did not patronize the local ones very often."

"No, she doesn't," Nan agreed. "My darling Bron has not had much time for things like that since she came here. But I'm determined she will have her hair done properly for the Show tomorrow."

Bronwen was thoroughly embarrassed by the personal trend of the conversation. "It's not much use having it done, Nan," she said, "because it will all get squashed down when I wear my nurses' cap."

Lewis looked interested. "What's all this about a nurse's cap?"

"Bronwen is going to do nurse-aide work at the Show."

"Well, you are noble," said Sarah. "I'd hate it. You will probably find yourself having to look after hundreds of bawling brats. Can you really do first aid on me if I fall off Lady Pearl?"

"I hope so," said Bronwen.

"Sure and I'm not going to give you the chance, anyway," laughed Sarah. "We are all set to win all our events, and, if I do win, Lewis says I can go to a gymkhana in Johannesburg, next week. Isn't that exciting?"

"Only if you behave yourself, sweetie," grinned Lewis.

"He adores her," thought Bronwen. "They are two of a kind, but it seems completely fatherly or elder brotherly."

"Are you riding in the events, Lewis?" asked Nan.

"Yes, I'm entering on Cara Mia for a couple of jumping events. She's a bit temperamental as yet, but I think she will shape up."

"I can't ride her. She just won't let me," said Sarah. "But she adores Lewis, like most women do."

She gave Bronwen a mischievous glance, but whether it was just because of high spirits or it was meant to convey a knowledge of her infatuation, Bronwen dared not surmise. As they rose to go back to their task, Lewis said, "I hope you two will join us at Lion's Rest before the Ball, if you haven't made any other arrangements. We have a couple of friends coming from the Transvaal; a farmer, and a chap from the University who is interested in Bushman paintings, Nan. You would be doing me a favor by coming to meet them."

"That will be fun, won't it, Bron?" asked Nan. And Bronwen perforce had to agree. She had already told Douglas she thought it best not to accompany him to the Ball. Accepting this second invitation would make her refusal seem a little churlish, but she would have to explain to him as best she could. He was determined to be there, and in any case she thought he would be happier without a partner. If he were alone, he might get his opportunity to approach Sarah again.

Bronwen had made herself a very simple evening dress in preparation for Show week. It was made of an uncrushable white cotton material that was inexpensive yet looked like crepe. It was perfectly plain, sleeveless, and scoop-necked. With it she would wear Nan's amethyst necklace that was set in silver.

She had seen the elaborate, expensive dresses that had appeared in the stores during the last few weeks, but they were not for her. The homemade dress would be adequate, she thought wryly, for someone who looked as if they never visited a hairdresser.

It was quite a good idea to be a volunteer nurse, she decided next day, as she sat on a bench to the side of the crowded spectator stand, her view unimpeded. There was little call for their services. They bandaged a few knees for small children and disinfected grazes for the riders, but the farming crowd were evidently a healthy lot. For most of the time Bronwen had leisure to watch the events of the ring.

Sarah, looking immaculate in tailored riding habit, the peaked, black velvet cap contrasting with her bright hair, easily led the field in all her jumping and riding events.

"She rides most beautifully," thought Bronwen. "That must be because Lewis taught her." And she looked forward eagerly to seeing him ride in the men's events.

But now came the contest which everyone had been waiting for; the parade of girls and judging of the Show Queen. Sarah came to sit near Bronwen.

"What a yell!" she said. "Lewis was asked to help judge, but he had to decline because it didn't seem fair when Carlotta, who is his guest, seems such a sure thing."

The girls had to make their appearance on a podium, erected specially in the middle of the spacious grounds. They were interviewed by a male commentator in front of a microphone, and Bronwen felt a lively compassion toward the small group of pretty, nervous girls.

They were so fresh, so young looking, and had obviously taken enormous trouble to dress becomingly. But they were no match for the sparkling charm of Carlotta; whose beauty, self-confidence, perfect figure and face, were enhanced by the attraction of a low sweet voice with a broken accent. Her gorgeous dress of golden brocade, as it reflected beams of light, seemed to be the very essence of the sun itself.

"She looks heavenly, doesn't she?" said Sarah, and Bronwen agreed that this was so.

"Where is Ramon?" she asked.

"He has had to go off on some tiresome business, but

he will be back soon. I'll die if he isn't back in time for the Ball. Oh, Bronwen, wasn't he a clever actor the way he pretended to be so attracted to you that night? It completely hoodwinked Lewis."

"Yes, it seemed so," agreed Bronwen, dryly. "But why do you want to keep it from him, Sarah? Surely it would be better. . . ."

"No, it wouldn't," Sarah declared adamantly. "He's so stuffy about me, I daren't say anything until . . . well, anyway, it won't be for much longer. I'm going to give everyone a surprise soon, but don't say anything."

Sarah gave her a secretive smile. Bronwen did not have time to surmise what she meant by this, because they were interrupted by a roar of applause as Carlotta stepped down from the podium. She looked around and finding Lewis standing nearby slipped her arm through his and chattered excitedly as the judges conferred together.

Then the announcement came. Carlotta had won, and Bronwen saw her fling her arms around Lewis and kiss him, to the roaring approval of the crowd. He led her back to the podium, and she bowed right and left waving with a regal gesture before the Mayor crowned her with the golden circlet and pinned on the white sash with its golden lettering.

Now she was in the Mayoral Rolls-Royce, but still she clung to Lewis and insisted on his sitting on one side of her while the Mayor sat on the other, as they slowly circled the showgrounds to the cheers of the enormous crowd.

"Lewis doesn't seem to mind now that she has won," said Sarah, biting a piece of grass. "They had lots of arguments about whether she should enter for it. She will have a fabulous time at the Ball tonight. Everyone will want to dance with her. Lewis will hardly get a look in. He won't like that. You had better be there to console him, Bron," and she glanced mischievously at Bronwen, sedate in her nurse's uniform.

"Here's Douglas arriving," she said in a different tone of voice. "Now what does he want?"

"Hello, Bron. Hello, Sarah. Bron, will you be able to get off duty for an hour, do you think, while we have our big moment?"

"What big moment is this?" asked Sarah, sounding a little nettled that her ex-suitor should seem more interested in Bronwen.

"Bron is riding with me in the *Concours d'Elegance*. Any objections?"

"No, none at all, if that's how you want it," replied Sarah, sharply.

Bronwen felt like a bone seized upon by two warring puppies.

"I must go to change," she said, having already arranged for someone to take her place on casualty duty.

The temporary dressing room that had been erected for the Show Queen contestants and anyone else who needed it was deserted when she arrived there, and she had space and leisure to change into her Edwardian costume. It was really most becoming. She was surprised at her own transformation when she gazed into the long mirror.

The full leg o' mutton sleeves emphasized the slenderness of her small waist and the feminine moulding of the bodice below the high boned collar. The bright yellow dress with its sweeping folds of skirt adorned with brown velvet braid was offset by a wide brown velvet plumed hat, set horizontally upon her head and tied down under the chin with yards of pale tulle. She brushed down the curls onto her forehead to give the effect of Edwardian bangs.

The canvas walls of the dressing tent were not soundproof. Bronwen could hear the sounds of people talking as they went past, and sometimes heard amusing snatches of conversation. Then suddenly near at hand as if immediately on the other side of the canvas, she heard voices that she recognized as those of Ramon and Carlotta.

"Well, it's all arranged. We will take a trip to the Transvaal next week." This was Ramon.

"But Ramon, I cannot leave here . . . Lewis. . . ."

"That is not as important as my affair. Absence will increase his feeling for you, if it is there, of course, little sister?"

"What do you mean?"

"I mean he is taking quite a long time to make up his mind, this strong silent man. Perhaps a little too silent for you, eh, Carlotta? Maybe a little parting would do the trick, who knows? Meanwhile you cannot stay here next week while this other business is brewing. It would be most unwise. You must come with me. I have arranged it all. You must provide a cover for my plans."

"But, Ramon, I do not like. Your plans interfere with mine, maybe will spoil my future, who knows?"

"For you with your great beauty there are other fish in the sea, Carlotta. But for me the matter is urgent, you know that. I must satisfy Papa, otherwise. . . ." The voices drifted away, and a little while later Carlotta came into the dressing room. She looked brilliantly beautiful in the golden dress, but her face was flushed, her eyes shining with unshed tears. When she saw Bronwen, she looked somewhat disconcerted.

"Bronwen, how charming you look!" but her voice was distrait.

"Congratulations, Carlotta. I'm so glad you won."

This was the effect Carlotta had. One hated the idea of her in connection with Lewis and yet now, seeing her distressed and near to tears, Bronwen could only feel the sympathetic pity she would feel for a charming child.

"Yes, it was exciting, no?" She smiled through her tears at the glamorous memory of her recent triumph. "And Lewis . . . I do not think he was too displeased."

"I'm sure he wasn't. He must be very proud of you."

"You think? Oh, Bronwen, me, I think I understand men, but this Lewis . . ." she shook her head.

Bronwen felt reluctant to be involved in her confidences. "I must go," she said, "Douglas is waiting for me."

"No, no, Bronwen, I . . ." and the storm that had been threatening to overwhelm her finally broke. Carlotta laid her head on the bench before the mirror and sobbed bitterly.

"Carlotta, what is it?"

Through her sobs, Bronwen heard Carlotta murmur Ramon's name and Lewis's, but she could not understand what the girl was trying to say. She put her arm around Carlotta and tried to calm her as one would soothe a distressed child.

"Carlotta, I don't know what this is all about, but try not to be so upset. Just think, you are the Show Queen. You are going to have a glorious time at the Ball, because you will be the most beautiful, the most important person there."

Like a flower unfolding to the sun after being dashed down by a storm of rain, Carlotta's lovely face gradually brightened.

"And Lewis will love me? You think, Bronwen, that I have some chance of gaining Lewis's love?"

"Of course," said Bronwen firmly.

Ignoring her own hurt, she could not however stop herself from adding, "Do you love him?"

"Oh yes, indeed. He is so handsome, so rich, so suitable. Papa approves of him."

These seemed to Bronwen rather flimsy reasons for loving. She sighed. Was this doll-like creature really suitable for a man like Lewis? But her heart melted again as Carlotta clasped her hands, raising those lovely eyes to thank Bronwen.

"You are so good, Bronwen, so independent. Me—I have always been brought up to obey my father's wishes and now my brother's. I cannot help myself."

If Lewis wanted a pliant bride, he would get one if he married Carlotta. Bronwen thought regretfully of the differences of opinion that seemed to occur every time she met Lewis. She heard Douglas calling her name and hurried to join him, leaving Carlotta repairing the damage the storm of tears had wrought upon her beauty.

"Why, Bron, you look perfectly lovely," exclaimed Douglas. He tucked her arm into his and laughing companionably they turned toward the refurbished veteran Ford.

"One moment, Bronwen, have you seen Carlotta?"

It was Lewis, in search of the Show Queen, who was expected to be upon the stand for this event. Bronwen went back to tell her Lewis was waiting and returned to find Douglas and Lewis standing side by side in stony silence. But when Lewis looked at Bronwen, his grim expression relaxed a little.

"That outfit is a bit of a change from your usual slacks, Bronwen. I had no idea you could look so sedate."

"Well, I think she looks terrific," asserted Douglas, who seemed, with the successful appearance of his car and of his partner, to have lost his awe of Lewis. He himself was dressed in old-fashioned tweed breeches, a motoring cap and goggles. Carlotta came running toward them showing no sign of her former tears.

"Lewis, how lovely that you did come. Me—I am so shy to sit on stand by myself. You will come with me, no?" She stood on tiptoe to kiss him on the cheek.

"If you use such persuasive methods, I don't see that I have any alternative. Goodbye, Bron, and good luck, Watson."

"That was decent of him," said Douglas, surprised.

"He is decent," said Bronwen. "I wish you could be friendly with him now that. . . ."

"Now that there's no reason to be otherwise—is that what you were going to say? Yes, Bron, I realize I seem to have lost Sarah's interest, but it doesn't mean that I've lost interest in her. Old faithful, that's me. If she ever needs me, I'm there."

"That's a good name for the car," said Bronwen. "Old Faithful."

"Good idea. Let's announce it that way."

The car with a name seemed to capture the crowd's imagination. There were beautiful old Bentleys, Daimlers, and even one stately, high Rolls, but the bright yellow Ford with its picturesque young passenger was greeted with roars of applause each time it made its laborious way around the course.

When Douglas had to crank the engine and dash up onto the driver's seat as quickly as he could before it started to move forward, the audience thought this was rehearsed and cheered heartily. Bronwen's fresh pretty looks in her bright Edwardian costume, and the modest popularity she had gained in the village since she came here, helped them in the contest too. Nobody was surprised when they were declared the winners.

Carlotta as Show Queen was asked to present the prizes: a small silver plaque and a check for 1000 rand. At her insistence Lewis came along with her, and the cheering rose to a crescendo as she gave Douglas the envelope and kissed him.

The young man was quite overwhelmed by the fulfillment of his dreams. "I owe it all to you, Bron," he said, turning to her, and in front of the vast crowd, he flung his arms around her, kissing and hugging her until she was quite breathless.

Then Lewis came forward to tender his congratulations. "Well done, Watson," he said. "Charming performance, Bronwen. You certainly deserved your partner's enthusiastic thanks."

His words were kind, but Bronwen, sensitive to his slightest reaction, detected some disapproval in his tone of voice.

"Thank you for the congratulations," she said. "But I will have to be like Cinderella now. Back to the nurse's uniform!"

A while later she was sitting in her old place at the side of the track, watching Lewis perform upon Cara Mia. How graceful it was, the poetic motion of man and horse. His immaculate riding habit of russet tweed harmonized with the creamy coloring of the beautiful Palomino with its red-gold mane. As he lifted his hard hat acknowledging the cheers of his audience, his chestnut hair was sunflecked to a coppery gold.

Bronwen held her breath as he negotiated the high barriers with the artificial ditches below them. Each time a horse stumbled, the crowd gasped, but Cara Mia never faltered. Rider and horse were completely at one.

The accident happened so quickly that nothing could

have been done to prevent it. A little child, strayed from his parents, ran across the arena, with a steward, momentarily caught napping, running in pursuit. But the child, imagining this was a game, laughed joyously and ran even faster right into the path of Lewis's oncoming horse.

The pounding hooves sounded like thunder in Bronwen's ears. It seemed too late for Lewis to take any avoiding action, impossible to divert the sensitive, highly strung filly from its course in that short distance.

She saw Lewis desperately trying to rein the horse in; the child a bare three feet from the lethal hooves. Instinctively she closed her eyes. There were screams and a concerted groan from the vast crowd.

"Are you all right, miss? We'd better get going."

It was the ambulance attendant at her side. Bronwen opened her eyes, ashamed of her momentary weakness. The child was clasped unharmed in the arms of the pursuing steward, while Cara Mia nosed at the still figure upon the ground.

"Better take the stretcher. It looks pretty bad. He took a bad fall. Why the devil can't people look after their children at a show like this?"

A doctor had emerged from the audience by the time they reached Lewis. "Let's get him under cover, where I can examine him more closely," he said, when he had completed his preliminary examination.

In those few minutes when she looked at the beloved craggy features, the ashen face, its freckles standing out in sharp relief, the thick eyelashes over the closed eyes, Bronwen seemed to die a thousand deaths.

"No bones broken, it seems," the doctor said cheerfully when they had brought Lewis to the first aid hut. A little concussion maybe, but I think he's just had a bad jolt. Don't look so worried, nurse. He'll survive, but I don't know about you. You look as if you need a drop of sal volatile yourself. Let him rest quietly. He's pretty tough, you know, he'll soon come around. Call me if you need me. I won't be far away. He may have a bit of a headache when he comes to, but he'll be right as rain tomorrow."

Bronwen sat calmly for less than five minutes. Lewis

looked so quiet and still. Surely the doctor had been a little casual? He looked so pale and helpless. She leaned over him, filled with dreadful panic.

"Lewis, my darling, please wake up. Please listen to me." He was so still. "Don't be ill, you are so alive always. It's dreadful to see you like this."

Seized by an ungovernable impulse, she stooped and kissed him, then, shocked at her own behavior, sat back and tried to think calmly.

His eyes flickered, and he gave a long sigh.

"What happened. Cara Mia. . . ." he tried to sit up.

Bronwen was immediately at his side.

"Lie quietly, Lewis. It's quite all right. You had a bit of a fall, but the doctor says there are no bones broken."

"Bronwen," he looked puzzled. "I thought . . . must have been dreaming."

"Don't talk, Lewis. I'll get the aide to call the doctor."

"No, not yet. Come here, Bronwen."

She approached the couch. He took her hand and held it to his brow.

"Beautifully cool. I thought they would be. Little Bronwen, so calm, so efficient. You would make a good. . . ." His voice trailed off.

"Lewis, please stop talking."

". . . a good, a good . . . what was I going to say?"

"You were telling me I would make a good nurse," said Bronwen, trying to pacify him.

"Not a good nurse, Bronwen," his speech was slurred. "No . . . no . . . I meant . . . for some lucky fellow . . . a good wife."

"He hardly knows what he is saying," thought Bronwen, but all the same for her it was as if a hundred singing birds made music in the quiet first-aid room.

"Carlotta. . . ." Bronwen's exhilaration faded. "Where is she, poor child; did she get a fright?"

Until now Bronwen had not given Carlotta a thought. Now she looked out of the hut to where Carlotta was still sitting upon the stand, surrounded now by several admirers who, because of Lewis's absence, had taken the opportunity of approaching her. She was laughing and chatting, her beautiful small hands gesticulating to emphasize her words.

"She seems to have got over it quite well," said Bronwen.

CHAPTER TWELVE

By the next day, as the doctor had optimistically predicted, Lewis had fully recovered from his fall. The plans for the Ball were not disrupted.

"Why are we going to Lewis's to eat beforehand, if we intend to eat all this food later on?" asked Bronwen. She and Nan had come to help with the preparation of supper for the Ball.

"We don't eat until about midnight, and you will have to do a lot of dancing before then," replied Nan.

The Town Hall was a little gem. Built during the 19th century, when the settler population had begun to thrive, it was like a small old-fashioned theater, with red-curtained boxes looking onto the stage and a lofty roof adorned with elaborate plaster mouldings from which were suspended huge beautiful crystal chandeliers.

Portraits of worthies who had served the town over the last century adorned the cream and gold walls. But the farmers' wives were not content with such mundane decorations for their Ball. Those fortunate enough to have sunsoaked valleys free from frost had brought armfuls of flowering peach and plum blossom. This was mixed with festoons of shining evergreens and red, yellow and pink poinsettia. The stage was transformed into a garden with a small fountain in the middle, live goldfish, and a dovecot with cooing, bowing, white doves.

In the kitchen and supper room there was the same mad activity that Bronwen had experienced at the Show. Women in cotton dresses, aprons, and with hair sometimes adorned with curlers and scarves, cut up meat, roast chicken and duck, great hams and saddles of lamb, mixed gargantuan salads of tomatoes and lettuce, or stirred giant-sized bowls full of sliced paw-paw, oranges, grenadillas, bananas and pineapples.

"Angel's Food," said Nan. "A Ball would not be

complete without Angel's Food, accompanied by trifle and ice cream."

"What fun it all is," thought Bronwen. "And how bitterly I will regret leaving it."

As she cut and sliced at the long trestle table and listened to the laughing badinage of her neighbors, she felt a part of this easy-going, warm, good-natured life.

Sarah came in with Ramon to deliver the Lion's Rest contribution to the feast; numerous cooked chickens, several roast suckling pigs, and a whole basket of hard-boiled eggs for making savories. Ramon looked rather disdainfully at the crowd of busy women and waited a little impatiently for Sarah as she displayed the new elaborate coiffure the hairdresser had just concocted for this evening.

"Lewis is flourishing," she assured Nan and Bronwen. "I must fly. Ramon says he wants to try the new cocktail bar before we go back to lunch."

"In that case, I hope you stick to lemonade, Sarah," said Nan, with unaccustomed sharpness.

"Don't worry, Nan dear. I'm saving my thirst for the champagne tonight. I'll just have a vermouth on the rocks with Ramon."

Nan shook her head as Sarah danced away to rejoin Ramon. She frowned as she watched the young girl laughing with head upturned toward him and eyes unashamedly adoring.

"I feel a little worried about Sarah, Bron. Do you think there's anything in this infatuation? Do you think Lewis realizes how she feels? I wonder whether I should speak to him about it."

"I think Sarah is sensible enough basically. She is just a bit carried away with Ramon's glamor."

"I don't want to start anything before the Ball and spoil everyone's evening. We will see how things go tonight."

This had been spoken in an undertone, and now they woke up to the fact that their neighbors were gossiping on the same subject. But it was far from disapproving. All the world loves a lover, and the sight of Ramon looking so handsome, and Sarah looking so unusually attractive and sophisticated had set all the middle-aged hearts beating it seemed.

"What a handsome pair!"

"I always said Sarah would marry young."

"She'll make a lovely bride."

"He must be well off too, doing all that traveling."

"In any case she will have enough for the two of them. She comes into her parents' money as soon as she marries. In that case she doesn't have to wait until she is 21."

"Is that a fact? My goodness, some people have all the luck, don't they?"

An uneasy feeling niggled at the back of Bronwen's mind as she listened to this gossip. Why? It was all very good-natured. Why did she have this feeling that something disastrous was pending?

"It is just that I have come to a decision about telling Nan we must give up the farm," she thought to herself. "But no, it isn't that. I've known for ages I would have to face up to that."

This feeling of gloom seemed definitely to be centered upon Sarah, and yet who could feel sad about Sarah with her bright head and merry nature? Surely she was destined for a golden future? There would be many men in love with her vivacious temperament before she made her choice. After all she was still almost a child. This interest in Ramon would soon be over. He could not stay forever, even though it seemed likely that his sister might make her home here.

The dark wood paneling of Lion's Rest made a perfect foil for Carlotta's loveliness, thought Bronwen. That evening she watched her pause at the head of the stairs as if awaiting a tribute to her own beauty. Her white chiffon dress was classical in design, beautifully simple save for a motif of silver Greek keys around the draped folds of the skirt and upon the square-cut bodice.

Her lovely neck was bare, but long brilliant earrings swept almost to her shoulders. Silver Italian sandals revealed an elaborate triangular design of crystals upon the instep, and a small bolero of silver mink swung from her arm.

Bronwen's own white cotton dress with which she had felt well pleased, now seemed extremely humdrum. The fluffy blue bolero Nan had unearthed and lent to her for the cold journey by car was old-fashioned and dowdy.

"I'm jealous," she admitted to herself. "I want to be beautiful, glamorous, well dressed, and fascinating—all for Lewis. But I'm not. I'm Cinderella without any godmother this evening, so I'd better be contented with the fact that I can stay up until after midnight strikes, but unfortunately the prince will not even notice that I am there because he will be very much involved with a fairy princess."

Carlotta, evidently well satisfied with the stunned silence her appearance had produced, gracefully descended the stairs and was introduced to the two guests. Professor Roberts hardly paused from his conversation with Nan. He had buttonholed her straight away to tell him about the Bushman paintings in the district. But Tom Ransom, the Transvaal farmer, a bluff, hearty man, simple and good-natured, seemed completely bowled over by Carlotta's attraction. With a determined air, he stayed like a limpet at her side, as if he intended to claim priority for the rest of the evening.

Bronwen found herself being offered a drink by Lewis. "Have some, Bron, it's great," said Sarah, whose simple pale green dress enhanced her sophisticated coiffure.

"Not too much for you, young lady, remember," warned Lewis. "Only one glass."

It was a champagne cup with whole strawberries floating on the top.

"Unfortunately frozen ones," said Lewis. "The best we could do in midwinter."

The snacks were delicious, small pancakes stuffed with tasty savory fillings, slices of toast piled with caviare and decorated with lemon slices, lobster patties, thinly-rolled Parma ham and smoked salmon on skewers, tiny clams upon hot biscuits. It was difficult to remember that later one still had to do justice to the large supper at the Ball.

Sipping her champagne, standing beside Lewis, Bronwen was again overwhelmingly conscious of his attraction. Casual dress was all very well, but a tall man still looked his best in white tie and tails. The conventionality of the white carnation was strangely contradicted by the bandage on his head that gave a rakish, piratical look to his otherwise staid appearance.

"Doesn't Lewis look devastating tonight?" asked Sarah, giving Bronwen a mischievous look. Lewis laughed and the resemblance to a swashbuckling hero of some other age was even more pronounced.

"Bronwen prefers me in a riding habit, isn't that so?"

Bronwen glanced at him sharply. Surely he could not know anything about her emotional behavior of the previous day? She must be imagining that there was an added significance behind the wicked, knowing grin?

If she thought he had heard her she would feel like running home and hiding her head in a pillow like a child in disgrace . . . but she was being too sensitive and mistaking his usual teasing manner for something more significant.

There was a cheer for the Show Queen when she arrived at the Ball, and a special table had been reserved for their party at the head of the hall. Lewis had ordered orchids as being appropriate for his South American guests; a beautiful flamboyant Cattleya for Carlotta, a lavender spray for Nan, an exotic greenish one for Sarah, and for Bronwen small exquisite starlike blooms of amber, yellow and brown.

"Do you like them?" he asked Bronwen, after he had received Carlotta's demonstrative gratitude.

"They are really exquisite," she said, gently touching the small brownish blooms, each one a miracle of perfection.

"It seemed to me they would suit you much better than something more exotic. Do you mind?"

She wanted to say, "I do mind, of course, I do—that I haven't got a hauntingly lovely face, an indefinable allure, but only because if I had I might stand a chance with you."

But she smiled and said a little shyly, "Of course you are right, Lewis. I could never live up to a Cattleya. I do honestly prefer these."

"Shall I tell you a secret? So do I."

She glanced up startled, and what she saw in his eyes both puzzled and thrilled her. She had a sensation of breathlessness, and the hall with its gay decorations seemed to whirl in a dizzying rainbow of shimmering colors. Then the officating stewards came to ask if the Queen was ready to open the Ball with her chosen partner, and Carlotta came to Lewis, her arms outstretched, alluring as a Lorelei, in her shimmering draperies of white and silver.

To the haunting nostalgic strains of a Strauss waltz, Lewis and Carlotta swayed in a graceful solo dance around the pale yellow shining floor. Crystal chandeliers shimmered above and below in their own shining reflection. Like moths to a flame, the dancers clustered around the pair. Then, the solo finished, the rest began to dance as if their patience had been tried beyond endurance by the evocative waltz rhythm and the gleaming temptation of the dance floor.

"Glamorous night . . ." sang the violinist, and Bronwen was whirled away by Lewis's friend, Tom Ransom, the visiting farmer from the Transvaal.

"Always a good show, this," he said. "Splendid chap, Lewis. Have you known him long?"

"A few months," said Bronwen.

"Jolly good farmer. Knows a lot about horses. That's a beauty he was riding yesterday. He was lucky she didn't break a leg. Knows how to pick a filly," he said, obviously searching the room for a glimpse of Carlotta.

"Horses or girls?" asked Bronwen.

"Ha-ha, little card, aren't you?" and he swung Bronwen around to the strains of the waltz. As soon as the dance had ended, and they had seated themselves at the table, he looked around and made some excuse to join Carlotta. He was deeply attracted to her, that was plain, and had no scruples about trying to take Lewis's girl. He was a handsome, bluff, simple fellow who seemed to be able to make Carlotta laugh a great deal.

Lewis's other guest, Professor Roberts, was an older man and seemed to find enjoyment in Nan's company. Lewis was joining in their conversation too, and Bronwen was glad that his attention seemed to be diverted to his guests, for Sarah's behavior with Ramon was far from discreet. Ramon himself seemed to realize this, and, after a dance during which Sarah had gazed at him in particularly amorous fashion, he whispered to her and came to ask Bronwen to be his partner.

Sarah looked displeased and certainly after the dinner episode Bronwen did not care if she never saw Ramon again, but she accepted his request with good grace and soon found herself involved in the intricate steps of a South American tango. Even though she disliked Ramon, his dancing was a joy to follow, and she returned to the table smiling and exhilarated.

"I'm afraid my dancing will seem a little sober after that. The doctor said I'd better not prance around too much. But let's have a go, shall we, Bronwen?" said Lewis.

And now Bronwen gave herself up to the joy of being in his arms. She did not speak for words would break the spell. "I know what Cinderella felt like," she thought, smiling to herself and looking up, found him regarding her with the same odd quizzical expression she had noticed before.

"I amuse him tonight," she thought. "For some silly reason, I appeal to his teasing sense of humor. Well, I suppose that is better than making him angry."

When the music stopped, he whirled her away into a small side room that was screened by ferns and had been made to resemble an old-fashioned conservatory. No one had discovered this hideaway so early in the evening, or else everyone was still intent upon dancing.

"Come, little one, we are usually surrounded by people or eland or horses, and I never get a chance to talk to you."

"If you want to talk about the farm, Lewis, I can't tell you anything until I have had a discussion with Nan—and that will be soon, I hope."

"Who said anything about the farm? Why do we always have to be practical together, you and I? Here we are at a Ball. You are young, and looking, if I may say so, very lovely. No, I don't want to talk about the farm. Nothing was farther from my mind."

"Looking, if I may say so, very lovely." The words seemed to dance in front of Bronwen's eyes in letters of fire.

"Sit down," he said, indicating a small sofa "and tell me about yourself."

"There's very little to tell," said Bronwen, smiling.

Seating himself beside her, he took her hand in his and watched intently as a delicate pink swept up from neck to brow.

"How charming to see a girl blush. I didn't know they could these days. You say there's nothing to tell, but, little one, there must be something. What kind of a life did you lead before you came here? All I know about you is that you seem to spend your life doing things for other people, trying to run the farm for Nan and helping lame ducks like this Douglas Watson."

"He isn't much of a lame duck now. With his check from the *Concours d'Elegance*, he hopes to go to the Agricultural College."

"Really? You surprise me. But we are getting away from the subject, which is you, Bronwen. Tell me what you did in England."

Yesterday Bronwen would not have believed it possible, but now she found herself telling Lewis all kinds of things about herself and her family.

"I suppose they must be eager to see you again. How do you feel about it? How have you liked it here? Could you make you life here?"

"I do . . . love it here," Bronwen stammered. "In spite of all the difficulties, I have been very happy."

It was true, she thought. Knowing that he was here, that she might see him, gave her a kind of bittersweet contentment. She knew that for the rest of her life, however far away she traveled, she could never love another person with the exacting passion she felt for this man, who was able to arouse her emotions so easily. At times she felt a stranger to the staid girl who had left London only a few months ago.

Lewis put his arms around her and kissed her gently on the mouth.

"Don't look so surprised. That's in return for the lovely kiss that roused me from my sleeping beauty state yesterday. It was a most sweet awakening."

Bronwen was enormously confused. She sat feeling wave upon wave of vivid color mantling her cheek.

"You said something too, but I didn't quite get that. What did you say, Bronwen?"

He laughed and kissed her again, giving her a little shake. "Don't look so stricken. There's no harm done. You are a very sweet thing, Bron. No wonder Ramon and Douglas fought over you."

"I . . . they. . . ." Bronwen stopped. How could she explain to Lewis that Ramon's apparent interest was nothing but a pretense, when it was intended to hoodwink Lewis himself?

"I don't think I blame them now. Whoever wins your affection will be a lucky man, Bronwen."

Back in the ballroom, no one seemed to have missed them. Bronwen was surprised to see Sarah dancing with Douglas, talking earnestly and not looking too pleased. Nan was still getting on well with Professor Roberts, and Carlotta was whirling around the dance floor with Tom Ransom.

The thought crossed Bronwen's mind that perhaps Lewis had taken an interest in her because of Carlotta's temporary defection. But no, he would never be so petty. She hugged the odd bittersweet conversation to herself, knowing that when she was alone, she would take it out, examine it, analyze it, and blame herself for leaving many things unsaid.

CHAPTER THIRTEEN

"It's Lewis for you," said Nan, holding the phone a few days later. The main events of the Show week were past, and tomorrow the results of a year's organization would disappear. Hundreds of animals would be loaded onto trucks to be returned to their natural habitat, and the Show grounds would be deserted for another 12 months.

There was only one event left, a spectacular torchlight procession arranged to take place upon the mountain. Its climax was to be the spelling out of the centenary dates of the little town.

"Hello, it's me," said Bronwen, a little breathlessly, as Lewis's deep attractive voice came over the line.

"You sound as if you have been running. How are you this morning? I'm deserted."

"Why's that?"

"Sarah has gone to Johannesburg, and Ramon and Carlotta have taken a trip to Tom's Transvaal farm for a few days. I myself have to go away tomorrow to inspect my other farm, but I was wondering if you would like to take up that long-standing invitation to try Joe's paella this evening?"

"That would be fun. I'll ask Nan," said Bronwen.

"Oh, er—yes, do that."

Bronwen had taken it for granted that Lewis meant the invitation was for both of them, but from Lewis's tone it appeared that he had not. Bronwen's heart gave a lurch of disappointment, but it was too late now. She went to ask Nan while Lewis held on. But Nan surprised her by saying Professor Roberts had said he would like to come over this evening to see some of her drawings.

"You go, Bronwen. It will be fun, and I think we are both old enough not to need a chaperon. It would have been a bit boring for you in any case because you have seen them all before."

Lewis sounded pleased. "Right. I'll phone José and tell

him to produce the best paella he can. And I'll buy a bottle of white wine. José's place isn't licensed but you are allowed to bring your own. Have you any preference?"

"I know very little about South African wines. I've liked most of the ones I've tasted."

"Then we'll have a Late Harvest. That should suit your palate, white but not too dry."

Lewis's careful choice of wine was rather lost on her this evening, she thought, as she faced him across the red checked tablecloth. In her present mood, vinegar would have tasted like nectar. All day, to quell the excitement this invitation had aroused, she had kept telling herself that this was simply a kindly gesture. He had found himself at a loose end, alone after weeks of being surrounded by pleasant company, and he had recollected the half promise forced upon him by José that some day they would dine together in the little café.

Earlier during the week, when she had learned she had won a cash prize for her exhibit, Nan had insisted upon a small spending spree for both of them. Now Bronwen was wearing a plain dark skirt with a pretty, warm blue sweater. Nan had bought Bronwen a creamy coat of long piled mohair material. She said icy winds would soon sweep in across the country, gathering their coldness from the mountain snowfields of the Drakensberg and the Maluti range of Basutoland. The creamy fluffy coat gave an extra glow to Bronwen's golden skin, and the blue sweater enhanced the gentian color of her eyes.

"You are looking very lovely, this evening, little one," said Lewis, as he took her arm when he had parked the car in front of the little café. José was on the doorstep to greet them, his rotund figure covered by a voluminous white apron, the downward droop of his luxuriant moustache belied by the upward turn of his mouth with its flashing brilliant teeth. His brown eyes rolled frantically in his efforts to make Bronwen feel she was the most welcome guest he had ever received.

"*Mama mia*," he called, "see who has arrived."

His plump wife came running into the café, clutching

her latest baby, a child like a cherub from an old Italian painting.

"Isn't she a honey?" said Lewis.

She went to him without hesitation, cooing and gurgling in some strange language of her own.

"I can see she will be a real beauty," Lewis assured the proud parents.

"He is so natural and has a genuine interest in people," thought Bronwen. "No wonder he is popular. He makes you feel valuable and important to him. He does that with everyone, so I mustn't let myself think that there's anything special about his attitude to me lately. I'd only be storing up heartbreak for myself if I did."

But it was difficult not to respond to his attraction, for tonight it really seemed as if he had set out to charm her. José brought the paella, serving it in true Spanish style from a metal pan with handles; a delicious mixture of rice, green peppers, onion, tomatoes, chicken, crayfish, prawns and mussels. He insisted upon finding what he thought were the most succulent titbits for Bronwen's plate.

"Is Spanish dish," he told them. "But I can do Italian cuisine too. Some day you must bring the young lady to try my cannelloni, or my chicken risotto. Mama mia, that melts in mouth and brings good feeling in stomach," and he rubbed his rounded figure reminiscently.

"This tastes good enough for me," declared Lewis appreciatively.

They lingered for a long while over the wine before Lewis summoned José to bring the cassata and coffee. With this José gave them his own homemade liqueur made from alcohol and honey. It was breathtaking in its effect, but they assured José it tasted good, and he was delighted.

"You are honored indeed," Lewis assured Bronwen. "José must have taken a fancy to you. He only produces this for his favorite customers. He didn't even give any to Carlotta."

Bronwen felt as if a sudden shower of hail had fallen upon a summer garden. Of course he had brought

Carlotta here. Why ever not? It was the natural thing to do if they had wanted to be alone together away from the household.

"Poor sweet, I'm afraid she didn't like it much. She was indignant at my familiarity with 'peons' as she called them and thought the food and tablecloths only fit for a peasant's home. She is like a kitten who has always been used to a satin cushion and a saucer of cream. She gets no fun from things that she feels are commonplace."

Bronwen was astonished at Lewis's outspoken criticism of Carlotta. "He must be feeling jealous because she had gone to visit the Transvaal admirer," she thought.

"I expect it is the way she has been brought up," she said. "You can't expect her to be chummy and democratic like people are here. She is so beautiful she has probably always been made to feel important and special."

"You may be right, my dear. Do you like her then? Do you consider she would make a good wife?"

"What a question!" thought Bronwen. "If I say 'no,' it will lower his opinion of me, if I say 'yes' . . . oh, what on earth difference can it make? He obviously intends to marry her anyway."

"I think she would make a most beautiful, charming wife for someone who could give her lovely clothes and plenty of luxury," she said. "She needs that, Lewis. She has always been used to it. She is very lovable, like a child. Marriage and children would probably make her more mature. She would make a lovely chatelaine for a great house."

"Yes, you are right. Now she is like a child who grabs at the shining baubles on the Christmas tree. But she will become more mature, I am sure of it."

The red candle in its basketed Chianti bottle had burned right down. And the happiness with which Bronwen had started the evening had almost gone.

José came running from the front of the shop. "The torchlight procession—it has started!"

"Let's take the car up the mountain road," suggested Lewis. "I know a place where we should get a good view. It won't be crowded. Not many people know of it."

And now she put aside thoughts of Carlotta and gave herself up to the thrilling experience of driving along the narrow, winding, mountain road. There was no moon, and the road was lit only by the powerful headlights which picked up the silver thorn trees, the strangely shaped boulders, the red aloes thrusting up their candles of red flowers between the rocks. Sometimes a rabbit sat hypnotized by the light before clumsily loping away. Once a small buck raised its head from its grassy hide, its eyes dark and terrified.

Halfway up the mountain the road widened to a view point. Lewis stopped the car and drew to the side. From here they could see across the small valley to the next rise situated just above the little town. Farther down they could see the lamps of the main street in a parallel row, then a scattering of more subdued lights amongst the surrounding avenues of houses.

In the valley at the foot of the road where it led to the neighboring hill, there was some activity going on: flickers of light, an occasional glimpse of a figure partly illuminated by a red glow. Then the procession seemed to become organized; torches were lit and slowly a long line of figures bearing flaring brands could be seen moving up the mountain.

There was something magical and moving about the sight of the flaming torches, something a little frightening too. Bronwen gave a small shudder.

"What is it?" asked Lewis.

"There is something so primitive and thrilling about the sight of fire. I felt for a moment as if we had gone back in time, as if those people were going to the top of the mountain to celebrate some ancient ceremony."

"Don't be scared, little one. If you were a bit nearer you would see it's really not so romantic. You would see Milly, the postmistress, and our local butcher, and many of the neighbors all taking part in the procession. That's why I thought it would be more picturesque if we saw it from a distance."

"Now you have made it seem too prosaic. Milly carrying a torch, when I'm imagining primitive priestesses in gorgeous robes!"

The procession had reached the top of the mountain that had the flat top peculiar to the geological strata of this district. To simplify matters, stones painted white had been placed in the position spelling out the two dates, and there the torchbearers took up their positions. The dates of the centenary stood out from the blackness in letters of fire, and cheers from the watching crowd echoed up the valley.

"What a pity Sarah had to miss this," said Lewis. "She is still such a child in lots of ways. She would have been so excited."

"She's a darling," said Bronwen, warmly. "She has such a very happy nature."

"I'm glad she strikes you that way. It's a battle for a bachelor to bring up a sensitive, temperamental, little person without spoiling her. It has been hard to be strict with her sometimes. She has always had a very special place in my heart. I suppose I was over-strict about young Watson. I know you thought so. But if anyone ever harmed her, I think I would kill him."

Lewis said this quite simply. But Bronwen felt as if iced water were trickling down her spine.

"He really means it," she thought. "He guards her so, and yet he has not recognized the fact of her infatuation for Ramon. Have we been wise not to draw his attention to it? Nan said she intended to do something about it. But Ramon has gone away now, so perhaps it will all work out for the best."

"When is Sarah going to Switzerland?" she asked.

"As soon as I can persuade her to go. I'm going to miss her terribly, but in a way I'll be glad when she is safely installed at finishing school. She seems to attract men already, and I wouldn't like her to make the mistake of marrying too young. She comes in for a good deal of money from her parents' will, but I think she has the sense to fend off fortune hunters."

"Girls don't have a great deal of sense when they fall in love," said Bronwen, voicing her thoughts aloud.

"You speak as if from experience, my dear. Tell me, have you ever been in love?"

"Hundreds of times," laughed Bronwen, trying to brush away the emotion that came crowding into her breathless heart at his intimate question.

She tried to laugh it off for she was desperately afraid that at any moment now he must sense her feelings: the wild passion he aroused in her that seemed to be enmeshed with the strange night; the vast bowl of the starlit African sky above them, the flaming torches upon the further hill, the lonely but exultant call of the curlew winging home to its mate.

But he who usually teased her stayed silent. She was left with a feeling that she had given the wrong answer, that she had been flippant when for once he had meant his question seriously.

"Lewis. . . ." she said tentatively, but he started the car and began to drive back the way they had come. Bronwen sighed. The lovely evening was finished now, and tomorrow he would be going away. He had seemed more friendly during the last few days, and yet perhaps it was due to the fact that he was lonely and lacked company after the hectic preceding weeks.

He must be missing Carlotta. Certainly she had seemed reluctant to leave him. It was Ramon who had insisted upon going to the Transvaal. She recalled Lewis's words about marriage in connection with the South American girl. There seemed to be no doubt of his feelings in that direction.

On the farther hillside the torches had gone out, and one by one the lights were vanishing in the valley below. The Show was over for another year, and when that time came she would be far away.

CHAPTER FOURTEEN

That night she dreamed that she was walking in a garden with Lewis, but it was high summer with the roses all in bloom.

"Dearest," laughed Lewis, indicating a bush laden with radiant pink flowers, and with fearful joy she realized he was about to kiss her. But suddenly the scene changed; the sky was stormy with great clouds hanging green above the horizon. The sound of icy hail drummed in her ears.

She woke with a start, and at once realized the cause of her dream. A shower of pebbles had struck her window. Someone was trying to attract her attention. Who on earth could it be? She glanced at the illuminated dial of her clock. Three a.m.! It could hardly be a burglar making all that noise. She tiptoed to the window and peered out.

"Bron, are you awake?"

"Douglas, what in the world. . . ."

"Sorry to do this to you. Can you come down? It's urgent."

With thoughts of all kinds of farming emergencies, Bronwen pulled on slacks and a heavy sweater and tiptoed down the stairs letting herself out quietly. It was the coldest time of night. The moon had risen, and frost sparkled on the shining corrugated roof of the barn.

"We can't stand here," said Bronwen, shivering. "Come inside."

"No, I don't want Nan to hear us. We can sit in Old Faithful in the barn. There's a traveling rug in the trunk."

"But what's wrong? Is it the lambing? But they aren't due yet."

"No, it's nothing to do with the farm. I'm worried about Sarah."

Bronwen felt sleepy, cold, and thoroughly exasperated.

"Good heavens, Douglas, have you wakened me at three a.m. to tell me that?"

"I don't mean worried in general. I mean worried right now about where she is, and what she's doing."

"But she is in Johannesburg, taking part in the gymkhana. That's what Lewis said."

"Is she? Bron, we had a bit of a row at the Ball the other night. I told her a few home truths about her infatuation for Ramon. She was very angry with me; told me it was none of my business, that Ramon was a mature man and I was just a boy, and that she knew very well what she was doing, that she had every intention of marrying him whether Lewis liked it or not."

"Well naturally I was upset, but when I thought it over I knew it had been stupid of me to tackle her about it, that she was right. It was none of my business really since she never even pretended to love me, so I felt badly about it and decided to phone and try to make up.

"I just felt I couldn't wait until she came back. I phoned the place where she usually stays, friends of hers. They didn't know anything about her coming to Johannesburg.

"Of course she might just have decided not to stay with them this time, but they had not heard from her. What's more they had been at the gymkhana, and as yet she had not taken part in any of the events."

"But what about her horse and groom?"

"She could easily give the groom some excuse, that she was ill or something. All the Africans adore her—he would do just whatever she asked."

"But I don't understand. What do you think she is doing? Where is she?"

"I think that she and Ramon plan to elope. She hinted as much, but I didn't take it seriously. I thought she only intended to provoke me. She thinks that if their marriage is an accomplished fact, there is nothing Lewis could do about it."

"But that's impossible. She is under age, and Ramon is not a citizen of this country. They would run into trouble straight away."

"That's what I thought, but Sarah might not realize it. She is such a child in some ways."

"You mean . . . ?"

"To be frank, Bronwen, I don't trust Ramon one inch. They have gone so far that if they can't marry I'm scared to death Ramon will involve her in an affair with him so that Lewis will have no alternative, but to give his consent to their marraige."

Bronwen thought of the incidents with Ramon that had involved herself. Certainly he was very unrestrained. If he desired Sarah for a wife he would not scruple about his method of bringing this about.

"What do you want to do?" she asked Douglas.

"Bronwen, I know it's a lot to ask, but I wonder whether you would come with me to Johannesburg."

"Now?" asked Bronwen, startled.

"I've borrowed a car from a friend in town. It will take about seven hours of driving."

"But what about the farm?"

"I've been training Gumede as you know for when I leave. He's quite reliable. I'll get him up and give him instructions while you get ready. We shouldn't be away for more than two days."

"But Douglas, suppose we are going on a wild goose chase, suppose this is all in your imagination?"

"I don't think it is, Bron. Do you honestly?"

"No, I'm afraid you may be right."

"She is so obstinate, but she would listen to you, whereas she might quarrel with me. That's why I need you to come along too, Bron."

"What am I to do about telling Nan? I will have to wake her."

"No, don't do that. She might think she must tell Lewis; then the fat will be in the fire. I'd rather deal with this in my own way. If we get going now, Lewis maybe need never know. For everyone's sake, Lewis's included, that would be best."

Thinking of Lewis's words upon the mountain, "If anyone harmed her I really think I would kill him," Bronwen heartily agreed.

"But I can't just disappear."

"You can phone from a garage as soon as it gets light."

Bronwen crept quietly back into the house and packed

an overnight bag. She changed into her skirt, blue sweater, and the fluffy coat. It would be cold on the high passes between here and Johannesburg. Last night the radio had reported a slight sprinkling of snow upon the ridges with a promise of more to come. She dared not make coffee because she was afraid of disturbing Nan, but she took a thermos flask so that she could have it filled at some wayside café.

At the last moment she felt she must leave some indication of her intentions to Nan so she wrote a brief note: "I'm so sorry to give you a shock, but Douglas has persuaded me to drive with him to Johannesburg on some very personal business. I will phone as soon as I can and explain everything to you. Please don't tell Lewis."

She made up her mind she would phone as soon as she thought Nan would be awake. Douglas had left the car some way from the house, and they made their way quietly over the frozen grass to where Gumede was by the side of the car. The old African was still a little sleepy and bewildered, but he promised to look after everything to the best of his ability while they were away.

There was no one beside themselves upon the ribbon of main road that gradually rose until it reached a high mountain pass. It was very cold. As they climbed higher, flakes of snow began to fall, and the windshield wiper had to work hard to dislodge the layer of ice.

"I didn't know it could be like this in South Africa," said Bronwen.

"Yes, in these parts you get sudden falls of snow three or four times during the winter even as far into spring as September. That's what makes the winter lambing such a risky business, but if the lambs were born in the hot summer, they would be too weak."

But Bronwen's thoughts were not on the lambs.

"Douglas, how will you know where to look for Sarah? Johannesburg is a big place."

"I realize that, of course. I'm not going to look for Sarah first. I'm going after Ramon. I know where Tom Ransom's farm is: about 100 miles on this side of Johannesburg, not far in this country. We will go there, call in on some excuse. I knew Tom when he lived in this district. If Ramon and Carlotta are there then we'll know we have come on a wild goose chase. If Ramon is absent, we will find out from Carlotta where he is."

Judging from his expression, Bronwen thought he would have little trouble with the pliant Carlotta, but the whole adventure filled her with dreadful misgiving. Now that it was too late to turn back, she began to have doubts about the wisdom of their action in taking all the responsibility of interfering in Sarah's affairs by themselves.

But when she thought of Lewis, she was determined to protect him if possible from any disillusion about this girl who as he said, held a special place in his heart, and in addition to guard him from himself. She thought of the cold words, "I would not hesitate to kill him," and she shuddered.

"Are you cold, Bron? Wrap the rug around you. There's a cushion on the back seat. Put it behind your head and try to get some sleep. I'll be all right. I'm used to driving in bad weather. Farm roads are good training for this kind of thing."

Bronwen thought she could never sleep. The car was sliding about the road and visibility was almost nil, but to her surprise she dropped off, lulled by the steady sound of the engine and only awoke as a cold late dawn was painting a few red streaks over the dark grey sky.

The sleet and rain had ceased. They were driving through the Free State now, through flat, monotonous farm lands. A group of stunted trees or a farm windmill were the only features in this fenced dull landscape. It might look vast and impressive under an arch of blue sky in high summer when the maize crops were ripe, but now, cold, frosty, colorless brown, it looked like miles and miles of nothing.

They stopped at a garage to pick up gas and inquire about the road to the farm which must be nearby now. Stretching her cramped limbs after freshening up in the washroom, Bronwen noticed a telephone booth. She made up her mind to phone Nan from here, despite

Douglas's protests that it would take up too much time and that she could easily phone from the farm.

The local exchange took the number and said they would phone back. She waited anxiously. The sun was rising now, large and red upon the horizon, transforming the dismal scene with its promise of daytime warmth. The garage attendants hastened to find patches of sun where they stood swinging gloved hands against leather jackets, only their dark eyes showing in the slit of their woollen balaclava caps.

The phone rang shrilly above the sound of their deep-voiced sociable jests. "Nan . . ." said Bronwen hopefully. But it was the exchange. "We are sorry we can't get your number. The lines are down in that area because of the snowfall. They won't be repaired for 24 hours."

"Thank you," said Bronwen, replacing the receiver. She felt terribly depressed that she had not been able to explain the situation to Nan. What bad luck! But she should have remembered when she set out the lines were often out of order. She regretted now that they had not wakened Nan. But, she consoled herself, at least she had left the note. And haste was the essential thing in this business; whether they succeeded or failed in bringing Sarah to her senses, it should not take long.

They drove away from the isolated gas pumps and were once more on the ribbon of road that led straight as an arrow across the flat farm country.

"We shouldn't have much difficulty finding Tom's place," said Douglas. After a few more miles they came to the turn off that led to "Hunter's Hill."

"What a hopeful name for this flat country," exclaimed Bronwen. But when they approached nearer they found there was a small *kopje* behind the house, and this presumably was what gave the place its imposing name. It looked a farm as prosperous if not as interesting as Lion's Rest. Ploughed ground showed where land was being prepared for maize. Amongst the stubble Afrikander cattle with humped backs and long magnificent horns lifted their heads from the bales of winter fodder that had been distributed in the bare pastures.

The house was new and very modern with its oddly shaped roof and metallic pillars. It did not seem to worry Douglas that they were descending unannounced upon someone they hardly knew on a rather dubious errand. He rang the bell, and they stood watching the winter sunlight finding its way through the grove of leafless trees that made a windbreak to the side of the house.

Tom's housekeeper came to the door, and in reply to their inquiries informed them that Tom was out already in the farther farmlands, but would be back later in the morning. Carlotta was still in bed. She looked puzzled when Douglas inquired for Ramon. The young lady's brother brought her here and then departed for Johannesburg. She informed them that Mr. Ransom's aunt was staying here as well, so there was no question of the young lady being alone with Mr. Ransom. It seemed these South American ladies were very well brought up, and a very good thing too. Mr. Tom asked his aunt especially so she could be a chaperon. It would be all very *comme il faut* as they say.

"May we see Carlotta?" asked Douglas.

The housekeeper looked doubtful.

"She doesn't usually get up much before 11. I was just taking her breakfast now."

"May I take it?" asked Bronwen, looking at Douglas. "It will give her a surprise."

She intercepted the sudden grin on Douglas's face. "It certainly will," he whispered as the housekeeper left to bring the tray. "Do your best, Bron. I'm trusting in you."

Lewis's house had the settled comfort of a place where generations of people had made their home. It was like a shell that has grown accretions over the years, and its character belonged to its gradual growth. But Tom's house was the very acme of modern luxury. Bronwen was shown to the elevator; she did not even have to ascend the stairs with her tray, and walking along the wide close-carpeted passageway she reflected that Carlotta must love this place where everything spoke of comfort.

She knocked at the door indicated by the housekeeper, and a sleepy voice bade her enter. The circular bed set on a small platform was fit for a princess. Its curving headboard was of pink quilted satin, and from a white crownlike projection above the bed a gauzy curtain was looped back with satin ribbon.

Carlotta lay under a rosy quilt, the pink silk sheets enhancing her beautiful coloring and the blush white of her lacy nightgown. Her dark hair streamed loose over the pillow, and her eyes with their wonderful dark lashes were closed.

She stretched one beautiful arm out of the coverlet and yawned like a kitten, the pink jonquil tongue curving in a delicious unself-conscious way. Once more Bronwen experienced a pang half of envy, half of admiration, at Carlotta's loveliness. The curly lashes flickered upward, the huge dark eyes were suddenly startled. Then as realization dawned their expression changed to wariness and something else . . . was it fear?

"Bronwen, what on earth . . . Lewis . . . did he send you? Is he here?" Was there a note of hope in her voice.

"No, Carlotta. I've come with Douglas. He was worried because he could not get in touch with Sarah at the place where she usually stays. He heard she had not been seen at the gymkhana. He thought she might be with Ramon. Is she?"

Carlotta gave a little gasp. One white pink-tipped hand flew to her mouth.

"I said something would go wrong. I told him he couldn't do it."

"What do you mean? Carlotta, you have to tell me what you know!"

"No, I dare not."

Bronwen had a primitive desire to shake the doll-like creature into confession, but she controlled her exasperation and spoke gently.

"Carlotta dear, we have come a long way to find Sarah. Surely you would not wish her to come to any harm. Please tell me where they are."

Carlotta shook her head and tears rolled silently from those lovely eyes like a statue weeping.

"If Lewis gets to know about this, he will be very

angry. You would not want to upset Lewis, would you?"

Carlotta seemed to come to life. She flung herself against Bronwen, dragging her down to sit upon the bed and nestling a damp warm perfumed face into her neck. Bronwen stroked the fragrant silky hair as she would have done to a distressed child.

"No, I would not like if Lewis was angry with me. Lewis is very handsome, very passionate—you think so?"

For a few moments Bronwen felt a stark jealousy, a desire to slap the beautiful face with the large luminous eyes looking questioningly into her own.

"Tom is not so thrilling, you agree? But richer, yes? And he adores me. It is difficult, no?"

"Carlotta," said Bronwen, forcing herself to be patient, "we haven't time now to discuss your affairs. It is most important that we find Sarah and Ramon."

Carlotta shrugged lacy shoulders. "I do not care about Ramon. He has always been big bully, and it is nothing to me whether he marries Sarah or no, though it is pity really, if not, for she will be wealthy, yes?"

Bronwen sighed. "Carlotta, where can we find them, do you know?"

"Of course. Ramon has borrowed small apartment from friend, a *pied-à-terre*, you understand. But, Bronwen, they plan to marry very soon. I think with Ramon so passionate and Sarah so in love it will be too late, no?" Her expression changed from that of an ingenuous child to a woman with all the wisdom of Eve.

"We will see," said Bronwen grimly. "Now give me the address."

Carlotta groped in her black suede purse to find an address book tooled in gold. Bronwen wrote the address down, wondering how long it would take them to find it.

"You won't tell Ramon I told you?" asked Carlotta plaintively.

"I'll do what I can to shield you," Bronwen assured her.

"But it does not matter too much now I am here," said Carlotta, stretching luxuriously. "Tom will not let anyone harm me. Bronwen darling, when you go down, please tell the housekeeper to send me some more hot chocolate. This pot has become quite cold."

Bronwen delivered the message and, when she had rejoined Douglas, they set off in the direction of Johannesburg.

Leaving the farming country behind, they were soon driving through small satellite towns. All around were signs of mining activity, the towerlike headgear and great sandy white artifical hills amassed from the waste products of the goldmining industry. As they reached the numbered route into the city, Bronwen admired the skilful way in which Douglas steered his course through the heavy traffic.

"What a determined person he is," she thought. "He has quite got over whatever faults Lewis found in him. Lewis was unreasonable to object to him so strongly."

But he was not reasonable. He was difficult, passionate, quick-tempered. Anything that threatened Sarah aroused his deepest feelings. She did not blind herself to his faults. Yet he was the only man in the world that she could ever love.

He had said he would be away for a few days, so he need never know about Sarah, provided that she had not surrendered completely to her mad infatuation. No, surely if they were trying to arrange a marriage, she would have the strength of mind to wait. She would not want to spoil it. If only they could arrive in time to persuade her from this course of action!

Their directions led them to a district that was obviously a concrete jungle, a place of towering apartment houses set in narrow streets, echoing with the reverberations of mopeds, and the sound of jazz loudly blaring from stereo systems in radio stores. Long-haired youths lounged at every corner, and oddly dressed girls emerged with their escorts from coffee bars. Nothing could have been farther from the peace and timeless atmosphere of Lion's Rest.

Finding a parking garage, Douglas drove the car up a twisting ramp to the eighth floor of the building. Then they were ready to search for the apartment. A group of small boys directed them, running along beside them and begging for cigarettes. "Let me go first," said Bronwen when they arrived at the apartment building.

It was a soulless place, she thought, as she took the elevator to the 15th floor; not shabby or poor, but simply completely without character, without hope. There must be people living happy lives behind those drab green doors, but it was hard to believe it.

Bronwen's heart beat faster as she rang the doorbell. What would she find, and could Sarah possibly be amenable to persuasion? There was the jangle of a chain, and the door opened cautiously.

"Who is it?" asked Sarah's voice. She sounded subdued and quiet.

"It's Bronwen."

"Bron!"

The door was flung open, and Sarah dragged her in. "But how . . . how?" The sudden shock of meeting Bronwen had enlivened Sarah's expression until she looked vivid and welcoming. But now her face changed.

"Are you with Lewis? Is he here?"

"No. Promise you won't be angry, Sarah. I'm with Douglas."

"Douglas?" Sarah's expression hardened. "I might have known. But, oh, Bron, I'm so pleased to see you, you don't know. . . ." and suddenly she burst into tears. "It's so wonderful to see you again. I felt so lonely. I didn't know what to do. I've been such a fool. Oh, Bron, you don't know what a fool I've been!"

CHAPTER FIFTEEN

Bronwen thought fleetingly of Douglas waiting downstairs, surrounded by their small raucous guides, but her first duty was to Sarah.

The apartment was drab; one-roomed, furnished in the manner of a low grade hotel, with a striped bedcover, one threadbear rug, and two uncomfortable chairs. Everything looked shabby and down at heel.

"Ramon borrowed it from a friend. It's pretty grim, isn't it?" said Sarah, as Bronwen glanced around. "Not exactly one's idea of a honeymoon suite . . ." and she began to weep again.

Sitting on the bed, Bronwen put her arm around Sarah and gave her a little shake. "Try to tell me about it, Sarah. I've come to help you. What is going on here? Where is Ramon?"

"He has gone."

"Gone?"

"Bron, you know . . . you must have known that I was crazy about him. I've never met anyone like him before. He was so sophisticated, so handsome. He knew so much about the world. I found him tremendously exciting because the boys in the district are all so dull."

"Poor Douglas," thought Bronwen, but she kept silent.

"I must have been mad. There seemed nothing in the world I wanted so much as to marry him, and I knew Lewis would never consent, or would insist on a long engagement, hoping it would fizzle out. But, Bron, I felt I couldn't wait. I don't know whether you have ever felt this, but it was like a lovely firework. I just wanted to have all the thrilling romance now, not wait for a million years.

"When Ramon suggested we should take the opportunity to marry when I came to Johannesburg, I thought it was the most romantic proposal possible. I guess I should have had the sense to know there would be lots of complicated legal problems, but I never thought of it. But Ramon must have known. I don't think he believed for a moment that we would be able to get married. He just wanted to seduce me so that Lewis would think we had to marry."

She started to weep all over again, and Bronwen felt unutterably depressed. Did Sarah mean that she and Ramon were already having an affair? If this was so, it did not seem to be making her very happy.

"But I don't understand. Where is Ramon?" she asked for the second time.

"I have sent him away. I never want to see him again. He brought me to this ghastly place last night and started to make love to me. He said it was crazy to wait; we were going to marry anyway. But Bron, somehow I had changed. It just seemed awful, not romantic at all, so hole in the corner. I thought of Lewis, of what he would think of me, and Ramon didn't seem a charming lover any more. It was just all horribly sordid. The firework had gone out, and all the glamor had vanished, I guess.

"Ramon was furious with me, but I didn't care. I told him I never wanted to see him again, and he went off to stay at a hotel. He told me if I changed my mind I should phone him. He said he would come back this evening if he didn't hear from me before then.

"I've been sitting here for hours not knowing what to do. I want to go home, but Lewis will know there is something wrong if I haven't been to the gymkhana. Oh, Bron, I am so glad to see you. Please tell me what I should do."

All her pseudo-sophistication had vanished. She was just a child once more, and a badly frightened one at that.

"I must go to fetch Douglas," said Bronwen. "We can decide between us what would be the best plan."

Sarah gave a little gulp of dismay, but did not protest when Bronwen left her. She even went toward the washbasin, presumably to bathe her eyes. Bronwen took the scratched, shabby elevator down to the ground floor where Douglas was pacing anxiously. She quickly explained the situation to him, and between them they decided upon a course of action. Then they went back to join Sarah.

Sarah did not greet Douglas with much enthusiasm, but Bronwen hardly expected it. Without Douglas, they would not have been here, but Sarah was too childlike to be grateful for his help. Bronwen on the other hand was glad of his sound common sense as they decided what to do.

"It seems to me that the best thing you can do is to go to the gymkhana. Say you have had flu or something."

"But what about Ramon? I'm afraid he will come after me. You don't know what he was like last night."

Sarah shuddered, clasping her arms and pushing up the sleeves of her blouse. For the first time Bronwen noticed bruises on the white skin. Douglas had seen them too. She saw his face flush red and his mouth compress, but he did not remark upon it.

"Go to stay with your friends. They were expecting you anyway. Tell them you had flu and didn't want to upset them, so went to a hotel at first. Ramon would hardly dare to create a scene there," said Bronwen.

"Leave Ramon to me. I'll deal with him," said Douglas. "You have the name of his hotel, Sarah?"

"Yes, but you mustn't fight," said Sarah, hastily. "If you do, Lewis is bound to hear of it."

"I promise you I won't fight. We will just have a little talk. I'll threaten him with a lawsuit for abduction if he ever comes near you again. That is if you are sure you are quite serious about not wanting to see him, Sarah?"

"I am quite serious," said Sarah. She suddenly seemed to lose her animosity toward Douglas and smiled at him.

"Poor Douglas," thought Bronwen, as she saw the look of adoration return to the boy's eyes. "He has as much chance of falling out of love with her as I have with Lewis."

"Do you think I have been an awful fool, Douglas?" said Sarah softly, her clear gray eyes like the limpid cloud reflection in a pool after rain.

"Of course I do," said Douglas, gruffly. "What do you expect, Sarah?"

"Well, I have been foolish, I know I have, but all the same you mustn't say so. You mustn't ever remind me about it either."

"As if I would!" said Douglas.

"Oh, Douglas, let's go," demanded Sarah. "Let's get out of this beastly place. I'm so hungry I could eat . . . no, not a horse . . . my poor Lady Pearl, what can she be thinking of me? Oh, it will be fun to ride in the gymkhana!"

She was well on the way to forgetting about her sordid experience with Ramon, thought Bronwen with relief. She was essentially a spirited person, easily revitalized, not pressed down for long by anything unpleasant. Lewis need never know what she had been through. There was no harm done, and after Douglas's warning Ramon would never dare to come back to the farm.

Everything had turned out much better than likely, she thought as they relaxed in the sun at the Zoo Lake. Douglas had insisted they should go to some place to eat while he went to interview Ramon. Although there was a slight chill in the breeze, they sat in the warm sunshine at the open air restaurant. The air was thin, dry, invigorating; it seemed 1000 miles from the snowstorm of the night before, and the green lawns and ordered gardens of the zoo seemed a far cry from the sordid apartment in which Sarah's girlish dreams of romance had been shattered.

Bronwen watched her feeding peanuts to the monkeys and laughing at the antics of the penguins as if she had not a care in the world.

"Unhappiness has only brushed against her," she thought. "But if we had not come, being lonely, uncertain and afraid to come home, she might easily have yielded to Ramon's persuasions. On his return he would have been more skilful in his handling of her."

Douglas did not say much about his talk with Ramon, but he told her briefly that he had managed to see him and had arranged everything satisfactorily. He told Bronwen a little more about it when they had left Sarah at her lodgings.

"He won't try anything in the way of blackmail," he

assured Bronwen. "He actually hinted at that, but I let him have it. He said that if Sarah would not marry him he would tell Lewis she had spent the night with him. It's her money he's after, of course. Funny, that! It's just the thing that stands in my way. I'll never be able to marry her with that stumbling block. Oh well, I guess she would never have me anyway."

Bronwen took the wheel while Douglas snatched some sleep. Once they were away from the Reef towns it was easy to drive on the long straight road. Its direct course cut through ploughed maize fields and short stubble that stretched in an endless plain to the low blue hills upon the horizon.

In the late afternoon, Douglas awoke, stretching and saying, "Gosh, that was good. I sure needed it." He looked at his watch. "Bron, I think we had better turn in later at a motel. We have both done enough driving and lost enough sleep over this. We both need a rest; you look dead beat. There's no point in arriving and having to wake Nan in the middle of the night. We can get up early tomorrow morning and be home before breakfast."

It seemed the wisest thing to do in the circumstances. Certainly they were both weary in the extreme. As the early winter darkness fell, they pulled in to a motel that had small separate buildings with overhanging shelters for cars, around a large central block of public rooms. They were allocated a chalet with two rooms and a bathroom off the small stoep between them.

It was wonderful to relax in a hot bath after the long wearisome hours of driving. Bronwen had packed an extra blouse and before bathing brushed her dusty suit well. Flushed from the bath, with eyes shining, she looked a very different person from the tired girl who had driven so many miles.

Douglas too had a scrubbed clean look as he greeted her cheerfully in the large bar lounge.

"We need a drink, I guess," he said, ordering brandy. When she protested, "Purely medicinal," he said. "Honestly it will do you good."

The building had a high pitched roof with the interior

beams visible. Much use had been made of the natural quarried stone in the large fireplace and the floors that were covered with gay, handwoven rugs. On one wall was a mural of an African scene; red aloes, round beehive huts, a train of blanketed women carrying pots upon their heads. The other walls were hung with African masks and shelves of animal carvings.

Bronwen had put through a call to Nan, and now a waiter called her to the phone. At last she was able to speak to Nan who sounded very relieved to hear from her.

"Bron, where are you? What's going on?"

"Nan, I'll be home tomorrow morning. I can't say much now. I'll tell you all about it when I get there."

It was awkward to try to explain because the farm phones were on party lines. Anyone picking up the receiver could hear the conversation.

But at least Nan was able to convey some important news.

"Bron," she said, "there's a telegram here for Douglas asking him to go for an interview to that agriculture school."

"Oh, that's great. I'll tell him. He will be thrilled. 'Bye, Nan. See you tomorrow."

Returning to Douglas, Bronwen told him the good news. Despite her weariness, she had a feeling of satisfaction, for they seemed to have solved Sarah's troubles successfully. She did not think there would be any more trouble from Ramon.

She smiled across at Douglas as he sat on the other side of the big log fire with his drink cradled in his hands. His eyes were half-closed, and his head nodded a little.

"Put your drink on the table, Douglas. You look as if you are going to drop it at any moment."

"Yes, I'm pretty weary. It's the reaction, I guess. We'll turn in as soon as we've had dinner. I'm always awake early, so you can just relax and sleep in peace. I'll give you a shout when I get up. It's a good thing we decided to get a night's sleep if I have to go for that interview tomorrow."

Bronwen could scarcely keep her eyes open as dinner was set before them. Very soon she was stumbling into bed. For a few minutes, still half awake, she was aware that there were several late arrivals at the motel. She had forgotten to close the curtains and watched the lights of the cars flashing over the ceiling. Then the noise of chattering and throbbing engines was drowned for her in waves of sleep.

It seemed only about an hour later when she was aroused by someone sitting on her bed and gently shaking her shoulder. Then the bedside light was turned on. She struggled up through receding mists of sleep to find Douglas at her bedside.

"I'm sorry, Bron," he said. "I knocked, but you didn't hear. You looked so sound asleep, I hated to wake you, but I guess we had better get on. The sooner we get back to Bushman's Fountain, the sooner I can be on my way again."

"Oh gosh, Douglas, I'm sorry. Just give me ten minutes, and I'll be with you."

"I don't want to rush you too much," said Douglas apologetically. "I still have to dress. Shall I pull the curtains together before you get up? You will need to keep your light on. It's still pitch dark outside."

"Thanks, Douglas," murmured Bronwen, still befogged by sleep. As he turned his back and crossed to the window, she reached for her dressing gown and slipping into it, made her way to the adjoining bathroom. She stumbled at the doorstep. Douglas put his arm around her and prevented her from falling.

"Upsy daisy, you're still half-asleep. I'll see you in a few minutes."

She dressed hurriedly. Going to the window she pulled aside the curtain again and took deep breaths to try to get rid of the heavy feeling this abrupt awakening had given her.

"We aren't the only people making an early start," she thought. The red tail lights of a large car were vanishing along the drive. As she watched she saw the powerful headlights flooding the darkness as it turned into the main road. It was going in the same direction that they would take.

"Well, thank goodness they went first. I'd hate to have those headlights behind us," she thought.

"Ready to go home?" asked Douglas behind her.

"Home . . ." she thought. "If only it could be. . . ."

CHAPTER SIXTEEN

"I think it would be best to keep the whole thing from Lewis if we can," said Bronwen, when she had confided Sarah's story to Nan.

"Yes, I agree. Normally I don't like secrets but sometimes it's more advisable not to tell. Lewis would be so stricken if he knew Sarah had acted so foolishly. I'm afraid he might feel he had to seek out Ramon. Let sleeping dogs lie, I say."

Douglas had gone off immediately after breakfast for his interview. He hoped to do a 12 months' course with his prize money, and then he would see what happened next. "I'll play it by ear," he confided to Bronwen. "I've had such fantastic luck as it is, meeting you people, winning the prize . . . if only. . . ." He sighed.

Bronwen knew he was thinking of Sarah.

"I'm worried that I may have to leave you when the lambing season is just getting going, but Gumede is pretty efficient now. I dare say our neighbor will be willing to give you advice."

"Don't worry, Douglas, we'll manage."

But she knew that soon she must talk to Nan about selling the farm. There was little time to brood however as she supervised the milking, inspected and dosed the sheep, and put out food for the poultry.

How lovely the farm looked to her this morning! And how bitterly she would regret leaving it. The sky was a dome of pale winter blue; the seeded grass yellow as butter. The old thorn trees near the house etched a silver pattern against its white walls, and a japonica bush was covered with the bright pink bloom that came in winter before the leaves. In the sheltered flower bed below the stoep, Iceland poppies were opening their petals, pink, yellow and flame to the growing warmth of the sun. The first green spikes of spring bulbs could be seen thrusting their way through the frosty soil.

She heard a commotion and down the hillside came the two little herdboys, shouting long drawn-out messages across the half mile of countryside.

"What do they say?" she asked Gumede.

"They say eland out again in Baas Lewis's land."

"Oh, bother!" she thought. She had so many tasks to do, and with Lewis still away she could not expect any help, but she could hardly leave the eland to roam over his pastures and down to his winter oats without trying to do something about it.

"Saddle the horse," she instructed Gumede. "It will be quicker."

"I could go, Miss Bron," he offered, but she knew she could manage the sensitive animals better. Besides Gumede had plenty of work to do here.

It was wonderful to be riding up the hillside in the sparkling morning. The strong little pony, a similar breed to the Basuto type, picked its way surefootedly across the tussocks of grass and large rocks until they arrived on the ridge.

She was relieved to find that a few of Lewis's farm hands were already there, helping to drive the animals toward the gap and to build up the stones again. She helped them with the animals and then turned to thank the Africans.

"How did you know they had got out?" she asked.

"The baas saw them and told us to come."

"Has he come back?" she asked, surprised.

"Yes, miss, he came back this morning. Here he comes now."

He was riding swiftly up the hillside. It was so like their first encounter that the sight of him aroused in her an intense emotion. Her heart thudded, and she had difficulty controlling the trembling of her whole body. The sturdy pony shifted restlessly sensing her unaccustomed nervousness, so she slid down and stood at its side. But when Lewis saw that she was there, he stopped his horse in full career. What could be wrong? She could not understand why he stood like some equestrian statue with clear-cut rigid pose.

For a few moments they both stood regarding each other, and then the spell seemed to break as he dismounted and slowly approached her. He had been so friendly toward her of late, why now was he not smiling? As he came nearer she could see that his eyes were like blue ice; his mouth set and grim, his whole expression one of cold dislike.

"So," he said, "you have come back from your little jaunt."

"I don't understand," stammered Bronwen. Thoughts raced madly through her brain. Had he found out about Sarah? But how could that be? The accusing glance seemed to be directed against herself.

"My grapevine tells me that young Watson was to go away this morning. He must have been sorry to leave so soon after your little trip to the Welcome Inn Motel, or was that just in the nature of a last fond farewell?"

Bronwen was struck dumb with dismay and astonishment. Obviously someone had seen them together at the motel. The gossip, so usual in a small place, had winged home to Lewis. What was she to do? For Sarah's sake, she could not explain why she and Douglas had been together, but at least she could rid his mind of these preposterous suspicions. She attempted to smile.

"But, Lewis, you can't believe . . . certainly Douglas and I were at the motel together, but it was perfectly innocent. Someone must have seen us, but you know how people gossip. You couldn't possibly believe that Douglas and I . . . why, he has always been like a young brother to me!"

"A brother!" Lewis's voice was furious, and she could not meet his expression as he towered above her. She turned her face away, but he grabbed her by the shoulders.

"Look at me!" Her eyes were dark and dilated as she gazed into the fierce blue eyes.

"You are right! Someone did see you there at the motel. Someone whose word and eyesight I cannot doubt. Myself!"

"You!" said Bronwen. Under his furious gaze she

found it difficult to think clearly. How could she explain the circumstance of the journey with Douglas without involving Sarah?

"Don't attempt to deny anything, Bronwen. It's no use. With my own eyes, I saw Douglas sitting on your bed in the early hours of this morning. I even saw him put his arms around you as you both came out of the door. I was going to my car. The window framed you as if in a picture. You should exercise a little caution about drawing your curtains if you intend to entertain your lover so early in the morning."

"Douglas is not my lover. Oh, Lewis, this is ridiculous. Douglas was waking me to resume our journey. We were coming home."

"Your journey from where?" Bronwen was silent. "You didn't tell me you expected to be away when we parted that evening."

"Why should I have told you?" Bronwen was stung to retort, raw from the injustice of his accusations. Lewis's hands dropped from her shoulders, but she could still feel the burning imprint of his grasp. He gave a bitter laugh.

"Yes, I suppose you are right. It is entirely your own affair what kind of life you choose to lead. I should have realized what you were after that scene with Ramon, but in spite of that I could have sworn that you were as pure, as innocent as Sarah."

"You once implied to me that our ideas of love were different, that mine was a fliratious kind. Well, let me tell you you were wrong. You are the light one."

There was no answer she could offer. She had given Sarah her promise not to betray her. She turned away from Lewis and slowly like an old woman started to climb the hill toward her horse. When she grasped the bridle, she ventured one swift glance at the man below her.

He had remounted his horse, but was still standing as if carved out of granite, gazing up the slope in her direction. Then suddenly he started to gallop at a wild breakneck speed across the veld. She heard the farm hands talking amongst themselves. There were shouts of "Indoda!"— "A man!" The tears were still trickling down her cheeks as she returned slowly to the homestead.

CHAPTER SEVENTEEN

Bronwen did not go straight back. She felt she could not face Nan, so rode over to see the sheep in the far pasture. It was typical of her life here that even in this extreme distress, she thought of the farm work. In fact she seized upon the idea that she should see how the ewes were faring, for she was numb with shock and could not bring herself to go over the scene with Lewis.

She rode doggedly on, attempting to think only of her immediate duties and trying to ignore the painful constriction of her throat as she fought back her tears. The ewes were nearly ready to lamb, moving heavily about the pasture. How was she to manage with only Gumede to help her now that Douglas had gone? Since Lewis had seemed more friendly she had thought she could rely on him for help. But now she wished she need never see him again. If only she could get away. But how could she leave Nan without help? She would have to discuss it with her and the farm would have to be sold, for there was no alternative.

Here she was at the stream where she and Douglas had found the mushrooms. She washed her face in the clear water. It was very cold, coming from the snow in the far mountains. "Now I can face Nan," she thought and turned to go back.

In spite of Nan's vagueness, she had a sharp sensitivity where emotions were concerned. Bronwen dreaded having to appear normal when her whole being was crying out for consolation.

And yet she could not endure discussing Lewis's suspicions even with Nan, so she must appear her usual cheerful self even though her world had been torn apart. But Nan's interest had been distracted by a letter she had received during the morning. She was looking out for Bronwen from the stoep, and as soon as she saw the horse she came across to the stables and was there before Bronwen had unsaddled the pony.

Bronwen noticed that she was walking more quickly now. She had almost completely recovered from her broken leg.

"Bron . . ." she cried, waving a piece of paper. "The most astounding thing! I've had a letter from Professor Roberts offering me a job at the University. It's illustrating work—you remember he was so interested in my paintings."

"But, Nan, that's wonderful. Are you pleased?"

"Yes, of course. Come onto the stoep. Tabitha has just brought me some hot coffee."

For the first time she seemed to take in Bronwen's appearance. "You look as if you need it, Bron. You look very pale and tired."

"I am pleased," admitted Nan, when they were sipping the hot coffee. "When Patrick died, I thought I wanted to stay here forever, but I realize now that one can't stay in the past. This is a marvelous opportunity to live my own kind of life. The University is in a small pleasant town. I will meet people who are interested in the same kind of things that I am. I will take a small apartment or cottage there. But, Bron darling, here I am running on about myself and not giving a thought to you."

"Will you sell the farm?" asked Bronwen.

"Yes, I phoned Mr. Prothero about it, and he sounded very relieved. Don't think I haven't realized, Bron, how hard you have been working to keep the farm going. I'm only sorry you haven't been better rewarded. But it isn't really your kind of life, either, is it? You were just thrown into it, and you have been wonderful. But I expect you will be glad to get back to your own life in London, now you haven't your old aunt to fret about."

Bronwen realized with a shock that by this one letter Nan's troubles had been solved, but her own world had been turned upside down.

"Of course," she assured herself. "It's exactly what I wanted. I was wishing I could get away, and now I can. I have my wish. I need never see Lewis again."

But beneath her practical thoughts, beneath her self-congratulation, her heart cried out, "Why? Why did I ever have to meet him?"

Life on the farm could not come to a sudden halt just because it was to be sold as soon as possible. A broken heart was no excuse when cows had to be milked, hens fed, and one had to play midwife to sheep who had to be persuaded to appreciate their own maternal roles.

Bronwen booked her passage home. There was nothing to keep her now. She would go by ship because it was less expensive than by air.

Lewis sent his manager over to discuss the sale of the farm with Bronwen who knew more about it than its owner.

"I wonder why Lewis didn't come himself. It seems strange," said Nan.

"I expect he's busy," Bronwen replied.

But Sarah came, riding up to the front door on her moped with great sound and fury. The white overalls and red helmet looked as gay as ever. She peeled them off to stand revealed in emerald green tights and a short black tunic.

"Morning, Nan. Hi, Bron. Isn't it wonderful about your new job, Nan? Are you pleased? Perhaps you'll marry the Prof. I though he looked rather a honey, didn't you, Bron?"

Nan asked her how the gymkhana went.

"It was super," she said, without batting an eyelid. "I missed a couple of days though . . . had flu," she glanced swiftly at Bronwen, "so I didn't get any of the big awards, but Lady Pearl did pretty well for herself during the rest of the week."

Later she made the opportunity to speak to Bron alone. "Everything's all right, Bron, thanks to you."

"And Douglas?"

"Yes, of course. You must give me his college address. I'll send him a postcard."

"Bron," she added, "Ramon is going back to South America soon. I heard from Carlotta. She is going to marry Tom, of course. But please don't ever tell Lewis what a fool I was. He's in such a bad mood lately, I hate to think what he would be like if he knew about me.

"I can't understand it. I didn't really ever think he cared for Carlotta in that way, but he's such a bear since she left. I tried to persuade him that he should get Douglas to run this farm when he has finished his course, but he just about took off into space. I thought he felt better about Douglas since he realized I wasn't really interested in him."

"Aren't you?" asked Bronwen. She had had a vague hope that if Douglas and Sarah came together it would demonstrate that Lewis's suspicions were unfounded.

"I'm tired of men," said Sarah.

Bronwen could not help smiling. "Poor Sarah, that sounds rather world-weary."

"For the time being, I mean," Sarah added, hastily. "I can't wait to get to this Swiss nunnery."

"Are you really going there?" asked Bronwen, surprised.

"Yes, Lewis seems dead set on it and I thought . . . well, to tell you the truth, Bron, after that awful fiasco, even though Lewis doesn't know about it, I thought I'd like to do something that would please him. And I don't think it will be so bad anyway. It might even be quite fun."

"When are you going?"

"As soon as it can be arranged. Next week perhaps. Lewis will drive me to Johannesburg, and I will fly from there."

"I hope to go home next week too," said Bronwen. "But I will be going by ship. The travel agents say they think they will be able to get me a berth."

"That's great! Maybe I'll see you if I come to London. You must give me your address."

She would make some excuse, thought Bronwen, if Sarah ever attempted to get in touch with her. Once she was home she wanted to forget everything about her few months in this bright wilderness. Oh yes, it had been a name more apt than she had realized at the time. At first the bright joy of her deep love for Lewis had changed her life, but now she felt as if she had been abandoned in a desolate wilderness of the spirit.

She watched Sarah hop jauntily onto her bike and hurtle over the bumpy track. "She will fall on her feet wherever she goes," she thought and remembered Sarah saying she had a red-haired angel to take care of her.

The days raced by to the time of her departure. There was so much to do. Lewis's agent came over frequently to check things over with her. He assured her that he would take over as soon as she wished. Nan would not have any trouble.

But some streak of obstinacy made Bronwen determined to go on running the farm until it was actually time for her to leave. One or two lambs had appeared in the pastures: small, leggy, stumbling objects, looking like cuddlesome toys beside their clumsy mothers. But the weather had taken a springlike turn, and it was ideal for lambing.

Lewis did not come although Nan phoned him and remarked on his absence.

"He says he is very busy with the lambing and with arrangements for Sarah's departure. He will come over later when she has gone to say goodbye to me. I told him that might mean he would miss seeing you, because you are to sail a couple of days after Sarah leaves. He will hardly be back from Johannesburg by then. Don't you think, Bronwen, you could find time to go over there, if he can't come here?"

"I'm busy too, Nan," said Bronwen, quietly.

"I wish you two could have got on better," said Nan, twisting the knife. "I had an idea once that you would suit each other. I suppose matchmaking for other people is always a bit foolish, isn't it?"

"Yes, it never usually works," said Bronwen.

So she was never to see him again. She had to get through the rest of her life with the knowledge that somewhere in the world he was there with his craggy features and his fierce blue eyes that could soften to tenderness, but not, alas, for her.

Always in her mind there would be a picture of him riding like a mythical god over the bright wilderness that was his home, but she herself would be on the other side of the earth.

CHAPTER EIGHTEEN

Bronwen's few possessions were packed. Tomorrow she would start her journey to the coast to embark on the liner that in two weeks' time would bring her to Southampton. In her wardrobe there still hung the old leather jacket, the blue sweater, and the slacks stained with sheep dip and paint.

"You can burn them when I've gone," she said to Nan.

"Tabitha's granddaughter would probably be glad of the jacket," said Nan.

"It will fall to pieces if it is sent to be cleaned. One thing is certain, I won't need it in London."

Nan had insisted upon a small celebration this last evening and opened the last bottle of Lewis's wine. Even Tabitha had excelled herself at cooking a savory goulash and served it while wiping away tears with the corner of her apron. She was to go with Nan to keep house for her in the University town. Nan had ruefully, laughingly accepted the fact that she was to have Tabitha to tyrannize over her forever. So it was for Bronwen's sake that Tabitha was mourning, and for all the changes that were to take place in their lives.

"Who will cook and wash for you, Miss Bron, when you are in that big town?" she asked.

"I will do it myself, Tabitha. They do not have servants there."

"Hau, no servants!"

It was a way of life very foreign to Tabitha.

After dinner they wandered out onto the stoep. The evening was very mild. A large silver ring had formed around the full moon.

"That's supposed to be a sign of snow to come," Nan informed Bronwen.

"Snow!" exclaimed Bronwen. "Why, Nan, how can there be snow? It seems warm enough for summer."

"It usually gets warm before it snows," said Nan.

"I can't believe it. It seems incredible that it could become cold again after the warm weather we have had during the last few days," said Bronwen.

They stood together looking over the silver veld. Near at hand a poplar rustled its dry branches and an owl hooted, but farther away came the haunting moaning cry of a jackal. Bronwen remembered the night in the Bushman's cave.

"Don't look so sad, Bron," said Nan, taking her hand. "You will come again. You must come to visit me in a couple of years' time. But I was forgetting, you will probably be married by then."

"Married?"

"Well, for heaven's sake, you don't expect to stay single all your life, do you? You are very attractive, Bron. I only wish I could have given you more social life, let you meet more people, while you were here, then perhaps I could have kept my favorite niece in this country."

"I could never come back again," thought Bronwen. "Once I have gone, I will try to put all thought of this life behind me. I mustn't brood on what might have been."

Nan looked at her watch. "Sarah must be well on her way over Africa by now. Her plane was to go at seven. Lewis said he would be staying in Johannesburg for a couple of days after she had gone. Poor Lewis, he will be lonely without her. No wonder Sarah said he has seemed moody and depressed lately. It's strange for him. He's usually so vigorous and full of life."

When Gumede came calling at her window a few hours later, Bronwen was glad that she had not as yet burned the slacks, jersey and jacket. She looked amazed onto a landscape swirling with large snowflakes that were rapidly blotting out familiar landmarks.

"You will have to bring the sheep to the *kraal* nearer the house, Gumede," she instructed him. "We can't leave them so far away."

"I tried, Miss Bron. I've been there already. But there are six ready to lamb tonight. I can't move them. They will have to stay there."

"All right, I'll come," said Bronwen with sinking heart.

She phoned through to Lewis's manager. After all the sheep really belonged to him now, but his wife's sleepy voice told her that he also had gone to care for Lewis's flock. She would not be able to give him a message until he returned.

She would never forget the next few hours. She and Gumede struggled through the blizzard on foot until they reached the far pasture. Her old boots squelched and slithered in the slushy mud left by the snow. Gumede had left his son at the place, and the sheep had been driven into a small hut.

There was scarcely room for the panic-stricken animals and the three human beings, but the Africans had contrived to bring in a brazier to keep the place warm. From freezing cold, Bronwen was switched to stifling heat. The combined smell of woodsmoke, sheep's wool, and damp clothing was quite suffocating.

"I'm going to lose them" she thought despairingly an hour or so later. "I'm going to lose them because I don't know enough about the complications that can arise when lambs are born. How did I think I could manage this on my own? Of course I didn't really think so, but there was no one to turn to, and I had to try."

In the hot little hut the sheep seemed very weak. Gumede had relapsed into exclamations of despair. Someone had ill-wished the sheep, he said. Someone must have buried bad charms in this pasture. Nothing could be done about it. His resigned, fatalistic attitude drove Bronwen to desperation again. The air in the hut was fetid, stifling.

The blizzard had quietened now. Far away over the pasture, low on the horizon, she could see a star. But it could not be a star, for it was moving. A lantern! She prayed hard that it might be Lewis's manager, MacDonald. He had received her message. He was coming to help. She stumbled over the rough ground toward the yellow light, swinging now and quite near. The man in the helmeted cap was tall and broad. Mr. MacDonald was a small, slight man.

"Lewis!" Not able to hide her joy, she ran toward him,

and he . . . he was opening his arms to her. She ran into them and was swung up against a solid wall of damp snowy cloth and wet wool. Then he was kissing her with the snow swirling all around them. His eyebrows were white with snow, his helmet covered. But there he was, comforting, loving, acting as if she were the most important person in the world.

"But how . . . why . . . ?" she said.

"I'll tell you later," he said as he strode toward the hut and with that she had to be satisfied.

Hours later, it seemed, they were back at the homestead in front of a log fire. A lamb bleated plaintively in a box beside the warmth. They had been unable to save its mother, but all the rest were thriving and had been brought to the pastures beside the house.

"It will be a 'hans' lamb for you. Since you are going to bottle feed it, it will believe you are its mother. It will live around the house until it is far too big for comfort. Did you know that a lamb in the house always brings happiness?" asked Lewis.

"You seem to have forgotten, Lewis, that I am due to sail tomorrow."

"You can forget about that too!" said Lewis adamantly. "Do you think for one moment that I intend to let you go?"

He sounded so sure of himself, but all at once he was on his knees, burying his head in her lap, talking in a muffled voice as she timidly stroked his springing chestnut hair.

"Bronwen, little one, I've been such a fool. My only excuse is that I was wild with jealousy. How could I have been so dense? On the way to Johannesburg, Sarah was so sweet. I wouldn't see her, I knew, for a long time again and it made me feel very lonely. The life I had to look forward to seemed infinitely bleak and depressing.

"Sarah spoke of Carlotta, asked if I minded that she had decided to marry Tom. When I told her I had never loved Carlotta she said that she was glad, that you were a much more suitable person for me, didn't I think so? It was then that I told her about you and Douglas. She looked very startled at first. And then she told me what you and Douglas had done for her.

"She said that she had been wanting to tell me all the time before she left me, but she had been afraid to do it. But she would rather I had a bad opinion of her than that I should think ill of you after all you had done for her."

He raised his head and put his arms around Bronwen, looking at her with more tenderness than she had dreamed possible in those fierce blue eyes. He grinned reminiscently.

"Young Sarah! She berated me pretty solidly for doubting you. Didn't give me a chance to say what I thought of her. She said if you had told me that Douglas was waking you that was what he was doing and nothing else, that you had saved her from being an absolute idiot, and she was sure that you certainly would not be so idiotic yourself. Bronwen, can you ever forgive me for thinking such a thing?"

The love in her eyes was answer enough as he took her in his arms.

"I'm a foolish man, a bad-tempered man, an impatient man, I warn you," he said. "But I love you, Bronwen. Do you dare to take on such a bad marriage prospect, my own darling?"

"I'll risk it," said Bronwen as she kissed him with all her heart.